SNOW FALLING ON CEDARS

&

EAST OF THE MOUNTAINS

SNOW FALLING ON CEDARS

ON CEDARS

&

EAST OF THE MOUNTAINS

DAVID GUTERSON

BLOOMSBURY

Snow Falling on Cedars first published in Great Britain 1995
Copyright © 1995 by David Guterson

East of the Mountains first published in Great Britain 1999
Copyright © 1999 by David Guterson

This paperback edition published 2004
Copyright © 2004 by David Guterson

The moral right of the author has been asserted

Bloomsbury Publishing Plc, 38 Soho Square, London W1D 3HB

A CIP catalogue record for this book
is available from the British Library

ISBN 0 7475 7455 3

10 9 8 7 6 5 4 3 2 1

All papers used by Bloomsbury Publishing are natural, recyclable
products made from wood grown in well-managed forests.
The manufacturing processes conform to the
environmental regulations of the country of origin.

Printed in Great Britain by Clays Ltd, St Ives plc

www.bloomsbury.com/davidguterson

SNOW FALLING ON CEDARS

To my mother and father,
with gratitude

ACKNOWLEDGMENTS

I thank the many people who contributed to the writing of this book: Mike Hobbs at Harborview Hospital in Seattle, for his help with matters of forensic pathology; Phil McCrudden for taking me salmon fishing and for carefully reading a draft of the novel; Steve Shapiro for his insights about gill-netting; Leonard Hayashida for his gentle and precise commentary; Walt and Millie Woodward for their courage and conviction as owner-editors of the *Bainbridge Review*; Ann Radwick for assistance with local sources; Murray Guterson and Rob Crichton for their assistance regarding legal esoterica; Frank Kitamoto and Hisa Matsudaira for help in my research and interviews; the Bainbridge Historical Society for access to its archives and museum; the University of Washington's Suzzallo Library for assistance with its microfilm collection; Captain Alan Gill for his expertise regarding ships and shipping and for his comments about the book; and Robin Guterson for her willingness to discuss this story with me over the course of many years.

I would also like to acknowledge my debt to the following sources: Dudley Witney's fine book *The Lighthouse*, an architectural and pictorial history; Charles F. Chapman's *Piloting, Seamanship and Small Boat Handling* and Brandt Aymar and John Marshall's *Guide to Boatmanship*; Jim Gibbs's *Disaster Log of Ships*, a pictorial account of shipwrecks from California to Alaska; Hazel Heckman's *Island in the Sound*, a psychologically and culturally accurate portrait of island life in Washington; Joe Upton's marvelous *Alaska Blues*, a beautifully written book about commercial fishing in coastal waters; and Sallie Tisdale's *Stepping Westward*, with its brilliant and exacting descriptions of the Pacific Northwest woods.

Also, James L. Stokesbury's *A Short History of World War II*, Richard F. Newcomb's *Iwo Jima*, Rafael Steinberg's *Island Fighting*, Edwin P. Hoyt's *The Battle of Leyte Gulf*, Studs Terkel's *The Good War*, and Eric M. Hammel and John E. Lane's *76 Hours: The Invasion of Tarawa*, all of which were troubling and helpful.

I am further indebted to Ronald Takaki's brilliant book, *Strangers from a Different Shore*, a history of Asian Americans; to Monica Sone's *Nisei Daughter* and Akemi Kikumura's *Through Harsh Winters*, two moving accounts of Japanese-American families before, during, and after World War II; to Seymour Wishram's *Anatomy of a Jury*, an exacting account of our criminal justice system; to Peter Irons's *Justice at War* for its insight into the internment years; to *Japanese Americans: From Relocation to Redress*, edited by Roger Daniels, Sandra C. Taylor, and Harry H. L. Kitano; to John Armor and Peter Wright's *Manzanar*, with photographs by Ansel Adams and commentary by John Hersey; and to Karlfried Graf von Durckheim's *The Japanese Cult of Tranquility*, Julia V. Nakamura's *The Japanese Tea Ceremony*, and Alan W. Watts's The *Way of Zen*.

Local sources to which I owe a debt include Elsie Franklund Warner's *Bainbridge Through Bifocals*, Katy Warner's *A History of Bainbridge Island*, the Bainbridge School District's *They Cast a Long Shadow*, Junkoh Harui's "Garden Nostalgia" column in the Bainbridge Gardens' *Garden News*, and the Bainbridge Island Japanese American Community Association's "For the Sake of the Children" photograph exhibit.

To those whose contributions I have neglected to note here from sheer failure of memory or character, please accept my apologies. I owe all a great debt.

In the middle of the journey of our life I came to myself
within a dark wood where the straight way was lost.
Ah, how hard a thing it is to tell what a wild,
and rough, and stubborn wood this was,
which in my thought renews the fear!

DANTE
The Divine Comedy

Harmony, like a following breeze
at sea, is the exception.

HARVEY OXENHORN
Turning the Rig

1

The accused man, Kabuo Miyamoto, sat proudly upright with a rigid grace, his palms placed softly on the defendant's table – the posture of a man who has detached himself insofar as this is possible at his own trial. Some in the gallery would later say that his stillness suggested a disdain for the proceedings; others felt certain it veiled a fear of the verdict that was to come. Whichever it was, Kabuo showed nothing – not even a flicker of the eyes. He was dressed in a white shirt worn buttoned to the throat and gray, neatly pressed trousers. His figure, especially the neck and shoulders, communicated the impression of irrefutable physical strength and of precise, even imperial bearing. Kabuo's features were smooth and angular; his hair had been cropped close to his skull in a manner that made its musculature prominent. In the face of the charge that had been leveled against him he sat with his dark eyes trained straight ahead and did not appear moved at all.

In the public gallery every seat had been taken, yet the courtroom suggested nothing of the carnival atmosphere sometimes found at country murder trials. In fact, the eighty-five citizens gathered there seemed strangely subdued and contemplative. Most of them had known Carl Heine, a salmon gill-netter with a wife and three children, who was buried now in the Lutheran cemetery up on Indian Knob Hill. Most had dressed with the same communal propriety they felt on Sundays before attending church services, and since the courtroom, however stark, mirrored in their hearts the dignity of their prayer houses, they conducted themselves with churchgoing solemnity.

This courtroom, Judge Llewellyn Fielding's, down at the end

1

of a damp, drafty hallway on the third floor of the Island County Courthouse, was run-down and small as courtrooms go. It was a place of gray-hued and bleak simplicity – a cramped gallery, a bench for the judge, a witness stand, a plywood platform for the jurors, and scuffed tables for the defendant and his prosecutor. The jurors sat with studiously impassive faces as they strained to make sense of matters. The men – two truck farmers, a retired crabber, a bookkeeper, a carpenter, a boat builder, a grocer, and a halibut schooner deckhand – were all dressed in coats and neckties. The women all wore Sunday dresses – a retired waitress, a sawmill secretary, two nervous fisher wives. A hairdresser accompanied them as alternate.

The bailiff, Ed Soames, at the request of Judge Fielding, had given a good head of steam to the sluggish radiators, which now and again sighed in the four corners of the room. In the heat they produced – a humid, overbearing swelter – the smell of sour mildew seemed to rise from everything.

Snow fell that morning outside the courthouse windows, four tall, narrow arches of leaded glass that yielded a great quantity of weak December light. A wind from the sea lofted snowflakes against the windowpanes, where they melted and ran toward the casements. Beyond the courthouse the town of Amity Harbor spread along the island shoreline. A few wind-whipped and decrepit Victorian mansions, remnants of a lost era of seagoing optimism, loomed out of the snowfall on the town's sporadic hills. Beyond them, cedars wove a steep mat of still green. The snow blurred from vision the clean contours of these cedar hills. The sea wind drove snowflakes steadily inland, hurling them against the fragrant trees, and the snow began to settle on the highest branches with a gentle implacability.

The accused man, with one segment of his consciousness, watched the falling snow outside the windows. He had been exiled in the county jail for seventy-seven days – the last part of September, all of October and all of November, the first week of December in jail. There was no window anywhere in his basement cell, no portal through which the autumn light could

2

come to him. He had missed autumn, he realized now – it had passed already, evaporated. The snowfall, which he witnessed out of the corners of his eyes – furious, wind-whipped flakes against the windows – struck him as infinitely beautiful.

San Piedro was an island of five thousand damp souls, named by lost Spaniards who moored offshore in the year 1603. They'd sailed in search of the Northwest Passage, as many Spaniards did in those days, and their pilot and captain, Martín de Aquilar of the Vizcaíno expedition, sent a work detail ashore to cull a fresh spar pole from among the hemlocks at water's edge. Its members were murdered almost immediately upon setting foot on the beach by a party of Nootka slave raiders.

Settlers arrived – mostly wayward souls and eccentrics who had meandered off the Oregon Trail. A few rooting pigs were slaughtered in 1845 – by Canadian Englishmen up in arms about the border – but San Piedro Island generally lay clear of violence after that. The most distressing news story of the preceding ten years had been the wounding of an island resident by a drunken Seattle yachtsman with a shotgun on the Fourth of July, 1951.

Amity Harbor, the island's only town, provided deep moorage for a fleet of purse seiners and one-man gill-netting boats. It was an eccentric, rainy, wind-beaten sea village, downtrodden and mildewed, the boards of its buildings bleached and weathered, their drainpipes rusted a dull orange. Its long, steep inclines lay broad and desolate; its high-curbed gutters swarmed, most winter nights, with traveling rain. Often the sea wind made its single traffic light flail from side to side or caused the town's electrical power to flicker out and stay out for days. Main Street presented to the populace Petersen's Grocery, a post office, Fisk's Hardware Center, Larsen's Pharmacy, a dime-store-with-fountain owned by a woman in Seattle, a Puget Power office, a chandlery, Lottie Opsvig's apparel shop, Klaus Hartmann's real estate agency, the San Piedro Cafe, the Amity Harbor Restaurant, and a battered, run-down filling station owned and operated by the Torgerson brothers. At the wharf a fish packing plant exuded the odor of salmon bones, and the creosoted pilings of the state ferry terminal lay in among a fleet of mildewed boats. Rain, the spirit of the place, patiently beat down everything man-made. On winter evenings it roared in sheets against the pavements and made Amity Harbor invisible.

San Piedro had too a brand of verdant beauty that inclined its residents toward the poetical. Enormous hills, soft green with cedars, rose and fell in every direction. The island homes were damp and moss covered and lay in solitary fields and vales of alfalfa, feed corn, and strawberries. Haphazard cedar fences lined the careless roads, which slid beneath the shadows of the trees and past the bracken meadows. Cows grazed, stinking of sweet dung and addled by summer blackflies. Here and there an islander tried his hand at milling sawlogs on his own, leaving fragrant heaps of sawdust and mounds of cedar bark at roadside. The beaches glistened with smooth stones and sea foam. Two dozen coves and inlets, each with its pleasant muddle of sailboats and summer homes, ran the circumference of San Piedro, an endless series of pristine anchorages.

Inside Amity Harbor's courthouse, opposite the courtroom's four tall windows, a table had been set up to accommodate the influx of newspapermen to the island. The out-of-town reporters – one each from Bellingham, Anacortes, and Victoria and three from the Seattle papers – exhibited no trace of the solemnity evident among the respectful citizens in the gallery. They slumped in their chairs, rested their chins in their hands, and whispered together conspiratorially. With their backs only a foot from a steam radiator, the out-of-town reporters were sweating.

Ishmael Chambers, the local reporter, found that he was sweating, too. He was a man of thirty-one with a hardened face, a tall man with the eyes of a war veteran. He had only one arm, the left having been amputated ten inches below the shoulder joint, so that he wore the sleeve of his coat pinned up with the cuff fastened to the elbow. Ishmael understood that an air of disdain, of contempt for the island and its inhabitants, blew

4

from the knot of out-of-town reporters toward the citizens in the gallery. Their discourse went forward in a miasma of sweat and heat that suggested a kind of indolence. Three of them had loosened their ties just slightly; two others had removed their jackets. They were reporters, professionally jaded and professionally immune, a little too well traveled in the last analysis to exert themselves toward the formalities San Piedro demanded silently of mainlanders. Ishmael, a native, did not want to be like them. The accused man, Kabuo, was somebody he knew, somebody he'd gone to high school with, and he couldn't bring himself, like the other reporters, to remove his coat at Kabuo's murder trial. At ten minutes before nine that morning, Ishmael had spoken with the accused man's wife on the second floor of the Island County Courthouse. She was seated on a hall bench with her back to an arched window, just outside the assessor's office, which was closed, gathering herself, apparently. 'Are you all right?' he'd said to her, but she'd responded by turning away from him. 'Please,' he'd said. 'Please, Hatsue.'

She'd turned her eyes on his then. Ishmael would find later, long after the trial, that their darkness would beleaguer his memory of these days. He would remember how rigorously her hair had been woven into a black knot against the nape of her neck. She had not been exactly cold to him, not exactly hateful, but he'd felt her distance anyway. 'Go away,' she'd said in a whisper, and then for a moment she'd glared. He remained uncertain afterward what her eyes had meant – punishment, sorrow, pain. 'Go away,' repeated Hatsue Miyamoto. Then she'd turned her eyes, once again, from his.

'Don't be like this,' said Ishmael.

'Go away,' she'd answered.

'Hatsue,' said Ishmael. 'Don't be like this.'

'Go away,' she'd said again.

Now, in the courtroom, with sweat on his temples, Ishmael felt embarrassed to be sitting among the reporters and decided that after the morning's recess he would find a more anonymous seat in the gallery. In the meantime he sat facing the wind-driven

5

snowfall, which had already begun to mute the streets outside the courthouse windows. He hoped it would snow recklessly and bring to the island the impossible winter purity, so rare and precious, he remembered fondly from his youth.

2

The first witness called by the prosecutor that day was the county sheriff, Art Moran. On the morning Carl Heine died – September 16 – the sheriff was in the midst of an inventory at his office and had engaged the services of the new court stenographer, Mrs. Eleanor Dokes (who now sat primly below the judge's bench recording everything with silent implacability), as an aide in this annual county-mandated endeavor. He and Mrs. Dokes had exchanged surprised glances when Abel Martinson, the sheriff's deputy, reported over the newly purchased radio set that Carl Heine's fishing boat, the *Susan Marie*, had been sighted adrift in White Sand Bay.

'Abel said the net was all run out and drifting along behind,' Art Moran explained. 'I felt, well, concerned immediately.'

'The *Susan Marie* was on the move?' asked Alvin Hooks, the prosecutor, who stood with one foot perched on the witnesses' podium as if he and Art were talking by a park bench.

'That's what Abel said.'

'With its fishing lights on? Is that what Deputy Martinson reported?'

'That's right.'

'In *day*light?'

'Abel called in nine-thirty A.M., I believe.'

'Correct me if I'm wrong,' Alvin Hooks asked. 'Gill nets, by law, must be on board by nine o'clock – is that right, Sheriff Moran?'

'That's correct,' said the sheriff. 'Nine A.M.'

The prosecutor swiveled with a faintly military flourish and executed a tight circle over the courtroom's waxed floor, his

7

hands against the small of his back neatly. 'What did you do then?' he inquired.

'I told Abel to stay put. To stay where he was. That I would pick him up in the launch.'

'You didn't call the coast guard?'

'Decided I'd hold off just yet. Decided to have a look myself.'

Alvin Hooks nodded. 'Was it your jurisdiction, sheriff?'

'It's a judgment call, Mr. Hooks,' Art Moran said. 'I felt it was the right thing to do.'

The prosecutor nodded one more time and surveyed the members of the jury. He appreciated the sheriff's answer; it cast a favorable moral light on his witness and gave him the authority of the conscientious man, for which there was ultimately no substitute.

'Just tell the court your whole story,' Alvin Hooks said. 'The morning of September 16.'

The sheriff stared at him doubtfully for a moment. By nature Art Moran was an uneasy person, nervous in the face of even trivial encounters. He'd come to his vocation as if driven ineluctably; he had never formed the intention of being sheriff, yet, to his astonishment, here he was. In his liver-colored uniform, black tie, and polished shoes he looked inevitably miscast in life, a man uncomfortable with the accoutrements of his profession, as if he had dressed for a costume party and now wandered about in the disguise. The sheriff was a lean figure, unimposing, who habitually chewed a stick of Juicy Fruit gum (though he wasn't chewing any at the moment, mostly out of deference to the American legal system, which he believed in wholeheartedly despite its flaws). He'd lost much of his hair since turning fifty, and his belly, always undernourished in appearance, now suggested a shriveled emaciation.

Art Moran had lain awake the night before fretting about his role in this trial and remembering the sequence of events with his eyes shut, as if they were occurring in a dream. He and his deputy, Abel Martinson, had taken the county launch into White

8

Sand Bay on the morning of September 16. The tide, steadily on the rise, had turned about three and a half hours before, at six-thirty; by midmorning sunlight lay like a glaze over the water, warming his back pleasantly. The preceding night a fog as palpable as cotton had hung suspended over Island County. Later it gently separated at the seams and became vast billows traveling above the sea instead of a still white miasma. Around the launch as it churned toward the *Susan Marie* the last remnants of this night fog sailed and drifted in shreds of vapor toward the sun's heat.

Abel Martinson, one hand on the launch's throttle, the other on his knee, told Art that a Port Jensen fisherman, Erik Syvertsen – Erik the younger, he pointed out – had come across the *Susan Marie* adrift off the south side of White Sand Point with her net set and, it appeared, no one on board. It was more than an hour and a half past dawn and the running lights had been left on. Abel had driven to White Sand Point and walked out to the end of the community pier with his binoculars dangling from his neck. Sure enough, the *Susan Marie* lay drifting on the tide well into the bay on an angle north by northwest, he'd found, and so he'd radioed the sheriff.

In fifteen minutes they came abreast of the drifting boat and Abel turned back the throttle. In the calm of the bay their approach went smoothly; Art set the fenders out; and the two of them made fast their mooring lines with a few wraps each around the forward deck cleats. 'Lights're *all* on,' observed Art, one foot on the *Susan Marie*'s gunnel. 'Every last one of 'em, looks like.'

'He ain't here,' replied Abel.

'Doesn't look like it,' said Art.

'Went over,' Abel said. 'I got this bad feeling.'

Art winced at hearing this. 'Let's hope not,' he urged. 'Don't say that.'

He made his way just abaft of the cabin, then stood squinting up at the *Susan Marie*'s guys and stays and at the peaks of her stabilizer bars. The red and white mast lights had been left on all morning; the picking light and the jacklight at the end of the net both shone dully in the early sun. While Art stood there, pondering this, Abel Martinson dragged the hatch cover from the hold and called for him to come over.

'You got something?' Art asked.

'Look here,' answered Abel.

Together they crouched over the square hold opening, out of which the odor of salmon flew up at them. Abel maneuvered his flashlight beam across a heap of inert, silent fish. 'Silvers,' he said. 'Maybe fifty of 'em.'

'So he picked his net least once,' said Art.

'Looks like it,' answered Abel.

Men had been known to fall into empty holds before, crack their heads, and pass out even in calm weather. Art had heard of a few such incidents. He looked in at the fish again.

'What time you figure he put out last night?'

'Hard to say. Four-thirty? Five?'

'Where'd he go, you figure?'

'Probably up North Bank,' said Abel. 'Maybe Ship Channel. Or Elliot Head. That's where the fish been running.'

But Art already knew about these things. San Piedro lived and breathed by the salmon, and the cryptic places where they ran at night were the subject of perpetual conversation. Yet it helped him to hear it aloud just now – it helped him to think more clearly.

The two of them crouched by the hold a moment longer in a shared hiatus from their work. The still heap of salmon troubled Art in a way he could not readily articulate, and so he looked at it wordlessly. Then he rose, his knees creaking, and turned away from the dark hold.

'Let's keep looking,' he suggested.

'Right,' said Abel. 'Could be he's up in his cabin, maybe. Knocked out one way or t'other.'

The *Susan Marie* was a thirty-foot stern-picker – a standard, well-tended San Piedro gill-netter – with her cabin just abaft of midship. Art ducked through its stern-side entry and stood to port for a moment. In the middle of the floor – it was the first thing he noticed – a tin coffee cup lay tipped on its side. A marine battery lay just right of the wheel. There was a short bunk made up with a wool blanket to starboard; Abel ran his flashlight across it. The cabin lamp over the ship's wheel had been left on; a ripple of sunlight, flaring through a window, shimmered on the starboard wall. The scene left Art with the ominous impression of an extreme, too-silent tidiness. A cased sausage hanging from a wire above the binnacle swayed a little as the *Susan Marie* undulated; otherwise, nothing moved. No sound could be heard except now and again a dim, far crackle from the radio set. Art, noting it, began to manipulate the radio dials for no other reason than that he didn't know what else to do. He was at a loss.

'This is bad,' said Abel.

'Take a look,' answered Art. 'I forgot – see if his dinghy's over the reel.'

Abel Martinson stuck his head out the entry. 'It's there, Art,' he said. 'Now what?'

For a moment they stared at one another. Then Art, with a sigh, sat down on the edge of Carl Heine's short bunk.

'Maybe he crawled in under the decking,' suggested Abel. 'Maybe he had some kind of engine trouble, Art.'

'I'm sitting on top of his engine,' Art pointed out. 'There's no room for anyone to crawl around down there.'

'He went over,' said Abel, shaking his head.

'Looks like it,' answered the sheriff.

They glanced at each other, then away again.

'Maybe somebody took him off,' suggested Abel. 'He got hurt, radioed, somebody took him off. That – '

'They wouldn't let the boat drift,' put in Art. 'Besides, we'd a heard about it by now.'

'This is bad,' repeated Abel Martinson.

Art tucked another stick of Juicy Fruit between his teeth and wished this was not his responsibility. He liked Carl Heine, knew Carl's family, went to church with them on Sundays.

11

Carl came from old-time island stock; his grandfather, Bavarian born, had established thirty acres of strawberry fields on prime growing land in Center Valley. His father, too, had been a strawberry farmer before dying of a stroke in '44. Then Carl's mother, Etta Heine, had sold all thirty acres to the Jurgensen clan while her son was away at the war. They were hard-toiling, quiet people, the Heines. Most people on San Piedro liked them. Carl, Art recalled, had served as a gunner on the U.S.S. *Canton*, which went down during the invasion of Okinawa. He'd survived the war – other island boys hadn't – and come home to a gill-netter's life.

On the sea Carl's blond hair had gone russet colored. He weighed two hundred and thirty-five pounds, much of it carried in his chest and shoulders. On winter days, picking fish from his net, he wore a wool cap knitted by his wife and an infantryman's battered field jacket. He spent no time at the San Piedro Tavern or drinking coffee at the San Piedro Cafe. On Sunday mornings he sat with his wife and children in a back pew of the First Hill Lutheran Church, blinking slowly in the pale sanctuary light, a hymnbook open in his large, square hands, a calm expression on his face. Sunday afternoons he squatted on the aft deck of his boat, silently and methodically untangling his gill net or knitting its flaws up patiently. He worked alone. He was courteous but not friendly. He wore rubber boots almost everywhere, like all San Piedro fishermen. His wife, too, came from old island people – the Varigs, Art remembered, hay farmers and shake cutters with a few stump acres on Cattle Point – and her father had passed away not so long ago. Carl had named his boat after his wife, and, in '48, built a big frame house just west of Amity Harbor, including an apartment for his mother, Etta. But – out of pride, word had it – Etta would not move in with him. She lived in town, a stout, grave woman with a slight Teutonic edge to her speech, over Lottie Opsvig's apparel shop on Main. Her son called at her door every Sunday afternoon and escorted her to his house for supper. Art had watched them trudge up Old Hill together, Etta with her umbrella turned against the winter rain, her free hand clutching at the lapels of a coarse winter coat, Carl with his hands curled up in his jacket pockets, his wool cap pulled to his eyebrows. All in all, Art decided, Carl Heine was a good man. He was silent, yes, and grave like his mother, but the war had a part in that, Art realized. Carl rarely laughed, but he did not seem, to Art's way of thinking, unhappy or dissatisfied. Now his death would land hard on San Piedro; no one would want to fathom its message in a place where so many made their living fishing. The fear of the sea that was always there, simmering beneath the surface of their island lives, would boil up in their hearts again.

'Well, look,' said Abel Martinson, leaning in the cabin door while the boat shifted about. 'Let's get his net in, Art.'

'Suppose we better,' sighed Art. 'All right. We'd better do it, then. But we'll do it one step at a time.'

'He's got a power takeoff back there,' Abel Martinson pointed out. 'You figure he hasn't run for maybe six hours. And all these lights been drawing off the battery. Better choke it up good, Art.'

Art nodded and then turned the key beside the ship's wheel. The solenoid kicked in immediately; the engine stuttered once and then began to idle roughly, rattling frantically beneath the floorboards. Art slowly backed the choke off.

'Okay,' he said. 'Like that?'

'Guess I was wrong,' said Abel Martinson. 'She sounds real good and strong.'

They went out again, Art leading. The *Susan Marie* had veered off nearly perpendicular to the chop and angled, briefly, to starboard. With the thrust of the engine she'd begun to bobble a little, and Art, treading across the aft deck, stumbled forward and grabbed at a stanchion, scraping his palm at the heel of the thumb, while Abel Martinson looked on. He rose again, steadied himself with a foot on the starboard gunnel, and looked out across the water.

The morning light had broadened, gained greater depth, and lay in a clean sheet across the bay, giving it a silver tincture. Not

13

a boat was in sight except a single canoe traveling parallel to a tree-wreathed shoreline, children in life jackets at the flashing paddles a quarter mile off. *They're innocent*, thought Art.

'It's good she's come about,' he said to his deputy. 'We'll need time to get this net in.'

'Whenever you're ready,' answered Abel.

For a moment it occurred to Art to explain certain matters to his deputy. Abel Martinson was twenty-four, the son of an Anacortes brick mason. He had never seen a man brought up in a net before, as Art had, twice. It happened now and then to fishermen – they caught a hand or a sleeve in their net webbing and went over even in calm weather. It was a part of things, part of the fabric of the place, and as sheriff he knew this well. He knew what bringing up the net really meant, and he knew Abel Martinson didn't.

Now he put his foot on top of the beaver paddle and looked across at Abel. 'Get over there with the lead line,' he said softly. 'I'll bring her up real slow. You may need to pick some, so be ready.'

Abel Martinson nodded.

Art brought the weight of his foot down. The net shuddered for a moment as the slack went out of it, and then the reel wound it in against the weight of the sea. Surging, and then lowering a note, the engine confronted its work. The two men stood at either end of the gunnel roller, Art with one shoe on the beaver paddle and Abel Martinson staring at the net webbing as it traveled slowly toward the drum. Ten yards out, the float line fell away and bobbled in a seam of white water along the surface of the bay. They were still moving up the tide about north by northwest, but the breeze from the south had shifted just enough to bring them gently to port.

They had picked two dozen salmon from the net, three stray sticks, two dogfish, a long convoluted coil of kelp, and a number of ensnarled jellyfish when Carl Heine's face showed. For a brief moment Art understood Carl's face as the sort of illusion men are prone to at sea – or hoped it was this, rather, with a fleeting

14

desperation – but then as the net reeled in Carl's bearded throat appeared too and the face completed itself. There was Carl's face turned up toward the sunlight and the water from Carl's hair dripped in silver strings to the sea; and now clearly it *was* Carl's face, his mouth open – Carl's *face* – and Art pressed harder against the beaver paddle. Up came Carl, hanging by the left buckle of his rubber bib overalls from the gill net he'd made his living picking, his T-shirt, bubbles of seawater coursing under it, pasted to his chest and shoulders. He hung heavily with his legs in the water, a salmon struggling in the net beside him, the skin of his collarbones, just above the highest waves, hued an icy but brilliant pink. He appeared to have been parboiled in the sea.

Abel Martinson vomited. He leaned out over the transom of the boat and retched and cleared his throat and vomited again, this time more violently. 'All right, Abel,' Art said. 'You get ahold of yourself.'

The deputy did not reply. He wiped his mouth with a handkerchief. He breathed heavily and spat into the sea a half-dozen times. Then, after a moment, he dropped his head and pounded his left fist against the transom. 'Jesus Christ,' he said.

'I'll bring him up slow,' answered Art. 'You keep his head back away from the transom, Abel. Get ahold of yourself. Keep his head back and away now.'

But in the end they had to rattle up the lead line and pull Carl fully into the folds of his net. They cupped the net around him like a kind of hammock so that his body was borne by the webbing. In this manner they brought Carl Heine up from the sea – Abel yarding him over the net roller while Art tapped gingerly at the beaver paddle and squinted over the transom, his Juicy Fruit seized between his teeth. They laid him, together, on the afterdeck. In the cold salt water he had stiffened quickly; his right foot had frozen rigidly over his left, and his arms, locked at the shoulders, were fixed in place with the fingers curled. His mouth was open. His eyes were open too, but the pupils had disappeared – Art saw how they'd revolved backward and now

15

looked inward at his skull. The blood vessels in the whites of his eyes had burst; there were two crimson orbs in his head.

Abel Martinson stared.

Art found that he could not bring forward the least vestige of professionalism. He simply stood by, like his twenty-four-year-old deputy, thinking the thoughts a man thinks at such a time about the ugly inevitability of death. There was a silence to be filled, and Art found himself hard-pressed in the face of it to conduct himself in a manner his deputy could learn from. And so they simply stood looking down at Carl's corpse, a thing that had silenced both of them.

'He banged his head,' whispered Abel Martinson, pointing to a wound Art hadn't noticed in Carl Heine's blond hair. 'Must have banged it against the gunnel going over.'

Sure enough, Carl Heine's skull had been crushed just above his left ear. The bone had fractured and left a dent in his head. Art Moran turned away from it.

3

Nels Gudmundsson, the attorney who had been appointed to defend Kabuo Miyamoto, rose to cross-examine Art Moran with a slow and deliberate geriatric awkwardness, then roughly cleared the phlegm from his throat and hooked his thumbs behind his suspenders where they met their tiny black catch buttons. At seventy-nine, Nels was blind in his left eye and could distinguish only shades of light and darkness through its transient, shadowy pupil. The right, however, as if to make up for this deficiency, seemed preternaturally observant, even prescient, and as he plodded over the courtroom floorboards, advancing with a limp toward Art Moran, motes of light winked through it.

'Sheriff,' he said. 'Good morning.'

'Good morning,' replied Art Moran.

'I just want to make sure I'm hearing you right on a couple of matters,' said Nels. 'You say the lights on this boat, the *Susan Marie*, were all on? Is that right?'

'Yes,' said the sheriff. 'They were.'

'In the cabin, too?'

'That's right.'

'The mast lights?'

'Yes.'

'The picking lights? The net lights. *All* of them?'

'Yes, sir,' said Art Moran.

'Thank you,' Nels said. 'I thought that was what you said, all right. That they were all on. All the lights.'

He paused and for a moment seemed to study his hands, which were riddled with liver spots and trembled at times:

Nels suffered from an advancing neurasthenia. Its foremost symptom was a sensation of heat that on occasion flamed in the nerve endings of his forehead until the arteries in his temples pulsed visibly.

'You say it was foggy on the night of September 15?' Nels asked. 'Is that what you said, sheriff?'

'Yes.'

'Thick fog?'

'Absolutely.'

'Do you remember this?'

'I remember, yes. I've thought about it. Because I went out on my porch about ten o'clock, see. Hadn't seen fog for more than a week. And I couldn't see more than twenty yards.'

'At ten o'clock?'

'Yes.'

'And then?'

'I went to bed, I guess.'

'You went to bed. What time did you get up, sheriff? Do you remember? On the sixteenth?'

'I got up at five. At five o'clock.'

'You remember this?'

'I'm always up at five. Every morning. So on the sixteenth, yes, I was up at five.'

'And was the fog still there?'

'Yes, it was.'

'Just as thick? As thick as at ten o'clock the night before?'

'Almost, I'd say. Almost. But not quite.'

'So it was still foggy in the morning, then.'

'Yes. Until nine or so. Then it started burning off – was mostly gone by the time we set out in the launch, if that's what you're driving at, sir.'

'Until nine,' answered Nels Gudmundsson. 'Or thereabouts? Nine?'

'That's right,' replied Art Moran.

Nels Gudmundsson raised his chin, fingered his bow tie, and

18

pinched experimentally the wattles of skin at his neck – a habit of his when he was thinking.

'Out there on the *Susan Marie*,' he said. 'The engine started right up, sheriff? When you went to start it you had no trouble?'

'Right away,' said Art Moran. 'No trouble at all.'

'With all those lights drawing, sheriff? Batteries still strong?'

'Must have been. Because she started with no trouble.'

'Did that strike you as odd, sheriff? Do you remember? That with all those lights drawing, the batteries still had plenty of charge, enough to turn the engine over with no trouble, as you say?'

'Didn't think about it at the time,' said Art Moran. 'So no is the answer – it didn't strike me as odd, at least not then.'

'And does it strike you as odd now?'

'A little,' said the sheriff. 'Yes.'

'Why?' Nels asked.

'Because those lights do a lot of drawing. I'd reckon they can run a battery down quick – just like in your car. So I have to wonder a little, yes.'

'You have to wonder,' said Nels Gudmundsson, and he began to massage his throat again and pull at the dewlaps of skin there.

Nels made his way to the evidence table, selected a folder, and brought it to Art Moran. 'Your investigative report,' he said. 'The one just admitted into evidence during Mr. Hooks's direct examination. Is this it, sheriff?'

'It is.'

'Could you turn to page seven, please?'

The sheriff did so.

'Now,' said Nels, 'is page seven an inventory of items found on board Carl Heine's boat, the *Susan Marie*?'

'Could you read for the court the item listed as number twenty-seven?'

'Of course,' said Art Moran. 'Item twenty-seven. A spare D-8 battery, six celled.'

'A spare D-8 battery, six celled,' said Nels. 'Thank you. A D-8. Six celled. Would you turn now to item forty-two, sheriff? And read one more time for the court?'

'Item forty-two,' replied Art Moran. 'D-8 and D-6 batteries in battery well. Each six celled.'

'A 6 and an 8?' Nels said.

'Yes.'

'I did some measuring down at the chandlery,' said Nels. 'A D-6 is wider than a D-8 by an inch. It wouldn't fit into the *Susan Marie*'s battery well, sheriff. It was an inch too large for that.'

'He'd done some on-the-spot refitting,' Art explained. 'The side flange was banged away to make room for a D-6.'

'He banged out the side flange?'

'Yes.'

'You could see this?'

'Yes.'

'A metal flange that had been banged aside?'

'Yes.'

'Soft metal?'

'Yes. Soft enough. It'd been banged back to make room for a D-6.'

'To make room for a D-6,' Nels repeated. 'But sheriff, didn't you say that the spare was a D-8? Didn't Carl Heine have a D-8 available that would have fit into the existing well with none of this banging and refitting?'

'The spare was dead,' Art Moran said. 'We tested it after we brought the boat in. It didn't have any juice to it, Mr. Gudmundsson. Didn't have any juice at all.'

'The spare was dead,' Nels repeated. 'So, to summarize, you found on the deceased's boat a dead spare D-8 battery, a working D-8 down in the well, and beside it a working D-6 that was in fact too large for the existing space and which forced someone to do some refitting? Some banging at a soft metal flange?'

'All correct,' said the sheriff.

'All right now,' said Nels Gudmundsson. 'Would you please turn to page twenty-seven of your report? Your inventory of items aboard the *defendant's* boat? And read for the court item twenty-four, please?'

Art Moran turned the pages. 'Item twenty-four,' he said after a while. 'Two D-6 batteries in well. Each six celled.'

'Two D-6s on Kabuo Miyamoto's boat,' Nels said. 'And did you find a spare aboard, sheriff?'

'No. We didn't. It isn't in the inventory.'

'The defendant had no spare battery aboard his boat? He'd gone out fishing without one?'

'Apparently, yes, sir, he did.'

'Well, then,' Nels said. 'Two D-6s in the well and no spare to be found. Tell me, sheriff. These D-6s on the defendant's boat. Were they the same sort of D-6 you found in the deceased's battery well? On board the *Susan Marie*? The same size? The same make?'

'Yes,' replied the sheriff. 'All D-6s. The same battery.'

'So the D-6 in use on the deceased's boat could have – hypothetically, since it was identical – made a perfect spare for the defendant's batteries?'

'I suppose so.'

'But, as you say, the defendant *had* no spare on board. Is that right?'

'Yes.'

'All right, sheriff,' Nels said. 'Let me ask you about something else, if you don't mind, for a moment. Tell me – when you brought the deceased in was there some sort of trouble? When you hauled him up from the sea in his fishing net?'

'Yes,' said Art Moran. 'I mean, he was heavy. And, well, his lower half – his legs and feet? – they wanted to slide out of the net. He was hanging by one of his rain gear buckles. And we were afraid if we pulled him out of the water maybe we'd lose him altogether, he'd come out and the buckle would give or the rubber around it would and he'd be gone. His legs were hanging in the water, you understand. His legs weren't quite in the net.'

'And,' said Nels Gudmundsson, 'can you tell us what you and Deputy Martinson did about this?'

'Well, we cupped the webbing. And then we pulled on the lead line. We made a sort of cradle with the net, got his legs inside it. Then we brought him in.'

'So you had some trouble,' Nels said.

'A little, yes.'

'He didn't come in cleanly?'

'Not at first, no. We had to jerk the net around, work it. But once we had him in and the webbing grabbed it was fairly smooth from there, yes.'

'Sheriff,' said Nels Gudmundsson, 'with all of this jerking of the net and this trouble you're mentioning now – is it possible the deceased hit his head on the transom of the boat as you were bringing him in? Or somewhere else? On the stern gunnel, say, or on the net roller? Is it possible?'

'I don't think so,' said Art Moran. 'I would have seen it if we did.'

'You don't think so,' said Nels Gudmundsson. 'What about when you pulled him out of the net? When you laid him on the deck? He was a big man, as you say, two hundred and thirty-five pounds, and stiff, as you've pointed out. Was he difficult to move around, sheriff?'

'He was heavy, yes, real heavy. But there were two of us and we were careful. We didn't hit him on anything.'

'Are you sure of this?'

'I don't remember hitting him on anything, no, Mr. Gudmundsson. We were careful, as I've said already.'

'But you don't remember,' Nels said. 'Or to put it another way, do you have any uncertainty at all about this? That in moving this awkward and heavy corpse about, in operating this winch equipment you'd rarely operated before, in doing this difficult job of bringing in a drowned man of two hundred and thirty-five pounds – is it possible, Sheriff Moran, that the deceased banged his head sometime *after* his death? Is that possible?'

'Yes,' said Art Moran. '*Possible*. I guess it is – but not likely.'

Nels Gudmundsson turned toward the jury. 'No more questions,' he said. And with a slowness that embarrassed him – because as a young man he had been lithe and an athlete, had always moved fluidly across the floorboards of courtrooms, had always felt admired for his physical appearance – he made his way back to his seat at the defendant's table, where Kabuo Miyamoto sat watching him.

4

Judge Lew Fielding called for a recess at ten forty-five that first morning. He turned to observe the silent sweep of the snowfall, rubbed his graying eyebrows and the tip of his nose, then rose in his black robe, slid his hands through his hair, and lumbered into his chambers.

The accused man, Kabuo Miyamoto, leaned to his right and nodded just perceptibly while Nels Gudmundsson spoke into his ear. Across the aisle Alvin Hooks rested his chin in his hands, drumming the floorboards with the heel of his shoe, impatient but not dissatisfied. In the gallery the citizens stood and yawned, then wandered off into the less stultifying atmosphere of the hallway or gazed out the windows with awed expressions, watching the snow lash toward them in parabolas before it struck against the leaded panes. Their faces, bathed in the attenuated December light from the tall windows, appeared quiet and even faintly reverent. Those who had driven into town felt fretful about getting home.

The jurors were led away by Ed Soames to drink cone-shaped cups of lukewarm cooler water and to make use of the lavatory. Then Soames reappeared and plodded about like a parish beadle, backing down the steam radiator valves. Yet it remained too hot in the courtroom despite this; the trapped heat wouldn't dissipate. Steam began to coalesce in a film of vapor on the upper reaches of the windows, closing the courtroom in a little, muffling the pale morning light.

Ishmael Chambers found a seat in the gallery and sat tapping his pencil's eraser against his bottom lip. Like others on San Piedro Island, he'd first heard about the death of Carl Heine on the afternoon of September 16 – the day the body was discovered. He'd been calling the Reverend Gordon Groves of the Amity Harbor Lutheran Congregation to ask about the sermon topic for Sunday in order that he might paraphrase the reverend's answer in his 'At Our Island Churches' column, a weekly feature in the *San Piedro Review* that ran beside the Anacortes ferry schedule. The Reverend Groves was not in, but his wife, Lillian, informed Ishmael that Carl Heine had drowned and been found tangled in his gill net.

Ishmael Chambers did not believe her: Lillian Groves was a gossip. He was not inclined to believe such a thing and when he hung up sat brooding over it. Then, disbelieving, he dialed the sheriff's office and asked Eleanor Dokes, a person he did not entirely trust either: yes, she replied, Carl Heine had drowned. He'd been fishing, yes. He'd been found in his net. The sheriff? Not in just now. She supposed he was seeing the coroner.

Ishmael immediately called the coroner, Horace Whaley. That's right, said Horace, you'd better believe it. Carl Heine was dead. Terrible thing, wasn't it? The man had survived Okinawa. Carl *Heine*, it was *unbelievable*. He'd hit his head on something.

The sheriff? said Horace. You just barely missed him. He and Abel both; just barely gone. Heading for the docks, they said.

Ishmael Chambers put down the receiver and sat with his forehead held in his palm, remembering Carl Heine from high school. They had both graduated in '42. They had played on the football team together. He remembered riding the team bus with Carl to a game against Bellingham in the fall of '41. They rode wearing their uniforms, their helmets in their laps, each boy carrying his own towel. He remembered how Carl looked sitting beside him with his gym towel draped around his thick German neck, glaring out the window at the fields. It was dusk, a brief November twilight, and Carl was watching snow geese land in low flooded wheat, his square chin set, his head tilted up, a man's blond stubble on his jaw. 'Chambers,' he'd said. 'You see the geese?'

Ishmael slid a notepad into the pocket of his pants and went outside into Hill Street. Behind him he left unlocked the office of the *Review* – three rooms that had once housed a book and magazine shop and still contained its many wall shelves. The bookshop had ultimately not been profitable because of the steep hill on which it was situated; Hill Street discouraged tourists. Ishmael, though, liked this feature of it. He had nothing in principle against the vacationers from Seattle who frequented San Piedro all summer long – most islanders disliked them because they were city people – but on the other hand he did not especially enjoy seeing them as they wandered up and down Main Street. Tourists reminded him of other places and elicited in him a prodding doubt that living here was what he wanted.

He had not always been so ambivalent about his home. Once he'd known how he felt about it. After the war, a man of twenty-three with an amputated arm, he'd left San Piedro without reluctance to attend school in Seattle. He'd lived in a boardinghouse on Brooklyn Avenue and taken, at first, history classes. He had not been particularly *happy* in this period, but in that regard he was like other veterans. He was keenly aware of his pinned-up sleeve, and troubled because it troubled other people. Since they could not forget about it, neither could he. There were times when he visited taverns near campus and allowed himself to act gregarious and animated in the manner of younger students. Afterward he inevitably felt foolish, however. It was not in him to drink beer and shoot pool. His more natural domain was a high-backed booth near the rear of Day's Restaurant on University Way where he sipped coffee and read his history.

The next fall Ishmael took up American literature. Melville, Hawthorne, Twain. He was prepared, in his cynicism, to find *Moby Dick* unreadable – five hundred pages about chasing a whale? – but, as it turned out, it was entertaining. He read the whole thing in ten sittings in his booth at Day's and began pondering the whale's nature at an early juncture. The narrator, he found upon reading the first sentence, bore his own name –

Ishmael. Ishmael was all right, but Ahab he could not respect and this ultimately undermined the book for him.

Huckleberry Finn he had read as a child, but he couldn't remember much of it. He recalled only that it was funnier then – everything was funnier – but the story had fled his mind. Other people spoke fondly and knowingly of books they had read decades before. Ishmael suspected this was pretense. He sometimes wondered what had become of the books he'd read many years earlier – if they were still somewhere inside him. James Fenimore Cooper, Sir Walter Scott, Dickens, William Dean Howells. He didn't think any of them were still there. He couldn't remember them, anyway.

The Scarlet Letter he read in six sittings. He closed down Day's finishing it. The cook came out from behind the swinging doors and told him it was time to leave. Ishmael was on the last page when this occurred and ended up reading 'ON A FIELD, SABLE, THE LETTER A, GULES,' while standing on the sidewalk outside. What did it mean? He could only guess what it might fully mean, even with the explanatory footnote. People hurried past him while he stood there with his book open, an October gust blowing in his face. He felt troubled by this ending to the story of Hester Prynne; the woman, after all, deserved better.

All right, he decided, books were a good thing, but that was all they were and nothing else – they couldn't put food on his table. And so Ishmael turned to journalism.

His father, Arthur, had been a logger at Ishmael's age. Wearing a handlebar mustache and calf-high caulk boots, frayed suspenders and woolen long johns, he'd labored in the service of the Port Jefferson Mill Company for four and a half years. Ishmael's grandfather had been a Highland Presbyterian, his grandmother an Irish zealot from the bogs above Lough Ree; they met in Seattle five years before the Great Fire, wed, and raised six sons. Arthur, the youngest, was the only one to remain on Puget Sound. Two of his brothers became mercenary soldiers, one died of malaria on the Panama Canal, one became a surveyor in Burma and India, and the last made tracks for the eastern seaboard at seventeen, never to be heard from again.

The *San Piedro Review*, a four-page weekly, was the invention of Arthur's early twenties. With his savings he acquired a printing press, a box camera, and a damp, low-ceilinged office in the rear of a fish-processing warehouse. The inaugural edition of the *Review* displayed a banner headline: JURY ACQUITS SEATTLE'S GILL. Brushing shoulders with reporters from the *Star*, the *Times*, the *Evening Post*, the *Daily Call*, and the *Seattle Union-Record*, Arthur had covered the trial of Mayor Hiram Gill, accused in a liquor scandal. He ran a long feature on George Vandeveer, charlatan attorney for the Wobbly defense in the Everett Massacre deliberations. An editorial pleaded for the exercise of common sense as Wilson moved to declare war; another celebrated the recent extension of ferry service to the leeward side of the island. A meeting of the Rhododendron Society was announced, as was an evening of square dancing at the Grange and the birth of a son, Theodore Ignatius, to the Horatio Marches of Cattle Point. All of this appeared in Centurion bold type – already antiquated in 1917 – with delicate hairlines separating seven columns and subheads in bold serif relief.

Shortly thereafter Arthur was drafted to serve in General Pershing's army. He fought at Saint-Mihiel and Belleau Wood, then came home to his newspaper. He married a Seattle woman of Illini stock, corn blond, svelte, and somber eyed. Her father, a haberdasher on Seattle's First Avenue and a real estate speculator, frowned on Arthur, who seemed to him a lumberjack posing as a reporter, a man without prospects and unworthy of his daughter; nevertheless the two were married and settled down to the business of rearing children. They had only one, though, after much effort; they lost a second at birth. They built a house at South Beach with a view of the sea and cleared a path to the beach. Arthur became an astute and deliberate vegetable gardener, an inveterate observer of island life, and gradually a small-town newspaperman in the truest sense: he came to

28

recognize the opportunity his words provided for leverage, celebrity, and service. For many years he took no vacations. He put out extra editions on Christmas Eve, during election week, and on the Fourth of July. Ishmael remembered running the press with his father every Tuesday evening. Arthur had bolted it to the floor of a boat-building warehouse on Andreason Street, a dilapidated barn that smelled permanently of lithographic ink and of the ammonia in the typesetting machine. The press was an enormous lime green contraption, rollers and conveyor pulleys in a cast-iron housing; it started with the hesitancy of a nineteenth-century locomotive and shrieked and bleated while it ran. It was Ishmael's job to set the impression meters and water fountains and to act in the role of fly boy; Arthur, who had formed over the years a symbiotic relationship with the machine, ducked in and out inspecting the plates and printing cylinders. He stood mere inches from the clattering rollers, seemingly oblivious to the fact that – as he'd explained to his son – were he caught by a sleeve he'd be instantly popped open like a child's balloon and splattered across the walls. Even his bones would disappear – this was part of Arthur's warning – until somebody found them scattered among the stained newsprint on the floor, looking like strips of white confetti.

A group of businessmen from the chamber of commerce had tried to persuade Arthur to run for the Washington state legislature. They came to the house dressed in overcoats and checkered scarves, reeking of pomade and shaving soap, and sat down to snifters of blackberry cordial, after which Arthur declined to run for office, telling the gentlemen from Amity Harbor that he harbored no illusions, that he preferred to turn sentences and prune his mulberry hedges. The sleeves of his striped oxford shirt lay rolled to his elbows so that the hairs on his forearms showed; his back formed a long hard wedge of muscle against which his suspenders rode tautly. On his nose, a bit low, sat his steel-rimmed full moons, gently prosthetic and handsomely discordant with the sinewy length of his jawline. The cartilage in his nose was twisted – it'd been broken by the lash of a wayward logging cable in the winter of 1915. The men from Amity Harbor couldn't argue with this or with the fixed upward tilt of his chin and jaw. They left unsatisfied.

An unflagging loyalty to his profession and its principles had made Arthur, over the years, increasingly deliberate in his speech and actions, and increasingly exacting regarding the truth in even his most casual reportage. He was, his son remembered, morally meticulous, and though Ishmael might strive to emulate this, there was nevertheless this matter of the war – this matter of the arm he'd lost – that made such scrupulosity difficult. He had a chip on his shoulder: it was a sort of black joke he shared with himself, a double entendre, made silently. He didn't like very many people anymore or very many things, either. He preferred not to be this way, but there it was, he was like that. His cynicism – a veteran's cynicism – was a thing that disturbed him all the time. It seemed to him after the war that the world was thoroughly altered. It was not even a thing you could explain to anybody, why it was that everything was folly. People appeared enormously foolish to him. He understood that they were only animated cavities full of jelly and strings and liquids. He had seen the insides of jaggedly ripped-open dead people. He knew, for instance, what brains looked like spilling out of somebody's head. In the context of this, much of what went on in normal life seemed wholly and disturbingly ridiculous. He found that he was irritated with complete strangers. If somebody in one of his classes spoke to him he answered stiffly, tersely. He could never tell if they were relaxed enough about his arm to say what they were really thinking. He sensed their need to extend sympathy to him, and this irritated him even more. The arm was a grim enough thing without that, and he felt sure it was entirely disgusting. He could repel people if he chose by wearing to class a short-sleeved shirt that revealed the scar tissue on his stump. He never did this, however. He didn't exactly want to *repel* people. Anyway, he had this view of things – that most human activity was utter folly, his own included, and that his existence in the world made others nervous. He could not help but possess this unhappy perspective, no matter how much he might not want it. It was his and he suffered from it numbly.

Later, when he was no longer so young and back home on San Piedro Island, this view of things began to moderate. He learned to be cordial to everyone – a sophisticated and ultimately false front. Add to the cynicism of a man wounded in war the inevitable cynicism of growing older and the professional cynicism of the journalist. Gradually Ishmael came to view himself as a one-armed man with a pinned-up sleeve, past thirty and unmarried. It was not so bad, and he was not so irritated as he had once been in Seattle. Still, though, there were those tourists, he thought, as he walked down Hill Street toward the docks. All summer they looked at his pinned-up sleeve with the surprised, unaccustomed faces his fellow islanders had stopped making. And with their ice cream and clean faces they elicited in his gut again that bilious, unwanted irritation. The strange thing was, he wanted to like everyone. He just couldn't find a way to do it.

His mother, who was fifty-six and lived alone in the old family house on the south end of the island – the house where Ishmael had lived as a child – had pointed out to him when he'd come home from the city that this cynicism of his, while understandable, was on the other hand entirely unbecoming. His father before him had had it, she said, and it had been unbecoming in him, too.

'He loved humankind dearly and with all his heart, but he disliked most human beings,' she'd told Ishmael. 'You're the same, you know. You're your father's son.'

Art Moran was standing with one foot up on a piling, talking to half a dozen fishermen, when Ishmael Chambers arrived that afternoon on the Amity Harbor docks. They were gathered in front of Carl Heine's gillnetter, which was moored between the *Erik J* and the *Tordenskold* – the former a bow-picker owned by Marty Johansson, the latter an Anacortes purse seiner. As Ishmael came their way a south breeze blew and caused the mooring lines of boats to creak – the *Advancer*, the *Providence*, the *Ocean Mist*, the

Torvanger – all standard San Piedro gill-netters. The *Mystery Maid*, a halibut and black cod schooner, had fared badly of late and was in the process of being overhauled. Her starboard hull plate had been removed, her engine dismantled, and her crankshaft and rod bearings lay exposed. On the dock at her bow lay a pile of pipe fittings, two rusted diesel barrels, a scattering of broken plate glass, and the hulk of a marine battery on which empty paint cans were stacked. A sheen of oil lay on the water just below where scraps of rug had been nailed down to act as dockside bumpers.

Today there were a lot of seagulls present. Normally they foraged around the salmon cannery, but now they sat on drag floats or buoy bags without stirring a feather, as if made of clay, or rode the tide in Amity Harbor, occasionally flaring overhead, riding the winds with their heads swiveling. Sometimes they alighted on unattended boats and scavenged desperately for deck scraps. Fishermen sometimes shot duck loads at them, but for the most part the gulls were given free rein on the docks; their gray white droppings stained everything.

An oil drum had been turned onto its side before the *Susan Marie*, and on it sat Dale Middleton and Leonard George, dressed in mechanics' grease suits. Jan Sorensen leaned against a plywood garbage Dumpster; Marty Johansson stood with his feet planted wide, his forearms folded across his bare chest, his T-shirt tucked into his pants waist. Directly beside the sheriff stood William Gjovaag with a cigar lodged between his fingers. Abel Martinson had perched himself on the bow gunnel of the *Susan Marie* and listened to the fishermen's conversation with his boots dangling above the waterline.

San Piedro fishermen – in those days, at least – went out at dusk to work the seas. Most of them were gill-netters, men who traveled into solitary waters and dropped their nets into the currents salmon swam. The nets hung down like curtains in the dark water and the salmon, unsuspecting, swam into them.

A gill-netter passed his night hours in silence, rocking on the sea and waiting patiently. It was important that his character be adapted to this, otherwise his chances of success were dubious.

At times the salmon ran in such narrow waters that men had to fish for them in sight of one another, in which case arguments brewed. The man who'd been cut off by another man up tide might motor abreast of the interloper in order to shake a gaff at him and curse him up and down as a fish thief. There were, on occasion, shouting matches at sea, but far more often a man was alone all night and had no one, even, to argue with. Some who had tried this lonely sort of life had given up and joined the crews of purse seiners or of long-line halibut schooners. Gradually Anacortes, a town on the mainland, became home to the big boats with crews of four or more, the Amity Harbor fleet home to one-man gill-netters. It was something San Piedro prided itself on, the fact that its men had the courage to fish alone even in inclement weather. An ethic, with time, asserted itself in island souls, that fishing alone was better than fishing other ways, so that the sons of fishermen, when they dreamed at night, dreamed of going forth in their lonely boats and hauling from the sea with their nets large salmon that other men would find impressive.

Thus on San Piedro the silent-toiling, autonomous gill-netter became the collective image of the *good* man. He who was too gregarious, who spoke too much and too ardently desired the company of others, their conversation and their laughter, did not have what life required. Only insofar as he struggled successfully with the sea could a man lay claim to his place in things.

San Piedro men learned to be silent. Occasionally, though, and with enormous relief, they communicated with one another on the docks at dawn. Though tired and still busy, they spoke from deck to deck of what had happened during the night and of things only they could understand. The intimacy of it, the comfort of other voices giving credence to their private myths, prepared them to meet their wives with less distance than they might otherwise bring home after fishing. In short, they were lonely men and products of geography – island men who on occasion recognized that they wished to speak but couldn't.

Ishmael Chambers knew, as he approached the knot of men

gathered before the *Susan Marie*, that he was not a part of this fraternity of fishermen, that furthermore he made his living with words and was thus suspect to them. On the other hand he had the advantage of the prominently wounded and of any veteran whose war years are forever a mystery to the uninitiated. These latter were things that solitary gill-netters could appreciate and offset their distrust of a word shaper who sat behind a typewriter all day.

They nodded at him and with slight alterations in posture included him in their circle. 'Figure'd you'd a heard by now,' said the sheriff. 'Probably know more 'n I do.'

'Hard to believe,' answered Ishmael.

William Gjovaag tucked his cigar between his teeth. 'It happens,' he grunted. 'You go fishing, it happens.'

'Well, yeah,' said Marty Johansson. 'But Jesus Christ.' He shook his head and rocked on his heels.

The sheriff brought his left leg down from the piling, hitched his trousers at the thigh and brought his right up, then settled his elbow on his knees.

'You see Susan Marie?' asked Ishmael.

'I did,' said Art. 'Boy.'

'Three kids,' said Ishmael. 'What's she going to do?'

'I don't know,' said the sheriff.

'She say anything?'

'Not a word.'

'Well, what's she *going* to say?' put in William Gjovaag. 'What can she say? Jesus Christ.'

Ishmael understood by this that Gjovaag disapproved of journalism. He was a sunburned, big-bellied, tattooed gill-netter with the watery eyes of a gin drinker. His wife had left him five years before; William lived on his boat.

'Excuse me, Gjovaag,' said Ishmael.

'I don't need to excuse nothing,' Gjovaag answered. 'Fuck you anyhow, Chambers.'

Everybody laughed. It was all good-natured, sort of. Ishmael Chambers understood that.

'Do you know what happened?' he asked the sheriff.

'That's just what I'm trying to straighten out,' said Art Moran. 'That's just what we're talking about.'

'Art wants to know where we all was fishing,' Marty Johansson explained. 'He – '

'Don't need to know where *everyone* was at,' Sheriff Moran cut in. 'I'm just trying to figure out where Carl went last night. Where he fished. Who maybe saw him or talked to him last. That kind of thing, Marty.'

'I saw him,' said Dale Middleton. 'We ran out of the bay together.'

'You mean you *followed* him out,' said Marty Johansson. 'I bet you followed him out, didn't you?'

Younger fishermen like Dale Middleton were apt to spend considerable time each day – at the San Piedro Cafe or the Amity Harbor Restaurant – rooting for information. They wanted to know where the fish were running, how other men had done the night before, and where – exactly – they had done it. The seasoned and successful, like Carl Heine, ignored them as a matter of course. As a result he could count on being tailed to the fishing grounds: if a man wouldn't speak he was followed. On a foggy night his pursuers had to run in close and were more apt to lose their quarry altogether, in which case they turned to their radios, checking in with various compatriots whom they invariably found to be checking in with them: hapless voices tuned to one another in the hope of some shred of knowledge. The most respected men, in accordance with the ethos that had evolved on San Piedro, pursued no one and cultivated radio silence. Occasionally others would approach them in their boats, see who it was, and turn immediately away, knowing there would be neither idle conversation nor hard information about the fish they pursued. Some men shared, others didn't. Carl Heine was in the latter category.

'All right, I followed him,' said Dale Middleton. 'The guy'd been bringing in a lot of fish.'

'What time was that?' asked the sheriff.

35

'Six-thirty, around there.'

'You see him after that?'

'Yeah. Out at Ship Channel Bank. With a lot of other guys. After silvers.'

'It was foggy last night,' said Ishmael Chambers. 'You must have been fishing in close.'

'No,' said Dale. 'I just saw him setting. Before the fog. Maybe seven-thirty? Eight o'clock?'

'I saw him, too,' said Leonard George. 'He was all set. Out on the bank. He was in.'

'What time was that?' said the sheriff.

'Early,' said Leonard. 'Eight o'clock.'

'Nobody saw him later than that? Nobody saw him after eight?'

'I was outa there by ten myself,' Leonard George explained. 'There was nothing doing, no fish. I ran up to Elliot Head real slow like. A fog run. I had my horn going.'

'Me, too,' said Dale Middleton. 'Most everybody took off 'fore long. We came over and got into Marty's fish.' He grinned. 'Had a pretty fair night there, too.'

'Did Carl go up to Elliot?' asked the sheriff.

'Didn't see him,' Leonard said. 'But that don't mean nothing. Like I said, fog soup.'

'I doubt he moved,' put in Marty Johansson. 'I'm just guessing on that, but Carl never moved much. He made up his mind 'n' stuck where he was. Probably pulled some fish off Ship Channel, too. Never did see him at the head, no.'

'Me neither,' said Dale Middleton.

'But you saw him at Ship Channel,' said the sheriff. 'Who else was there? You remember?'

'Who else?' said Dale. 'There was two dozen boats, easy. Even more, but Jesus, who knows?'

'Soup,' said Leonard George. 'Real thick fog. You couldn't see nothing out there.'

'Which boats?' asked Art Moran.

'Well, okay,' said Leonard, 'let's see now. I saw the *Kasilof*, the

Islander, the *Mogul*, the *Eclipse* – this was all out at Ship Channel I'm talking about – '

'The *Antarctic*,' said Dale Middleton. 'She was out there.'

'The *Antarctic*, yeah,' said Leonard.

'What about over the radio?' said Art Moran. 'You hear anybody else? Anybody you didn't see?'

'Vance Cope,' said Leonard. 'You know Vance? The *Providence*? I talked with him a little.'

'You talked with him a lot,' said Marty Johansson. 'I heard you guys all the way over to the head. Jesus Christ, Leonard –'

'Anybody else?' said the sheriff.

'The *Wolf Chief*,' answered Dale. 'I heard Jim Ferry and Hardwell. The *Bergen* was out at Ship Channel.'

'That it?'

'I guess,' said Leonard. 'Yeah.'

'The *Mogul*,' said Art. 'Whose boat is that?'

'Moulton,' replied Marty Johansson. 'He got it from the Laneys last spring.'

'What about the *Islander*? Who's that?'

'The *Islander* is Miyamoto,' said Dale Middleton. 'Ain't that right? The middle one?'

'The oldest,' Ishmael Chambers explained. 'Kabuo – he's the oldest. The middle is Kenji. He's working at the cannery.'

'Suckers all look alike,' said Dale. 'Never could tell them guys apart.'

'Japs,' William Gjovaag threw in. He tossed the stub of his cigar into the water beside the *Susan Marie*.

'All right, look,' said Art Moran. 'You see those guys like Hardwell or Cope or Moulton or anybody, you tell them they ought to come talk to me. I want to know if anybody spoke with Carl last night, from all those guys – you got this? From every last one of them.'

'Sheriff's sounding like a hard-ass,' said Gjovaag. 'Ain't this just a accident?'

'Of course it is,' said Art Moran. 'But still, a man's dead, William. I've got a report to write up.'

'A gud man,' said Jan Sorensen, who spoke with a hint of Danish in his voice. 'A gud fisherman.' He shook his head.

The sheriff brought his leg down from the piling and with care repaired the tuck of his shirt. 'Abel,' he said. 'Why don't you square away the launch and meet me back up at the office? I'm going to walk up with Chambers here. Me and him've got things to discuss.'

But it was not until they'd left the docks altogether and turned onto Harbor Street that Art Moran quit speaking idly and came to the point with Ishmael. 'Look,' he said. 'I know what you're thinking. You're gonna do an article that says Sheriff Moran suspects foul play and is investigating, am I right?'

'I don't know what to say,' said Ishmael Chambers. 'I don't know anything about it yet. I was hoping you'd fill me in.'

'Well, sure, I'll fill you in,' said Art Moran. 'But you got to promise me something first. You won't say anything about an investigation, all right? If you want to quote me on the subject here's my quote: Carl Heine drowned by accident, or something like that, you make it up, but don't say anything about no investigation. Because there isn't one.'

'You want me to lie?' asked Ishmael Chambers. 'I'm supposed to make up a phony quote?'

'Off the record?' said the sheriff. 'Okay, there's an investigation. Some tricky, funny little facts floating around – could mean anything, where we stand now. Could be murder, could be manslaughter, could be an accident – could be *anything*. Point is, we just don't know yet. But you go telling everyone that on the front page of the *Review*, we aren't ever going to find out.'

'What about the guys you just talked to, Art? You know what they're going to do? William Gjovaag's going to be telling everyone he can you're snooping around looking for a killer.'

'That's different,' insisted Art Moran. 'That's a rumor, isn't it? And around here there's always going to be rumors like that even if I'm *not* investigating *anything*. In this case we want to leave it to the killer – if there *is* a killer, remember – to figure what he

38

hears is just gossip. We'll just let rumor work for us, confuse him. And anyway I've got to be asking questions. I don't have much choice about that, do I? If people want to guess what I'm driving at it's their business, I can't help it. But I'm not going to have any announcement in the newspaper about any sheriff's investigation.'

'Sounds like you think whoever it is, he lives right here on the island. Is that what – '

'Look,' said Art Moran, halting. 'As far as the *San Piedro Review* is concerned there *is* no "whoever", okay? Let's you and I be clear on that.'

'I'm clear on it,' said Ishmael. 'All right, I'll quote you as calling it an accident. You keep me posted on what develops.'

'A deal,' said Art. 'A deal. I find anything, you're the first to know. How's that? You got what you want now?'

'Not yet,' said Ishmael. 'I've still got this story to write. So will you give me a few answers about this *accident*?'

'Now you're talking,' said Art Moran. 'Fire away. Ask.'

5

After the morning recess had drawn to a close, Horace Whaley, the Island County coroner, swore softly on the courtroom Bible and edged into the witness box, where he seized the oak armrests between his fingers and blinked behind steel-rimmed spectacles at Alvin Hooks. Horace was by inclination a private man, nearing fifty now, with a sprawling portwine stain on the left side of his forehead that he often fingered unconsciously. In appearance he was tidy and meticulous, storklike and slender – though not so thin as Art Moran – and wore his starched trousers high on his narrow waist and his scant hair slicked from right to left with pomade. Horace Whaley's eyes bulged – his thyroid gland was overactive – and swam, too, behind his spectacles. Something attenuated, a nervous caution, suggested itself in all his movements.

Horace had served as a medical officer for twenty months in the Pacific theater and had suffered in that period from sleep deprivation and from a generalized and perpetual tropical malaise that had rendered him, in his own mind, ineffective. Wounded men in his care had died, they'd died while in his sleepless daze Horace was responsible for them. In his head these men and their bloody wounds mingled into one recurring dream.

Horace had been at his desk doing paperwork on the morning of September 16. The evening before, a woman of ninety-six had died at the San Piedro Rest Home, and another of eighty-one had expired while splitting kindling wood and had been discovered sprawled across her chopping block, a milk goat nuzzling her face, by a child delivering apples in a wheelbarrow. And so Horace was filling in the blanks on two certificates of death, and doing so in triplicate, when the phone beside him rang. He brought the receiver to his ear irritably; since the war he could not do too many things at once and at the moment, busier than he liked to be, did not wish to speak to anyone.

It was under these circumstances that he heard about the death of Carl Heine, a man who had endured the sinking of the *Canton* and who, like Horace himself, had survived Okinawa – only to die, it now appeared, in a gill-netting boat accident.

The body, on a canvas stretcher, its booted feet sticking out, had been borne in by Art Moran and Abel Martinson twenty minutes later, the sheriff wheezing under his end of the load, his deputy tight-lipped and grimacing, and laid on its back on Horace Whaley's examination table. It was wrapped by way of a shroud in two white wool blankets of the type issued to navy men and of which there was a great surplus nine years after the war, so that every fishing scow on San Piedro Island seemed to have half a dozen or more. Horace Whaley peeled back one of these blankets and, fingering the birthmark on the left side of his forehead, peered in at Carl Heine. The jaw had set open, he saw, and the vast mouth was a stiffened maw down which the dead man's tongue had disappeared. There were a large number of broken blood vessels in the whites of the deceased's eyes.

Horace pulled the blanket over Carl Heine again and turned his attention to Art Moran, who stood immediately at his side.

'Goddamn,' he said. 'Where'd you find him?'

'White Sand Bay,' Art replied.

Art told the coroner about the drifting boat, the silence and the lights on board the *Susan Marie* and about bringing the dead man up in his net. How Abel went to fetch his pickup truck and the canvas stretcher from the fire station and how together, while a small crowd of fishermen looked on and asked questions, they'd loaded Carl up and brought him in. 'I'm going over to see his wife,' Art added. 'I don't want word to reach her some other way. So I'll be back, Horace. Real soon. But I've got to see Susan Marie first.'

Abel Martinson stood at the end of the examination table

exerting himself, Horace observed, to grow accustomed to this idea of conversing in the presence of a dead man. The toe of Carl Heine's right boot poked out of the blankets just in front of him.

'Abel,' said Art Moran. 'Maybe you better stay here with Horace. Give him a hand, if he needs it.'

The deputy nodded. He took the hat he held in his hand and placed it beside an instrument tray. 'Good,' he said. 'Okay.'

'Fine,' said the sheriff. 'I'll be back soon. Half an hour to an hour.'

When he was gone Horace peered in at Carl Heine's face again – letting Art's young deputy wait in silence – then washed his glasses at the sink. 'Tell you what,' he said at last and shut the water off. 'You go on across the hall and sit in my office, all right? There's some magazines in there and a radio and a thermos of coffee if you want it. And if it comes about I've got to shift this body around and I need your help, I'll call for you. Sound fair enough, deputy?'

'Okay,' said Abel Martinson. 'You call me.'

He picked up his hat and carried it out with him. *Damn kid*, Horace said to himself. Then he dried his steel-rimmed glasses on a towel and, because he was fastidious, got his surgical gown on. He pulled on his gloves, removed the shroud of blankets from Carl Heine, and then, methodically, using angled scissors, cut away the rubber bib overalls, dropping pieces of them in a canvas bin. When the overalls were gone he began on the T-shirt and cut away Carl Heine's work pants and underwear and pulled off Carl's boots and socks, out of which seawater ran. He put all the clothes in a sink.

There was a pack of matches, mostly used, in one pocket, and a small shuttle of cotton twine stuffed in another. A knife sheath had been knotted to a belt loop on his work pants, but no knife was in it. The sheath had been unsnapped and left open.

In Carl Heine's left front pocket was a watch that had stopped at one forty-seven. Horace dropped it into a manila envelope.

The body – despite the two hours it had spent in transport

from White Sand Bay to the dock east of the ferry terminal and from there in the back of Abel Martinson's truck up First Hill and into the alley behind the courthouse (where the morgue and the coroner's office could be found beyond a set of double doors that gave onto the courthouse basement) – had not thawed perceptibly, Horace noted. It was pink, the color of salmon flesh, and the eyes had turned back in the head. It was also blatantly and exceedingly powerful, stout and thick muscled, the chest broad, the quadriceps muscles of the thighs pronounced, and Horace Whaley could not help but observe that here was an extraordinary specimen of manhood, six foot three and two hundred thirty-five pounds, bearded, blond, and built in the solid manner of a piece of statuary, as though the parts were made of granite – though, too, there was something apelike, inelegant, and brutish in the alignment of the arms and shoulders. Horace felt a familiar envy stirring and despite himself noted the girth and heft of Carl Heine's sexual organs. The fisherman had not been circumcised and his testicles were taut and hairless. They had pulled up toward his body in the frigid seawater, and his penis, at least twice as large as Horace's own, even frozen, lay fat and pink against his left leg.

The Island County coroner coughed twice, dryly, and circumnavigated his examination table. He began, consciously, for this would be necessary, to think of Carl Heine, a man he knew, as *the deceased* and not as Carl Heine. The deceased's right foot had locked itself behind the left, and Horace now exerted himself to free it. It was necessary to pull hard enough to tear ligaments in the deceased's groin, and this Horace Whaley did.

A coroner's job is to do certain things most people would never dream of doing. Horace Whaley was ordinarily a family physician, one of three on San Piedro. He worked with fishermen, their children, their wives. His peers were unwilling to examine the dead, and so the job had fallen to him, by default as it were. Thus he'd had these *experiences*; he'd seen things most men couldn't look at. The winter before he'd seen a crabber's body recovered out of West Port Jensen Bay after two full months' immersion. The crabber's skin resembled soap more than anything; he seemed encased in it, a kind of ambergris. On Tarawa he had seen the bodies of men who had died facedown in shallow water. The warm tides had washed over them for days, and the skin had loosened from their limbs. He remembered one soldier in particular from whose hands the skin had peeled like fine transparent gloves; even the fingernails had come away. There were no dog tags, but Horace had been able to obtain excellent fingerprints and make an identification anyway.

He knew a little about drowning. He had seen a fisherman in '49 who had been eaten about the face by crabs and crayfish. They'd fed steadily on the softest portions – the eyelids, the lips, to a lesser extent the ears – so that in these areas the face was intensely green. This he had seen in the Pacific war, too, along with other men who had died in tidal pools, astonishingly intact beneath the waterline but entirely eaten – to the bone – by sand flies wherever flesh lay exposed to air. And he had seen a man half-mummy, half-skeleton, floating in the waters of the China Sea, eaten from below while his back side, sun dried, gradually turned brown and leathery. After the sinking of the *Canton* there were parts of men floating around for miles that even the sharks had forsaken. The navy had not taken time to collect these parts; there were living men to attend to.

Carl Heine was the fourth deceased gill-netter Horace had examined in five years. Two others had died in a fall storm and washed up on the mud flats of Lanheedron Island. The third, recalled Horace, was an interesting case – the summer of '50, four years earlier. A fisherman named Vilderling – Alec Vilderling. His wife typed for Klaus Hartmann, who sold real estate in Amity Harbor. Vilderling and his partner had set their net and underneath the summer moon had shared in the lee of their bow-picker's cabin a bottle of Puerto Rican rum. Then Vilderling, it seemed, had decided to empty his bladder into the salt water. With his pants undone he had fallen in and, to his partner's horror, had thrashed once or twice before disappearing altogether beneath the surface of the moon-addled sea. Vilderling, it appeared, could not swim.

His partner, a boy of nineteen named Kenny Lynden, hurled himself in after him. Vilderling, hung up in his net, struggled as the boy tried to free him. Though bleary with rum, Kenny Lynden somehow managed to cut Vilderling loose with a pocketknife and haul him back to the surface. But that was all he could do. Vilderling had ceased to live.

The interesting thing, Horace Whaley recalled, was that in the purely technical sense Alec Vilderling had not drowned. He had inhaled a large volume of seawater, yet his lungs were entirely dry. Horace had at first offered the conjecture in his notes that the deceased's larynx had clamped down – a spastic closure – to prevent liquid from reaching the deeper air passages. But this could not explain the clear distension of the lungs, which had to have been caused by the pressure of the sea, and so he revised his initial hypothesis and entered in his final report that the salt water swallowed by Alec Vilderling had been absorbed into his blood-stream while he yet lived. In this case the official cause of death, he wrote, was anoxia – a deprivation of oxygen to the brain – as well as an acute disturbance to the composition of the blood.

Chief among his current considerations as he stood brooding over Carl Heine's naked form was to determine the precise cause of Carl's demise – or rather to determine how the deceased had become the deceased, for to think of the slab of flesh before him as *Carl*, Horace reminded himself, would make doing what he had to do difficult. Only the week before, the deceased, in rubber boots and a clean T-shirt – perhaps the T-shirt just now cut to pieces with a pair of angled surgical scissors – had carried his eldest, a boy of six, into Horace's office in Amity Harbor and pointed out a cut on the boy's foot, sliced open against the metal strut of an overturned wheelbarrow. Carl had held the boy against the table while Horace put in the sutures. Unlike other fathers to whom this task had fallen, he gave no instructions to his son. He did not allow the boy to move, and the boy cried only when the first stitch went in and thereafter held his breath. When it was over Carl lifted the boy from the table and held him in the cradling manner one holds an infant. Horace had said that the foot must be elevated and went for a set of crutches. Then, as was his habit, Carl Heine paid for the work in cash, taking neat bills from his wallet. He was not profusely thankful and there was that silence about him, that bearded, gruff, and giant silence, that unwillingness to engage the protocols of island life. A man of his size, Horace thought, must take it as a duty to imply no menace or risk that his neighbors will be wary of him. Yet Carl did little to assuage the natural distrust an ordinary man feels for a man of physical stature. He went about his life deliberately instead, taking no time and making no gestures to suggest to others his harmlessness. Horace remembered seeing him one day flicking his lock blade open and then shutting it against the flank of his leg, flicking and shutting it again and again, but as for whether this was a habit or a threat, a nervous tic or an announcement of his prowess, Horace Whaley couldn't tell. The man seemed to have no friends. There was no one who could insult him in jest or speak lightly with him about unimportant matters, though on the other hand he was on courteous terms with almost everyone. And furthermore other men admired him because he was powerful and good at his work, because on the sea he was thoroughly competent and even in his rough way elegantly so; still, their admiration was colored by their distrust of his size and his brooding deliberation.

No, Carl Heine was not amiable, but neither was he a bad sort. He had once, before the war, been a boy on the football team, like other schoolboys in most ways: he'd had a large group of friends, he'd worn a letterman's jacket, he'd spoken when there was no reason to speak, for fun. He had been that way and then the war had come – the war Horace himself had been to. And how to explain? What could he say to others? There was no longer any speaking for the hell of it, no opening one's mouth just to have it open, and if others would read darkness into his silence, well then, darkness was there, wasn't it? There'd been the darkness of the war in Carl Heine, as there was in Horace himself.

But – *the deceased*. He must think of Carl as the deceased, a bag of guts, a sack of parts, and not as the man who had so recently brought his son in; otherwise the job could not be done.

Horace Whaley placed the heel of his right hand against the solar plexus of the dead man. He placed his left hand over it and began to pump in the manner of someone attempting to resuscitate a drowning victim. And as he did so a foam, something like shaving cream though flecked with pink-hued blood from the lungs, mushroomed at the deceased's mouth and nose.

Horace stopped and inspected this. He leaned down over the deceased man's face, scrutinizing the foam closely. His gloved hands were still clean, they had touched nothing except the chilled skin of the deceased's chest, and so he took from beside his instrument tray a pad and pencil and noted for himself the color and texture of this extruded foam that was abundant enough to cover the deceased's bearded chin and his mustache almost entirely. It was a result, Horace knew, of air, mucus, and seawater all mingled by respiration, which meant the deceased had been alive at submersion. He had not died first and then been cast beneath the waves. Carl Heine had gone in breathing.

But anoxia, like Alec Vilderling, or a waterlogged, choking asphyxiation? Like most people, Horace felt the need not merely to know but to envision clearly whatever had happened; furthermore it was his obligation to envision it clearly so that in the official register of Island County deaths the truth, however painful, might be permanently inscribed. Carl Heine's dark struggle, his effort to hold his breath, the volume of water that had filled the vacuum of his gut, his profound unconsciousness and final convulsions, his terminal gasps in the grip of death as the last of the air leaked out of him and his heart halted and his brain ceased to consider anything – they were all recorded, or not recorded, in the slab of flesh that lay on Horace Whaley's examination table. It was his duty to find out the truth.

For a moment Horace stood with his hands linked across his belly and debated silently the merits of opening the deceased man's chest so as to get at the evidence in the heart and lungs. It was in this posture that he noted – how had he missed it before? – the wound to the skull over the dead man's left ear. 'I'll be damned,' he said aloud.

With a pair of barber's shears he cut hair out of the way until the outlines of this wound emerged cleanly. The bone had fractured and caved in considerably over an area of about four inches. The skin had split open, and from the laceration of the scalp a tiny strand of pink brain material protruded. Whatever had caused this wound – a narrow, flat object about two inches wide – had left its telltale outline behind in the deceased man's head. It was precisely the sort of lethal impression Horace had seen at least two dozen times in the Pacific war, the result of close-in combat, hand to hand, and made by a powerfully wielded gun butt. The Japanese field soldier, trained in the art of *kendo*, or stick fighting, was exceptionally proficient at killing in this manner. And the majority of Japs, Horace recalled, inflicted death over the left ear, swinging in from the right.

Horace inserted a razor into one of his scalpels and poked it into the deceased's head. He pressed the razor to the bone and guided it through the hair, describing an arc across the top of the deceased's skull literally from ear to ear. It was a skillful and steady incision, like drawing a curved line with a pencil across the crown of the head, a fluid and graceful curve. In this manner he was able to peel back the dead man's face as though it were the skin of a grapefruit or an orange and turn his forehead inside out so that it rested against his nose.

Horace peeled down the back of the head, too, then lay his scalpel in the sink, rinsed his gloves, dried them, and brought out a hacksaw from his instrument cupboard.

He set about the work of sawing through the dead man's skullcap. After twenty minutes it became necessary to turn the body over, and so with reluctance Horace crossed the hall to Abel Martinson, who sat in a chair doing nothing at all, his legs crossed, his hat in his lap.

'Need a hand,' said the coroner.

The deputy rose and put his hat on his head. 'Sure,' he said. 'Glad to help.'

'You won't be glad,' said Horace. 'I've made an incision across the top of his head. His skull is exposed. It isn't pretty.'

'Okay,' said the deputy. 'Thanks for telling me.'

They went in and without speaking turned the body over, Abel Martinson pushing from one side, the coroner reaching across and pulling from the other, and then, with his head hung over the sink, Abel Martinson vomited. He was dabbing his mouth with the corner of his handkerchief when Art Moran came through the door. 'Now what?' asked the sheriff.

Abel, in answer, pointed a finger at Carl Heine's corpse. 'I puked again,' he said.

Art Moran looked at Carl's face turned inside out, the skin of it peeled back like a grape, a bloody foam that looked like shaving cream clinging to his chin. Then he turned away from seeing it.

'Me, too,' said Abel Martinson. 'I got no stomach for this neither.'

'I'm not blaming you,' the sheriff answered. 'Jesus H. Christ. *Jesus Christ.*'

But he stood there watching anyway while Horace, in his surgical gown, worked methodically with his hacksaw. He watched while Horace removed the dead man's skullcap and placed it beside the dead man's shoulder.

'This is called the dura mater.' Horace pointed with his scalpel. 'This membrane here? Right under his skull? This right here is the dura mater.'

He took the dead man's head between his hands and with some effort – the ligaments of the neck were extremely rigid – twisted it to the left.

'Come over here, Art,' he said.

49

The sheriff seemed aware of the necessity of doing so; nevertheless, he didn't move. Certainly, thought Horace, he had learned in his work that there were distasteful moments about which he had no choice. In the face of these it was best to move quickly and without reservations, as Horace himself did as a matter of principle. But the sheriff was a man of inherited anxieties. It was not really in him to go over there and see what was under Carl Heine's face.

Horace Whaley knew this: that the sheriff did not want to see what was inside of Carl Heine's head. Horace had seen Art this way before, chewing his Juicy Fruit and grimacing, rubbing his lips with the ball of his thumb and squinting while he thought things over. 'It'll just take a minute,' Horace urged him. 'One quick look, Art. So you can see what we're up against. I wouldn't ask if it wasn't important.'

Horace indicated for Art Moran the blood that had clotted in the dura mater and the tear in it where the piece of brain protruded. 'He got hit pretty hard with something fairly flat, Art. Puts me in mind of a type of gun butt wound I saw a few times in the war. One of those *kendo* strikes the Japs used.'

'*Kendo*?' said Art Moran.

'Stick fighting,' Horace explained. 'Japs are trained in it from when they're kids. How to kill with sticks.'

'Ugly,' said the sheriff. 'Jesus.'

'Look away,' said Horace. 'I'm going to cut through the dura mater now. I want you to see something else.'

The sheriff turned his back deliberately. 'You're pale,' he said to Abel Martinson. 'Why don't you go sit down?'

'I'm okay,' answered Abel. He stood looking into the sink with his handkerchief in his hand and leaned hard against the counter.

Horace showed the sheriff three fragments of the deceased's skull that had lodged in the tissue of his brain. 'That what killed him?' Art asked.

'That's complicated,' answered Horace Whaley. 'Could be he took a hit to the head, then went over the side and drowned.

Or maybe he hit his head *after* he drowned. Or *while* he was drowning. I don't know for sure.'

'Can you find out?'

'Maybe.'

'When?'

'I have to look inside his chest, Art. At his heart and lungs. And even that might not tell me much.'

'His chest?'

'That's right.'

'What're the possibilities?' said the sheriff.

'Possibilities?' said Horace Whaley. 'All kinds of possibilities, Art. Anything could have happened, and all kinds of things *do* happen. I mean, maybe he had a *heart* attack that pitched him over the side. Maybe a stroke, maybe alcohol. But all I want to know just now is did he get knocked in the head first and *then* go over? Because I know from this foam' – he pointed at it with his scalpel – 'that Carl went in breathing. He was respiratory when he hit the water. So my guess right now is that he drowned, Art. With the head wound an obvious contributing factor. Banged himself on a fairlead, maybe. Setting his net and got a little careless – hung up his buckle and went over. I'm inclined to put all that in my report just now. But I don't know for sure yet. Maybe when I see his heart and lungs everything is going to change.'

Art Moran stood rubbing his lip and blinked hard at Horace Whaley. 'That bang to the head,' he said. 'That bang to the head is sort of . . . *funny*, you know?'

Horace Whaley nodded. 'Could be,' he said.

'Couldn't it be somebody hit him?' asked the sheriff. 'Isn't that a possibility?'

'You want to play Sherlock Holmes?' asked Horace. 'You going to play detective?'

'Not really. But Sherlock Holmes isn't here, is he? And this wound in Carl's head is.'

'That's true,' said Horace. 'You got that part right.'

Then – and afterward he would remember this, during the

trial of Kabuo Miyamoto, Horace Whaley would recall having spoken these words (though he would not repeat them on the witness stand) – he said to Art Moran that if he were inclined to play Sherlock Holmes he ought to start looking for a Jap with a bloody gun butt – a right-handed Jap, to be precise.

6

Horace Whaley scratched the birthmark on his forehead and watched the falling snow beyond the courtroom windows. It was coming harder now, much harder, wind whipped and silent, though the wind could be heard pushing against the beams in the courthouse attic. *My pipes*, thought Horace. *They'll freeze.*

Nels Gudmundsson rose a second time, slipped his thumbs behind his suspenders, and noted with his one good eye that Judge Lew Fielding appeared half-asleep and was leaning heavily on the palm of his left hand, as he had throughout Horace's testimony. He was listening, Nels knew; his tired demeanor shielded an active mind from view. The judge liked to mull things soporifically.

Nels, as best he could – he had arthritis in his hips and knees – made his way to the witness stand. 'Horace,' he said. 'Good morning.'

'Morning, Nels,' answered the coroner.

'You've said quite a bit,' Nels Gudmundsson pointed out. 'You've told the court in detail about your autopsy of the deceased, your fine background as a medical examiner, and so forth, as you've been asked to do. And I've been listening to you, Horace, like everybody else here. And – well – I'm troubled by a couple of matters.' He stopped and pinched his chin between his fingers.

'Go ahead,' urged Horace Whaley.

'Well, for example, this *foam*,' said Nels. 'I'm not sure I understand about that, Horace.'

'The foam?'

'You've testified to having applied pressure to the deceased's

53

chest and that shortly thereafter a peculiar foam appeared at his mouth and nostrils.'

'That's right,' said Horace. 'I would say this is usually the case with drowning victims. It may not appear when they're first recovered from the water, but almost as soon as someone starts removing their clothing or attempting resuscitation there it is, generally in copious amounts.'

'What would cause that?' Nels asked.

'Pressure brings it up. It results from a chemical reaction in the lungs when water mixes with air and mucus.'

'Water, air, and mucus,' said Nels. 'But what causes them to mix, Horace? This chemical reaction you speak of – what is it?'

'It's caused by breathing. It happens in the presence of respiration. It – '

'Now this is where I got confused,' interrupted Nels. 'Earlier, I mean. When you were testifying. You say this foam is *only* produced when you've got water, mucus, and air all mixed together by a person's breathing?'

'That's right.'

'But a drowned person doesn't breathe,' said Nels. 'So how does this foam . . . you can see why I'm confused.'

'Oh, sure,' said Horace. 'I think I can make this clear. It's formed – this foam – in the *early* stages. The victim is submerged and begins to struggle. Finally he begins to swallow water, you see, and as he does the air in his lungs is forced out under pressure – and this gives rise to the foam I've testified about. The chemical reaction occurs at the time the drowning victim is *ceasing* to breathe. Or breathing his final breaths.'

'I see,' said Nels. 'So this foam, then, tells you Carl Heine in fact drowned, doesn't it?'

'Well – '

'It tells you, for example, that he wasn't murdered first – say on the deck of his boat – and then thrown overboard? Because if he was, there would be no foam, would there? Am I understanding the chemical reaction correctly? It can't happen unless the victim is breathing at the time of submersion? Is that what you said about it, Horace?'

'Yes,' said Horace. 'It tells you that. But – '

'Excuse me,' said Nels. 'Just wait a moment, now.' He made his way to where Mrs. Eleanor Dokes sat poised over her stenograph. He worked past her and nodded at the bailiff, Ed Soames, then picked out a document from the evidence table and made his way back to the witness stand.

'All right, Horace,' he said now. 'I'm returning to you the exhibit you identified earlier, in direct examination, as your autopsy report, which you've testified accurately reflects your findings and conclusions. If you would kindly take it and read back to yourself paragraph four on page four, please, we'll all wait.'

While Horace did so Nels returned to the defendant's table and sipped from a glass of water. His throat had begun to bother him; his voice had gone hoarse and reedy.

'All right,' said Horace. 'Done.'

'All right,' said Nels. 'Am I correct in saying, Horace, that paragraph four on page four of your autopsy report identifies *drowning* as the cause of Carl Heine's death?'

'Yes, it does.'

'So your conclusion was that he drowned?'

'Yes.'

'Was that unequivocal? Was there any doubt?'

'Yes, of course there's doubt. There's always doubt. You're not – '

'Just a minute, Horace,' said Nels. 'Do you wish to say that your report is inaccurate? Is that what you're trying to tell us?'

'The report is accurate,' said Horace Whaley. 'I – '

'Can you read for the court the last sentence of paragraph four, page four, of the autopsy report you have in front of you?' said Nels Gudmundsson. 'The paragraph you read silently just a moment ago? Please go ahead and read.'

'All right,' answered Horace. 'It says this, and I quote: "The presence of foam in the airway and around the lips and nose indicates beyond doubt that the victim was alive at the time of submersion." Unquote.'

'*Beyond doubt* that he was alive at the time of submersion? Is that what it says, Horace?'

'Yes, it does.'

'*Beyond doubt*,' said Nels Gudmundsson, and turned toward the jurors. 'Thank you, Horace. That's important. That's good. But there is something else I'd like to ask about now. Something in that autopsy report.'

'Okay,' said Horace, removing his glasses and biting one stem. 'Go ahead and ask.'

'Well, page two, then,' said Nels. 'At the top? The second paragraph, I believe?' He went to the defendant's table and leafed through his own copy. 'Paragraph two,' he said. 'Yes, that's it. If you could read that back for the court, please? Just the first line will do, Horace.'

'Quote,' answered Horace Whaley stiffly. '"A secondary and minor laceration of the right hand is noted, of recent origin, and extends laterally from the fold between the thumb and forefinger to the outside of the wrist."'

'A cut,' said Nels. 'Is that right? Carl Heine cut his hand?'

'Yes.'

'Any idea how?'

'None, really. I could speculate, though.'

'That won't be necessary,' Nels said. 'But this cut, Horace. You say in your report that it's of "recent origin". Any idea how recent?'

'Very. Very recent, I'd say.'

'Very,' said Nels. 'How much is "very"?'

'*Very* recent,' repeated Horace. 'I would say he cut his hand on the night he died, and in the hour or two just preceding his death. *Very* recent, okay?'

'Hour or two?' said Nels. 'Two hours is possible?'

'Yes.'

'What about three? Or four, Horace? What about *twenty-four*?'

56

'Twenty-four is out of the question. The wound was fresh, Nels. Four hours – maybe, at the outside. No more than four, absolutely.'

'All right,' said Nels. 'He cut his hand, then. No more than four hours before he drowned.'

'That's correct,' said Horace Whaley.

Nels Gudmundsson began to pull, once again, at the wattles of skin at his throat. 'Just one more thing, Horace,' he said. 'I have to ask about something else that confused me during your testimony. This wound to the deceased's head you mentioned.'

'Yes,' said Horace Whaley. 'The wound. All right.'

'Can you tell us again what it looked like?'

'Yes,' repeated Horace. 'It was a laceration about two and a half inches long just slightly above the left ear. The bone under it had fractured over an area of about four inches. There was also a small bit of brain material showing through the laceration. It was evident from the impression left behind in the skull that something narrow, something flat, had caused this injury. That's about everything, Nels.'

'Something narrow and flat had caused it,' Nels repeated. 'Is that what you saw, Horace? Or is that an inference?'

'It's my *job* to infer,' insisted Horace Whaley. 'Look, if a night watchman is struck over the head with a crowbar during the course of a robbery, the wounds you're going to see in his head will look like they were made with a crowbar. If they were made by a ball-peen hammer you can see that, too – a ball-peen leaves behind a crescent-shaped injury, a crowbar leaves, well, linear wounds with V-shaped ends. You get hit with a pistol butt, that's one thing; somebody hits you with a bottle, that's another. You fall off a motorcycle at forty miles an hour and hit your head on gravel, the gravel will leave behind patterned abrasions that don't look like anything else. So yes, I *infer* from the deceased's wound that something narrow and flat caused his injury. To infer – it's what coroners *do*.'

'The motorcyclist is an interesting example,' Nels Gudmundsson pointed out. 'Are you saying it isn't necessary to be struck by anything to produce one of these telltale wounds? That if the victim is *propelled* against an object – let's say it's gravel – his own forward motion might produce the observed injury?'

'It might,' said Horace Whaley. 'We don't know.'

'So in the present case,' said Nels Gudmundsson, 'might the injury in question, the injury to Carl Heine's skull you've spoken of, might it have been the result of *either* a blow to the head *or* the propulsion of the victim against some object? Are both possible, Horace?'

'There's no way to tell them apart,' argued Horace. 'Only that whatever made contact with his head – whether it was moving toward him or he toward it – was flat, narrow, and hard enough to fracture his skull.'

'Something flat, narrow, and hard enough to fracture his skull. Like the gunnel of a boat, Horace? Is that possible?'

'Possible, yes. If he was moving fast enough toward it. But I don't see how he might have been.'

'What about a net roller? Or one of these fairleads at the stern of a gill-netter? Are they also flat and narrow?'

'Yes. That is, flat *enough*. They – '

'Might he have hit his head on these? Is that at least a possibility?'

'Sure it's a possibility,' agreed Horace. 'Any – '

'Let me ask you something else,' said Nels. 'Is there any way a coroner can determine if a wound like this one occurred before or after death? I mean – to return to your earlier example – couldn't I poison the night watchman, watch him die, then club his lifeless corpse over the head with a crowbar and leave behind precisely the same sort of injury as if I had *killed* him by the latter method?'

'Are you asking about Carl Heine's wound?'

'I am. I want to know if *you* know something. Did he sustain the injury and then die? Or is it possible the wound to the head occurred postmortem? That he sustained it – or should we say his *corpse* sustained it – *after* Carl Heine drowned? Perhaps, say, when he was being brought up in his net by Sheriff Moran and Deputy Martinson?'

Horace Whaley thought about it. He took off his glasses; he massaged his forehead. Then he fixed the stems of his glasses once again behind his earlobes and folded his arms across his chest.

'I don't know,' he said. 'I can't answer that, Nels.'

'You don't know whether the wound to the head preceded death or not? Is that what you're saying, Horace?'

'That's what I'm saying, yes.'

'But the cause of death – unequivocally – was drowning. Is that right? Am I correct?'

'Yes.'

'It was not a wound to the head, then, that killed Carl Heine?'

'No. But – '

'No more questions,' said Nels Gudmundsson. 'Thank you, Horace. That's all.'

Art Moran, from his place in the gallery, felt a peculiar satisfaction watching Horace Whaley suffer. He remembered the insult: *Sherlock Holmes*. He remembered leaving Horace's office, hesitating before going up to Mill Run Road to bring the news to the dead man's wife.

He'd leaned against the fender of Abel Martinson's truck inspecting the hand he'd scraped that morning against a stanchion on Carl Heine's gill-netting boat. Then he'd dug in his pocket for a stick of Juicy Fruit – first his shirt pockets, next, vaguely irritated, his pants. Two remained; he'd gone through eight already. He popped one in his mouth, saved the other, then slid behind the wheel of Abel's pickup. His own car was parked in town near the docks; he'd left it there earlier that same morning when he'd gone to the harbor for the launch. It made him feel like a fool driving Abel's truck because the boy, frankly, had put too much time into it. It was a high-stacked Dodge painted burgundy in Anacortes, elaborately pin-striped and with decorative exhaust extensions pillared just behind the gleaming cab – a schoolboy's play truck, in short. Just the sort of pickup you saw in mainland towns like Everett or Bellingham, the kind kids drove around after football games or on Saturday nights, late. Art had to figure that in his high school days Abel Martinson had been moderately restless, that in the interim between then and now he had changed, and that this truck was the last vestige of his former self: thus he was loath to part with it. But he would, Art predicted, and soon. That was how things went.

Driving up to see Susan Marie Heine, Art muddled out his words in silence, revising as he went and planning his demeanor, which ought, he decided, to have a vaguely military architecture with certain nautical decorative touches – to report a man's death at sea to his widow was a task done gravely but with tragic stoicism for centuries on end, he figured. *Excuse me, Mrs. Heine. I am sorry to report that your husband, Carl Gunther Heine, was killed last night in an accident at sea. May I express the condolences of the entire community and . . .*

But this would not do. She was not unknown to him; he couldn't treat her like a stranger. After all, he saw her at church every Sunday after services pouring tea and coffee in the reception room. She always dressed impeccably for her duties as hostess, in a pillbox hat, tweed suit, and beige gloves: taking coffee from her sure hand he'd found pleasurable. She wore her blond hair pinned up under her hat and a double strand of costume pearls around her neck, a neck that reminded him of alabaster. In short she was, at twenty-eight, attractive in a way that disturbed him. Pouring coffee she called him 'Sheriff Moran' and afterward pointed out the cake and mints down the table with a gloved index finger, as if he had not noted them himself. Then she would smile at him prettily and set the coffee service down on its tray while he helped himself to the sugar.

The prospect of telling her about Carl's death was more than just unsettling to Art, and as he drove he struggled to find the proper words, the formula of phrases that would free him without too much fumbling from the message he carried to this woman. But it seemed to him there were none.

Just before the Heine place on Mill Run Road there was a turnout where in August the sheriff had picked blackberries. Here he pulled in impulsively, because he was not ready to do what was required, and with the engine of Abel's Dodge idling in neutral he popped the last stick of Juicy Fruit between his teeth and looked down the road toward the Heines'.

It was precisely the sort of home Carl *would* build, he thought – blunt, tidy, gruffly respectable, and offering no affront to the world, though at the same time inviting nobody. It sat back fifty yards from the road on three acres of alfalfa, strawberries, raspberries, and orderly vegetable gardens. Carl had cleared the land himself with a characteristic rapidity and thoroughness – he'd sold the timber to the Thorsen brothers, burned his slash piles, and poured his footing all in the space of a single winter. By April the berries were in and a post-and-beam shed-barn, and by summer Carl could be seen framing up walls and mortaring clinker brick. He had meant – or so word at church had it – to build an elaborate bungalow of the sort his father had built years before on the family farm at Island Center. He'd wanted inglenooks, somebody had said, and an overscaled fireplace and alcoves, built-in window seats and wainscoting, a battered porch base and low stone walls along his entrance walk. But in time, as he worked, he'd found himself too straightforward for all of that – he was a builder, an exacting one, but not an artist, as his wife had put it – the wainscoting, for example, was left out entirely, and he had not built the sort of river rock chimney that stood up so prominently at his father's old place (now owned by Bjorn Andreason), preferring clinker brick. What he ended up with was a blunt, sturdy house sheathed carefully with cedar shingles, testimony to its builder's exacting nature.

Art Moran, his foot on the brake, chewing his gum and fretting in silence, took in the gardens first, then the front porch with its tapered posts, and finally the overscaled trusses in the gable roof; he took in the pair of shed-roofed dormers that had, despite the original intent of asymmetry, been built formally and in tandem. And he shook his head and recollected having been inside this house, with its exposed roof rafters in the upstairs rooms and Susan Marie's oversized furniture downstairs – he'd attended, last October, an autumn church social there – but he knew he would not go inside this time. He knew that suddenly. He'd stand on the porch to deliver his news with his cap resting against one thigh, and then leave without ever entering. He understood that this was not *right*, but on the other hand what else could he do? It was too difficult; it wasn't in him. He would call Eleanor Dokes at his office when he was done, and she would alert Susan Marie's older sister, and the sister would come here before long. But he himself? There wasn't any way he could think of. It wasn't in him to sit with her through this. He would ask this widow to understand that there were matters he must attend to . . . urgent matters of a professional nature . . . he would deliver his message, offer condolences, and then in the spirit of one who knows his place simply leave Susan Marie Heine alone.

He coasted down and turned into Susan Marie's drive with Abel's truck still in neutral. From here, looking east across the rows of trained raspberry canes, the sea was visible beyond the tops of the cedars falling away along the hill. It was a fine September day of the sort they saw rarely, cloudless and June warm if you stood where there was no shade, the sunlight glinting among the whitecaps in the far distance, so that Art Moran understood what he hadn't before that Carl had built here not just for the sun it afforded but for the long view to the north and west. While Carl had cultivated his raspberries and strawberries he'd kept one eye always on the salt water.

Art pulled in behind the Heines' Bel-Air and shut the ignition down. And as he did so Carl's sons came around the corner of the house running – a boy of three or four, Art guessed, followed by another of about six, who limped. They stood beside a rhododendron bush staring, in shorts, shirtless and barefoot.

Art took a wrapper out of his shirt pocket and spit his Juicy Fruit into it. He did not want to say what he had to say with Juicy Fruit in his mouth.

'Hey there, men,' he called cheerfully through the window frame. 'Your mother home a-tall?'

The two boys didn't answer. They stared at him instead. A German shepherd came stalking around the corner of the house, and the older boy caught him by the collar and held him. 'Stay,' he said, but nothing else.

Art Moran shoved his door partway open, then took his hat from off the seat and put it on the back of his head. 'Policeman,' said the younger boy, and stepped in beside his brother. 'It's not a policeman,' answered the older boy. 'It's the sheriff or somebody like that.'

'That's right,' said Art. 'I'm Sheriff Moran, boys. Is your mother home a-tall?'

The older boy gave his brother a shove. 'Go get Mom,' he said.

They looked like their father. They were going to be big like their father, he could see that. Sun-browned, thick-limbed German children.

'You go ahead and play,' he said to them. 'I'll just go knock. You play.' He smiled down at the younger one.

But they didn't go. They watched from beside the rhodo-dendron bush while he climbed to the porch with his hat in his hand and rapped his knuckles against the front door, which was thrown open to reveal Carl's living room. Art looked in, waiting. The walls had been paneled with varnished pine board in which the knots shone luminously; Susan Marie's curtains were of a clean, smooth yellow, tied off crisply behind careful bows, ruffled, valenced, and undertiered. The concentric circles of a braided wool rug concealed most of the floorboards. In one far corner an upright piano loomed; in another sat a rolltop desk. There were twin oak rockers with embroidered cushions, twin walnut end tables astride a worn bench sofa, and a plush easy chair beside a gilt brass floor lamp. The chair had been pulled

63

up to the oversized fireplace Carl had built, inside of which stood tall, fluted andirons. The sheriff was impressed by the order of this room, its bronze, quiet, and syrupy light, and by the photographs on the wall of the various Heines and assorted Varigs who had preceded Carl and Susan Marie in the world: stout, impressive, blunt-faced Germans who never smiled for photographers.

It was a fine living room, clean and quiet. He gave Susan Marie credit for that, just as he had given Carl credit for the chimney and dormers, and while he stood there admiring her hand in everything she appeared at the top of the stairs.

'Sheriff Moran,' she called. 'Hello.'

He knew then that she hadn't heard. He knew it was up to him to say it. But he couldn't just yet – couldn't bring himself – and so he only stood there with his hat in his hand, rubbing his lips with the ball of his thumb and squinting while she came down the stairs. 'Hello,' he said. 'Mrs. Heine.'

'I was just putting the baby down,' she answered.

It was a far different woman from the one at church – the winsome fisher wife serving tea and coffee. Now she wore a dull skirt, no shoes, and no makeup. She had a diaper draped over her left shoulder, spittle stained, and her hair had not recently been washed. In her hand was a baby bottle.

'What can I do for you, sheriff?' she asked. 'Carl hasn't come home yet.'

'That's why I'm here,' Art replied. 'I'm afraid I have some . . . bad news to report. The worst sort of news, Mrs. Heine.'

She seemed at first not to understand. She looked at him as if he'd spoken in Chinese. Then she pulled the diaper from her shoulder and smiled at him, and it was his duty to make clear this mystery.

'Carl is dead,' said Art Moran. 'He died last night in a fishing accident. We found him this morning tangled in his net out in White Sand Bay.'

'Carl?' said Susan Marie Heine. 'That can't be.'

'It is, though. I know it can't be. I don't want it to be.

Believe me, I wish it wasn't true. But it is true. I've come to tell you.'

It was strange, the way she reacted. There was no way to have predicted it ahead of time. Suddenly she backed away from him, blinking, sat down hard on the bottom stair, and set the baby bottle on the floor beside her toes. She dug her elbows into her lap and began to rock with the diaper between her hands, wringing it between her fingers. 'I knew this would happen one day,' she whispered. Then she stopped rocking and stared into the living room.

'I'm sorry,' Art said. 'I'm . . . I'm going to call your sister, I think, and ask her to come on over. Is that all right with you, Mrs. Heine?'

But there was no answer, and Art could only repeat that he was sorry and step past her in the direction of the telephone.

In the back of Judge Lew Fielding's courtroom sat twenty-four
islanders of Japanese ancestry, dressed in the clothes they
reserved for formal occasions. No law compelled them to
take only these rear seats. They had done so instead because
San Piedro required it of them without calling it a law.

Their parents and grandparents had come to San Piedro as
far back as 1883. In that year two of them – Japan Joe and
Charles Jose – lived in a lean-to near Cattle Point. Thirty-nine
Japanese worked at the Port Jefferson mill, but the census taker
neglected to list them by name, referring instead to Jap Number
1, Jap Number 2, Jap Number 3, Japan Charlie, Old Jap Sam,
Laughing Jap, Dwarf Jap, Chippy, Boots, and Stumpy – names
of this sort instead of real names.

By century's turn over three hundred Japanese had arrived on
San Piedro, most of them schooner hands who jumped ship in
Port Jefferson Harbor in order to remain in the United States.
Many swam ashore with no American currency and wandered
island trails eating salmonberries and matsutake mushrooms
until they found their way to 'Jap Town': three bathhouses, two
barbershops, two churches (one Buddhist, the other a Baptist
mission), a hotel, a grocery store, a baseball diamond, an ice
cream parlor, a tofu shop, and fifty unpainted and slatternly
dwellings all fronting onto muddy roads. Within a week the
ship jumpers possessed mill jobs – stacking lumber, sweeping
sawdust, hauling slab wood, oiling machines – worth eleven
cents an hour.

Company books preserved in the Island County historical
archives record that in 1907 eighteen Japanese were injured

or maimed at the Port Jefferson mill. Jap Number 107, the books indicate, lost his hand to a ripping blade on March 12 and received an injury payment of $7.80. Jap Number 57 dislocated his right hip on May 29 when a stack of lumber toppled over.

In 1921 the mill was dismantled: all of the island's trees had been fed to the saws, so that San Piedro resembled a bald stump desert. The mill owners sold their holdings and left the island behind. The Japanese cleared strawberry fields, for strawberries grew well in San Piedro's climate and required little starting capital. All you needed, the saying went, was one horse, one plow, and a lot of children.

Soon some Japanese leased small plots of land and entered into business for themselves. Most, though, were contract farmers or sharecroppers who worked in fields owned by *hakujin*. The law said they could not own land unless they became citizens; it also said they could not become citizens so long as they were Japanese.

They saved their money in canning jars, then wrote home to their parents in Japan requesting wives be sent. Some lied and said they'd gotten rich, or sent pictures of themselves as younger men; at any rate, wives came across the ocean. They lived in cedar slat huts lit by oil lamps and slept on straw-filled ticks. The wind blew in through the cracks in the walls. At five o'clock in the morning bride and groom both could be found in the strawberry fields. In the fall, squatting between the rows, they pulled weeds or poured fertilizer out of buckets. They spread slug and weevil bait in April. They cut back the runners on the yearlings first and then on the two- and three-year-old plants. They weeded and watched for fungus and spit bugs and for the mold that grew when it rained.

In June, when the berries ripened, they took their caddies into the fields and began the task of picking. Canadian Indians came down each year to join them at working for the *hakujin*. The Indians slept at the verges of fields or in old chicken houses or barns. Some worked in the strawberry cannery. They stayed for two months, through raspberry season, then they were gone again.

But for at least a solid month each summer there were endless strawberries to pick. By an hour after dawn the first flats were mounded over, and the foreman, a white man, stood writing Roman numerals in a black book beside the name of each picker. He sorted the berries in cedar bins while men from the packing company loaded them onto flatbed trucks. The pickers went on filling flats, squatting in the numbered rows.

When the harvest was over in early July they were given a day off for the Strawberry Festival. A young girl was crowned Strawberry Princess; the *hakujin* put on a salmon bake; the Volunteer Fire Department played a softball game against the Japanese Community Center team. The Garden Club displayed strawberries and fuchsia baskets, and the chamber of commerce awarded trophies for a float competition. In the dance pavilion at West Port Jensen the night lanterns were kindled; tourists from Seattle poured forth from the excursion steamers to perform the Svenska polka, the Rhinelander, the schottische, and the hambone. Everybody came out – hay farmers, clerks, merchants, fishermen, crabbers, carpenters, loggers, net weavers, truck farmers, junk dealers, real estate brigands, hack poets, ministers, lawyers, sailors, squatters, millwrights, cedar rats, teamsters, plumbers, mushroom foragers, and holly pruners. They picnicked at Burchillville and Sylvan Grove, listened while the high school band played sluggish Sousa marches, and sprawled under trees drinking port wine.

One part bacchanal, one part tribal potlatch, one part vestigial New England supper, the entire affair hinged on the coronation of the Strawberry Princess – always a virginal Japanese maiden dressed in satin and dusted carefully across the face with rice powder – in an oddly solemn ceremony before the Island County Courthouse at sundown of the inaugural evening. Surrounded by a crescent of basketed strawberries, she received her crown with a bowed head from Amity Harbor's mayor, who wore a red sash from shoulder to waist and carried a decorated scepter.

In the hush that ensued he would announce gravely that the Department of Agriculture – he had a letter – credited their fair island with producing America's Finest Strawberry, or that King George and Queen Elizabeth, on a recent visit to the city of Vancouver, had been served San Piedro's Best for breakfast. A cheer would fly up as he stood with scepter high, his free hand about the young maiden's shapely shoulder. The girl, it turned out, was an unwitting intermediary between two communities, a human sacrifice who allowed the festivities to go forward with no uttered ill will.

The next day, at noon traditionally, the Japanese began picking raspberries.

Thus life went forward on San Piedro. By Pearl Harbor Day there were eight hundred and forty-three people of Japanese descent living there, including twelve seniors at Amity Harbor High School who did not graduate that spring. Early on the morning of March 29, 1942, fifteen transports of the U.S. War Relocation Authority took all of San Piedro's Japanese-Americans to the ferry terminal in Amity Harbor.

They were loaded onto a ship while their white neighbors looked on, people who had risen early to stand in the cold and watch this exorcising of the Japanese from their midst – friends, some of them, but the merely curious, mainly, and fishermen who stood on the decks of their boats out in Amity Harbor. The fishermen felt, like most islanders, that this exiling of the Japanese was the right thing to do, and leaned against the cabins of their stern-pickers and bow-pickers with the conviction that the Japanese must go for reasons that made sense: there was a war on and that changed everything.

During the morning recess the accused man's wife had come alone to the row of seats behind the defendant's table and asked permission to speak with her husband.

'You'll have to do it from back there,' said Abel Martinson. 'Mr. Miyamoto can turn and face you all right, but that's about it, you see. I'm not supposed to let him move around much.'

Once each afternoon, for seventy-seven days, Hatsue Miyamoto had appeared at the Island County Jail for a three o'clock visit with her husband. At first she came alone and spoke with him through a pane of glass, but then he asked her to bring the children. Thereafter she did so – two girls, eight and four, who walked behind her, and a boy of eleven months whom she carried in her arms. Kabuo was in jail on the morning their son began to walk, but in the afternoon she brought the boy and he took four steps while his father watched from behind the visiting room windowpane. Afterward she'd held him up to the glass and Kabuo spoke to him through the microphone. 'You can go further than me!' he'd said. 'You take some steps for me, okay?'

Now, in the courtroom, he turned toward Hatsue. 'How are the kids?' he said.

'They need their father,' she answered.

'Nels is working on that,' said Kabuo.

'Nels is going to move away,' said Nels. 'Deputy Martinson ought to do the same. Why don't you stand where you can watch, Abel? But give these people some privacy.'

'I can't,' replied Abel. 'Art'd kill me.'

'Art won't kill you,' Nels said. 'You know darn well Mrs. Miyamoto isn't going to slip Mr. Miyamoto any kind of weapon. Back off a little. Let them talk.'

'I can't,' said Abel. 'Sorry.'

But he sidled back about three feet anyway and pretended not to be listening. Nels excused himself.

'Where are they staying?' asked Kabuo.

'They're at your mother's. Mrs. Nakao is there. Everybody is helping out.'

'You look good. I miss you.'

'I look terrible,' answered Hatsue. 'And you look like one of Tojo's soldiers. You'd better quit sitting up so straight and tall. These jury people will be afraid of you.'

He fixed his gaze directly on hers, and she could see he was thinking about it. 'It's good to be out of that cell,' he said. 'It feels great to be out of there.'

Hatsue wanted to touch him then. She wanted to reach out and put her hand on his neck or place her fingertips against his face. This was the first time in seventy-seven days that they had not been separated by a pane of glass. For seventy-seven days she'd heard his voice only through the filter of a microphone. During this time she had never once felt composed, and she had stopped imagining their future. At night she'd brought the children into her bed, then exerted herself fruitlessly toward sleep. She had sisters, cousins, and aunts who called mornings and asked her to come for lunch. She went because she was lonely and needed to hear the sound of voices. The women made sandwiches, cakes, and tea and chattered in the kitchen while the children played, and this is how the autumn passed, with her life arrested, on hold.

Sometimes in the afternoons, Hatsue fell asleep on a sofa. While she slept these other women cared for her children, and she didn't neglect to thank them for it; but in the past she would never have done such a thing, fall asleep, drop away in the middle of a visit while her children ran about recklessly.

She was a woman of thirty-one and still graceful. She had the flat-footed gait of a barefoot peasant, a narrow waist, small breasts. She very often wore men's khaki pants, a gray cotton sweatshirt, and sandals. It was her habit in the summer to work at picking strawberries in order to bring home extra money. Her hands were stained in the picking season with berry juice. In the fields she wore a straw hat low on her head, a thing she had not done consistently in her youth, so that now around her eyes there were squint lines. Hatsue was a tall woman – five foot eight – but nevertheless able to squat low between the berry rows for quite some time without pain.

Recently she had begun to wear mascara and lipstick. She was not vain, but she understood that she was fading. It was all right with her, at thirty-one, if she faded, for it had come to her slowly over the years, an ever-deepening realization, that there was more to life than the extraordinary beauty she had always been celebrated for. In youth she had been so thoroughly

71

beautiful that her beauty had been public property. She had been crowned princess of the Strawberry Festival in 1941. When she was thirteen her mother had dressed her in a silk kimono and sent her off to Mrs. Shigemura, who taught young girls to dance *odori* and to serve tea impeccably. Seated before a mirror with Mrs. Shigemura behind her, she had learned that her hair was *utsukushii* and that to cut it would be a form of heresy. It was a river of iridescent onyx – Mrs. Shigemura described it in Japanese – the salient feature of her physical being, as prominent and extraordinary as baldness might have been in another girl of the same age. She had to learn that there were many ways to wear it – that she might tame it with pins or weave it in a thick plait hanging over one breast or knot it intricately at the nape of her neck or sweep it back in such a manner that the broad, smooth planes of her cheeks declared themselves. Mrs. Shigemura lifted Hatsue's hair in her palms and said its consistency reminded her of mercury and that Hatsue should learn to play her hair lovingly, like a stringed musical instrument or a flute. Then she combed it down Hatsue's back until it lay opened like a fan and shimmered in unearthly black waves.

Mrs. Shigemura, on Wednesday afternoons, taught Hatsue the intricacies of the tea ceremony as well as calligraphy and scene painting. She showed her how to arrange flowers in a vase and how, for special occasions, to dust her face with rice powder. She insisted that Hatsue must never giggle and must never look at a man directly. In order to keep her complexion immaculate – Hatsue, said Mrs. Shigemura, had skin as smooth as vanilla ice cream – she must take care to stay out of the sun. Mrs. Shigemura taught Hatsue how to sing with composure and how to sit, walk, and stand gracefully. It was this latter that remained of Mrs. Shigemura: Hatsue still moved with a wholeness of being that began in the balls of her feet and reached right through to the top of her head. She was unified and graceful.

Her life had always been strenuous – field work, internment, more field work on top of housework – but during this period

72

under Mrs. Shigemura's tutelage she had learned to compose herself in the face of it. It was a matter in part of posture and breathing, but even more so of *soul*. Mrs. Shigemura taught her to seek union with the Greater Life and to imagine herself as a leaf on a great tree: The prospect of death in autumn, she said, was irrelevant next to its happy recognition of its participation in the life of the tree itself. In America, she said, there was fear of death; here life was separate from Being. A Japanese, on the other hand, must see that life embraces death, and when she feels the truth of this she will gain tranquillity.

Mrs. Shigemura taught Hatsue to sit without moving and claimed that she would not mature properly unless she learned to do so for extended periods. Living in America, she said, would make this difficult, because here there was tension and unhappiness. At first Hatsue, who was only thirteen, could not sit still for even thirty seconds. Then later, when she had stilled her body, she found it was her mind that would not be quiet. But gradually her rebellion against tranquillity subsided. Mrs. Shigemura was pleased and claimed that the turbulence of her ego was in the process of being overcome. She told Hatsue that her stillness would serve her well. She would experience harmony of being in the midst of the changes and unrest that life inevitably brings.

But Hatsue feared, walking home over forest trails from Mrs. Shigemura's, that despite her training she was not becalmed. She dallied and sometimes sat under trees, searched for lady's slippers or white trilliums to pick, and contemplated her attraction to the world of illusions – her craving for existence and entertainment, for clothes, makeup, dances, movies. It seemed to her that in her external bearing she had succeeded only in deceiving Mrs. Shigemura; inwardly she knew her aspiration for worldly happiness was frighteningly irresistible. Yet the demand that she conceal this inner life was great, and by the time she entered high school she was expert at implying bodily a tranquillity that did not in fact inhabit her. In this way she developed a secret life that disturbed her and that she sought to cast off.

Mrs. Shigemura was open and forthright with Hatsue about matters of a sexual nature. With all the seriousness of a fortune-teller she predicted that white men would desire Hatsue and seek to destroy her virginity. She claimed that white men carried in their hearts a secret lust for pure young Japanese girls. Look at their magazines and moving pictures, Mrs. Shigemura said. Kimonos, sake, rice paper walls, coquettish and demure geishas. White men had their fantasies of a passionate Japan – girls of burnished skin and willowy long legs going barefoot in the wet heat of rice paddies – and this distorted their sex drives. They were dangerous egomaniacs and utterly convinced that Japanese women worshiped them for their pale skin and for their ambitious courage. Stay away from white men, said Mrs. Shigemura, and marry a boy of your own kind whose heart is strong and good.

Her parents had sent Hatsue to Mrs. Shigemura with the intent that the girl would not forget that she was first and foremost Japanese. Her father, a strawberry farmer, had come from Japan, from people who had been pottery makers for as long as anyone in his prefecture could remember. Hatsue's mother, Fujiko – the daughter of a modest family near Kure, hardworking shopkeepers and rice wholesalers – had come to America as Hisao's picture bride on board the *Korea Maru*. The marriage was arranged by a *baishakunin* who told the Shibayamas that the potential groom had made a fortune in the new country. But the Shibayamas were owners of a respectable house, and it seemed to them that Fujiko, the daughter in question, could do better than to marry a hired hand in America. Then the *baishakunin*, whose work was to procure brides, showed them twelve acres of prime mountain land, which, he said, the potential bridegroom intended to purchase upon his return from America. There were peach and persimmon trees there, and slender, tall cedars, and a beautiful new home with three rock gardens. And finally, he pointed out, Fujiko *wanted* to go: she was young, nineteen, and wished to see something of the world beyond the sea before settling into her married life.

74

But she had been sick all the way across the ocean, prostrate, clench bellied, and vomiting. And once in the new country, arriving in Seattle, she found she had married a pauper. Hisao's fingers were callused and sun blistered, and his clothing smelled powerfully of field sweat. He had nothing, it turned out, but a few dollars and coins, for which he begged Fujiko's forgiveness. At first they lived in a Beacon Hill boardinghouse where the walls were plastered with pictures from magazines and where the white people on the streets outside treated them with humiliating disdain. Fujiko went to work in a waterfront cookhouse. She, too, sweated beneath her clothes and cut her palms and knuckles working for the *hakujin*.

Hatsue was born, the first of five daughters, and the family moved to a Jackson Street boardinghouse. It was owned by people from Tochigiken prefecture who had done astoundingly well for themselves: the women among them wore silk crepe kimonos and scarlet, cork-soled slippers. Jackson Street, though, smelled of rotting fish, cabbages and radishes fermenting in sea brine, sluggish sewers and diesel streetcar fumes. Fujiko cleaned rooms there for three years, until one day Hisao came home with the news that he had procured jobs for them with the National Cannery Company. In May the Imadas boarded a boat for San Piedro, where there was work to be had in the many strawberry fields.

It was hard work, though – Hatsue and her sisters would do a lot of it in their lives – stoop labor performed in the direct sun. But despite that it was infinitely better than Seattle: the neat rows of strawberries flowed up and down the valleys, the wind brought the smell of the sea to their nostrils, and in the morning the gray light evoked something of the Japan Hisao and Fujiko had left behind.

At first they lived in the corner of a barn they shared with an Indian family. Hatsue, at seven, cut ferns in the forest and pruned holly trees beside her mother. Hisao sold perch and made Christmas wreaths. They filled a grain sack with coins and bills, leased seven acres of stumps and vine maple, purchased a plow horse, and started clearing. Autumn came, the maple leaves curled into fists and dropped away, and the rain ground them into an auburn paste. Hisao burned piles and pried stumps from the earth in the winter of 1931. A house of cedar slats went up slowly. The land was tilled and the first crop planted in time for the pale light of spring.

Hatsue grew up digging clams at South Beach, picking blackberries, collecting mushrooms, and weeding strawberry plants. She was mother, too, to four sisters. When she was ten a neighborhood boy taught her how to swim and offered her the use of his glass-bottomed box so that she could look beneath the surface of the waves. The two of them clung to it, their backs warmed by the Pacific sun, and together watched starfish and rock crabs. The water evaporated against Hatsue's skin, leaving a residue of salt behind. Finally, one day, the boy kissed her. He asked if he might, and she said nothing either way, and then he leaned across the box and put his lips on hers for no more than a second. She smelled the warm, salty interior of his mouth before this boy pulled away and blinked at her. Then they went on looking through the glass at anemones, sea cucumbers, and tube worms. Hatsue would remember on the day of her wedding that her first kiss had been from this boy, Ishmael Chambers, while they clung to a glass box and floated in the ocean. But when her husband asked if she had kissed anyone before, Hatsue had answered *never*.

'It's coming down hard,' she said to him now, lifting her eyes to the courtroom windows. 'A big snow. Your son's first.'

Kabuo turned to take in the snowfall, and she noticed the thick sinews in the left side of his neck above where his shirt was buttoned. He had not lost any of his strength in jail; his strength, as she understood it, was an inward matter, something he tuned silently to the conditions of life: in his cell he had composed himself to preserve it.

'Check the root cellar, Hatsue,' he said. 'You don't want anything to freeze.'

'I've been checking,' she answered. 'Everything's fine.'

'Good,' said Kabuo. 'I knew you would.'

He watched the snow for a silent moment, the needles of it blurring past the leaded panes, then turned again to look at her. 'Do you remember that snow at Manzanar?' he said. 'Whenever it snows I think of that. The drifts and the big wind and the potbellied stove. And the starlight coming through the window.'

It was not the sort of thing he would normally have said to her, these romantic words. But perhaps jail had taught him to release what otherwise he might conceal. 'That was jail, too,' said Hatsue. 'There were good things, but that was jail.'

'It wasn't jail,' Kabuo told her. 'We thought it was back then because we didn't know any better. But it wasn't jail.'

She knew, as he spoke, that this was true. They'd been married at the Manzanar internment camp in a tar paper Buddhist chapel. Her mother had hung woolen army blankets to divide the Imadas' cramped room in half and had given them, on their wedding night, two cots adjacent to the stove. She had even pushed the cots together to form one bed and smoothed their sheets with her palms. Hatsue's sisters – all four of them – had stood beside the curtain watching while their mother went about her silent business. Fujiko loaded coal into the potbellied stove and wiped her hands on her apron. She nodded and said they should close the damper when forty-five minutes had gone by. Then she took her daughters out with her and left Hatsue and Kabuo behind.

They stood beside the window in their wedding clothes and kissed, and she smelled his warm neck and throat. Outside snow had drifted against the barracks wall. 'They'll hear everything,' Hatsue whispered.

Kabuo, his hands at her waist, turned and spoke to the curtain. 'There must be something good on the radio,' he called. 'Wouldn't some music be nice?'

They waited. Kabuo hung his coat on a peg. In a little while a station from Las Vegas came on – country-and-western music. Kabuo sat down and removed his shoes and socks.

He put them under the bed neatly. He unknotted his bow tie.

Hatsue sat down beside him. She looked at the side of his face for a moment, at the scar on his jaw, and then they kissed. 'I need help with my dress,' she whispered. 'It unhooks in the back, Kabuo.'

Kabuo unclasped it for her. He ran his fingers along her spine. She stood and pulled the dress from her shoulders. It dropped to the floor, and she picked it up and hung it on the peg beside his coat.

Hatsue came back to the bed in her bra and slip and sat down beside Kabuo.

'I don't want to make a lot of noise,' she said. 'Even with the radio. My sisters are listening.'

'Okay,' said Kabuo. 'Quietly.'

He unbuttoned his shirt, stripped it off, and set it on the end of the cot. He pulled his undershirt off. He was very strong. She could see the muscles flowing in his abdomen. She was glad to have married him. He, too, came from strawberry farmers. He was good with the plants and knew which runners to cut. His hands, like hers, were berry stained in the summer months. The red fruit mingled with his skin and scented it. She knew that in part because of this smell she wanted to tie her life to his; it was something she understood in her nose, finally, as odd as that might seem to others. And she knew that Kabuo wanted what she wanted, a San Piedro strawberry farm. That was all, there was nothing more than that, they wanted their farm and the closeness at hand of the people they loved and the scent of strawberries outside their window. There were girls Hatsue's age she knew very well who felt certain their happiness was something other, who wanted to go to Seattle or Los Angeles. They could not say in any precise way exactly what it was they sought in the city, only that they wanted to go there. It was something Hatsue herself had once felt but had since emerged from as if from a dream, discovering the truth of her private nature: it was in her to have the composure and tranquillity of an island strawberry farmer. She knew in her bones what she wanted, and she knew why she wanted it, too. She understood the happiness of a place where the work was clear and there were fields she could enter into with a man she loved purposefully. And this was what Kabuo felt, too, and what he wanted from life. And so they made plans together. When the war was over they would return to San Piedro. Kabuo was rooted there just as she was, a boy who understood the earth and the working of it and how it was a good thing to live among people one loved. He was precisely the boy Mrs. Shigemura had described for her so many years ago when she'd spoken of love and marriage, and now she kissed him, hard, because of that. She kissed his jaw and forehead more softly, and then she put her chin against the top of his head and held his ears between her fingers. His hair smelled like wet earth. Kabuo put his hands against her back and pulled her deeply to him. He kissed the skin just over her breasts and put his nose against her bra.

'You smell so good,' he said.

He drew away and stripped his pants off and laid them next to his shirt. They sat there beside each other in their underwear. His legs shone in the light from the window. She could see beneath the fabric of his underpants how his penis stood erect. The end of it pushed his shorts into the air.

Hatsue brought her feet up onto the bed and propped her chin on her knees. 'They're listening,' she said. 'I know they are.'

'Could you turn the radio up?' Kabuo called. 'We can't hear it so well in here.'

The country-and-western music grew louder. And they were very quiet at first. They lay on their sides and faced one another, and she felt his hardness against her belly. She reached down and touched it beneath the fabric of his shorts, the tip of it and the ridge just below. She could hear the coal burning in the potbellied stove.

She remembered how she had kissed Ishmael Chambers, clinging to that wooden box. He was a brown-skinned boy who lived down the road – they'd picked blackberries, climbed trees, fished for perch. She thought of him while Kabuo kissed the undersides of her breasts, and then her nipples through the fabric of her bra, and she recognized Ishmael as the beginning of a chain, that she had kissed a boy when she was ten years old, had even then felt something strange, and that tonight, soon, she would feel another boy's hardness deep inside of her. But it was not difficult for her, on her wedding night, to then cast Ishmael out of her mind completely; he had only crept in by accident, as it were, because all romantic moments are associated willy-nilly – even when some are long dead.

In a little while her husband took off her slip and underpants and unhooked her bra, and she pulled down his shorts. They were naked, and she could see his face in the starlight from the window. It was a good face, strong and smooth. The wind was blowing hard outside now, and the sound of it whistled between the boards. She put her hand around Kabuo's hardness and squeezed it, and it pulsed once in her hand. Then, because she wanted it this way, she fell onto her back without letting go, and he was on top of her with his hands on her buttocks.

'Have you ever done this before?' he whispered.

'Never,' answered Hatsue. 'You're my only.'

The head of his penis found the place it wanted. For a moment he waited there, poised, and kissed her – he took her lower lip between his lips and gently held it there. Then with his hands he pulled her to him and at the same time entered her so that she felt his scrotum slap against her skin. Her entire body felt the rightness of it, her entire body was seized to it. Hatsue arched her shoulder blades – her breasts pressed themselves against his chest – and a slow shudder ran through her.

'It's right,' she remembered whispering. 'It feels so right, Kabuo.'

'*Tadaima aware ga wakatta*,' he had answered. '*I understand just now the deepest beauty*.'

Eight days later he left for Camp Shelby, Mississippi, where he joined the 442nd Regimental Combat Team. He *had* to go to the war, he told her. It was necessary in order to demonstrate his bravery. It was necessary to demonstrate his loyalty to the United States: his country.

'You can die demonstrating all of that,' she told him. '*I* know you are brave and loyal.'

He went despite these words of hers. She had spoken them many times before their wedding, often she'd urged him not to go, but he had not been able to bring himself to stay away from the fighting. It was not only a point of honor, he'd said, it was also a matter of having to go because his face was Japanese. There was something extra that had to be proved, a burden this particular war placed on him, and if he would not carry it, who would? She saw that in this he would not be swayed and recognized the hardness buried in him, the part of her husband that was attracted to the fighting and wanted to enter it desperately. There was a place in him she could not reach where he made his choices in solitude, and this made her not only uneasy about him but afraid for their future, too. Her life was joined to his now, and it seemed to her that every corner of his soul should be opened to hers because of this. It was the war, she persistently told herself, it was the prison of camp life, the pressures of the times, their exile from home, that explained his distance. Many men were going off to the war against the wishes of women, a lot of them leaving the camp each day, droves of young men going. She told herself she must endure it in the way her mother and Kabuo's mother counseled her and not struggle against those larger forces that could not be struggled against. She was in the stream of history now, as her mother before her had been. She must travel in it easily or her own heart would devour her and she would not endure the war unwounded, as she still hoped to do.

Hatsue settled into missing her husband and learned the art of waiting over an extended period of time – a deliberately controlled hysteria that was something like what Ishmael Chambers felt watching her in the courtroom.

Ishmael Chambers, watching Hatsue, remembered digging geoduck clams with her below the bluff at South Beach. Hatsue, carrying a garden shovel and a metal pail rusted through in its bottom, dripped water behind her as she walked the tide flats; she was fourteen and wore a black bathing suit. She went barefoot, avoiding barnacles, picking her way along the flats with the tide drawn out and the salt chuck grass sleek against the mud in sun-dried fans. Ishmael wore rubber boots and clutched a gardener's hand spade; the sun struck his shoulders and back as he walked and dried the mud on his knees and hands.

They wandered for nearly a mile. They stopped to swim. At the turning of the tide the geoducks emerged, shooting jets of water like miniature geysers hidden among the eelgrass. Down the mud flats small fountains erupted, dozens of them, spurting two feet or more, then again, then lower, then dwindling and stopping. The geoducks raised their necks from the mud and aimed their lips at the sun. The siphons at the ends of their necks glistened. They blossomed delicately white and iridescent out of the tidal morass.

The two of them knelt beside a clam siphon to discuss the particulars of its appearance. They were quiet and made no sudden movements – movement inspired shyness among clams and encouraged them to withdraw. Hatsue, her bucket beside her, her shovel in one hand, pointed out the darkness of the exposed clam's lip, its size, its hue and tone, the circumference of its watery dimple. She decided they'd stopped beside a horse clam.

They were fourteen years old; geoducks were important. It was summer and little else really mattered.

They came to a second siphon and knelt again. Hatsue, sitting on her ankles, twisted the salt water out of her hair so that it dripped along her arm. She lofted her hair out neatly behind her and let it spread against her back to catch the sun.

'Geoduck,' she said quietly.

'A good one,' Ishmael agreed.

Hatsue bent forward and slipped a forefinger inside the siphon. They watched while the clam seized up around it and drew its neck into the mud. She followed its retreating path with the point of an alder stick; its two feet of length disappeared. 'He's way down there,' she said, 'and he's big.'

'My turn to dig,' answered Ishmael.

Hatsue handed him her shovel. 'The handle's coming loose,' she warned. 'Be careful it doesn't break.'

The shovel brought butter clams, sticks, and sea worms up with it. Ishmael built a dike against the turning of the tide; Hatsue bailed with the leaking pail, stretched out flat against the warm mud, the backs of her legs smooth and brown.

When the alder stick fell over, Ishmael dropped down beside her and watched while she scraped with the hand spade. The clam's siphon came into view; they saw the aperture through which its neck had retreated. They lay at the edge of the hole together, each with a muddy arm hung in, and excavated around it until a third of the shell showed. 'Let's pull it now,' suggested Ishmael.

'We'd better get under it,' answered Hatsue.

He had taught her to dig geoducks, and they had dug them for four summers, but in the end she'd surpassed him in it. There was this way she had of speaking with certainty that he found entirely convincing. 'He's still got a good grip,' she pointed out. 'He'll break if we start pulling. Let's be patient and dig some more. It's better if we keep digging.'

When the time came to pull he slid his hand down as far as he could so that the side of his face lay against the mud, turned toward Hatsue's knee. He was close enough so that her knee was his whole view of things, and he smelled the salt on her skin.

'Gentle,' she urged. 'Slow. Easy is the way. Don't hurry it. Slow is best.'

'He's coming,' Ishmael grunted. 'I can feel him.'

Afterward she took the clam from between his fingers and rinsed it off in the shallows. She rubbed the shell with the heel of her palm and cleaned the long neck and foot. Ishmael took the clam back and put it in the bucket. Clean and delicate, as large as any he had seen, it was approximately the size and shape of a turkey breast carved away from the bone. He admired it, turned it in his hand. He was always surprised at the thickness and heft of a geoduck. 'We found a good one,' he said.

'He's huge,' answered Hatsue. 'Enormous.'

She stood in the shallows rinsing mud from her legs while Ishmael filled in the hole. The tide skated in over sun-heated flats, and the water was as warm as a lagoon. The two of them sat side by side in the shallows, facing out toward the expanse of the ocean, kelp draped across their legs. 'It goes forever,' said Ishmael. 'There's more water than anything in the world.'

'It ends somewhere,' answered Hatsue. 'Or it just goes around and around.'

'That's the same thing. It's forever.'

'There's a shore somewhere right now where the tide is up,' explained Hatsue. 'And that's the end of the ocean.'

'It doesn't end. It meets another one and pretty soon the water is back and it all mixes together.'

'Oceans don't mix,' said Hatsue. 'They're different temperatures. They have different amounts of salt.'

'They mix underneath,' said Ishmael. 'It's all really just one ocean.' He lay back on his elbows, draped a strand of seaweed across his thighs, and settled in again.

'It's not one ocean,' said Hatsue. 'It's four oceans – Atlantic, Pacific, Indian, Arctic. They're different from each other.'

'Well, how are they different?'

'They just are.' Hatsue lay back on her elbows beside him and let her hair fall behind. 'Just because,' she added.

'That's not a good reason,' Ishmael said. 'The main thing is, water is water. Names on a map don't mean anything. Do you think if you were out there in a boat and you came to another ocean you'd see a sign or something? It – '

'The color would change, I've heard that,' said Hatsue. 'The Atlantic Ocean is brown, sort of, and the Indian Ocean is blue.'

'Where'd you hear that?'

'I don't remember.'

'It isn't true.'

'Yes, it is.'

They were silent. There was the lapping of the water and no other sound. Ishmael was aware of her legs and arms. The salt had dried at the corners of her lips and left a residue behind. He noticed her fingernails, the shape of her toes, the hollow place at her throat. He had known her for six years and he had not known her. The detached part of her, the part she kept to herself, had begun to interest him deeply.

It made him unhappy when he thought about her lately, and he had passed a lot of time, all spring long, mulling how to tell her about his unhappiness. He'd sat on top of the bluff at South Beach thinking about it in the afternoons. He'd thought about it during school. His thoughts, however, yielded no clue as to how to talk to Hatsue. Words evaded him completely. He felt in her presence that to reveal himself would be a mistake he might never correct. She was closed up and offered him no opening for talk, though for years now they had walked from the school bus together, met on the beach and in the woods to play, picked berries on the same nearby farms. They had played together as children in a group that included her sisters and other kids – Sheridan Knowles, Arnold and Bill Kruger, Lars Hansen, Tina and Jean Syvertsen. They had passed autumn afternoons when they were nine years old in the hollowed-out base of a cedar tree, where they sprawled on the ground looking out at the rain as it pummeled the sword ferns and ivy. At school they were strangers for reasons unclear to him, though at the same time he understood it had to be that way because she was

Japanese and he wasn't. It was the way things were and there was nothing to be done about such a basic thing.

She was fourteen and her breasts were beginning to show beneath her bathing suit. They were small and hard, like apples. He could not put his finger on how else she had changed, but even her face was different. The texture of its skin had changed. He had watched her change, and when he sat close to her, as he did now in the water, he felt driven and nervous.

Ishmael's heart began the fretful pounding he'd experienced of late in her presence. There were no words for what he had to say and his tongue felt paralyzed. He couldn't stand another moment without explaining his heart to her. A knot of pressure was building inside him to declare the love he felt. It was not only that her beauty moved him but that they already had a history together that included this beach, these waters, the very stones, and the forest at their backs, too. It was all theirs and always would be, and Hatsue was the spirit of the place. She knew where to find matsutake mushrooms, elderberries, and fern tendrils, and she had found them now for years at his side, and they had taken each other for granted, they had been as easy as friends about it all – until these last few months. Now he was in pain about her, and he understood that he would continue in his pain unless he did something about it. It was up to him. It took courage and it made him feel ill, this unasked-for thing. It was too hard. He shut his eyes.

'I like you,' he confessed with his eyes still shut. 'Do you know what I mean? I've always liked you, Hatsue.'

She didn't answer. She didn't even look at him; she looked down. But having started it he moved into the warmth of her face anyway and put his lips against hers. They were warm, too. There was the taste of salt and the heat of her breathing. He pushed too hard, and she planted one hand beneath the water behind her to keep from falling over. She pushed back against him, and he felt the pressure of her teeth and smelled the inside of her mouth. Their teeth clashed a little. He shut his eyes and

86

then opened them again. Hatsue's eyes were tightly shut, she wouldn't look at him.

Just as soon as they were no longer touching she leapt up and went for her geoduck pail and ran away down the beach. She was very fast, he knew that. He stood up only to watch her go. Then, after she had disappeared into the woods, he lay in the water for another ten minutes feeling the kiss many times. He decided then that he would love her forever no matter what came to pass. It was not so much a matter of deciding as accepting the inevitability of it. It made him feel better, though he felt perturbed, too, worried that this kiss was *wrong*. But from his point of view, at fourteen years old, their love was entirely unavoidable. It had started on the day they'd clung to his glass box and kissed in the sea, and now it must go on forever. He felt certain of this. He felt certain Hatsue felt the same way.

For ten days after that Ishmael worked – odd jobs and stray chores, weeding and window washing – and worried about Hatsue Imada. She stayed away from the beach intentionally, it seemed to him in his fretfulness, and gradually he became dark and morose. He battened down the guy wires over which Mrs. Verda Carmichael's raspberries were trellised, straightened out the contents of her shadowy toolshed, and bundled up her cedar kindling – all of it permeated by thoughts about Hatsue. He helped Bob Timmons scrape paint from his shed and weeded flower beds with Mrs. Herbert Crow, a woman who concerned herself with flower arrangements and treated Ishmael's mother formally. Now, seated on a knee pad, Mrs. Crow worked beside Ishmael with a maple-handled claw, stopping every now and then to wipe sweat from her brow with the back of her forearm and to exclaim that he seemed blue. Later she decided they would sit on the back porch and sip tall glasses of iced tea and lemon wedges. She pointed to a fig tree and told Ishmael she'd planted it more years ago than she could remember; against all odds it had taken hold and produced enormous quantities of sweet figs.

Mr. Crow greatly approved of figs, she added. She sipped her tea, then changed the subject: the families up and down South Beach, she said, were thought of by folks in Amity Harbor as self-styled aristocrats and malcontents, seclusion seekers and eccentrics – Ishmael's family included. Did he know that his grandfather had helped to drive the pilings for the wharf at South Beach Bay landing? The Papineaus, she said, were dirt poor for a reason: none of them did any work. The Imadas, on the other hand, were consistently hard workers, including the five little girls. The Eberts hired professional gardeners and various domestic troubleshooters – plumbers, electricians, and handymen arrived in step vans to do *their* dirty work – but the Crows always hired neighborhood people. For forty years, she reminded Ishmael, she and Mr. Crow had lived right there at South Beach. Mr. Crow had been in coal mining and the manufacturing of pallet boards but had recently gone into the shipbuilding business and was right now in Seattle financing the construction of frigates and minesweepers for Roosevelt's navy (though he didn't care a lick for Roosevelt, she said) – but why was Ishmael so blue? Cheer up, urged Mrs. Crow, and sipped her tea. Life was wonderful.

Fishing with Sheridan Knowles that Saturday – rowing the shoreline and worrying about Hatsue – Ishmael saw Mr. Crow, with his hands on his knees, peering into a telescope mounted on a tripod in the center of his terraced lawn. From this vantage point he jealously inspected the yachts of the Seattlites who cruised past South Beach on their way to anchorages in Amity Harbor. Mr. Crow was a man of uncertain temper with a high, severe forehead like Shakespeare's. His vista of the sea was a wide and windy one; his gardens were planted with low azalea hedges, camellias, starina roses, and espaliered boxwoods, all framed by the white-caps on the shuffling waters and the annealed gray of the beach stones. His house turned a great, immaculate wall of shuttered windows to the sun, cedars surrounding it on three sides imperiously. Mr. Crow had entered into a sort of border war with Bob Timmons, his neighbor to the north, claiming that Bob's grove of western hemlocks actually grew on his property. One morning when Ishmael was eight years old a pair of surveyors had showed up with their transits and alidades and knotted red flagging everywhere. This ceremony was repeated at odd intervals over the years, and while the faces of the surveyors changed nothing else did except that the hemlocks grew taller, their limber tips bent like green whips against the sky. Bob Timmons – a transplanted son of the New Hampshire uplands and a pale, wordless, determined man of puritanical sensibilities – looked on without expression, hands braced against his hips, while Mr. Crow grumbled and paced with his high forehead glistening.

Ishmael worked, too, for the Etheringtons, who were vigorous summer people from Seattle. In June each year the summer people arrived *en force* to take up balmy residence along South Beach. Here they meandered in their tiny sailboats, tacking and coming about; they painted, hoed, swept, and planted when the mood for therapeutic work struck them, and lolled on the beach when they felt like it. In the evenings there were bonfires and steamer clams, mussels, oysters, and perch, the boats dragged up beyond the tide line, the shovels and rakes hosed off and put away. The Etheringtons drank gin-and-tonics.

At the head of Miller Bay, beyond the mud flats, lived Captain Jonathan Soderland, who'd plied his decrepit windjammer, the *C. S. Murphy*, to the Arctic each year on trading expeditions. He had finally gotten too old for it and spent his time telling lies to the summer people – stroking his snowy beard, dressed in woolen long johns and ragtag suspenders – and posing for photographs at the wheel of the *Murphy*, which was permanently lodged in the mud flats. Ishmael helped him split firewood.

The only viable profit-seeking concern on South Beach – other than the Imadas' strawberry enterprise – was Tom Peck's Great American Blue Fox Farm. On the far side of Miller Bay, in the shadows of madrona trees, Tom Peck tugged at his burnt-red goatee, sucked on his pipe stem, and raised American blue foxes for their varnished pelts in sixty-eight overcrowded breeding pens. The world left him thoroughly alone in this, although Ishmael and two other boys were hired that June to clean the cages with wire brushes. Peck had accumulated a personal mythology that included Indian wars, gold mining, and mercenary executions, and was known to carry a derringer pistol in a hidden shoulder holster. Farther up the bay, on the dead-water east arm known as Little House Cove, the Westinghouse family had built a Newport-style mansion on thirty acres of Douglas fir trees. Troubled by the general moral demise of the East – manifest, particularly, in the Lindbergh kidnapping – the well-known home appliance magnate and his high-born Bostonian wife had brought their three sons, a maid, a cook, a butler, and a pair of private tutors to San Piedro's secluded shores. Ishmael, one long afternoon, helped Dale Papineau – self-appointed caretaker for half a dozen summer families – prune back the alder branches overarching their long drive.

Ishmael worked with Dale, too, to clean the Etheringtons' gutters. The Etheringtons mostly humored him, it seemed to Ishmael – for them he was a colorful island character, part of the charm of the place. After a freeze or two days of hard rain, Dale would plod from house to house with a flashlight in hand – limping because the hip he'd dislocated at the creosote plant ached when it was damp or cold or both together, and squinting because he was too vain to wear glasses – and poke around garages and basements, clearing mud from the drains. In the fall he burned brush piles and raked leaves for Virginia Gatewood, a stick figure at twilight in cloth gloves and a threadbare mackinaw coat ragged at the elbows. The veins in his cheeks were broken and smashed flat and appeared as a sort of blue paste beneath his skin; his Adam's apple bulged like a toad's. He looked, to Ishmael, vaguely like an alcoholic scarecrow.

Four days after the kiss on the beach, just after dusk – it was dark in the woods, but the strawberry fields lay in twilight – Ishmael crouched at the edge of the Imadas' farm and watched for half an hour. To his surprise no boredom overtook him and so he stayed for an hour more. It was a kind of relief to rest his cheek against the earth underneath the stars and to have some hope of seeing Hatsue. The fear of being discovered and labeled a Peeping Tom urged him to move on finally, and he had almost convinced himself to leave, was getting up in fact, when the screen door creaked open, light slipped across the porch, and Hatsue crossed to one of the corner posts. She lifted a wicker basket to the cedar railing and began drawing in her family's laundry.

Ishmael watched Hatsue pull sheets from the line, standing in a pool of muted porch light with her arms illuminated and elegant. Clenching clothespins between her teeth, she folded towels, pants, and work shirts before dropping them into the wicker basket. When she finished she leaned against the corner post for a moment, scratching her neck and looking at the stars, then smelling the dampness in the fresh laundry. Then she took her basket of sheets and clothes and melted back into the house.

Ishmael returned the following evening; five nights in a row he spied religiously. Each night he told himself not to return, but on the next he would take a walk at dusk, his walk would become a pilgrimage, he would feel guilt and shame, he would top the groundswell that buttressed her strawberries and pause before the sweep of her fields. He wondered if other boys did this sort of thing, if his voyeurism constituted a disease. He was sustained, though, by seeing her once more reel in laundry – elegant hand over elegant hand – drop the clothespins in a bucket on the railing, then fold shirts, sheets, and towels. Once she stood on the porch for a moment brushing the dust from her summer dress. She corralled the long sweep of her hair in deftly and knotted it before going inside.

On the last night of his spying he saw her empty a bucket of kitchen scraps not fifty yards from where he crouched. She appeared in the porch light, as always, without warning and shut the door behind her gently. As she moved in his direction his heart lurched before freezing altogether in his chest. He could see her face now and hear the *thock* of her sandals. Hatsue turned down between strawberry rows and upended her bucket on the compost heap, glanced at the moon so that its blue light caught her face, then returned to the house by a different route. He caught a glimpse of her through the interstices of raspberry canes before she emerged in front of her porch with one hand knotting her hair at her neck and the bucket dangling from the other. He waited, and in a moment she was at the kitchen window with a nimbus of light around her head. Moving closer, keeping low, Ishmael saw her smoothing hair from her eyes while soapsuds ran from her fingers. There were young strawberries growing on the plants around him and their fragrance filled up the night. He moved closer until the Imadas' dog came loping around the corner of the house and then he froze, prepared to bolt. The dog sniffed for a moment, whined, sidled toward him and allowed him to stroke her head and ears and licked his palm and lay down. She was a jaundiced, stain-toothed, and lopsided old hound, leathery looking and swaybacked, and her sad eyes wept miserably. Ishmael rubbed her belly. The dog's gray tongue lolled in the dust and her rib cage pumped up and down.

A moment later Hatsue's father came onto the porch and called to the dog in Japanese. He called again, a low guttural command, and the dog raised her head, barked twice, sprang to her feet, and limped away.

That was the last time Ishmael spied at the Imada place.

At the start of the strawberry season, at five-thirty in the morning, Ishmael saw Hatsue on the South Beach wood path underneath silent cedars. They were both of them going to work for Mr. Nitta – he paid better than any berry farmer on the island – for thirty-five cents a flat.

He walked behind her, his lunch in hand. He caught up and said hello. Neither said anything about their kiss on the beach two weeks before. They walked the path quietly, and Hatsue suggested there was a chance they'd see a black-tailed deer out feeding on fern tendrils – she'd seen a doe the previous morning.

Where the path met the beach the madrona trees leaned out over the tidal water. Slender and sinuous, olive green, mahogany red, scarlet, and ash, they were weighted with broad, gleaming leaves and velvet berries and shaded the beach stones and mud flats. Hatsue and Ishmael flushed a roosting blue heron with feathers the hue of beach mud; it squawked once and, elongated wing tips wide, graceful even in sudden flight, crossed Miller Bay at a soaring angle to perch in the dead top of a far tree.

The path looped around the head of the bay, then down into a swale known as Devil's Dip – ground fog shrouded its thimbleberry and devil's club, such was the clammy, low wetness of the place – then climbed among cedars and the shadows of spruces before descending into Center Valley. The homesteads here were old and productive ones – the Andreasons, the Olsens, the McCullys, the Coxes; oxen had been used to cultivate their fields, descendants of the oxen brought to San Piedro in the old, log-skidding days. They were enormous, pungent, and hoary beasts, and Ishmael and Hatsue stopped to stare at one rubbing his hindquarters against a fence post.

At Nitta's farm the Canadian Indians were already busy when they arrived. Mrs. Nitta, a small woman with a waist no larger than a soup tin, darted up and down the rows like a hummingbird beneath her straw picking hat. Her mouth – like her husband's – was full of gold fillings and when she smiled the sun glinted in among them. In the afternoons she sat beneath a canvas umbrella with a pencil between her fingers, her accounts laid out on a cedar crate before her, one palm laid against her forehead. Her handwriting was impeccable – small, soft, and elegant numbers filled the pages of her account book. She wrote with the quiet deliberation of a court scribe, sharpening her pencil often.

Ishmael and Hatsue went their separate ways to pick among their friends. The farm was so large that a leased, battered school bus carried workers to its dusty gate at the height of picking season. An aura of manic purpose hung over the fields, for in them went forward a gleeful harvest performed by children only just freed from school. San Piedro children delighted in their field toil in part because of the social life it provided, in part because it furnished the illusion that a job had been included in the summer's proceedings. The rich heat, the taste of berries on the tongue, the easy talk, and the prospect of spending money on soda pop, firecrackers, fishing lures, and makeup all seduced them toward Mr. Nitta's. All day the children knelt beside one another in the fields, hunkered down close against the earth beneath the heat of the sun. Romances began and ended there; children kissed at the verges of fields or walking home through the woods.

Ishmael, from three rows off, watched Hatsue at her work. Her hair soon came loose from its arrangement, and a sheen of sweat appeared against her collarbones. She picked deftly and had a reputation for speed and efficiency; she filled two flats in the time it took other pickers to fill one and a half. She was among friends – a half-dozen Japanese girls squatting in the rows together, their faces shrouded by straw hats – and would not acknowledge that she knew him when he passed her with his own flat mounded high. He passed her again with his emptied flat and saw how intent she was on her picking, never hurrying but never stopping. He squatted again in his spot three rows distant and tried to concentrate on his own work. When he looked up she was sliding a berry into her mouth, and he stopped to watch her eat it. Hatsue turned and met his eyes, but he could not discern in this her feelings and it seemed to him wholly an accident; she meant nothing by it. Looking away, she ate another berry with no embarrassment, slowly. Then, adjusting herself on her haunches for a moment, she went back to her methodical work.

Late in the afternoon, at about four-thirty, heavy clouds shadowed the strawberry fields. The clean June light went softly gray and a breeze came up in the southwest. It was possible, then, to smell the rain coming and to feel the cool pause before the first drops fell. The air turned thick; sudden gusts caught the cedars at the edge of the fields and flailed their tops and branches. The pickers hurried their last flats in and waited in line while Mrs. Nitta put marks beside their names and paid them from underneath her umbrella. The pickers craned their necks to watch the clouds and held their palms out to check for rain. At first just a few drops raised tiny wisps of dust around them and then, as if a hole had been punched in the sky, an island summer rain poured hard against their faces, and the pickers began moving toward shelter of any kind – the doorway of a barn, the inside of a car, the berry storage sheds, the cedar woods. Some stood with flats held over their heads and let their picked strawberries catch the water.

Ishmael saw Hatsue cross the Nittas' upper fields and slip into the cedar woods, going south. He found himself following, slowly at first, letting the rain pound him as he moved through the strawberries – he was already soaked so what difference could it make?; the rain was warm and felt good on his face – and then he was trotting through the forest. The South Beach trail, with its canopy of cedars, was as good a place as any in a rainstorm, and he wanted to walk it home with her, saying nothing if that was what she desired. But when he caught sight of her below the McCullys' farm it occurred to him to slow to a walking pace and follow along at fifty yards. The rain would cover any noise he made and besides, he didn't know what to say. It would be enough merely to see her, as it had been in the fields or when he'd hid behind the cedar log and watched her fold her family's laundry. He would follow along behind, listening to the rain pelt the trees, and watch her wind her way home.

Where the trail hit the beach on Miller Bay – there was a wall of honeysuckle just past blossom, salmonberries hanging in among it and a few last wild roses blooming – Hatsue cut into the cedar woods. Ishmael followed her through a dell of ferns where white morning glory blossoms dotted the forest floor. A fallen cedar log hung with ivy bridged the dell; she slipped under it and turned up a side path that followed a shallow creek where three years before they'd sailed driftwood boats together. The path made three bends, and then Hatsue crossed the water on a log, hiked halfway up the cedar hillside, and ducked into the hollow tree they'd played in together when they were only nine years old.

Ishmael squatted beneath branches in the rain and watched the tree's entry for half a minute. His hair hung wet in his eyes. He tried to understand what had brought her here; he himself had forgotten about the place, which was a good half mile from his home. He remembered, now, how they'd packed moss underneath their legs and lolled in the tree looking up. It was possible to kneel but not to stand, though on the other hand the room inside the tree was wide enough to lie down in. They'd gone there with other kids and imagined they were hiding out, sharpening alder sticks with pocketknives to be used in their defense. The inside of the tree had been filled with a stock of arrows to be used in a fantasy battle at first, then in a battle fought amongst themselves. From twine and yew wood they'd made miniature bows; they'd used the hollow cedar as a kind of fort and run up and down the hillside shooting at each other. Ishmael squatted there remembering playing war on this hillside and how that had ultimately driven the Syvertsen girls away, and then the Imada sisters, and then he saw that Hatsue was looking at him from the entry of the hollow cedar tree.

He looked back; there was no point in hiding. 'You'd better come in,' she said. 'It's wet.'

'All right,' he answered.

Inside the tree he knelt on the moss with water dripping beneath his shirt. Hatsue sat on the moss in her damp summer dress, her broad-rimmed picking hat beside her. 'You followed me,' she said. 'Didn't you.'

'I didn't mean to,' Ishmael apologized. 'It just happened, sort of. I was going home. You know what I mean? I saw you turn off and . . . it just happened, sort of. Sorry,' he added. 'I followed you.'

She smoothed her hair back behind her ears. 'I'm all wet,' she said. 'I'm soaked.'

'So am I. It feels good, sort of. Anyway it's dry in here. Remember this place? It seems smaller.'

'I've been coming here all along,' said Hatsue. 'I come here to think. Nobody else comes around. I haven't seen anybody here in years.'

'What do you think about?' Ishmael asked. 'When you're here, I mean. What do you think about?'

'I don't know. All sorts of things. You know, a place to think.'

Ishmael lay down with his hands propping up his chin and looked out at the rain. The inside of the tree felt private. He felt they would never be discovered here. The walls surrounding them were glossy and golden. It was surprising how much green-tinted light entered from the cedar forest. The rain echoed in the canopy of leaves above and beat against the sword ferns, which twitched under each drop. The rain afforded an even greater privacy; no one in the world would come this way to find them inside this tree.

'I'm sorry I kissed you on the beach,' said Ishmael. 'Let's just forget about it. Forget it happened.'

There was no answer at first. It was like Hatsue not to answer. He himself was always in need of words, even when he couldn't quite muster them, but she seemed capable of a brand of silence he couldn't feel inside.

She picked up her straw hat and looked at it instead of him. 'Don't be sorry,' she said with her eyes down. 'I'm not sorry about it.'

'Me, neither,' said Ishmael.

She lay down on her back beside him. The green-tinted light caught her face. He wanted to put his mouth against hers and leave it there forever. He knew now that he might do so without regretting it. 'Do you think this is wrong?' she asked.

'Other people do,' said Ishmael. 'Your friends would,' he added. 'And your parents.'

'So would yours,' said Hatsue. 'So would your mother and father.'

'Yours more than mine,' said Ishmael. 'If they knew we were out here in this tree together . . .' He shook his head and laughed softly. 'Your father'd probably kill me with a machete. He'd slice me into little pieces.'

'Probably not,' said Hatsue. 'But you're right – he would be angry. With both of us, for doing this.'

'But what are we doing? We're talking.'

'Still,' said Hatsue, 'you're not Japanese. And I'm alone with you.'

'It doesn't matter,' answered Ishmael.

They lay beside each other in the cedar tree talking until half an hour had gone by. Then, once again, they kissed. They felt comfortable kissing inside the tree, and they kissed for another half hour. With the rain falling outside and the moss softly under him Ishmael shut his eyes and breathed the smell of her fully in through his nostrils. He told himself he had never felt so happy, and he felt a sort of ache that this was happening and would never again happen in just this way no matter how long he lived.

Ishmael found himself sitting in the courtroom where Hatsue's husband was on trial for murder. He found he was watching her as she spoke to Kabuo, and he exerted himself to look away.

The jurors returned, and then Judge Fielding, and Carl Heine's mother took the stand. Despite living in town a full ten years she retained the look of a farmer's wife: stout, faded, and wind worn. Etta adjusted her girth in the witness chair so that the hitching and sliding of her undergarments was heard – heavy nylons, a girdle purchased in Lottie Opsvig's shop, a back brace prescribed by a doctor in Bellingham for the sciatica she attributed to her farm days. For twenty-five years she had worked in all weather beside her husband, Carl senior. Winters, with steam puffing from her mouth, she'd worn mud boots, a greatcoat, and a scarf over her head firmly knotted below her heavy chin. In fingerless wool gloves knitted late at night – sitting up in bed while Carl snored – she'd perched on a stool, milking cows. In summer she'd sorted berries, cut runners, pulled weeds, and kept one eye on the Indians and Japanese who yearly picked on the Heine farm.

She'd been born in Bavaria – still carried its accent – on a dairy farm near Ingolstadt. She'd met her husband when he came to her father's wheat farm near Hettinger, North Dakota. They'd eloped on the Northern Pacific to Seattle – she remembered eating breakfast in the dining car – where he worked for two years in a Harbor Island foundry and for one loading lumber on the waterfront. Etta, a farmer's daughter, found Seattle to her liking. She was a seamstress on Second Avenue and made Klondike coats at piece rate. The strawberry farm on San Piedro, where they visited at Christmas, belonged to Carl's father, a portly man; Carl'd left it at seventeen, seeking adventure in the world. When his father died he migrated back, bringing Etta with him.

She tried to like San Piedro. It was damp, though, and she developed a cough, and her lower back began to bother her. She had four children and raised them to work hard, but the oldest went off to Darrington to set choker cables, and the second and third went off to war. Only the second – Carl junior – returned. The fourth was a girl who, like Etta herself, eloped and went off to Seattle.

Etta grew tired, gut weary, of strawberries: she didn't even like to eat them. Her husband was a true lover of the fruit, but Etta couldn't feel anything for it. To him strawberries were a holy mystery, jewels of sugar, deep red gems, sweet orbs, succulent rubies. He knew their secrets, the path they took, the daily responses they made to sunlight. The rocks between the rows collected heat, he said, and kept his plants warmer at night than they would otherwise have been – but to this sort of thing she made no answer. She brought him his eggs and went to the barn for milk. Threw feed from her apron pockets to the turkeys and chickens. Scrubbed the field muck from the mudroom floor. Filled the hog trough and walked through the pickers' cabins to see that they hadn't relieved themselves in pilfered canning jars.

Carl's heart failed him one clear October night in 1944. She'd found him on the toilet with his head against the wall, his pants clumped around his ankles. Carl junior was away at the war, and Etta took advantage of this circumstance to sell the farm to Ole Jurgensen. That gave Ole sixty-five acres in the middle of Center Valley. It also provided Etta with enough money to get by on, if she was mindful of her pennies. Fortunately this mindfulness accorded with her nature: it brought her the same depth of pleasure Carl had derived from nurturing his strawberries.

Alvin Hooks, the prosecutor – he appeared more nimble than ever in her presence – was keenly interested in Etta's finances. He paced in front of her with his left elbow cradled in his right palm neatly and his chin resting on his thumb. Yes, she said, she'd kept the books for the farm. No, it had never been very profitable, but the thirty acres had gotten them by for twenty-five years – better some years than others, she added: depended what the cannery was paying out. They'd cleared their debts by '29, that helped, but then the Depression came along. The price of berries dropped, the Farmall needed a rod bearing from Anacortes, the sun didn't shine every year. One spring a touch of night cold ruined the fruit, another you couldn't get the fields to dry out and the low-hanging berries rotted. One year the fungus got you, another you couldn't keep the spit bugs down. On top of all that Carl broke his leg in '36 and spent his time hobbling up and down the rows, chasing after posts or buckets he couldn't carry on account of his homemade crutches. Then he went and put five acres into raspberries and dumped money into *that* experiment – wire and cedar posts, labor to build trellises – it set them back until he figured how to cull the canes and train them to produce. Another time he tried a new variety – Rainiers – that wouldn't take because he used too much nitrogen: lots of green, plants high and fluffy, but small hard fruit, a piddling harvest.

Yes, she'd known the defendant, Kabuo Miyamoto, for a good long time, she figured. It was more than twenty years since his family came to pick – the defendant, his two brothers, his two sisters, his mother and father – she remembered them well enough. They were hard workers, kept to themselves mostly. They brought their caddies in mounded up, she marked them off and paid out. They lived in one of the pickers' cabins at first: she could smell the perch they cooked there. She saw them some evenings sitting under a maple tree eating rice and fish off of tin plates. They would have their laundry strung between two saplings in a field of fireweed and dandelions. They had no automobile for getting about, she didn't know how they did it. In the mornings, early, two or three of their children went down to Center Bay with hand lines and fished from the pier or swam out to the rocks and tried for cod. She'd seen them on the road at seven in the morning coming home with their strings of fish or with mushrooms, with fern tendrils, butter clams, searun trout if they got lucky. They walked barefoot; they kept their faces down. All of them wore woven straw pickers' hats.

Oh, yes, she remembered them well. How was it she was supposed to forget such people? She sat in the witness stand staring at Kabuo, and tears pooled in her eyes.

Judge Fielding called for a recess then, seeing that her emotions had overwhelmed her, and Etta followed Ed Soames into the anteroom, where she sat in silence, remembering.

Zenhichi Miyamoto had appeared at her door at the end of his family's third picking season. Etta had been at the kitchen sink, and from there, looking through the parlor, she saw him watching her. He nodded at her, and she stared at him and then went back to her dishes. Then Carl – her husband – came to the door and spoke to Zenhichi with his pipe between his thumb and forefinger. It was difficult to hear exactly what they were saying so she turned the water off. Etta stood quietly and listened.

In a little while the two men left the doorway and went out into the fields together. From the window over the sink she could see them: they would stop, one of them would point, they would move on. They stopped again, pointed, swept their arms this way and that. Carl lit his pipe and scratched behind his ear, and Zenhichi pointed with his hat to the west, made a sweep, put his hat on his head. The two men walked between the rows some more, made the crest of the rise, and turned west behind some raspberry canes.

When Carl returned she'd put coffee on the table. 'What did *he* want?' she said.

'Land,' said Carl. 'Seven acres of it.'

'Which seven?'

Carl had set his pipe on the table. 'Due west seven, middle west seven. Leaves plots north and south. I told him better the northwest seven. If I was going to sell. It's hilly anyway.'

Etta poured coffee for both of them. 'We ain't going to sell,' she said firmly. 'Not in such times as these, when land is cheap. Not until better times come.'

'It's hilly,' repeated Carl. 'Hard to work. Good sun, bad drainage. Least productive acres on the property. He knows that. That's why he asked for it. Knows it's the only piece I'd think of letting go.'

'He wanted the *middle* seven,' Etta pointed out. 'Figured he might get a good two acres 'thout your noticing it.'

'Maybe,' said Carl. 'Anyway, I noticed.'

They drank their coffee. Carl ate a slice of bread spread with butter and sugar. He ate another. He was always hungry. Feeding him was a challenge. 'So what did you tell him?' she asked.

'Told him I'd think on it,' answered Carl. 'I was getting ready to let five of them west acres go to weeds, you know, they're so choresome to keep the thistle out of.'

'Don't sell,' said Etta. 'You do, you'll regret it, Carl.'

'They're decent folks,' answered Carl. 'You can bet it'd be quiet over there. Nobody carousing or carrying on. Somebody you can work with when you have to. Better than a lot of other people that way.' He picked up his pipe and fiddled with it; he liked the feel of it in his hand. 'Anyway, I told him I'd think on it,' said Carl. 'Doesn't mean I have to sell to him, does it? Just means I'm going to think.'

'Think hard,' warned Etta. She got up and started in clearing the coffee things. She felt willing to push and pull about this; seven acres was near one-quarter of the property, one-quarter of their holdings. 'That seven will be worth plenty more later,' she advised. 'You're better off keeping a good hold to it.'

'Maybe,' said Carl. 'I'll have to think about that, too.'

Etta stood at the sink with her back to him. She did her dishes hard.

'Sure be nice to have the money, though, wouldn't it?' Carl said after a while. 'There's things we've been needing and – '

'If you're going to get on to *that*,' Etta told him, 'it won't do any good by *me*. Don't try waving new church clothes at me,

Carl. I can get myself clothes when I need them. We're not such paupers as to sell to Japs, are we? For new clothes? For a pouch of fancy pipe tobacco? I say you'd better keep hold of your land, keep a tight hold, Carl, and a new frilly hat from Lottie's won't change that. Besides,' she added, turning toward him now and wiping her hands on her apron, 'you think that man's got a treasure chest or something buried in the fields somewhere? That what you think? You think he's going to slap it down all at once in front of you or some such like? Do you? He doesn't have a thing but what we give him for picking and what he gets cutting firewood for Thorsens and those Catholic people – who are they? – on South Beach, by the pier. He doesn't *have* it, Carl. He's going to pay up two bits at a time, and you're going to carry it for pocket change to town. Pipe tobacco aplenty. Magazines to read. Your seven acres is going to be swallowed up by the dime store in Amity Harbor.'

'Them Catholic people is the Hepplers,' returned Carl. 'Miyamoto don't do any work for them anymore, I don't think. Last winter he cut cedar bolts for Torgerson, made good money would be my guess. He works hard, Etta. You know that. You've seen him in the fields. Don't have to tell you that. He don't spend none of it either. Eating sea perch all the time, big sack wholesale rice from Anacortes.' Carl scratched beneath his arm, massaged his chest with his thick, heavy fingers, picked up his pipe again and fiddled with it. 'Miyamotos live clean,' he pressed on. 'You never been in their cabin? Person could eat off the floor in there, kids sleep on mats, somebody even been scrubbing mildew off the walls. Kids don't run around their faces all stained. Laundry all strung out neat with clothespins somebody *carved*. Don't wake up late, don't holler, don't complain, don't ask for nothing – '

'Like the Indjuns do,' put in Etta.

'Don't treat the Indians like dirt, neither,' Carl said. 'Kind to 'em. Showed 'em to the latrine, showed them new ones the trail to the salt chuck, showed 'em the best place for butter clams. Now,' said Carl, 'to me it don't make one bit of difference which way it is their eyes slant. I don't give a damn 'bout that, Etta. People is people, comes down to it. And these are clean-living people. Nothing wrong with them. So the question is, do we want to sell? Because Miyamoto, what he said, he's got five hundred to put down *now*. Five *hundred*. And the rest we can spread over ten years.'

Etta turned to her sink again. If this wasn't Carl all over! She thought. Liked to wander in his fields, chat with his pickers, taste his berries, smack his lips, smoke his pipe, go to town for a sack of nails. Put himself on the board for the Strawberry Festival Association, judged the floats, helped barbecue the salmon. Got himself all involved buying up the new fairgrounds, getting folks in Amity Harbor to donate lumber and whatnot for the dance pavilion at West Port Jensen. Joined the Masons and the Odd Fellows both, helped out with the record keeping at the Grange. Stood around evenings up at the pickers' cabins jawing with the Japs and taking pains with the Indians, watching the women weave sweaters and such, drawing the men out on the subject of the old days before the strawberry farms went in. Carl! Come end of picking season, he'd wander out to some old lonely place they'd told him about and look for arrowheads and bits of old bones, clamshell, and whatnot. Once some old chief went with him; they came back with arrowheads and sat on the porch smoking pipes until two o'clock in the morning. Carl gave the man rum to drink – she could hear them going at it from the bedroom, the both of them getting tipsy. She lay there with her eyes open and her ears tuned to the night and listened to Carl and his chief do their rum, some horse laughs, all the while the chief telling stories about totem poles and canoes and an old potlatch he'd been to where some other chief's daughter had gotten married and the old chief himself had won a spear-throwing contest and the next day the other chief died suddenly in his sleep, just like that he was dead and his daughter married, and the others went and punched a hole in his canoe and stuck him in it and put it up in a tree for some god-awful reason.

Etta had come to the door at two A.M. in her robe and told the chief to get on home, it was late, there were stars to walk by, she didn't like the smell of rum in her house.

'Well,' she said to Carl now, folding her arms in the kitchen doorway, where she knew she would have the last word. 'You're the man of the house, you wear the pants, go ahead and sell our property to a Jap and see what comes of it.'

The arrangement, she explained at the behest of Alvin Hooks when the court had been called into session again, included a five-hundred-dollar down payment and an eight-year 'lease-to-own' contract. Carl to collect two hundred and fifty dollars every six months, June 30 and December 31, with six and a half percent interest figured annually. Papers to be held by Carl, another set by Zenhichi, a third set for any inspector wanted to see them. The Miyamotos – this was back in '34, said Etta – couldn't really own land anyway. They were from Japan, both of them *born* there, and there was this law on the books prevented them. Carl'd kept the title in his own name, held it for them, called it a lease in case they got checked. *She* hadn't figured it, Carl had – she just kept track, was all. Watched the money come and go, made sure the interest was right. *She* didn't ever arrange no such thing.

'One moment,' Judge Fielding interrupted. He smoothed his robe and blinked at her. 'Excuse me for interrupting, Mrs. Heine. The court has a few things to say about these matters. Pardon me for interrupting.'

'All right,' said Etta.

Judge Fielding nodded at her, then turned his attention toward the jury. 'We'll skip all the whispering at the bench,' he began. 'Mr. Hooks and I might discuss matters for a bit, but if we did, no doubt it would come down to this – I'm going to have to interrupt the witness in order to explain a point of law.'

He rubbed his eyebrows, then drank some water. He put down his glass and began again. 'The witness makes reference to a currently defunct statute of the State of Washington which made it illegal at the time of which she speaks for an alien, a noncitizen, to hold title to real estate.

This same statute furthermore stipulated that no person shall hold title *for* an alien – a noncitizen – in any way, shape, or form. Furthermore, in 1906, I believe it was, the U.S. attorney general ordered all federal courts to deny naturalized citizenship to Japanese aliens. Thus it was impossible, in the strict legal sense, for Japanese immigrants to own land in Washington state. Mrs. Heine has told us that her deceased husband, in joint *conspiracy* with the defendant's deceased father, entered into an agreement which, shall we say, was predicated on a rather liberal, albeit mutually satisfying, interpretation of these laws. They quite simply made their way *around* them. At any rate, the witness's husband and the defendant's father entered into a so-called "lease" agreement that concealed an actual purchase. A substantial down payment changed hands, false papers were drawn up for state inspection. These papers, in fact – along with the others Mrs. Heine has described, the ones her husband and his "buyer" held – were entered, as you may recall, as state's evidence in this trial. The *perpetuators* of all this, as Mrs. Heine has taken pains to point out, are no longer among us, so their culpability is not at issue. If counsel or witness feel any further explanation is required they may inquire further,' the judge added. 'However,' he said, 'let it be known that this court is not concerned with any perpetuators of violations against our state's now – blessedly so – defunct Alien Land Law. Mr. Hooks, you may proceed.'

'One thing,' said Etta.

'Yes, of course,' the judge answered.

'Them Japanese couldn't own land,' said Etta. 'So I don't see how them Miyamotos could think they owned ours. They – '

'Mrs. Heine,' said the judge. 'Excuse me one more time. I apologize for interrupting. But I must remind you that Mr. Miyamoto here is on trial for murder in the first degree, that such is the focus of this court's concern, and that any contentiousness about legal ownership of land will have to be addressed in a civil court, madam. You will confine yourself, please, to answering the questions put to you. Mr. Hooks,' said the judge. 'Proceed.'

'Thank you,' Alvin Hooks replied. 'For the record let me point out that the witness has attempted only to reconstruct the facts about ownership of her land in direct response to a question put to her in the course of examination. That furthermore such information is vital to the state's case and that a clear portrait of the agreement between the defendant and the witness will illuminate the defendant's motive for committing murder. That – '

'That's enough,' said Judge Fielding. 'You've made your opening statement, Alvin. Let's get on with it.'

Alvin Hooks nodded and paced again. 'Mrs. Heine,' he said. 'Let's back up just a moment. If the law, as you say, prevented the Miyamotos from owning land, what was the point of this sale agreement?'

'So they could make payments,' said Etta. 'The law let 'em own land if they were citizens. Them Miyamoto kids were born here so they're citizens, I guess. When they turned twenty the land'd go over into their name – law said they could do that, put it in their kids' name at twenty.'

'I see,' Alvin Hooks replied. 'And they – the defendant's family, the Miyamotos, that is – had no children in 1934 who were twenty years of age, Mrs. Heine? As far as you know, ma'am?'

'Oldest one's sitting right there,' said Etta, pointing a finger at Kabuo. 'He was twelve, I believe, back then.'

Alvin Hooks turned to look at the defendant as though he was uncertain who she meant. 'The defendant?' he asked. 'In '34?'

'Yes,' said Etta. 'The defendant. That's what the eight-year lease was all about. When eight years was up, he'd be twenty.'

'In '42,' said Alvin Hooks.

'Forty-two, that's right,' said Etta. 'November of '42 he'd be twenty, they'd make the last payment December 31, the land'd go over into his name, that was going to be that.'

108

'*Going* to be?' said Alvin Hooks.

'Missed the last payment,' said Etta. 'Missed the last *two* payments, in fact. Never made 'em. The last two. Out of sixteen total.'

She folded her arms across her chest. She set her mouth and waited.

Nels Gudmundsson coughed.

'Now Mrs. Heine,' said Hooks. 'When they missed two successive payments in 1942, what did you do about that?'

It took her awhile to answer. She rubbed her nose. She adjusted her arms. She remembered how Carl'd come home one afternoon with a posting he'd picked up in Amity Harbor. He'd sat at the table, smoothed it down in front of him, and read every word slowly. Etta had stood over him reading, too.

'INSTRUCTIONS TO ALL PERSONS OF JAPANESE ANCESTRY LIVING IN THE FOLLOWING AREAS,' it said, and then it listed Anacortes and Bellingham, San Juan and San Piedro, a lot of other places in the Skagit Valley; she forgot the others. At any rate, it told the Japs they had to leave by noon on March 29. They were to be evacuated by the Fourth Army.

Etta had counted on her fingers. The Japs had eight days exactly. They could bring bedding, linen, toilet articles, extra clothing, knives, spoons, forks, plates, bowls, cups. They had to tie it in neat bundles and put their names on everything. The government would give them a number. The Japs could bring what they could carry, but no pets. The government said it would store their furniture. The furniture would stay, the Japs had to report to an assembly center at the Amity Harbor dock on March 29, eight A.M. The government would provide transportation.

'By God,' said Carl. He smoothed the bill with his thumb, shook his head.

'Won't be pickers this year,' replied Etta. 'Maybe get some Chinamen from Anacortes, the Japs aren't going to be around.'

'Plenty of time for that,' said Carl. 'By God, Etta.' He shook his head.

Carl took his fingers from the bill on the table. It rolled up of its own accord. 'By God,' he repeated. 'Eight days.'

'They'll be selling everything off,' said Etta. 'Just you wait and see. All their knickknacks, pots and pans. A lot of yard sales – you watch. That's what those people'll do with their things – sell them off as fast as they can to whoever'll take them off their hands.'

'People are going to take advantage, too,' said Carl, still wagging his big head. He sat with his forearms on the table. Soon, she knew, he was going to eat something, spread crumbs across her kitchen. He looked as though he was ready to eat, as if he was contemplating food. 'It's too bad,' he said. 'It ain't *right.*'

'They're Japs,' answered Etta. 'We're in a war with them. We can't have spies around.'

Carl shook his head and, heavy as he was, swiveled in his chair to face her.

'We ain't right together,' he told Etta flatly. 'You and me, we just ain't right.'

She knew, indeed, what he meant by that. But just the same she didn't answer. Anyway, he had said this sort of thing before. It didn't hurt very much.

For a moment Etta stood with her wrists against her hips, letting him know how she felt about matters, but Carl didn't look away. 'Have some Christian compassion,' he said. 'My grace, Etta. Don't you feel nothing?'

She went out. There was weeding to be done, and she had to fill the hog trough. She stopped in the mudroom, hung her apron on a hook, sat down to pull her boots on. She was sitting there like that, struggling with a boot, worrying over what Carl had said – the two of them not being right for each other, that old thing – when Zenhichi Miyamoto came to the door, took his hat off, and nodded.

'We heard,' she said, 'about you people.'

'Is Mr. Heine home, Mrs. Heine?' Miyamoto propped his hat against his leg, but then he shifted it behind his back.

110

'He's here,' said Etta. 'Yes.'

She stuck her head around the mudroom door and called loudly for Carl. 'Someone's here!' she added.

When Carl showed she said to him, 'You may as well talk about it right here in front of me, I'm a part of this.'

'Hello, Zenhichi,' said Carl. 'Why don't you come on in?'

Etta pried her boots off. She followed the Jap into the kitchen.

'Sit down, Zenhichi,' Carl said. 'Etta will get you some coffee.'

He stared at her and she nodded. She took a fresh apron from its hook and put it on. She filled the coffeepot.

'We saw the posting,' said Carl. 'Eight days just isn't near enough time. How can a body be ready in eight days? It ain't right,' he added. 'It just ain't right.'

'What can we do?' Zenhichi said. 'We will put boards with nails on our windows. Leave everything. If you will like, Mr. Heine, you can work our fields. We are grateful that you have sold them to us. Good two-year plants now, most. We will have plenty berries. You pick them, please. Sell them to the cannery, keep what money. Otherwise they rot, Mr. Heine. And nobody gets nothing.'

Carl began to scratch his face. He sat across from Zenhichi scratching. He looked large and coarse, the Japanese man smaller and clear-eyed. They were about the same age, but the Jap looked younger, fifteen years younger at least. Etta put cups and saucers on the table, opened the sugar bowl. *Pretty shrewd, for openers*, she thought. Offer the berries, they're worth nothing to him now. Real clever. Then talk about payments.

'I'm obliged,' said Carl. 'We'll pick them, then. I'm much obliged, Zenhichi.'

The Japanese man nodded. He was always nodding, thought Etta. It was how they got the better of you – they *acted* small, thought big. Nod, say nothing, keep their faces turned down; it was how they got things like her seven acres. 'How are you going to make your payments if me and Carl's picking your berries?' she asked from her place by the stove. 'It's not – '

'Just hold on now, Etta,' Carl broke in. 'We don't need to talk about that just yet.' He turned his attention back to the Jap. 'How is everyone to home?' he said. 'How is everyone taking it?'

'Very busy at home,' said Miyamoto. 'Packing everything, making ready.' He smiled; she saw his big teeth.

'Can we help somehow?' said Carl.

'You pick our berries. That is big help.'

'But can we help? Can we do something else?'

Etta brought the coffeepot to the table. She saw that Miyamoto had his hat in his lap. Well, Carl was being a real gracious host, but he'd forgotten about that, hadn't he? The Jap had to sit there with his hat under the table like a man who'd wet his pants.

'Carl will pour,' she announced. She sat down, smoothed her apron. She folded her hands on the tabletop.

'Let it sit a minute,' answered Carl. 'Then we'll have our coffee.'

They were sitting there like that when Carl junior barged through the kitchen door. Home from school already. Three thirty-five and home already. Must've *run* or something. Had one book with him – mathematics. His jacket was grass stained, his face ruddy with the wind, a little sweaty, too. She could see he was hungry, like his father that way, ate everything in sight. 'There's some apples in the pantry,' she pointed out.

'You may get one, Carl. Get a glass of milk and go outside. Somebody's here, we're talking.'

'I heard about it,' said Carl junior. 'I – '

'Go on and get your apple,' said Etta. 'Somebody's here, Carl.'

He went. He came back with two apples. Went to the refrigerator, took out the milk pitcher, poured himself a glass of milk. His father reached for the coffeepot and filled Miyamoto's cup, then Etta's, then his own. Carl junior looked at them, the apples in one hand, the glass of milk in the other. He went on into the living room.

'You go outside,' called Etta. 'Don't you eat in there.'

The boy came back and stood in the doorway. There was a bite taken out of one of the apples. The milk was gone from his glass. He was already near as big as his father. He was eighteen. It was hard to believe how big he was. He took another bite from the apple. 'Is Kabuo home?' he asked.

'Kabuo just home,' replied Miyamoto. 'Yes, he is there.' He smiled.

'I'm going over,' said Carl junior. He walked across the kitchen and put his glass in the sink. He banged out through the kitchen door.

'Come back for your schoolbook!' Etta called.

The boy came back and took his book up the stairs. He went into the pantry, got another apple, waved as he went by them. 'I'll be back,' he announced.

Carl pushed the sugar bowl toward the Japanese man. 'Take some,' he said. 'Cream, too, if you like.'

Miyamoto nodded. 'Thank you,' he said. 'Very good. Sugar only, please.'

He stirred in half a spoon of sugar. He used his spoon carefully, set it in his saucer. He waited until Carl picked up his cup, then picked up his own and sipped. 'Very good,' he said. He looked over at Etta and smiled her way – a little smile, that was all he ever gave.

'Your boy is very big now,' he said. He was still smiling. And then he lowered his head. 'I want to make payment. Two more payment, everything done. Today I have one hundred twenty dollar. I – '

Carl senior was shaking his head. He put his coffee down, shook his head some more. 'Absolutely not,' he said. 'Absolutely not, Zenhichi. We'll get your harvest in, see what comes of that July. Maybe then we can work out something. Maybe, where you're going, they'll have work for you to do. Who knows? It'll turn out. Point is, though, no way am I going to take your savings off your hands at a time like this, Zenhichi. Don't even *talk* about that now.'

The Jap put his one hundred and twenty dollars on the table – a lot of tens, some fives, ten ones; he spread them out in a fan. 'You take this, please,' he said. 'I send more from where I am going. Make payment. Maybe payment is not enough, you still have seven acres strawberries this year. Then, December, there is one more payment. You see? One more.'

Etta folded her arms across her chest; she *knew* he wasn't giving his strawberries for nothing! 'Your berries,' she said. 'What can we figure? After all, nobody sets the price 'til June. All right, say you've got good plants, two-year plants, like you say you do. Everything goes right. We get people in there weeding. No spit bugs, good sun, everything comes out right, berries come in, good crop. All right, after labor and what we put into fertilizer maybe you've got two hundred worth of berries? In a good year? If the price is good? If everything goes right? But let's just say it's a bad year. An average year. Fungus gets 'em, too much rain, any one of a dozen things – now we're talking about a hundred, maybe a hundred twenty worth of berries. Okay? What then? I'll tell you what. It won't be enough to cover your payment, two hundred and fifty dollars.'

'You take this,' said Zenhichi. He made a stack of the bills, moved them toward her. 'This one hundred and twenty dollar. Strawberries bring one hundred and thirty, next payment is made.'

'Thought you was *giving* the berries,' said Etta. 'Didn't you come in here giving them away? Didn't you tell us to sell them to the cannery and keep whatever comes from that? Now what you want is one hundred thirty.' She reached out and took his neat stack of bills, counted the money while she spoke. 'One hundred and thirty on the risk they bring it, plus this here as an early payment, the risk in exchange for getting this March instead of us waiting on all of it 'til June? Is that what you came here hoping on?'

The Japanese man blinked at her steadily. He said nothing, didn't touch his coffee either. He'd gone rigid, gone cold. She could see that he was angry, that he was holding it in, not

114

exposing his rage. *He's proud*, she thought. *I just spit on him, he's pretending it didn't happen that way. Blink away*, she thought.

Etta finished counting his money, set the stack of bills back on the table, and folded her arms across her chest again. 'More coffee?' she asked.

'No, thank you,' the Jap replied. 'You take money, please.'

Carl's big hand slid across the table. His fingers covered the stack of bills and pushed it in front of the Jap's coffee. 'Zenhichi,' he said. 'We won't take this. Don't matter what Etta says, we won't. She's been rude to you and I apologize for that.' He looked at her then and she looked right back. She knew how he felt, but it didn't matter very much – she wanted Carl to know what was up, how he was being duped. She wasn't going to hang her head. She stared back at him.

'I am sorry,' the Jap said. 'Very sorry.'

'We'll worry about this come picking season,' said Carl. 'You get where you're going, you write to us. We'll get your berries in, write back, we'll go from there. We'll just play this by ear a little bit, far as I'm concerned. One way or another you get your payments finished, maybe down the road somewhere, everything comes out like it should in the long run. Everything comes out satisfactory. But right now you got deeper things to think about. You don't need us bending your ear about payments. You got plenty to do 'thout that. And anything I can do, help you get your things all ready, you let me know, Zenhichi.'

'I make payments,' Zenhichi answered. 'I find a way, I send you.'

'That's fine,' said Carl and put his hand out. The Japanese man took it.

'Thank you, Carl,' he said. 'I make payments. No worry.'

Etta watched Zenhichi. It occurred to her that he had not grown old – she noticed this more clearly than ever. For ten years he'd been working these very same fields, his eyes were still clear, his back was straight, his skin was taut, his belly remained lean and hard. Ten years he had worked in the same

115

fields she had, and yet he hadn't aged a day. His clothes were clean, his head erect, his complexion brown and healthy. And all of this was part of his mystery, his distance from what *she* was. Something he knew about kept him from aging while she, Etta, grew worn and weary – something he knew about yet kept to himself, bottled up behind his face. Maybe it was Jap religion, she thought, or maybe it was in his blood. There didn't seem any way to know.

She remembered, on the witness stand, that Carl junior had returned that evening with a bamboo fishing rod. How he had looked to her coming through the door with his hair rumpled by the wind. How big and young, like a Great Dane puppy, bounding into her kitchen. Her son, a big young man.

'Look at this,' he'd said to her. 'Kabuo loaned it to me.'

He began to explain it to her. She'd been at the sink peeling supper potatoes. He said it was a good rod for sea-run cutthroat. Split bamboo, made by a Mr. Nishi, the ferrules smooth, silk wrapped. Figured he'd go trolling with it, get Erik Everts or somebody, one of his friends, to take him out in a canoe. Rig it up with light tackle, see how it played. Where was Dad? He'd go show it to him.

Etta didn't stop peeling her potatoes while she said to her son what she had to say: take the fishing rod back to the Japs, they owed them money, the rod confused that.

She remembered how the boy had looked at her. Hurt and trying to hide it. Wanted to argue, didn't want to argue – wouldn't win and already knew it. The look of the defeated – his father's look – big, plodding strawberry farmer. Subdued, pinned to the earth. The boy spoke like his father and moved like his father, but he had a broad brow, small ears, there was a set to his eyes, some of her in him. The boy was not all Carl's. Her son, too, she felt that.

'You turn around and take it right on back,' she'd said again, and pointed with the peeler. And in this, she saw now, on the witness stand, her feelings had not been wrong. He'd taken the rod back, some months had passed, he'd gone to the war,

116

he'd come on home, that Japanese boy had *killed* him. She'd been right about them all along; Carl, her husband, had been wrong.

They didn't meet their payments, she told Alvin Hooks. Simple as that. Didn't meet them. She sold the place off to Ole Jurgensen, sent their equity on down to them in California, didn't try to hold back their money. Gave every penny back. She moved into Amity Harbor Christmastime '44. That was that, she'd figured. Looked, now, like she was wrong about one thing: you were never shut of people where money was concerned. One way or another, they *wanted*. And on account of that, she told the court, her son had been murdered by Kabuo Miyamoto. Her son was dead and gone.

10

Alvin Hooks skirted the edge of his table and resumed the slow, fluid pacing of the floorboards that had been part of his strategy all morning. 'Mrs. Heine,' he said. 'In December of '44 you moved to Amity Harbor?'

'That's right.'

'Your husband had recently passed away?'

'That's right, too.'

'You felt that without him you could not work your land?'

'Yes.'

'So you moved to Amity Harbor,' said Alvin Hooks. 'Where exactly, Mrs. Heine?'

'On Main Street,' said Etta. 'Up above Lottie Opsvig's shop.'

'Lottie Opsvig's? An apparel shop?'

'That's right.'

'In an apartment?'

'Yes.'

'A big apartment?'

'No,' said Etta. 'Just one bedroom.'

'One bedroom above an apparel shop,' said Alvin Hooks. 'So you took a one-bedroom apartment then. And may I ask about your monthly rent?'

'Twenty-five dollars,' said Etta.

'A twenty-five-dollar-a-month apartment,' Alvin Hooks said. 'You're still living there? You currently reside there?'

'Yes.'

'Still paying twenty-five dollars?'

'No,' said Etta. '*Thirty*-five. Price has gone up since '44.'

'Forty-four,' Alvin Hooks repeated. 'The year you moved in? The year you sent the Miyamotos their equity and came to live in Amity Harbor?'

'Yes,' said Etta.

'Mrs. Heine,' said Alvin Hooks, and stopped pacing. 'Did you hear again from the Miyamotos after that? After you sent them their money?'

'I heard from them,' said Etta.

'When was that?' Alvin Hooks asked.

Etta bit her lip and thought it over; she squeezed her cheeks between her fingers. 'It was July of '45,' she answered finally. 'That one there showed up at my door.' And she pointed at Kabuo Miyamoto.

'The defendant?'

'Yes.'

'He came to your door in 1945? To your apartment door in Amity Harbor?'

'That's right.'

'Did he call ahead? Were you expecting him?'

'No. Just showed up. Just like that.'

'Just showed up unannounced? Out of nowhere, as it were?'

'That's right,' replied Etta. 'Out of nowhere.'

'Mrs. Heine,' said the prosecutor. 'What did the defendant indicate was the nature of his business with you?'

'He wanted to talk about land, he said. Had a few things to say about my land I sold to Ole.'

'Exactly what did he say, Mrs. Heine? Can you remember? For the benefit of the court?'

Etta folded her hands in her lap and glanced at Kabuo Miyamoto. She could see in his eyes – they didn't fool *her* – that he remembered everything. He'd stood in her doorway, neatly dressed, his hands clasped, unblinking. It was July and the heat in her apartment was unbearable; the doorway felt much cooler. They'd stared at each other, and then Etta had folded her arms across her chest and asked him what he wanted.

'Mrs. Heine,' he'd said. 'Do you remember me?'

119

"Course I do,' Etta had answered.

She hadn't seen him since the day the Japs left – more than three years before, in '42 – but she recollected him clearly enough. He was the boy who'd tried to give Carl a fishing rod, the boy she used to see from her kitchen window practicing in the fields with his wooden sword. He was the oldest of the Miyamoto children – she knew his face but didn't remember his name – the one her son used to hang around with.

'I've been back home three days,' he'd said. 'I guess Carl isn't home yet.'

'Carl's passed on,' replied Etta. 'Carl junior's fighting the Japs.' She stared at the man in the doorway. 'They're just about licked,' she added.

'Just about,' Kabuo had replied. He unclasped his hands and put them at his back. 'I was sorry to hear about Mr. Heine,' he said. 'I heard about it in Italy. My mother sent me a letter.'

'Well, I told you people about it when I sent on down the equity,' returned Etta. 'Said in my letter Carl'd passed on and that I'd had to go and sell the place.'

'Yes,' said Kabuo. 'But Mrs. Heine, my father had an agreement with Mr. Heine, didn't he? Didn't – '

'Mr. Heine was passed away,' Etta interrupted. 'I had to make a decision. Couldn't farm the place myself, could I? I sold to Ole and that's that,' she said. 'You want to talk about that piece of land, you're going to have to talk to *Ole*. I don't have nothing to do with it.'

'Please,' replied Kabuo. 'I talked to Mr. Jurgensen already. I got back to the island just last Wednesday and went out to see what had become of the place. You know, have a look around. Mr. Jurgensen was out there, up on his tractor. We talked for a while about things.'

'Well, good,' said Etta. 'So you talked to him.'

'I talked to him,' said Kabuo. 'He said I'd better talk to you.'

Etta folded her arms more tightly. '*Humpf*,' she said. 'It's his land, isn't it? Go on back and tell him that. Tell him I said so. You tell him.'

'He didn't *know*,' said Kabuo. 'You didn't tell him we were one payment away, Mrs. Heine. You didn't tell him Mr. Heine had – '

'He didn't know,' sneered Etta. 'Is that what Ole told you? He didn't know – is that it? Was I supposed to say, "Ole, there's these folks made an illegal agreement with my husband hands over seven acres to them"? Is that what I was supposed to say? He didn't *know*,' repeated Etta. 'Most ridiculous thing I ever heard. I'm supposed to tell someone's buying up my land there's an illegal contract muddling matters up? And what if I did? Huh? Fact is you people didn't meet your payments. That's a fact. And just suppose you done that to a bank 'round here. Just suppose. You don't make your payments, what do you think happens? Somebody waits real polite on you? No. Bank repossesses your land, that's what happens. I haven't done anything a bank wouldn't do. I haven't done anything wrong.'

'You haven't done anything *illegal*,' the Jap replied. 'Wrong is a different matter.'

Etta blinked. She stepped back and put her hand on the doorknob. 'Get out of here,' she said.

'You sold our land,' the Jap continued. 'You sold our land out from under us, Mrs. Heine. You took advantage of the fact that we were gone. You – '

But she'd shut the door so as not to listen. *Carl made such a mess*, she'd thought. *Now I have to clean it all up.*

'Mrs. Heine,' said the prosecutor, Alvin Hooks, when she'd finished telling of these things. 'Did you see the defendant thereafter? Did he approach you again about these land matters?'

'Did I see him?' asked Etta. 'Sure I saw him. Saw him in town, saw him at Petersen's, here and there . . . I saw him now and again, yes.'

'Did he speak to you?'

'No.'

'Ever?'

'No.'

'There was no further communication between you?'

'None I can think of. 'Less you want to call dirty looks a way of speaking.' And she glanced at Kabuo again.

'Dirty looks, Mrs. Heine? What exactly do you mean?'

Etta smoothed the front of her dress and sat more erectly in the witness stand. 'Ever time I saw him,' she insisted, 'there he'd be with his eyes narrowed at me. You know, watchin', *glarin*'.'

'I see,' said the prosecutor. 'And how long did this continue?'

'Been going on ever since,' said Etta. 'Never stopped. I never saw a sociable look from him, not once in all the times I saw him. Always narrowin' his eyes at me, giving me his *mean* face.'

'Mrs. Heine,' said Alvin Hooks. 'Did you ever have a conversation with your son about the defendant in this regard? Did you tell Carl junior that Kabuo Miyamoto had come to your door and argued with you about the sale of your family's land?'

'My son knew all about it. When he got back, I told him.'

'Got back?'

'From the war,' said Etta. 'Couple months later, 'bout October, I think it was.'

'And you told him then the defendant had come to your door?'

'Yes.'

'Do you recall his response?'

'Yes,' said Etta. 'He said he'd keep an eye on it. Said that if Kabuo Miyamoto was giving me dirty looks he'd keep an eye on him.'

'I see,' said Alvin Hooks. 'And did he?'

'Yes. Far as I know, yes.'

'He kept an eye out for Kabuo Miyamoto?'

'Yes, he did. He watched for him.'

'To your knowledge, Mrs. Heine, were the two of them on unfriendly terms? They were both fishermen, they shared that in common. They were, as you have said, neighbors in adolescence. And yet there was this . . . dispute. This family dispute over land. So were they, the defendant and your son, on friendly or unfriendly terms from 1945 on?'

122

'No,' said Etta. 'The defendant wasn't no friend of my son's. Isn't that obvious? They were enemies.'

'Enemies?' said Alvin Hooks.

'Carl told me more 'n once he wished Kabuo would forget about his seven acres and stop lookin' at me cross-eyed.'

'When you told him the defendant had given you dirty looks your son reacted exactly how, Mrs. Heine?'

'Said he wished Kabuo'd stop doing that. Said he'd have to keep an eye out for Kabuo.'

'*Keep an eye out*,' Alvin Hooks repeated. 'He saw some danger from Mr. Miyamoto?'

'Objection,' cut in Nels Gudmundsson. 'The witness is being asked to speculate as to her son's state of mind and his emotional status. He's – '

'All right, all right,' said Alvin Hooks. 'Tell us what you *observed*, Mrs. Heine. Tell us what your son said or did – was there anything to suggest he saw some kind of danger from Kabuo Miyamoto?'

'Said he'd keep an eye out for him,' repeated Etta. 'You know, he'd watch out.'

'Did your son say he felt he had to watch for Mr. Miyamoto? That there was danger from him of some kind?'

'Yes,' said Etta. 'He kept an eye on him. Every time I told him that man was glarin' at me, that's what he said – he'd watch out.'

'Mrs. Heine,' said Alvin Hooks. 'Do you think that the term "family feud" could be accurately applied to the relationship between your family and that of the defendant? Were you enemies? Was there a feud?'

Etta looked directly at Kabuo. 'Yes,' she said. 'We're enemies all right. They've been botherin' us over those seven acres for near ten years now. My son was killed over it.'

'Objection,' said Nels Gudmundsson. 'The witness is speculating as to – '

'Sustained,' agreed Judge Fielding. 'Witness will confine herself to answering questions put to her without further speculation. I hereby instruct you jury members to disregard her last words. Witness's comment will furthermore be struck from the record. Let's move on, Mr. Hooks.'

'Thank you,' Alvin Hooks said. 'But I can't think of anything else I want to ask, Your Honor. Mrs. Heine, I want you to know that I appreciate your coming down, though, what with this weather we've been having. Thank you for testifying in a snowstorm.' He swiveled, now, on the toe of one shoe; he pointed a forefinger at Nels Gudmundsson. 'Your witness,' he said.

Nels Gudmundsson shook his head and frowned. 'Just three questions,' he grumbled, without getting up. 'I've done some calculating, Mrs. Heine. If I've multiplied correctly, the Miyamoto family purchased seven acres from you for forty-five hundred dollars – is that right? Forty-five hundred dollars?'

'Tried to buy it for that much,' said Etta. 'Never finished their payments.'

'Second question,' Nels said. 'When you went to Ole Jurgensen in 1944 and told him you wanted to sell him your land, what was the price per acre?'

'A thousand,' said Etta. 'Thousand per acre.'

'I guess that makes what would have been forty-five hundred dollars into seven thousand dollars instead, doesn't it. A twenty-five-hundred-dollar increase in the land's value if you sent the Miyamotos their equity and sold the land to Ole Jurgensen?'

'Is that your third question?' said Etta.

'It is,' said Nels. 'Yes.'

'You done your math right. Twenty-five hundred.'

'That's all then, thank you,' Nels replied. 'You may step down, Mrs. Heine.'

Ole Jurgensen came out of the gallery leaning hard on his cane. Alvin Hooks held the swinging door for him, and Ole shuffled past with his cane in his right hand and his left at the small of his back. He shuffled half sidewise, an injured crab, making his way toward where Ed Soames stood proffering the Holy Bible.

When Ole arrived he bobbled his cane from hand to hand before settling on the expediency of hanging it from his wrist. The stroke he'd suffered in June caused his hands to tremble. He'd been out among his pickers, sorting berries in a bin, when the sensation that the earth was tilting under his feet grew on him out of a more general dizziness and nausea that had inhabited him all morning. Ole reared up and made a last desperate effort to shrug off what was happening, but the sky seemed to crowd around his head, the earth buckled, and he keeled over into a strawberry bin. There he lay blinking up at the clouds until two Canadian Indian pickers pulled him out by the armpits. They took him up to his house in the tractor bucket and laid him on his porch like a corpse. Liesel shook him until he grunted at her and drooled, and in the face of this she began a hysterical interrogation into the nature of his symptoms. When it became apparent he didn't intend to answer she stopped talking and kissed his forehead. Then she hurried in and called Dr. Whaley.

Since then he had withered rapidly. His legs were stilts, his eyes leaked water, his beard ended in wisps at the third button of his vest, his skin appeared pink and chafed. He perched in the stand, both hands wrapped around the head of his cane now, a tremulous and gangling old man.

'Mr. Jurgensen,' Alvin Hooks began. 'You were for many years a neighbor of the Heine family in Center Valley? Is that correct, sir?'

'Yes,' said Ole Jurgensen.

'How many years?'

'Yust always,' said Ole. 'Why, I can remember back fo-forty years to when Carl – old Carl – cleared his land next to mine.'

'Forty years,' said Alvin Hooks. 'For forty years you were a berry farmer?'

'Yes, sir. More than forty.'

'How many acres did you own, Mr. Jurgensen?'

Ole seemed to think about it. He licked his lips and squinted at the courthouse ceiling; his hands roamed up and down the length of his cane. 'Thirty-five, start out,' he said. 'Then I ac-acquired thirty more from Etta, you see, like Etta tell before when she was up here. So that brought me up–up to sixty-five acre; big farm, it was.'

'Yes,' said Alvin Hooks. 'So you purchased thirty acres from Etta Heine, then?'

'Yes, sir. I did so.'

'And when was that, Mr. Jurgensen?'

'Yust like she tell. Nineteen hundred and forty-four.'

'She handed over to you the property deed at that time?'

'Yes, sir.'

'In your mind, Mr. Jurgensen, did the deed read free and clear? That is, were there any encumbrances or conditions? Easements? Liens? That sort of thing?'

'No,' said Ole Jurgensen. 'No ting like that. The contract was good. Every ting look right with it.'

'I see,' said Alvin Hooks. 'So you were not aware of any claim, then, that the Miyamotos might have had to any seven of your newly purchased thirty acres?'

'Not aware, no,' said Ole. 'I bring it up with Etta, you see, because the Miyamoto family, they have–have a house on the property, I know seven acres has been sold to them. But Etta says to me they don' make no payment so she is . . . to repossess. She don' have any choice after Carl passed away, says she. Every ting looks good with the contract, says she. The Miyamoto family away in the camp, says she, maybe they won' come b–back. She is going to give them their money, says she. They don' have any claim, no, sir.'

'So you heard nothing about any claim the Miyamotos might have had to seven acres of your newly purchased land?'

'No. I hear no ting about it until that man' – he aimed his nose at the defendant – 'come round about and tell me.'

'Do you mean the defendant there – Kabuo Miyamoto?'

'Him,' said Ole. 'Yes, that's right.'

'He came around when, Mr. Jurgensen?'

'Let's see,' said Ole. 'He come summer of '45, he does. He sh–shows up at my place and say Mrs. Heine robbed him,

126

Mr. Heine never would have let no such ting like that happen, he says.'

'I'm not following,' said Alvin Hooks. 'The defendant showed up at your farm in the summer of 1945 and accused Etta Heine of *robbing him?*'

'*Yes, sir. That's what I remember.*'

'*And what did you say?*'

'*I say no to him, she sell the land to me, and I don't see his* name any place on the contract.'

'Yes?'

'He wants to know will I sell it back to him.'

'Sell it back?' said Alvin Hooks. 'The thirty acres?'

'He don't want all thirty,' answered Ole. 'He just want the seven in the northwest, where his family was one time living. Before the war.'

'And did you talk about that? Did you consider selling?'

'He didn't have no money,' said Ole. 'Anyway, I'm not thinking of s-selling then. It was before . . . my stroke. I had a good farm, sixty-five acres. I don't want to sell one piece to anybody.'

'Mr. Jurgensen,' said Alvin Hooks. 'When you purchased Etta Heine's thirty acres did you acquire her home as well?'

'No. She sold it separate. Just the house, to Bjorn Andreason. And he is still living there now.'

'And the house the *defendant's* family had lived in, Mr. Jurgensen?'

'This one,' said Ole, 'I bought.'

'I see,' said Alvin Hooks. 'And what did you do with it?'

'I use it for my pickers, you see,' said Ole. 'My f-farm was so big now, I need to have a manager with me year around. So he is living there, plus room for pickers come picking time.'

'Mr. Jurgensen,' Alvin Hooks said. 'Did the defendant say anything else to you during his visit in the summer of 1945? Anything you can remember?'

Ole Jurgensen's right hand left the head of his cane. It clawed its way into the side pocket of his coat and fumbled about for something. 'Yes, one ting,' said Ole. 'He said some day he would get his land back.'

'That he would get it back?'

'Yes, sir. And he is angry.'

'And what did you say?'

'I said to him why is he angry to *me*? I don't know any ting about this land, except that I don't want to sell it to nobody.' Ole lifted a handkerchief to his mouth and dried his lips with it. 'I say to him go talk with Etta Heine, she is moved into Amity Harbor. I tell him where he can look for her, she is the person to talk to.'

'And did he leave then?'

'Yes.'

'And did you see him again?'

'I see him, yes. This island is small. You live hereabouts you see everybody.'

'All right,' Alvin Hooks said. 'You've had a stroke, Mr. Jurgensen, as you say. And that was in June of this year?'

'Yes, sir. June 28.'

'I see,' said Alvin Hooks. 'And it incapacitated you? So that you felt you could no longer run your farm?'

Ole Jurgensen didn't answer at first. His right hand, with the handkerchief in it, returned to the head of his cane. He chewed on the inside of his cheek; his head shook. Ole struggled to speak.

'I – I . . . yes,' he said. 'I yust couldn't do it, you see.'

'You couldn't run your farm?'

'N-no.'

'So what did you do?'

'I – I put it on the market. For sale,' said Ole Jurgensen. 'September 7. Yust after Labor Day.'

'Of this year?'

'Did you list your property with a real estate agent, Mr. Jurgensen?'

'Yes, sir.'

'With Klaus Hartmann?'

128

'Yes, sir.'

'Did you advertise in any other way?'

'We had a sign on the barn,' said Ole. 'That was everyting.'

'And what happened then?' asked Alvin Hooks. 'Did anybody come to look?'

'Carl Heine came,' said Ole. 'C-Carl Heine, Etta's son.'

'When was that?' Alvin Hooks asked.

'That was September 7,' said Ole. 'Round about comes Carl Heine, wantin' to buy my farm.'

'Tell us about that,' Alvin Hooks asked gently. 'Carl Heine was a . . . successful fisherman. He owned a fine place on Mill Run Road. What did he want with your farm?'

Ole Jurgensen blinked half a dozen times. He dabbed at his eyes with his handkerchief. The young man, he remembered, Carl junior, had driven into his yard that morning in a sky blue Bel-Air, scattering chickens before him. Ole, from his place on the porch, knew who it was immediately; he guessed what it was he wanted. The young man had come by each picking season; he'd brought along his wife and children. They'd taken their caddies into the fields and picked berries together. Ole had always refused Carl's money, but Carl'd pressed it on him. When Ole shook his head Carl put the bills on the weighing table next to the scales, beneath a stone. 'Don't care if it was my father's land once,' he'd say. 'It's yours now. We'll pay.'

Now here he was, big, like his father, with his father's stature and his mother's face, dressed like a fisherman in rubber boots – he *was* a fisherman, Ole recalled, had named his boat after his wife: the *Susan Marie*.

Liesel had given the young man a glass of iced tea. He'd sat down so that from where they looked the strawberry fields spread out before them. Way in the distance they could just make out the broad side of Bjorn Andreason's house – where Carl junior had once lived.

Small talk, Ole explained now to the court. Carl had asked about the strawberries this year, Ole had asked about the salmon runs. Liesel had inquired as to Etta's health, and then she had asked Carl how the fishing life suited him. 'It doesn't,' Carl had answered.

It'd been, thought Ole, an odd thing for the young man to say aloud. It must have hurt his pride to say it. He'd been admitting something, Ole understood, and admitting it for a reason. He'd wanted to make a point.

The young man had put his glass down, just in front of his rubber boots, and leaned toward them, his elbows on his knees, as if he was about to confess something. He'd looked at the floorboards of the porch for a moment. 'I want to buy your farm,' he'd said.

Liesel had explained to him how Bjorn Andreason had the old Heine house – there was nothing to be done about it. Liesel had explained that she and Ole didn't want to leave the farm at all – but there was nothing to be done about that either. And the young man had nodded and scratched the bristles along his jaw. 'I'm sorry for that,' he'd said quietly. 'I feel bad to take advantage of your health, Mr. Jurgensen. But if you have to sell, I guess . . . well, I'm interested.'

Ole had said, 'I am happy. You have lived here, you know this place. We do what is fair. I am happy.' And he'd reached his hand toward the young man.

The young man took it solemnly. 'It's the way I feel, too,' he'd said.

They'd spoken in the kitchen of the arrangements they would make together. Carl's money was tied up in the *Susan Marie* and in his house on Mill Run Road. In the meantime there was a thousand dollars in earnest money – Carl put it on the table. Ten one-hundred–dollar bills. Come November the boat would sell, then the house, said Carl. 'Your wife will be happy,' said Liesel with a smile. 'Fishermen are always gone at night.'

Ole Jurgensen leaned on his cane and remembered another visitor later that same day. Kabuo Miyamoto had come to see him.

'The defendant?' asked Alvin Hooks. 'On September 7 of this year?'

130

'Yes, sir,' said Ole.

'The same day Carl Heine came to see you to inquire about the sale of your land?'

'Yes, sir.'

'In the afternoon of that same day?'

'Round abouts lunch,' said Ole. 'We were yust about sitting down to lunch, it was. Miyamoto knocked on our door.'

'And did he say, Mr. Jurgensen, what he wanted?'

'Same as Etta's son,' said Ole. 'He wanted to buy my land.'

'Tell us about that,' said Alvin Hooks. 'What exactly did he say to you?'

They'd sat down on the porch together, explained Ole. The defendant had seen the sign on the barn and wanted to buy Ole's farm. Ole had remembered the Japanese man's promise: how he'd stood in the fields and vowed that one day he would get his family's land back. The Japanese man had slipped his mind altogether. Nine years had passed.

He'd remembered, too, that the Japanese man had worked for him years before, part of a crew that put in his raspberries in 1939. Ole remembered him pounding home cedar posts for raspberry canes, standing in the bed of a pickup truck, shirtless, swinging a maul. He must have been sixteen or seventeen.

He remembered seeing him early in the morning, too, swinging a wooden sword in the fields. The boy's father, he remembered, was Zeneechee, something like that. He never could pronounce it.

On the porch he'd asked Kabuo about his father, but the man had long passed away.

The Japanese man had asked about the land then, and asserted his wish to buy the seven acres his family had once held.

'I'm afraid it isn't for sale,' Liesel had said. 'It's already been sold, you see. Somebody else came by this morning. I'm sorry to tell you, Kabuo.'

'Yes,' said Ole. 'We're sorry.'

The Japanese man had stiffened. In a moment the politeness

went from his face so that Ole could no longer read him. 'It's sold?' he said. 'Already?'

'Yes,' said Liesel. 'Just like that. We're sorry to disappoint you.'

'All of it?' asked the Japanese man.

'Yes,' said Liesel. 'We're very sorry. We didn't even have time to take our sign down.'

The stiff expression of Kabuo Miyamoto's face didn't change even for a second. 'Who bought it?' he said. 'I want to talk to them.'

'Etta Heine's son Carl,' said Liesel. 'He came by around ten o'clock.'

'Carl Heine,' the Japanese man answered, with a hint of anger in his voice.

Ole had suggested that Kabuo Miyamoto go to see Carl Heine about the matter. Perhaps something could be worked out.

Liesel shook her head and wrung her hands in her apron. 'We've sold it,' she'd repeated apologetically. 'Ole and Carl shook hands, you see. We accepted earnest money. We're bound to our agreement. It's sold, you see. We're sorry.'

The Japanese man had stood then. 'I should have come earlier,' he said.

The next day Carl had come by again – Liesel phoned him about Kabuo Miyamoto – to take the sign down from the barn. Ole, leaning on his cane, stood below and told him about the Japanese man's visit. Carl, he remembered, had been interested in the details of it. He nodded his head and listened closely. Ole Jurgensen told everything – the way the politeness had gone out of the Japanese man, the unreadable Japanese expression on his face when he heard that the land he coveted had been sold. Carl Heine nodded again and again and then came down from the ladder with the sign. 'Thanks for telling me,' he'd said.

11

After the noon recess was called that day Kabuo Miyamoto ate lunch in his cell, as he had seventy-seven times. The cell was one of two in the courthouse basement and had neither bars nor windows. It was big enough for a low military surplus bunk, a toilet, a sink, and a nightstand. There was a drain in the corner of its concrete floor and a foot-square grate in its door. Other than this there were no openings or apertures through which light could seep. A naked bulb hung overhead, and Kabuo could turn it on and off by screwing and unscrewing it in its socket. Yet before the first week was over he'd discovered in himself a preference for darkness. His eyes adjusted to it. He was less troubled by the closeness of his cell walls with the naked light put out, less conscious that he was jailed.

Kabuo sat on the edge of his bunk with his lunch perched in front of him on the nightstand. A peanut-butter-and-jelly sandwich, two carrot sticks, a mound of lime gelatin, a tin cup of milk, served on a cafeteria tray. At this particular moment his light was on. He'd turned it on in order to see what he was eating but also in order to look at his face in a hand-held shaving mirror. His wife had said he looked like one of Tojo's soldiers. He wanted to see if this was so.

He sat with his tray just in front of his knees, confronting his reflection in the hand mirror. He could see how his face had once been a boy's face and how on top of this was laid the face of his war years – a face he was no longer surprised to see, though it had astonished him greatly in the beginning. He had come home from the war and seen in his own eyes the disturbed empty reaches he'd seen in the eyes of other soldiers he'd known.

They did not so much seem to stare right through things as to stare past the present state of the world into a world that was permanently in the distance for them and at the same time more immediate than the present. Kabuo remembered much in this manner. Under the surface of his daily life was a life he lived as if underwater. Kabuo remembered how under the helmet of the soldier on the wooded hillside, underneath the steady droning of the bees, it had turned out to be a very young boy he had shot directly through the groin. When Kabuo approached from one side the boy had stared up at him and spoke through clenched teeth in tremulous German. Then the boy panicked and moved his hand toward his gun, and Kabuo shot him one more time in the heart at point-blank range. Yet still the boy refused to die and lay on his back between two trees while Kabuo stood five feet away, frozen, his rifle shouldered still. The boy held his chest in both of his hands and exerted himself to raise his head from the ground, at the same time gathering himself to take a breath, and sucked in the hot afternoon air. Then he spoke again, between his teeth, and it was clear to Kabuo that he was begging, pleading, that he wanted the American who had killed him to save him – he had no choice but to ask him for this, nobody else was present. All of it was too much, and when the boy stopped talking his chest twitched a half-dozen times and blood ran from his mouth and down his cheeks. Then Kabuo went forward with his rifle and squatted beside the German boy, on his right, and the boy put his hand on Kabuo's boot and shut his eyes and gave out. The tension stayed in his mouth for a while, and Kabuo watched until it faded. The smell of breakfast soon rose from the German boy's bowels.

Kabuo sat in his prison cell now and examined his reflection carefully. It was not a thing he had control over. His face had been molded by his experiences as a soldier, and he appeared to the world seized up inside precisely because this was how he felt. It was possible for him all these years later to think of the German boy dying on the hillside and to feel his own heart pound as it had as he squatted against the tree, drinking from his canteen, his ears ringing, his legs trembling. What could he say to people on San Piedro to explain the coldness he projected? The world was unreal, a nuisance that prevented him from focusing on his memory of that boy, on the flies in a cloud over his astonished face, the pool of blood filtering out of his shirt and into the forest floor, smelling rank, the sound of gunfire from the hillside to the east – he'd left there, and then he hadn't left. And still there had been more murders after this, three more, less difficult than the first had been but murders nonetheless. So how to explain his face to people? After a while, motionless in his cell, he began to feel objective about his face, and then he saw what Hatsue did. He had meant to project to the jurors his innocence, he'd wanted them to see that his spirit was haunted, he sat upright in the hope that his desperate composure might reflect the shape of his soul. This was what his father had taught him: the greater the composure, the more revealed one was, the truth of one's inner life was manifest – a pleasing paradox. It had seemed to Kabuo that his detachment from this world was somehow self-explanatory, that the judge, the jurors, and the people in the gallery would recognize the face of a war veteran who had forever sacrificed his tranquillity in order that they might have theirs. Now, looking at himself, scrutinizing his face, he saw that he appeared defiant instead. He had refused to respond to anything that happened, had not allowed the jurors to read in his face the palpitations of his heart.

Yet listening to Etta Heine on the witness stand had moved Kabuo to bitter anger. He had felt his carefully constructed exterior crumbling when she spoke to the court so insultingly about his father. The desire had come over him to deny what she said, to interrupt her testimony with the truth about his father, a strong and tireless man, honest to a fault, kind and humble as well. But all of this he suppressed.

Now, in his jail cell, he stared into the mirror at the mask he wore, which had been arranged by its wearer to suggest his war and the strength he'd mustered to face its consequences but which instead communicated haughtiness, a cryptic superiority not only to the court but to the prospect of death the court confronted him with. The face in the hand mirror was none other than the face he had worn since the war had caused him to look inward, and though he exerted himself to rearrange it – because this face was a burden to wear – it remained his, unalterable finally. He knew himself privately to be guilty of murder, to have murdered men in the course of war, and it was this guilt – he knew no other word – that lived in him perpetually and that he exerted himself not to communicate. Yet the exertion itself communicated guilt, and he could see no way to stop it. He could not change how his face arranged itself while he sat with his hands on the defendant's table with his back to his fellow islanders. In his face, he knew, was his fate, as Nels Gudmundsson had asserted at the start of things: 'There are facts,' he said, 'and the jurors listen to them, but even more, they watch you. They watch to see what happens to your face, how it changes when witnesses speak. For them, at bottom, the answer is in how you appear in the courtroom, what you look like, how you act.'

He liked this man, Nels Gudmundsson. He had begun to like him on the September afternoon when he first appeared at his cell door carrying a folded chessboard beneath his arm and a Havana cigar box full of chess pieces. He'd offered Kabuo a cigar from his shirt pocket, lit his own, then brought two candy bars out of the box and dropped them on the bunk beside Kabuo without acknowledging that he had done so. It was his way of being charitable.

'I'm Nels Gudmundsson, your attorney,' he said. 'I've been appointed by the court to represent you. I – '

'I didn't do it,' Kabuo had said. 'I'm not guilty of anything.'

'Look,' said Nels. 'I'll tell you what. We can worry about that later, all right? I've been trying to find someone with the free time to play chess for fifty years now, even more. Seems to me you just might be the fellow.'

'I am,' said Kabuo. 'But – '

'You were in the service,' said Nels. 'My guess is you play a mean game of chess. Chess, checkers, rummy, bridge, hearts, dominoes, cribbage. And what about solitaire?' added Nels. 'Solitaire might be the thing for you in here.'

'Never liked solitaire,' Kabuo answered. 'Besides, a guy who starts playing solitaire in jail is just asking to get depressed.'

'Never thought of that,' said Nels. 'We'll have to get you out of here, that's all there is to it.' He smiled.

Kabuo nodded. 'Can you?'

'They're not budging just now on anything, Kabuo. You're here until your trial, I think.'

'There shouldn't even *be* a trial,' said Kabuo.

'Alvin Hooks would disagree,' said Nels. 'He's putting his case together. He's serious about murder in the first degree, and he's serious about asking for the death penalty. We should be, too – we should get serious. We have a lot of work to do, you and I. But first, what about chess?'

The death penalty, Kabuo said to himself. He was a Buddhist and believed in the laws of karma, so it made sense to him that he might pay for his war murders: everything comes back to you, nothing is accidental. The fear of death grew in him. He thought of Hatsue and of his children and it seemed to him he must be exiled from them – because he felt for them so much love – in order to pay his debts to the dead he had left on the ground in Italy.

'You sit on the bunk,' he said to Nels, trying to calm himself. 'We'll draw up the nightstand for the board.'

'Fine,' Nels said. 'Just fine.'

The old man's hands fumbled setting up the chess pieces. They were darkly spotted, and the skin, translucent in appearance, was prominently veined.

'White or black?' Nels asked.

'Advantages to both,' replied Kabuo. 'You choose, Mr. Gudmundsson.'

'Most players prefer to open,' Nels said. 'Why is that, anyway?'

'Must see some advantage in going first,' said Kabuo. 'Must believe in taking the offensive.'

'And you don't?' inquired Nels.

Kabuo took up a pawn in each hand and put them behind his back. 'Best way to settle the problem,' he said. 'This way, all you have to do is guess.' He held his closed fists in front of Nels.

'Left,' the old man said. 'If we're going to leave it to chance, left is as good as right. They're both the same, this way.'

'You don't prefer it?' asked Kabuo. 'You prefer white? Or black?'

'Open your hands,' Nels answered, and tucked his cigar in between his teeth high up on the right side – dentures, it occurred to Kabuo.

As it turned out, the first move was Nels's. As it turned out, the old man never castled. He had no interest in an endgame. His strategy was to give up points for position, to give up men in the early going in return for an undefeatable board posture. He'd won, even though Kabuo could see what he was doing. There was no fiddling around. The game, quite suddenly, was over.

Kabuo set the hand mirror on his tray of food now and ate half of the lime gelatin. He chewed down his carrot sticks and what remained of his sandwich, then poured out the tin cup of milk and filled it twice with water. He washed his hands, removed his shoes, and lay down on the jail bed. After a while he stood up again and turned the lightbulb in its socket. Then in the darkness the accused man lay down again, shut his eyes, and dreamed.

He dreamed without sleeping – daydreams, waking dreams, as had come to him often in his jail cell. In this manner he escaped from its walls and roamed in freedom along San Piedro's wood paths, along the verges of its autumn pastures crusted over with skins of hoarfrost; he followed in his mind certain remnants of trail that gave out suddenly in blackberry riots or in fields of unexpected Scotch broom. In his thoughts were vestiges of old skid roads and forgotten farm paths that bled into vales of

138

ghost fern and hollows filled with skunk cabbage. Sometimes these trails faded at mud bluffs overlooking the sea; other times they wandered down onto beaches where thick cedars, sapling alders, and vine maples, toppled by winter tides, lay with the tips of their desiccated branches buried in sand and gravel. The waves brought seaweed in and draped it across the downed trees in thick oozing skeins. Then his mind moved outward, and Kabuo was at sea again, his net set, the salmon running, and he was standing on the foredeck of the *Islander* with the breeze in his face, the phosphorus in the water brilliant before him, the whitecaps silver in the moonlight. From his bunk in the Island County Jail he felt the sea again and the swells under his boat as it rode over the foam; with his eyes shut he smelled cold salt and the odor of salmon in the hold, heard the net winch working and the deep note of the engine. Rafts of seabirds rose off the water, making way in the first misty light with the *Islander* bound for home on a cool morning, half a thousand kings in her hold, the whine of wind in her rigging. At the cannery he held each fish in his hands before tossing it up and over the side – lambent chinooks, lithe and sleek, as long as his arm and weighing a fourth what he did, slick, glassy eyes held open. He could feel them in his hands again while overhead the gulls flew tangents. When he put off and motored for the docks the gulls followed on high with their breasts opened to the wind. Then he was amid a flock of gulls while he swabbed the deck of the *Islander*. He heard their squawking and watched them circle low, angling for scraps, while Marlin Teneskold or William Gjovaag shot at them with a side-by-side so that the gulls settled out on the water. The gun's report echoed from the hills of Amity Harbor, and then Kabuo remembered what he had missed this year: the birch and alder going golden, the red autumn hue of the vine maples, the rust and russet colors of October, the cider press, pumpkins, and baskets of young zucchini squash. The smell of dying leaves in the motionless gray morning as he shambled up onto the porch after a night's fishing, and the full, fine growth in the cedar trees. The *scritching* sound of leaves underfoot; leaves mashed into paste after rains. He'd *missed* fall rains, the water dripping along the knobs of his spine and mixing with the sea spray in his hair – things he hadn't known he'd miss.

In August he'd taken his family to Lanheedron Island. They'd tied off to a float, and he'd rowed them up onto Sugar Sand Beach in the skiff. His daughters stood in the surf and poked at jellyfish with sticks and collected sand dollars; then they followed the beach creek up through a dell, Kabuo carrying the baby on his right arm, until they came to a waterfall, a cascade tumbling from a wall of moss. They ate their lunch there in the shadows of the hemlocks and gathered salmonberries. Hatsue found under birch trees a half-dozen destroying angels and pointed them out to her daughters. They were pure white and lovely, she explained, but fatal to eat. She pointed out, too, the maidenhair fern nearby; the black stems, she said, retained their shine in a pine needle basket's weave.

He'd admired her fully on that day. She collected the stems of wild ginger for seasoning rice and yarrow leaves for tea. On the beach she dug butter clams with a pointed stick, raking an arc in front of her. She found sea glass and a fossilized crab leg embedded in a concretion. She doused the baby with seawater. The girls helped Kabuo gather beach wood for a fire when evening came up. At the last of dusk they launched their skiff again. His oldest daughter hooked a true cod in the kelp beds off Lanheedron. He filleted it on the deck while Hatsue caught another on a hand line. They ate at sea – the cod, the clams, ginger rice, yarrow tea. His middle daughter and the baby slept on his bunk, his oldest daughter manned the wheel. Kabuo and Hatsue went forward. He stood with his chest against her back and his hands in the rigging until the lights of Amity Harbor came up to the south, and then he went in and repositioned the *Islander* in order to take the channel head on. His daughter leaned against him after he took the wheel from her, and he came into the harbor that way at midnight, the girl's head against his arm.

Then he remembered strawberry fields from before Manzanar

and he was in them as he'd always been, a sea of strawberries, rows and rows, a labyrinth of runners as intricate as a network of arteries feeding on the surface of a dozen farms he knew from childhood. He was in these mounded rows, stooped and picking with the sun on his neck, low against the land in a sea of green and red with the smell of the earth and its berries rising like a mist, filling by the labor of his hands the twelve woven pine baskets in his caddy. He saw his wife before she'd married him, he saw her picking at Ichikawas' farm, how he'd come toward her carrying his caddy and as if by accident, by happenstance, how she hadn't seen him coming, intent on her work, bent to it, but at the last minute lifted her black eyes, lissome as ever, continuously picking – berries lay gently like red gems between her fingers – and while she met his eyes fed one of her woven pine baskets, three of which already lay full on the caddy, mounded over with ripened fruit. He'd squatted down across from her and, picking, took her in – how she squatted with her chin near her kneecaps, her hair woven tautly into a long, thick rope, the sweat against her forehead and the tendrils of hair that had escaped from their arrangement – loose strands fell across her cheeks and nose. She was sixteen. Low to the ground, folded together with her breasts against her thighs, she wore woven sandals and a red muslin summer dress, its narrow straps running over her shoulders. He saw again the strength of her legs, the brown of her ankles and calves, the suppleness of her spine, the film of sweat at her throat. Then it was evening, and he'd left the South Beach wood path to look at her home of worn cedar slats and across the fields to where she lived: fields circumscribed by tall cedar trees and lit by spindly moonlight. A kerosene lantern flickered orange in the window of Hatsue's home, her door stood open, ajar ten inches, and an angle of lantern light spilled across her porch. Crickets and night toads, the brattle of a dog, laundry billowing on a line against the night breeze. And again he breathed in the green in the strawberry runners, the rain in the cedar duff, and the salt water. She padded toward him with a bucket full of kitchen scraps, her sandals squeaking, moving toward the compost heap, and on her return trip she'd passed between the rows of raspberries. He watched while she held her hair back with one hand, the other moving in search of the sweetest fruit, grazing among the canes. Her heels lifted from the sandals now and then. She slid the berries in between her lips, still holding her hair, the canes rebounding in quiet arcs when she freed the berry caps from their cores. He stood watching and imagined that if he kissed her that night the taste of the raspberries would be cool in his mouth.

He saw her just as he had seen her in history class, a pencil between her teeth, one hand laid against the nape of her neck, lost behind her effusive hair. She walked through the halls with her books pressed against her breasts, in pleated skirt, argyle sweater, white bobby socks folded down crisply above the polished onyx buckles of her shoes. She looked at him and then away again quickly, saying nothing when he passed by.

He remembered Manzanar, the dust in the barracks, in the tarpapered shacks and cafeteria; even the bread tasted gritty. They'd worked tending eggplants and lettuces in the camp garden. They'd been paid little, the hours were long, they'd been told it was their duty to work hard. He and Hatsue spoke of little things at first, then of the San Piedro fields they'd left behind and the smell of ripening strawberries. He had begun to love her, to love more than just her beauty and grace, and when he saw that in their hearts they shared the same dream he felt a great certainty about her. They kissed in the back of a crew truck coming into camp one night, and the warm wet taste of her, however brief, brought her down for him from the world of angels and into the world of human beings. In this way his love deepened. Working in the gardens he would pass her by and, for a moment, slide one hand around her waist. She would squeeze his hand between her fingers, which had grown more callused and hard at Manzanar, and he would squeeze back, and they would return to their weeding. The wind blew desert dust in their faces and dried their skin and turned their hair to wire.

He remembered the expression on Hatsue's face when he told her he had enlisted. It was not the being gone, she said – though the being gone was a horrible thing – it was more that he might not ever return, or that he might return not himself. Kabuo had not made promises to her – he could not say if he was coming back, or if he would come back the same man. There was this matter of honor, he'd explained to her, and he had no choice but to accept the duty the war required of him. At first she had refused to understand this and had insisted that duty was less important than love and she hoped Kabuo felt the same way. But he could not bring himself to agree with this; love went deep and meant life itself, but honor could not be turned from. He was not who he was if he didn't go to war, and would not be worthy of her.

She turned from him and tried to stay away, and for three days they didn't speak. At last he'd come to her, at dusk, in the gardens, and said that he loved her more than anything in the world and that he hoped only that she would understand why it was he had to leave. He asked for nothing else from her, only this acknowledgment of who he was, how his soul was shaped. Hatsue stood with her long-handled hoe and said that she had learned from Mrs. Shigemura that character was always destiny. He would have to do what he must do, and she would have to do the same.

He'd nodded and exerted himself to show nothing. Then he turned and walked between the rows of eggplants. He was twenty yards off when she called his name and asked if he would marry her before leaving. '*Why do you want to marry me?*' he asked, and her answer came back, '*To hold a part of you.*' She dropped the hoe and walked the twenty yards to hold him in her arms. '*It's my character, too,*' she whispered. '*It's my destiny now to love you.*'

It had been, he saw now, a war marriage, hurried into because there was no choice and because both of them felt the rightness of it. They had not known each other more than a few months, though he had always admired her from a distance, and it seemed to him, when he thought about it, that their marriage had been meant to happen. His parents approved, and hers approved, and he was happy to leave for the war in the knowledge that she was waiting for him and would be there when he returned. And then he had returned, a murderer, and her fear that he would no longer be himself was realized.

He remembered, too, his father's face, and the sword his father kept inside a wooden chest in the days before Pearl Harbor. A *katana* made by the swordsmith Masamune, it had been in the Miyamoto family, it was said, for six centuries. His father kept it sheathed and rolled in cloth, an undecorated and highly useful weapon. Its beauty lay in its simplicity, the plainness of its curve; even its wooden scabbard was spare and plain. His father had taken it, along with other things – his wooden *kendo* practice swords, his *sageo*, his *obi*, his *naginata*, his *hakama* pants, his *bokken* – and buried them one night in a strawberry field, laid them carefully wrapped in a hole along with the dynamite he'd used to clear stumps, a case full of books and scrolls written in Japanese, and a photograph taken of Kabuo at the San Piedro Japanese Community Center dressed in the feudal costume of a *bugeisha* and wielding a *kendo* stick.

Kabuo's training at *kendo* had begun when he was seven. His father had taken him one Saturday to the community center hall, where a *dojo* had been established in a corner of the gym. They knelt before an alcove at the back of the room and contemplated a shelf on which small bowls of uncooked rice had been neatly arranged. Kabuo learned to bow from a seated position. While he sat on his heels his father explained softly the meaning of *zenshin*, which the boy understood to mean a constant awareness of potential danger. His father finished by repeating the word twice – '*zenshin! zenshin!*' – then took down a wooden pole from the wall and, before Kabuo knew what had happened, slammed him with it in the solar plexus.

'*Zenshin!*' said Zenhichi, while the boy caught his breath. 'Didn't you say you understood?'

His father said that if he was to learn *kendo* more would be

144

expected of him than of the average person. Did he wish to learn anyway? The choice was his. He should take some time to consider it.

When Kabuo was eight his father put a weapon in his hands for the first time – a *bokken*. They stood in the strawberry fields early one July morning just after picking season was finished. The *bokken*, a curved piece of cherry wood three feet long, had been Kabuo's great-grandfather's, a man who had been a samurai before the Meiji Restoration and later – after the wearing of swords was outlawed – a farmer of government rice lands on Kyushu for ten days before he joined two hundred other rebellious samurai in Kumamoto. They formed themselves into the League of the Divine Tempest and attacked an imperial garrison with swords aloft, having fasted for three days. Its defenders, wielding rifles, killed all but twenty-nine with their opening volley; the survivors committed suicide on the battlefield, including Kabuo's great-grandfather.

'You come from a family of samurai,' Kabuo's father said to him in Japanese. 'Your great-grandfather died because he could not stop being one. It was his bad fortune to live at a time when the samurai were no longer necessary. He could not adapt to this, and his anger at the world overwhelmed him. I remember what an angry man he was, Kabuo. He lived for revenge against the Meiji. When they told him he could no longer wear his sword in public he conspired to kill men he hardly knew – government officials, men with families who lived near us, who were kind to us, whose children we played with. He became irrational in his behavior and spoke of purifying himself in such a manner that he would afterward be invulnerable to the Meiji rifles. He was always gone at night. We didn't know where he went. My grandmother bit her nails. She argued with him when he came home in the mornings, but he wouldn't change his ways or explain. His eyes were red, his face rigid. He sat eating from his bowl in silence, wearing his sword in the house. It was said that he had joined other samurai who had been displaced by the Meiji. They roamed the roads disguised, swords in hand, killing government officials. They were bandits, thieves, and renegades. My grandfather – I remember this – was happy to hear of Okubo Toshimichi's assassination, the man who had been responsible for the confiscation of his master's castle and the destruction of his master's army. He smiled, showed his teeth, and drank.

'My grandfather was an expert swordsman,' Zenhichi had explained, 'but his anger overwhelmed him in the end. It is ironic, because how often did he tell me, when I was your age and he was a contented and peaceful man, of the kind of sword a man should wield? *"The sword that gives life, not the sword that takes life, is the goal of the samurai,"* my grandfather said then. The goal of the sword is to give life, not to take it.

'You can be very good with the *bokken* if you concentrate,' said Kabuo's father. 'You have it in you. You have only to decide to learn – now, when you are eight.'

'I want to,' replied Kabuo.

'I know you do,' his father said. 'But look, your hands.'

Kabuo adjusted them.

'Your feet,' said his father. 'The front turned in more. Too much weight on the back.'

They began to work on the vertical stroke, moving along between the strawberries, the boy advancing, the man retreating, the two of them together in it. 'The *bokken* strikes,' Kabuo's father said. 'The hips and stomach cut. You must tighten the stomach muscles as the stroke advances. No, you're locking your knees – they must give when you strike. Elbow soft, too, or there is no follow-through, the *bokken* is cut off from the power of the body. Hips sink, knees and elbows go soft, stomach is hard, cut, turn, again, strike . . .'

Kabuo's father showed him how to hold the wooden sword so that the wrists were flexible and liberated. An hour went by, and then it was time for field work and they put the *bokken* away. Thereafter, each morning, Kabuo practiced his *kendo* strokes – the vertical slash that would split a man's head down the bridge of the nose, leaving one eye on each side, the skull cleaved into two parts; the four diagonal strokes – from left and right, upward and downward – that would cleave a man beneath a rib or disjoin an arm deftly; the horizontal stroke swinging in from the left that could sever a man just above the hips; and, finally, the most common of *kendo* strokes, a horizontal thrust a right-handed man could propel with great force against the left side of his enemy's head.

He practiced these until they were natural to him, part of who he was, the *bokken* an extension of his hands. By the time he was sixteen there was no one any longer at the community center who could defeat him, not even the half-dozen grown men on the island for whom *kendo* was a serious hobby, not even his father, who acknowledged his son's triumph without shame. It was said by many in the Kendo Club that Zenhichi, despite his years, remained the superior practitioner, the more pure between father and son, but that the boy, Kabuo, had the stronger fighting spirit and a greater willingness to draw on his dark side in order to achieve a final victory.

It was only after he'd killed four Germans that Kabuo saw how right they were, how they had seen deeply into his heart with the clarity of older people. He was a warrior, and this dark ferocity had been passed down in the blood of the Miyamoto family and he himself was fated to carry it into the next generation. The story of his great-grandfather, the samurai madman, was his own story, too, he saw now. Sometimes, when he felt his anger rising because he had lost his family's strawberry land, he gathered it up into the pit of his gut and stood in the yard with his *kendo* stick rehearsing the black choreography of his art. He saw only darkness after the war, in the world and in his own soul, everywhere but in the smell of strawberries, in the good scent of his wife and of his three children, a boy and two girls, three gifts. He felt he did not deserve for a moment the happiness his family brought to him, so that late at night, when he couldn't sleep, he imagined that he would write them a note explicating his sin completely. He would leave them and go to suffer alone, and his unhappiness would overwhelm his anger. The violence might at last die out of him and set him free to contemplate his destiny and his next life on the Great Wheel.

Sitting where he sat now, accused of the murder of Carl Heine, it seemed to him he'd found the suffering place he'd fantasized and desired. For Kabuo Miyamoto was suffering in his cell from the fear of his imminent judgment. Perhaps it was now his fate to pay for the lives he had taken in anger. Such was the nature of cause and effect, such was the impermanence of all things. What a mystery life was! Everything was conjoined by mystery and fate, and in his darkened cell he meditated on this and it became increasingly clear to him. Impermanence, cause and effect, suffering, desire, the precious nature of life. Every sentient being straining and pushing at the shell of identity and distinctness. He had the time and the clarity about suffering to embark on the upward path of liberation, which would take him many lives to follow. He would have to gain as much ground as possible and accept that the mountain of his violent sins was too large to climb in this lifetime. He would still be climbing it in the next and the next, and his suffering inevitably would multiply.

12

Outside the wind blew steadily from the north, driving snow against the courthouse. By noon three inches had settled on the town, a snow so ethereal it could hardly be said to have settled at all; instead it swirled like some icy fog, like the breath of ghosts, up and down Amity Harbor's streets – powdery dust devils, frosted puffs of ivory cloud, spiraling tendrils of white smoke. By noon the smell of the sea was eviscerated, the sight of it mistily depleted, too; one's field of vision narrowed in close, went blurry and snowbound, fuzzy and opaque, the sharp scent of frost burned in the nostrils of those who ventured out of doors. The snow flew up from their rubber boots as they struggled, heads down, toward Petersen's Grocery. When they looked out into the whiteness of the world the wind flung it sharply at their narrowed eyes and foreshortened their view of everything.

Ishmael Chambers was out walking aimlessly in the snow, admiring it and remembering. The trial of Kabuo Miyamoto had brought that world back for him.

Inside their cedar tree, for nearly four years, he and Hatsue had held one another with the dreamy contentedness of young lovers. With their coats spread against a cushion of moss they'd stayed as long as they could after dusk and on Saturday and Sunday afternoons. The tree produced a cedar perfume that permeated their skin and clothes. They would enter, breathe deeply, then lie down and touch each other – the heat of it and the cedar smell, the privacy and the rain outside, the slippery softness of their lips and tongues inspired in them the temporary illusion that the rest of the world had disappeared;

there was nobody and nothing but the two of them. Ishmael pressed himself against Hatsue while they held each other, and Hatsue pressed back, her hips leaving the moss, her legs open beneath her skirt. He felt her breasts and grazed the waistband of her underwear, and she stroked his belly and chest and back. Sometimes when he was walking home through the forest Ishmael would stop in some lonely place and, because he had no choice in the matter, take himself in his hand. He would think about Hatsue while he touched himself. He would shut his eyes and lean his head against a tree; afterward he felt better and worse.

Sometimes at night he would squeeze his eyes shut and imagine how it might be to marry her. It did not seem so farfetched to him that they might move to some other place in the world where this would be possible. He liked to think about being with Hatsue in some place like Switzerland or Italy or France. He gave his whole soul to love; he allowed himself to believe that his feelings for Hatsue had been somehow preordained. He had been meant to meet her on the beach as a child and then to pass his life with her. There was no other way it could be.

Inside their cedar tree they spoke of everything in the intense and overwrought manner of teenagers and he found that she had many moods. There were times when she went cold and silent and he felt her distance from him so completely that it seemed impossible to reach her. Even when he held her it seemed to him there was a place in her heart he couldn't get to. At times he worked himself up to discussing this, gradually revealing to her how it hurt him to feel there was a part of her love she withheld. Hatsue denied that this was so and explained to him that her emotional reserve was something she couldn't help. She had been carefully trained by her upbringing, she said, to avoid effusive displays of feeling, but this did not mean her heart was shallow. Her silence, she said, would express something if he would learn to listen to it. Yet his suspicion that he loved more deeply than

150

she did nevertheless remained with him, and he worried about it perpetually.

Hatsue, he found, had a religious side he had only sensed when they'd been younger. He drew her out in conversation on this matter, and she told him how she tried to keep in mind certain basic articles of her faith. All of life was impermanent, for example – a thing she thought about every day. It was important for a person to act carefully, for every action, Hatsue explained, had consequences for the soul's future. She confessed to experiencing a moral anguish over meeting him so secretly and deceiving her mother and father. It seemed to her certain that she would suffer from the consequences of it, that no one could maintain such deceit for so long without paying for it somehow. Ishmael argued at length about this, asserting that God could not possibly view their love as something wrong or evil. God, replied Hatsue, was personal; only she could know what God wanted from her. Motive, she added, was very important: what was her motive in concealing from her parents the time she spent with Ishmael? This was the question that worried her most: determining for herself her motive.

Ishmael, at school, feigned detachment in her presence and ignored her in the casual way she gradually taught him to use. Hatsue was a master of the art of false preoccupation; she would pass him in the hallway, in her plaid blouse with its neat tucks, puffed sleeves, and ruffled collar, with a bow in her hair, pleats in her skirt, and books hiked up against her breast, and move on with an apparently artless indifference that in the beginning painfully astonished him. How was it possible for her to feign such coldness without feeling it at the same time? By degrees he learned to enjoy these encounters, though his indifference always appeared more studied than hers and he was always anxious, in a barely concealed way, to meet her gaze. He even said hello to her now and again as one element in his pretense. 'Hard test,' he'd say at the end of a class. 'How'd you do, anyway?'

'I don't know. I didn't study enough.'

'Did you do the essay for Sparling?'

'I tried. It's about a page long.'

'Mine, too. A little longer.'

He would move on, collect his books, and leave the room with Sheridan Knowles or Don Hoyt or Denny Horbach.

At the Strawberry Festival in 1941 he'd watched while the mayor of Amity Harbor had crowned Hatsue Strawberry Princess. The mayor had placed a tiara on her head and hung a sash over her left shoulder. Hatsue and four other girls made a promenade through the crowd and tossed strawberry-flavored candy to the children. Ishmael's father – owner, publisher, editor, chief reporter, photographer, and printer of the *San Piedro Review* – had a special interest in these proceedings. Year after year they provided a lead story, complete with a portrait of the crowned and comely maiden, candids of picnicking families ('The Maltons of Protection Point enjoy Saturday's strawberry festival'), and a beneficent editorial or boilerplate column approving the efforts of local organizers ('. . . Ed Bailey, Lois Dunkirk, and Carl Heine, Sr., without whom none of this would have been possible . . .'). Arthur wandered the picnic grounds in bow tie and suspenders, a porkpie hat pulled low over his forehead and the enormous weight of his camera slung from a thick leather thong around his neck. Ishmael stood beside him while he photographed Hatsue – he winked at her when his father put one eye to the camera, and she gave back the faint trace of a smile.

'Neighbor girl,' his father said. 'South Beach ought to be proud.'

He followed his father that afternoon, and they joined in the tug-of-war and the three-legged race. The strawberry floats, festooned with staghorn ferns, zinnias, and forget-me-nots – and with the royal court of the Strawberry Festival draped theatrically under cherry sprays and spruce boughs trained to wire guy lines – passed like ships before the somber eyes of the Strawberry Festival Association, which included the mayor, the chairman of the chamber of commerce, the fire chief, and Arthur Chambers. Again Ishmael stood beside his father while Hatsue, on board her float, passed by waving to everybody majestically with her crepe paper scepter in hand. Ishmael waved back and laughed.

September came; they were high school seniors. A gray green stillness settled into things, and the summer people left for their city homes again: soft overcast, night fog, low mists in the dips between hills, road mud, vacant beaches, empty clamshells scattered among rocks, silent shops folded in on themselves. By October San Piedro had slipped off its summer reveler's mask to reveal a torpid, soporific dreamer whose winter bed was made of wet green moss. Cars slumped along the mud and gravel roads at twenty or thirty miles an hour like sluggish beetles beneath the overhanging trees. The Seattle people passed into memory and winter savings accounts; stoves were stoked, fires banked, books taken down, quilts mended. The gutters filled with rust-colored pine needles and the pungent effluvium of alder leaves, and the drainpipes splashed with winter rain.

Hatsue told him, one fall afternoon, about her tutelage under Mrs. Shigemura and the directive she'd been given as a girl of thirteen to marry a boy of her own kind, a Japanese boy from a good family. She repeated that it made her unhappy to deceive the world. Her secret life, which she carried with her in the presence of her parents and sisters at every moment, made her feel she had betrayed them in a way that was nothing less than *evil* – there was no other word for it, she told Ishmael. Outside, the rain dripped from the canopy of cedar boughs down into the under-growth of ivy. Hatsue sat with her cheek against her knees, looking out through the opening in the cedar tree, her hair a single braid down her spine. 'It isn't evil,' Ishmael insisted. 'How can this be evil? It wouldn't make any sense for this to be evil. It's the world that's evil, Hatsue,' he added. 'Don't pay it any mind.'

'That isn't so easy,' said Hatsue. 'I lie every day to my family, Ishmael. Sometimes I think I'll go crazy with it. Sometimes I think this can't go on.'

Later they lay side by side against the moss, looking up into the darkened cedar wood with their hands folded behind their heads. 'This can't go on,' whispered Hatsue. 'Don't you worry about that?'

'I know,' answered Ishmael. 'You're right.'

'What will we do? What's the answer?'

'I don't know,' said Ishmael. 'There isn't one, it looks like.'

'I heard a rumor,' Hatsue replied. 'There's a fisherman who claims to have seen a German submarine just off Amity Harbor. A periscope – he followed it for half a mile. Do you think that can be true?'

'No,' said Ishmael. 'It isn't true. People will believe anything – they're scared, I guess. It's just fear, is all. They're afraid.'

'I'm afraid, too,' said Hatsue. 'Everybody's afraid right now.'

'I'm going to be drafted,' answered Ishmael. 'It's something I just have to face.'

They sat in their cedar tree thinking about this, but the war still seemed far away. The war did not disturb them there, and they continued to view themselves as exceedingly fortunate in the particulars of their secret existence. Their absorption in one another, the heat of their bodies, their mingling smells and the movements of their limbs – these things shielded them from certain truths. Yet sometimes at night Ishmael Chambers would lie awake because there was a war on in the world. He would turn his thoughts toward Hatsue then and keep them there until at the verge of sleep the war swam back to spill forth horribly anyway in his dreams.

13

Hatsue Imada was standing in the foyer of the Amity Harbor Buddhist Chapel, buttoning her coat after services, when Georgia Katanaka's mother told the people gathered there the news about Pearl Harbor. 'It's very bad,' she said. 'A bombing raid. The Japanese air force has bombed everything. It is bad for us, terribly bad. There is nothing else on the radio. Everything is Pearl Harbor.'

Hatsue pulled her lapels more closely around her throat and turned her eyes toward her parents. Her father – he'd been busy helping her mother into her coat – only stood there blinking at Mrs. Katanaka. 'It can't be true,' he said.

'It's true,' he said.

'It's true,' she said. 'Find a radio. Just this morning. They bombed Hawaii.'

They stood in the reception room kitchen with the Katanakas, Ichiharas, Sasakis, and Hayashidas and listened to the Bendix sitting on the counter. Nobody spoke – they merely stood there. They listened for ten minutes without moving, their heads down, their ears turned toward the radio. Finally Hatsue's father began to pace and scratch his head and then to rub his chin, long strokes. 'We'd better get home,' he said.

They drove home and listened to the radio again, the five Imada girls and their parents. They kept the radio on all afternoon and late into the evening, too. Now and then the telephone would ring, and Hatsue's father, in Japanese, would discuss matters with Mr. Oshiro or Mr. Nishi. More than a half-dozen times he made calls himself to discuss matters with other people. He would hang up, scratch his head, then return to his seat by the radio.

Mr. Oshiro called again and told Hatsue's father that in Amity Harbor a fisherman named Otto Willets had put up a ladder in front of Shigeru Ichiyama's movie theater and unscrewed the lightbulbs in the marquee. While he was busy at it two other men had steadied the ladder for him and yelled curses at the Ichiyamas, who were not present. Otto Willets and his friends, on discovering this, had driven out to Lundgren Road and sat in front of the Ichiyamas' in a pickup truck, where they pounded on the horn until Shig came out and stood on his porch to see what they wanted. Willets had called Shig a dirty Jap and told him he ought to have smashed every light in the marquee – didn't he know there was a blackout? Shig said no, he hadn't known, he was glad to have been told, he was thankful to the men for unscrewing the marquee bulbs for him. He ignored Otto Willets's insults.

At ten o'clock Mr. Oshiro called again; armed men had posted themselves around Amity Harbor out of fear of a Japanese attack. There were men with shotguns behind logs along the beach just north and south of town. The defense of San Piedro was being organized; there were men meeting right now at the Masons' lodge. The Otsubos had driven by at eight o'clock and seen at least forty cars and pickup trucks parked along the road near the Masons'. Furthermore three or four gill-netters, it was said, had left the harbor to patrol San Piedro's waters. Mr. Oshiro had seen one drifting on the tide, its engine cut, its running lights out, below the bluff near his home on Crescent Bay, a mere silhouette in the night. Hatsue's father – he spoke in Japanese – asked Mr. Oshiro if in fact there were submarines and if the rumors of an invasion of Oregon and California were factual. 'Anything is possible,' answered Mr. Oshiro. 'You should be prepared for anything, Hisao.'

Hatsue's father took his shotgun from the closet and set it in the corner of the living room, unloaded. He got out a box of squirrel loads, too, and slipped three shells into his shirt pocket. Then he turned off every light but one and hung sheets across all the windows. Every few minutes he would leave his place by the radio to pull back a corner of one of these sheets and peer out into the strawberry fields. Then he would go out onto the porch to listen and to search the sky for airplanes. There were none, but on the other hand the sky was mostly overcast and a plane would not easily be seen.

They went to bed; nobody slept. In the morning, on the school bus, Hatsue looked directly at Ishmael Chambers as she passed him on the way to her seat. Ishmael looked back and nodded at her, once. The bus driver, Ron Lamberson, had an Anacortes newspaper tucked underneath his chair; at each stop he flung the door open with a flourish, then sat reading a section of the paper while the children boarded in silence. 'Here's the deal,' he called over his shoulder as the school bus wound down Mill Run Road. 'The Japanese are attacking all over the place, not just Pearl Harbor. They're making raids all over the Pacific Ocean. Roosevelt is going to declare war today, but what are we gonna do about these attacks? The whole fleet's been destroyed out there, is the deal. And they're arresting Jap traitors in Hawaii and other places – the FBI's in on it. They're getting them down in Seattle right now, in fact. Arresting the spies and everything. The government's frozen Jap bank accounts, too. Main thing, there's a blackout ordered for tonight all up and down the coast. The navy figures there's gonna be an air raid. Don't want to scare you kids, but could be right here – the transmitter station at Agate Point? The navy transmitter station? Your radio is gonna be off the air from seven tonight until tomorrow morning so the Japs don't pick up any signals. Everyone's supposed to put black cloth on their windows and stay inside, stay calm.'

At school, all day, there was nothing but the radio. Two thousand men had been killed. The voices that spoke were cheerless and sober and suggested a barely suppressed urgency. The young people sat with their books unopened and listened to a navy man describe in detail how to extinguish incendiary bombs, and then to reports of further Japanese attacks, Roosevelt's speech before the Congress, an announcement by Attorney General Biddle that Japanese fifth columnists were being arrested in Washington,

Oregon, and California. Mr. Sparling became restive and bitter and began to talk in a desolate monotone about his eleven months in France during the Great War. He said that he hoped the boys in his class would take their duty to fight seriously and that furthermore they should consider it an honor to meet the Japs head-on and do the job of paying them back. 'War stinks,' he added. 'But they started it. They bombed Hawaii on a Sunday morning. On a Sunday morning, of all things.' He shook his head, turned up the radio, and leaned morosely against the blackboard with his arms seized against his narrow chest.

By three o'clock that afternoon Ishmael's father had printed and distributed the first war extra in the history of his island newspaper, a one-page edition with a banner headline – ISLAND DEFENSE SET!

Only a few hours after the outbreak of hostilities between Japan and the United States, San Piedro Island late last night was prepared – temporarily at least – for an air raid bombing or other serious emergency.

A meeting of the local defense commission was called promptly by Richard A. Blackington, local defense commissioner, at the Masons' lodge yesterday afteroon and attended by all defense commission lieutenants. An air raid blackout signal system, details of which can be found elsewhere in this edition, was established. It will rely on church bells, industrial plant whistles, and automobile horns.

Defense leaders, taking the attitude that 'anything can happen,' warned islanders to be on the alert to black out electric lights on extremely short notice.

Island watchers for the Interceptor Command will be on duty on a twenty-four-hour basis. Meanwhile members of the island's Japanese community pledged their loyalty to the United States.

Guards were trebled at the U.S. Navy's Agate Point radio transmitter station and at the Crow Marine Railway

and Shipbuilding Company. The Pacific Telephone and Telegraph Company and the Puget Sound Power and Light Company indicated steps would be taken to guard their facilities here.

Arrangements were being made to bring summer fire-fighting equipment, stored for the winter in Anacortes, back to the island today.

Ensign R. B. Clawson, representing Comdr. L. N. Channing of the Agate Point radio transmitter station, addressed the defense commission meeting. Military and naval intelligence units, he said, have the situation well in hand and are taking proper local steps to guard against saboteurs and spies. 'The transmitter station went on prearranged war alert status immediately upon news of the Pearl Harbor attack,' added Ensign Clawson. 'Nevertheless, island civilians must do whatever they can independent of naval and military aid to safeguard their homes and businesses against sabotage or bombing.'

The following lieutenants of the defense commission were present at yesterday's meeting:

Bill Ingraham, communications; Ernest Tingstaad, transportation; Mrs. Thomas McKibben, medical supplies; Mrs. Clarence Wukstich, supplies and food; Jim Milleren, auxiliary police; Einar Petersen, roads and engineering; Larry Phillips, auxiliary fire force; Arthur Chambers, publicity.

Also present were Major O. W. Hotchkins, chairman of the separate local defense council; Bart Johannson, an assistant to Major Hotchkins; and S. Austin Coney, organizer of the island's Interceptor Command force.

At the bottom of the page, in bold sixteen-point type, was a message from the island defense commission:

AT THE SOUND OF PROLONGED RINGING OF CHURCH BELLS, THE PROLONGED SOUNDING OF AUTOMOBILE HORNS, AND THE

PROLONGED BLOWING OF WHISTLES AT THE CROW MARINE
RAILWAY AND SHIPBUILDING COMPANY, IMMEDIATELY TURN
OFF ALL ELECTRIC LIGHTS. THIS INCLUDES THE TURNING OFF
OF ALL PERMANENT NIGHT LIGHTS, SUCH AS STORE DISPLAY
LIGHTS, WHICH ARE UNDER YOUR CONTROL. KEEP LIGHTS OFF
UNTIL THE ALL-CLEAR SIGNAL, WHICH WILL BE A DUPLICATION
OF THE AIR RAID WARNING SIGNAL.

There was also a statement issued by Richard Blackington that
church bells and automobile horns should be used only in a manner consistent with the air raid warning system. Mrs. Thomas
McKibben, in charge of medical supplies, requested that any
islander with a station wagon available for use as an emergency
ambulance should contact her at Amity Harbor 172-R; she was
also registering emergency nurses and those with emergency
first-aid training. Finally, the island sheriff, Gerald Lundquist,
asked islanders to report suspicious activities or signs of sabotage
to his office with all due speed.

Arthur's war extra included an article entitled 'Japanese
Leaders Here Pledge Loyalty to America,' in which Masato
Nagaishi, Masao Uyeda, and Zenhichi Miyamoto, all strawberry men, made statements to the effect that they and all other
island Japanese stood ready to protect the American flag. They
spoke on behalf of the Japanese Chamber of Commerce, the
Japanese-American Citizens' League, and the Japanese Community Center, and their pledges, said the *Review*, were 'prompt
and unequivocal,' including Mr. Uyeda's promise that 'if there
is any sign of sabotage or spies, we will be the first ones to report
it to the authorities.' Arthur also ran his editor's column under
the usual heading of 'Plain Talk,' which he'd composed wearily
at two A.M. with a candle propped beside his typewriter:

**If ever there was a community which faced a local
emergency growing out of something over which it had
no control, it is San Piedro Island this Monday morning,
December 8, 1941.**

This is, indeed, a time for plain talk about things that matter to all of us.

There are on this island some 800 members of 150 families whose blood ties lie with a nation which yesterday committed an atrocity against all that is decent. That nation has committed itself to a war against us and has earned our swift and sure action. America will unite to respond courageously to the threat now facing us in the Pacific. And when the dust settles, America will have won.

In the meantime the task before us is grave and invites our strongest emotions. Yet these emotions, the *Review* must stress, should not include a blind, hysterical hatred of all persons who trace their ancestry to Japan. That some of these persons happen to be American citizens, happen to be loyal to this country, or happen to have no longer a binding tie with the land of their birth could all easily be swept aside by mob hysteria.

In light of this, the *Review* points out that those of Japanese descent on this island are not responsible for the tragedy at Pearl Harbor. Make no mistake about it. They have pledged their loyalty to the United States and have been fine citizens of San Piedro for decades now. These people are our neighbors. They have sent six of their sons into the United States Army. They, in short, are not the enemy, any more than our fellow islanders of German or Italian descent. We should not allow ourselves to forget these things, and they should guide us in our behavior toward all our neighbors.

So of all islanders – of all ancestries – the *Review* would seek as calm an approach as possible in this emergency. Let us so live in this trying time that when it is all over we islanders can look one another in the eye with the knowledge that we have behaved honorably and fairly. Let us remember what is so easy to forget in the mad intensity of wartime: that prejudice and

161

hatred are never right and never to be accepted by a just society.

Ishmael sat reading his father's words in the cedar tree; he was rereading them when Hatsue, in her coat and scarf, ducked in and sat down on the moss beside him. 'My father was up all night,' said Ishmael. 'He put this paper out.'

'My father can't get our money from the bank,' Hatsue replied to this. 'We have a few dollars, and the rest we can't get. My parents aren't citizens.'

'What will you do?'

'We don't know.'

'I have twenty dollars from picking season,' said Ishmael. 'You can have all of it – you can just have it. I'll bring it to school in the morning.'

'No,' said Hatsue. 'Don't bring it. My father will fig-ure out something pretty soon. I could never accept your money.'

Ishmael turned onto his side, toward her, and propped himself on his elbow. 'It's hard to believe,' he said.

'It's so unreal,' answered Hatsue. 'It just isn't fair – it's not *fair*. How could they do this, just like that? How did we get ourselves into this?'

'*We* didn't get ourselves in it,' said Ishmael. 'The Japanese *forced* us into it. And on a Sunday morning, when no one was ready. It's cheap, if you ask me. They – '

'Look at my face,' interrupted Hatsue. 'Look at my eyes, Ishmael. My face is the face of the people who did it – don't you see what I mean? My face – it's how the Japanese look. My parents came to San Piedro from Japan. My mother and father, they hardly speak English. My family is in bad trouble now. Do you see what I mean? We're going to have trouble.'

'Wait a minute,' said Ishmael. 'You're not Japanese. You're – '

'You heard the news. They're arresting people. They're calling a lot of people spies. Last night some men stopped at the Ichiyamas' and called them names, Ishmael. They sat out

162

front and honked their horn. How can this be happening?' she added. 'How did things get like this?'

'Who did that?' said Ishmael. 'Who are you talking about?'

'It was Mr. Willets – Otto Willets. Gina Willets's uncle and some other men. They were mad about the lights at the theater. The Ichiyamas left them on.'

'This is crazy,' said Ishmael. 'This whole thing is crazy.'

'They unscrewed his lightbulbs and then drove out to his house. They called him a dirty Jap.'

Ishmael had no answer for this. He shook his head instead.

'I went home after school,' said Hatsue. 'My father was talking on the telephone. Everyone is worried about the navy transmitter, the one on Agate Point. They think it's going to be bombed tonight. There are men going out there with shotguns to defend it. They're going to sit in the woods along the beaches. The Shirasakis have a farm on Agate Point, and some soldiers from the transmitter station came there. They took their radio and their camera and their telephone, and they arrested Mr. Shirasaki. And the rest of the Shirasakis can't leave their house.'

'Mr. Timmons was going down there,' Ishmael answered. 'I saw him, he was getting into his car. He said he was going to the Masons' first, where everything is being organized. They're telling people which beaches to watch. And my mother is painting these blackout screens. She's had the radio on all day.'

'Everyone's had their radios on. My mother can't move away from ours. She sits there and listens to everything and talks on the phone to people.'

Ishmael sighed. 'A war,' he said. 'I can't believe this is happening.'

'We'd better go,' replied Hatsue. 'It's getting dark already.'

They crossed the small torrent of the creek below their tree and followed the path down the hillside. It was dusk and the sea wind blew in their faces. Standing in the path with their arms around each other they kissed once and then again, the second time with greater force. 'Don't let this hurt us,' Ishmael said. 'I don't care about what's happening in the world. We're not going to let this hurt us.'

'It won't,' said Hatsue. 'You'll see.'

Ishmael, on Tuesday, went to work for his father. He answered the telephone in the office on Andreason Street and took notes on a yellow legal pad. His father told him to call certain people and made lists of questions to ask. 'Give me a hand?' his father had asked. 'I can't keep up with it all.'

Ishmael made a call to the naval station. The pilot of a daily reconnaissance plane, said an Ensign Clawson, had noticed something he'd never noticed before: the Japanese strawberry farms on San Piedro Island were planted in rows pointing straight toward the radio transmitter at the end of Agate Point. The rows of berry plants could guide Jap Zeroes straight to their target easily. 'But those fields have been there for thirty years,' said Ishmael. 'Not all of them,' replied Ensign Clawson.

The county sheriff called in. Dozens of Japanese farmers, he speculated, had stores of dynamite in their sheds and barns which could be used for sabotage. Others, he'd heard, had shortwave radios. The sheriff asked that as an act of goodwill these farmers turn in such dangerous items to his office in Amity Harbor. He wanted, he said, a message in the *Review*. He was thankful for Ishmael's help.

Arthur printed the sheriff's message. He printed a notice from the defense authority telling Japanese nationals on San Piedro that as of December 14 they could no longer ride the ferries. Twenty-four men, he wrote in a news article, had been named by Larry Phillips to the civilian defense auxiliary fire force, including George Tachibana, Fred Yasui, and Edward Wakayama. 'Yes, I did, I singled those three out,' he explained when Ishmael asked about it. 'Not every fact is just a fact,' he added. 'It's all a kind of . . . balancing act. A juggling of pins, all kinds of pins, that's what journalism is about.'

'That isn't journalism,' Ishmael answered. 'Journalism is just the facts.'

164

He had been learning about journalism at school, from a textbook, and it seemed to him that his father had abridged some basic journalistic principle.

'But which facts?' Arthur asked him. 'Which facts do we print, Ishmael?'

In the next issue Arthur reminded island businesses to extinguish display lights promptly at dusk; it was Christmas and the temptation was to leave them on. He announced that on New Year's Eve a public dance would be held under the slogan 'Remember Pearl Harbor – It Could Happen Here!'; men in uniform would be admitted at no charge; all islanders were encouraged to attend. Arthur informed his readers that a quota of $500 had been set by Mrs. Lars Heineman of the San Piedro Red Cross Relief Fund and that the Japanese-American Citizens' League had immediately donated $55 – the largest contribution to date. Another article reported that at the Japanese Community Center hall in Amity Harbor a reception had been held for Robert Sakamura, who'd been inducted into the army. Speeches were made and food was served; a salute to the American flag and the loud singing of 'The Star-Spangled Banner' rounded out the evening.

The *San Piedro Review* printed a reminder to its readers that it was pledged to remain silent on military news that might comfort or aid the enemy. It furthermore counseled islanders 'not to talk carelessly of army or navy maneuvers which may be observed.' The construction of the island's first fishing resort, at Protection Point, was delayed, Arthur wrote, because of the war. Nick Olafsen died while stacking wood; the George Bodines escaped death when their kitchen stove exploded, but Mrs. Bodine broke a leg and an arm. The PTA began a paper drive and took a special interest in Christmas wrappings. The island Grange committed itself to the defense of San Piedro and promised in a letter to the secretary of agriculture to 'see to the production of such fruits and vegetables as can be grown on our island and as our fighting forces might need.' The army asked owners of mules and horses on San Piedro to register

165

their animals with the county agent, describing the request in the pages of the *Review* as 'a patriotic obligation'; islanders were also asked to check their automobile tires and to drive in a manner consistent with preserving them: rubber was in short supply.

The navy warned islanders, in a message printed in the *Review*, 'to kill a rumor by refusing to carry it further.' Another benefit dance was held, and the enlisted men at the Agate Point station were invited as guests of honor. The defense fund committee came to the school board with a request that the high school auditorium be made available for two future dances; the board in return asked for written assurance that there would be no smoking or drinking. A draft registration desk was set up at Fisk's Hardware Center; meanwhile a sudden warm spell turned San Piedro's roads to mud and sank automobiles up to their running boards. Eve Thurmann, who was eighty-six, stalled out on Piersall Road in her '36 Buick, then showed up at Petersen's with mud caked on her knees; she'd walked two miles into town. Air raid rules, the *Review* reminded readers, were now posted on many electrical poles: keep calm and cool; stay home; put out lights; lie down; stay away from windows; don't telephone. Ray Ichikawa scored fifteen points for the Amity Harbor High School basketball team in its victory over Anacortes. A half-dozen residents of West Port Jensen claimed to have seen a mysterious creature sunning itself in the shallows; it appeared to have a swanlike neck, the head of a polar bear, and a cavernous mouth from which emerged puffs of steam. When islanders rowed out to get a closer look the creature disappeared beneath the waves.

'This doesn't go in the paper, does it?' Ishmael asked his father. 'A sea creature at West Port Jensen?'

'Maybe you're right,' answered Arthur. 'But do you remember the bear stories I ran last year? The bear who was responsible for everything, suddenly? Dead dogs, broken windows, missing chickens, scratched cars? A mysterious creature – that's news, Ishmael. The fact that people see it – that's news.'

In the following issue Arthur printed a public service advertisement urging islanders to buy war bonds. He explained that the civilian defense commission was registering boats that might be available in the event of an evacuation. William Blair, he told his readers – son of Zachary and Edith Blair of Amity Harbor – graduated in the U.S. Naval Academy's first emergency class and shipped out for the European theater. The island lost power for four hours one morning when a half-dozen of the army's captive balloons broke away and dragged down power lines. The defense commissioner, Richard Blackington, appointed nine district air raid wardens to be responsible for the effectiveness of an island blackout; he also attended, in Anacortes, a chemical warfare training class and afterward busied himself disseminating flyers about it. Meanwhile the children of San Piedro Island had been numbered and registered in their school classrooms against the possibility of separation from their families. Arthur published a War Department chart showing wing and tail markings of airplanes. He also printed a photograph of Japanese-Americans in Fresno, California, standing in line to get citizen registration cards.

Four more islanders of Japanese descent – this was a front-page article – enlisted in the United States Army. Richard Enslow, who taught wood shop at the high school, resigned his position and joined the navy. Mrs. Ida Cross of South Beach knitted socks for sailors, sent them off, and received a thank-you note from an antiaircraft gunner stationed near Baltimore. The coast guard banned fishing on the west side of the island and bore down on gill-netters in the middle of the night who had set nets near restricted areas. In late January islanders experienced a temporary fuel shortage and were made to turn their oil heaters down by order of the civilian defense commission. The commission asked farmers for ten thousand sandbag sacks – gunny, feed, or flour. One hundred and fifty islanders attended first-aid courses offered by the Red Cross auxiliary. Petersen's store cut back on deliveries, citing fuel and labor shortages.

'Seems like you're favoring the Japs, Art,' an anonymous

Review reader wrote one day. 'You're putting them on the front page every week and writing all about their patriotism and loyalty while saying nothing about their treachery. Well, maybe it's time you pulled your head from the sand and realized – there's a war on! And who are you siding with, anyway?'

In January fifteen islanders canceled their subscriptions, including the Walker Colemans of Skiff Point and the Herbert Langlies of Amity Harbor. 'The Japs are the enemy,' wrote Herbert Langlie. 'Your newspaper is an insult to all white Americans who have pledged themselves to purge this menace from our midst. Please cancel my subscription as of this date and send refund immediately.'

Arthur did so; he sent a full refund to each customer who canceled, and a personal note written in a cordial style. 'One day they'll be back,' he predicted. But then the Price-Rite store in Anacortes canceled its weekly quarter-page advertisement; then Lottie's Opsvig's apparel shop on Main Street, then Larsen's Lumberyard and the Anacortes Cafe. 'We won't worry about this,' Arthur told his son. 'We can always put out four pages instead of eight if that's what we have to do.' He printed the letter from Walker Coleman and another one like it from Ingmar Sigurdson. Lillian Taylor, who taught English at the high school, wrote back in angry condemnation of the 'spirit of small-mindedness evident in the letters of Mr. Walker Coleman and Mr. Ingmar Sigurdson, two well-known islanders who quite obviously have lost their grip on their senses while in the grip of war hysteria.' Arthur printed that, too.

14

Two weeks later, on February 4, a black Ford threaded through
the Imadas' fields, making for the house of cedar slats. Hatsue
was standing at the verge of the woodshed, filling her apron with
cedar kindling from a pile underneath a sheet of waxed canvas,
when she noticed – this was odd – that the Ford's headlights had
been blackened; she heard the car before she saw it. It came to
a halt just in front of her house; two men emerged in suits and
ties. They shut their doors gently and looked at each other; one
of them straightened his coat a little – he was bigger than the
other, and his sleeves were not long enough to cover even half
of his shirt cuffs. Hatsue stood silently with her apron full of
kindling while the men mounted the porch and knocked on the
door, holding their hats in their hands. Her father answered in
his sweater and sandals, his newspaper dangling from his left
hand neatly and his reading glasses perched on the bridge of his
nose; her mother stood just behind him.

'Allow me to introduce myself,' said the smaller of the men,
producing a badge from his coat pocket. 'Federal Bureau of
Investigation,' he announced. 'Are you He-say-o Imada?'

'Yes,' said Hatsue's father. 'Is something wrong?'

'Not wrong exactly,' said the FBI man. 'It's just that we've
been asked to search this place. You understand, we're going
to search. Now if you'll just step inside, please, we'll all sit
down.'

'Yes, come in,' said Hatsue's father.

Hatsue dropped her apron full of kindling back onto the pile
of cedar sticks. The two men turned to look at her; the larger one
came halfway down the porch steps. Hatsue walked out of the

shadow of the woodshed and into the glow of the porch light. 'You come in, too,' said the smaller man.

They crowded into the living room. While Hatsue and her sisters sat on the couch, Hisao brought chairs from the kitchen for the FBI men – the larger one followed him everywhere. 'Please, sit down,' offered Hisao.

'You're real polite,' replied the smaller man. Then he took an envelope from his coat pocket; he handed it over to Hisao. 'It's a warrant from the U.S. district attorney. We're going to search the premises – it's an order, see, an order.'

Hisao held the envelope between his fingers but made no move to open it. 'We are loyal,' he said. That was all.

'I know, I know,' said the FBI man. 'Still, we've got to look around.'

While he spoke the larger man stood and shot his cuffs, then calmly opened Fujiko's glass case and picked up the stack of *shakuhachi* sheet music she kept on the bottom shelf. He picked up Fujiko's bamboo flute, turned it over twice in his hands – small hands for such a thick, cloddish man – then set it on the dining room table. There was a magazine stand beside the wood stove, and he pawed through the magazines there. He picked up Hisao's newspaper.

'We've had some complaints from local citizens that certain enemy aliens on San Piedro Island have in their possession items declared illegal contraband,' said the smaller man. 'It's our job to search the premises for these. We ask for your cooperation.'

'Yes, of course,' said Hisao.

The larger man went into the kitchen. They could see him through the doorway peering beneath the sink and opening the oven door. 'We're going to have to search through your private effects,' the small FBI man explained. He stood and took the envelope from Hisao; he put it back in his coat pocket. 'I hope you won't mind,' he added.

He opened the *tansu* – a chest of drawers in one corner of the living room. He took out Fujiko's silk kimono with its gold

170

brocaded sash. 'That's very nice,' he said, holding it to the light. 'From the old country, it appears. High class.'

The larger man came through the living room from the pantry with Hisao's shotgun seized in one hand and four boxes of shells against his chest. 'The guy's all armed,' he said to his partner. 'There's a big old sword back there, too.'

'Put it all on the table,' said the small man. 'And tag everything, Wilson – did you bring the tags in?'

'They're in my pocket,' Wilson answered.

The youngest of the Imada girls began to whimper, covering her face with her hands. 'Hey, little girl,' said the FBI man. 'I know this is kind of scary – but guess what? There's nothing to cry about, you hear me? We'll be done and out of your way soon.'

The large man, Wilson, went back for Hisao's sword. Then he turned his attention to the bedrooms.

'Tell you what,' said the first man to Hisao. 'Let's just sit tight until Wilson is finished. Then you and me, we'll take a walk outside. We'll tag these things up and load them in the car. Then you can show me around your outbuildings. We have to check everything – that's the way it is.'

'I understand,' said Hisao. He and Fujiko were holding hands now.

'Don't be nervous,' said the FBI man. 'We'll be out of your hair in a few minutes.'

He stood at the table putting tags on things. For a while he waited in silence. He tapped his foot and put his mouth to the flute. 'Wilson!' he said finally. 'Get your paws off the underwear!' Then he chuckled and picked up Hisao's shotgun.

'We gotta take this,' he said apologetically. 'All this stuff, you understand. They'll hold it for a while – who knows why? – then they'll ship it all back to you. They'll ship it back when they're done with it. It's complicated, but that's the way it is. There's a war on and that's the way it is.'

'The flute is precious,' said Hisao. 'The kimono, the sheet music – you must take those things?'

171

'Anything like that, yeah,' said the FBI man. 'Any old-country stuff we have to take.'

Hisao was silent, his brow furrowed. Wilson came back from the bedrooms looking solemn; he carried Hatsue's scrapbook. 'Pervert,' said his partner. 'Come on.'

'Crap,' said Wilson. 'I was going through the drawers. You do it next time if you don't like it.'

'He-say-o and I are going out,' the small man said firmly. 'You can sit here with the ladies and finish up with these tags. And be polite,' he added.

'I'm always polite,' said Wilson.

Hisao and the small man went outside; Wilson worked on the tags. When he was done he browsed through Hatsue's scrapbook, chewing on his bottom lip. 'Strawberry Princess,' he said, looking up. 'You must a been flattered by that.'

Hatsue didn't answer. 'It's a good picture,' added Wilson. 'It looks like you. Looks just like you, in fact.'

Hatsue said nothing. She wished Wilson would get his hands off her scrapbook. She was thinking of asking him, politely, to put it down, when Hisao and the other man came through the door, the FBI man carrying a crate. 'Dynamite,' he said. 'Look at this, Wilson.' He set the crate lightly on the table. The two men stood pawing through the dynamite – twenty-four sticks of it. Wilson chewed on his cheek and stared.

'You must believe me,' insisted Hisao. 'This is for tree stumps, for clearing land.'

The smaller FBI man shook his head gravely. 'Maybe,' he said. 'But this is still bad. This stuff' – he pointed a finger at the crate – 'this is illegal contraband. You were supposed to have turned this stuff in.'

They took the gun, the shells, the sword, and the dynamite and put it all in the car trunk. Wilson came back with a duffel bag and stuffed in the scrapbook, the kimono, the sheet music, and finally the bamboo flute.

When everything was loaded in the trunk of their car the FBI men sat down again. 'Well,' said the smaller one. 'This is it. Guess what?' he said to Hisao.

Hisao didn't answer. He sat in his sandals and sweater, blinking, holding his glasses in his hand. He waited for the FBI man to speak.

'We gotta arrest you,' said Wilson. 'You're going on a trip to Seattle.' He unhooked a pair of handcuffs from his belt; they were clipped on next to his gun.

'You don't need those,' urged the smaller man. 'This guy here is a class act, a gentleman. There's no need for any handcuffs.' He turned his attention to Hisao. 'They're just going to ask you some questions, okay? We go down to Seattle, a few questions, a few answers, the whole thing is over.'

The two younger girls were both crying. The youngest buried her face in her hands, and Hatsue put an arm around her. She pulled her sister's head in close and stroked her hair gently. Hisao rose from his chair.

'Please not take him,' said Fujiko. 'He has done no bad things. He – '

'Nobody knows about that,' said Wilson. 'There's nobody who can say.'

'Probably in just a few days,' said the other man. 'These things take a little time, you see. We have to take him on down to Seattle. He's gotta be scheduled in and all. Maybe a few days, maybe a week.'

'A week?' said Fujiko. 'But what we do? What do you – '

'Think of it as a war sacrifice,' the FBI man interrupted. 'Figure to yourself there's a war on, you see, and everybody's making some sacrifices. Maybe you could look at it that way.'

Hisao asked if he could change out of his sandals and get his coat from the pantry. He wanted to pack a small bag, he added, if that would be acceptable. 'Both,' said Wilson. 'Go ahead. We're perfectly willing to accommodate.'

They allowed him to kiss his wife and daughters and to say good-bye to each. 'Call Robert Nishi,' Hisao told them. 'Tell him I am arrested.' But when Fujiko called it turned out that

Robert Nishi had been arrested as well. Ronald Kobayashi, Richard Sumida, Saburo Oda, Taro Kato, Junkoh Kitano, Kenzi Yamamoto, John Masui, Robert Nishi – they were all in a Seattle jail now. They had all been arrested on the same night.

The arrested men rode on a train with boarded windows – prisoners had been shot at from railroad sidings – from Seattle to a work camp in Montana. Hisao wrote a letter to his family each day; the food, he said, was not very good, but they were not really being mistreated. They were digging trenches for a water system that would double the size of the camp. Hisao had gotten a job in the laundry ironing and folding clothes. Robert Nishi worked in the camp kitchen.

Hatsue's mother gathered her five daughters together, Hisao's letter in her hand. She told her daughters, once again, the story of her odyssey from Japan on board the *Korea Maru*. She told them about the Seattle rooms she had cleaned, the sheets on which white men had vomited blood, the toilets full of their excrement, the stench of their alcohol and sweat. She told them about the waterfront cookhouse where she'd worked chopping onions and frying potatoes for *hakujin* stevedores who looked right through her as if she weren't even there. She knew, already, about hardship, she said – her life had long been difficult. She knew what it was to be alive without being alive; she knew what it was to be invisible. She wanted her daughters to know how to face this in a manner that would allow them their dignity. Hatsue sat motionless while her mother spoke, trying to guess at her meaning. She was eighteen now, and her mother's story held more weight than it had when she'd heard it earlier. She leaned forward and listened carefully. Her mother predicted that the war with Japan would force all her daughters to decide who they were and then to become more Japanese. Wasn't it true that the *hakujin* didn't really want them in their country? There were rumors that all the Japanese on the coast were going to be forced to leave. There was no point in trying to conceal anything or in trying to pretend they were not Japanese – the *hakujin* could see it in their faces; they were going to have to accept this. They were Japanese girls in America during a time when America was fighting a war with Japan – did any of them want to deny it? The trick was to live here without hating yourself because all around you was hatred. The trick was to refuse to allow your pain to prevent you from living honorably. In Japan, she said, a person learned not to complain or be distracted by suffering. To persevere was always a reflection of the state of one's inner life, one's philosophy, and one's perspective. It was best to accept old age, death, injustice, hardship – all of these were part of living. Only a foolish girl would deny this was so, thus revealing to the world her immaturity and the degree to which she lived in the world of the *hakujin* instead of in the world of her own people. And her people, insisted Fujiko, were Japanese – the events of the past months had proved it so; why else had their father been arrested? The events of the last two months should teach them something about the darkness in the hearts of the *hakujin* and the more general darkness that was part of living. To deny that there was this dark side to life would be like pretending that the cold of winter was somehow only a temporary illusion, a way station on the way to the higher 'reality' of long, warm, pleasant summers. But summer, it turned out, was no more real than the snow that melted in wintertime. Well, said Fujiko, now your father is gone, folding laundry in a camp in Montana, and we all must get by, endure. 'Do you understand?' she said in Japanese. 'There is no choice in the matter. We will all have to endure.'

'They don't all hate us,' Hatsue replied. 'You're exaggerating, mother – you know you are. They're not so different from us, you know. Some hate, others don't. It isn't all of them.'

'I know what you're saying,' said Fujiko. 'Not all of them hate – you're correct. But on this other matter' – she still spoke in Japanese – 'you don't think they are very much different? In some big way, Hatsue? Different from us?'

'No,' said Hatsue. 'I don't.'

'They are,' said Fujiko, 'and I can tell you how. The whites, you see, are tempted by their egos and have no means to resist.

175

We Japanese, on the other hand, *know* our egos are nothing. We bend our egos, all of the time, and that is where we differ. That is the fundamental difference, Hatsue. We bend our heads, we bow and are silent, because we understand that by ourselves, alone, we are nothing at all, dust in a strong wind, while the *hakujin* believes his aloneness is everything, his separateness is the foundation of his existence. He seeks and grasps, seeks and grasps for his separateness, while we seek union with the Greater Life – you must see that these are distinct paths we are traveling, Hatsue, the *hakujin* and we Japanese.'

'These people seeking union with the Greater Life,' argued Hatsue, 'are the ones who bombed Pearl Harbor. If they're so ready to bend and bow, then what are they doing attacking all over the world and taking over other countries? I don't feel I'm a part of them,' said Hatsue. 'I'm a part of *here*,' she added. 'I'm from this place.'

'Yes, you were born here, that's so,' said Fujiko. 'But your blood – you are still Japanese.'

'I don't want to be!' said Hatsue. 'I don't want anything to do with them! Do you hear me? I don't want to be Japanese!'

Fujiko nodded at her eldest daughter. 'These are difficult times,' she replied. 'Nobody knows who they are now. Everything is cloudy and unclear. Still, you should learn to say nothing that will cause you regret. You should not say what is not in your heart – or what is only in your heart for a moment. But you know this – silence is better.'

Hatsue knew immediately that her mother was right. Her mother, clearly, was serene and unruffled, and her voice carried the strength of truth. Hatsue fell silent, ashamed of herself. Who was she to say how she felt? What she felt remained a mystery, she felt a thousand things at once, she could not unravel the thread of her feelings with enough certainty to speak with any accuracy. Her mother was right, silence was better. It was something – one thing – she knew with clarity.

'I could say,' her mother went on, 'that living among the *hakujin* has tainted you, made your soul impure, Hatsue. This lack of purity envelops you – I see it every day. You carry it with you always. It is like a mist around your soul, and it haunts your face like a shadow at moments when you do not protect it well. I see it in your eagerness to leave here and walk in the woods in the afternoon. I cannot translate all of this easily, except as the impurity that comes with living each day among the white people. I am not asking you to shun them entirely – this you should not do. You must live in this world, of course you must, and this world is the world of the *hakujin* – you must learn to live in it, you must go to school. But don't allow living *among* the *hakujin* to become living *intertwined* with them. Your soul will decay. Something fundamental will rot and go sour. You are eighteen, you are grown now – I can't walk with you where you are going anymore. You walk alone soon, Hatsue. I hope you will carry your purity with you always and remember the truth of who you are.'

Hatsue knew then that her pretense had failed her. For four years now she had taken her 'walks' and come home offering fuki tendrils, watercress, crawfish, mushrooms, huckleberries, salmonberries, blackberries – even clusters of blue elderberries for making jam – anything to conceal her purpose. She had gone to dances with other girls and stood in a corner refusing requests, while Ishmael stood among his friends. Her girlfriends had sought to concoct dates for her; she was widely encouraged to make use of her beauty and to emerge from the shell of her apparent shyness. It had even been rumored for a while last spring that she had a secret boyfriend who was extraordinarily handsome, somebody she visited in Anacortes, but that rumor gradually evaporated. Through all of it Hatsue had struggled with the temptation to reveal the truth to her sisters and school friends, because the truth was a burden to carry in silence and she felt the need, like most young girls, to speak about love with other girls. But she never did. She persisted in the pretense that her shy demeanor in the presence of boys prevented her from dating them.

Now her mother seemed to know the truth, or to have some

inkling of it. Her mother's black hair was bound severely into a gleaming knot pinned to the back of her head. Her hands were folded majestically in her lap – she'd set her husband's letter on the coffee table – and she was perched with great dignity on the edge of her chair, blinking calmly at her daughter. 'I know who I am,' said Hatsue. 'I know exactly who I am,' she asserted again, but they were just more words to feel uncertain about; they were just more words to regret. Silence would have been better.

'You're fortunate,' said Fujiko evenly, in Japanese. 'You speak with great assurance, oldest daughter. The words fly from your mouth.'

Hatsue found herself walking in the woods later that afternoon. It was getting on toward the end of February, a time of only bleak light. In spring great shafts of sun would split the canopy of trees and the litter fall of the forest would come floating down – twigs, seeds, needles, dust bark, all suspended in the hazy air – but now, in February, the woods felt black and the trees looked sodden and smelled pungently of rot. Hatsue went inland to where the cedars gave way to firs hung with lichen and moss. Everything was familiar and known to her here – the dead and dying cedars full of punky heartwood, the fallen, defeated trees as high as a house, the upturned root wads hung with vine maple, the toadstools, the ivy, the salal, the vanilla leaf, the low wet places full of devil's club. These were the woods through which she had wandered on her way home from Mrs. Shigemura's lessons, the woods where she had cultivated the kind of tranquillity Mrs. Shigemura had demanded. She'd sat among sword ferns six feet tall or on a shelf above a vale of trilliums and opened her eyes to the place. As far back as she could recall the content of her days there had always been this silent forest which retained for her its mystery.

There were straight rows of trees – colonnades – growing out of the seedbed of trees that had fallen two hundred years before and sunk and become the earth itself. The forest floor was a map of fallen trees that had lived half a thousand years before collapsing – a rise here, a dip there, a mound or moldering hillock somewhere – the woods held the bones of trees so old no one living had ever seen them. Hatsue had counted the rings of fallen trees more than six hundred years old. She had seen the deer mouse, the creeping vole, the green-hued antlers of the white-tailed deer decaying underneath a cedar. She knew where lady fern grew and phantom orchids and warted giant puffballs.

Deep among the trees she lay on a fallen log and gazed far up branchless trunks. A late winter wind blew the tops around, inducing in her a momentary vertigo. She admired a Douglas fir's complicated bark, followed its grooves to the canopy of branches two hundred feet above. The world was incomprehensibly intricate, and yet this forest made a simple sense in her heart that she felt nowhere else.

She drew up for herself, in the silence of her mind, a list of the things now cluttering her heart – her father was gone, arrested by the FBI for keeping dynamite in his shed; there was talk going around that before too long everyone with a Japanese face on San Piedro would be sent away until the war was done; she had a *hakujin* boyfriend she could see only in secret, who in a few short months was sure to be drafted and sent to kill the people of her blood. And now, on top of these insoluble things, her mother had only hours before probed into the pit of her soul and discovered her deep uncertainty. Her mother seemed to know about the gulf that separated how she lived from what she was. And what was she anyway? She was of this place and she was not of this place, and though she might desire to be an American it was clear, as her mother said, that she had the face of America's enemy and would always have such a face. She would never feel at home here among the *hakujin*, and at the same time she loved the woods and fields of home as dearly as anyone could. She had one foot in her parents' home, and from there it was not far at all to the Japan they had left behind years before. She could feel how this country far across the ocean pulled on her and lived inside her despite her wishes to the contrary; it was something she could not deny. And at the same time her feet were planted on San Piedro Island, and she wanted only her own strawberry farm, the fragrance of the fields and the cedar trees, and to live simply in this place forever. And then there was Ishmael. He was as much a part of her life as the trees, and he smelled of them and of the clam beaches. And yet he left this hole inside of her. He was not Japanese, and they had met at such a young age, their love had come out of thoughtlessness and impulse, she had fallen into loving him long before she knew herself, though it occurred to her now that she might never know herself, that perhaps no one ever does, that such a thing might not be possible. And she thought she understood what she had long sought to understand, that she concealed her love for Ishmael Chambers not because she was Japanese in her heart but because she could not in truth profess to the world that what she felt for him was love at all.

She felt a sickness overtake her. Her late-afternoon walks had not concealed her meetings with a boy her mother had long had intuition of. Hatsue knew she had not fooled anybody, she had not fooled herself, as it turned out, either, she had never felt completely right. How could they say, she and Ishmael, that they truly loved each other? They had simply grown up together, been children together, and the proximity of it, the closeness of it, had produced in them love's illusion. And yet – on the other hand – what was love if it wasn't the instinct she felt to be on the moss inside the cedar tree with this boy she had always known? He was the boy of this place, of these woods, these beaches, the boy who smelled like this forest. If identity was geography instead of blood – if living in a place was what really mattered – then Ishmael was part of her, inside of her, as much as anything Japanese. It was, she knew, the simplest kind of love, the purest form, untainted by Mind, which twisted everything, as Mrs. Shigemura, ironically, had preached. No, she told herself, she'd merely followed her instincts, and her instincts did not make the kinds of distinctions having Japanese blood demanded. She didn't know what else love could be.

One hour later, inside the cedar tree, she brought this matter up with Ishmael. 'We've known each other forever,' she said. 'I can hardly remember not knowing you. It's hard to remember the days before you. I don't even know if there were any.'

'My memory is like that, too,' said Ishmael. 'Do you remember that glass box I had? The one we took into the water?'

'Of course,' she said. 'I remember it.'

'That must have been ten years ago,' said Ishmael. 'Hanging onto that box. Being out there in the ocean – that's what I remember.'

'That's what I want to talk about,' said Hatsue. 'A box in the ocean – what kind of a start is that? What, really, did we have in common? We didn't even know each other.'

'We knew each other. We've always known each other. We've never been strangers the way most people are when they meet and start going out.'

'That's another thing,' said Hatsue. 'We don't go out – that isn't the right word – we *can't* go out, Ishmael. We're trapped inside this tree.'

'We're going to graduate in three months,' answered Ishmael. 'I think we should move to Seattle after that. It'll be different in Seattle – you'll see.'

'They're arresting people like me there, too, just like here, Ishmael. A white and a Japanese – I don't care if it's Seattle – we couldn't just go walking down the street together. Not after Pearl Harbor. You know that. Besides, you're going to be drafted in June. That's the way it's going to be. You won't be moving to Seattle, either. Let's be honest with ourselves.'

'Then what will we do? You tell me. What's the answer, Hatsue?'

'There isn't one,' she said. 'I don't know, Ishmael. There isn't anything we can do.'

'We just have to be patient,' Ishmael replied. 'This war won't go on forever.'

They sat in silence inside their tree, Ishmael propped up against one elbow, Hatsue with her head perched against his

181

ribs and her legs up against the glossy wood. 'It's nice in here,' said Hatsue. 'It's always nice in this place.'

'I love you,' answered Ishmael. 'I'll always love you. I don't care what else happens. I'm always going to love you.'

'I know you do,' said Hatsue. 'But I'm trying to be realistic about this. It isn't that simple, is what I'm saying. There are all these other things.'

'They don't really matter,' said Ishmael. 'None of those other things make a difference. Love is the strongest thing in the world, you know. Nothing can touch it. Nothing comes close. If we love each other we're safe from it all. Love is the biggest thing there is.'

He spoke with such confidence and drama about it that Hatsue allowed herself to be convinced by him that nothing was greater than love. She wanted to believe this, and so she indulged herself and tried to be swept up in it. They began to kiss against the moss inside the tree, but the touch of it felt to her false somehow, an attempt to obliterate the truth of the world and to deceive themselves with their lips. 'I'm sorry,' she said, drawing away. 'Everything is complicated. I can't forget about things.'

He held her in his arms and stroked her hair. They didn't speak anymore. She felt safe there, as though she were hibernating at the heart of the forest with time suspended and the world frozen – the temporary safety of a quiet way station one must leave in the morning. They fell asleep with their heads against the moss until the light in the tree went from green to gray, and then it was time to go home.

'Everything is going to work out,' said Ishmael. 'You'll see – it'll work out.'

'I don't see how,' answered Hatsue.

The problem was resolved for them on March 21 when the U.S. War Relocation Authority announced that islanders of Japanese descent had eight days to prepare to leave.

The Kobayashis – they'd planted a thousand dollars' worth of rhubarb on five acres in Center Valley – negotiated an agreement with Torval Rasmussen to tend and harvest their crop. The Masuis weeded their strawberry fields and worked at staking peas in the moonlight; they wanted to leave things in good condition for Michael Burns and his ne'er-do-well brother Patrick, who'd agreed to take care of their farm. The Sumidas decided to sell at cut-rate and close their nursery down; on Thursday and Friday they held all-day sales and watched pruning tools, fertilizer, cedar chairs, birdbaths, garden benches, paper lanterns, fountain cats, tree wrap, caddies, and bonsai trees go out the door with whoever was willing to take them. On Sunday they put padlocks on the greenhouse doors and asked Piers Petersen to keep an eye on things. They gave Piers their flock of laying chickens as well as a pair of mallard ducks.

Len Kato and Johnny Kobashigawa traveled island roads in a three-ton haying truck hauling loads of furniture, packing crates, and appliances to the Japanese Community Center hall. Filled to the rafters with beds, sofas, stoves, refrigerators, chests of drawers, desks, tables, and chairs, the hall was locked and boarded up at six P.M. on Sunday evening. Three retired gill-netters – Gillon Crichton, Sam Goodall, and Eric Hoffman, Sr. – were sworn in as deputies by San Piedro's sheriff for the purpose of guarding its contents.

The War Relocation Authority moved into musty offices at the old W. W. Beason Cannery dock, just outside Amity Harbor. The dock housed not only the Army Transport Command but representatives of the Farm Security Administration and the Federal Employment Service. Kaspars Hinkle, who coached the high school baseball team, stormed into the war relocation office on a late Thursday afternoon – everyone was just then preparing to leave – and slammed his roster on the secretary's desk: his starting catcher, second baseman, and two outfielders, he said – not to mention his two best pitchers – were going to miss the whole season. Couldn't this matter be thought through again? None of these kids were spies!

On Saturday evening, March 28, the Amity Harbor High School senior ball – its theme this year was 'Daffodil Daze' –

went forward in the high school auditorium. An Anacortes swing band, Men About Town, played upbeat dance tunes exclusively; during an interlude the captain of the baseball team stood in front of the microphone on the bandstand and cheerfully handed out honorary letters to the seven team members departing Monday morning. 'We don't have much chance without you,' he said. 'Right now we don't even have enough guys to field a team. But any wins we do get, they're for you guys who are leaving.'

Evelyn Nearing, the animal lover – she was a widow who lived without a flush toilet or electricity in a cedar cabin on Yearsley Point – took goats, pigs, dogs, and cats from a half-dozen Japanese families. The Odas leased their grocery to the Charles MacPhersons and sold Charles their car and two pickup trucks. Arthur Chambers made arrangements with Nelson Obada to act as a special correspondent for his newspaper and to send reports to San Piedro. Arthur ran four articles on the imminent evacuation in his March 26 edition: 'Island Japanese Accept Army Mandate to Move,' 'Japanese Ladies Praised for Last-Minute PTA Work,' 'Evacuation Order Hits Prep Baseball Nine,' and a 'Plain Talk' column called 'Not Enough Time,' which roundly condemned the relocation authority for its 'pointless and merciless speed in exiling our island's Japanese-Americans.' The next morning, at seven-thirty, Arthur fielded an anonymous phone call – 'Jap lovers get their balls cut off,' a shrill tenor voice had explained. 'They get their balls stuffed down – ' Arthur had hung up and gone on typing a story for the next edition of his newspaper: 'Faithful to Praise Christ Easter Morn.'

On Sunday afternoon, at four o'clock, Hatsue told her mother she was going for a walk; her last walk before leaving, she pointed out. She wanted to sit in the forest, she said, and think about matters for a while. She left as if headed toward Protection Point, then circled through the woods to the South Beach trail and followed the path to the cedar tree. Ishmael, she found, was waiting for her there with his head propped up on his jacket. 'This is it,' she said to him, kneeling for a moment in the entry. 'Tomorrow morning we leave.'

'I've got something figured out,' answered Ishmael. 'When you get where you're going you write to me. Then when the school newspaper comes out I'll send you a copy with a letter from me inside it and put Journalism Class for a return address. What do you think of that plan? You think that will be safe?'

'I wish we didn't even need a plan,' said Hatsue. 'Why do we have to do this?'

'Write me at my house,' said Ishmael, 'but put Kenny Yamashita's name for the return address – my parents know I'm friendly with Kenny, you can write me at home with no problems.'

'But what if they want to see Kenny's letter? What if they ask how he's doing?'

Ishmael thought about this for a moment. 'What if they want to see Kenny's letter? What if you collect maybe half a dozen letters and stick them all in one envelope? One from Kenny, one from you, one from Helen, one from Tom Obata – tell them it's a request from the school newspaper. I'll call Kenny tonight and tell him about it so it doesn't sound suspicious when you bring it up. Collect them all, stick yours in last, send them all to me, I'll pull yours out and take the rest to school. That should work out perfectly.'

'You're like me,' said Hatsue. 'We've both gotten good at being devious.'

'I don't think it's devious,' said Ishmael. 'It's just what we have to do.'

Hatsue undid the belt on her coat, a herringbone wraparound from the Penney's in Anacortes. Underneath she wore an austelle dress with a broad embroidered collar. On this day she'd brushed her hair out long and tossed it to flow down the length of her back, unfettered by plaits, braids, or ribbons. Ishmael pressed his nose against it. 'It smells like cedar,' he said.

'So do you,' said Hatsue. 'It's your smell I'll miss as much as anything.'

They lay on the moss, not touching, in silence, Hatsue with her hair coiled over one shoulder now, Ishmael with his hands in his lap. The March wind came up outside the tree and they heard it tossing the ferns together and the suspiration of the wind joined with the sliding of the water in the little creek just below. The tree muted and softened these sounds, and Hatsue felt herself at the heart of things. This place, this tree, was safe.

They began to kiss and touch each other, but the emptiness she felt pervaded it and she found she couldn't put her thoughts away. She placed an index finger against Ishmael's lips and shut her eyes and let her hair fall back against the moss. The smell of the tree was his smell, too, and the smell of the place she was leaving the next day, and she began to understand how she would miss it. The ache of it filled her; she felt sorry for him and sorry for herself and began to cry so quietly that it was only behind her eyes, a tautness in her throat, a tightening of her rib cage. Hatsue pressed against him, crying in this silent way, and breathed in the smell of Ishmael's throat. She buried her nose beneath his Adam's apple.

Ishmael moved his hands beneath the hem of her dress, then slowly up her thighs and over her underpants to the curves of her waist, where they stayed. He held her lightly in the curves of her waist and after a while lower, at her hips, and pulled her hard against him. She felt herself lifted, and she felt how hard he was and she pressed back into his hardness. The length of it pushed against his trousers, and his trousers pressed against her underpants and their smooth, wet silk pushed pleasantly. They kissed harder now, and she began to move as if to gather him in. She could feel the hard length of him and the silk of her underpants and his cotton trousers between. Then his hands left her hips and traced the line of her waist and traveled along up under her dress to the clasp on her bra. She arched off the moss to make room for his hands, and he undid the clasp without struggling and pulled the shoulder straps down onto her arms and softly kissed her earlobes. His hands traveled down her body again, coming out from the dress to hold her neck under her hair, then her shoulder blades. She let her weight rest against his hands and arched her breasts to meet him. Ishmael kissed the front of her austelle dress and then began, from just below the embroidered collar, to undo its eleven buttons. It took time. They breathed into one another, and she took his upper lip between her lips while he worked on the buttons carefully. After a while the front of her dress came open, and he pulled her bra up onto her chest and moved his tongue against her nipples. 'Let's get married,' he whispered. 'I want to marry you, Hatsue.'

She was far too empty to answer this; there was no way she could speak. Her voice felt buried underneath her crying, and there was no way to bring it to the surface. So instead she ran her fingertips along his spine and against his hips, and then with both hands she felt his hardness through the fabric of his pants and felt how, for a moment, he seemed to stop breathing altogether. She squeezed with both hands and kissed him.

'Let's get married,' he said again, and she understood what he meant. 'I just . . . I want to marry you.'

She made no move to stop him when he slid his hand inside her panties. Then he was peeling them down her legs, and she was still crying silently. He was kissing her and pulling his own pants to his knees, the tip of his hardness was against her skin now and his hands were cupped around her face. 'Just say yes,' he whispered. 'Just tell me yes, tell me yes. Say yes to me. Say yes, oh God say yes.'

'Ishmael,' she whispered, and in that moment he pushed himself inside of her, all the way in, his hardness filling her entirely, and Hatsue knew with clarity that nothing about it was right. It came as an enormous shock to her, this knowledge, and at the same time it was something she had always known, something until now hidden. She pulled away from him – she pushed him. 'No,' she said. 'No, Ishmael. No, Ishmael. Never.'

He pulled himself out, away. He was a decent boy, a kind boy, she knew that. He pulled his trousers up, buttoned them, and helped her back into her panties. Hatsue straightened her bra and clasped it again and buttoned up her dress. She put her coat on and then, sitting up, began meticulously to brush the moss from her hair. 'I'm sorry,' she said. 'It wasn't right.'

'It seemed right to me,' answered Ishmael. 'It seemed like getting married, like being married, like you and me were married. Like the only kind of wedding we could ever have.'

'I'm sorry,' said Hatsue, picking moss from her hair. 'I don't want you to be unhappy.'

'I am unhappy. I'm miserable. You're leaving tomorrow morning.'

'I'm unhappy, too,' said Hatsue. 'I'm sick with it, I feel worse than I've ever felt. I don't know anything anymore.'

He walked her home, to the edge of her fields, where they stood for a moment behind a cedar tree. It was nearly dusk and a March stillness had seized everything – the trees, the rotting deadwood, the leafless vine maple, the stones littering the ground. 'Good-bye,' said Hatsue. 'I'll write.'

'Don't go,' said Ishmael. 'Stay here.'

When she finally did leave it was well past dusk, and she walked out of the woods and into the open with the intention of not looking back again. But after ten steps she did so despite herself – it was too hard not to turn around. It was in her to say good-bye forever and tell him she would never see him again, to explain to him that she'd chosen to part because in his arms she felt unwhole. But she didn't say it, that they had been too young, that they had not seen clearly, that they had allowed the forest and the beach to sweep them up, that all of it had been delusion all along, that she had not been who she was. Instead, unblinking, she looked at him, unable to hurt him in the way that was demanded and in some undefined way still loving what he was, his kindness, his seriousness, the goodness in his heart. He stood there, Ishmael, looking at her desperately, and that was the way she would remember him. Twelve years later she would still see him this way, standing at the edge of the strawberry fields beneath the cover of the silent cedars, a handsome boy with one arm outstretched, beckoning her to come back.

15

An army truck took Fujiko and her five daughters to the Amity Harbor ferry dock at seven o'clock on Monday morning, where a soldier gave them tags for their suitcases and coats. They waited among their bags in the cold while their *hakujin* neighbors stood staring at them where they were gathered on the dock between the soldiers. Fujiko saw Ilse Severensen there, leaning against the railing with her hands clasped in front of her; she waved at the Imadas as they passed by. Ilse, a Seattle transplant, had for ten years purchased strawberries from Fujiko and spoke to her as if she were a peasant whose role in life was to make island life pleasantly exotic for Ilse's friends who visited from the city. Her kindness had always been condescending, and she had always paid a bit extra for her berries with the air of doling out charity. And so, on this morning, Fujiko could not meet her eyes or acknowledge her despite the fact that Ilse Severensen had waved and called out her name in a friendly way – Fujiko studied the ground instead; she kept her eyes cast down.

At nine o'clock they were marched on board the *Kehloken*, with the white people gaping at them from the hill above, and Gordon Tanaka's daughter – she was eight years old – fell on the dock and began to cry. Soon other people were crying, too, and from the hill came the voice of Antonio Dangaran, a Filipino man who had married Eleanor Kitano just two months before. 'Eleanor!' he shouted, and when she looked up he let go a bouquet of red roses, which sailed gently toward the water in the wind and landed in the waves below the dock pilings.

They were taken from Anacortes on a train to a transit camp – the horse stables at the Puyallup fairgrounds. They lived in the horse stalls and slept on canvas army cots; at nine P.M. they were confined to their stalls; at ten P.M. they were made to turn out their lights, one bare bulb for each family. The cold in the stalls worked into their bones, and when it rained that night they moved their cots because of the leaks in the roof. The next morning, at six A.M., they slogged through mud to the transit camp mess hall and ate canned figs and white bread from pie tins and drank coffee out of tin cups. Through all of it Fujiko maintained her dignity, though she'd felt herself beginning to crack while relieving herself in front of other women. The contortions of her face as she moved her bowels deeply humiliated her. She hung her head as she sat on the toilet, ashamed of the noises her body made. The roof leaked in the latrine, too.

After three days they boarded another train and began a languid crawl toward California. At night the MPs who roamed from car to car came through telling them to pull down their window shades, and they passed the dark hours twisting in their seats and exerting themselves not to complain. The train stopped and started and jolted them toward wakefulness, and there was a constant line at the door to the toilet. Many people had lost control of their bowels altogether as a result of eating in the Puyallup transit camp, including Fujiko. Her rectum burned as she sat in her train seat, her brain felt light and unmoored inside her skull, and a cold sweat beaded on her forehead. Fujiko did her best not to give in to her discomfort by speaking of it to her daughters. She did not want them to know that she was suffering inwardly and needed to lie down comfortably somewhere and sleep for a long time. For when she slept at all it was with her hearing tuned to the bluebottle flies always pestering her and to the crying of the Takami baby, who was three weeks old and had a fever. The wailing of this baby ate at her, and she rode with her fingers stuffed inside her ears, but this did not seem to change things. Her sympathy for the baby and for all of the Takamis began to slip as sleep evaded her, and she secretly began to wish for the baby's death if such a thing could mean silence. And at the same time she hated herself for thinking this and fought against it while her anger grew at the fact that the baby could not just be flung from the window so that the rest of them might have some peace. Then, long past the point when she had told herself that she could not endure another moment, the baby would stop its tortured shrieking, Fujiko would calm herself and close her eyes, retreat with enormous relief toward sleep, and then the Takami baby would once again wail and shriek inconsolably.

The train stopped at a place called Mojave in the middle of an interminable, still desert. They were herded onto buses at eight-thirty in the morning, and the buses took them north over dusty roads for four hours to a place called Manzanar. Fujiko had imagined, shutting her eyes, that the sandstorm battering the bus was the rain of home. She'd dozed and awakened in time to see the barbed wire and the rows of dark barracks blurred by blowing dust. It was twelve-thirty, by her watch; they were just in time to stand in line for lunch. They ate standing up, from army mess kits, with their backs turned against the wind. Peanut butter, white bread, canned figs, and string beans; she could taste the dust in all of it.

They were given typhoid shots that first afternoon; they stood in line for them. They waited in the dust beside their luggage and then stood in line for dinner. In the evening the Imadas were assigned to Block 11, Barrack 4, and given a sixteen-by-twenty-foot room furnished with a bare lightbulb, a small Coleman oil heater, six CCC camp cots, six straw mattresses, and a dozen army blankets. Fujiko sat on the edge of a cot with cramps from the camp food and the typhoid shot gathering to a knot in her stomach. She sat with her coat on, holding herself, while her daughters beat flat the straw in the mattresses and lit the oil heater. Even with the heater she shivered beneath her blankets, still fully dressed in her clothes. By midnight she couldn't wait any longer and, with three of her daughters who were feeling distressed too, stumbled out into the darkness of the desert in the direction of the block latrine. There was, astonishingly, a long line at midnight, fifty or more women and girls in heavy coats with their backs braced against the wind. A woman up the line vomited heavily, and the smell was of the canned figs they'd all eaten. The woman apologized profusely in Japanese, and then another in the line vomited, and they were all silent again.

Inside they found a film of excrement on the floor and damp, stained tissue paper everywhere. All twelve toilets, six back-to-back pairs, were filled up near to overflowing. Women were using these toilets anyway, squatting over them in the semidarkness while a line of strangers watched and held their noses. Fujiko, when it was her turn, hung her head and emptied her bowels with her arms wrapped around her stomach. There was a trough to wash her hands in, but no soap.

That night dust and yellow sand blew through the knotholes in the walls and floor. By morning their blankets were covered with it. Fujiko's pillow lay white where her head had been, but around it a layer of fine yellow grains had gathered. She felt it against her face and in her hair and on the inside of her mouth, too. It had been a cold night, and in the adjacent room a baby screamed behind a quarter-inch wall of pine board.

On their second day at Manzanar they were given a mop, a broom, and a bucket. The leader of their block – a man from Los Angeles dressed in a dusty overcoat who claimed to have been an attorney in his former life but who now stood unshaven with one shoe untied and with his wire-rimmed glasses skewed on his face – showed them the outdoor water tap. Fujiko and her daughters cleaned out the dust and did laundry in a gallon-size soup tin. While they were cleaning more dust and sand blew in to settle on the newly mopped pine boards. Hatsue went out into the desert wind and returned with a few scraps of tar paper she'd found blown up against a roll of barbed wire along a firebreak. They stuffed this around the doorjamb and fixed it over the knotholes with thumbtacks borrowed from the Fujitas.

There was no sense in talking to anyone about things. Everyone was in the same position. Everyone wandered like ghosts beneath the guard towers with the mountains looming on either side of them. The bitter wind came down off the mountains and through the barbed wire and hurled the desert sand in their faces. The camp was only half-finished; there were not enough barracks to go around. Some people, on arriving, had to build their own in order to have a place to sleep. There were crowds everywhere, thousands of people in a square mile of desert scoured to dust by army bulldozers, and there was nowhere for a person to find solitude. The barracks all looked the same: on the second night, at one-thirty A.M., a drunk man stood in the doorway of the Imadas' room apologizing endlessly while the dust blew in; he'd lost his way, he said. Their room had no ceiling either, and it was possible to hear people squabbling in other barracks. There was a man who distilled his own wine three rooms down – he used mess hall rice and canned apricot juice – they heard him weeping late on their third night while his wife threatened him. On that same night the searchlights went on in the guard towers and swept across their single window. In the morning it turned out that one of the guards had become convinced of an escape in progress and had alerted the tower machine gunners. On the fourth night a young man in Barrack 17 shot his wife and then himself while they lay in bed together – somehow he had smuggled in a gun. '*Shikata ga nai*,' people said. 'It cannot be helped, it has to be.'

There was nowhere to put any clothing. They lived out of their suitcases and packing crates. The floor was cold beneath their feet, and they wore their dusty shoes until bedtime. By the end of the first week Fujiko had lost track of her daughters' whereabouts altogether. Everybody had begun to look alike, dressed in surplus War Department clothing – pea coats, knit caps, canvas leggings, army earmuffs, and wool khaki pants. Only her two youngest ate with her; the other three ran with packs of young people and ate at other tables. She scolded them, and they listened politely and then went out again. The older girls left early and came back late, their clothes and hair full of dust. The camp was an enormous promenade of young people milling and walking in the fire lanes and huddling in the lee of barracks. On her way to the washhouse one morning after breakfast Fujiko had seen her middle daughter – she was only fourteen – standing in a group that included four boys dressed nattily in Eisenhower coats. They were, she knew, Los Angeles boys; most people in the camp were from Los Angeles. The Los Angeles people were not very cordial and looked down on her for some inexplicable reason; she could not get a word in with them edgewise. Fujiko fell silent about everything, collapsed in on herself. She waited for a letter from Hisao to come, but a different letter came instead.

When Hatsue's sister Sumiko saw the envelope with Ishmael's false return address – *Journalism Class, San Piedro High School* – she did not resist her urge to tear it open. Sumiko had been a sophomore before her exile, and although she knew the envelope was Hatsue's this mail remained irresistible. This mail was word from home.

Sumiko read the letter from Ishmael Chambers in front of the tarpaper YMCA building; she read it again, savoring the more astonishing phrases, out by the camp hog pens.

April 4, 1942

My Love,

I still go to our cedar tree in the afternoons every day. I shut my eyes, waiting. I smell your smell and I dream of you and I ache for you to come home. Every moment I think of you and long to hold and feel you. Missing you is killing me. It's like a part of me has gone away.

I'm lonely and miserable and think of you always and hope you will write me right away. Remember to use Kenny Yamashita's name for a return address on the envelope so my parents won't get too curious.

Everything here is horrible and sad and life is not worth living. I can only hope that you find some happiness during the time we have to be apart – some happiness of some kind, Hatsue. Myself, I can only be miserable until you are in my arms again. I can't

*live without you, I know that now. After all these years that
we've been together, I find you're a part of me. Without you, I
have nothing.*

*All My Love Forever,
Ishmael*

After a half hour of walking and thinking and of reading
Ishmael's letter four more times, she took it regretfully to her
mother. 'Here,' she said. 'I feel like a creep. But I have to show
this to you.'

Her mother read Ishmael Chambers's letter standing in the
middle of the tar-paper hut with one hand on her forehead.
While she read her lips moved rapidly, her eyes blinked severely
and often. Finished, she sat down on the edge of a chair, dangled
the letter in her hand for a moment, then sighed and took off her
glasses. 'Surely not,' she said in Japanese.

She set the glasses in her lap wearily, placed the letter on top
of them, and pressed against her eyes with both palms.

'The neighborhood boy,' she said to Sumiko. 'The one who
taught her how to swim.'

'Ishmael Chambers,' answered Sumiko. 'You know who he
is.'

'Your sister has made a terrible mistake,' said Fujiko. 'One I
hope you will never make.'

'I never would,' said Sumiko. 'Anyway, it isn't a mistake I
could make in a place like this, is it?'

Fujiko picked up her glasses again and held them between her
thumb and forefinger. 'Sumi,' she said. 'Have you told anyone?
Have you shown this letter to anyone?'

'No,' said Sumi. 'Just you.'

'You must promise something,' said Fujiko. 'You must
promise not to tell this to anyone – don't tell anyone about
it. There's enough gossip here without something like this.
You must promise to keep your mouth closed and never tell
this again. Do you understand me?'

'All right. I promise,' said Sumiko.

'I'll tell Hatsue I found the letter. You don't have to take the blame.'

'Okay,' answered Sumiko. 'Good.'

'Go out now,' said her mother. 'Go and leave me alone.'

The girl went out to wander aimlessly. Fujiko perched her glasses on her nose once more and began to reread the letter. It was clear to her from the words in it that her daughter had been deeply entangled with this boy for a long time, for many years. It was evident that he had touched her body, that the two of them had been sexually intimate inside a hollow tree they'd used as a trysting place in the forest. Hatsue's walks had been a ruse, just as Fujiko had suspected. Her daughter had returned with *fuki* tendrils in her hands and a wetness between her thighs. *Deceitful girl*, thought Fujiko.

She thought for a moment of her own romantic life, how she'd been wed to a man she'd never seen before and passed the first night of her life with him in a boardinghouse where the pages of *hakujin* magazines had been substituted for wallpaper. She had refused, on that first night, to let her husband touch her – Hisao was unclean, his hands were rough, he had no money but a few coins. He'd spent those first hours apologizing to Fujiko and explaining in detail his financial desperation, pleading with her to work beside him and underscoring his talents and better traits – he was ambitious, hardworking, didn't gamble or drink, he had no bad habits and saved his money, but times were so hard, he needed someone at his side. He could understand, he said, having to earn her love, and he was willing to prove himself to her with time if she would agree to be patient. 'Don't even speak to me,' she'd replied.

He'd slept in a chair that first night, and Fujiko had stayed awake pondering ways to extricate herself from this situation. She did not have enough money to buy a return ticket, and at any rate, she knew in her bones, she could not return to her family in Japan – her parents had sold her and paid a percentage to the deceitful *baishakunin* who had assured them that Hisao had amassed great wealth during his years in America. She stayed awake growing angrier about this; by dawn she had begun to feel murderous.

In the morning Hisao stood at the foot of the bed and asked Fujiko if she'd slept well. 'I'm not talking to you,' she answered. 'I'm going to write home for the money I need and go back as soon as I can.'

'We'll save together,' pleaded Hisao. 'We'll go back together, if that's what you want. We'll – '

'What about your twelve acres of mountain land?' Fujiko said to him angrily. 'The *baishakunin* took me to see it – peach trees, persimmons, weeping willows, rock gardens. None of that turns out to be true.'

'You're right, it isn't true,' confessed Hisao. 'I don't have money – that's correct. I'm a pauper and I work my fingers to the bone. The *baishakunin* lied to you, I'm sorry for that, but – '

'Don't talk to me, please,' said Fujiko. 'I don't want to be married to you.'

It had taken her three months to learn how to sleep with him. When she did she found that she had learned to love him, if love was the proper word to use, and it occurred to her then, sleeping in his arms, that love was nothing close to what she'd imagined as a girl growing up near Kure. It was less dramatic and far more practical than her girlhood had led her to believe. Fujiko had cried when her hymen broke, in part because sacrificing her virginity to Hisao's need had not been what she had hoped for. But she was married now, and he was a steady sort of a man, and she grew, gradually, close to him. They'd been, already, through much hardship together, and he had never once complained.

Now she stood with this letter in her hand – a letter a *hakujin* boy had sent to her daughter about love inside a cedar tree, about his loneliness and misery and how horribly he missed her and how she should write to him with a false return address – '*use Kenny Yamashita's name*,' he'd written. She wondered if her daughter loved this boy or if she knew the first thing about love. It made sense to her now that Hatsue had been so silent and morose – more silent and morose than her other daughters – since the day they left San Piedro. Everybody had been unhappy and Hatsue had used this, the general unhappiness had been convenient, but still she had sulked more than anyone; she'd been listless and had gone about her chores with the sluggishness of someone grieving. She missed her father, she said when asked; she missed San Piedro Island. But she did not say to anyone that she missed the *hakujin* boyfriend who had been her secret lover. The depth of her deceit became vivid to Fujiko, and she felt in herself a mother's rage at the weight of this betrayal. The rage mingled with the general melancholy that had been growing in her steadily since the bombing of Pearl Harbor; it was one of the rare times in Fujiko's adult life when she felt inconsolable.

She reminded herself to behave with dignity no matter what the circumstances. It was a lesson she'd forgotten in her early days in America, but with time she had rediscovered it as something worthy passed down from her grandmother in Kure. *Giri* was her grandmother's word for it – it could not be precisely translated into English – and it meant doing what one had to do quietly and with an entirely stoic demeanor. Fujiko sat back and cultivated in herself the spirit of quiet dignity that would be necessary in confronting Hatsue. She breathed deeply and shut her eyes.

Well, she told herself, she would have a talk with Hatsue when the girl came back from wandering aimlessly around the camp. She would put an end to this business.

Three hours before dinner a group of San Piedro boys knocked on the door of her room. They had with them tools and scraps of lumber, and they were prepared, they said, to build for the Imadas whatever was wanted: shelves, a chest of drawers, chairs. She recognized all of them as the sons of island families – the Tanakas, the Kados, the Matsuis, the Miyamotos – and she told them yes, she could use all of those things, and the boys set about working in the lee of the barrack, measuring and cutting and sawing while the wind blew. Kabuo Miyamoto came inside and nailed up brackets while Fujiko sat on a cot with her arms crossed and the letter from the *hakujin* boy behind her back. 'There are some scraps of tin at the side of the block kitchen,' Kabuo Miyamoto said to her. 'We can nail them over those knotholes in the floor – they'll do a better job than tar paper.'

'Tar paper tears like *that*,' answered Fujiko in the English Kabuo used. 'And it not help keep cold out.'

Kabuo nodded and went back to work, his hammer striking efficiently. 'How is your family?' Fujiko said. 'Your mother? Your father? How everybody?'

'My father is ill,' Kabuo answered. 'The camp food is bad for his stomach.' He paused to slip another nail from his pocket. 'And you?' he said. 'How are all of the Imada women?'

'Dusty,' said Fujiko. 'We eat dust.'

At this moment Hatsue came through the door, her face reddened by the cold outside, and tugged the scarf from her head. Kabuo Miyamoto stopped his work for a moment to gaze at her while she shook her hair free. 'Hello,' he said. 'It's good to see you.'

Hatsue tossed her hair once more, gathered it in her hands swiftly, and smoothed it down the back of her head. Then she stuffed her hands in her overcoat and sat down beside her mother. 'Hello,' she said, but nothing more.

They sat for a moment watching in silence while Kabuo Miyamoto went about his work. He sat on his shins with his back to them, tapping carefully with a hammer. Another of the carpenters came through the door with a stack of freshly sawed pine boards. Kabuo Miyamoto laid each on the brackets and tested each with a level. 'They're straight,' he announced. 'They should work out well. I'm sorry we couldn't do better.'

'They're very nice,' said Fujiko. 'It's kind of you. Our thanks.'

'We're going to build you six chairs,' said Kabuo, looking at Hatsue now. 'We're going to build you two chests of drawers and a table you can eat on. We'll have them to you in a few days' time. As soon as we can get them built.'

'Thank you,' said Fujiko. 'You're very kind.'

'We're glad to do it for you,' said Kabuo Miyamoto. 'It isn't any trouble at all.'

Still holding his hammer, he smiled at Hatsue, and she dropped her eyes to her lap. He slipped the hammer into a cloth ring on his pants, then picked up his level and measuring tape. 'Good-bye, Mrs. Imada,' he said. 'Good-bye, Hatsue. It's good to see you.'

'Our thanks again,' said Fujiko. 'Your help is greatly appreciated.'

When the door had shut she reached behind her and handed Hatsue the letter. 'Here,' she spat. 'Your mail. I don't know how you could have been so deceitful. I'll never understand it, Hatsue.'

She had planned to discuss the matter right there and then, but she understood suddenly that the strength of her bitterness might prevent her from saying what she really meant. 'You will not write again to this boy or accept his letters,' she said sternly from the doorway.

The girl sat with the letter in her hand, tears gathering in her eyes. 'I'm sorry,' Hatsue said. 'Forgive me, Mother. I've deceived you and I've always known it.'

'Deceiving me,' said Fujiko in Japanese, 'is only half of it, daughter. You have deceived yourself, too.'

Then Fujiko went out into the wind. She walked to the post office and told the clerk there to hold all mail for the Imada family. From now on, she herself would come for it. It should be handed to her only.

That afternoon she sat in the mess hall and wrote her own letter addressed to the parents of the boy Ishmael Chambers. She told them about the hollow tree in the woods and how Ishmael and Hatsue had deceived the world for a number of years successfully. She revealed to them the contents of the letter their son had written to her daughter. Her daughter, she said, would not be writing back, now or at any time in the future. Whatever had been between them was over, and she apologized for her daughter's role in it; she hoped that the boy would see his future in a new light and give no more thought to Hatsue. She understood, she wrote, that they were only children; she knew children were often foolish. Still, both of these young people were culpable and must look to themselves now, examine their souls, consider this a matter of conscience. It was no crime to find oneself attracted to another, she wrote, or to believe what one felt was love. The dishonor lay instead in concealing from one's family the nature of one's affections. She hoped that the parents of Ishmael Chambers would understand her position. She did not wish for any further communication to pass between her daughter and their son. She had expressed her feelings clearly to her daughter and asked her not to write to the boy or accept his letters in the future. She added that she admired the Chambers family and had great respect for the *San Piedro Review*. She wished them well, all of them.

She showed this letter to Hatsue when it was folded and ready to go in its envelope. The girl read it over twice, slowly, with her left cheek resting on her left hand. When she was done she held it tightly in her lap and looked blandly at her mother. Her face, strangely, was drained of emotion; she had the look of one exhausted from the inside, too tired to feel. Fujiko saw that she had gotten older in the three weeks since they'd left San Piedro. Her daughter was suddenly grown up, a woman, weary from the inside. Her daughter had suddenly grown hardened.

'You don't have to send this,' she said now to Fujiko. 'I wasn't going to write him again anyway. I was on the train, coming down here, and all I could think about was Ishmael Chambers and whether I should write him a letter. Whether I loved him anymore.'

'Love,' spat Fujiko. 'You not know about love. You – '

'I'm eighteen,' replied Hatsue. 'I'm old enough. Stop thinking of me as a little girl. You have to understand – I've grown up.'

Fujiko removed her glasses carefully and, as was her habit, rubbed her eyes. 'On the train,' she said. 'What you decide?'

'Nothing, at first,' said Hatsue. 'I couldn't think very clearly.

There were too many things to think about, Mother. I was too depressed to think.'

'And now?' said Fujiko. 'What now?'

'I'm done with him,' said Hatsue. 'We were children together, we played on the beach, and it turned out to be something bigger. But he isn't the husband for me, Mother. I've known that all along. Anyway I wrote him, I said that whenever we were together it seemed like something was wrong. I always knew, deep inside, it was wrong, I felt it down inside somewhere – this feeling like I loved him and at the same time couldn't love him – I was always confused, every day, ever since we met. He's a good person, Mother, you know his family, he's really a very good person. But none of that matters, does it? I wanted to tell him it was over, Mother, but I was *leaving* . . . it was all *confused*, I couldn't get the words out, and, besides, I didn't really know what I felt. I was confused. There was too much to think about. I needed to straighten it all out.'

'And is it straighten out now, Hatsue? Is it straighten?'

The girl was silent for a moment. She ran a hand through her hair and let it fall, then the other hand, too. 'It's straight,' she said. 'I have to tell him. I have to put an end to it.'

Fujiko took her letter from her daughter's lap and ripped it neatly down the middle. 'Write your own letter,' she said in Japanese. 'Tell him the truth about things. Put all of this in your history. Tell him the truth so you can move forward. Put this *hakujin* boy away now.'

In the morning Sumiko was reminded of the importance of revealing nothing about this episode. She promised her mother she would keep silent. Fujiko took Hatsue's letter to the post office and paid the postage on it. She licked the envelope shut herself and, because the notion took hold of her suddenly – a kind of caprice and nothing more – she pressed the stamp on upside down before putting the letter in the mailbox.

When Kabuo Miyamoto brought his chests of drawers, Fujiko asked him to stay for tea, and he sat with them for more than two hours, and again on the next night when he delivered the table, and on the following night when he delivered the chairs. Then on the fourth night he came to their door with his hat in his hand and asked Hatsue if she would go for a walk with him underneath the stars. She said no on that occasion and did not speak to him for another three weeks, and yet she saw that he was polite and handsome, the clear-eyed son of strawberry farmers, and anyway she couldn't grieve over Ishmael Chambers until the end of her days.

When the time came, a few months later, that Ishmael was mostly a persistent ache buried beneath the surface of her daily life, she spoke to Kabuo Miyamoto in the mess hall and sat beside him to eat lunch. She admired his impeccable table manners and the graciousness of his smile. He spoke softly to her, asked her about her dreams, and when she said she wanted an island strawberry farm he said he wanted the same thing precisely and told her about how his family's seven acres would soon be transferred to his name. When the war was over he planned to farm strawberries back home on San Piedro Island.

When she kissed him for the first time, she felt the grip of her sadness, how it seized more tightly around her, and how different his mouth was from Ishmael's. He smelled of earth and his body's strength was far greater than her own. She found she couldn't move within the circle of his arms and struggled against him, breathless. 'You'll have to be more gentle,' she'd whispered. 'I'll try,' Kabuo had answered.

16

Ishmael Chambers trained as a marine rifleman with seven hundred and fifty other recruits at Fort Benning, Georgia, in the late summer of 1942. In October he fell ill with fever and dysentery and was hospitalized for eleven days, during which he lost considerable weight and passed his time reading Atlanta newspapers and playing chess with other boys. Sprawled in his bed with his knees up and his hands behind his head, he listened to radio news accounts of the war and studied the diagrams of troop movements in the papers with a lazy, unruffled fascination. He grew a mustache for six days, then shaved it, then let it grow again. Through almost every afternoon he slept, waking in time to feel dusk settle in and to watch the light die beyond the window three beds away to his right. Other boys came and went, but he stayed. The war wounded came to the hospital but convalesced on two other floors he had no access to. He lived in his T-shirt and underwear, and the smell from the open window was of dying leaves and of rain in the dirt and turned fields, and it began to seem to him strangely apt that he lay so many thousand miles from home and was so alone in his sickness. It was the kind of suffering, after all, he'd yearned for during the last five months, since receiving Hatsue's letter. It was an easy, sleepy kind of languid fever, and so long as he did not try to move too much or exert himself unnecessarily he could live this way indefinitely. He surrounded himself with his illness thoroughly and embedded himself in it.

In October he trained a second time, as a radioman, and was sent to a staging area on the North Island of New Zealand as part of the Second Marine Division. They assigned him to B

Company in the Second Marine Regiment, Third Battalion, and he soon met men who'd been at Guadalcanal, and he replaced a radio operator who'd been shot during the fighting in the Solomons. One night a lieutenant named Jim Kent recollected how the former radioman had taken an interest in a dead Japanese boy with his pants turned inside out around his muddy ankles. The radioman, a Private Gerald Willis, had propped the boy's penis up by placing a stone under it, then had lain down carefully in the dirt and shot carbine rounds until he'd blown the head of it off. He'd been proud of himself afterward and had bragged about his aim for a half hour or more, describing for others how the boy's penis had looked with the head of it severed and how the head itself had looked lying on the ground. Private Willis had been killed two days later on patrol, by friendly mortar fire he'd called for at the direction of Lieutenant Kent himself, who'd given the correct coordinates. Seven men in the platoon had died on that occasion, and Kent had lowered himself into a foxhole and watched a Private Wiesner toss a grenade unsuccessfully toward a pillbox while at the same moment a stream of machine-gun fire caught Wiesner at the waist and forced his viscera out. A piece of it had landed on Kent's forearm, blue, fresh, and glistening.

They trained incessantly and practiced landing maneuvers at Hawkes Bay, where the tides were bad. Men died during these exercises. Ishmael tried to take maneuvers seriously, but the veterans in his squad went through them hung over or bored or both simultaneously, and their attitude of indifference had its influence. On liberty he drank ale and at other times gin with boys who like him were new to the war, and they played pool in Wellington together. Even at those times, drunk at one o'clock in the morning, leaning against his pool cue in the smoky light while another boy lined up a shot and a Wellington band played dance tunes he didn't recognize, Ishmael felt a peculiar detachment from everybody. He was numb to it all, uninterested in drinking and pool and other people, and the more drunk he became the more lucid his mind was and the colder he felt toward everyone. He did not understand the laughter of his compatriots or their ease or anything else about them. What were they doing here, drinking and shouting at one o'clock in the morning in a country so far from the homes they knew; what were they so feverishly happy about? One morning, in a heavy downpour, he wandered back to his Wellington hotel at four-thirty and lay down heavily with his writing tablet to compose a letter to his parents. After he'd written to them he wrote one to Hatsue, and then he took both letters and ripped them up and fell asleep with some of the pieces jammed into his coat pocket and the rest scattered across the floor. He slept with his shoes on and at six-fifteen awoke to vomit in the toilet closet down the hall.

On the first day of November the Second Division left Wellington, presumably on maneuvers at Hawkes Bay again, but ending up instead at Nouméa on the French island of New Caledonia. By the thirteenth Ishmael's regiment was on board the *Heywood*, a transport ship traveling with more than half of the Third Fleet – frigates, destroyers, light and heavy cruisers, half a dozen battleships – all headed for an unknown destination. On the second day his company was assembled on the top deck and told that they were moving toward Tarawa atoll, where they would go ashore at Betio, a strongly defended island. A major stood in front of them sucking on his pipe stem, with his right elbow tucked into his left palm. The idea, he explained, was to let the navy obliterate the place – it was less than two square miles of coral sand – then wade in and mop up the leftovers. The Jap commander, he said, had boasted that Betio could not be successfully invaded by even a force of a million soldiers with a thousand years to do battle. The major pulled his pipe from his mouth and proclaimed the Japanese commander laughable in this regard. He predicted a battle lasting two days at most, with few if any marine casualties. It was a matter the navy guns would take care of, he repeated, a tailor-made place for shipboard artillery to do the dirty work.

On the night of the nineteenth a quarter moon rose over the sea while the fleet stood seven miles off Tarawa. Ishmael ate a last meal on the *Heywood's* messing deck with Ernest Testaverde, a boy he liked, an anti-tank gunner from Delaware. They ate steak and eggs, fried potatoes and coffee, and then Testaverde put down his plate and took a pad of paper and a pen from his pocket. He began to write a letter home.

'You better write one yourself,' he said to Ishmael. 'Last chance you're going to get, you know.'

'Last chance?' answered Ishmael. 'There's no one I really want to write to in that case. I – '

'It isn't up to you,' said Testaverde. 'So just in case – write a letter.'

Ishmael went below and got his pad of paper. He sat on the top deck with his back against a stanchion and composed a letter to Hatsue. From where he sat he could see twenty other men, all of them writing intently. It was warm for so late at night, and the men all looked comfortable with their collars open and the sleeves of their uniform shirts rolled up. Ishmael told Hatsue how he was about to go ashore on an island in the South Pacific and that his job was to kill people who looked like her – as many of them as he could. What did she think about that? he wrote. How did that make her feel? He said that his numbness was a terrible thing, he didn't feel anything except that he looked forward to killing as many Japs as possible, he was angry at them and wanted their deaths – all of them, he wrote; he felt hatred. He explained to her the nature of his hatred and told her she was as responsible for it as anyone in the world. In fact, he hated *her* now. He didn't want to hate her, but since this was a last letter he felt bound to tell the truth as completely as he could – he hated her with everything in his heart, he wrote, and it felt good to him to write it in just that way. '*I hate you with all my heart,*' he wrote. '*I hate you, Hatsue, I hate you always.*' It was at this point that he ripped the sheet from his writing pad, crumpled it, and threw it into the sea. He watched it floating on the water for a few seconds, then threw his pad in after it.

At 3:20 in the morning, wide awake in his bunk, Ishmael heard the order delivered to the troop hold: 'All marines lay topside to your debarkation stations!' He sat up and watched Ernest Testaverde lace his boots and then began to lace his own, stopping once to drink from his canteen – 'Dry mouth,' he said to Ernest. 'You want some water before we die?'

'Lace up,' said Ernest. 'Get topside.'

They went up, dragging their gear along with them, and Ishmael felt wide awake now. There were already more than three hundred men squatting and kneeling on the top deck of the *Heywood*, rearranging their equipment in the dark – C rations, canteens, entrenching tools, gas masks, rounds of ammunition, steel helmets. There had been no firing yet, and it did not feel so much like war – another nighttime exercise in tropical waters. Ishmael heard the whine of the landing craft plummeting over the sheaves of the boat blocks; then men were going overboard into them, snaking their way down the cargo nets with packs on their backs and their helmets strapped on and timing their lunges to coincide with the bobbing of the boats below.

Ismael watched a half-dozen navy corpsmen busily packing medical field kits and stacking ambulatory litters. This was something he hadn't seen on maneuvers, and he pointed it out to Testaverde, who shrugged and went back to counting antitank rounds. Ishmael turned on his TBX, listened for a moment to the static in the headphones, then switched it off and waited. He did not want to strap it to his back too early, then have to stand around with its weight burdening him until his turn came to crawl down the cargo net. Sitting beside his gear, peering out to sea, he tried to make out Betio, but the island could not be seen. Each of the LCP landing craft that had left the *Heywood* in the past half hour appeared as a dark spot against the water, though – Ishmael counted three dozen of them.

The three squads of Third Platoon were briefed on the top deck by a First Lieutenant Pavelman from San Antonio, who explained in detail the role of B Company in the larger scheme of things. He had before him a relief model of the island made out of three square sections of rubber and with a pointer began to point out its topographical features, doing so with no flourishes. Amtracs, he said, were going in first, followed by waves of Higgins boats. There was going to be air cover – dive-bombers and Hellcats on strafing runs, then B-24s from out of Ellice Island, right up to the point of attack. B Company would go ashore at a place called Beach Red Two, he said, and the mortar section would place itself at the disposal of the weapons platoon leader, a Second Lieutenant Pratt, for the purpose of establishing a base of fire. Second Platoon would come in simultaneously on Pratt's right and advance over the seawall behind its light machine guns, then collect on higher ground and move inland. There were bunkers and pillboxes, said Lieutenant Pavelman, directly south of Beach Red Two; marine intelligence was furthermore of the opinion that the Jap command bunker was perhaps located in this area, possibly at the eastern end of the airfield. Second Platoon should look for it and fix the location of air vents for the demolitions teams, who would come in directly behind. Three minutes after Second went ashore, Third Platoon – Ishmael's – would beach and come in close or, according to the judgment of Lieutenant Bellows, go to the support of whichever platoon appeared to have made a solid advance. The platoon could expect support from K Company, which was scheduled to come in with the headquarters group and a heavy machine-gun platoon just behind the Third. They would land from more amtracs, which could be used against the seawall; the theory, said Lieutenant Pavelman, was to come in fast and hard with full support behind the initial wave of riflemen. 'Another name for it is suckers first,' someone in Third Platoon called out bitterly, but no one laughed at this. Pavelman pushed on mechanically with his briefing: rifle platoons, he explained, would cut a careful but persistent advance, followed by reinforcements in the second wave, command and support in the third tractor wave, then more rifle companies and more support and command, until the beachhead was well established. Then, with his hands at his belt, Lieutenant Pavelman called on a Chaplain Thomas to lead them in a recitation of the twenty-third psalm and in the singing of 'What a Friend We Have in Jesus.' When they were done, everyone fell silent on the deck and the chaplain called on the men to contemplate their relationship to God and Jesus. 'That's fine,' a soldier called out in the darkness. 'But, look here, I'm an atheist, sir, the exception to the rule that there ain't no atheists in foxholes or firefights, and I'm gonna stay a goddamn atheist to the goddamn end, goddamn it!'

'So be it,' Chaplain Thomas answered softly. 'And may God bless you just the same, my friend.'

Ishmael began to wonder how any of this would direct him once he hit the beach. He had listened to Lieutenant Pavelman as closely as he could but had not discerned the relationship between his words and the specific direction in which his own feet should move once he landed on Betio. Why was he going there? To do what exactly? The chaplain was passing out pieces of lucky candy and rolls of military toilet paper, and Ishmael took one of each from him chiefly because everyone else had done so. The chaplain, a Colt .45 strapped to his belt, encouraged him to take more of the candy – 'It's good stuff,' he said. 'Come on.' They were peppermints, and Ishmael popped one in his mouth, then strapped his radio onto his back and pulled himself into a standing position. The entire weight of his equipment, he guessed, was more than eighty-five pounds.

It was not easy to crawl down the cargo net so loaded, but Ishmael had been able to practice on maneuvers and had taught himself to relax. Halfway down he spit out the peppermint and leaned out over the water. A whistling had begun to sound in his ears, growing louder by the second. He turned to look, and at the same moment a shell plunged into the sea seventy-five feet to stern. A spray of salt water broke across the boat, dousing the soldiers there; the phosphorescence boiled up green and luminous against the darkness. The boy next to Ishmael, a Private Jim Harvey from Carson City, Nevada, swore softly under his breath twice, then leaned in against the net. 'Shit,' he said. 'A goddamn shell. I don't believe this shit.'

'Me neither,' said Ishmael.

'I thought they blew the shit out of this place,' Jim Harvey complained. 'I thought they dusted all the big guns off before we had to go in. Jesus fucking Christ,' he added.

'The big boys are still coming out from Ellice,' Walter Bennett down the net pointed out. 'They're gonna dust the Japs with daisy cutters before we ever hit the sand.'

'That's bullshit,' said another voice. 'There aren't going to be no daisy cutters coming. You're a motherfucking dreamer, Walter.'

'A fucking Jap shell,' Jim Harvey said. 'Goddamn it to shit, I – '

But another shell came whistling down and slammed into the water a hundred yards in front of them, sending up a momentary geyser.

'Fuckers!' Private Harvey yelled. 'I thought they softened the bastards up! Thought we was just mopping up!'

'They been fucking up for days, lobbing 'em long,' a boy named Larry Jackson explained calmly. 'All that softening-up bullshit don't mean a rat's ass. They fucked it all up, and now we're going in, and there's all sorts of fucking Jap fire.'

'Jesus,' said Jim Harvey. 'I can't *believe* this bullshit. What the fuck is going on here?'

The LCP pushed on toward Betio with Third Platoon aboard. Ishmael could hear the whistling of shells now distantly across the water. He sat low beneath a plywood gunnel a navy crew had jury-rigged during down time in Nouméa. He was weighted down now heavily by his pack, with his helmet pulled to his brow. He could hear Jim Harvey chattering hopefully: 'The fuckers been pounding 'em up for days, right? There ain't nothing left there but sand and bullshit and a whole lot of little Jap pieces. That's what *everyone's* been hearing. Madsen read it off the radio and Bledsoe was right there in the room with him, it's no bullshit, they fucking dusted 'em . . .'

The seas, as it turned out, contrary to all plans, were running high and choppy. Ishmael did not stand up well on high seas and had become addicted to Dramamine. He swallowed two with water from his belt canteen and peered out over the plywood gunnel with his helmet on but not strapped. The boat thrummed under him, and he saw that they were running alongside three other transports immediately off to the left. He could see the men in the boat next to his; one of them had lit a cigarette and the glow of its tip was visible, though he'd tucked it down inside his cradled palm. Ishmael lowered himself against his pack again, shut his eyes, and put his fingers in his ears. He tried not to think about any of it.

For three hours they pushed toward Betio, the waves coming in constantly over the gunnels and soaking everybody on board. The island became visible as a low black line almost on the horizon. Ishmael stood to stretch his legs now. There were fires glowing all up and down Betio, and a man beside him with a waterproof watch was attempting to time the battleship salvos being fired on the island. On the other side two men were complaining bitterly about an Admiral Hill who was in charge of things and who had timed matters such that they were going in at daylight instead of under cover of darkness. They could see that the navy was firing heavily – black smoke rose from the island in great billows – and this began to have a positive influence on the disposition of Third Platoon. 'There ain't gonna be nothing left of the fuckers,' Private Harvey asserted. 'Them five-inch guns'll do the trick. They're pounding the shit out of them.'

Fifteen minutes later they ran the big current at the entrance to Tarawa lagoon. They bobbed past two destroyers, the *Dashiell* and the *Ringgold*, both of which were firing in waves at the beach; the noise of it was deafening, louder than anything Ishmael had ever heard. Strapping his helmet on now, he decided he was done looking over the gunnel. He had peered up once and seen three amphibious tractors going up on the beach far ahead. They were taking a lot of machine-gun fire; one fell down into a shell hole; another caught fire and halted. There were no more divebombers coming in at all, and the B-24s had not appeared. The best thing to do was to tuck down, strap up, and keep well out of the line of fire. Ishmael had somehow arrived at the war moment little boys are prone to dream about. He was storming a beach, he was a marine radioman, and he felt like shitting his pants, literally. He could feel his rectum puckering.

'Holy shit,' Jim Harvey was saying. 'Goddamn it to hell, the motherfuckers, goddamn those assholes, the fucking shitheads, goddamn it, this ain't *right*!'

The squad leader, a man named Rich Hinkle from Yreka, California, who had made Ishmael an excellent chess partner in New Zealand, was the first among them to die. The transport ground up suddenly on the reef – they were still more than five hundred yards from the beach – and the men sat looking at one another for thirty seconds or more while artillery pinged off the LCP's port side. 'There's bigger stuff coming,' Hinkle yelled above the din. 'We'd better get the hell out of here. Let's move it! Move! Let's go!' 'You first,' somebody answered.

Hinkle went over the starboard gunnel and dropped down into the water. Men began to follow him, including Ishmael Chambers, who was manuevering his eighty-five-pound pack over the side when Hinkle was shot in the face and went down, and then the man just behind him was shot, too, and the top of his head came off. Ishmael wrestled his pack into the lagoon and splashed in hard behind it. He submerged himself for as long as he could, came up only for a single breath – he could see small-arms fire flashing along the shore – then went deep again. When he came up he saw that everybody – the ammo carriers, the demolitions guys, the machine gunners, *everybody* – they were all dropping everything into the water and going under like Ishmael.

He swam back behind the LCP with three dozen other soldiers. The navy coxswain was still exerting himself, cursing and ramming the throttle back and forth, to free the landing craft from the reef. Lieutenant Bellows was screaming at the men on board who had refused to go over the gunnels. 'Fuck you, Bellows,' somebody kept saying. 'You go first!' screamed someone else. Ishmael recognized the voice of Private Harvey, now at a hysterical pitch.

The LCP took more small-arms fire, and the crowd of men who had crouched behind it began to wade toward shore. Ishmael kept to the middle of the group, swimming and keeping low, breaststroking, and tried to think of himself as a dead marine floating harmlessly in Betio's lagoon, a corpse borne by the current. The men were in chest-high water now, some of them carrying rifles above their heads, and they were dropping into seas already tinged pink by the blood of other men in front of them. Ishmael saw men go lurching down, saw the machine-gun fire whipping the water's surface, and lowered himself even farther. In the shallows ahead of him a Private Newland stood up to run for the seawall, and then another man he didn't know made a run for it and was shot dead in the surf, and then a third man ran for it. The fourth, Eric Bledsoe, was shot in the knee and lay down again in the shallows. Ishmael stopped and watched the fifth and sixth men draw fire, then gathered himself and thrashed out of the water while the men ahead of him ran for it. All three of them made the seawall unharmed and crouched there watching Eric Bledsoe; his knee had been shot away.

Ishmael saw Eric Bledsoe bleed to death. Fifty yards away he lay in the surf pleading in a soft voice for help. 'Oh, shit,' he said. 'Help me, you guys, come on, you guys, fucking help me, please.' Eric had grown up in Delaware with Ernest Testaverde; they'd gotten drunk together a lot in Wellington. Robert Newland wanted to run out to save him, but Lieutenant Bellows held him back; there was nothing to be done about it, Bellows pointed out, there was far too much gunfire for something like that, the upshot of it all would be two dead men, and everyone silently agreed. Ishmael pushed his body up against the seawall; he was not going to run down the beach again to drag a wounded man to safety, though a part of him wanted to try. What could he have done about it anyway? His equipment was floating in the lagoon. He could not even offer Eric Bledsoe a bandage, much less save his life. He sat there and watched Eric roll over in the surf so that his face was pointing toward the sun. His legs were only partly in the water, and Ishmael could see plainly where one of them had come off and was moving with the undulations of the surf. The boy bled to death and then his leg floated away a few feet on the waves while Ishmael crouched behind the seawall.

At ten o'clock he was still there, unarmed and without a job to do, hunkered down with hundreds of other men who had come ashore and been shot at. There were plenty more dead marines on the beach now, and plenty more of the wounded, too, and the men behind the seawall tried not to listen when they moaned or called out for help. Then a sergeant from J Company, from out of nowhere, it seemed, was suddenly standing above them on the seawall with a cigarette hanging from the corner of his mouth, calling them 'a bunch of chickenshits.' He berated them relentlessly, a stream of invective, characterizing them as 'the sorts of cowards who ought to have your balls chewed off real slow and painful like when this goddamn battle is over,' men who'd let 'other men do the dirty work to save your own sorry asses,' men who 'aren't men at all but cornhole-fuckers and jack-off artists with half-inch hard-ons on those days once a year when you can get your sorry dicks to stand at half-mast,' and so on and so forth, while the men below pleaded with him to take cover and save himself. He refused and was shot through the spine with a shell that ripped open his shirt front and dropped some of his guts onto the beach. The sergeant had no time to be surprised and simply fell over face first into the sand and squarely on top of his own intestines. Nobody said anything.

A tractor at last breached a hole in the seawall, and a few men began to go through. All of them were shot immediately. Ishmael was commandeered to help dig free a half-track that had been deposited on Betio by a tank lighter and had promptly buried itself. He dug on his knees with an entrenching tool while the man beside him threw up in the sand before lying down with his helmet across his face and fainting. A radioman from K Company had set up against the seawall and was railing loudly about interference; every time battleship guns were fired offshore even the static died out, he complained. He couldn't raise anybody.

Ishmael realized, in the early afternoon, that the sweetish smell coming at him from off the beach was the odor of dead marines. He, too, vomited, then drank the last of his water. As far as he knew, no one else in his squad was even alive anymore. He had not seen any of them in over three hours, but he had been given a carbine, an ammo pack, and a field machete by a crew of cargo handlers moving down the wall with resupply orders. He fieldstripped the carbine – it was full of sand – and cleaned it as carefully as he could under the conditions, sitting against the base of the seawall with his steel helmet unstrapped. He was sitting there like that with the trigger assembly in hand, dabbing at it with the tail of his shirt, when a new wave of amtracs came up on the beach and began drawing mortar fire. Ishmael watched them with interest for a while, men spilling out and falling to the sand – some dead, some wounded, some screaming as they ran – then lowered his head and, refusing to look, went back to cleaning his carbine. He was still there, huddled in the same place with his carbine in hand, his machete in a sheath that hung from his belt, when darkness fell four hours later.

A colonel came down the beach with his entourage, exhorting the noncoms and junior officers to re-form and improvise squads. At 1900 hours, he said – less than twenty minutes from now – every man there was going over the top; anyone who stayed behind would be court-martialed; it was time, he added, to act like marines. The colonel moved on, and a Lieutenant Doerper from K Company asked Ishmael where his squad was and what the hell he thought he was doing dug in by himself against the seawall. Ishmael explained how he had lost his equipment going over the gunnel of an LCP and how everyone around him had died or been wounded; he didn't know where anyone was. Lieutenant Doerper listened impatiently, then told Ishmael to pick out a man along the wall, and then pick out another, and then some more, until he had himself a squad formed, and then to report to the command post Colonel Freeman had set up beside the buried half-track. He had, he said, no time for bullshit.

Ishmael explained matters to two dozen boys before he'd gathered enough of a squad. One boy told him to go fuck himself; another claimed to have an incapacitating leg wound; a third said he'd be along in a minute but never moved. There was gunfire coming from off the water suddenly, and Ishmael surmised that a Jap sniper had swum out and was manning the machine gun left behind on an amtrac destroyed in the lagoon. The seawall was no longer safe.

Moving down the wall, staying low and talking rapidly to people, he came at last on Ernest Testaverde, who was returning fire over the coconut logs with his gun held high and his head down. 'Hey,' said Ishmael. 'Jesus.'

'Chambers,' said Ernest. 'Jesus fucking Christ.'

'Where is everybody?' asked Ishmael. 'What about Jackson and those guys?'

'I saw Jackson get hit,' Ernest answered. 'All the demolitions guys and the mine detector guys got hit coming up onto the beach. And Walter,' he added. 'And Jim Harvey. And that guy Hedges, I saw him go down. And Murray and Behring got hit, too. They all got hit in the water.'

'So did Hinkle,' said Ishmael. 'And Eric Bledsoe – his leg came off. And Fitz – he got hit on the beach, I saw him go down. Bellows made it, but I don't know where he is. Newland, too. Where are those guys?'

Ernest Testaverde didn't answer. He pulled at his helmet strap and set his carbine down. 'Bledsoe?' he said. 'You sure?'

Ishmael nodded. 'He's dead.'

'His leg came off?' said Ernest.

Ishmael sat down with his back to the seawall. He did not want to talk about Eric Bledsoe or remember how he had died. It was difficult to know what the point would be of talking about such a thing. There was no point to anything, that was clear. He couldn't think straight about anything that had happened since the landing craft had ground onto the coral reef. The situation he

218

found himself in now had the sodden quality of a dream in which events repeated themselves. He was dug in against the seawall, and then he found himself there again, and again he was still dug in beneath the seawall. Occasionally a flare lit things well enough so that he saw the details of his own hands. He was weary and thirsty, and he could not really focus, and the adrenalin had died inside of him. He wanted to live, he knew that now, but everything else was unclear. He could not recollect his reason for being there – why he had enlisted to fight in the marines, what the point of it was. 'Yeah,' he said. 'Bledsoe's dead.'

'Goddamn it,' answered Ernest Testaverde. He kicked the first log in the seawall twice, then a third time, then a fourth. Ishmael Chambers turned away from him.

At 1900 hours they went over the seawall along with three hundred other men. They were met by mortar and machine-gun fire from straight ahead in the palm trees. Ishmael never saw Ernest Testaverde get hit; later he found out, on making inquiries, that Ernest had been found with a hole in his head roughly the size of a man's fist. Ishmael himself was hit in the left arm, squarely in the middle of his biceps. The muscle tore when the round entered – a single round from a Nambu machine gun – and the bone cracked jaggedly into a hundred splinters that were driven up against his nerves and veins and lodged into the meat of his arm.

Four hours later, when the light came up, he became aware of two medical corpsmen kneeling beside the man next to him. The man had been hit in the head, it seemed, and his brains were leaking out around his helmet. Ishmael had maneuvered behind this dead man and taken the sulfa pills and a roll of bandages from the medical kit at his belt. He'd wrapped his arm and had used the weight of his body to keep his blood from spilling out. 'It's okay,' one of the corpsmen told Ishmael. 'We're bringing up a litter team and a squad of bearers. The beach is secured. Everything's fine. We're going to get you shipboard pronto.'

'Fucking Japs,' said Ishmael.

Later he lay on the deck of some ship or other, seven miles

219

out to sea from Betio, one boy in the middle of rows and rows of wounded, and the boy on the litter to his left died from the shrapnel that had pierced his liver. On the other side was a boy with buckteeth who'd been shot squarely in the thighs and groin; the blood had soaked his khaki pants. The boy could not speak and lay with his back arched; every few seconds he groaned mechanically between forced, shallow breaths. Ishmael asked him once if he was all right, but the boy only went on with his groaning. He died ten minutes before the bearers came around to take him down to surgery.

Ishmael lost his arm on a shipboard operating table to a pharmacist's mate who had done only four amputations in his career, all of them in the past few hours. The mate used a handsaw to square up the bone and cauterized the stump unevenly, so that the wound healed more slowly than it would have otherwise and the scar tissue left behind was thick and coarse. Ishmael had not been fully anesthetized and awoke to see his arm where it had been dropped in a corner on top of a pile of blood-soaked dressings. Ten years later he would still dream of that, the way his own fingers curled against the wall, how white and distant his arm looked, though nevertheless he recognized it there, a piece of trash on the floor. Somebody saw him staring at it and gave an order, and the arm was scooped up inside a towel and dumped into a canvas bin. Somebody else pricked him once again with morphine, and Ishmael told whoever it was that 'the Japs are . . . the fucking Japs . . .' but he didn't quite know how to finish his words, he didn't quite know what he meant to utter, '*that fucking goddamn Jap bitch*' was all he could think to say.

17

By two o'clock on the first afternoon of the trial, snow had covered all the island roads. A car pirouetted silently while skating on its tires, emerged from this on a transverse angle, and slid to a stop with one headlight thrust into the door of Petersen's Grocery, which somebody opened at just the right moment – miraculously – so that no damage was done to car or store. Behind the Amity Harbor Elementary School, a girl of seven bending over to pack a snowball was rammed from behind by a boy skidding down a hill on a piece of cardboard box. She broke her right arm – a greenstick fracture. The principal, Erik Karlsen, wrapped a blanket around her shoulders and sat her down next to a steam radiator before going out to run his car engine. Then, gingerly, peering out through the crescents of glass his defroster had carved from the icy windshield, he drove her down First Hill into town.

On Mill Run Road Mrs. Larsen of Skiff Point ran her husband's De-Soto into a ditch. Arne Stolbaad overloaded his wood-burning stove and ended up with a chimney fire. The volunteer fire department was called out by a neighbor, but the pumper truck driver, Edgar Paulsen, lost traction on Indian Knob Hill and had to halt to put on tire chains. In the meantime Arne Stolbaad's chimney fire expired; when the firemen showed up at last he expressed to them his delight at having burned clean the flue creosote.

At three o'clock five school buses left Amity Harbor with their windshield wipers batting ice from the windshields and their headlights casting into the snowfall. High school students walking home hurled snowballs at them; the South Beach bus slid off the road shoulder just beyond Island Center. The schoolchildren climbed out and walked home in the snow-storm with Johnny Katayama, the bus driver, escorting them from behind. As each child turned off toward home, Johnny handed him or her a half stick of spearmint gum.

A boy on a sled that afternoon broke his ankle against the base of a cedar tree. He had not quite understood how to make the thing turn, and the tree had come up on him suddenly. He'd put his foot out to ward it off.

A retired dentist, old Doc Cable, slipped hard on the way to his firewood shed. Something in his tailbone twisted when he went down, so that Doc Cable winced and curled fetally in the snow. After a while he hauled himself up, lurched inside, and reported to his wife through clenched teeth that he'd injured himself. Sarah put him on the couch with a hot-water bottle, where he took two aspirins and fell asleep.

Two teenagers engaged in a snowball-throwing contest from the dock at Port Jefferson Harbor. The point was to hit a mooring buoy at first, then a piling on the next dock. One of the teenagers, Dan Daniels's son Scott, took a three-step running start, threw out to sea, then pitched headlong into the salt water. He was out again in five seconds, steam rising off his clothes. Running home, racing through the snowfall, his hair froze into icy tufts.

The citizens of San Piedro made their run on Petersen's and cleared the shelves of canned goods. They brought so much snow into the store on their boots that one of the box boys, Earl Camp, stayed busy all afternoon with a mop and a towel, cleaning up after them. Einar Petersen took a box of salt from his shelf and spread its contents outside the door, but two customers slipped despite this. Einar decided to offer free coffee to shoppers and asked one of his checkers, Jessica Porter – who was twenty-two and cheerful looking – to stand behind a folding table and serve.

At Fisk's Hardware Center the citizens of San Piedro bought snow shovels, candles, kerosene, kitchen matches, lined gloves, and flashlight batteries. The Torgerson brothers sold out their supply of tire chains by three o'clock, as well as most of their ice scrapers and antifreeze. Tom pulled ditched cars free with his freshly painted two-ton wrecker; Dave sold gasoline, batteries, and motor oil and advised his customers to go home and *stay* home. Dozens of islanders stopped in to listen while Dave pumped their gas or put on their tire chains and made grim predictions about the weather. 'Three-day blow,' he'd say. 'Folks'd better be ready.'

By three o'clock the branches of the cedars were loaded down with snow. When the wind came up it blew right through them, whirling flurries to the ground. San Piedro's strawberry fields became fields of white, as untouched and flawless as desert. The noise of living things was not so much muted as halted – even the seagulls were silenced. Instead there was the wind and the collapse of waves and the withdrawing of the water down the beaches.

Everywhere on San Piedro Island a grimness set in, accompanied by a strained anticipation. Who knew what might happen now that a December storm had started? The homes of these islanders might soon lie in drifts so that only the sloped roofs of the beach cabins would show and only the upper stories of the larger houses. The power might fizzle when the wind blew hard and leave them all in darkness. Their toilets might not flush, their well pumps might not draw, they would live close to their stoves and lanterns. Yet on the other hand the snowstorm might mean a respite, a happy wintertime vacation. Schools would shut down, roads would close, no one would go off to their jobs. Families would eat large breakfasts late, then dress for snow and go out in the knowledge that they'd return to warm, snug houses. Smoke would curl from chimneys; at dusk lights would come on. Lopsided snowmen would stand sentinel in yards. There would be enough to eat, no reason for worry.

Still, those who had lived on the island a long time knew that the storm's outcome was beyond their control. This storm might well be like others past that had caused them to suffer, had *killed* even – or perhaps it might dwindle beneath tonight's stars and give their children snowbound happiness. Who knew? Who could predict? If disaster, so be it, they said to themselves. There was nothing to be done except what could be done. The rest – like the salt water around them, which swallowed the snow without any effort, remaining what it was implacably – was out of their hands, beyond.

When the afternoon recess was over that day, Alvin Hooks called Art Moran again. The sheriff had left the courtroom for two and a half hours in order to contact the volunteer fire department and to call out his volunteer deputies, men who could be counted on in times of trouble. Generally their role was to keep order at the Strawberry Festival and other public occasions; now they would divide up the island terrain according to the locations of their homes and businesses and assist those stranded on the roads.

Art fidgeted in the witness stand for the second time that day. The snowstorm, just now, preoccupied him. He understood that Alvin's case necessitated his appearing twice at the trial, but on the other hand he wasn't glad about it. He'd eaten a sandwich during the fifteen-minute recess, sat in Alvin's office with a piece of wax paper laid across his knees and an apple on the edge of the desk. Hooks had reminded him to tell his story methodically, to pay attention to those minor details that might seem to him irrelevant. Now, on the witness stand, pinching the knot of his tie together and checking the corners of his lips for crumbs, Art waited impatiently while Alvin asked the judge to admit four pieces of rope into evidence. 'Sheriff Moran,' Hooks said at last. 'I have in my hand four lengths of rope of the sort fishermen use for mooring lines. May I ask you to inspect them, please?'

Art took the pieces of rope in his hand and made a show of looking at them carefully. 'Okay,' he said after a moment.

'Do you recognize them?'

'Yes, I do.'

'Did you refer to these pieces of mooring line in your report,

Sheriff Moran? Are they the same four referred to in your report?'

'Yes, they are. They're the ones I wrote about in my report, Mr. Hooks. These are them.'

The judge admitted the lines as evidence, and Ed Soames put a tag on each. Alvin Hooks put them back in Art's hands and asked him to explain where he'd found them.

'Well,' said the sheriff. 'This one here, marked with an A, came from the defendant's boat. It came off the port side cleat, to be exact, *third* cleat up from the stern. It matches all his other mooring lines, you see? Matches 'em all except the one on the port side cleat *second* up from the stern. That's this one here, the one marked B – that one was new, Mr. Hooks, but the rest were worn. They were all three-strand manila lines with a bowline knotted into one end, pretty well worn down, too. That's how Mr. Miyamoto kept his mooring lines – bowlined and pretty well worn out, except the one. It was brand-new but had the bowline in it.'

'And the other two?' asked Alvin Hooks. 'Where did you find them, sheriff?'

'I found them on Carl Heine's boat, Mr. Hooks. This one here – the one marked C' – the sheriff held the line up for the benefit of the jury – 'is exactly the same as every other line I found on Mr. Heine's, the deceased's, boat. You see here? It's a three-strand manila rope in new condition with a fancy eye braided in at one end – braided in by hand, Mr. Hooks, the way Carl Heine was known to do them. All his lines were braided up in loops, none of them had bowlines.'

'The fourth line you have there,' Alvin Hooks pushed on. 'Where did you find it, sheriff?'

'Found it on Carl Heine's boat, too, but it doesn't match up with the rest of them. Found it on the starboard side, second cleat back from the stern. Peculiar thing is, it *does* match up with the lines I found on board the defendant's boat. It's pretty well worn, and it's got the bowline in it just like the other one I showed you, just like *all* his mooring lines except the new one.

It looks so much like all the others, it's clear it came from the same set. Worn down just the same.'

'This line looks like the ones on the defendant's boat?'

'Exactly.'

'But you found it on the deceased's boat?'

'That's right.'

'On the starboard side, second cleat from the stern?'

'Yes.'

'And the defendant's boat – do I understand this right? – had a new line on the port side, sheriff – again the second cleat from the stern?'

'That's right, Mr. Hooks. There was a new line there.'

'Sheriff,' Alvin Hooks said. 'If the defendant had tied up to Carl Heine's boat would these two cleats in question line up?'

'You bet they'd line up. And if he – Miyamoto there – had gotten in a hurry to cast off from the deceased's boat, he could have left a line behind tied off to that second cleat.'

'I see,' said Alvin Hooks. 'Your inference is that he left a line behind, then replaced it with that new one – exhibit B, right there in your hand – replaced it when he got back to the docks.'

'It is,' said Art Moran. 'Exactly. He tied up to Carl's boat and left a line on it. That seems to me pretty clear.'

'But sheriff,' said Alvin Hooks. 'What led you to investigate the defendant in the first place? Why did you think to look around his boat and to notice something like a new mooring line?'

Art pointed out that his investigation into the death of Carl Heine had led him, quite naturally, to ask questions of Carl's relatives. He'd gone to see Etta Heine, he said, and explained to her that even in the case of a fishing accident there was a formal investigation to proceed with. Did Carl have any enemies?

After Etta, he said, the path to Ole Jurgensen was clear, and from Ole to Judge Lew Fielding's chambers: Art had needed a search warrant. He intended to search Kabuo Miyamoto's boat, the *Islander*, before it left that night for the salmon grounds.

18

It had been the judge's bailiff, Ed Soames, who'd answered the door when Art Moran knocked at five after five on the evening of the sixteenth and asked to see Lew Fielding. The bailiff wore his coat and held his lunchbox in his hand; he'd been on his way out, he explained; the judge was still working at his desk.

'This about Carl Heine?' inquired Ed.

'I guess you heard,' the sheriff answered. 'But, no, this isn't about him. And if you go down to the cafe and say it is, you know what? You'll be wrong, Ed.'

'I'm not that way,' said the bailiff. 'Maybe others are, but I'm not.'

''Course you're not,' said Art Moran.

The bailiff knocked at the door to the judge's chambers, then opened it and said that the sheriff was present on business he wished to keep private. 'All right,' answered the judge. 'Send him in.'

The bailiff held the door open for Art Moran and stood aside to let him pass. 'Good night, judge,' he said. 'See you in the morning.'

'Good night, Ed,' the judge replied. 'Could you lock up on your way out, please? The sheriff here is my last visitor.'

'Will do,' said Ed Soames, and shut the door.

The sheriff sat and adjusted his legs. He set his hat on the floor. The judge waited patiently until he heard the lock click. Then he looked the sheriff in the eye for the first time. 'Carl Heine,' he said.

'Carl Heine,' the sheriff answered.

Lew Fielding put his pen down. 'A man with kids, with a wife,' he said.

'I know,' Art answered. 'I went out this morning and told Susan Marie about it. Christ,' he added bitterly.

Lew Fielding nodded. He sat morosely with his elbows on his desk, cradling his chin in his hands. As always he looked to be on the verge of sleep; his eyes were those of a basset hound. His cheeks were creviced, his forehead furrowed, his silver eyebrows grew in fat tufts. Art remembered when he had been more spry, remembered him pitching horseshoes at the Strawberry Festival. The judge in his suspenders with his sleeves rolled up, squinting and half bent over.

'How is she?' the judge asked. 'Susan Marie?'

'Not good,' Art Moran replied.

Lew Fielding looked at him and waited. Art picked his hat up, set it in his lap, and began fiddling with its brim. 'Anyway, I came down to get you to sign a warrant. I want to search Kabuo Miyamoto's boat, maybe his house, too – I'm not sure yet.'

'Kabuo Miyamoto,' the judge said. 'What are you looking for?'

'Well,' the sheriff answered, leaning forward. 'I've got these *concerns*, judge. Five of 'em altogether. Number one, I've got men telling me Miyamoto worked the same waters Carl did last night when this thing happened. Number two, I've got Etta Heine saying Miyamoto and her son were enemies from way back – an old dispute over land. Three, I've got a piece of mooring line somebody left on Carl's boat wrapped around one of the cleats; seems like he could have been boarded, maybe, and I want to take a look at Miyamoto's mooring lines. Four, I've got Ole Jurgensen claiming both Carl and Miyamoto were out to see him recently 'bout buying his property, which Ole sold to Carl. 'Cording to Ole, Miyamoto went away hopping mad. Said he was going to have a talk with Carl. And, well, maybe he did. At sea. And things . . . got out of hand.'

'And what's the fifth?' asked Lew Fielding.

'Fifth?'

'You claimed to have five categories of cause. I've heard four. What's the fifth?'

'Oh,' said Art Moran. 'Horace did a . . . pretty thorough autopsy. There's a bad wound in the side of Carl's head. And Horace said something interesting about it that fits in with what I'm hearing from Ole. And from Etta, too, for that matter. Said he'd seen wounds like this one during the war. Said the Japs made 'em with their gun butts. Said they were trained to fight with sticks from the time they were kids. They were trained in *kendo*, Horace called it. And one of these *kendo* blows, I guess, would leave the kind of wound Carl has. Now at the time I didn't make nothing of it. I didn't even think of it when some of the guys down at the docks said Miyamoto'd been out on Ship Channel Bank last night – same place as Carl. Didn't even occur to me then. But I did think of it this afternoon when Etta told 'bout all the problems she'd had with Miyamoto, and I thought about it even more after Ole Jurgensen said his piece. And I decided I'd better follow this lead through and search Miyamoto's boat, Judge. Just in case. See what signs there are, if any.'

Judge Lew Fielding pinched the tip of his nose. 'I don't know, Art,' he said. 'First of all, you've got Horace's off-the-cuff-statement regarding a coincidental resemblance between this wound in Carl Heine's head and ones he saw inflicted by Japanese soldiers – now does *that* really point us toward Miyamoto? You've got Etta Heine, who I won't go into, but suffice it to say I don't trust that woman. She's hateful, Art; I don't trust her. And you've got at least fifty gill-netters out in the fog last night – any one of them as contentious as the next when he figures some other guy is cutting into his fish – and then you've got Ole Jurgensen. And I admit Ole is interesting. I admit you've got something worth thinking about with Ole. But – '

'Judge,' Art Moran cut in, 'can I say something? If you think about it *too* long we'll lose our chance altogether. The boats'll be going out soon.'

229

The judge pulled his sleeve back and squinted at his watch. 'Five-twenty,' he said. 'You're right.'

'I've got an affidavit here,' the sheriff pressed on, pulling it free of his shirt pocket. 'I did it up fast, but it's right, Judge. Lays it all out plain and simple. What I want to look for is a murder weapon, that's all, if there's a chance of that.'

'Well,' replied Lew Fielding. 'No harm, I suppose, if you do it properly, Art.' He leaned across his desk toward the sheriff. 'And for technicality's sake let's make *this* move, too: do you swear that the facts in this affidavit are true, so help you God – do you *swear*?'

The sheriff did.

'All right. You bring a warrant?'

The sheriff produced one from the opposite shirt pocket; the judge unfolded it beneath his desk lamp and picked up his fountain pen. 'I'm going to put this down,' he said. 'I'm going to allow you to search the boat but not Miyamoto's house. No intruding on his wife and children, I don't see there's any hurry to do something like that. And remember, now, this is a *limited* search. The murder weapon, Art, and nothing else. I won't have you running roughshod over this man's privacy.'

'Got it,' Art Moran said. 'The murder weapon.'

'You don't find anything on the boat, come see me in the morning. We'll talk about his house at that point.'

'All right,' said Art Moran. 'Thanks.'

He asked, then, if he might use the telephone. He dialed his office and spoke with Eleanor Dokes. 'Have Abel meet me down to the docks,' he said. 'And tell him to bring along his flashlight.'

San Piedro fishermen, in 1954, were apt to pay attention to signs and portents other men had no inkling of. For them the web of cause and effect was invisible and simultaneously everywhere, which was why a man could sink his net with salmon one night and catch only kelp the next. Tides, currents, and winds were one thing, the force of luck another. A fisherman didn't utter the words horse, pig, or hog on the deck of a gill-netter, for to do so was to bring bad weather down around his head or cause a line to foul in his propeller. Turning a hatch cover upside down brought a southwest storm, and bringing a black suitcase on board meant snarled gear and twisted webbing. Those who harmed seagulls risked the wrath of ship ghosts, for gulls were inhabited by the spirits of men who had been lost at sea in accidents. Umbrellas, too, were bad business, as were broken mirrors and the gift of a pair of scissors. On board a purse seiner only a greenhorn would ever think to trim his fingernails while sitting on a seine pile, or hand a shipmate a bar of soap as opposed to dropping it into his washbasin, or cut the bottom end off a can of fruit. Bad fishing and bad weather could result from any of these.

Kabuo Miyamoto, as he came up the south dock toward his boat that evening – carrying a battery for the *Islander* – saw a flock of seagulls perched on his net drum and stabilizer bars and sitting atop his cabin. When he moved to board they lofted themselves skyward, thirty or forty birds, it appeared at first, a clamor of wings, more of them than he imagined possible, half a hundred seagulls rising from the *Islander*, exploding out of her cockpit. They circled overhead a half-dozen times in arcs that took in the entire breadth of the docks, then settled on the swells to seaward.

Kabuo's heart worked hard in his chest. He was not particularly given to omens, but on the other hand he had never seen this before.

He went in and pried up the battery well cover. He slid his new battery into place and bolted the cables to it. Finally he started his boat engine. He let it run, then flicked the toggle for the number-one pump in order to run his deck hose. Kabuo stood on the edge of the hatch cover and washed gull droppings out the scupper holes. The gulls had disturbed his equilibrium, put him ill at ease. Other boats were pulling out, he saw, motoring past the buoys in Amity Harbor on their way to the salmon grounds. He looked at his watch; five-forty already. It occurred to him to try his luck at Ship Channel that evening; the good sets would be taken at Elliot Head.

When he looked up a lone gull had perched arrogantly on the port gunnel ten feet away and to stern. It was pearl gray and white winged, a young herring gull with a wide, flaring breast, and it seemed to be watching him, too.

Kabuo reached back delicately and turned the hose valve full open. The water shot harder against the aft deck and ricocheted to stern. When he had fixed in on the gull again he watched it for a moment out of the corners of his eyes, then shifted his weight to the left swiftly and aimed his hose at it. The stream caught the surprised bird broadside in the breast, and while it struggled to escape from the force of the water its head smashed against the gunnel of the *Channel Star*, which was moored in the adjacent berth.

Kabuo, the hose still in his hand, was standing beside the port gunnel staring at the dying gull when Art Moran and Abel Martinson appeared beside his boat, both carrying flashlights.

The sheriff, twice, slashed a hand across his throat. 'Cut your engine,' he called.

'What for?' asked Kabuo Miyamoto.

'I've got a warrant,' replied the sheriff, and took it out of his shirt pocket. 'We're going to search your boat tonight.'

Kabuo blinked at him, and then his face hardened. He shut the nozzle off and looked the sheriff in the eye. 'How long will it take?' he asked.

'I don't have any idea,' said the sheriff. 'It might take quite a while.'

'Well, what are you looking for?' asked Kabuo Miyamoto.

'A murder weapon,' answered Art Moran. 'We think you might be responsible for the death of Carl Heine.'

Kabuo blinked a second time and dropped the hose to the deck. 'I didn't kill Carl Heine,' he insisted. 'It wasn't me, sheriff.'

'Then you won't mind us searching, will you?' Art Moran said, and stepped up onto the boat.

He and Abel Martinson rounded the cabin and stepped down into the cockpit. 'You'll want to take a peek at this,' the sheriff said, and handed Kabuo the warrant. 'Meanwhile we're going to start looking around. We don't find anything, you're on your way.'

'Then I'm on my way,' Kabuo answered. 'Because there isn't anything to find.'

'Good,' answered Art. 'Now cut your engine.'

The three of them went into the cabin. Kabuo hit the kill switch beside the wheel. It was quiet now without the engine running. 'Have at it,' Kabuo said.

'Why don't you just take a load off?' replied Art. 'Have a seat on your bunk.'

Kabuo sat. He read the search warrant. He watched while the deputy, Abel Martinson, went through the tools in his toolbox. Abel picked up each wrench and examined it in the beam of his flashlight. He ran his beam along the galley floor, then knelt with a flathead screwdriver in his hand and pried ajar the battery well cover. His flashlight beam ran over the batteries and down into the recesses of the well. 'D-6s,' he said.

When Kabuo did not reply to this, Abel slid the cover back into place and put the screwdriver away. He turned his flashlight off.

'Engine under the bunk?' he said.

'That's right,' Kabuo answered.

'Stand up and haul the mattress,' said Abel. 'I'll have a look, if you don't mind.'

Kabuo stood, rolled the bedding aside, and opened the engine compartment hatch. 'There you go,' he said.

Abel flicked his flashlight on again and poked his head into the engine compartment. 'Clean,' he said after a while. 'Go ahead and put your mattress back.'

They went out onto the aft deck, Abel Martinson leading. The sheriff was laying hands on things – rain gear, rubber gloves, floats, lines, hose, life ring, deck broom, buckets. He moved slowly, pondering each. He circumnavigated the boat carefully, checking the mooring lines on each cleat as he went, kneeling to look at them closely. For a moment he went forward and knelt beside the anchor, brooding in silence over something. Then he made his way back to the stern and tucked his flashlight into his pants waist.

'I see you replaced a mooring line lately,' he said to Kabuo Miyamoto. 'One right there on that second cleat to port. It's a brand-new line, isn't it.'

'I've had that one around for a while,' Kabuo Miyamoto explained.

The sheriff stared at him. 'Right,' he said. 'Sure you have. Help me with this hold cover, Abel.'

They slid it to one side and peered in together. The stink of salmon flew up at them. 'Nothing,' said Abel. 'Now what?'

'Jump down in there,' urged the sheriff. 'Poke around a little.'

The deputy lowered himself into the hold. He knelt and flicked on his flashlight. He went through the motions of looking. 'Well,' he said. 'I don't see nothing.'

'There's nothing to see,' said Kabuo Miyamoto. 'You guys are wasting your time and mine. I need to get out there fishing.'

'Come on out,' said Art Moran.

Abel turned to starboard, his hands on the hatch combing. Kabuo watched while he peered up under the starboard gunnel at the long-handled gaff wedged against the wall. 'Look at this,' Abel said.

He pulled himself out of the hold and grabbed it – a stout three-and-a-half-foot gaff with a barbed steel hook on one end. He gave it to Art Moran.

'There's blood on it,' he pointed out.

'Fish blood,' said Kabuo. 'I gaff fish with that.'

'What's fish blood doing on the butt end?' Art asked. 'I'd expect maybe to see blood on the hook, but on the *butt* end? Where your hand goes? *Fish* blood?'

'Sure,' said Kabuo. 'It gets on your hands, sheriff. Ask any of these fishermen about that.'

The sheriff took a handkerchief from the rear pocket of his trousers and held the gaff with it. 'I'm going to take and have this tested,' he said, and handed it to Abel Martinson. 'The warrant allows me to do that. I wonder if I could get you to stay in tonight, stay off the water until you hear from me. I know you want to go out and fish, but I wonder if you shouldn't stay in tonight. Go home. Wait and see. Wait there until you hear from me. Because otherwise I'm going to have to arrest you now. Hold you in connection with all this.'

'I didn't kill him,' repeated Kabuo Miyamoto. 'And I can't afford not to fish. I can't let the boat sit idle on a night like this and – '

'Then you're under arrest,' cut in Art Moran. 'Because there's no way I'm letting you go out there. In a half hour you might be in Canada.'

'No, I wouldn't,' replied Kabuo. 'I'd fish and then I'd come home. And by the time I did, you'd know that gaff of mine has fish blood on it, not Heine's. I could go out and get my salmon, check with you in the morning.'

The sheriff shook his head and slipped his hands to his belt, where he hooked his thumbs over the buckle. 'No,' he said. 'You're under arrest. Sorry, but we're going to have to hold you.'

The investigation, it occurred to the sheriff, had thus far taken five hours. *Sherlock Holmes*, he remembered. Horace Whaley had laughed at his queasiness about the corpse, the peeled-back head, the bone splinters in Carl's brain. There was that diaper spread over Susan Marie's shoulder, and her gloved index finger pointing out the church cake, that white finger inviting him to slide a mint between his lips. She'd collapsed on the stairs with her feet splayed out, the baby bottle beside her toes. All right, in the end he had played Sherlock Holmes, yes: it had been a sort of game. He had not really expected to find anything other than that Carl Heine had drowned. Fallen into the sea like other men before him and died because that was the nature of things. Art Moran was a believer in circumstances. To him the occasional misfortunes of life were simply part of things. The misfortunes he'd seen in the course of his work remained painful and vivid in his memory, and because he had seen them for so many years he knew that more would come his way; that was how things went. Island life was like life anywhere in this regard: bad things now and then happened.

Now he began to believe, for the first time, that he had a murder on his hands. He should have expected that sooner or later the course of things would bring him to this pass. He was satisfied to have conducted himself, in the face of it, professionally; he had pursued his investigation as well as anyone could have. Horace Whaley would not ridicule him now about playing Sherlock Holmes.

It occurred to him, too, that for all his arrogance Horace Whaley had been right. For here was the Jap with the bloody gun butt Horace had suggested he look for. Here was the Jap he'd been led to inexorably by every islander he'd spoken with.

Art Moran looked into the Jap's still eyes to see if he could discern the truth there. But they were hard eyes set in a proud, still face, and there was nothing to be read in them either way. They were the eyes of a man with concealed emotions, the eyes of a man hiding something. 'You're under arrest,' repeated Art Moran, 'in connection with the death of Carl Heine.'

19

By eight-thirty on the morning of December 7, Judge Fielding's courtroom was filled with citizens who were thankful for the heat from the boilers. They'd left damp overcoats hanging in the cloakroom but still carried the smell of snow in their hair and on their pants, boots, and sweaters. Ed Soames had again turned the heat up; he did so because the foreman of the jury had reported that certain of the jurors had passed a cold night in the Amity Harbor Hotel. Groans from the hapless radiators, coupled with the slamming of the wind against their windows, had kept them awake through the dark hours. They had been sequestered on the second floor and had speculated before going to bed, said the foreman, that the snowstorm would interrupt the trial. They'd been sleepless, most of them, and had shivered in their beds while the storm rattled the hotel.

Ed Soames apologized to the members of the jury for the inferior nature of their accommodations and pointed out to them the urn of coffee in the anteroom, which they were welcome to serve themselves from – the coffee was hot – at any time during the day's recesses. He showed them, as he had the day before, a cabinet inside which fourteen coffee cups hung on angles from brass hooks. He pointed out the sugar dispenser and apologized to them for the fact that there was no way to make cream available: Petersen's had run out. He hoped they could make do despite this.

The foreman indicated that the jurors were ready, so Ed Soames led them to the courtroom. The reporters found their places, the defendant was brought in, Eleanor Dokes took her seat at the stenograph. Ed Soames asked all of them to rise, and as they did so Lew Fielding emerged from his chambers and strode to the bench as if no one were present. As always he looked disinterested. He propped the weight of his head against his left fist and nodded at Alvin Hooks. 'A new day,' he told him, 'but still your day in court, Mr. Prosecutor. Have at it. Call your witness.'

Alvin Hooks rose and thanked Judge Fielding. He was fresh looking and clean shaven, neat in his serge suit with its exaggerated shoulders. 'The state calls Dr. Sterling Whitman,' he announced, and then a man stood up in the gallery whom nobody had seen before, passed through the low gate, and approached the witness box, where he was sworn in by Ed Soames. He was tall, six foot five at least, and seemed too large for the suit he wore; a large portion of each shirt cuff showed; the coat bunched at the armpits.

'Dr. Whitman,' said Alvin Hooks. 'We thank you for battling the elements this morning in order to give your testimony. I understand that only a handful of mainlanders were brave enough to travel the waters to San Piedro on the 6:25 ferry run – is that correct, sir?'

'That's right,' said Dr. Whitman. 'There were six of us.'

'A thrilling ride through a blinding snowstorm,' added Alvin Hooks.

'That's right,' repeated Dr. Whitman.

He was entirely too large for the witness box and had the appearance of a stork or crane packed into a crate.

'Dr. Whitman,' said the prosecutor. 'You are a specialist in hematology employed by the Anacortes General Hospital – is that correct? Do I have that right?'

'That's correct.'

'And you have been employed there for how long?'

'Seven years.'

'And during this time, doctor, what precisely has been the nature and content of your work?'

'I've been a hematologist for the past six and a half years. Strictly a hematologist.'

'A hematologist,' said Alvin Hooks. 'A hematologist does what exactly?'

Dr. Whitman scratched the back of his head, then above and below the left stem of his glasses. 'I specialize in the pathology and therapeutics of the blood,' he said. 'Mostly blood testing and analysis. I consult with attending physicians.'

'I see,' said Alvin Hooks. 'So for six and a half years it has been your profession – let me find a way to put this simply – to perform blood tests? And to analyze the results of those tests, doctor? Is that correct?'

'In a nutshell,' said Sterling Whitman.

'Very good then,' said Alvin Hooks. 'Now, Dr. Whitman, could we accurately characterize you as an expert in the matter of blood testing? Given your six and a half years of experience? Would you say you have gained a degree of expertise in, for example, determining human blood type?'

'By all means,' said Sterling Whitman. 'Blood type is a . . . standard matter. A standard procedure for any hematologist – typing blood.'

'All right,' said Alvin Hooks. 'On the evening – the late evening – of September 16 of this year, the sheriff of this county brought you a fishing gaff, did he not, and asked you to test a bloodstain he found on it. Is that correct, Dr. Whitman?'

'It is.'

Alvin Hooks swiveled and looked at Ed Soames; Ed handed him the fishing gaff.

'Now, Dr. Whitman,' said the prosecutor. 'I'm showing you what has already been admitted into evidence as state's exhibit 4–B. I'm going to hand it to you and ask you to look it over.'

'All right,' said Sterling Whitman.

He took the gaff and examined it – a long-handled gaff with a barbed hook at one end, tagged as admitted around the butt.

'Okay,' he said. 'I've looked at it.'

'Very good,' said Alvin Hooks. 'Do you recognize this fishing gaff, Dr. Whitman?'

'I do. It's the one Sheriff Moran brought in on the evening

239

of September 16. It was bloodstained, and he asked me to do some tests on it.'

Alvin Hooks took the gaff and placed it on the evidence table in full view of the jurors. Then he selected a folder from among his papers and returned to the witness stand.

'Dr. Whitman,' he said. 'I'm now handing you what has been marked as state proposed exhibit 5-A. Would you please tell me whether you recognize it, whether you can identify it for the court?'

'I can,' said Sterling Whitman. 'It's my investigative report. The one I wrote after Sheriff Moran brought me the fishing gaff.'

'Examine it for a moment,' said Alvin Hooks. 'Is it in the same condition as it was when you prepared it?'

Sterling Whitman went through the motions of turning pages 'It is,' he said after a moment. 'It seems to be. Yes.'

'And do you recognize your signature thereon?'

'I do.'

'Thank you, doctor,' Alvin Hooks said, and took the folder in his hand again. 'The state moves the introduction of exhibit 5-A, Your Honor.'

Nels Gudmundsson cleared his throat. 'No objection,' he said.

Lew Fielding admitted the exhibit. Ed Soames, with a flourish, stamped it. Then Alvin Hooks returned it to Sterling Whitman.

'All right,' he said. 'Now, Dr. Whitman. I'm returning to you what is now in evidence as exhibit 5-A: your investigative report concerning this fishing gaff, among other things. Would you please summarize for the court your findings?'

'Certainly,' Sterling Whitman said, pulling uncomfortably at a cuff. 'Number one was that the blood on the fishing gaff I received from Sheriff Moran was human blood, it reacted immediately to human antibodies. Number two was that the blood was of a sort we can describe as B positive, Mr. Hooks. I obtained a clear identification in this regard, without any difficulties, under a microscope.'

'Anything else significant?' asked Alvin Hooks.

'Yes,' said Sterling Whitman. 'The sheriff asked me to check our hospital records as to the blood type of a fisherman named Carl Heine, Jr. I did so. We had the records on file. Mr. Heine had been admitted after the war at our hospital for a series of physicals, and we had obtained his medical records. I looked these over and have included them in my investigative report. Mr. Heine's blood type was B positive.'

'B positive,' said Alvin Hooks. 'Do you mean to say that the blood of the deceased *matched* the blood found on the fishing gaff?'

'Yes,' said Sterling Whitman. 'It did.'

'But, Dr. Whitman,' said Alvin Hooks. 'Many people must have this type of B positive blood. Can you say with any certainty that it was Carl Heine's?'

'No,' said Dr. Whitman. 'I can't say that. But let me add that B positive is a relatively rare blood type. Statistically rare. Ten percent of Caucasian males, at best.'

'One out of every ten Caucasian males? No more?'

'That's right.'

'I see,' said Alvin Hooks. 'One out of ten.'

'That's right,' said Sterling Whitman.

Alvin Hooks crossed in front of the jurors and approached the defendant's table. 'Dr. Whitman,' he said. 'The defendant's name here is Kabuo Miyamoto. I am wondering if his name appears in your report.'

'It does.'

'In what regard?' asked Alvin Hooks.

'Well, the sheriff asked me to check his records, too. As long as I was checking on Carl Heine, he asked, could I bring out Miyamoto's records? I did so and examined them at his request. Again, service medical records were available. Kabuo Miyamoto had been typed upon entering the service as O negative: he has an O negative blood type.'

'O negative?' said Alvin Hooks.

'That's right. Yes.'

241

'And the blood on the fishing gaff that Sheriff Moran brought you, the one he found while searching the defendant's boat – the one you held in your hands a moment ago – was B positive, doctor?'

'Yes. B positive.'

'So the blood on the gaff was not the defendant's?'

'No.'

'It was not salmon blood?'

'No.'

'It was not fish blood or animal blood of any kind?'

'No.'

'It was of the same type as the deceased's? As Carl Heine, Jr.?'

'Yes.'

'A blood type that you would characterize as rare?'

'Yes.'

'Thank you, Dr. Whitman. That's all.'

Nels Gudmundsson now tottered to his feet in order to cross-examine Sterling Whitman. By the morning of this second day he had become an amusement to the newspapermen, who smiled to themselves each time he cleared his throat and at his awkward attempts to stand or sit. He was an old man in suspenders, one useless eye wandering loose in its socket, poorly shaven wattles of skin at his throat – raw, chafed, and pinkish folds with sparse silver bristles poking out of them. Yet, though Nels Gudmundsson was at times vaguely laughable, the reporters fell serious when he passed in front of them and allowed them to see up close how his temples pulsed, the depth of the light in his good eye.

'All right,' said Nels. 'Dr Whitman, sir. Do you mind if I ask you a few questions?'

Sterling Whitman said he didn't mind at all; that was what he'd come to San Piedro for.

'Well, then,' said Nels. 'About this fishing gaff. You say you found blood on it?'

'Yes,' said Sterling Whitman. 'I've testified to that effect. Yes, I did.'

'This blood,' said Nels. 'Where *exactly* did you find it?' He picked up the gaff and brought it to the witness. 'On what part, Dr. Whitman? The butt end? The hook?'

'The butt,' the doctor answered. 'This end' – he pointed – '*opposite* the hook.'

'Right here?' said Nels, and put his hand on it. 'You found blood on this wooden handle?'

'Yes.'

'It hadn't soaked in?' Nels Gudmundsson asked. 'Wouldn't wood of this sort absorb blood, doctor?'

'Some soaking had occurred, yes,' said Sterling Whitman. 'But I was still able to obtain a blood sample.'

'How?' said Nels, still holding the gaff.

'By scraping. It's the procedure with dried blood. You have to scrape.'

'I see,' said Nels. 'You used a blade, doctor?'

'Yes.'

'You scraped it onto a microscope slide? You placed the slide under a microscope?'

'Yes.'

'And you saw what? Blood and wood scrapings?'

'Yes.'

'Anything else?'

'No.'

'Nothing. Only blood and wood scrapings?'

'That's right.'

'Doctor,' said Nels Gudmundsson. 'Were there no bits of bone, or strands of hair, or particles of scalp, on this fishing gaff?'

Sterling Whitman shook his head firmly. 'None,' he said. 'It was just as I have said. As I testified. As I wrote in my investigative report. Blood and wood scrapings only.'

'Doctor,' said Nels. 'Does this seem odd to you? If this fishing gaff were in fact used to inflict a head wound, would you not expect to see evidence of that? In the shape of, say, strands of hair? Or bits of skull bone? Or particles of scalp? The sort of

243

things we might normally associate with a head wound, Dr. Whitman? As evidence that the instrument in question had been used to inflict such a wound?'

'Sheriff Moran asked me to perform two blood tests,' said the witness. 'I did so. We determined that – '

'Yes, yes,' Nels Gudmundsson cut in. 'As you have testified previously. The blood on the gaff was of the type known as B positive: no one is contesting *that*, doctor. What I want to know is, to the best of your knowledge as a man who has for six and a half years made his living looking at blood under a microscope, would you not expect to see hair or bone or scalp particles as *well* as blood if this gaff were used to inflict a head wound? Would you not, doctor? Would it seem logical?'

'I don't know,' said Sterling Whitman.

'You don't know?' asked Nels Gudmundsson. He still carried the gaff in his hand, but now he perched it on the ledge of the witness box between himself and the expert hematologist.

'Doctor,' he said. 'The coroner who examined the deceased in question included mention in his report of, if I remember it correctly, a "secondary and minor laceration of the right hand extending laterally from the fold between the thumb and forefinger to the outside of the wrist." A cut on the palm, in other words. An ordinary cut on Carl Heine's right palm. Would it be possible, Dr. Whitman, that a cut like this – if the hand were wrapped around the butt end of this gaff here – that a cut like this might have caused the B positive blood you spoke of to soak into the wood? Would that be possible, doctor? *Possible?*'

'Possible, yes,' said Sterling Whitman. 'But I don't know anything about that. My only job was to perform the blood tests that Sheriff Moran asked me to perform. I found B positive blood on this fishing gaff. How it got there, I have no idea.'

'Well,' said Nels Gudmundsson. 'It's good of you to say so. Because, as you've said, one of every ten Caucasian males has blood of the B positive type, don't they? And on an island like this one that means, probably, two hundred men, doctor? Would that be about right?'

'Yes. I suppose. Ten percent of the island's Caucasian male population. It – '

'And isn't the percentage even higher, doctor, for males of Japanese descent? A higher percentage of B positives among the island's Japanese – Americans?'

'Yes, it is. Somewhere around twenty percent. But – '

'Twenty percent – thank you, doctor. That's quite a large number of island men we're talking about who have B positive blood. But let's suppose, for purposes of argument, that the blood on the fishing gaff *was* in fact Carl Heine's, even though it might have come from hundreds of other men – let's just suppose that hypothetically for a moment. It might have gotten there, it seems to me, in at least one of two ways. It might have come from the deceased man's head, or it might have come from this ordinary cut on his hand – his head or his hand, doctor, either one. Now, given the fact that the blood is on the *butt* end of this gaff where a person would normally place their *hand*, and given the fact that you found only blood there and no bone or skin or hair, doctor – the probable evidence of a head wound, I would think – what seems to you to be likely? That the blood on the gaff, if it came from Carl Heine at all, came from his head or his hand?'

'I have no idea,' said Sterling Whitman. 'I'm a hematologist, not a detective.'

'I'm not asking you to be a detective,' Nels said. 'I just want to know which is more *probable*.'

'The hand, I suppose,' Sterling Whitman confessed. 'The hand, I guess, would be more probable than the head.'

'Thank you,' answered Nels Gudmundsson. 'I appreciate your having battled the elements to come here and tell us so.' He turned away from the witness, made his way to Ed Soames, and handed him the fishing gaff. 'You can put that away, Mr. Soames,' he said. 'Thank you very much. We're done with that.'

Three fishermen – Dale Middleton, Vance Cope, and Leonard George – all testified for the court that on the evening of

September 15 they'd seen Carl Heine's boat, the *Susan Marie*, with her net set on the fishing grounds at Ship Channel Bank; furthermore they'd seen Kabuo Miyamoto's boat, the *Islander*, in the same vicinity at approximately the same time. Ship Channel, Leonard George explained, was like many other places island men netted salmon: a narrow and limited seafloor topography which forced you to fish within sight of other men and to move about with care lest, in the night fog general to Island County in early autumn, you motor across a set net and destroy it by winding it up in your propeller. That was why, even in the fog, Leonard had made out both the *Susan Marie* and the *Islander* between eight and eight-thirty at Ship Channel Bank: he recalled that as he cruised past he'd seen the *Islander* come about, that ten minutes later he'd come across the *Susan Marie* and seen that Carl Heine was backing net off his drum by motoring away from his jacklight. They'd been fishing, in short, the same waters, with Carl a bit farther toward the north and down current: a thousand yards closer to the shipping lanes that gave Ship Channel Bank its name.

Nels Gudmundsson asked Leonard George if it was common among gill-netters to board another's boat at sea. 'Absolutely not,' replied Leonard. 'There aren't many reasons why a guy'd do that. If you're stalled out and somebody's bringing you a part maybe – that's about it, no other reason. Maybe if you was hurt or broke down or somethin'. Otherwise you don't tie up to nobody. You do your job, keep to yourself.'

'Do men argue at sea?' said Nels. 'I've heard they do. That gill-netters do. Are there arguments out there, Mr. George?'

'You bet there are,' said Leonard. 'A guy gets corked off he – '

'Corked off?' interrupted Nels. 'Can you explain that for us briefly?'

Leonard George answered that a gill net was constructed to have a top and a bottom; that the bottom of the net was called the lead line – bits of lead were crimped onto it in order to weight

246

it down – and that the top was known as the cork line: cork floats allowed it to stay on the surface, so that from a distance a gill net appeared as a line of cork with the stern of the boat at one end and a warning jacklight at the other. When a man set his wall of net up current from your own he'd 'corked you off,' stolen your fish by getting to them before they could get to you. It meant trouble, said Leonard: you had to pick up, motor past him, and set your net somewhere up current, in which case the other guy might decide to play leapfrog and force both of you to waste your fishing time. Still, in all of this, Leonard pointed out, no man ever boarded another's boat. It wasn't done; he'd never heard of it. You kept to yourself unless you had some kind of emergency and needed another man's help.

Alvin Hooks called Army First Sergeant Victor Maples to the stand after that morning's recess. Sergeant Maples wore his green dress uniform and the insignia of the Fourth Infantry Division. He wore his expert marksmanship and combat infantryman's badges. The brass buttons on Sergeant Maples's coat, the insignia on his collar, and the badges on his chest all caught the meager courtroom light and held it. Sergeant Maples was overweight by thirty-five pounds but still looked distinguished in his dress uniform. The extra weight was nicely distributed; Maples was a powerful man. He had short, thick arms, no neck, and a pudgy, adolescent face. His hair stood up in a razor cut.

First Sergeant Maples explained to the court that since 1946 he had been assigned to Fort Sheridan, Illinois, where he specialized in the training of combat troops. Prior to that he'd trained troops at Camp Shelby, Mississippi, before taking part in the Italian campaign in 1944 and '45. Sergeant Maples had been wounded in fighting on the Arno River – he'd taken a German round in the small of his back which narrowly missed his spine – and had been awarded the Silver Star on account of it. He'd also, he said, been at Livorno and Luciana and seen the 442nd – the Nisei regiment to which the defendant had been attached – in action along the Gothic Line.

Sergeant Maples had in his time trained thousands of men in hand-to-hand combat. Hand-to-hand was his specialty, he said; he'd worked in other areas of basic training but generally found his way back to it. Sergeant Maples recollected for the court his astonishment in early 1943 when the 442nd – composed of Nisei boys – began training at Camp Shelby. These were boys from the internment camps, enlistees headed for the European theater, and among them, Sergeant Maples recalled, was the defendant, Kabuo Miyamoto.

He remembered Kabuo from among the thousands who'd come his way because of a . . . peculiar episode. Ten squads of trainees had surrounded Sergeant Maples on the drill field at Camp Shelby one February afternoon – ten squads composed of Nisei boys, so that he found himself in the midst of a hundred Japanese faces while he explained the particulars of the bayonet. Sergeant Maples informed his trainees that it was the policy of the United States Army to preserve their lives until they reached the battlefield; that was why a wooden staff would be substituted for an actual weapon during drill sessions. Helmets would be worn as well.

The sergeant began to demonstrate bayonet thrusts, then asked for a volunteer. It was at this point, he told the court, that he came face to face with the defendant. A young man stepped forward into the ring of trainees and presented himself to the sergeant, bowing slightly before saluting and calling out loudly, 'Sir!' 'First off,' Sergeant Maples scolded him, 'you don't have to salute me or call me sir. I'm an enlisted man, just like you – a sergeant, not a warrant officer or a major. Second, nobody in this army bows to nobody. There's plenty of officers who'll expect a salute, but a bow? It isn't *military*. Not *American* military. It isn't done.'

Sergeant Maples gave Miyamoto a wooden staff and tossed him a sparring helmet. There was something aggressive in the way the boy had spoken, and Sergeant Maples had heard it.

He was vaguely aware of this particular young man, who had built a reputation during basic training as a thoroughly eager warrior, ready to kill and businesslike every bit of the time. Maples had seen many such boys come his way and was never cowed by their youthful swagger; he was only on rare occasions impressed or prepared to view them as his equal. 'In combat your enemy won't be stationary,' he said now, looking the boy in the eye. 'It's one thing to work out on a dummy or a bag, another to spar with a trained human being who represents more accurately live movement. In this case,' he told the gathered recruits, 'our volunteer will seek to avoid the model bayonet thrusts put to him this afternoon.'

'Yes, sir,' said Kabuo Miyamoto.

'No more "sir,"' Sergeant Maples replied. 'That's the last time with that.'

He explained to the court how astonished he was – how thoroughly astonished – to find he couldn't hit the defendant. Kabuo Miyamoto hardly moved, and yet he slipped every thrust. The one hundred Nisei trainees looked on in silence and gave no indication that they approved of either man. Sergeant Maples fought on with his wooden staff until Kabuo Miyamoto knocked it from his hands.

'Excuse me,' said Miyamoto. He knelt, picked up the staff, and handed it to the sergeant. Once again, he bowed.

'There's no need to bow,' the sergeant repeated. 'I already told you about that.'

'I do it out of habit,' said Kabuo Miyamoto. 'I'm used to bowing when I'm sparring somebody.' Then, suddenly, he brought his wooden staff up. He looked Sergeant Maples in the eye and smiled.

Sergeant Maples acquiesced to the inevitable and did combat with the defendant that afternoon. It lasted all of three seconds. On his first rush the sergeant was swept off his feet, then felt his head pinned to the ground with the point of the staff, then the staff was withdrawn, the defendant bowed and picked him up. 'Excuse me, sergeant,' he'd said afterward. 'Your staff, sergeant.' He'd handed it to him.

After that Sergeant Maples availed himself of the opportunity to study *kendo* with an expert. Sergeant Maples wasn't stupid – he told the court this about himself without a trace of irony – and so he learned all he could from Miyamoto, including the importance of bowing. Sergeant Maples became a master with time and after the war taught *kendo* techniques to the army rangers at Fort Sheridan. From his point of view as an expert in the ancient Japanese art of stick fighting, Sergeant Maples could say with certainty that the defendant was eminently capable of killing a man far larger than himself with a fishing gaff. In fact, there were few men known to him who could ably defend themselves against such an attack by Kabuo Miyamoto – certainly a man with no training in *kendo* had little chance of warding him off. He was, in Sergeant Maples's experience, a man both technically proficient at stick fighting and willing to inflict violence on another man. He had made, the record showed, an excellent soldier. No, it would not surprise Sergeant Victor Maples to hear that Kabuo Miyamoto had killed a man with a fishing gaff. He was highly capable of such a deed.

20

Susan Marie Heine had been a widow for nearly three months by the time of Kabuo Miyamoto's murder trial but had not grown very much accustomed to it yet and still passed long hours – especially at night – during which she could think of nothing but Carl and the fact that he had gone out of her existence. In the gallery, with her sister on one side and her mother on the other, dressed in black from head to foot and with her eyes shrouded behind a chenille-dot veil, Susan Marie looked mournfully attractive: she exuded a blond, woeful distress that caused the reporters to turn in her direction and ponder the propriety of speaking intimately with her under the guise of professional necessity. The young widow's thick hair had been plaited and pinned up beneath her hat so that the alabaster neck Art Moran so much admired when Susan Marie poured coffee at church socials lay exposed to the crowded courtroom. The neck and the plaits of hair and the white hands folded decorously in her lap all stood in sharp contrast to her black mourning outfit and gave Susan Marie the air of an unostentatious young German baroness who had perhaps just recently lost her husband but had not in the face of it forgotten how to dress well, even when she dressed to suggest grief. And it was grief, foremost, that Susan Marie suggested. Those who had known her for a long while recognized that even her face had changed. The superficial among them attributed this to the fact that she'd neglected to eat heartily since Carl died – shadows had formed just under her cheekbones – but others recognized it as a deeper alteration, one that involved her spirit. The pastor at the First Hill Lutheran Church had on four successive Sundays asked his congregation to pray not only for Carl Heine's soul but for Susan Marie's 'deliverance from grief in the course of time' as well. In pursuit of this latter end, the church women's auxiliary had provided Susan Marie and her children with a straight month's worth of hot suppers in casserole dishes, and Einar Petersen had seen to it that groceries were delivered to her kitchen door. It was through food that the island expressed its compassion for Susan Marie in her widowhood.

Alvin Hooks, the prosecutor, knew well the value of a Susan Marie Heine. He had called to the witness box the county sheriff and the county coroner, the murdered man's mother and the bent-over Swede from whom the murdered man had planned to buy his father's old farm. He had proceeded to a variety of secondary witnesses – Sterling Whitman, Dale Middleton, Vance Cope, Leonard George, Sergeant Victor Maples – and now he would finish matters by presenting the wife of the murdered man, a woman who had already done much good merely sitting in the gallery where the jurors could view her. The men especially would not wish to betray such a woman with a not-guilty verdict at the end of things. She would persuade them not precisely with what she had to say but with the entirety of who she was.

On the afternoon of Thursday, September 9, Kabuo Miyamoto had stood at her doorstep and asked to speak with her husband. It was a cloudless day of the sort San Piedro rarely saw in September – this year there'd been an early string of them, though – a day of deep heat but with an onshore breeze that tossed the leaves in the alders and even ripped a few loose to fall earthward. One minute it was silent, the next a rush of wind came up from off the water smelling of salt and seaweed, and the roar of the leaves in the trees was as loud as waves breaking on a beach. A gust caught Kabuo Miyamoto's shirt as he stood on the porch so that the collar of it brushed his neck for a moment and the shoulders ballooned out, filled with air. Then the wind died and his shirt settled, and she asked him to come in and sit in the front room; she would go, she said, to find her husband.

The Japanese man had seemed uncertain about entering her house that afternoon. 'I can wait on the porch, Mrs. Heine,' he suggested. 'It's a nice afternoon. I'll wait outside.'

'Nonsense,' she replied, and stepped aside from the door. She gestured in the direction of the living room. 'You come in and make yourself comfortable. Get out of the sun and sit, why don't you? It's nice and cool inside.'

He looked at her, blinked, but took only one step. 'Thank you,' he said. 'It's a beautiful house.'

'Carl built it,' Susan Marie answered. 'Please come in now. Sit.'

The Japanese man passed her, turned to his left, and perched on the edge of the bench sofa. His back was straight, his demeanor formal. It was as if he considered making himself comfortable an insult of some kind. With a deliberation that bordered, to her thinking, on something stylized, he folded his hands together and waited at attention. 'I'll go after Carl,' said Susan Marie. 'It'll only take me a minute.'

'Fine,' said the Japanese man. 'Thank you.'

She left him there. Carl and the boys were out culling raspberry canes, and she found them down among the southward trellises, Carl cutting free the older stock, the boys filling the wheelbarrow. She stood at the end of the row and called to them. 'Carl!' she said. 'There's someone to see you. It's Kabuo Miyamoto. He's waiting.'

They all turned to look at her, the boys shirtless and small against the walls of raspberries, Carl bent at the knees, his knife in hand. He, a giant with a russet beard, closed the knife, and slipped it into the sheath at his belt. 'Where?' he said. 'Kabuo?'

'In the living room. He's waiting.'

'Tell him I'm coming,' said Carl. And he swung both boys into the wheelbarrow and planted them on top of the culled canes. 'Watch out for thorns,' he said. 'Here we go.'

She went back to the house and informed the Japanese man that her husband would be with him shortly; he'd been out among the raspberry canes working. 'Would you care for coffee?' she added.

'No, thank you,' replied Kabuo Miyamoto.

'It's no trouble,' she urged. 'Please have some.'

'It's very nice of you,' he said. 'You're very kind.'

'Will you have some, then?' Susan Marie asked. 'Carl and I were planning on a cup.'

'All right, then,' said Kabuo. 'Thank you. I will. Thank you.'

He was still seated in the same position, perched on the edge of the worn bench sofa precisely as she'd left him minutes before. Susan Marie found his immobility disquieting and was about to suggest that he sit back and relax, make himself at home, get comfortable, when Carl came through the front door. Kabuo Miyamoto stood up.

'Hey,' Carl said. 'Kabuo.'

'Carl,' said the Japanese man.

They came together and locked hands, her husband half a foot taller than his visitor, bearded and heavy through the shoulders and chest and wearing a sweat-stained T-shirt. 'What do you say we go out,' he suggested. 'Take a walk 'round the property or something? Get out of the house, go outside?'

'That sounds fine,' said Kabuo Miyamoto. 'I hope this is a good time,' he added.

Carl turned and looked at Susan Marie. 'Kabuo and me are going out,' he said. 'Be back after a while. Going to walk.'

'All right,' she said. 'I'll put coffee on.'

When they were gone she went upstairs to check her baby. She leaned over the side of the crib and smelled the girl's warm breath and let her nose brush against the girl's cheek. From the window she could see her boys in the yard, the tops of their heads as they sat in the grass beside the overturned wheelbarrow. They were tying knots in the culled raspberry canes.

Susan Marie knew Carl had spoken with Ole Jurgensen and had put down earnest money on Ole's farm; she knew how Carl felt about the old place at Island Center and his passion for

254

growing strawberries. Still, she didn't want to leave the house on Mill Run Road with its bronze light, varnished pine boards, and exposed roof rafters in the upstairs room, its view of the sea beyond the raspberry canes. From the window of her baby's room, looking out across the fields, it was more clear to her than ever that she didn't want to move. She'd grown up the daughter of a hay farmer and shake cutter, a man who couldn't get ends to meet; she'd cut thousands of shakes, had hunched over a cedar block with a froe and a mallet, her blond hair hanging in her eyes. She was the second of three daughters and remembered how her younger sister had died of tuberculosis one winter; they'd buried her on Indian Knob Hill in the Lutheran part of the cemetery. The ground had been frozen, and the men had difficulty digging Ellen's grave. It had taken the better part of a December morning.

She'd met Carl Heine because she'd wanted to meet him. On San Piedro a woman with her looks could do such a thing if she did it with the proper innocence. She'd been twenty and employed at Larsen's Pharmacy, where she clerked from behind an oak sales counter. One Saturday evening at eleven-thirty, on a hill above the dance pavilion at West Port Jensen, she stood beneath the branches of a cedar tree while Carl ran his hands up under her blouse and caressed her breasts with his fisherman's fingers. The woods were lit with lanterns, and far below in the bay, through the interstices of trees, she could make out the deck lights of moored pleasure boats. Some of the light came to where they stood so that his face was visible to her. This was their third dance together. By now she knew definitely that she admired his face, which was large, weathered, and durable. She held his face between her hands and looked at it from a distance of six inches. It was an island boy's face and at the same time mysterious. He'd been to the war, after all.

Carl began to kiss her throat so that Susan Marie had to throw back her head to make room for him – him with his russet beard. She looked up into the branches of the cedars and breathed in their perfume, and he moved his lips over her collarbones and then down into the space between her breasts. She let him. She remembered clearly how she had let him, how it was not resignation as it had been with two other boys – one near the end of her senior year of high school, the other during the summer before this one – but instead intensely and deeply what she wanted, this bearded fisherman who had been to the war and on occasion, if she pressed him, spoke about it without exaggerating. She stroked the top of his head with her fingers and felt the odd sensation of his beard against her breasts. 'Carl,' she whispered, but there was nothing to follow that with, she didn't know what other words she wanted to speak. After a while he stopped and pressed his hands against the bark of the cedar tree behind her so that his blunt muscled arms passed on either side of her head. He looked at her closely, with an intimacy and seriousness that did not seem to embarrass him – this somber man – then tucked a strand of blond hair in behind her ear. He kissed her and then, still looking into her eyes, unbuttoned two of the buttons on her blouse and kissed her again so that she was caught gently between Carl and the tree. She pushed back against him with the muscles of her pelvis, something she'd never done with a man before. It was an admission of her desire, a revealing of it, and it surprised her to the root of her being.

Yet in another way she was not surprised at all to find herself, at the age of twenty, pressing herself against Carl Heine beneath a cedar above the West Port Jensen dance pavilion. After all, she had brought this about, willed it into being. She had discovered when she was seventeen that she could shape the behavior of men with her behavior and that this ability was founded on her appearance. She was no longer astonished to look in the mirror and find she had developed the breasts and hips of an attractive, grown-up woman. Her astonishment gave way quickly to happiness about it. There was a roundness and firmness to her, a clean, strong roundness, and her heavy blond hair cast a glow over her shoulders when she wore a bathing suit. Her breasts turned just slightly away from one another and brushed against the insides of her arms when she walked. They were large, and when she got over her embarrassment about them she was able to take pleasure in the fact that boys became unnerved in their presence. Yet Susan Marie never flirted. She did not let on she knew she was attractive. She went out with two boys before meeting Carl and insisted on their politeness and reserve. Susan Marie did not want to be foremost a pair of breasts, but on the other hand she was proud of herself. This pride remained with her into her mid-twenties, until she'd given birth to a second child and her breasts were no longer so important to her as the most visible locus of her sexuality. Two sons had tugged at them with their gums and lips, and her breasts appeared different to her now. She wore a bra with stiff wire along its base in order to lift them up.

Susan Marie knew within three months of marrying Carl that she'd made an excellent choice. In his grave, silent veteran's way he was dependable and gentle. He was gone nights fishing. He came home in the morning, ate and showered, and then they got into bed together. He kept his hands smooth with a pumice stone, so that even though they were fishermen's hands they felt good stroking her shoulders. The two of them moved from position to position, trying everything, the sunlight just behind the pulled shade, their bodies moving in morning shadow but plainly visible. She found she had married an attentive man whose pursuit as a lover was to ensure her satisfaction. He read all her movements as signs and when she was close to coming retreated just enough so that her excitement became more desperate. Then it was necessary for her to put him on his back and rock high with her spine arched while he, half-sitting now, his stomach muscles clenched, stroked her breasts and kissed them. She often came this way, in control of her sensations, guiding herself along Carl's body, and Carl timed matters so as to begin to come while she was and thus carry her back up so that when she was through she did not feel satisfied and was compelled to press on toward a second coming that the pastor at the First Hill Lutheran Church could neither approve nor disapprove of because – she felt certain of this – he had no idea that it was possible.

Carl would sleep until one o'clock in the afternoon, then eat again and go out to work on the property. He was happy when she told him she was pregnant. He did not stop making love to her until she asked him to stop at the beginning of the ninth month. Sometime after their first son was born Carl bought his own boat. When he named it for her she was pleased and came aboard, and they took the baby out into the bay and west until the island was nothing but a low black line on the horizon. She sat on the short bunk nursing their son while Carl stood at the wheel. She sat there looking at the back of his head, his short, tousled hair, the broad muscles in his back and shoulders. They ate a can of sardines, two pears, a bag of filberts. The baby slept on the bunk, and Susan Marie stood on a pallet board piloting the boat while Carl, behind her, massaged her shoulders and the small of her back and then her buttocks. She gripped the wheel more tightly when he lifted her skirt and slid her under-pants out of the way, and then, leaning forward against the boat's wheel and reaching back to slide her hands along her husband's hips, she shut her eyes and rocked.

These were the things Susan Marie remembered. In her estimation of it, their sex life had been at the heart of their marriage. It had permeated everything else between them, a state of affairs she sometimes worried over. If it went bad, would they go bad? Somewhere down the road, when they were older and less passionate, when their desire for one another had staled and worn out – then where would they be? She didn't even want to think about that or to mull how one day they might have nothing except his silence and his obsession with whatever he was working on – his boat, their house, his gardens.

She could see her husband and Kabuo Miyamoto walking the border of the property. Then they went over a rise out of view, and she leaned downstairs again.

In twenty minutes' time Carl returned alone, changed into a

fresh T-shirt, and hunkered down on the front porch with his head in his hands.

She came out with a cup of coffee in each hand and sat down next to him, on his right. 'What did he want?' she asked.

'Nothing,' answered Carl. 'We had some things to talk about. Nothing much. No big deal.'

Susan Marie handed him a coffee cup. 'It's hot,' she said. 'Be careful.'

'All right,' said Carl. 'Thanks.'

'I made him some,' said Susan Marie. 'I thought he was going to stay.'

'It was nothing,' said Carl. 'It's a long story.'

Susan Marie put her arm around his shoulder. 'What's the problem?' she said.

'I don't know,' sighed Carl. 'He wants seven of Ole's acres. He wants me to let Ole sell them to him. Or sell them to him myself. You know, step out of his way.'

'Seven acres?'

'The ones his family had. He wants them back. That thing my mother talks about.'

'That,' said Susan Marie. 'I had a feeling it was that when he showed up. *That*,' she added grimly.

Carl said nothing. It was like him at a moment like this not to say very much. He did not like to explain or elaborate, and there was a part of him she couldn't get to. She attributed this to his war experiences, and for the most part she let it be, this silence of his. But it irritated her at times.

'What did you tell him?' she asked now. 'Did he go off angry, Carl?'

Carl set down his coffee. He leaned his elbows against his knees. 'Damn,' he answered. 'What could I tell him? There's my mother to think about, you know her, I have to think about that business. If I let him get back in out there . . .' He shrugged and seemed hapless for a moment. She saw the lines the sea wind had etched at the corners of his blue eyes. 'I told him I'd have to think it over, have a talk with you. Told him

259

how upset my mother was with him – 'bout his dirty looks and mean faces. He froze when I brought that up. Real polite, but frozen. Wouldn't look at me no more. Wouldn't come back up to the house for coffee. I don't know, I guess it was my fault. We got into a scrap, I guess. I couldn't *talk* with him, Susan. I just . . . didn't . . . know how to do it. I didn't know what to say to him . . .'

He trailed off. She recognized it as one of his *moments*, thought it over, and held her tongue. It had never been very clear to her if Carl and Kabuo were friends or enemies. This was the first time she had seen them together, and it seemed to her – it was her impression – that there remained some measure of kind feelings between them, that after all this time they held inside at least the memory of their friendship. But there was no way, truly, of telling. It could be that their cordiality and hand-shaking had been nothing but stiff formality, that underneath they hated each other. She knew, anyway, that Carl's mother had nothing but ill feelings for all the Miyamotos; she sometimes spoke of them at the dinner table on Sundays, rattling on obsessively. Carl generally fell silent when she did, or agreed with her in a perfunctory fashion, afterward dismissing the subject. Susan Marie had grown accustomed to these dismissals and to Carl's reluctance to speak about the matter. She was accustomed to it, but it pained her, and she wished she could clear it all up right now, while they sat together on the porch.

The wind came up and tossed the tops of the alders, and she felt the odd fall warmth in it. Carl had told her more than once – he'd repeated it just the other day – how since the war he couldn't *speak*. Even his old friends were included in this, so that now Carl was a lonely man who understood land and work, boat and sea, his own hands, better than his mouth and heart. She felt sympathy for him and rubbed his shoulder gently and waited patiently beside him. 'Damn,' Carl said after a while. 'Anyway, I guess as far as you're concerned I could hand the whole business over to him and let him do what he wants with it. I guess you don't want to move out there anyway.'

'It's so beautiful here,' replied Susan Marie. 'Just look around for a minute, Carl.'

'Look around out *there*,' he said. 'That's sixty-five acres, Susan.'

She understood that. He was a man who needed plenty of space, a vast terrain in which to operate. It was what he'd grown up with, and the sea, despite its size, was no substitute for green fields. Carl *needed* room, far more room than his boat could offer, and anyway in order to put his war behind him – the *Canton* going down, men drowning while he watched – he would have to leave his boat for good and grow strawberries like his father. She knew this was the only way for her husband to grow sound; it was what made her willing, ultimately, to follow him out to Island Center.

'Supposing you sell him his seven acres,' Susan Marie said. 'What's the worst your mother can do?'

Carl shook his head emphatically. 'It doesn't really come down to her,' he said. 'It comes down to the fact that Kabuo's a *Jap*. And I don't hate Japs, but I don't like 'em neither. It's hard to explain. But he's a Jap.'

'He's not a Jap,' Susan Marie said. 'You don't mean that, Carl. I've heard you say nice things about him. You and he were friends.'

'Were,' said Carl. 'That's right. A long time ago. Before the war came along. But now I don't like him much anymore. Don't like how he acted when I told him I'd think it over, like he expected me to just hand those seven acres to him, like I owed it to him or – '

There was a boy's cry from the back of the house then, a cry of pain instead of argument or upset, and Carl was already moving toward it before Susan Marie could stand. They found their older boy sprawled on a flagstone with his left foot gripped in both his hands; he'd sliced it open against the sharp edge of a strut on the overturned wheelbarrow beside him. Susan Marie knelt and kissed his face and held him closely while his foot bled. She remembered how Carl had looked at the wound, tenderly, transformed. He was no longer a war veteran. They'd taken the boy in to Dr. Whaley, and then Carl had gone off fishing. The two of them hadn't discussed Kabuo Miyamoto again, and Susan Marie soon recognized that the subject was somehow forbidden. It was forbidden in her marriage to open up her husband's wounds and look at them unless he asked her to.

Their marriage, she understood after Carl was gone, had largely been about sex. It had been about sex right up to the end, until the day Carl went out of her life: that morning, while the children slept, they'd shut the bathroom door and pulled the latch and taken off their clothes. Carl showered, and Susan Marie joined him when the stink of salmon had been washed down the drain. She washed his large penis and felt it harden in her fingers. She put her arms around his neck, locked her feet at the small of his back. Carl held her up with his strong hands clenching the muscles in her legs and leaned the side of his face against her breasts and took to licking them. They moved that way, standing up in the bathtub with the water pouring over them and Susan Marie's blond hair pasted to her face and her hands clutched around her husband's head. They washed each other afterward, taking their time about it in the friendly way of certain married people, and then Carl got into bed and slept until one in the afternoon. At two, having eaten a lunch of fried eggs and Jerusalem artichokes, canned pears and bread spread with clover honey, he went out to change the oil in his tractor. She saw him from the kitchen window that afternoon gathering early windfall apples and dropping them in a burlap bag. At three forty-five he came up to the house again and said good-bye to the children, who were seated on the porch drinking apple juice and eating graham crackers and rolling pebbles back and forth. He came into the kitchen, wrapped himself around his wife, and explained that unless the fishing was excellent he was coming home early the next morning, would be home, he hoped, by four A.M.. Then he left for the Amity Harbor docks, and she never saw him again.

21

Nels Gudmundsson stood at a distance from the witness stand when it was his turn to question Susan Marie Heine: he did not want to appear lecherous by placing himself in close proximity to a woman of such tragic, sensual beauty. He was self-conscious about his age and felt that the jurors would see him as disgusting if he did not distance himself from Susan Marie Heine and appear in general detached from the life of his body altogether. The month before, Nels had been told by a doctor in Anacortes that his prostate gland had become moderately enlarged. It would have to be removed surgically and he would no longer be able to produce seminal fluid. The doctor had asked Nels embarrassing questions and he had been forced to reveal a truth about which he was ashamed: that he could no longer achieve an erection. He could achieve one briefly, but it would wither in his hand before he had a chance to take pleasure from it. The bad part was not really this so much as it was that a woman like Susan Marie Heine inspired a deep frustration in him. He felt defeated as he appraised her on the witness stand. It was no longer possible for him to communicate to *any* woman – even those his own age he knew in town – his merit and value as a lover, for he no longer had this sort of worth and had to admit as much to himself – as a lover he was entirely through.

Nels remembered as he watched Susan Marie Heine the finest years of his sex life, now more than a half a century behind him. He could not quite believe that this was so. He was seventy-nine and trapped inside a decaying body. It was difficult for him to sleep and to urinate. His body had betrayed him and most of the things he once took for granted were no longer even possible.

A man might easily be embittered by such circumstances, but Nels made it a point not to struggle unnecessarily with life's unresolvable dilemmas. He had indeed achieved a kind of wisdom – if you wanted to call it that – though at the same time he knew that most elderly people were not wise at all but only wore a thin veneer of cheap wisdom as a sort of armor against the world. Anyway, the kind of wisdom younger people sought from old age was not to be acquired in this life no matter how many years they lived. He wished he could tell them this without inviting their mockery or their pity.

Nels's wife had died from cancer of the colon. They had not gotten along particularly well, but nevertheless he missed her. Occasionally he sat in his apartment and wept in order to empty himself of self-pity and remorse. Occasionally he attempted unsuccessfully to masturbate in the hope of rediscovering that lost part of himself he deeply, achingly missed. He was convinced at rare moments that he could succeed and that his youth was still buried inside of himself. The rest of the time he accepted this as untrue and went about the business of consoling himself in various unsatisfying ways. He liked to eat. He enjoyed chess. He did not mind his work and knew himself to be quite good at it. He was a reader and recognized his habit of reading as obsessive and neurotic, and told himself that if he read something less frivolous than newspapers and magazines he might indeed be better off. The problem was that he could not concentrate on 'literature,' however much he might admire it. It wasn't that *War and Peace* bored him exactly, but rather that his mind couldn't *focus* on it. Another loss: his eyes provided him with only half a view of the world, and reading caused his neurasthenia to flare up and made his temples throb. His mind, too, was failing him, he felt – although one could not be sure of such a thing. Certainly his memory was not as good as it had been when he was younger.

Nels Gudmundsson tucked his thumbs in behind his suspenders and looked with studied detachment at the witness.

'Mrs. Heine,' he said. 'The defendant here appeared on your doorstep on Thursday, September 9? Is that what I heard you say?'

'Yes, Mr. Gudmundsson. That's right.'

'He asked to speak to your husband?'

'He did.'

'They walked outside in order to talk? They didn't speak in the house?'

'Correct,' said Susan Marie. 'They spoke outside. They walked our property for thirty or forty minutes.'

'I see,' said Nels. 'And you didn't accompany them?'

'No,' said Susan Marie. 'I didn't.'

'Did you hear any part of their conversation?'

'No.'

'In other words, you have no firsthand knowledge of its content – is that correct, Mrs. Heine?'

'What I know is what Carl told me,' answered Susan Marie. 'I didn't hear their conversation, no.'

'Thank you,' Nels said. 'Because that concerns me. The fact that you've testified about this conversation without having heard any part of it.'

He pinched the wattles of skin at his throat and turned his good eye on Judge Fielding. The judge, his head resting on his hand, yawned and looked back with detachment.

'Well then,' Nels said. 'To summarize, Mrs. Heine. Your husband and the defendant walked and talked, and you stayed behind. Is that right?'

'Yes, it is.'

'And after thirty to forty minutes your husband returned. Is that also right, Mrs. Heine?'

'Yes, it is.'

'You asked him about the content of his conversation with the defendant?'

'Yes.'

'And he replied that the two of them had discussed the land in question? The land that your mother-in-law sold to Ole

Jurgensen more than a decade ago? The land on which the defendant's childhood home sat? Is all of that right, Mrs. Heine?'

'Yes,' said Susan Marie. 'It is.'

'You and your husband had recently put down earnest money on this land. Is that correct, Mrs. Heine?'

'Yes. My husband did.'

'Let's see,' said Nels Gudmundsson. 'Monday, September 6, was Labor Day, Tuesday the seventh Mr. Jurgensen put his land up for sale . . . was it Wednesday, then – the eighth of September – that your husband signed the contract on Mr. Jurgensen's property?'

'It must have been,' said Susan Marie. 'Wednesday the eighth sounds right.'

'And the defendant visited the next day? On Thursday, the ninth of September?'

'Yes.'

'All right, then,' said Nels Gudmundsson. 'You've testified that on the afternoon of the ninth the defendant presented himself at your door and that he and your husband walked and talked, but that you were not present during their conversation. Do I have that right, Mrs. Heine?'

'Yes, you do.'

'And furthermore,' said Nels, 'after the defendant left that afternoon you and your husband sat on the porch and had your own conversation?'

'Yes.'

'Your husband indicated an unwillingness to talk about the content of his conversation with the defendant?'

'Correct.'

'You pressed him?'

'I did.'

'He reported to you that he had indicated to the defendant a willingness to think matters over? That he would ponder whether or not he might sell the seven acres to Mr. Miyamoto? Or allow Mr. Jurgensen to do so?'

'Yes.'

266

'He reported to you a concern about how his mother might react if he sold to the defendant? Did I hear you say that, Mrs. Heine?'

'You did.'

'But he was pondering such a sale anyway?'

'That's right.'

'And he had indicated as much to the defendant?'

'Yes.'

'So in other words Mr. Miyamoto left your residence on the ninth having heard from your husband there was at least a possibility your husband would sell the seven acres to him.'

'That's right.'

'Your husband reported to you that he had encouraged Mr. Miyamoto to believe in such a possibility?'

'Encouraged?' replied Susan Marie Heine. 'I don't know about that.'

'Let me put it this way,' Nels said. 'Your husband did not state an unequivocal no? He did not lead the defendant to believe that no hope existed for the reclaiming of his family's land?'

'He did not,' answered Susan Marie.

'In other words, he encouraged Mr. Miyamoto to believe that at the very least a possibility existed.'

'I guess so,' said Susan Marie.

'I guess you'd have to guess,' said Nels, 'having not been present at their conversation. Having to report to the court only, Mrs. Heine, what your husband reported to you. Words that might not be one hundred percent accurate, since your husband was aware of your disenchantment about the possibility of moving, as you've said, and may well have altered the tone and substance of his conversation with Mr. Miyamo – '

'Objection,' put in Alvin Hooks. 'Argumentative.'

'Sustained,' said the judge. 'Stop rambling, Mr. Gudmundsson. Your purpose here is to ask questions of the witness that refer directly to her testimony. You must refrain from doing anything else – but you know this. Get on with it.'

'Apologies,' Nels replied. 'All right, then. Mrs. Heine, forgive me. Your husband and the defendant – do I have this right? – had grown up together as boys?'

'As far as I know, yes.'

'Did your husband ever mention him as a neighbor, an acquaintance from his youth?'

'Yes.'

'Did he tell you how they'd gone fishing together as boys of ten or eleven? Or that they'd played on the same high school baseball and football teams? That they rode the same school bus for many years? Any of that, Mrs. Heine?'

'I suppose so,' Susan Marie said.

'Hmmm,' said Nels. He pulled the wattles of skin at his throat again and gazed at the ceiling for a moment. 'Mrs. Heine,' he said. 'You mentioned during the course of your testimony these "dirty looks" Mr. Miyamoto is supposed to have aimed at your mother-in-law. Do you remember mentioning that?'

'Yes.'

'You didn't mention that the defendant had aimed similar looks at you. Is that right? Do I remember right?'

'No, I didn't.'

'Or at your husband? Did I hear you say he aimed dirty looks at your husband? Or is it just something your mother-in-law reported as having occurred?'

'I can't speak for either of them,' answered Susan Marie. 'I don't know what they experienced.'

'Of course not,' said Nels. 'And I wouldn't want you to speak for them, either. It's just that earlier – when Mr. Hooks was questioning you? – you seemed happy to do so, Mrs. Heine. So I thought I'd take a flyer myself.' He smiled.

'All right,' Judge Fielding interrupted. 'That'll do, Mr. Gudmundsson. Get on with your questioning or sit down at once.'

'Judge,' replied Nels. 'There's been a lot of hearsay admitted as evidence. That bears pointing out.'

'Yes,' said the judge. 'A lot of hearsay – hearsay you didn't object to, Mr. Gudmundsson. Because you know that

Mrs. Heine is entitled under statute to report the nature and content of a conversation held with her deceased husband. The unfortunate fact is that he cannot do it himself. Mrs. Heine is under oath to tell the truth. As a court of law, we have no choice but to trust that what she tells us is accurate.' He turned slowly toward the jurors. 'For want of a gentler title, the legal institution in question here is known as the Deadman's Statute,' he explained. 'Normally it prohibits evidence from being entered into the record – it allows me to rule it inadmissible as hearsay – because the individual in question is deceased. In criminal cases, however, the Deadman's Statute does *not* bar such evidence from being presented, as Mr. Gudmundsson well knows. Nevertheless, and quite frankly, the Deadman's Statute creates a . . . shady legal area. This is, I believe, what Mr. Gudmundsson seeks to point out.'

'Yes,' said Mr. Gudmundsson. 'It is precisely what I seek to point out.' He bowed his head to the judge, glanced at the jurors, then turned and looked fully at Kabuo Miyamoto, who still sat erectly in his place at the defendant's table with his hands folded neatly in front of him. It was at this moment that the courtroom lights flickered in the storm, flickered again, and went out. A tree had fallen on Piersall Road and knocked the power wires down.

22

Well timed,' Nels Gudmundsson said when the lights went out in the Island County Courthouse. 'I have no further questions for Mrs. Heine, Your Honor. As far as we're concerned, she may step down.'

The four tall windows, frosted with vapor from the steam radiators, allowed a gray snowfall light to descend into the courtroom. Its timbre replaced that of the overhead lights and cast a subtle pall across the citizens in the gallery, who sat looking at one another and at the ceiling.

'Very well,' Judge Fielding replied. 'One thing at a time now. Patience, patience. Let's proceed methodically, lights or no lights. Mr. Hooks, will you redirect?'

Alvin Hooks rose and told the court that the prosecution had no further questions. 'In fact,' he added, winking at Nels, 'the timing of this power outage is even more propitious than my colleague for the defense suspects. Mrs. Heine is our last witness. The state rests at the same moment the county's power supply does.'

The jurors – some of them – stirred and smiled. 'The state rests,' repeated Lew Fielding. 'Very well, then. Very good. I was at any rate going to call for a lunch recess. We will get a report from the power company and take matters from there. We shall see what we shall see. In the meantime, I would like to ask Mr. Hooks and Mr. Gudmundsson to visit with me in my chambers.'

The judge picked his gavel up and dropped it again listlessly against its walnut plate. 'Go have lunch,' he advised. 'If we begin again at all, we'll begin at one sharp – one P.M. according to *my* watch, which now reads' – he peered at it – 'eleven fifty-three. The electric clocks in this building are useless, incidentally. Pay no attention to them.'

Ed Soames held the door open for him, and Judge Fielding disappeared into his chambers. The citizens in the gallery filed out; the reporters picked up their notepads. Soames followed the judge with the intention of lighting a pair of candles he knew to be lodged in the back of a desk drawer. Judge Fielding would need them, after all. It was dark in his chambers, darker than dusk, with only a pale light seeping through the windows. Ed had the candles lit by the time Nels Gudmundsson and Alvin Hooks had arrived and situated themselves across the desk from Judge Fielding. The candles sat between them so that they looked like three men preparing for a séance – the judge in his silk robe, Nels in his bow tie with its touch of the theatrical, Alvin Hooks dapper and elegant, his legs crossed, one knee over the other. Ed made his way to the door and excused himself for interrupting; was there anything more the judge required? If not, he would see to the jurors.

'Oh, yes,' Judge Fielding answered. 'Go and check on the boiler room, won't you? Find out how it looks to keep the radiators perking. And ring the power company and get a report. And, let's see, scare up as many candles as you can find around.' He turned his attention to the attorneys in front of him. 'What am I forgetting?' he added.

'The hotel,' Alvin Hooks answered. 'You'd better ask about their boiler, too, or the jurors aren't going to make it. They didn't fare well last night, recollect, and with the power out things will be worse.'

'Right,' Ed Soames said. 'Will do.'

'Very well, Ed,' the judge returned. Then: 'Quite solicitous of you, Alvin.'

'I'm a solicitous man,' Alvin Hooks replied.

Soames went out, grimly. The courtroom was empty except for Ishmael Chambers, who sat in the gallery with the look on his face of a man willing to wait forever. Eleanor Dokes had tended to the jurors; they were gathered in the anteroom getting coats on. 'The judge will be conferring throughout the lunch recess,' Ed told Ishmael Chambers. 'There's no point in waiting around to speak to him. An announcement will be made at one o'clock.'

The newspaperman stood and stuffed his notepad in his pocket. 'I'm not waiting,' he said softly. 'I was just thinking about things.'

'You'll have to think about them elsewhere,' said Ed. 'I'm going to lock up the courtroom.'

'All right,' said Ishmael. 'Excuse me.'

But he left slowly, preoccupied. Ed Soames watched him impatiently. A *strange bird*, he told himself. *'Bout half the man his father was.* Maybe the missing arm had something to do with it. Ed remembered Ishmael's father and shook his head, disconcerted. He and Arthur had been friendly enough, but the boy was not someone you could speak to.

Ishmael, with his shoulders hunched, his collar turned up, his pinned coat sleeve whipping in the wind, slogged through the snow to his office. The wind blew from off the water to the northwest and swept raucously down Hill Street. Ishmael had to keep his head lowered; when he raised it needles of snow lashed his eyes. He could see, nevertheless, that there were no lights anywhere in Amity Harbor; the power was out entirely. Four cars had been abandoned at haphazard angles along Hill Street, and one near the intersection of Hill and Ericksen had slid into a parked pickup truck, crumpling the driver's-side rear panel.

Ishmael pushed the door to his office open and shut it again with his shoulder. In his overcoat and snow-flecked hat he picked up the telephone to call his mother; she lived alone five miles from town, and he wanted to see how she was faring in the storm and find out if the south end was in as bad a state as Amity Harbor just now. If she stoked it up – and hung a curtain across the pantry door – the cookstove in the kitchen should keep her warm enough.

The phone in his office was dead, however, and gave him back only a hollow silence; so was his printing press dead, for that matter, he realized now with a start. The office, furthermore, was quickly going cold, giving up its electric heat, and he sat for a moment with his hand in his coat pocket and considered the snow whirling past his window. The stump of his amputated arm throbbed, or more precisely it was as if the arm were *there* again but half-numb, a phantom limb. His brain apparently did not fully grasp – or still disbelieved – that the arm was gone. At times past, just after the war, his missing arm had caused him a great deal of pain. A Seattle doctor had suggested sympathetic denervation of the limb – doing away with its ability to feel – but Ishmael had balked for unfathomable reasons. Whatever there was to feel in his arm, pain or anything else, he wanted to feel it, he didn't exactly know why. Now he reached up inside his coat, cupped the stump of his arm in his right hand, and thought of all he had to do on account of the power being out. He must see to his mother, first of all; he must use Tom Torgerson's ham radio set and put in a call to Anacortes about printing the paper there. He wanted to talk to Nels Gudmundsson and Alvin Hooks. He wanted to find out if the Anacortes ferry was running and if the power company would project a time for getting the wires up again. It would be good to find out where the lines were down and to go out to wherever it was for pictures. It would be good to drive out to the coast guard station, too, and get a full storm report, the speed of the wind, the height of the tides, the rate of snowfall. He should probably take his mother food from town and a can of kerosene. There was a kerosene heater in the shed she could use to keep her bedroom warm, but it needed a new wick. He'd have to stop in at Fisk's.

Ishmael slung his camera around his neck and shoved out into Hill Street to take pictures. Even in good conditions it was not easy for him, a one-armed man, to steady his camera in the way he would like. It was a large box camera with an accordion apparatus for the lens, unwieldy and as heavy as a stone around his neck, and he disliked it thoroughly. When he had a choice he bolted it to a tripod; when he didn't he propped it on the stump of his missing arm, turned his head to look over his left shoulder, and got his pictures as best he could. Doing this always embarrassed him. Twisted and turned, the camera perched precariously beside his ear, he felt like a circus grotesque.

Ishmael took three shots of the car that had plowed into the pickup truck. It was impossible to keep the snow off the lens, and after a time he gave up trying. He felt certain that he should carry his camera, though, since a blizzard like this one did not come along often – the last had hit in '36 – and was sure to do the sort of damage that constituted island news. Nonetheless, from Ishmael's perspective this inclement weather should not be allowed to overshadow the trial of Kabuo Miyamoto, which was an affair of a different sort entirely and of a greater magnitude. In the hearts of his fellow islanders, though, weather of this sort overwhelmed absolutely everything, so that even when a man stood trial for his life it was no doubt the destruction of docks and bulkheads, the trees fallen on homes, the burst pipes, the stranded cars, that would most interest San Piedro's citizens. Ishmael, a native, could not understand how such transitory and accidental occurrences gained the upper hand in their view of things. It was as if they had been waiting all along for something enormous to enter their lives and make them part of the news. On the other hand the trial of Kabuo Miyamoto was the first island murder trial in twenty-eight years – Ishmael had looked it up in back issues of the *Review* – and unlike the storm was a human affair, stood squarely in the arena of human responsibility, was no mere accident of wind and sea but instead a thing humans could make sense of. Its progress, its impact, its outcome, its meaning – these were in the hands of people. Ishmael intended to lead with it – with the trial of Kabuo Miyamoto – if somehow he could get Thursday's edition printed despite the storm.

He picked his way down to Tom Torgerson's filling station, where a half-dozen battered cars stood lined up along the fence, gathering snow on their hoods and roofs while Tom backed yet another into place – 'They're everywhere,' he told Ishmael from the wrecker's window. 'I've seen fifteen alone on Island Center Road and a dozen more up on Mill Run. It'll take me three days just to get to 'em.'

'Listen,' answered Ishmael. 'I know you're busy. But I need to get chains on my DeSoto. It's parked up on Hill Street and I can't bring it down to you. There are four stranded cars up there you'll need to move anyway. What do you say to heading up there next? I've got the chains sitting on the floor in the backseat. On top of that I've got to raise Anacortes on your radio, unless I can find a phone that's working. I've got no power to print my paper.'

'Whole island's down,' Tom Torgerson answered. 'Nobody's got power or phone anywhere. There's trees across lines in twenty different places. Crew's over on Piersall now trying to bring town back up – maybe by morning would be my guess. Anyway, okay, I'll get somebody on the DeSoto, but I just can't do it myself. We've got two high school kids working for us, I'll send one of 'em up, okay?'

'That's fine,' said Ishmael. 'The keys are in it. Any chance I can use your radio?'

'Took it home last week,' Tom answered. 'You want to head out to the house, that's fine. It's set up there – Lois'll show you.'

'I'm heading up to the coast guard station. Maybe I'll get them to put a call through for me if your radio isn't handy.'

'Either way,' Tom said. 'You're welcome to have at it, like I said. Just go on out to the house.'

Ishmael made his way down Main Street to Fisk's, where he bought a one-gallon can of kerosene and a wick for his mother's heater. Fisk had sold all of his size D batteries and all but one of his snow shovels. Three-quarters of his stock of candles had gone out the door and four-fifths of his supply of kerosene. Fisk, Kelton Fisk, had a highly developed sense of civic duty that had led him, at ten o'clock that morning, to refuse to sell more than a gallon of kerosene to any one island household. He stood with his feet planted wide beside the potbellied stove, polishing his glasses on the hem of his flannel shirt and, without having been prompted by Ishmael to do so, recited in detail an inventory of items that had gone out his door since eight o'clock. He also reminded Ishmael that the wick he had purchased would have to be cut after six uses.

Ishmael stopped in at the Amity Harbor Restaurant and asked Elena Bridges to put two cheese sandwiches in a paper sack for him; he didn't have time to stay and eat. The restaurant, though half-dark, was full and loud with conversation – people sat in booths and at the counter wrapped in coats and scarves, with bags of groceries underfoot, and turned their glances toward the snowfall beyond the windows. They were glad to have found a place to come in from the storm. Later, when they were done eating, it would be difficult for them to go outside again. Ishmael, waiting, listened to the conversation of two fishermen hunkered down at the counter. They were lapping up tomato soup that had been warmed on the gas stove and speculating on when the power might come on again. One wondered if high tide, with the wind behind it at fifty-five knots, might not swamp the town docks. The other said that a wind out of the northwest would bring down a lot of trees that were used to southerlies, including a white fir he feared mightily that grew on a bluff behind his cabin. He had gone out that morning and tied his boat off to a mooring buoy with tripled lines and through his binoculars could see it from his living room swinging about when the wind gusted down the bay. The first man cursed and said he wished he'd done the same with his boat, which would have to take its chances moored on slack lines with a dozen fenders out, six on either side; it was too tricky in these winds to move it.

At a quarter to one Ishmael stopped in at the office of the Island County Power & Light Company on the corner of Second Street and Main. He was loaded down now with the sack of sandwiches stuffed into one coat pocket and the new heater wick in the other, the camera dangling around his neck, and the can of kerosene carried in his hand. The report, which had been posted on the door for San Piedro's citizens to read, listed Piersall Road, Alder Valley Road, South Beach Drive, New Sweden Road, Mill Run Road, Woodhouse Cove Road, and at least a half-dozen others as blocked by fallen trees that had brought down power lines. It projected that power would be restored to Amity Harbor by eight o'clock the following morning and requested patience on the part of citizens. The repair crew had the help of the volunteer fire department and intended to work through the night, it said; all that could be done was being done as speedily as possible.

Ishmael returned to the courthouse. He ate one of his sandwiches in the second-floor corridor, sitting on a bench with his camera beside him and the can of kerosene on the floor. The corridor, he noticed, was slick with the snow that had melted from the shoes of passersby. Those who came down it did so carefully, treading their way like novice ice-skaters – the only light was whatever passed through the windows of offices and from there through the translucent glass panels of doors. The same was true of the public cloakroom – a damp, slippery, dark place full of dripping coats, bags, hats, and gloves. Ishmael left his kerosene and his camera there on the shelf above his coat. He knew no one would steal the camera, and he hoped no one would steal the kerosene. With the power out, the latter, he supposed, was suddenly a possibility.

Judge Fielding's announcement to the gathered court was terse. The trial would adjourn until eight o'clock the following morning, at which time the power company expected to have the lights on. There were high seas between San Piedro and the mainland that were preventing the Anacortes ferry from running, so it was not possible to house the members of the jury anywhere but where they had been housed the previous evening – the cold, dark rooms of the Amity Harbor Hotel, where they would have to make the best of things, since circumstances were now beyond Judge Fielding's control and other accommodations were not available. He hoped that the elements would not divert the jurors from the crucial and difficult matters at hand. They had an obligation, Judge Fielding said, to brave the storm and power outage as best they could, in order to keep their minds fully on the facts of the trial and the testimony of its witnesses. The judge folded his arms in front of him and leaned from the bench so that the members of the jury could see, through the shadows, his shaggy, exhausted face. 'The thought of a retrial makes me weary,' he sighed. 'I think that with a little effort we can avoid one, can't we? I hope you will pass a relatively pleasant night at the Amity Harbor Hotel, but if you do not, then be brave about it and return tomorrow with your thoughts centered on the case at hand. This is a murder trial, after all,' the judge reminded them, 'and snow or no snow, we have got to keep that foremost in our hearts and minds.'

At two thirty-five that afternoon, Ishmael Chambers put his can of kerosene, the heater wick, and two bags of groceries into the trunk of his DeSoto. Tom Torgerson's high school kid had gotten the chains on his tires, and Ishmael, bending low, checked now to see that they were tightly bound. He scraped ice from the DeSoto's windows and ran the defroster before inching out into the snow. The trick, he knew, was to stay off the brake and to keep his traveling speed low and steady, backing off the accelerator at the crests of hills and evenly gaining momentum in the dips. On First Hill he heard his chains, felt them biting, and made his way down cautiously, in first gear, leaning forward in his seat. He did not stop when he got to Main but turned immediately left instead, skidding a little, in the direction of Center Valley Road. He was less worried now. The snow had compacted under the wheels of other cars. The roads were passable if you were patient and paid attention. His chief concern was not the snow but other, more careless drivers. It would be important to watch his rearview mirror and to pull over, if that was possible, when he was being gained on.

Ishmael took Lundgren Road out of Amity Harbor because it made a steady ascent, without curves or coils, on a grade more reasonable than Mill Run's or Piersall's, and because it had not been listed on the power company door as blocked by fallen trees. He did see, at George Freeman's place, a Douglas fir that had toppled over so that its root wad now stood twelve feet high beside George's mailbox. The top section of the tree had crushed a piece of George's split-rail cedar fence. George was out there with a chisel-toothed bucksaw, his wool hat perched on top of his balding head, working on it in the storm.

Ishmael pushed on down the back side of Lundgren and turned onto Scatter Springs Drive. In the first curve a Hudson was nosed into a ditch; in the second a Packard Clipper sedan had flipped onto its roof and sat in the brambles beside the road with its undercarriage facing toward the sky. Ishmael stopped and took photographs of it, setting his tripod on the road verge. The straight lines of the alders and maples behind the Packard, blunt and clean against a sea of snow, the hard, grayish quality of the snowstorm light, the forlorn and helpless car itself with its upturned tires gathering soft mounds of white, its passenger compartment nuzzled into the frozen undergrowth so that only the bottom halves of the windows showed – this was a storm scene if ever there was one, and Ishmael shot it with an eye toward its pathetic aspect and because it seemed to him to embody what the storm was about: a world in which a Packard Clipper lost its meaning and became unmoored from whatever purpose it originally had; it had no more practical value now than a ship on the bottom of the sea.

Ishmael was glad to see that the driver's side window had been rolled down and that no one was still in the car. He thought he recognized it as Charlie Torval's – Charlie lived on New Sweden Road and made his living building bulkheads and docks and anchoring mooring buoys. He owned a lot of driving equipment, a barge on which a crane had been mounted, and – if Ishmael remembered it right – this rust brown Packard. Perhaps it would be an embarrassment to him if an image of his upturned car appeared in the pages of the *Review*. Ishmael decided to talk to him about it before going ahead with the photograph.

In the third bend in Scatter Springs Drive – a hairpin turn where the road rolled down out of cedar woods and onto the breaks over Center Valley – Ishmael saw three men busying themselves with a snowbound Plymouth half in the road: one jumped up and down on its bumper, another squatted and kept an eye on its spinning tires, a third sat behind the wheel with his door thrown open and worked the accelerator. Ishmael threaded past without stopping and swiveled, skidding – a little gleefully, his stomach leaping – onto Center Valley Road. An odd enthusiasm for this drive and its dangers had been growing in him ever since he'd left First Hill.

The DeSoto, he knew, was a dubious snow car. Ishmael had mounted a cherry wood knob on its steering wheel in order to ease the difficulties driving presented to a man with only one arm. He had changed nothing else, though, and didn't intend to. The DeSoto, strictly an island car for more than a decade, had been purchased by Ishmael's father fifteen years before, a four-speed with a semiautomatic transmission, hypoid rear axle, and column shift. Arthur had traded in his Ford Model A plus five hundred dollars cash for it in 1939 at a lot in Bellingham. It was a modest vehicle, square and bulky in the manner of a Dodge, so long in front as to look out of balance and with its radiator grille low over the bumper. Ishmael had hung on to it in part from sheer inertia, in part because driving it reminded him of his father. Sitting behind the wheel he felt his father's contours in the way the seat molded under him.

Center Valley's strawberry fields lay under nine inches of powder and were as fuzzy through the snowfall as a landscape in a dream, with no discernible hard edges. On Scatter Springs Drive the trees had closed the road in so that the sky was little more than an indistinct, drab ribbon overhead, but down here the dramatic expanse of it was visible, chaotic and fierce. Looking out past the windshield wipers Ishmael saw billions of snowflakes falling in long tangents, driven southward, the sky shrouded and furious. The wind propelled the snow against the sides of barns and homes, and Ishmael could hear it whistling through the wing window's rubber molding, which had been loose now for many years: it had been loose back when his father was alive, one of the car's small idiosyncrasies, part of the reason he was loath to part with it.

He passed Ole Jurgensen's house, where white wood smoke furled from the chimney and disappeared on the wind – Ole, apparently, was keeping warm. The snowfall obliterated the borders between the fields and made Kabuo Miyamoto's long-cherished seven acres indistinguishable from the land that surrounded them. All human claims to the landscape were superseded, made null and void by the snow. The world was one world, and the notion that a man might kill another over some small patch of it did not make sense – though Ishmael knew that such things happened. He had been to war, after all.

At the intersection of Center Valley Road and South Beach Drive Ishmael spied, ahead of him in the bend, a car that had failed to negotiate the grade as it coiled around a grove of snow-hung cedars. Ishmael recognized it as the Willys station wagon that belonged to Fujiko and Hisao Imada; in fact, Hisao was working with a shovel at its rear right wheel, which had dropped into the roadside drainage ditch.

Hisao Imada was small enough most of the time, but he looked even smaller bundled up in his winter clothes, his hat pulled low and his scarf across his chin so that only his mouth, nose, and eyes showed. Ishmael knew he would not ask for help, in part because San Piedro people never did, in part because such was his character. Ishmael decided to park at the bottom of the grade beside Gordon Ostrom's mailbox and walk the fifty yards up South Beach Drive, keeping his DeSoto well out of the road while he convinced Hisao Imada to accept a ride from him.

Ishmael had known Hisao a long time. When he was eight years old he'd seen the Japanese man trudging along behind his swaybacked white plow horse: a Japanese man who carried a machete at his belt in order to cut down vine maples. His family lived in two canvas tents while they cleared their newly purchased property. They drew water from a feeder creek and warmed themselves at a slash pile kept burning by his children – girls in rubber boots, including Hatsue – who dragged branches and brought armfuls of brush to it. Hisao was lean and tough and worked methodically, never altering his pace. He wore a shoulder strap T-shirt, and this, coupled with the sharp-honed weapon at his belt, put Ishmael in mind of the pirates he'd read about in illustrated books his father had brought him from the Amity Harbor Public Library. But all of this was more than twenty years ago now, so that as he approached Hisao Imada in the South Beach Drive, Ishmael saw the man in another light: hapless, small in the storm, numb with the cold and ineffective with his shovel while the trees threatened to come down around him.

Ishmael saw something else, too. On the far side of the car, with her own shovel in hand, Hatsue worked without looking up. She was digging through the snow to the black earth of the cedar woods and throwing spadefuls of it underneath the tires.

Fifteen minutes later the three of them walked down the road toward his DeSoto. The Willys station wagon's rear right tire had been perforated by a fallen branch still wedged up under both axles. The rear length of exhaust pipe had been crushed, too. The car wasn't going anywhere – Ishmael could see that – but it took Hisao some time to accept this truth. With his shovel he'd struggled defiantly, as if the tool could indeed change the car's fate. After ten minutes of polite assistance Ishmael wondered aloud if his DeSoto wasn't the answer and persisted in this vein for five minutes more before Hisao yielded to it as an unavoidable evil. He opened his car door, put in his shovel, and came out with a bag of groceries and a gallon of kerosene. Hatsue, for her part, went on with her digging, saying nothing and keeping to the far side of the car, and throwing black earth beneath the tires.

At last her father rounded the Willys and spoke to her once in Japanese. She stopped her work and came into the road then, and Ishmael was granted a good look at her. He had spoken to her only the morning before in the second-floor hallway of the

Island County Courthouse, where she'd sat on a bench with her back to an arched window just outside the assessor's office. Her hair had been woven then, as now, into a black knot against the nape of her neck. She'd told him four times to go away.

'Hello, Hatsue,' said Ishmael. 'I can give you a lift home, if you want.'

'My father says he's accepted,' Hatsue replied. 'He says he's grateful for your help.'

She followed her father and Ishmael down the hill, still carrying her shovel, to the DeSoto. When they were well on their way down South Beach Drive, easing through the flats along the salt water, Hisao explained in broken English that his daughter was staying with him during the trial; Ishmael could drop them at his house. Then he described how a branch had hurled down into the road in front of him; to avoid it he'd hit his brake pedal. The Willys had fishtailed while it climbed the snapped branch and nudged down into the drainage ditch.

Only once, driving and listening, nodding politely and inserting small exclamations of interest – '*I see, I see, yes, of course, I can understand*' – did Ishmael risk looking at Hatsue Miyamoto in the rectangle of his rear-view mirror: a risk that filled all of two seconds. He saw then that she was staring out the side window with enormous deliberation, with intense concentration on the world outside his car – she was making it a point to be absorbed by the storm – and that her black hair was wringing wet with snow. Two strands had escaped from their immaculate arrangement and lay pasted against her frozen cheek.

'I know it's caused you trouble,' Ishmael said. 'But don't you think the snow is beautiful? Isn't it beautiful coming down?'

The boughs in the fir trees hung heavy with it, the fence rails and mailboxes wore mantles of it, the road before him lay filled with it, and there was no sign, anywhere, of people. Hisao Imada agreed that it was so – *ah, yes, beautiful,* he commented softly – and at the same moment his daughter turned swiftly forward so that her eyes met Ishmael's in the mirror. It was the cryptic look, he recognized, that she'd aimed at him fleetingly on the second floor of the courthouse when he'd tried to speak to her before her husband's trial. Ishmael still could not read what her eyes meant – punishment, sorrow, perhaps buried anger, perhaps all three simultaneously. Perhaps some sort of disappointment.

For the life of him, after all these years, he couldn't read the expression on her face. If Hisao wasn't present, he told himself, he'd ask her flat out what she was trying to say by looking at him with such detached severity and saying nothing at all. What, after all, had he done to her? What had she to be angry about? The anger, he thought, ought to be his own; yet years ago now the anger about her had finished gradually bleeding out of him and had slowly dried up and blown away. Nothing had replaced it, either. He had not found anything to take its place. When he saw her, as he sometimes did, in the aisles of Petersen's Grocery or on the street in Amity Harbor, he turned away from seeing her with just a little less hurry than she turned away from seeing him; they avoided one another rigorously. It had come to him one day three years before how immersed she was in her own existence. She'd knelt in front of Fisk's Hardware Center tying her daughter's shoelaces in bows, her purse on the sidewalk beside her. She hadn't known he was watching. He'd seen her kneeling and working on her daughter's shoes, and it had come to him what her life was. She was a married woman with children. She slept in the same bed every night with Kabuo Miyamoto. He had taught himself to forget as best he could. The only thing left was a vague sense of waiting for Hatsue – a fantasy – to return to him. How, exactly, this might be achieved he could not begin to imagine, but he could not keep himself from feeling that he was waiting and that these years were only an interim between other years he had passed and would pass again with Hatsue.

She spoke now, from the backseat, having turned again to look out the window. 'Your newspaper,' she said. That was all.

'Yes,' answered Ishmael. 'I'm listening.'

'The trial, Kabuo's trial, is unfair,' said Hatsue. 'You should talk about that in your newspaper.'

'What's unfair?' asked Ishmael. 'What exactly is unfair? I'll be happy to write about it if you'll tell me.'

She was still staring out the window at the snow with strands of wet hair pasted against her cheek. 'It's all unfair,' she told him bitterly. 'Kabuo didn't kill anyone. It isn't in his heart to kill anyone. They brought in that sergeant to say he's a killer – that was just prejudice. Did you hear the things that man was saying? How Kabuo had it in his heart to kill? How horrible he is, a killer? Put it in your paper, about that man's testimony, how all of it was unfair. How the whole trial is unfair.'

'I understand what you mean,' answered Ishmael. 'But I'm not a legal expert. I don't know if the judge should have suppressed Sergeant Maples's testimony. But I hope the jury comes in with the right verdict. I could write a column about that, maybe. How we all hope the justice system does its job. How we hope for an honest result.'

'There shouldn't even *be* a trial,' said Hatsue. 'The whole thing is wrong, it's *wrong*.'

'I'm bothered, too, when things are unfair,' Ishmael said to her. 'But sometimes I wonder if unfairness isn't . . . part of things. I wonder if we should even expect fairness, if we should assume we have some sort of right to it. Or if – '

'I'm not talking about the whole universe,' cut in Hatsue. 'I'm talking about people – the sheriff, that prosecutor, the judge, you. People who can do things because they run newspapers or arrest people or convict them or decide about their lives. People don't have to be unfair, do they? That isn't just *part of things*, when people are unfair to somebody.'

'No, it isn't,' Ishmael replied coldly. 'You're right – people don't have to be unfair.'

When he let them out beside the Imadas' mailbox he felt that somehow he had gained the upper hand – he had an emotional advantage. He had spoken with her and she had spoken back, wanting something from him. She'd volunteered a desire. The strain between them, the hostility he felt – it was better than nothing, he decided. It was an emotion of some sort they shared. He sat in the DeSoto and watched Hatsue trudge away through the falling snow, carrying her shovel on her shoulder. It occurred to him that her husband was going out of her life in the same way he himself once had. There had been circumstances then and there were circumstances now; there were things beyond anyone's control. Neither he nor Hatsue had wanted the war to come – neither of them had wanted that intrusion. But now her husband was accused of murder, and that changed things between them.

23

The coast guard lighthouse on the rocks at Point White was a tower built out of reinforced concrete that rose a hundred feet above the sea. In the thirty years before it went up, eleven ships came aground at the point – two mail steamers, seven timber schooners, a Norwegian freighter, and a four-masted bark with a cargo of Newcastle coal on board, inbound for Seattle in a windstorm. There was no sign of them at all anymore – they'd broken up and, over the years, washed away into the ocean. There was only a jumble of barnacle-encrusted sea rock and a view of the water stretching to the horizon, unbroken, gray, and blurred in the distance at the place where the ocean and the sky met.

On occasions when the tide ran exceptionally high, waves washed perilously close to the lighthouse, dashing its base with salt-tinged algae, which clung to it now like sea moss. Underneath the lighthouse's copper dome lay sixteen reflecting prisms and four projecting lenses floating in a bath of mercury. The coast guard kept the clockworks greased, and the lenses revolved twice each minute. And yet there were still accidents, despite everything. There seemed no way to prevent them. In a thick fog the light could not be seen and boats continued to come aground. The coast guard installed sounding boards along island beaches and anchored numbered buoys at intervals in the shipping channel, and these measures seemed sufficient to islanders until the next accident came along. A tug towing a diesel ferry from San Francisco broke up on the rocks a mile to the north; then a tug towing a barge full of peeler logs; then a salvage steamer working out of Victoria. News of such wrecks was received by islanders with a grim brand of determinism; it seemed to many that such things were ordained by God, or at any rate unavoidable. They came out in large numbers in the aftermath of a shipwreck to stand on the beach and stare in awe at the latest foundering vessel; some brought binoculars and cameras. Old fishermen with time on their hands built bonfires out of driftwood and warmed themselves while the sea made breaches in the hulls of ships that had come hard aground. There was much discussion and finger pointing. Working without a single hard fact, islanders drew a variety of conclusions: pilot error, pilot inexperience, misread charts, crossed signals, fog, wind, tide, ineptitude. When after days a ship broke apart, or the pieces of it sank, or a salvage company gave up in despair after off-loading one twenty-fifth of its cargo, islanders watched blankly with their mouths hard-set and shook their heads once or twice. For a week or so they spoke cautiously of what they'd seen, and then it faded out of the realm of the discourse they shared together. They thought of it only at private moments.

Ishmael Chambers, in the last light of day, found himself seated in the office of the lighthouse chief petty officer, a large man named Evan Powell. The place was lit by kerosene lanterns and heated by a cast-iron wood stove. Outside a generator powered the lighthouse, so that each thirty seconds the beacon flashed against the glass of the office window. Petty Officer Powell kept an immaculate desk – a calendar blotter, twin upright pen stands, a nearly full ashtray, a telephone. He sat back in a reclining desk chair with a lit cigarette between his fingers, scratching his face and coughing. 'I've got a cold,' he explained to Ishmael hoarsely. 'I'm not firing on every cylinder right now. But I'll help you out if I can, Mr. Chambers. You need something for your newspaper?'

'I do,' said Ishmael. 'I'm putting an article together on this storm. I'm wondering if you have archives of some kind, weather records from way back, maybe, something I could take a look at. Go through old logs, something like that, try to make some comparisons. I can't remember a storm like this one, but that doesn't mean it never happened.'

'We do a *lot* of record keeping,' Petty Officer Powell replied. 'The lighthouse has been here longer than the coast guard – I don't know how far back there's reliable information – anyway you can have a look, if you want. There's more stuff around than you'd ever want to get into. I'd be interested in seeing what you find out.'

Petty Officer Powell fell forward in his chair and carefully snubbed out his cigarette. He picked up the telephone and, dialing a single number, drew a handkerchief out of his pocket. 'Who's this?' he said gruffly into the receiver. 'I want you to see if you can find Levant. Find Levant and tell him to come down here. Tell him to bring a couple kerosene lanterns. Tell him I need him right away.'

He put his hand over the receiver mouth, blew his nose, and looked at Ishmael. 'How much time you got?' he said. 'I can spare Levant to help you out for a couple of hours, tops.'

'That's all right,' said Ishmael. 'I don't want to trouble anybody here. Just point me in the right direction.'

Evan Powell slipped his hand from the receiver. 'Smoltz,' he said. 'Get Levant. Tell him I need him right away. Find Levant for this.'

He hung up and blew his nose one more time. 'There's no shipping in this weather,' he said. 'We raised Neah Bay an hour ago. We figure the snow isn't going to let up until tomorrow afternoon.'

The radioman named Levant arrived. Levant was tall enough to be a basketball player, six five or six six, with a large Adam's apple and tightly curled black hair, and he carried a lantern and a flashlight. 'This man here is Ishmael Chambers,' Petty Officer Powell explained. 'He runs the newspaper down in town and needs to take a look into our weather records. I want you to set things up for him, get him squared away, help him out. Give him what he needs, set him up a couple lanterns.'

'Anything else?' Levant said.

'Don't miss your radio watch over it,' Powell said. 'There's two hours before you're on.'

'Listen,' said Ishmael. 'Just point me in the right direction. I don't want to take anybody's time.'

Levant led the way to the records room on the second floor, which was stacked floor to ceiling with wooden crates, file cabinets, and stacked duffel bags. It smelled of brittle paper and of mimeograph ink and had not been dusted recently. 'Everything's dated,' Levant pointed out, finding a place for a lantern. 'That's how we do things – by dates, mainly. Radio transmissions, shipping log, weather reports, maintenance – everything's in here by date, I guess. There's a date on everything.'

'You have a radio watch?' Ishmael asked. 'Are you the radioman?'

'I am now,' Levant said. 'I have been for the last couple months or so – last guys got transferred, I moved up.'

'Is there a lot of record keeping with your job? Does a radioman contribute to all of this?'

'There's a guy shorthands all the radio transmissions,' Levant explained to him. 'He writes 'em up, files 'em, they end up here in a cabinet. And that's all they're good for, seems like. They just take up space, is all. No one pays any attention.'

Ishmael picked up a manila folder and turned it toward the lantern light. 'Looks like I'm going to be awhile,' he said. 'Why don't you go about your business? If I need something I can find you.'

'I'll bring another lantern,' Levant replied.

He was alone then with the fog of his breath in the lantern light and the crates of maritime records. The room smelled of salt water and snow and of the past – it was full of the scent of lost days. Ishmael tried to concentrate on his work, but the image of Hatsue in the backseat of his car – her eyes meeting his in the rearview mirror – carried him away into his memories.

The first time he'd seen her after the war she'd tried, he recalled, to be amiable, but he had not been capable of accepting this.

290

He'd stood behind her with his milk and crackers, waiting in line at Petersen's. He'd stood in silence, hating her, and she'd turned toward him with a baby on her shoulder and said with a detached formality that she was very sorry to have heard about his arm, how he had lost it in the war. She was, he remembered, as beautiful as ever, a little older and harder around the eyes, and it hurt him to look at her face and at her hair, which she wore in a braid down her back. Ishmael stood there looking pale and ill – he had a cold and a mild fever – with the sleeve of his mackinaw coat pinned up, his milk and crackers clutched in his hand, and stared long and hard at Hatsue's baby while the grocery checker, Eleanor Hill, pretended not to notice that Hatsue had spoken of what others, including Eleanor, would not acknowledge – that Ishmael was missing an arm. 'The Japs did it,' Ishmael said flatly, still staring hard at the baby. 'They shot my arm off. *Japs.*'

Hatsue looked at him a moment longer, then turned toward Eleanor Hill again and opened up her coin purse. 'I'm sorry,' said Ishmael immediately. 'I didn't mean that. I didn't mean what I said.' But she showed no sign of having heard, and so he put down the crackers and milk and put his hand on her shoulder. 'I'm sorry,' he said a second time, but she still didn't turn to look at him, and she moved away from his hand. 'I'm more than sorry. I'm miserable. Do you understand? I don't mean what I say. You can't trust me when I speak anymore. I just say things. I – '

Eleanor Hill was pretending, busily, that Ishmael, a war veteran, wasn't standing in her presence speaking the words he was speaking. It was what he'd gotten when he spoke about himself, when he'd tried to say what he had to say; there was nothing he could easily explain to anyone, and nobody who wanted to listen. There were other boys who had been to the war, and he found that on occasion he could speak to them, but that didn't mean anything. 'I'm sorry, Hatsue,' he said one more time. 'I'm sorry about everything. All of it.'

He'd left without buying the milk and crackers. He went home and wrote an apologetic letter, explaining at length that he was not himself, that he sometimes said what he did not mean, that he wished he had never said *Jap* in front of her, that he would never do so again. The letter sat in his desk drawer for two weeks before he threw it away.

Despite himself he knew where she lived and which car she drove and when he saw her husband, Kabuo Miyamoto, he felt something tighten around his heart. He felt himself grow tight inside, and for a long time he could not sleep at night. He would lie awake until two o'clock in the morning, then turn a light on and attempt to read from a book or magazine. Gradually dawn came and he would not have slept. He would go out to wander the island's trails in the early morning, at a slow pace. Once, so doing, he came across her. She was down on the beach at Fletcher's Bay, raking for steamer clams busily. Her baby slept on a blanket beside her, underneath an umbrella. Ishmael had come up the beach deliberately, and squatted beside Hatsue while she raked clams free and dropped them into a bucket. 'Hatsue,' he'd pleaded. 'Can I talk to you?'

'I'm married,' she'd said, without looking at him. 'It isn't right for us to be alone. It will look bad, Ishmael. People will talk.'

'There's no one here,' answered Ishmael. '*I've got* to talk to you, Hatsue. You owe me that much, don't you? Don't you think you do?'

'Yes,' said Hatsue. 'I do.'

She turned away from him and looked at her baby. The sun had crept up onto the child's face; Hatsue adjusted the beach umbrella.

'I'm like a dying person,' Ishmael said to her. 'I haven't been happy for a single moment since the day you left for Manzanar. It's like carrying a weight around in my gut, a ball of lead or something. Do you know how that feels, Hatsue? Sometimes I think I'm going to go crazy, end up in the hospital in Bellingham. I'm crazy, I don't sleep, I'm up all night. It never leaves me alone, this feeling. Sometimes I don't think I can stand it. I tell myself this can't go on, but it goes on anyway. There isn't anything I can do.'

Hatsue pushed the hair from her eyes with the back of her left wrist. 'I'm sorry for you,' she said softly. 'I don't want your unhappiness. I never meant for you to suffer. But I don't know what I can do for you now. I don't know how I can help you.'

'You'll think this is crazy,' Ishmael said. 'But all I want is to hold you. All I want is just to hold you once and smell your hair, Hatsue. I think after that I'll be better.'

Hatsue had looked at him, hard, for a long moment, the clamming rake clutched in her hand. 'Look,' she said. 'You know I can't. I can never touch you, Ishmael. Everything has to be over between us. We both have to put it all behind us and go on, live our lives. There's no halfway, from my point of view. I'm married, I have a baby, and I can't let you hold me. So what I want you to do right now is get up and walk away from here and forget about me forever. You have to let go of me, Ishmael.'

'I know you're married,' Ishmael had said. 'I want to forget about you, I do. I think if you hold me I can start, Hatsue. Hold me once, and I'll walk away and never speak to you again.'

'No,' she'd said. 'It can't be. You'll have to find some other way. I'm not going to hold you, ever.'

'I'm not talking about love,' he said. 'I'm not asking you to try to love me. But just as one human being to another, just because I'm miserable and don't know where to turn, I just need to be in your arms.'

Hatsue sighed and turned her eyes from his. 'Go away,' she'd said. 'I hurt for you, I honestly do, I feel terrible for your misery, but I'm not going to hold you, Ishmael. You're going to have to live without holding me. Now get up and leave me alone, please.'

The years had passed, and now her husband was on trial for the murder of a man at sea. It dawned on Ishmael, in the coast guard record room, that perhaps something pertinent to Kabuo's case could be found right here among these files. And suddenly he put aside his weather records and began to search the cabinets, and a strange excitement grew in him.

It took Ishmael all of fifteen minutes to find what it was he wanted. It was in a file cabinet to the right of the door, near the front of the third drawer down – records for September 15 and 16 of 1954. No wind, moderate tides, thick fog, balmy. One ship through at 0120 hours, the S.S. *West Corona*, Greek owned, Liberian flag; she'd called in her position from out to the west, headed southbound toward Seattle. The radio transmissions were in shorthand: the *Corona* had put in a call from northwest of sounding board 56, looking for a fix from the lighthouse radio signal. She'd come down the strait plotting soundings as she went, but the pilot would not put his faith in this, and at 0126 hours that morning, in heavy fog, had radioed the lighthouse for assistance. There was interference and the signal was weak, so the radioman on duty had advised the *Corona*'s navigator to take a reading off sounding board 56, which lay on the north shore of Lanheedron Island, and to plot his position accordingly. The *Corona*'s navigator had ordered a whistle blast and timed the interval of the echo. He did his division and his multiplication and relayed his position to the radioman. The *Corona* was out of the lane, he reported, somewhere south of buoy 56, and would have to dogleg to the northeast, bisecting Ship Channel Bank.

Ship Channel Bank. Where Dale Middleton, Vance Cope, and Leonard George had all seen Carl Heine with his net out on the night he went into the sea. On that night an enormous freighter had plowed right through the fishing grounds, throwing before it a wake large enough to knock even a big man overboard.

At 0142, on pilot's orders, the *Corona* made its corrective dogleg while the navigator fixed twice more on the sounding board. Later the navigator took three more insurance readings – boards 58, 59, and 60. It seemed to the *Corona*'s radioman that they were safely back in the shipping lane. In the vicinity of White Sand Bay he picked up the lighthouse's radio beacon and, gaining confidence by the moment, made the big swing to the south. The *Corona* locked onto the lighthouse radio signal and made headway for Seattle.

Everything was in triplicate – military standard carbon copies. They were signed by the radioman's assistant, a Seaman Philip Milholland – he'd transcribed the radio transmissions. Ishmael slipped three center pages of Seaman Milholland's notes free and folded them into quarters. The pages fit neatly into his coat pocket, and he let them sit there, feeling them, composing himself a little. Then he grabbed one of the lanterns and went out.

At the bottom of the stairs, in an anteroom, he found Levant slowly paging through the *Saturday Evening Post* beside a kerosene floor heater. 'I'm done,' he pointed out. 'There's just one more thing. Is Philip Milholland around somewhere? I want to talk to him.'

Levant shook his head and put the magazine on the floor. 'You know Milholland?' he said.

'Sort of,' said Ishmael. 'An acquaintance.'

'Milholland's gone. He got transferred out to Cape Flattery, Milholland and Robert Miller. That's when we moved up.'

'We?' asked Ishmael. 'Who's we?'

'Me and Smoltz, the two of us, we started in together. Smoltz.'

'When was that? When did Milholland leave?'

'That was back in September,' said Levant. 'Me and Smoltz started in September 16 as dogwatch radio team.'

'Dogwatch? Like at night?'

'Night shift, yes,' Levant said. 'Me and Smoltz work the night shift.'

'So Milholland's gone,' said Ishmael. 'He left September 15?'

'He couldn't have left the fifteenth,' said Levant. ''Cause he worked the night of the fifteenth. So he must have left on the sixteenth – that's it. He and Miller went out to Flattery the sixteenth of September.'

Nobody knows, thought Ishmael. The men who'd heard the *Corona*'s radio transmissions had gone somewhere else the next day. They'd done their watch on the night of the fifteenth, slept through the morning of the sixteenth, and then they'd left San Piedro. The transcribed transmissions had gone into a manila folder, and the folder had gone into a file cabinet in a room stuffed full of coast guard records. And who would find them there? They were as good as lost forever, it seemed to Ishmael, and no one knew the truth of the matter: that on the night Carl Heine had drowned, stopping his watch at 1:47, a freighter plowed through Ship Channel Bank at 1:42 – just five minutes earlier – no doubt throwing before it a wall of water big enough to founder a small gillnetting boat and toss even a big man overboard. Or rather one person, he himself, knew this truth. That was the heart of it.

24

Ishmael's mother had the woodstove in the kitchen going – he could see the smoke rising thick from the chimney, a ghostly white against the hard-falling snow – and was standing at the sink in her overcoat and scarf when Ishmael passed in front of her window carrying his can of kerosene. A fog of condensation had formed on the inside of the pane, so that her image appeared to him as a kind of silhouette, a vague impression of his mother at the sink, refracted and fragmented, a wash of color. As he passed by, peering through the window mist and snowfall, he saw her hand work with sudden clarity to wipe a circle of the pane dry, and then her eye met his and she waved. Ishmael held up the can of kerosene, still moving steadily toward the kitchen door. His mother had shoveled clear a path to the woodshed, but the snowfall was already covering it. Her shovel stood propped against the fence railing.

He stood in the kitchen doorway, set the kerosene down, and felt the place in his coat pocket where Philip Milholland's coast guard notes lay folded against his leg. He took his hand out and then returned it and touched the notes again. Then he picked up the kerosene and went in.

His mother had on rubber boots, unbuckled, and had used small finishing nails to tack a wool blanket across the entry to the living room. The light in the kitchen came opaquely through the wet windows; the room was warm, and on the table, neatly arranged, lay a collection of candles, a kerosene lantern, two flashlights, and a box of wooden matches. His mother had set a soup kettle full of snow on the woodstove; it hissed and snapped as Ishmael shut the door behind him. 'I've got some food in the car,' he said, setting the can of kerosene against the wall, 'and a new wick for the heater.' He put it on the table beside the candles. 'Did you freeze last night?' he asked.

'Not at all,' replied his mother. 'I'm really glad to see you, Ishmael. I tried to call, but the phone is out. The lines must all be down.'

'They are,' said Ishmael. 'Everywhere.'

She finished pouring snowmelt water from a second kettle into jugs in the sink, then dried her hands and turned to him. 'Are people stranded?' she said.

'I must have seen fifty cars along the roads between here and town,' said Ishmael. 'I saw Charlie Torval's car upside down in the blackberry stickers up on Scatter Springs. Trees are down all over the place; there's no power anywhere. They're trying to get town back up by morning – they're doing town first, like always. If they do get it lit again you should come stay with me; we'll shut this place up and move to town, there's no need to stay out here and freeze to death. I – '

'I'm not freezing,' his mother said, pulling the scarf from her head. 'In fact, it's a little *too* hot just now. I just got done shoveling and bringing stove wood around. I'm perfectly comfortable except for my worry about what's going to happen when the plumbing thaws out. The last thing I need is a burst pipe.'

'We'll open the taps,' answered Ishmael. 'You shouldn't have any problems. There's a pressure valve in the line on the east wall in the cellar – Dad put it in, remember?' He sat down at the table and cupped the stump of his amputated arm in his hand, then rubbed and squeezed it gently. 'Thing aches when it gets this cold,' he said.

'It's twelve degrees,' said his mother. 'Are those groceries up in your car going to freeze? Maybe we should go for them.'

'All right,' said Ishmael. 'Let's.'

'When your arm is ready,' said his mother.

They brought the two bags of groceries down, as well as Ishmael's camera. His mother's flower beds were all covered over, and the snow was lining up on her holly trees and mulberry and frosting the tops of her rhododendrons. She was, she said, worried about her flowers, whether the less hardy of them would survive the freeze – she'd lost flowers in lesser weather, she pointed out. Ishmael saw where she had worked with the wheelbarrow at bringing cordwood from the shed to the kitchen door; there were splinters around the wood block where she'd cut kindling.

His mother, at fifty-six, was the sort of country widow who lives alone quite capably; he knew that she rose at a quarter after five every morning, made her bed, fed her chickens, showered, dressed, cooked herself a poached egg and toast, steeped strong tea and sipped it at the table, then got immediately at her breakfast dishes and whatever housework needed doing. By nine o'clock, he speculated, there was nothing left she felt obligated to do, and so she read or tended her flowers or drove in to Petersen's Grocery. It was unclear to him, though, exactly how she passed her time. He knew she read incessantly – Shakespeare, Henry James, Dickens, Thomas Hardy – but he did not think this could fill her days. On Wednesday evenings twice a month she attended a meeting of her book circle, five other women who enjoyed discussing *Benito Cereno*, *Flowers of Evil*, *The Importance of Being Earnest*, and *Jane Eyre*. She was on friendly terms with Lillian Taylor, with whom she shared a passion for flowers and for *The Magic Mountain* and *Mrs. Dalloway*. The two of them would stoop or stand in the garden picking the seeds from the feathery spires of astilbes a few weeks past their prime, then sit at a garden table shaking the seeds clean and collecting them in small manila packets. They drank lemon-scented water and ate sandwiches with the crusts cut off at three o'clock in the afternoon. 'We're dainty old ladies,' he heard Lillian exclaim once. 'We'll wear painters' smocks and blue berets and do watercolors next – what do you say to that, Helen? Are you ready to be an old biddy with her paints?'

Helen Chambers was homely and dignified in the manner of

Eleanor Roosevelt. Her homeliness composed a form of beauty; she was quite impressive to look at. Her nose was broad and her forehead stately. For her shopping trips to town she wore a camel's-hair coat and a boater festooned with ribbon and striped lace. Her husband's death had inspired in her a greater attentiveness to her books and flowers and a greater need for people. Ishmael had stood beside her at church while she greeted her friends and acquaintances with the sort of cordiality and genuine feeling he couldn't muster in himself. Often he ate lunch with her afterward. He had explained to his mother, when she asked him to say grace, that like his father before him he was an incorrigible agnostic and suspected God was a hoax. 'Suppose you had to choose right now,' his mother had once replied. 'Supposing somebody put a gun to your head and forced you to choose, Ishmael. Is there a God or isn't there?'

'Nobody has a gun to my head,' Ishmael had answered her. 'I don't *have* to choose, do I? That's the whole point. I don't have to know for certain one way or the other if – '

'Nobody *knows*, Ishmael. What do you *believe*'

'I don't believe anything. It isn't in me. Besides, I don't know what you mean by God. If you tell me what he is, Mom, I'll tell you if I think he exists.'

'Everybody knows what God is,' said his mother. 'You feel what God is, don't you?'

'I don't feel what God is,' answered Ishmael. 'I don't feel anything either way. No feeling about it comes to me – it's not something I have a choice about. Isn't a feeling like that supposed to *happen*? Isn't it just supposed to happen? I can't make a feeling like that up, can I? Maybe God just chooses certain people, and the rest of us – we can't feel Him.'

'You felt Him as a child,' his mother said. 'I remember, Ishmael. You felt Him.'

'That was a long time ago,' Ishmael answered. 'What a child feels – that's different.'

Now, in the twilight, he sat in the kitchen of his mother's house with Philip Milholland's notes in his coat pocket and tried to feel that intimation of God he had felt as a younger person. It was not something he could conjure up again. After the war he had tried to feel God, to take solace in Him. It hadn't worked, and he had dismissed the attempt when he could no longer ignore that it felt like a pathetic falsehood.

The wind shuddered against the window behind him and the snow outside fell fast. His mother had a soup they could eat, she said: five kinds of beans, onions and celery, a ham shank, two small turnips. Was he hungry now or did he want to wait? She was happy either way, she could eat or not eat, it didn't matter to her. Ishmael pushed two slabs of fir heartwood into the fire in the cook stove. He put a kettle of water on, then sat down again at the table. 'It's plenty warm in here,' he pointed out. 'You don't have to worry about getting cold.'

'Stay,' replied his mother. 'Spend the night. I've got three extra comforters. Your room will be cold, but your bed should be fine. Don't go back out into all of that snow. Stay and be comfortable.'

He agreed to stay and she put the soup on. In the morning he would see about printing his newspaper; for now he was warm where he was. Ishmael sat with his hand in his coat pocket and wondered if he shouldn't just tell his mother about the Coast Guard notes he had stolen from the lighthouse and then drive carefully back into town to hand the notes over to Judge Fielding. But he did nothing. He sat watching the twilight fade beyond the kitchen windows.

'That murder trial,' his mother said finally. 'I suppose you've been busy with that.'

'It's all I think about,' said Ishmael.

'It's a shame,' said his mother. 'I have to think it's a travesty. That they arrested him because he's Japanese.'

Ishmael made no reply to this. His mother lit one of the candles on the table and placed a saucer under it. 'What do you think?' she asked him. 'I haven't been there listening, so I'm interested in what you have to say.

'I've covered every minute,' Ishmael answered. And he felt

himself growing cold now, and the depth of his coldness was not a surprise, and he closed his hand around Milholland's notes.

'I have to think he's guilty,' lied Ishmael. 'The evidence is very solidly against him – the prosecutor has a good case.'

He explained to her about the blood on the fishing gaff, the wound on the left side of Carl Heine's head, the sergeant who had testified that Kabuo Miyamoto was an expert when it came to killing with a stick. He told her about Ole Jurgensen's testimony and the long dispute over land. He told her how three different fishermen had reported seeing Kabuo Miyamoto fishing near Carl Heine on the night the murder happened, and he told her about the length of mooring rope. The accused man sat so rigorously in his chair, so unmovable and stolid. He did not appear remorseful. He did not turn his head or move his eyes, nor did he change his expression. He seemed to Ishmael proud and defiant and detached from the possibility of his own death by hanging. It reminded him, he told his mother, of a training lecture he'd listened to at Fort Benning. The Japanese soldier, a colonel had explained, would die fighting before he would surrender. His allegiance to his country and his pride in being Japanese prevented him from giving in. He was not averse to dying at war in the way Americans were. He did not have the same feeling about death on the battlefield that American soldiers felt. To the Japanese soldier a life in defeat was not for a moment worth living; he knew he could not return to his people having suffered the humiliation of losing. He could not meet his Maker afterward, either – his religion demanded he die with honor. Understand, the colonel added: the Jap preferred to die with honor intact, and in this the infantryman should indulge him. In other words, take no prisoners: shoot first and ask questions later. The enemy, you see, has no respect for life, his own or anyone else's. He doesn't play by the rules. He'll put up his hands, pretend to surrender, and all the while he's rigged himself to booby-trap as you approach. It's characteristic of the Jap to be sly and treacherous. He won't show what he's thinking in his face.

302

'It was all propaganda,' added Ishmael. 'They wanted us to be able to kill them with no remorse, to make them less than people. None of it is fair or true, but at the same time I find myself thinking about it whenever I look at Miyamoto sitting there staring straight ahead. They could have used his face for one of their propaganda films – he's that inscrutable.'

'I know who he is,' said Ishmael's mother. 'He's a striking man, his face is powerful. Like you, Ishmael, he served in the war. Have you forgotten – that – that he fought in the war? That he risked his life for this country?'

'All right,' said Ishmael, 'he served. Is that a fact pertinent to the murder of Carl Heine? Is it relevant to the case at hand? I grant you the man is "striking", as you say, and that he served in the war – are those things relevant? I don't understand what makes them relevant.'

'They're at least as relevant as your propaganda lecture,' Ishmael's mother replied. 'If you're going to remember something like that and connect it in some way to the defendant's expression – well then, you'd better be remembering other things, too, just to keep yourself fair. Otherwise you're being subjective in a way that is not at all fair to the accused. You're allowing yourself an imbalance.'

'The defendant's expression isn't part of it,' said Ishmael. 'Impressions aren't part of it; feelings aren't part of it. The facts are all that matter,' said Ishmael, 'and the facts weigh in against him.'

'You said yourself the trial isn't over,' Ishmael's mother pointed out. 'The defense hasn't made its case yet, but you're all ready to convict. You've got the prosecutor's set of facts, but that might not be the whole story – it never is, Ishmael. And besides, really, facts are so cold, so horribly cold – can we depend on facts by themselves?'

'What else do we have?' replied Ishmael. 'Everything else is ambiguous. Everything else is emotions and hunches. At least the facts you can cling to; the emotions just float away.'

'Float away with them,' said his mother. 'If you can remember how, Ishmael. If you can find them again. If you haven't gone cold forever.'

She got up and went to the woodstove. He sat in silence with his forehead in his hand, breathing through his nose and suddenly empty – a great, airy space had blown up inside of him, a bubble of ether expanding against his rib cage – he was empty now, emptier than he had been just a moment earlier, before his mother had spoken. What did she know about the vast region of emptiness that inhabited him all of the time? What did she know about him anyway? It was one thing for her to have known him as a child; it was another for her to come to terms with the nature of his adult wounds. She didn't know, finally; he couldn't explain himself. He did not want to explain to her his coldness or reveal himself in any way. He had watched her, after all, mourn her husband's death and it had been for her in part the discovery that grief could attach itself with permanence – something Ishmael had already discovered. It attached itself and then it burrowed inside and made a nest and stayed. It ate whatever was warm nearby, and then the coldness settled in permanently. You learned to live with it.

His mother had gone cold when Arthur died; her grief for him was fixed. But this had not stopped her from taking pleasure in life, it now occurred to Ishmael. There she stood at the stove ladling soup with the calm ease of one who feels there is certainly such a thing as grace. She took pleasure in the soup's smell, in the heat of the woodstove, in the shadow of herself the candlelight now cast against the kitchen wall. The room had gone dark and tranquil now, the one warm place in all the world, and he felt empty in it.

'I'm unhappy,' he said. 'Tell me what to do.'

His mother made no reply at first. Instead she came to the table with his bowl of soup and set it down in front of him. She brought her own bowl to the table, too, and then a loaf of bread on a cutting board and a dish of creamery butter and spoons. 'You're unhappy,' she said, seating herself. She put her elbows down on the table and rested her chin against her palms.

'That you are unhappy, I have to say, is the most obvious thing in the world.'

'Tell me what to do,' repeated Ishmael.

'Tell you what to do?' his mother said. 'I can't tell you what to do, Ishmael. I've tried to understand what it's been like for you – having gone to war, having lost your arm, not having married or had children. I've tried to make sense of it all, believe me, I have – how it must feel to be you. But I must confess that, no matter how I try, I can't really understand you. There are other boys, after all, who went to war and came back home and pushed on with their lives. They found girls and married and had children and raised families despite whatever was behind them. But you – you went numb, Ishmael. And you've stayed numb all these years. And I haven't known what to do or say about it or how I might help you in some way. I've prayed and I've talked to Pastor – '

'There were guys who prayed at Tarawa,' said Ishmael. 'They still got killed, Mother. Just like the guys who didn't pray. It didn't matter either way.'

'But just the same I've prayed for you. I've wanted you to be happy, Ishmael. But I haven't known what to do.'

They ate their soup and bread in silence while the kettle on the wood-stove hissed. The candle on the table cast an arc of light across their food, and outside, through the misty windowpane, the snow on the ground caught the moonlight beyond the clouds and held it so that it suffused everything. Ishmael tried to enjoy the small pleasures of warmth and light and bread. He did not want to tell his mother about Hatsue Miyamoto and how he had, many years ago, felt certain they would be married. He did not want to tell her about the hollow cedar tree where they'd met so many times. He had never told anybody about those days; he had worked hard to forget them. Now the trial had brought all of that back.

'Your father fought at Belleau Wood,' his mother told him suddenly. 'It took him years to get over it. He had nightmares and he suffered just as you do. But it didn't stop him from living.'

'He didn't get over it,' said Ishmael. 'Getting over it isn't possible.'

'It didn't stop him from living,' his mother insisted. 'He went right on with his life. He didn't let self-pity overwhelm him – he just kept on with things.'

'I've kept on,' said Ishmael. 'I've kept his newspaper going, haven't I? I – '

'That isn't what I mean,' his mother said. 'That isn't what I'm getting at. You know as well as I do what I'm trying to say. Why on earth don't you go out with someone? How can you stand your loneliness? You're an attractive man, there are a lot of women who – '

'Let's not go over all of this again,' said Ishmael, putting down his spoon. 'Let's talk about something else.'

'For you, what else is there?' said his mother. 'When it comes down to it – to answer your question – here's what you should do about being unhappy: you should get married and have some children.'

'That isn't going to happen,' said Ishmael. 'That's not the answer to the question.'

'Yes, it is,' said his mother. 'It genuinely, surely is.'

After dinner he lit the kerosene heater and put it in her bedroom. His parents' grandfather clock still ticked away after all these years with a maniacal endurance. It reminded him now of Saturday mornings when his father would read to him under the sheets with the clock thundering in the background. They'd read *Ivanhoe* together, taking turns, and then *David Copperfield*. Now, he saw in his flashlight beam, his mother slept under eiderdown quilts that were just beginning to yellow. He was surprised to find beside her bed the antique RCA turntable that had, until recently, resided in his father's old study. She'd been listening to Mozart's *Jupiter* Symphony as performed by the Vienna Symphony Orchestra in 1947, and Ishmael, seeing it on the turntable, imagined her in bed with that melancholy music playing and a cup of tea beside her. He imagined her with the Mozart on at nine o'clock at night.

He opened the taps in the sink and bathtub and went out to check on her chickens. There were twelve of them, all Rhode Island Reds, huddled into a ball at one end of the chicken house his father had built years before. For a moment Ishmael caught them in the beam of his flashlight; then he reached in and took up a nearby egg left untended in the cold. It was hard to the touch and he knew that inside the embryo was solidly frozen. He warmed it for a moment in the palm of his hand, then rolled it gently in the direction of the chickens. They rearranged themselves in the face of this, panicking and fluttering just a little.

He went back in and, still wearing his coat and hat, wandered through the rooms of the cold house. His breath came forth in jets of fog and disappeared into the darkness. Ishmael put his hand on the newel post at the bottom of the stairway, then removed it and shone the flashlight beam upward. Shallow moons had been worn into the risers; the bannister, he saw, had lost its luster. Upstairs, the room he'd slept in as a boy had been converted by his mother into a place to sew and iron and to store her clothes. Ishmael went up and, sitting on his old bed, tried to remember how it had once been. He recollected that on a good day in winter, when the maple trees stood bare, he could look through his dormer window out beyond the trees and see the green salt water to the southwest.

He'd had a button and a pennant collection, a thousand pennies in a large mason jar, a fishbowl, and a model tin lizzie hung from a strand of wire in one corner. They were all gone now, he didn't know where. He'd kept his glass underwater box in the corner of the closet, his mitt on top of it. On certain nights the moonlight had flooded through his dormer window and bathed everything in blue, beguiling shadows that prevented him from sleeping. He'd sit up listening to crickets and frogs and on some nights to the radio at his bedside. He'd listened mostly to baseball games –

the Seattle Rainiers of the Pacific Coast League – and he could still remember the voice of Leo Lassen barely audible beyond a field of static: '*White leads off first, dancing, dancing, ready to break, he's driving Gittelsohn ab-so-lute-ly crazy. . . . Strange is at the plate now after taking his practice cuts . . . hum, baby, hear this fine crowd on hand at Sick's Stadium greet Strange as he digs in, he's a real favorite, isn't he? Oh, you should be here tonight! Mount Rainier is out beyond the rightfield fence looming up like a great big ice cream cone. Gittelsohn is into his windup now and . . . there goes White no time for a throw White is standing up safe at second base hoooo boy! White is safe! He's stolen second base! White is safe at second base!*'

His father, too, had liked baseball. Ishmael had sat with him by the Bendix in the living room, and they had both been mesmerized by the urgency Leo Lassen imparted to a battle so many miles away in Seattle, Portland, or Sacramento. The voice from the radio – it had dropped an octave, altered pitch, slowed and lengthened measurably – was now that of someone's wayward uncle confiding the secrets of his golf game; now it miraculously glided through a tongue twister; now it suddenly sensed great depths of meaning in an ordinary double play. Arthur would slam the armrest of his chair in satisfaction at a fortunate turn of events; he was saddened when errors in judgment or carelessness cast the team into a hole. At lulls in the game he would stretch his legs out, twine his hands across his lap, and stare at the radio as it spoke to him. Eventually he slept with his head lolled forward and stayed that way until Leo Lassen went shrill again in ecstasy about the game. Freddy Mueller had hit a double.

Ishmael remembered his father half-asleep, the crescent of warm light thrown by the table lamp containing only his figure, that of the radio, and the turned-back pages of a magazine in his lap – *Harper's* or *Scientific Agriculture*. By the late innings of the game the rest of the room – a few laggard coals glowed orange beneath the fireplace grate – lay sleeping in soft, quiescent shadows. Coats hung from polished brass hooks in the foyer, and his father's books, arranged by size, stood neatly along the glassed-in shelves of two vaultlike oak bookcases. When something momentous came to pass – a home run, a stolen base, a double play, a run batted in – his father would stir, blink two or three times, and by dint of habit bring his hand to rest on the spectacles sitting atop his magazine. His hair lay close to his skull in gray twists, and his chin tilted slightly heavenward. Gray hairs sprouted from his ears and nostrils, and more straggled forth from his eyebrows. When the game was over he would shut off the radio and fix his spectacles carefully in place by curling their stems behind his ears. They were antique steel full moons, and when he put them on he invariably underwent a quiet transformation, becoming suddenly professorial, handsome in the way that some outdoorsmen are yet scholarly at the same time. He would pick up his magazine and begin to read as if the game had never happened.

Ishmael's father had died in Seattle at the Veterans Administration Hospital. He'd had cancer of the pancreas and in the end of the liver, and Ishmael had not been there at the final moment. One hundred and seventy islanders turned out for Arthur's funeral, which was held on a warm, cloudless day in June at the San Piedro Memorial Cemetery. Masato Nagaishi, Ishmael recalled, had presented himself in the funeral's aftermath to offer condolences on behalf of the Japanese-American Citizens' League and the Japanese Community Center. 'I wish to say,' said Masato Nagaishi, 'that the Japanese people of San Piedro Island are saddened by the death of your father. We have always had great respect for him as a newspaperman and as a neighbor, a man of great fairness and compassion for others, a friend to us and to all people.' Masato Nagaishi took Ishmael's hand and gripped it in his own tightly. He was a large man with a broad face and no hair on his head, and he blinked often behind his spectacles. 'We know you will follow in your father's footsteps,' Mr. Nagaishi said forcefully, shaking Ishmael's hand. 'We are certain you will honor his legacy. For now, like you, we are all sad. We mourn with you and honor your father. We think of you in your grief.'

Ishmael opened the closet door and looked in at the boxes stacked there. He had not gone through the things he'd packed in them in more than eight years' time. He was no longer very interested in what they contained – his books, his arrowheads, his essays from high school, his pennant collection, his penny jar, his buttons and sea glass and beach stones; they were the things of another time. He had it in mind, though, to dig out the letter Hatsue had written him from Manzanar and read it again after all these years in the spirit of an indulgence. Ever since he'd stopped to pick her up in the snowstorm he'd been indulging himself foolishly. Beneath the surface of everything else he'd been thinking about her with pleasure.

It was buried in a box, just where he'd left it, between the pages of a book on boatmanship he'd been given on his thirteenth birthday. The return address on the envelope was Kenny Yamashita's, and the stamp, curiously, was upside down. The envelope, now brittle with age, felt dry and cold to the touch. Ishmael tucked the flashlight under his armpit and sat down again on the edge of the bed with the envelope held between his fingers. The letter inside had been written on rice paper that after all these years was fast deteriorating, and he held it with the care he felt it deserved, moving it now into the flashlight beam, where he saw her delicate handwriting.

Dear Ishmael,

These things are very difficult to say – I can't think of anything more painful to me than writing this letter to you. I am now more than five hundred miles away, and everything appears to me different from what it was when I was with you last on San Piedro. I have been trying to think clearly about everything and to use all this distance to advantage. And here is what I've discovered.

I don't love you, Ishmael. I can think of no more honest way to say it. From the very beginning, when we were little children, it seemed to me something was wrong. Whenever we were together I knew it. I felt it inside of me. I loved you and I didn't love you at the very same moment, and I felt troubled and confused. Now, everything is obvious to me and I feel I have to tell you the truth. When we met that last time in the cedar tree and I felt your body move against mine, I knew with certainty that everything was wrong. I knew we could never be right together and that soon I would have to tell you so. And now, with this letter, I'm telling you. This is the last time I will write to you. I am not yours anymore.

I wish you the very best, Ishmael. Your heart is large and you are gentle and kind, and I know you will do great things in this world, but now I must say good-bye to you. I am going to move on with my life as best I can, and I hope that you will too.

Sincerely,
Hatsue Imada

He read it over a second time, and then a third, and then he turned off the flashlight. He thought of how she'd had her revelation at the very moment he'd entered her, how the invasion of his penis had brought with it a truth she could discover in no other way. Ishmael shut his eyes and thought back to that moment in the cedar tree when he had moved, briefly, inside of her and how he had not been able to predict how pleasurable that would feel. He had no way of knowing what it would feel like to be inside, all the way in where he could feel the heat of her, and his surprise at the sensation had been overwhelming, and then she had suddenly pulled away. He had not come, he had been there for less than three seconds altogether, and in that time – if her letter was right – she'd discovered she didn't love him anymore while he'd come to love her even more. Wasn't that the strangest part? That by entering her he'd granted her the means to understand the truth? He'd wanted to be inside of her again, and he'd wanted her to ask him to be there again, and on the next day she'd gone away.

In his Seattle years he'd slept with three different women, two of whom he felt briefly hopeful about, wondering if he might in fact fall in love with them, but this had never happened. The women he slept with asked often about his arm, and he told them about his war experiences, and he decided before long that he didn't respect them and a kind of disgust developed. He was a war veteran with a missing arm, and this fascinated a certain type of woman in her early twenties who fancied herself mature beyond her years and was serious about herself. He slept with each for a few more weeks after deciding he wanted nothing to do with them – he slept with them angrily and unhappily and because he was lonely and selfish. He came inside them hard and often, keeping each up until the middle of the night, and in the late afternoons, too, before dinner. He knew that when he asked them to walk out of his life he would be even lonelier than he'd been before, and so he waited for a few weeks, both times, just to have someone around at night, just to come inside someone, just to hear someone breathing under him while he moved his hips with his eyes shut. Then his father came down to the city because he was dying, and Ishmael forgot about women. His father died one afternoon while Ishmael was in the newsroom at the *Seattle Times* banging away with his five fingers at a typewriter. Ishmael went back to San Piedro for the funeral and to tie up his father's business affairs; he stayed to run his father's paper. He lived in an apartment in Amity Harbor and kept to himself insofar as that was possible for a newspaperman on a small island. Once every two weeks or so he masturbated into the folds of his handkerchief, and that was the extent of his sex life.

Yes, he decided, he would write the article Hatsue wanted him to write in the pages of the *San Piedro Review*. It was perhaps not the manner in which his father would proceed, but so be it: he was not his father. His father, of course, would have gone hours earlier directly to Lew Fielding in order to show him the coast guard shipping lane records for the night of September 15. But not Ishmael, not now – no. Those records would stay in his pocket. Tomorrow he would write the article she wanted him to write, in order to make her beholden to him, and then in the trial's aftermath he would speak with her as one who had taken her side and she would have no choice but to listen. That was the way, that was the method. Sitting by himself in the cold of his old bedroom, her letter held uneasily in his hand, he began to imagine it.

25

At eight in the morning on the third day of the trial – a dozen tall candles now lighting the courtroom in the manner of a chapel or sanctuary – Nels Gudmundsson called his first witness. The wife of the accused man, Hatsue Miyamoto, came forward from the last row of seats in the gallery with her hair tightly bound to the back of her head and tucked up under an unadorned hat that threw a shadow over her eyes. As she passed through the swinging gate Nels Gudmundsson held open for her she stopped to look for a moment at her husband, who sat at the defendant's table immediately to her left with his hands folded neatly in front of him. She nodded without altering her calm expression, and her husband nodded back in silence. He unclasped his hands, laid them on the table, and watched her eyes intently. The wife of the accused man appeared, briefly, as if she might turn in his direction and go to him, but instead she proceeded without hurry toward Ed Soames, who stood in front of the witness stand proffering the Old Testament patiently.

When Hatsue Miyamoto had seated herself, Nels Gudmundsson coughed three times into his fist and cleared the phlegm from his throat. Then he passed in front of the jury box with his thumbs once again hooked inside of his suspenders and his one good eye leaking tears. The arteries in his temples had begun to pulse, as they often did when he'd been sleepless. Like others there he'd passed a difficult night with no electricity or heat. At two-thirty, bitter with cold, he'd struck a match and held it close to the face of his pocket watch; he'd padded in his socks to the unlit bathroom and found the toilet water frozen in its bowl. Nels, flailing, his breath issuing forth in vaporous grunts, had

314

broken out the ice with the handle of his toilet plunger, propped himself against the wall – his lumbago plagued him mercilessly – and dribbled night water unsteadily. Then he'd climbed into bed again, curled up like an autumn leaf, every blanket in the house thrown over him, and lain without sleeping until dawn came. Now, in the courtroom, the jurors could see that he had not shaved or combed his hair; he looked at least ten years older. His blind left pupil seemed especially transient and beyond his control this morning. It traveled in its own eccentric orbit.

The gallery was as crowded as it had been throughout the trial. Many of the citizens gathered there wore overcoats, shoe rubbers, and woolen scarfs, having elected not to leave these things in the cloakroom: there'd been a rush to find a place to sit. They'd carried the smell of wet snow into the room – it had melted against the wool in their coats – and were grateful to be in a warm place where something of interest was going forward. Stuffing their mittens and wool caps into their pockets, they settled in conscious of their extraordinary good fortune in having escaped temporarily from the snowstorm. As always their demeanor was formally respectful; they took the law seriously and felt its majesty emanating toward them from the bench where Lew Fielding sat with his eyes halfshut, inscrutable and meditative, and from the way in which the jurors sat ruminating in rows on their elevated podium. The reporters, for their part, had focused their attention on the wife of the accused man, who wore a knife-pleated skirt on this day and a blouse with long darts through the shoulders. Her hand where it lay atop the Bible was graceful, and the planes of her face were smooth. One of the reporters – he'd lived in Japan just after the war, training automotive engineers to write manuals – was reminded of the calm of a geisha he'd witnessed performing the tea ceremony at Nara. The sight of Hatsue's face in profile elicited in him the smell of pine needles strewn in the courtyard outside the tearoom.

But inwardly Hatsue felt no serenity; her calm was a practiced disguise. For her husband, she knew, was a mystery to her, and had been ever since he'd returned from his days as a soldier nine years before. He'd come home to San Piedro, and they'd rented a cottage out on Bender's Spring Road. It was a dead-end road overhung with alders; they could see no other homes. At night Kabuo was subject to disturbing dreams that sent him to the kitchen table in his slippers and bathrobe, where he sat drinking tea and staring. Hatsue found that she was married to a war veteran and that this was the crucial fact of her marriage; the war had elicited in him a persistent guilt that lay over his soul like a shadow. For her this meant loving him in a manner she hadn't anticipated before he'd left for the war. There was nothing of charity in it and she did not step lightly around his heart or indulge his sorrow or his whims. Instead she brought herself to his sorrow completely, not to console him but to give him time to become himself again. Without regrets she honored the obligation she felt to him and was happy to efface herself. This gave her life a shape and meaning that were larger than her dream of farming strawberries from island soil, and at the same time giving herself over to his wounds was both disturbing and rewarding. She sat across from him at the kitchen table at three o'clock in the morning, while he stared in silence or talked or wept, and she took when she could a piece of his sorrow and stored it for him in her own heart.

The advent of her pregnancy had been good for Kabuo; he'd taken a job at the cannery, where he packed salmon beside his brother Kenji. He began to talk about buying a farm and drove her up and down island roads where property was for sale. Something was wrong with each, however – drainage, sunlight, clay soil. Kabuo pulled into a turnout one rainy afternoon and explained to her in grave tones that he intended to repurchase his parents' property as soon as the chance arose. He told the story, once again, of how they had been within one last payment of owning the seven acres outright. How Etta Heine had pulled out from under them and sold their land to Ole Jurgensen. How the land was to have gone over into his name, because he was the eldest son and the first of the Miyamotos to become a citizen.

They'd lost everything because of Manzanar. His father had died of stomach cancer; his mother had gone to live in Fresno, where Kabuo's sister had married a furniture merchant. Kabuo struck the steering wheel with the side of his fist and cursed the injustice of the world. 'They stole from us,' he said angrily, 'and they got away with it.'

One night six months after his return from the war she woke up to find him gone from their bed and nowhere to be found in the house. Hatsue sat in the dark of the kitchen, where she waited for seventy-five minutes uneasily; it was raining outside, a windy night, and the car was gone from the garage.

She waited. She ran her hands across her belly, imagining the shape of the baby inside, hoping to feel it move. There was a leak in the shed roof over the pantry, and she got up to empty the pan she'd placed under it. Sometime after four A.M. Kabuo came in with two burlap sacks; he was rain soaked, there was mud on his knees. He turned on the light to find her there, sitting motionless at the kitchen table, staring at him in silence. Kabuo, staring back, set one sack on the floor, hauled the other up onto a chair, and took the hat from his head. 'After Pearl Harbor,' he said to her, 'my father buried all of this.' Then he began to pull things out – wooden swords, *hakama* pants, a *bokken*, a *naginata*, scrolls written in Japanese – and placed each carefully on the kitchen table. 'These are my family's,' he said to her, wiping the rain from his brow. 'My father hid them in our strawberry fields. Look at this,' he added.

It was a photograph of Kabuo dressed like a *bugeisha* and wielding a *kendo* stick in both hands. In the photograph he was only sixteen years old, but he already looked wrathful and fierce. Hatsue studied the photograph for a long time, particularly Kabuo's eyes and mouth, to see what she might discern there. 'My great-grandfather,' said Kabuo, pulling off his coat, 'was a samurai and a magnificent soldier. He killed himself on the battlefield at Kumamoto – killed himself with his own sword, *seppukku*' – Kabuo pantomimed disemboweling himself, the imaginary sword plunged deep into his left side and drawn steadily to the right. 'He came to battle wielding a samurai's sword against the rifles of an imperial garrison. Try to imagine that, Hatsue,' said Kabuo. 'Going to battle with a sword against rifles. Knowing you are going to die.'

He'd knelt beside the wet sack on the floor then and took a strawberry plant from it. The rain bellowed against the roof and struck against the side of their house. Kabuo took out another strawberry plant and brought them both into the light over the table where she could look at them closely if she wanted to. He held them out to her, and she saw how the veins and arteries in his arms flowed in ridges just beneath his skin and how strong his wrists and fingers were.

'My father planted the fathers of these plants,' Kabuo said to her angrily. 'We lived as children by the fruit they produced. Do you understand what I am saying?'

'Come to bed,' answered Hatsue. 'Take a bath, dry yourself, and come back to bed,' she said.

She got up and left the kitchen table. She knew that he could see in profile the new shape their baby was making. 'You're going to be a father soon,' she reminded him, halting in the doorway. 'I hope that will make you happy, Kabuo. I hope it will help you to bury all of this. I don't know how else I can help you.'

'I'll get the farm back,' Kabuo had answered over the din of the rain. 'We'll live there. We'll grow strawberries. It will be all right. I'm going to get my farm back.'

That had been many years ago – nine years, or nearly. They'd saved their money insofar as that was possible, putting away as much as they could, until they had enough to buy their own house. Hatsue wanted to move from the dilapidated cottage they rented at the end of Bender's Spring Road, but Kabuo had convinced her the better move was to purchase a gill-netting boat. Within a year or two, he said, they would double their money, own the boat outright, and have enough left over for a land payment. Ole Jurgensen was getting old, he said. He would want to sell before long.

Kabuo had fished as well as he could but he was not really born to fish. There was money in fishing and he wanted the money, he was ambitious, strong, and a zealous worker, but the sea, in the end, made no sense to him. They had not doubled their money or even come close, and they did not own the *Islander* outright. Kabuo only pressed himself harder and measured his life according to his success at bringing salmon home. On every night that he did not catch fish he felt his dream recede before him and the strawberry farm he coveted moved further into the distance. He blamed himself and grew short with her, and this deepened the wounds in their marriage. Hatsue felt she did him no favors by indulging his self-pity, and he resented her for this. It was difficult for her to distinguish these moments from the deeper anguish of his war wounds. Besides, she had three children now, and it was necessary to turn her attention toward them and to give to them a part of what she had once given to her husband. The children, she hoped, would soften him. She hoped that through them he might become less obsessed with the dream of a different life. She knew that had happened in her own heart.

Yes, it would be nice to live in a nicer house and to walk out into the perfume of berries on a June morning, to stand in the wind and smell them. But this house and this life were what she had, and there was no point in perpetually grasping for something other. Gently she tried to tell him so, but Kabuo insisted that just around the corner lay a different life and a better one, that it was simply a matter of catching more salmon, of waiting for Ole Jurgensen to slow down, of saving their money, of waiting.

Now Hatsue sat upright with her hands in her lap in order to give her testimony. 'I'm going to ask you to think back,' said Nels, 'to events that occurred about three months ago, in early September of this year. Would it be fair to say that at that time your husband became interested in purchasing land that was for sale at Island Center? Do you recollect, Mrs. Miyamoto?'

319

'Oh, yes,' answered Hatsue. 'He was very interested in buying land out there. He had always been interested in buying land out there. It had been his family's land – strawberry land – and he badly wanted to farm it again. His family had worked very hard to buy it, and then, during the war, they lost everything, their land was taken from them.'

'Mrs. Miyamoto,' said Nels. 'Think back specifically now to Tuesday, September 7, if you will do that for me. A Mr. Ole Jurgensen, you might recall, a retired strawberry farmer from out at Island Center, has testified that your husband came to see him on that date to inquire about purchasing seven acres of his land, the strawberry land you mentioned. Does this ring a bell with you?'

'It does,' said Hatsue. 'I know about it.'

Nels nodded and began to knead his forehead; he sat down on the edge of the defendant's table. 'Did your husband mention he'd gone out there? Did he tell you about his conversation with Mr. Jurgensen regarding the purchase of these seven acres?'

'Yes,' said Hatsue. 'He did.'

'Did he say anything about this conversation? Anything you can remember?'

'He did,' said Hatsue. 'Yes.'

Hatsue recounted that on the afternoon of September 7 she'd driven with her children past the old farm at Island Center and seen Ole Jurgensen's sign. She'd turned the car around and driven over Mill Run into Amity Harbor, where she used the public telephone booth beside Petersen's to call her husband and tell him. Then she'd gone home and waited for an hour until Kabuo returned with the unhappy news that Carl Heine had purchased Ole's farm.

'I see,' said Nels. 'This unhappy news – this was on the evening of September 7 that your husband told you about this?'

'Afternoon,' said Hatsue. 'We talked about it in the late afternoon, I remember, before he went out fishing.'

'Late afternoon,' Nels repeated. 'Did your husband seem

disappointed, Mrs. Miyamoto, that he had not succeeded in purchasing his seven acres? Did he seem to you disappointed?'

'No,' said Hatsue. 'He was not disappointed. He was hopeful, Mr. Gudmundsson, as hopeful as I'd seen him. To his way of thinking the important thing was that Ole Jurgensen had decided to retire from farming strawberries and sell off all his holdings. Something, he said, had been set in motion – there'd been no opportunity, now there was one. He'd waited many years for this moment to arrive – now the opportunity was at hand. He was very eager, very hopeful?'

'Let's skip forward one day,' said Nels, raising his head from his hand. 'On the next day, September 8, did he talk about it? Was he still feeling, as you say, hopeful?'

'Oh, yes,' answered Hatsue. 'Very much so. We talked about it again the following day. He'd decided to go have a talk with Carl Heine, to see him about purchasing the seven acres.'

'But he didn't go. Until the next day. He waited a day, is that right?'

'He waited,' said Hatsue. 'He was nervous about it. He wanted to plan what he would say.'

'It's now Thursday, September 9,' Nels Gudmundsson said to her. 'It's two days since your husband spoke with Ole Jurgensen; two long days have passed. What, as you recall it, happened?'

'What happened?'

'He went to talk to Carl Heine – am I correct? – as Susan Marie Heine testified yesterday. According to Susan Marie Heine's testimony your husband showed up at their residence on the afternoon of Thursday, September 9, asking to talk to Carl. According to Susan Marie Heine they spoke for thirty or forty minutes as they walked about the property. She did not accompany them or overhear their words, but she has testified as to the content of a conversation she held with her husband after your husband left that day. She said that the two of them had discussed the seven acres and the possibility that your husband might purchase them. Susan Marie Heine has testified under cross-examination that Carl did not give your husband an unequivocal no answer regarding the purchase of these seven acres. Carl did not lead your husband to believe no hope existed for reclaiming his family's property. It was her understanding that Carl had encouraged your husband to believe that a possibility existed. Now, does that seem accurate to you, Mrs. Miyamoto? On the afternoon of September 9, in the aftermath of his talk with Carl Heine, did your husband still seem hopeful?'

'More hopeful than ever,' said Hatsue. 'He came home from his conversation with Carl Heine more hopeful and more eager than ever. He told me that he felt closer to getting the family land back than he had in a long, long time. I felt hopeful, too, at that point. I was hopeful it would all work out.'

Nels pushed himself upright again and began, slowly, to pace before the jurors, brooding in silence for a moment. In the quiet the wind pushed against the window sashes; steam hissed and boiled through the radiators. With no overhead lights the courtroom, always pallid, seemed grayer and duller than ever. The smell of snow was in the air.

'You say, Mrs. Miyamoto, that you felt hopeful. And yet, as you well know, the deceased man's mother and your husband over there were not on the best of terms. There had been, shall we say, words between them. So on what grounds did you hold out hope, if I might ask? What made you optimistic?'

Yes, said Hatsue, she understood this question. She'd brought it up with Kabuo herself: would such people agree to sell him the land they'd once stolen so eagerly? 'Etta and Carl are two different people,' Kabuo had replied to this. It was up to Carl, not his mother, this time. And Carl had been his friend long ago. Carl would do what was right.

'Mrs. Miyamoto,' Nels continued. 'Your husband had his conversation with Carl Heine on the afternoon of Thursday, September 9. On the following Thursday, September 16, Carl Heine was found drowned in his fishing net out in White Sand Bay. A week intervened between the two events – six full days passed, and seven nights. A full week, or nearly a week anyway.

322

My question is whether during this week your husband spoke to you about Carl Heine or the seven acres in question. If he said anything to you about the seven acres or about his attempts to reacquire them. Do you recall your husband having spoken about this or having done anything pertinent to reacquiring his family's land during the week between the ninth and the sixteenth?'

Well, explained Hatsue, Kabuo felt there was nothing to do, that the next move was Carl's, that it was Carl who had to come forward. It was Carl who had to think about things and come to some conclusion. It was Carl's heart that was now in question, whether he wanted to redress a wrong his own mother had perpetrated. Did Carl feel responsible for the actions of his family? Did he understand his obligations? It was dishonorable, anyway, added Kabuo, to approach Carl once again with the same tired question; he did not wish to beg, to place himself at Carl's mercy. He did not wish to appear weak in Carl's presence or reveal a humiliating eagerness. No, it was best to be patient in such a matter. There was nothing to be gained by putting oneself forward or revealing oneself too fully. He would wait instead. He would wait one week, he explained to Hatsue, and then he would decide what to do.

On the morning of the sixteenth, while she boiled tea water, he pushed through the door in his rubber boots and rubber bib overalls and explained how he had seen Carl out at sea, helped Carl with a dead battery in the fog, and the two of them had shaken about the matter. They'd come to an agreement about the seven acres. Eighty-four hundred dollars, eight hundred down. The Miyamotos' land was Kabuo's again, after all these years.

But later that day, at one o'clock in the afternoon, a clerk at Petersen's – it was Jessica Porter – told Hatsue about the terrible accident that had befallen Carl Heine while he fished the preceding evening. He'd been found tangled in his net, dead, out in White Sand Bay.

26

Alvin Hooks began his cross-examination by perching himself on the edge of the prosecutor's table and crossing his well-shined shoes in front of him as though he were relaxing on a street corner. His hands in his lap, his fingers intertwined, he cocked his head to the right for a moment and studied Hatsue Miyamoto. 'You know,' he said, 'it's been interesting hearing from you. On this matter of the morning of the sixteenth in particular. This story you've just told us about boiling tea water when the defendant burst through your kitchen door, just terribly excited, and told you about his conversation at sea, how he and Carl Heine came to some sort of agreement? I found this all quite interesting.'

He stopped and studied her for another moment. Then he began to nod. He scratched his head and turned his eyes toward the ceiling. 'Mrs. Miyamoto,' he sighed. 'Was I fair just now in describing your husband's state of mind as "terribly excited" on the morning of the sixteenth – the morning Carl Heine was murdered? Have I by any chance misinterpreted your testimony? Did he come home on that morning "terribly excited"?'

'I would use that phrase, yes,' said Hatsue. 'He was terribly excited, certainly.'

'He didn't seem himself? His state of mind was – agitated? He seemed to you somehow . . . different?'

'Excited,' answered Hatsue. 'Not agitated. He was excited about getting his family's land back.'

'All right, so he was "excited",' Alvin Hooks said. 'And he told you this story about stopping at sea to help Carl

Heine with a . . . dead battery or something. Is that correct, Mrs. Miyamoto?'

'That's correct.'

'He said that he tied up to Carl Heine's boat and came aboard to loan Carl a battery?'

'That's right.'

'And that in the course of this charitable maneuver on his part he and Carl discussed the seven acres they'd been arguing about until that point? Is that right? And that somehow Carl agreed to sell it to him? For eighty-four hundred dollars or something? Is that all correct? Do I have it right?'

'You do,' said Hatsue. 'That's what happened.'

'Mrs. Miyamoto,' said Alvin Hooks. 'Did you, by any chance, repeat this story to anyone? Did you, for example, call a friend or a relative to deliver the happy news? Did you let your friends and family know that your husband had come to terms with Carl Heine in the middle of the night on his fishing boat – that you would soon be moving to seven acres of strawberry land, starting a new life, anything like that?'

'No,' said Hatsue. 'I didn't.'

'Why not?' asked Alvin Hooks. 'Why didn't you tell anyone? It seems like the sort of thing that would constitute news. It would seem you might tell your mother, for example, or your sisters, perhaps – someone.'

Hatsue adjusted herself in her chair and brushed uneasily at her blouse front. 'Well,' she said. 'We heard about how Carl Heine had . . . passed away just a few hours after Kabuo came home. Carl's accident – that changed how we thought. It meant there was nothing to tell anyone. Everything was up in the air again.'

'Everything was up in the air,' said Alvin Hooks, settling his arms across his chest. 'When you heard that Carl Heine had died, you decided not to talk about the matter? Is that what you're saying, am I correct?'

'You're misinterpreting,' complained Hatsue. 'We just – '

'I'm not interpreting or misinterpreting,' Alvin Hooks cut

in. 'I merely want to know what the facts are – we all want to know what the facts are, Mrs. Miyamoto, that's what we're doing here. You're under oath to give us the facts, so please, ma'am, if I might ask again, did you decide not to talk about your husband's night at sea, his encounter with Carl Heine? Did you decide not to talk about this matter?'

'There was nothing to talk about,' said Hatsue. 'What news could I announce to my family? Everything was up in the air.'

'Worse than up in the air,' said Alvin Hooks. 'On top of your husband's real estate deal going sour, a man, we might note, had died. A man had died, let us understand, the side of his skull bashed in. Did it occur to you, Mrs. Miyamoto, to come forward with the information you had about this and notify the sheriff? Did you ever think it might be proper to share what you knew, your husband's night at sea, this battery business, and so on and so forth, with the sheriff of Island County?'

'We thought about it, yes,' said Hatsue. 'We talked about it all afternoon that day, if we should go to the sheriff and tell him, if we should talk about things. But in the end we decided not to, you see – it looked very bad, it looked like murder, Kabuo and I understood that. We understood that he could end up here, on trial, and that's exactly what has happened. That's exactly how it has turned out, you see. You've charged my husband with murder.'

'Well, of course,' said Alvin Hooks. 'I can see how you felt. I can see how you might be very concerned that your husband would be charged with murder. But if, as you imply, the truth was on your side, what in the world were you worried about? Why, if the truth was really with you – why on earth, Mrs. Miyamoto – why not go immediately to the sheriff and tell him everything you know?'

'We were afraid,' said Hatsue. 'Silence seemed better. To come forward seemed like a mistake.'

'Well,' said Alvin Hooks, 'that's an irony. Because the mistake, it seems to me, was in *not* coming forward. The

326

mistake was in your having been deceitful. In having deliberately concealed information during the course of a sheriff's
investigation.'

'Maybe,' said Hatsue. 'I don't know.'

'But it *was* a mistake,' said Alvin Hooks, pointing a forefinger
at her. 'A very serious error in judgment, don't you think, in
retrospect? Here we have a death under suspicious circumstances, the sheriff is out and about gathering information,
and you're not coming forward to help. You're in a position
to be of assistance and you're not coming forth or being honest.
Frankly, it makes you suspect, Mrs. Miyamoto, I'm sorry to say
it but it's true. If you can't be trusted to come forward at such a
time with what you know, with vital information, how can we
trust you now – you see? How on earth can we trust you?'

'But,' said Hatsue, leaning forward in her chair, 'there wasn't
time to come forward. We heard about Carl's accident in the
afternoon. Within hours of that, my husband was arrested.
There just wasn't very much time.'

'But Mrs. Miyamoto,' Alvin Hooks replied. 'If in fact you felt
it was an accident, why not come forward immediately? Why
not come forward that very afternoon and tell the good sheriff
what you know about this *accident*? Why not help him with the
details of his investigation? Why not lend him a hand? Why not
tell him your husband had boarded Carl Heine's boat to help him
with – what was it now? – a dead battery, was that it? I hope you
can understand how I just have to say that I just don't understand
this at all. I'm stumped, I'm confused, I'm completely at a loss.
I don't know what to believe and what not to believe. I'm at a
loss with all of this, I really am.'

Alvin Hooks tugged at the seams of his pants, rose and
swiveled around the edge of the table, then settled in his
chair and pressed his palms together. 'No more questions,
Your Honor,' he said abruptly. 'The witness is through. She
may step down.'

'Wait a minute,' answered Hatsue Miyamoto. 'I – '

'That's enough, you'll stop right there,' Judge Fielding cut in

327

sternly. He glared without wavering at the wife of the accused man, and she glared at him in return. 'You've answered the questions put to you, Mrs. Miyamoto. I understand that you must be upset, but your state of mind, your emotional condition, these are not considerations I can legally contemplate under the rules governing these proceedings. The fact that you wish to speak, that you would like to give Mr. Hooks over there a piece of your mind just now – I don't blame you for having strong feelings – this just isn't allowed. You've answered the questions put to you and now, I'm afraid, you must step down. I'm afraid you have no other choice.'

Hatsue turned toward her husband. He nodded at her, and she nodded back, and in the next moment she composed herself deliberately. She stood up without saying another word and went to her seat at the rear of the courthouse where, adjusting her hat, she sat down. A few citizens in the gallery – including Ishmael Chambers – turned impulsively to look at her, but she made no move to acknowledge them. She stared straight ahead and said nothing.

Nels Gudmundsson called Josiah Gillanders, the president of the San Piedro Gill-Netters Association, a man of forty-nine with a walrus mustache and the watery, dull eyes of an alcoholic. Short, broad, and powerful, Josiah had fished alone for thirty years from the cockpit of his boat, the *Cape Eliza*. Islanders knew him as a nautical sot who affected the gait and mannerisms of a sea captain: he tipped his captain's hard-billed blue cap wherever he went on San Piedro. He wore wool dungarees and shetland sweaters and often got *dead mucked* – his term – with Captain Jon Soderland at the San Piedro Tavern. The two of them would trade stories in voices that grew louder with each pint of beer they hoisted. Captain Soderland would stroke his beard; Josiah would wipe the froth from his mustache and clap the captain on the shoulder blade.

Now, on the witness stand, he held his hard-billed captain's hat between his fingers, crossed his arms over his barrel chest, and pointed his cleft chin at Nels Gudmundsson, who wavered unsteadily before him, blinking.

'Mr. Gillanders,' Nels said. 'How long have you been president of the San Piedro Gill-Netters Association?'

'Eleven years,' Josiah answered. 'Been fishing thirty, though.'

'Fishing for salmon?'

'Yes. Mostly.'

'On board a gill-netter, Mr. Gillanders? Thirty years an island gill-netter?'

'That's correct. Thirty years.'

'Your boat,' said Nels. 'The *Cape Eliza*. Ever had a hand aboard?'

Josiah shook his head. 'Never,' he said. 'I work alone. Always have, always will. I fish by myself, like it.'

'Mr. Gillanders,' Nels said. 'In your thirty years of fishing have you ever had occasion to board another man's boat, sir? Have you ever, while at sea, tied up to another gill-netter and come aboard for any reason?'

'Just about never,' said Josiah Gillanders, primping his mustache as he spoke. 'Maybe, at best, a half-dozen times in all my years – half-dozen times, no more 'n that. Five or six – that's all.'

'Five or six times,' Nels said. 'Can you recall for us, Mr. Gillanders, what occasioned these at-sea boardings? Do you remember what your purpose might have been, on each of these occasions, for tying up to another man's boat? Can you recollect for the benefit of the court?'

Josiah worked on his mustache again; it was a habit of his when he was thinking. ''Thout going into too much detail, I guess it was always some fellow was broke down. Some fellow had engine problems or couldn't run and needed help. Or – all right now – there was one fellow needed a hand with things on account of he'd broke his hip, I believe it was. I tied up and boarded on that one, too. Helped him out, got things squared away. But 'thout going into too much detail, you board, see, in an emergency. You board if a fellow needs a hand.'

'You board if a fellow needs a hand,' said Nels. 'In your thirty years of gill-netting, Mr. Gillanders, have you ever boarded another man's boat for some reason other than an emergency? For some reason other than the fact that the fellow on the other boat, as you say, needs a hand?'

'Never,' said Josiah. 'Fishing's fishing. Let 'em fish and don't bother me neither. We all got work to do.'

'Yes,' said Nels. 'And in your thirty years of gill-netting, sir, and in your capacity as president of the association – as a man who reviews, I would presume, various incidents between gill-netters at sea – have you ever heard of a boarding for a reason other than an emergency? Can you recall any such thing?'

'Doesn't happen,' said Josiah. 'Unwritten rule of the sea, Mr. Gudmundsson. Code of honor among fishermen. You keep to yourself and I'll keep to myself. We got nothing to say to one another out there. We're busy working, got no time for jawing, can't sit on the deck drinking rum and telling stories while someone else hauls fish. No, you don't board for no other reason than a good one – other guy's in need, he's got an emergency, his engine ain't running, his leg's broke. Then, go on ahead and board.'

'You don't suppose, then,' Nels asked, 'that the defendant here, Mr. Miyamoto, would have boarded Carl Heine's boat on September 16 for any reason other than to help him in an emergency? Does that make sense to you?'

'I never heard of no boarding for no other reason, if that's what you're asking, Mr. Gudmundsson. Only kind I know about is what I said – a man's got engine problems, his leg's broke.'

Nels set himself down precariously against the edge of the defendant's table. With a forefinger he attempted to check the erratic movement of his bad eye, but to no avail; it continued. 'Mr. Gillanders,' he said. 'Isn't it tricky to tie up at sea? Even in calm weather, in good light?'

'A bit,' said Josiah. 'It can be.'

'A night tie-up on open water? Can this be done speedily, in the manner of an attack? Could a man who wanted to make a boarding against another's will even do so? Is it possible?'

'Never heard of it,' replied Josiah, throwing up his hands. 'Two willing skippers helps mightily, yes. Takes a bit of maneuvering, you see. Tying up against another man's will – I'd think that impossible, Mr. Gudmundsson. I never heard of no such thing.'

'You've never heard of one gill-netter boarding another's boat against his will, sir? You see such an act as physically impossible? Is that an accurate summary of what you've told us? Am I getting all of this right?'

'You're getting it right,' Josiah Gillanders said. 'Can't be done. The other man'd throw you off. Wouldn't let you line up, tie off.'

'Only in an emergency,' said Nels. 'There'd be no other logical reason for boarding. Is that correct, Mr. Gillanders?'

'That's correct. Emergency boardings. I never heard of no other kind.'

'Supposing you wanted to kill a man,' Nels said emphatically. 'Do you think you'd try boarding his boat against his will and hitting him with your fishing gaff? You're a man with many years of experience at sea, so I'm asking you to imagine this. Would that plan be a sensible one, a good one, in your estimation, sir? Would you think it workable to tie up to his boat and board him for the purpose of committing murder? Or would you try something else, some other approach, something other than a forced boarding in the fog on the open sea, in the middle of the night, against the other man's will – what do you think, Mr. Gillanders?'

'You couldn't board him if he didn't want you to,' Josiah answered. 'I just don't see that happening. Carl Heine in particular. He wouldn't be an easy man to board against – darn tough, big, and strong. There's just no way, Mr. Gudmundsson, that Miyamoto here could have made a forced boarding. It just isn't possible. He didn't do that.'

'It isn't possible,' Nels said. 'In your estimation, as a veteran gillnetter, as president of the San Piedro Gill – Netters Association, it isn't possible that the defendant boarded Carl Heine's boat for the purpose of committing murder? The problem of a forced boarding precludes that – makes it impossible?'

'Miyamoto there didn't board Carl Heine against his will,' Josiah Gillanders said. 'Tie-up's too tricky, and Carl was no slouch. Had to be, if he boarded at all, some kind of emergency, engine problem or something. Battery, that's what his missus said. Carl had battery problems.'

'All right,' said Nels. 'Battery problems. Let's say you had a battery problem. You couldn't run. No lights. You're dead in the water. What would you do about it, Mr. Gillanders? Would you, say, put a spare in?'

'Don't carry a spare,' Josiah answered. 'Be like carrying a spare in your car. Just doesn't happen much, does it?'

'But, Mr. Gillanders,' said Nels Gudmundsson. 'If you will recall from the county sheriff's testimony, as well as from his written report, there was, in fact, a spare on board Carl Heine's boat when it was found adrift in White Sand Bay. There was a D-8 and a D-6 in his battery well, in use, and a D-8 sitting on the floor of his cabin – a third battery, albeit dead, which might presumably be thought of as a spare.'

'Well,' said Josiah. 'All of that's mighty strange. Three batteries – that's mighty strange. A dead spare – that's mighty strange, too. Everybody I know runs off two batteries, a main and the other, an auxiliary. One goes bad you can run off the other 'til you get to the docks again. And something else here, a D-8 and a D-6 side by side in the well – I never heard of that before neither, in all my time on the water. I never heard of no such arrangement – a guy'd use just one size battery – and I don't think Carl Heine would've run that way, you see, so irregular and all. I think Mrs. Miyamoto there had it true – Carl had battery problems, probably pulled his D-8, set it on his cabin floor dead, and borrowed a D-6 from Miyamoto, who ran off his other the rest of the night – that's the most likely explanation.'

'I see,' said Nels. 'Say you're dead in the water and in need of help. What would be your next move?'

'I'd get on the radio,' said Josiah. 'Or I'd hail somebody in sight distance. Or if my net was set and I was doing all right I'd wait for somebody to come into sight distance and hail them at that point.'

'Your first choice would be the radio?' Nels asked. 'You'd call for help on your radio? But if your battery's dead do you even *have* a radio? What's powering it, Mr. Gillanders, sir, what's powering your radio if you have no battery? Can you really put a call out on your radio?'

'You're right,' said Josiah Gillanders. 'Radio's dead. I can't call. You're dead to rights.'

'So what do you do?' Nels asked. 'You hail someone, if it isn't too foggy. But if it is foggy, as it was on the night Carl Heine drowned – sometime on the morning of September 16, a very foggy morning, you might recall – well then, you have to hope – don't you? – that someone passes closely by, and you have to hail whoever it is, because the chances of your seeing another boat are not too good, are they? You have to take whatever help comes along because otherwise you're in big trouble.'

'You're straight all the way,' said Josiah Gillanders. 'Spot like that, you'd better get some help, drifting along in the fog and all, right up next to the shipping lanes out there at Ship Channel Bank. Dangerous spot to be dead in the water. Big freighters come right through all the time. You'd better get yourself some help if you can – whoever, like you say, shows up out of the fog when you start blowing on your horn. All right, I'm ahead of you on this one,' Josiah added. 'Carl'd have aboard a compressed-air horn, see. He didn't need no battery to give his emergency blow. He'd be out there with his hand horn blowing away. He didn't need no battery to blow his horn.'

'Well,' said Nels. 'All right then. He's drifting in the fog near the shipping lanes, no engine, no lights, no radio, no spare battery – do you think he would welcome it if help came along?

Do you think he'd be thankful if another gill-netter came along and offered to tie up to him, help him out?'

'Of course,' said Josiah. 'Sure he'd welcome it. He's stranded at sea, he can't get under way, he can't even bring his net in, pick fish. He'd better be pretty damn thankful, you bet. If he isn't, he's off his rocker.'

'Mr. Gillanders.' Nels coughed into his hand. 'I want you to think back to a question I asked you just a few moments ago, sir. I want you to ponder this matter of murder – of first-degree murder, premeditated. Of planning to kill someone in advance of the fact, then executing the following strategy: approaching your victim while he fished at sea, tying up to his boat against his will, leaping aboard, and hitting him in the head with the butt of a fishing gaff. I want to ask you – I'm asking you again – from the perspective of a man who has been fishing for thirty years, from the perspective of the gill-netters association president – a man who presumably hears about almost everything that happens out there on the sea at night – would you, sir, consider this a good plan? Is this the plan a fisherman would make if he wanted to kill someone?'

Josiah Gillanders shook his head as if offended. 'That, Mr. Gudmundsson,' he said emphatically, 'would be the most cockeyed procedure imaginable. Absolutely the most cockeyed, see. If one fellow wanted to kill another he could find a way less foolhardy and dangerous, I guess you'd have to say. Boardin' another man's boat against his will – that, I've told you, isn't possible. Leapin' at him with a fishing gaff? That's just laughable, sir. That's pirates and stories and such like. I guess if you could get close enough to tie up – you couldn't – you'd also be close enough to shoot him, wouldn't you? Just shoot him, you see, then tie up to him real easy, then toss him overboard and wash your hands. He's going down hard to the bottom of the sea and twon't be seen again. I'd shoot him, I would, and skip being the first gill-netter in the history of the profession to make a successful forced boarding. No, sir, if there's anyone in this court thinks Kabuo Miyamoto there boarded Carl Heine's boat against his will, bashed him in the head with a fishing gaff, and tossed him over-board – well, they're just daft, that's all. You'd have to be daft to believe that.'

'All right, then,' Nels said. 'I have no further questions for you, Mr. Gillanders. I thank you, however, for coming down here this morning. It's snowing hard outside.'

'It's snowing hard, yes,' said Josiah. 'But it sure is warm in here, Mr. Gudmundsson. It's mighty warm for Mr. Hooks there, in fact. It – '

'Your witness,' interrupted Nels Gudmundsson. He sat down next to Kabuo Miyamoto and put his hand on Kabuo's shoulder. 'I'm all through, Mr. Hooks,' he said.

'Well then, I suppose it's my turn,' Alvin Hooks answered calmly. 'I have just a few questions, Mr. Gillanders. Just a few things we need to turn about in all this heat – is that all right with you sir?'

Josiah shrugged and clasped his hands over his belly. 'Turn 'em then,' he advised. 'I'm all ears, cap'n.'

Alvin Hooks stood and strolled casually to the witness box with his hands deep in his trousers pockets. 'Well,' he said. 'Mr. Gillanders. You've been fishing for thirty years.'

'That's right, sir. Thirty. Count 'em.'

'Thirty years is a long time,' said Alvin Hooks. 'A lot of lonely nights at sea, yes? Plenty of time to think.'

'Landlubber might see it as lonely, I s'pose. A man like you might get lonely out there – a man who talks for a living. I – '

'Oh, yes,' said Alvin Hooks. 'I'm a landlubber, Mr. Gillanders. I'm the sort of man who would feel lonely at sea – all of that's true, yes. Fine, fine, perfectly fine – my personal life is out of the way, then. So let's talk about the case instead and skip these other matters for just right now – would that be all right with you, sir?'

'You're calling the shots here,' said Josiah Gillanders. 'Ask me whatever you want to ask me and let's be done with it.'

Alvin Hooks passed in front of the jurors with his hands clasped at the small of his back neatly. 'Mr. Gillanders,' he said. 'I understood you to say earlier that no gill-netter would board another's boat except in the case of an emergency. Is this correct, sir? Did I hear you right?'

'Correct,' said Josiah Gillanders. 'You got me.'

'Is it a matter of principle among gill-netters, then, to help out another in distress? That is, Mr. Gillanders, would you consider yourself duty bound to assist a fellow fisherman in an emergency at sea of some sort? Is that about the size of it?'

'We're men of honor,' said Josiah Gillanders. 'We fish alone but we work together. There's times at sea when we need each other, see? Any man worth his salt out there is going to come to the aid of his neighbor. It's the law of the sea – you bet it is – to put away whatever you're doin' and answer any distress call. I can't think of a single fisherman on this island who wouldn't make it his business to help another man in an emergency out there on the water. It's a law, see – not written anywhere exactly, but just as good as something written. Gill-netters help each other.'

'But Mr. Gillanders,' said Alvin Hooks. 'We've heard here in previous testimony, sir, that gill-netters don't always get along very well, they're silent men who fish alone, they argue about the placement of their boats at sea, about who is stealing fish from who, and so forth, et cetera, et cetera. They're not known to be particularly friendly men, and they prefer to fish alone, keep their distance. Now, sir, even with all of this – with this atmosphere of isolation, of competition, of disregard for the company of others – is it fair to say that a gill-netting man will always help another in an emergency? Even if he doesn't like the other man, even if they have argued in the past, even if they are enemies? Does all of that get pushed aside, become suddenly irrelevant, in the face of distress at sea? Or do men harbor grudges and ignore one another, even take pleasure in the difficulties of a stranded enemy – illuminate us, sir.'

'Bah,' said Josiah. 'We're good men through and through. Don't matter what sort of scrap there's been, we help each other, that's the way we do things – why, a man'll even help his enemy. We all know that someday we could need a hand, too; we all know we're subject to grief, see. Much as you get fried with someone else, much as he gets under your skin, you don't just let him drift away – that'd be plain sour, wouldn't it? We help each other in an emergency, it don't matter what else is going on.'

'Well then,' said Alvin Hooks. 'We'll take you at your word, Mr. Gillanders, and move on to other matters. We'll take you at your word that even enemies help each other in an emergency at sea. Now, did I understand you to say earlier that a forced boarding at sea was impossible? That conditions prevent a gill-netting man from boarding the boat of another gill-netter unless there is mutual consent? Unless the two of them agree and work together? Is that, sir, also correct? Did I understand you clearly on this?'

'You got me plain,' said Josiah Gillanders. 'That's exactly what I said – you won't see no forced boardings.'

'Well,' said Alvin Hooks. 'Mr. Gudmundsson here, my esteemed colleague for the defense, asked you earlier to imagine a scenario at sea in which one man seeks to kill another in a premeditated fashion. He asked you to imagine a forced boarding, a leap, a thrust of a fishing gaff. You, sir, said it wasn't possible. You said such a murder couldn't happen.'

'It's a sea yarn if it includes a forced boarding, and that's that. It's a pirate story and that's all.'

'All right, then,' said Alvin Hooks. 'I'll ask you to imagine another scenario – you tell me if it sounds plausible. If this sort of thing could have happened, sir, or if it's just another sea yarn.'

Alvin Hooks began to pace again, and as he paced he looked at each juror. 'Number one,' he began. 'The defendant here, Mr. Miyamoto, decides he wishes to kill Carl Heine. Is that part plausible – so far?'

'Sure,' Josiah answered. 'If you say so.'

'Number two,' said Alvin Hooks. 'He goes out to fish on September 15. There's a bit of mist but no real fog yet, so he has no trouble motoring out within sight distance of his intended

victim, Carl Heine. He follows him out to Ship Channel Bank –
how's all of that, so far?'

'I guess,' said Josiah Gillanders.

'Number three then,' continued Alvin Hooks. 'He watches
Carl Heine set his net. He sets his own not too far off,
deliberately up current, and fishes until late in the evening.
Now the fog comes in thick and strong, a big fog, obscuring
everything from sight. He can't see anything or anybody, but
he knows where Carl Heine is, two hundred yards off, down
current in the fog. It's late now, two A.M. The water is
very quiet. He has listened over his radio while other men
have motored off to fish at Elliot Head. He is not sure how
many are still in the area, but he knows it can't be more than
a handful. And so Mr. Miyamoto at last makes his move. He
hauls in his net, cuts his motor, makes sure his trusty fishing gaff
is handy, and drifts down current toward Carl Heine, perhaps
even blowing his foghorn. He drifts nearly right into Carl, it
seems, and lies to him, says his engine is dead. Now you tell
me – you told us earlier – wouldn't Carl Heine feel bound to
help him?'

'Sea yarn,' Josiah Gillanders spat. 'But a ripping good one.
Go ahead.'

'Wouldn't Carl Heine feel bound to help him? As you said
earlier – men help their enemies? Wouldn't Carl Heine have
helped?'

'Yes, he'd have helped. Go ahead.'

'Wouldn't the two men have tied their boats together?
Wouldn't you have the mutual consent necessary – an emergency
situation, even if feigned – for a successful tie-up at sea? Wouldn't
you, Mr. Gillanders?'

Josiah nodded. 'You would,' he answered. 'Yes.'

'And at this point, sir, in the scenario, could the defendant
not – a trained *kendo* master, remember, a man proficient at
killing with a stick, lethal and experienced at stick fighting –
could the defendant not have leapt aboard and killed Carl Heine
with a hard blow to the skull, hard enough to crack it open? As

338

opposed to doing the job with a gunshot? Which potentially – which might – be heard across the water by somebody else out there fishing? Am I, sir, still plausible? Does my scenario sound plausible to a man of your expertise? Is all of that, sir, plausible?'

'It could have happened,' said Josiah Gillanders. 'But I don't much think it did.'

'You don't much think it did,' said Alvin Hooks. 'Your opinion is otherwise, it appears. But on what do you base your opinion, sir? You have not denied that my scenario is plausible. You have not denied that this premeditated murder might have happened in precisely the fashion I have just described, have you, Mr. Gillanders – *have* you?'

'No, I haven't,' Josiah said. 'But – '

'No further questions,' said Alvin Hooks. 'The witness can sit down. The witness can sit in the pleasant warmth of the gallery. I have no further questions.'

'Bah,' said Josiah Gillanders. But the judge held his hand up, and Josiah, seeing this, left the stand carrying his hat between his fingers.

27

The storm winds battered the courtroom windows and rattled them in their casements so vigorously it seemed the glass would break. For three days and nights the citizens in the gallery had listened to the wind beat against their houses and echo violently inside their ears as they struggled against it to make their way to and from the courthouse. They had not at all grown accustomed to it. They were habituated to the sea winds that blew across the island each spring when the mud was up and the rain fell steadily, but a wind of this magnitude, so frigid and elemental, remained foreign to them. It seemed improbable that a wind should blow so consistently for days on end. It made them irritable and impatient. The snow was one thing, falling as it did, but the whine of the storm, the stinging force of it against their faces – everyone wished unconsciously that it would come to an end and grant them peace. They were tired of listening to it.

Kabuo Miyamoto, the accused man, had not heard the wind at all from his cell, not even a murmur of it. He had no inkling of the storm outside except when Abel Martinson led him up the stairs – handcuffed for his journey to Judge Fielding's courtroom – so that emerging into the twilight of the courthouse's ground floor he felt the wind shaking the building. And he saw through the windows in each of the stairwells how the snow fell hard out of a glowering sky and boiled, borne by the wind. The cold, cottony light of a winter storm was something he gave thanks for after living without windows for seventy-seven days. Kabuo had passed the preceding night wrapped in blankets – his concrete cell was especially cold – and pacing and shivering endlessly. The deputy appointed to watch him through the dark hours – a retired sawyer named William Stenesen – had shone a flashlight on him just before midnight and inquired if he was faring well. Kabuo had asked for extra blankets and a glass of tea, if possible. 'I'll see about that,' William Stenesen had answered. 'But Jesus, man, if you hadn't gotten yourself into this mess, neither of us would be here in the first place.'

And so Kabuo had pondered the mess he'd indeed gotten himself into. For when Nels Gudmundsson had asked for his side of the story after their chess game two and a half months ago he'd stuck with the lie he'd told Sheriff Moran: he didn't know anything about it, he'd insisted, and this had deepened his problems. Yes, he'd spoken with Carl about the seven acres, yes, he'd had an argument with Etta Heine, yes, he'd gone to see Ole. No, he hadn't seen Carl out at Ship Channel Bank on the night of September 15. He had no idea what had happened to Carl and could offer no explanation to anyone, no information about Carl's drowning. He, Kabuo, had fished through the night, then gone home and gone to bed, that was all there was to it. That was all he'd had to say.

Nels Gudmundsson, in the beginning, had been satisfied with this and seemed to take him at his word. But then he came again on the following morning with a yellow legal pad tucked beneath his arm and, a cigar between his teeth, settled down on Kabuo's bed. The cigar ashes fell into the lap of his pants, but he did not seem to mind or notice, and Kabuo felt sorry for him. His back was bent and his hands trembled. 'The sheriff's report,' he said with a sigh. 'I read it, Kabuo. The whole thing.'

'What does it say?' Kabuo asked.

'It contains a few facts I'm concerned about,' said Nels, pulling a pen from his coat pocket. 'I hope you won't mind if I ask you, once more, to give me your side of the story. Can you do that for me, Kabuo? Tell me everything all over again? Your story about the seven acres, et cetera? Everything that happened?'

Kabuo moved to the door of his cell and put his eye to the

opening. 'You don't believe what I've told you,' he said softly. 'You think I'm lying, don't you.'

'The blood on your fishing gaff,' Nels Gudmundsson replied. 'They had it tested in Anacortes. It matches Carl Heine's blood type.'

'I don't know anything about it,' said Kabuo. 'I told that to the sheriff and I'm telling it to you. I don't know anything about it.'

'Another thing,' insisted Nels, pointing his pen at Kabuo. 'They found one of your mooring lines on Carl's boat. Wrapped around a cleat on the *Susan Marie*. One of your lines, clearly, they say. Matched all your other lines with the exception of a new one. That's in the report, too.'

'Oh,' said Kabuo, but nothing more.

'Look,' said Nels Gudmundsson. 'I can't help you with this unless I know the truth. I can't build a case around an answer like "oh" when I've brought to your attention such damning evidence as your mooring line being found by the sheriff of Island County on the boat of a suspiciously dead fisherman. What good can I do you if all I get is "oh"? How am I going to help you, Kabuo? You've got to level with me, that's all there is to it. Otherwise, I can't help you.'

'I've told you the truth,' said Kabuo. He turned around and faced his attorney, an old man with one eye and trembling hands, appointed to his case because he, Kabuo, had refused to honor the prosecutor's point of view by purchasing his own defense. 'We talked about my family's land, I argued with his mother years ago, I went to see Ole, I went to see Carl, and that was the end of it. I've said what I have to say.'

'The mooring line,' Nels Gudmundsson repeated. 'The mooring line and the blood on the fishing gaff. I – '

'I can't explain those things,' insisted Kabuo. 'I don't know anything about them.'

Nels nodded and stared at him, and Kabuo held his gaze. 'You could hang, you know,' Nels said bluntly. 'There's no attorney

342

in the world who can help you with this if you're not going to tell the truth.'

And the next morning Nels had come yet again, carrying a manila folder. He smoked his cigar and paced the length of the cell with the folder tucked beneath his arm. 'I've brought you the sheriffs report,' he said, 'so you can see exactly what we're up against. Problem is, once you read the thing, you may decide to concoct a *new* story – you may pretend you want to level with me by concocting a more defensible lie. Once you've read this report, Kabuo, you can make something up that's consistent with it and I'll go ahead and work with that, mainly because I'll have no choice. I don't like that. I'd rather it didn't turn out that way. I'd rather know I can trust you. So before you read what's in that thing, tell me a story that squares with its details and exonerate yourself in my eyes. Tell me the story you should have told the sheriff right off the bat, when it wasn't too late, when the truth might still have given you your freedom. When the truth might have done you some good.'

Kabuo, at first, said nothing. But then Nels dropped the manila folder on the mattress, dropped it and stood directly over him. 'It's because you're from Japanese folks,' he said softly; it was more a question than a statement. 'You figure because you're from Japanese folks nobody will believe you anyway.'

'I've got a right to think that way. Or maybe you've forgotten that a few years back the government decided it couldn't trust any of us and shipped us out of here.'

'That's true,' said Nels. 'But – '

'We're sly and treacherous,' Kabuo said. 'You can't trust a Jap, can you? This island's full of strong feelings, Mr. Gudmundsson, people who don't often speak their minds but hate on the inside all the same. They don't buy their berries from our farms, they won't do business with us. You remember when somebody pitched rocks through all the windows at Sumida's greenhouses last summer? Well, now there's a fisherman everybody liked well enough who's dead and drowned in his net. They're going to figure it makes sense a Jap killed him. They're going to want to see me hang no matter what the truth is.'

'There are laws,' said Nels. 'They apply equally to everyone. You're entitled to a fair trial.'

'There are men,' said Kabuo, 'who hate me. They hate anyone who looks like the soldiers they fought. That's what I'm doing here.'

'Tell the truth,' Nels said. 'Decide to tell the truth before it's too late.'

Kabuo lay down on his bed with a sigh and twined his fingers behind his head. 'The truth,' he said. 'The truth isn't easy.'

'Just the same,' Nels said. 'I understand how you feel. There are the things that happened, though, and the things that did not happen. That's all we're talking about.'

It seemed to Kabuo a lushly textured dream, fogbound, still, and silent. He thought about it often in his darkened cell, and the smallest details were large for him and every word was audible.

On the night in question he'd checked the *Islander*'s engine oil and quickly greased the net drum's reel drive before putting out for Ship Channel Bank in the hour just before dusk. Ship Channel, he'd understood, had been fished hard and happily on two consecutive evenings. He'd spoken to Lars Hansen and Jan Sorensen about it and made the decision to fish at Ship Channel on account of their information. The silvers were running in immense schools, they said, mostly on the flood tide. There were fish to be had on the ebb tide, too, though nowhere near as many. It would be possible to take two hundred or more working the flood alone, Kabuo hoped, and perhaps a hundred more on the ebb if he was lucky – and luck, he knew, was what he needed. Elliot Head, on the previous night, had barely covered his costs. He'd come away with eighteen fish and had furthermore set his net in the dark beside a large and labyrinthine kelp island. The tide drift had taken him down into the kelp, and he'd wasted four hours extricating himself so as not to rip his gill

344

net. Now, tonight, he would have to do better. He would need to have fortune on his side.

In the blue light of dusk he'd made the turn out of the harbor and run for open water. From his vantage point at the wheel of the *Islander* he saw the soft cedars of San Piedro Island, its high, rolling hills, the low mist that lay in long streamers against its beaches, the whitecaps riffling its shoreline. The moon had risen already behind the island and hung just over the big bluff at Skiff Point – a quarter moon, pale and indefinite, as ethereal and translucent as the wisps of clouds that traveled the skies, obscuring it. Kabuo, his radio on, checked his barometer; it still held steady despite talk of rough weather, cold squalls of sleet reported to the north, out of the Strait of Georgia. When he looked up again a raft of seabirds was scattering, gray silhouettes off the chop a hundred yards out, rising and then skimming over the surface of the waves in the manner of surf scoters, though there were too many to be surf scoters – he didn't know what they might be, maybe murres, he couldn't tell. Steering wide of Harbor Rocks, bucking the sea wind head-on at seven knots, he ran with the tide race pushing hard behind him and fell in with the *Kasilof*, the *Antarctic*, and the *Providence*, all of which were making for Ship Channel, too: half the fleet was headed there. Half the fleet was spread out before him, running hard for the fishing grounds at dusk and throwing wide silver wakes.

Kabuo drank the green tea in his thermos and ran through the radio channels. It was his habit to listen but not to speak, to gather what he could about men by the manner in which they expressed themselves, and to discern what he could about the fishing.

At full dusk or thereabouts he ate three rice balls, a slab of rock cod, and two windfall apples from a wild tree behind Bender's Spring. The night mist hovered on the water already, so he backed the throttle down and ran with his spotlight broadcasting over the waves. The prospect of a blind fog, as always, concerned him. A fisherman could become so lost in a blind fog he'd set his own net in a circle without knowing it or end up working the middle of the shipping lane where the big freighters ran toward Seattle. It was better in such conditions to fish Elliot Head, since the head lay far from the shipping lane and well to the lee side of Elliot Island, out of the big water breezes.

But by eight-thirty he'd idled his engine at the bank and stood in the cockpit beside the net drum, listening, with the fog settling all around him. From the lighthouse station far to the east he could hear the low, steady intonation of the fog signal diaphone. It was the sound he associated with blind nights at sea – lonely, familiar, hushed, and so melancholy he could never listen without emptiness. Tonight, he knew, was what old-timers called *ghost time*, with fog as immobile and dense as buttermilk. A man could run his hands through such a fog, separating it into tendrils and streamers that gathered themselves languidly once more into the whole and disappeared seamlessly, without a trace. Drifting on the tide, a gill-netter moved through it as though it composed its own netherworld medium halfway between air and water. It was possible on such a night to become as disoriented as a man without a torch in a cave. Kabuo knew that other fishermen were out there, drifting as he was and peering into the fog, blindly gliding across the bank in the hope of establishing their locations. The shipping lane boundaries were marked by numbered buoys, and the hope was to stumble across one fortuitously so as to orient oneself.

Kabuo, giving up, propped a buoy bag between the stern fairleads and lit a kerosene lantern with a wooden kitchen match. He waited until the wick held strong, pumped in some air, adjusted the fuel, then set the lantern carefully in its life ring and bent down over the *Islander*'s transom to place the buoy bag on the water. With his face so close to the surface of the sea he imagined he could smell the salmon running. He shut his eyes, put a hand in the water, and in his own manner he prayed to the gods of the sea to assist him by bringing fish his way. He asked for good luck, for a respite from the fog; he prayed that the gods would clear the fog away and keep him safe from the freighters in the shipping lane. Then he stood again in the stern of the *Islander*, square-knotted his buoy bag line to his net line, and released the brake on the net drum.

Kabuo laid his net out north to south by motoring away from it on a true blind heading as slowly as was possible. It seemed to him the lane lay to the north, though he couldn't be certain about that. The tidal drift, running east, would keep his net taut, but only if he laid it on the right bearing; if he quartered to the current, even slightly, on the other hand, he'd end up having to tow all night just to keep his net from collapsing. There was no way of knowing in dense fog how true a net lay; he couldn't see twenty corks down his line and would have to run it every hour or so with his spotlight seeking it out. Kabuo could not see the surface of the sea more than five yards beyond the bow of his boat from his place at the wheel in his cabin. The *Islander*, in fact, divided the fog, the bow literally peeling it open. The fog was dense enough to make him ponder running for Elliot Head before long; for all he knew he was setting his net in the Seattle-bound shipping lane. Besides, he had to hope no one had set due south, particularly at an angle to his own set. In this fog he'd no doubt miss the man's jacklight and twist his net up in the *Islander*'s prop, a long diversion from the night's fishing. Any number of things could go amiss.

In the stern the net slipped free from the drum and rolled over the fairleads easily toward the sea until at last the whole of it was out of the boat, three hundred fathoms long. Kabuo went back and hosed the net gurry out the scupper holes. When he was done he shut the engine down and stood on the hatch with his back against the cabin, listening for the blasts of passing freighters. Nothing, though – there was no sound now but lapping water and the distant sound from the lighthouse. The tidal current carried him gently east, just as he'd predicted. He felt better about things with his net in. He could not be certain he was not in the shipping lane, but he knew he was drifting at the same speed as every other gill-netter fishing these fogbound waters. He imagined there were thirty or more boats out there, all hidden and silent in the dense sea fog, moving to the same tidal rhythm that moved under him, keeping everyone equi-distant. Kabuo went in and flicked his mast light on: red over white, the sign of a man night fishing, not that it did any good. Not that the light was worth anything. But on the other hand he'd done all he could about matters. He'd set his net as well as possible. There was nothing to do now but be patient.

Kabuo brought his thermos into the cockpit, then sat on the port gunnel and sipped green tea, listening into the fog uneasily. Farther south he could hear someone idling, the sound of net unraveling from a drum, a boat under way at a crawl. There was an occasional dim crackle from his radio set, but other than that nothing. In the silence he sipped tea and waited for the salmon: as on other nights he imagined them in motion, swift in pursuit of the waters they'd sprung from, waters that held both past and future for them, their children and their children's children and their deaths. When he picked his net and held them pinched at the gills he felt in their silence how desperate their sojourn was, and he was moved in the manner a fisherman is moved, quietly, without words. Their rich silver flanks would feed his dreams and for this he was thankful and sorrowful. There was something tragic in the wall of invisible mesh he'd hung to choke the life from them while they traveled to the rhythm of an urging they could not deny. He imagined them slamming against his net in astonishment at this invisible thing that finished their lives in the last days of an urgent journey. Sometimes, hauling net, he came across a fish thrashing hard enough to elicit a cracking *thump* when it banged off the *Islander*'s transom. Like all the others, it went into the hold to die over the course of hours.

Kabuo put his thermos together and took it into the cabin. Once again he flipped through the radio channels, and this time he caught a voice – Dale Middleton's – chattering away in a slow island drawl: 'I done just got the bug out of my squelch,' it said, and then someone answered, 'What for?' Dale replied he'd had just about enough of setting by the shipping lane in soup fog for a dozen silvers, a few dogfish, a couple of hake, and what's

348

more taking flack off his radio. 'I near can't see my own hands,' he said. 'I near can't see the nose on my own face.' Somebody, a third party, agreed the fishing had gone sour, the bank seemed all dried up real sudden, he'd been thinking on fishing at Elliot Head, couldn't tell but maybe things was better there. 'Leastwise off this shipping lane,' replied Dale. 'One good swing I got laid out now, that'll do it for me here. Hey, Leonard, your net coming up clear? Mine here's lookin' like a oil rag. Damn thing's darker 'n burnt toast.'

The fishermen on the radio discussed this for a while, Leonard saying his net was fairly clean, Dale asking him if he'd greased it lately, Leonard claiming to have seen a buoy marker, number 57, off to port. He'd worked off it for a half hour or so but never came on to 58 or 56, never fixed himself properly. Far as he was concerned he was lost in the fog and intended to stay that way – leastwise 'til his net was up, then he'd think about matters. Dale asked him if he'd picked once yet, and Leonard sounded disappointed. Dale described the fog again and said he guessed it was as thick as it gets, and Leonard, agreeing, said he remembered one last year at Elliot Head in rougher seas – a bad scene, he'd added. 'The Head'd be good about now,' replied Dale. 'Let's fog-run our way on down there.'

Kabuo left his radio on; he wanted to hear about it if a freighter came down the strait and put in a call to the lighthouse. He slid the cabin door open and stood listening, and in time came the air blasts, both muted and melancholy, of boats moving off the fishing grounds, the fog whistles of gill-netters running blindly east, farther off all the time and so less audible. It was time to pick, he decided, and then if necessary to make his own fog run to the fishing grounds off Elliot Head – a run he preferred to make alone. The boats out there now were moving on blind bearings, and he didn't necessarily trust their skippers. He'd wait an hour more, then pick and run if he came up short on fish.

At ten-thirty he stood on the beaver paddle in the cockpit, picking his net and stopping now and then to throw strands of kelp into the water. The net, under tension, rained seawater onto the deck along with sticks and kelp. He was happy to find there were salmon coming up as well, big silvers mostly over ten and eleven pounds, a half-dozen ten-pound chums, too, even three resident black-mouth. Some dropped to the deck coming over the transom, others he deftly maneuvered free. He was good at this part of things. His hands found their way through the folds of the net to the long flanks of dead and dying salmon. Kabuo lofted them into the hold along with three hake and three pale dogfish he intended to take home to his family. There were fifty-eight salmon, he counted, for this first set, and he felt grateful about them. Kneeling for a moment beside the hold, he looked down at them with satisfaction and calculated their worth at the cannery. He thought of the journey they'd made to him and how their lives, perhaps, would buy his farm back.

Kabuo watched for one long moment – an occasional fish flaring at the gills or jerking – then pulled the hatch cover over them and sprayed sea slime out the scupper holes. It was a good haul for a first set, enough to keep him fishing the bank – there was no reason for him to go elsewhere. Chances were that, fog and all, he'd made his drift dead center by happenstance; he'd had the luck he'd prayed for earlier. So far everything had gone right.

It was close to eleven-thirty, if his watch was right, the last of the flood still carrying him east, and he decided to motor west again in order to fish the tide turn. On the turn the salmon would pile up, milling on the bank by the hundreds, in schools, and some to the east would back in on the ebb so that his net would load up going both ways. He hoped for another hundred fish from his next set; it seemed a reasonable prospect. He was glad to have stuck it out in the fog and felt vindicated somehow. He'd made his drift successfully. There were fish in his hold, more to be had, and small competition to get them. He guessed more than two-thirds of the fishermen in the area had made the fog run for Elliot Head with their horns sounding across the water.

Kabuo stood at the wheel in his cabin with a cup of green tea on the table behind him and flipped once more through the radio channels. There was no talk now. All the men who couldn't help talking had moved on, it appeared. Out of habit he checked his engine gauges and took a reading from his compass. Then he throttled up, turned tight, and motored west, adjusting to the north less than five degrees in the hope of stumbling across a buoy marker.

The bow of the *Islander* cut through the fog for ten minutes or more. One eye on the binnacle, the other on the spotlighted water before his bow, Kabuo inched forward on blind faith. He was, he knew, motoring against the grain of boats drifting down the bank. The protocol among gill-netters in such conditions was to lay on one's foghorn at one-minute intervals and to keep a sharp ear turned toward the fog on the chance of receiving a reply. Kabuo, moving into the tidal drift, had signaled his position a half-dozen times when an air horn replied off his port bow. Whoever it was, he was close.

Kabuo backed into neutral and drifted, his heart beating hard in his chest. The other man was too near, seventy-five yards, a hundred at best, out there in the fog, his motor cut. Kabuo laid on his horn again. In the silence that followed came a reply to port – this time a man's voice, calm and factual, a voice he recognized. 'I'm over here,' it called across the water. 'I'm dead in the water, drifting.'

And this was how he had found Carl Heine, his batteries dead, adrift at midnight, in need of another man's assistance. There Carl stood in the *Islander*'s spotlight, a big man in bib overalls poised in his boat's bow, a kerosene lantern clutched in one hand and an air horn dangling from the other. He'd raised his lantern and stood there like that, his bearded chin set, expressionless. 'I'm dead in the water,' he'd said again, when Kabuo pulled up against his starboard side and tossed him a mooring line. 'My batteries are drawed down. Both of them.'

'All right,' said Kabuo. 'Let's tie up. I've got plenty of juice.'

'Thank God for that,' answered Carl. 'It's good luck to have run across you.'

'Kick your fenders out,' Kabuo said. 'I'll drift right up in close.'

They tied their boats together in the fog, underneath the *Islander*'s spotlight. Kabuo shut his engine down while Carl stepped across both gunnels and came aboard his boat. He stood in the doorway shaking his head; 'I drawed 'em both down,' he repeated. 'Volt meter's down around nine somewhere. Alternator belts were loose, I guess. I got 'em tightened up better now, but meanwhile I'm dead in the water.'

'Hope we're not in the lane,' said Kabuo, peering up at the *Susan Marie*'s mast. 'Looks like you put a lantern up.'

'Lashed it up there just a bit ago,' said Carl. 'Best I could do, seems like. Lost my radio when the juice ran out, couldn't call anyone. Couldn't do anything to help myself, just drifting along this last hour. Lantern's probably useless in this fog, but anyway I've got it up there. It's all the lights I got just now, that and the one I've been carrying. Probably isn't worth nothing to nobody.'

'I've got two batteries,' Kabuo answered. 'We'll pull one and get you started.'

''Preciate that,' said Carl. 'Thing is I run D-8s, you see. S'pose you run off 6s.'

'I do,' said Kabuo. 'But it'll work if you've got room. Anyway, we can refit your well. Or rig up some longer cables? It should go in just fine.'

'I'll measure,' said Carl. 'Then we'll know.'

He crossed back over the boat gunnels then, and Kabuo hoped that underneath his facade there was part of him wanting to discuss the land that lay between them silently. Carl would *have* to say something one way or the other simply because the two of them were at sea together, moored boat to boat but to nothing else, adrift and battling the same problem.

Kabuo had known Carl for many years; he knew that Carl avoided circumstances in which he had to speak. He spoke mostly of the world of tools and objects when he had to speak at all. Kabuo remembered trolling for cutthroat with

352

Carl – they were twelve years old, long before the war – in a borrowed, weathered rowboat. It was just after sunset and the phosphorescence in the water boiling underneath Carl's rowing oars inspired him to comment – a boy so moved by the beauty of the world he could not keep himself from utterance: 'Look at those colors,' he'd said. And even at twelve Kabuo had understood that such a statement was out of character. What Carl felt he kept inside, showing nothing to anyone – as Kabuo himself did, for other reasons. They were more similar in their deepest places than Kabuo cared to admit.

Kabuo pried the cover from his battery well and loosened the cables from the terminals. He lifted one of his batteries out – twice as large as a car battery and twice as heavy as well – and carried it out to where he could rest it on his gunnel and pass it to Carl Heine. They stood each on his own boat, and the battery passed between them. 'It'll fit,' said Carl. 'There's a flange in the way. It's soft. I can bang it back.'

Kabuo reached down and took his gaff in his hand. 'I'll bring this,' he said. 'We can hammer with it.'

They passed into Carl's tidy cabin together, Kabuo carrying a lantern and the gaff, Carl in front with the battery. A cased sausage hung from a wire beside the binnacle; the cot was neatly made up. Kabuo recognized Carl's neat hand in things, his way of establishing a rigid order, the force that had driven him, years before, to keep his tackle box shipshape. Even his clothes, no matter how worn-out, were conspicuously neat and well kept.

'Give me that gaff,' Carl said now.

He knelt on one knee beside his battery hold and banged with the gaff at the metal flange. Kabuo, beside him, was aware of his strength and of the facility with which he approached this problem; he made each stroke count, put his shoulders into each, and did not hurry his blows. Once his right hand slipped, though, and grazing the soft metal came away bloody, but Carl did not halt. He gripped Kabuo's fishing gaff harder and only afterward, when the battery was in the well, did he put his palm to his mouth and hold it there, taking back his blood in silence. 'Let's try starting up,' he said.

'You sure,' asked Kabuo, 'you got those belts tight? No point in starting up otherwise, you know. You'll just run this battery down, too, and we'll have another problem.'

'They're tight now,' said Carl, working on his palm. 'I put a wrench on 'em good.'

He pulled out the choke and threw his toggle switches. The *Susan Marie's* engine wheezed twice below the floorboards, then coughed, rattled, and fired up when Carl backed down the choke.

'Tell you what,' said Kabuo. 'You keep that battery for the rest of the night. I can't wait around 'til you draw back up, so I'll just run off the one I've got and catch you back at the docks.'

Carl slid the dead battery out of the way, tucked it in to the right of the wheel, then snapped on the cabin light and took a volt meter reading with his handkerchief pressed against his hand. 'You're right,' he said. 'I'm charging now, but this'll take awhile. Maybe I'll find you later.'

'Catch fish,' said Kabuo. 'Don't worry about it. I'll see you back at the docks.'

He worked the battery hold cover into place. He picked up his gaff and waited there. 'I'm off,' he said finally. 'I'll see you.'

'Hold on,' answered Carl, still working on his hand – looking at it and not Kabuo. 'You know as well as I do we both got something to talk about.'

'All right,' replied Kabuo, his gaff in his hand. And then he stood and waited.

'Seven acres,' said Carl Heine. 'I'm wonderin' what you'd pay for 'em, Kabuo. Just curious, that's all.'

'What are you selling them for?' Kabuo asked. 'Why don't we start with what you want for them? I guess I'd rather start there.'

'Did I say I was selling?' Carl asked. 'Didn't say one way or the other, did I? But if I was, I guess I'd have to figure they're mine and you want 'em pretty bad. Guess I'd ought to charge

354

you a small fortune, but then maybe you'd want your battery back, leave me out here stranded.'

'The battery's in,' Kabuo answered, smiling. 'That's separate from the rest of things. Besides, you'd do the same for me.'

'I *might* do the same for you,' said Carl. 'I have to warn you about that, chief. I'm not screwed together like I used to be. It isn't like it was before.'

'All right,' said Kabuo. 'If you say so.'

'Hell,' said Carl. 'I'm not saying what I mean. Look, goddamn it, I'm sorry, okay? I'm sorry over this whole damn business. I'd a been around, it wouldn't have happened how it did. My mother pulled it off, I was out at sea, fighting you goddamn Jap sons a – '

'I'm an American,' Kabuo cut in. 'Just like you or anybody. Am I calling you a Nazi, you big Nazi bastard? I killed men who looked just like you – pig-fed German bastards. I've got their blood on my soul, Carl, and it doesn't wash off very easily. So don't you talk to me about Japs, you big Nazi son of a bitch.'

He still held the gaff gripped tightly in one hand, and he became aware of it now. Carl put one boot on the *Susan Marie's* port gunnel and spat hard into the water. 'I am a bastard,' he said finally, and stared out into the fog. 'I'm a big Hun Nazi son of a bitch, and you know what else, Kabuo? I still got your bamboo fishing rod. I kept it all these years. I hid it in the barn after my mother tried to make me go and return it over to your house. You went off to prison camp, I caught a mess of sea runs. Damn thing's still in my closet.'

'Leave it there,' said Kabuo Miyamoto. 'I forgot all about that fishing rod. You can have it. To hell with it.'

'To hell with that,' said Carl. 'It's been driving me crazy all these years. I open up my closet and there it is, your goddamn bamboo rod.'

'Give it back, if you want,' said Kabuo. 'But I'm telling you you can keep it, Carl. That's why I gave it to you.'

'All right,' said Carl. 'Then that settles it. Twelve hundred an acre and that's final. That's what I'm paying Ole, see.

That's the going price on strawberry land, go and have a look around.'

'That's eighty-four hundred for the lot,' answered Kabuo. 'How much are you going to want down?'

Carl Heine spat into the water one more time, then turned and put out his hand. Kabuo put the gaff down and took it. They did not shake so much as grip like fishermen who know they can go no further with words and must communicate in another fashion. So they stood there at sea in the fog, floating, and locked their hands together. Their grip was solid, and there was the blood from Carl's cut palm in it. They did not mean for it to say too much overtly, and at the same time they wished for it to say everything. They moved away from this more quickly than they desired but before embarrassment overtook them. 'A thousand down,' said Carl Heine. 'We can sign papers tomorrow.'

'Eight hundred,' said Kabuo, 'and it's a deal.'

28

When Kabuo had finished telling his story on the witness stand, Alvin Hooks rose and stood before him insistently working on a hangnail. Studying his fingers as he delivered his words, he attended in particular to his cuticles. 'Mr. Miyamoto,' he began. 'For the life of me I can't understand why you didn't tell this story from the start. After all, don't you think it might have been your citizenly duty to come forward with all of this information? Don't you think you should have gone to the sheriff and told him about this battery business you claim occurred on the high seas? I would think you would, Mr. Miyamoto. I would think you would go to Sheriff Moran and tell him all of this just as soon as you heard that Carl Heine had died so horribly.'

The accused man looked at the jurors now, ignoring Alvin Hooks entirely, and answered quietly and evenly in their direction, as if there were no one else present. 'You must understand,' he said to them, 'that I heard nothing about the death of Carl Heine until one o'clock on the afternoon of September 16 and that within just a few hours of my having heard of it Sheriff Moran arrested me. There was no time for me to voluntarily come forward with the events as I have just delivered them. I – '

'But,' Alvin Hooks intervened, placing himself between Kabuo and the jurors, 'as you've just said yourself, Mr. Miyamoto, you had in fact – what did you say? – a few *hours* in which to seek out the sheriff. You heard about this death, an afternoon passed, and then you went down to the Amity Harbor docks with the intent of putting out to sea. You intended to fish until the morning of the seventeenth, at which time, if you'd decided to come forward, at least *sixteen* hours would have passed since you'd heard of the death of Carl Heine. So let me put this another way, a bit more consistent with reality – did you, Mr. Miyamoto, *intend* to come forward? Were you about to come forward with your battery story at the time of your arrest?'

'I was thinking about it,' said Kabuo Miyamoto. 'I was trying to decide just what I should do. The situation was difficult.'

'Oh,' answered Alvin Hooks. 'You were thinking about it. You were weighing whether or not to come forward and tell Sheriff Moran, in a voluntary way, about this battery incident.'

'That's right,' said Kabuo Miyamoto. 'I was.'

'But then, as you say, Sheriff Moran came to you. He appeared at your boat on the evening of the sixteenth with a search warrant, is that correct?'

'He did.'

'And you were still considering, at that point in time, whether or not you should tell him your battery story?'

'I was.'

'But you didn't tell him your battery story.'

'I guess not. No, I didn't.'

'You didn't tell him your battery story,' Alvin Hooks repeated. 'Not even in the face of imminent arrest did you offer any sort of explanation. Here stood Sheriff Moran with your fishing gaff in hand, telling you he intended to have the blood on it tested, and you didn't tell him about Carl Heine's cut palm – wasn't that what you told the court, that Carl cut his palm using your fishing gaff? And that this is the explanation for the blood on it?'

'That's what happened,' said Kabuo Miyamoto. 'He cut his palm, yes.'

'But you didn't offer that as an explanation to the sheriff. You said nothing about having seen Carl Heine. Now why was this, Mr. Miyamoto? Why did you claim complete ignorance?'

'You must understand,' said Kabuo. 'The sheriff had appeared with a warrant in hand. I found myself under suspicion of murder. It seemed to me best not to say anything. To wait until I . . . had a lawyer.'

'So you didn't tell the sheriff your battery story,' Alvin Hooks said again. 'Nor did you tell it after your arrest, even when you *had* an attorney. Instead you claimed – am I correct about this? – you claimed to know nothing about the death of Carl Heine, you claimed not to have seen him on the night of the fifteenth at the Ship Channel Bank fishing grounds. These claims of yours, these claims of ignorance, were all recorded in the sheriff's investigative report, which has been admitted as evidence in this trial. Your story, then, immediately *after* your arrest, differs from the one you've told today, Mr. Miyamoto. So I ask you – where lies the truth?'

Kabuo blinked; his lips tightened. 'The truth,' he said, 'is as I have just described it. The truth is that I loaned Carl a battery, helped him get his boat started, made arrangements for my family's seven acres with him, then motored away and fished.'

'I see,' said Alvin Hooks. 'You wish to retract the story of complete ignorance you told Sheriff Moran in the wake of your arrest and replace it with this new one you've just now told us? You wish us to believe this new story?'

'Yes, I do. Because it's true.'

'I see,' said Alvin Hooks. 'Well, then. On the morning of September 16 you returned from a night's fishing and informed your wife of your at-sea conversation with Carl Heine. Is that correct, Mr. Miyamoto?'

'It is.'

'And then?' asked the prosecutor. 'What next?'

'I slept,' said Kabuo. 'Until one-thirty. My wife woke me up at one-thirty or thereabouts with the news about Carl's death.'

'I see,' said Alvin Hooks. 'And then what?'

'We sat and talked,' said Kabuo. 'I ate lunch and took care of some bills I had to pay. About five I headed down to the docks.'

'About five,' said Alvin Hooks. 'And did you stop anywhere along the way? Errands, perhaps? Did you visit anyone or go anywhere? Speak to anybody about anything?'

'No,' said Kabuo. 'I left around five and went straight to my boat. That was all there was to it.'

'You didn't, say, stop at the store to stock up on supplies? Nothing of that sort, Mr. Miyamoto?'

'No.'

'At the docks,' said Alvin Hooks.. 'Did you see anyone? Did you stop at another boat for any reason, speak to any other fishermen?'

'Straight to my boat,' said Kabuo Miyamoto. 'I didn't stop for anything, no.'

'Straight to your boat,' Alvin Hooks repeated. 'And there you were, preparing for a night of fishing, when the sheriff came along with his warrant.'

'That's right,' said Kabuo. 'He searched my boat.'

Alvin Hooks crossed over to the evidence table and selected a folder from it. 'The sheriff indeed searched your boat,' he agreed. 'And the details of his search, Mr. Miyamoto, are recorded in this investigative report I'm holding right here in my hand. In fact, in the course of cross-examining the sheriff, your counsel – Mr. Gudmundsson – made reference to this report, including an item on page twenty-seven which says – 'Alvin Hooks shuffled through the pages, then stopped and tapped his forefinger against it, tapped it three times, emphatically. Once again he turned toward the jurors, swiveling the sheriff's report in their direction as if to suggest they read along with him despite their distance across the courtroom.

'Now this is highly problematic,' Alvin Hooks said. 'Because the sheriff's report states that in your battery well there were two D-6 batteries. "Two D-6 batteries in well. Each six celled" – that's what it says, right here.'

'My boat runs on D-6s,' answered Kabuo. 'There are many boats that do so.'

'Oh, yes,' said Alvin Hooks. 'I know about that. But what

about the fact that there were *two* batteries? *Two* batteries, Mr. Miyamoto. If your story is true, if you loaned one to Carl Heine as you say you did – if you pulled one out of your own battery well in order to loan it to Carl Heine – shouldn't there have been just *one* present when the sheriff made his search? I've asked you about the course of your day, how you spent your afternoon, and at no point did you tell us that you stopped at the chandlery to purchase yourself a new battery, at no point did you say anything suggestive of time spent purchasing or finding a new battery. You didn't tell us that you spent any time getting another battery down in your well – so why, Mr. Miyamoto, why did the sheriff find *two* batteries on your boat if you'd loaned one to Carl Heine?'

The accused man looked once again at the jurors and let a moment of silence pass. Once again his face showed nothing; it was impossible to know what he was thinking. 'I had a spare battery in my shed,' he said evenly. 'I brought it down and put it in before the sheriff showed up with his warrant. That's why he found two batteries when he searched. One of them had just gone in.'

Alvin Hooks put the sheriff's report in its place on the evidence table. With his hands behind his back, as though contemplating this answer, he made his way toward the jurors' platform, where he stopped and turned to face the accused man, nodding at him slowly.

'Mr. Miyamoto,' he said, and his tone suggested admonition. 'You are under oath here to tell the truth. You're under oath to be honest with the court, to be forthcoming with the truth about your role in the death of Carl Heine. And now it seems to me that once again you wish to change your story. You wish to say that you brought a battery from home and inserted it in your battery well during the hour before your boat was searched, or something of that sort – you're adding this now to what you said before. Well then, all right, that's all well and good, but why didn't you tell us this earlier? Why do you change your battery story every time a new question is raised?'

'These things happened almost three months ago,' said Kabuo. 'I don't remember every detail.'

Alvin Hooks held his chin in his fingers. 'You're a hard man to trust, Mr. Miyamoto,' he sighed. 'You sit before us with no expression, keeping a poker face through – '

'Objection!' cut in Nels Gudmundsson, but Judge Lew Fielding was already sitting upright and looking sternly at Alvin. 'You know better than that, Mr. Hooks,' he said. 'Either ask questions that count for something or have a seat and be done with it. Shame on you,' he added.

Alvin Hooks crossed the courtroom one more time and sat down at the prosecutor's table. He picked up his pen and, revolving it in his fingers, looked out the window at the falling snow, which seemed to be slowing finally. 'I can't think of anything more,' he said. 'The witness is free to step down.'

Kabuo Miyamoto rose in the witness box so that the citizens in the gallery saw him fully – a Japanese man standing proudly before them, thick and strong through the torso. They noted his bearing and the strength in his chest; they saw the sinews in his throat. While they watched he turned his dark eyes to the snowfall and gazed at it for a long moment. The citizens in the gallery were reminded of photographs they had seen of Japanese soldiers. The man before them was noble in appearance, and the shadows played across the planes of his face in a way that made their angles harden; his aspect connoted dignity. And there was nothing akin to softness in him anywhere, no part of him that was vulnerable. He was, they decided, not like them at all, and the detached and aloof manner in which he watched the snowfall made this palpable and self-evident.

29

Alvin Hooks, in his final words to the court, characterized the accused man as a murderer in cold blood, one who had decided to kill another man and had executed his plan faithfully. He told the court that Kabuo Miyamoto had been driven by hatred and cold desperation; that after so many years of coveting his lost strawberry fields he had found himself, in early September, in a position to lose them for good. And so he'd gone to Ole Jurgensen and heard from Ole that the land was sold, and then he'd gone to Carl Heine and Carl had turned him away. He'd pondered this crisis during his hours at sea and come to the conclusion that unless he acted, his family's land – for from his point of view it *was* his family's land – would slip from his grasp forever. Like the man he was – a strong man of bold character, trained from an early age at the art of stick fighting; a man Sergeant Victor Maples had described for the court as not only capable of committing murder but willing to commit it as well – this strong, cold, unfeeling man decided to solve his problem. He decided to end the life of another man who stood between him and the land he coveted. He decided that if Carl Heine was dead, Ole would sell him the seven acres.

So it was that he trailed Carl to the fishing grounds at Ship Channel Bank. He followed him out, set his net above him, and watched while the fog concealed everything. Kabuo Miyamoto was a patient man and waited until the deepest part of the night to do what he had in mind. He knew that Carl was not far off, a hundred and fifty yards at best; he could hear his engine in the fog. He listened and then finally, at about one-thirty, he laid hard on his foghorn. In this way he attracted his victim.

Carl, Alvin Hooks explained, came out of the fog towing his net behind – he'd been nearly ready to pick salmon from it – to find the accused man, Kabuo Miyamoto, 'adrift' and 'in need of help'. It was here, he said, that the treachery of the defendant was surely most horrible – for he relied on the code among fishermen to assist one another in times of trouble and on the residue of friendship he knew remained from the youth he and Carl had passed together. Carl, he must have said, I am sorry for what has come between us, but here on the water, adrift in the fog, I plead with you for your help. I beg you to tie up and help me, Carl. Please don't leave me like this.

Imagine, Alvin Hooks implored the jurors, leaning toward them with his hands outstretched like a man petitioning God – imagine this good man stopping to help his enemy in the middle of the night at sea. He moors his boat to his enemy's boat, and while he is busy making fast a line – you will note there is no sign, anywhere, of struggle, such was the treachery of the defendant over there – his enemy leaps aboard with a fishing gaff and strikes a blow to his head. And so this good man falls dead – or nearly dead, that is. He is unconscious and mortally wounded.

Let us imagine, too, said Alvin Hooks, the defendant rolling Carl Heine over a gunnel and the splash on the black night water. The sea closes over Carl Heine – it seeps into his pocket watch, stopping it at 1:47, recording the time of his death – and the defendant stands watching the place where it seals up, leaving no trace behind. But just under the surface the tidal current is working – stronger than the defendant had imagined it – and carries Carl into the folds of his own net, which still trails out behind. The buckle of his bib overalls catches in the webbing and Carl hangs there, under the sea, the evidence of Kabuo Miyamoto's crime waiting to be discovered. It is one of three things the defendant hasn't counted on – the body itself, the bloody fishing gaff, and the mooring line he'd left behind in his haste to leave this scene of murder.

Now he sits in this court before you, Alvin Hooks told

the jurors. Here he is in a court of law with the evidence displayed and the testimony given, the facts all aired and the arguments made and the truth of the matter manifest. There was no uncertainty any more and the jurors were bound to do their duty to the people of Island County. 'This is not a happy occasion,' Alvin Hooks reminded them. 'We are talking about convicting a man of murder in the first degree. We're talking about *justice*, finally. We're talking about looking clearly at the defendant and seeing the truth self-evident in him and in the facts present in this case. Take a good look, ladies and gentlemen, at the defendant sitting over there. Look into his eyes, consider his face, and ask yourselves what your duty is as citizens of this community.'

Just as he had throughout the trial, Nels Gudmundsson rose with a geriatric awkwardness that was painful for the citizens in the gallery to observe. By now they had learned to be patient with him as he cleared his throat and wheezed into his handkerchief. They had learned to anticipate how he would hook his thumbs behind the tiny black catch buttons of his suspenders. The jurors had noted how his left eye floated and how the light winked against its dull, glassy surface as it orbited eccentrically in its socket. They watched him now as he gathered himself up and cleared his throat to speak.

In measured tones, as soberly as he could, Nels recited the facts as he understood them: Kabuo Miyamoto had gone to Ole Jurgensen to inquire about his land. Mr. Jurgensen had directed him to Carl Heine, and Kabuo had sought out Carl. They had spoken and Kabuo had come to believe that Carl was pondering the matter. And so, believing this, he waited. He waited and on the evening of September 15 a circumstance of fate, a coincidence, brought him through the fog at Ship Channel Bank to where Carl was stranded at sea. Kabuo had done what he could in these circumstances to assist the friend he had known since childhood, a boy he'd fished with years earlier. And finally, said Nels, they spoke of the land and resolved this matter between them. Then Kabuo Miyamoto went his way again and fished on into the dawn. And the next day he found himself arrested.

There was no evidence presented, Nels Gudmundsson told the jurors, to suggest that the accused man had planned a murder or that he'd gone to sea in search of blood. The state had not produced a shred of evidence to suggest premeditation. Not a single witness had been brought forward to testify about the defendant's state of mind in the days prior to Carl's death. No one had sat beside Kabuo at a tavern and listened to him rail against Carl Heine or announce his intent to kill him. There were no receipts from any sort of shop where a murder weapon had been newly purchased; there were no journal entries or overheard phone calls or late-night conversations. The state had not proved beyond a reasonable doubt that the crime the defendant had been charged with had in fact occurred. There was more than reasonable doubt, added Nels, but reasonable doubt was all that was needed. There was reasonable doubt, he emphasized, so the jury could not convict.

'The counsel for the state,' added Nels Gudmundsson, 'has proceeded on the assumption that you will be open, ladies and gentlemen, to an argument based on prejudice. He has asked you to look closely at the face of the defendant, presuming that because the accused man is of Japanese descent you will see an enemy there. After all, it is not so long since our country was at war with the Empire of the Rising Sun and its formidable, well-trained soldiers. You all remember the newsreels and war films. You all recall the horrors of those years; Mr. Hooks is counting on that. He is counting on you to act on passions best left to a war of ten years ago. He is counting on you to remember this war and to see Kabuo Miyamoto as somehow connected with it. And, ladies and gentlemen,' Nels Gudmundsson pleaded, 'let us recall that Kabuo Miyamoto *is* connected with it. He is a much-decorated first lieutenant of the United States Army who fought for his country – the United States – in the European theater. If you see in his face a lack of emotion, if you see in him a silent pride, it is the pride and hollowness of a veteran of war who has returned home to *this*. He has returned to find himself the victim of prejudice – make no mistake about it, this trial is about prejudice – in the country he fought to defend.

'Ladies and gentlemen,' Nels pressed on, 'perhaps there is such a thing as fate. Perhaps for inscrutable reasons God has looked down and allowed the accused man to come to this pass, where his very life lies in your hands. An accident of some kind befell Carl Heine at a moment that could not be less propitious or less fortunate for the accused. And yet it happened. It happened and Kabuo Miyamoto has been accused. And here he sits awaiting your verdict, in the hope that although fate has acted against him, human beings will be reasonable. There are things in this universe that we cannot control, and then there are the things we can. Your task as you deliberate together on these proceedings is to ensure that you do nothing to yield to a universe in which things go awry by happen-stance. Let fate, coincidence, and accident conspire; human beings must act on *reason*. And so the shape of Kabuo Miyamoto's eyes, the country of his parents' birth – these things must not influence your decision. You must sentence him simply as an American, equal in the eyes of our legal system to every other American. This is what you've been called here to do. This is what you must do.

'I am an old man,' Nels Gudmundsson continued. 'I do not walk so well anymore, and one of my eyes is useless. I suffer from headaches and from arthritis in my knees. On top of all this I nearly froze to death last night, and today I am weary, having slept not a wink. And so, like you, I hope for warmth tonight and for an end to this storm we are enduring. I would wish for my life to continue pleasantly for many years to come. This final wish, I must admit to myself, is not something I can readily count on, for if I do not pass on in the next ten years I will certainly do so in the next twenty. My life is drawing to a close.

'Why do I say this?' Nels Gudmundsson asked, moving nearer

to the jurors now and leaning toward them, too. 'I say this because as an older man I am prone to ponder matters in the light of death in a way that you are not. I am like a traveler descended from Mars who looks down in astonishment at what passes here. And what I see is the same human frailty passed from generation to generation. What I see is again and again the same sad human frailty. We hate one another; we are the victims of irrational fears. And there is nothing in the stream of human history to suggest we are going to change this. But – I digress, I confess that. I merely wish to point out that in the face of such a world you have only yourselves to rely on. You have only the decision you must make, each of you, alone. And will you contribute to the indifferent forces that ceaselessly conspire toward injustice? Or will you stand up against this endless tide and in the face of it be truly human? In God's name, in the name of humanity, do your duty as jurors. Find Kabuo Miyamoto innocent as charged and let him go home to his family. Return this man to his wife and children. Set him free, as you must.'

Judge Lew Fielding looked down from the bench with the tip of his left forefinger set against his nose and his chin propped against his thumb. As always he had the air of a weary man; he looked reluctantly awake. He appeared to be half-alert at best – his eyelids drooped, his mouth hung open. The judge had been uncomfortable throughout the morning, annoyed by the sensation that he had not performed well, had not conducted the proceedings adroitly. He was a man of high professional standards, a careful and deliberate, exacting judge who held himself to the letter of the law, however soporifically. Having never presided over a trial of murder in the first degree before, he felt himself in a precarious position: if the jury returned a guilty verdict the decision would be his alone as to whether the accused man should hang.

Judge Lew Fielding roused himself and, pulling at his robe, turned his gaze toward the jurors. 'This case,' he announced, 'now draws to a close, and it will be your duty in just a few moments to retire to the room reserved for you and deliberate together toward a verdict. Toward that end, ladies and gentlemen, the court charges you to take into account the following considerations.

'First of all, in order to find the defendant guilty you must be convinced of every element of the charge beyond a reasonable doubt. *Beyond a reasonable doubt*, understand. If a reasonable doubt exists in your minds, you cannot convict the accused man. If there is in your minds a reasonable uncertainty regarding the truth of the charge made here, you must find the defendant not guilty. This is a duty you are bound to by law. No matter how strongly you feel yourselves compelled to act in any other manner, you can convict only if you are certain it is correct to do so beyond a reasonable doubt.

'Second,' said the judge, 'you must keep in mind the specificity of the charge and address that charge exclusively. You have only to determine one thing here: whether or not the defendant is guilty of murder in the first degree, and nothing else. If you determine that he is guilty of something else – of hatred, of assault, of manslaughter, of murder in self-defense, of coldness, of passion, of second-degree murder – none of that will be relevant. The question is whether the man brought before you is guilty of *first-degree* murder. And first-degree murder, ladies and gentlemen, implies a question of *planned intent*. It is a charge that suggests a state of mind in which the guilty party *premeditates a murder in cold blood*. That he thinks about it ahead of time and makes a conscious decision. And here,' said the judge, 'is a difficult matter for jurors in cases of this sort. For premeditation is a condition of the mind and cannot be seen directly. Premeditation must be inferred from the evidence – it must be seen in the acts and words of the human beings who have testified before you, in their conduct and conversation, and in the evidence brought to your attention. In order to find the defendant guilty, you must find that he *planned and intended* to commit the acts for which he has been charged. That he premeditated murder, understand. That he went forth in search of his victim with the conscious intent of committing a premeditated murder. That it did not happen in the heat of the moment or as the accidental result of escalating violence but was rather an act planned and executed by a man with murder on his mind. So once again the court charges you to consider only first-degree murder and absolutely nothing else. You must be convinced beyond a reasonable doubt of one thing and one thing exclusively: that the defendant in this case is guilty of murder in the first degree, premeditated.

'You were selected as jurors in this case,' Judge Lew Fielding continued, 'in the belief that each of you could, without fear, favor, prejudice, or sympathy, in sound judgment and clear conscience, render a just verdict on evidence presented in conformity with these instructions. The very object of our jury system is to secure a verdict by comparison of views and discussion among jurors – provided this can be done reasonably and in a way consistent with the conscientious convictions of each. Each juror should listen, with a disposition to be convinced, to the opinions and arguments of the other jurors. It is not intended under the law that a juror should go into the jury room with a fixed determination that the verdict shall represent his opinion of the case at that moment. Nor is it intended that he should close his ears to the discussions and arguments of his fellow jurors, who are assumed to be equally honest and intelligent. You must, in short, *listen* to one another. Stay objective, be reasonable.'

The judge paused and let his words sink in. He let his eyes meet the eyes of each juror, holding the gaze, momentarily, of each. 'Ladies and gentlemen,' he sighed. 'Since these are criminal proceedings, understand, your verdict – whether guilty or not so – must be a unanimous one. There is no call for haste or for anyone to feel that they are holding up the rest of us as you deliberate. The court thanks you in advance for having served in this trial. The power has gone out and you have passed difficult nights at the Amity Harbor Hotel. It has not been easy for you to concentrate on these proceedings while you are worried about the conditions of your homes and the welfare of your families and loved ones. The storm,' said the judge, 'is beyond our control, but the outcome of this trial is not. The outcome of this trial is up to you now. You may adjourn and begin your deliberations.'

30

At three o'clock in the afternoon the jurors in the trial of Kabuo Miyamoto filed out of the courtroom. Two of the reporters tipped their chairs back precariously and sat with their hands clasped behind their heads, speaking casually to one another. Abel Martinson handcuffed the accused man, then allowed his wife to speak to him once before urging his prisoner toward the basement. 'You're going to be free,' she said to Kabuo. 'They'll do the right thing – you'll see.'

'I don't know,' her husband replied. 'But either way, I love you, Hatsue. Tell the kids I love them, too.'

Nels Gudmundsson gathered his papers together and slid them into his briefcase. Ed Soames, in a generous mood, kept the courtroom open to the public. He understood that the citizens in the gallery had no warm place to go. Many of them sat languidly along the benches or milled in the aisles discussing the trial in hushed and speculative tones. Ed stood with his hands behind his back beside the door to Judge Fielding's chambers in the obsequious pose of a royal footman, watching everything impassively. Occasionally he checked his watch.

In the gallery Ishmael Chambers mulled over his notes, looking up every now and again to take in Hatsue Miyamoto. Listening to her testify that morning he'd been keenly aware of his private knowledge of this woman: he'd understood what each expression suggested, what each pause signified. What he wanted, he realized now, was to drink in the smell of her and to feel her hair in his hands. It was all the more acute for not having her and wanting, like the wish he had to be whole again and to live a different life.

372

Philip Milholland's notes were in Ishmael's front left pants pocket, and it was just a matter of standing up, crossing over to Ed Soames, and asking to see Judge Fielding. Then bringing the notes out and unfolding them, and watching the look on Soames's face, then taking them back from Soames again and pushing his way into the judge's chambers. Then Lew Fielding blinking down through his glasses, pulling the candelabra on his desk a little closer – the flickering taper dancing left and right – and at last the judge peering over his glasses at him as the weight of Philip Milholland's notes began to press against his mind. *The freighter began its dogleg at 1:42. Carl Heine's pocket watch stopped at 1:47.* It spoke for itself.

What was it Nels Gudmundsson had said in closing? '*The counsel for the state has proceeded on the assumption that you will be open, ladies and gentlemen, to an argument based on prejudice . . . He is counting on you to act on passions best left to a war of ten years ago.*' But ten years was not really such a long time at all, and how was he to leave his passion behind when it went on living its own independent life, as tangible as the phantom limb he'd refused for so long to have denervated? As with the limb, so with Hatsue. Hatsue had been taken from his life by history, because history was whimsical and immune to private yearnings. And then there was his mother with her faith in a God who stood at the wayside indifferently while Eric Bledsoe bled to death in the surf, and then there was that boy on the deck of the hospital ship with the blood soaking his groin.

He looked at Hatsue again where she stood in the midst of a small group of Japanese islanders who whispered softly to one another and peered at their watches and waited. He examined her knife-pleated skirt, the blouse she wore with long darts through the shoulders, her hair bound tightly to the back of her head, the plain hat held in her hand. The hand itself, loose and graceful, and the way her ankles fit into her shoes, and the straightness of her back and her refined, true posture that had been the thing to move him in the beginning, back when he was just a child. And the taste of salt on her lips that time when for a second he had touched them with his own boy's lips, clinging to his glass-bottomed box. And then all the times he had touched her body and the fragrance of all that cedar . . .

He got up to leave, and as he did so the courtroom lights flickered on. A mute kind of cheer went up from the gallery, an embarrassed, cautious island cheer; one of the reporters raised his fists into the air, Ed Soames nodded and smiled. The gray, sullen hue that had hung over everything was replaced by a light that seemed brilliant by comparison to what had gone before. 'Electricity,' Nels Gudmundsson said to Ishmael. 'Never knew I'd miss it so much.'

'Go home and get some sleep,' answered Ishmael. 'Turn your heater up.'

Nels snapped the clasps on his briefcase, turned it upright, and set it on the table. 'By the way,' he said suddenly. 'I ever tell you how much I liked your father? Arthur was one admirable man.'

'Yes,' said Ishmael. 'He was.'

Nels pulled at the skin of his throat, then took his briefcase in his hand. 'Well,' he said, with his good eye on Ishmael, the other wandering crazily. 'Regards to your mother, she's a wonderful woman. Let's pray for the right verdict in the meantime.'

'Yes,' said Ishmael. 'Okay.'

Ed Soames announced that the courtroom would remain open until such time as a verdict was reached or until six P.M., whichever came first. At six he would let the gathered court know about the current status of things.

In the cloakroom Ishmael found himself beside Hisao Imada as they both struggled into their overcoats. 'Many thanks for giving to us a help,' Hisao greeted him. 'It make our day much better than walking. We have our many thanks to you.'

They went out into the hallway, where Hatsue waited against the wall, her hands deep in her coat pockets. 'Do you need a ride?' asked Ishmael. 'I'm going out your way again. To my mother's house. I can take you.'

'No,' said Hisao. 'Thank you much. We have made for us a ride.'

Ishmael stood there buttoning his coat with the fingers of his one hand. He buttoned three buttons, starting at the top, and then he slipped his hand into his pants pocket and let it rest against Philip Milholland's notes.

'My husband's trial is unfair,' said Hatsue. 'You ought to put that in your father's newspaper, Ishmael, right across the front page. You should use his newspaper to tell the truth, you know. Let the whole island see it isn't right. It's just because we're Japanese.'

'It isn't my father's newspaper,' answered Ishmael. 'It's mine, Hatsue. I run it.' He brought his hand out and with some awkwardness slipped another button into place. 'I'll be at my mother's,' he told her. 'If you want to come speak to me about this there, that's where you can find me.'

Outside he found that the snow had stopped – only a few scattered flakes fell. A hard winter sunlight seeped through the clouds, and the north wind blew cold and fast. It seemed colder now than it had been that morning; the air burned in his nostrils. The wind and the snow had scoured everything clean; there was the sound of snow crunching under Ishmael's feet, the whine of the wind, and nothing else. The eye of the storm, he knew, had passed; the worst of it was behind them. And yet there was still a blind chaos to the world – cars turned front first to the curbs, abandoned where they had skidded unpredictably; on Harbor Street a white fir fallen against the snow, its branches snapped off at splintering angles, some of them piercing the ground. He walked on and found two cedars across the road, and beyond that the town docks were mostly swamped and under water. The outermost pilings had broken loose, the wind had shoved against the outside piers, and two dozen boats had piled up against one another and finally up onto the sunken piers, where they listed against their mooring ropes.

The white fir's root wad had pulled out of the ground and stood now like a wall more than twenty feet high with a tuft of snow-laden ferns and ivy sprouting over the top of it. Whitecaps roiled among the capsized boats and caused them and the docks to surge and roll, and the tops of the cabins and drum reels and gunnels were loaded down with snow. Occasionally sea foam broke across the boats and water washed through their cockpits. The tide and the wind were pushing in hard now, and the current funneled through the mouth of the harbor; the green boughs and branches of the fallen trees lay scattered across the clean snow.

It occurred to Ishmael for the first time in his life that such destruction could be beautiful.

The reckless water, the frenzied wind, the snow, the downed trees, the boats dashed against their sunken docks – it was harsh and beautiful and disorderly. He was reminded for a moment of Tarawa atoll and its seawall and the palms that lay in rows on their side, knocked down by the compression from the naval guns. It was something he remembered too often. He felt inside not only an aversion to it but an attraction to it as well. He did not want to remember and he wanted to remember. It was not something he could explain.

He stood there looking at the destruction of the harbor and knew he had something inviolable that other men had no inkling of and at the same time he had nothing. For twelve years, he knew, he had waited. He had waited without knowing he was waiting at all, and the waiting had turned into something deeper. He'd been waiting for twelve long years.

The truth now lay in Ishmael's own pocket and he did not know what to do with it. He did not know how to conduct himself and the recklessness he felt about everything was as foreign to him as the sea foam breaking over the snowy boats and over the pilings of the Amity Harbor docks, now swamped and under water. There was no answer in any of it – not in the boats lying on their sides, not in the white fir defeated by the snow or in the downed branches of the cedars. What he felt was the chilly recklessness that had come to waylay his heart.

*   *   *

It was a boat builder who lived out on Woodhouse Cove Road – a gray-bearded man named Alexander Van Ness – who was primarily responsible for holding up a verdict in the trial of Kabuo Miyamoto. For three hours – until six o'clock – he persisted in the same inexorable vein: that Judge Fielding's admonitions should be heeded with the utmost seriousness and that reasonable doubt existed. The twelve jurors had argued over the meaning of the word *doubt*, then over the meaning of the term *reasonable*, then over both put together. 'Well,' Alexander Van Ness had concluded, 'I guess it comes down to a feeling, doesn't it? If I feel uncertain, if I feel that I doubt, that's all that matters, right?'

It had seemed to the others that he would not budge, and they had prepared themselves, by five forty-five, for another long night at the Amity Harbor Hotel and for the necessity of taking the matter up with Alexander Van Ness at eight o'clock the next morning.

'Now look here,' Harold Jensen argued desperately. 'Nobody ain't ever sure about nothing. It's *un*reasonable to be so dog-headed stubborn. What's reasonable comes out of the rest of us, right here. You're what's unreasonable, Alex.'

'I can see what you're driving at,' Roger Porter added. 'I know what you're trying to say, Alex, and I've thought that way about it myself. But look here and think about the straight-off evidence. That mooring line come off his boat. That blood was on his fishing gaff. Mostly he lied about replacing his batt'ry, things like that, it was *fishy*. He just didn't show me nothin'.'

'Me neither,' put in Edith Twardzik. 'Didn't show me a thing, either. It was just suspicious how he sat there like that and said one thing about it to the sheriff one time and then later changed his melody. A person can't go changing his tune 'thout the rest of us thinking on it, Mr. Van Ness – don't you believe that man's a liar?'

Alex Van Ness agreed amiably; the defendant had indeed lied. But that made him a liar, not a murderer. He wasn't accused of lying.

'Now look again,' said Harold Jensen. 'What do you figure

drives a man to lie? You think a man's got to go and lie when he ain't done nothin' worth lying about? A lie's a cover-up every time, it's something a man says when he don't want the truth out. The lies that man's been telling about this, they tell us he's got to be hiding something, don't you agree with that?'

'All right,' answered Alexander Van Ness. 'Then the question is, what's he hiding? Is he necessarily hiding the fact he's a murderer? Does that follow for sure and nothing else? I'm telling you I have my doubts, and that's all I'm trying to tell you. Not that you're wrong, just that I have my doubts.'

'Now listen to this,' snapped Edith Twardzik. 'Supposing a man's got his gun to your son's head and 'nuther one at your wife. He tells you to take yourself exactly one minute and decide whether he ought to shoot your son or your wife, which should he shoot, and if you don't decide, he'll shoot them both. 'Course you're going to have some doubts no matter which way you decide. There's always something to fret about. But meanwhile, while you're fretting, the man's getting ready to pull both triggers, and that's all there is to it, all right? You aren't ever going to get past your doubt so you have to face it head-on.'

'It's a good example,' answered Alex Van Ness. 'But I'm not really in that situation.'

'Well, try looking at it another way, then,' said Burke Latham, a schooner deckhand. 'A big old comet or a chunk of the moon could come crashing down through the roof just now and fall on top of your head. So maybe you'd better move yourself case such a thing might happen. Maybe you'd better have your doubts 'bout whether your chair is safe. You can doubt everything, Mr. Van Ness. Your doubt ain't reasonable.'

'It'd be unreasonable for me to move to another chair,' Alex Van Ness pointed out. 'I'd run the same risk anywhere in the room – same risk you run from your seat, Burke. It's not worth worrying about.'

'We're not talking about the evidence anymore,' Harlan McQueen told them. 'All these hypothetical examples aren't getting us anywhere. How're we going to convince him what's reasonable without talking about the facts presented by the prosecutor, step by step, each one? Now, look here, Mr. Van Ness, don't you think that mooring line has to tell you something?'

'I think it does,' said Alex Van Ness. 'It tells me that Kabuo Miyamoto was probably on board Carl Heine's boat. I don't have much doubt about that.'

'That's one thing,' noted Edith Twardzik. 'That's something, anyway.'

'That fishing gaff,' said Harlan McQueen. 'It had a man's blood on it, Carl Heine's blood type. Can that slip past your doubt?'

'I don't much doubt it was Carl's blood,' Alex Van Ness agreed. 'But chances are it came from his hand. I think there's a chance of that.'

'There's a chance of everything. But you add a chance from here and a chance from there, too many things get to being a chance, they can't all be that way. The world ain't made a coincidences only. If it looks like a dog and walks like a dog,' Burke Latham asserted, 'then most prob'ly it is a dog, that's all there's going to be to it.'

'Are we talking about dogs now?' asked Alex Van Ness. 'How did we get on to dogs?'

'Well, what about this?' said Harlan McQueen. 'The defendant heard about Carl's body being found, but did he go to the sheriff and tell him how the night before he'd seen Carl out fishing? Even after they arrested him, he just kept saying he didn't even know a single thing about it. Then, later, he changed his story, came up with this battery explanation. Then he even altered that, said he put in a spare battery, but only on cross-examination. At this point it's his story against the prosecution's, and I'm finding him a little hard to believe.'

'I don't believe anything about him, either,' Ruth Parkinson said angrily. 'Let's get this done and over with, Mr. Van Ness. Stop being so unreasonable.'

Alex Van Ness rubbed his chin and sighed. 'It's not that I can't be convinced,' he said. 'I'm not so stubborn I can't be made to see the light. There's eleven of you and one of me. I'm all ears and I'll listen to anything. But I won't be in such a hurry as to go in there while I still have what I think are reasonable doubts and condemn the defendant to the hangman's rope or fifty years in prison. You ought to sit back and relax, Mrs. Parkinson. We can't hurry this.'

'Been here almost three hours,' said Burke Latham. 'You saying there's a way to move slower?'

'The mooring line and the fishing gaff,' Harlan McQueen repeated. 'Are you with us on those things, Mr. Van Ness? Can we push forward from there?'

'The mooring line, okay, I'll give you that. The fishing gaffs a maybe, but assume I'll go with you. Where do you take me from there?'

'The different stories he told. Prosecutor really cornered him on having two batteries on board. If he'd really loaned one to Carl Heine, there should have only been one.'

'He said he replaced it. He explained that well enough. He – '

'He added it in at the last minute,' cut in McQueen. 'Made it up only when he was cornered, didn't he? He had his story pretty well lined up, but he left that detail out.'

'True,' said Alexander Van Ness. 'There should have only been one battery. But let's suppose he did board Carl's boat – maybe it was to talk about the land business, maybe Carl attacked him, maybe it was selfdefense or manslaughter, an argument that got out of hand – how do we know this was murder in the first degree, planned out ahead of time? All right, it could be the defendant's guilty of something, but maybe not what he's charged with. How do we know he boarded Carl's boat with the intention of killing him?'

'You heard what all them fishermen said,' Roger Porter answered. 'No one ever boards a boat at sea except in an emergency. He wouldn't have come aboard just to talk, you see. Fishermen don't do things that way.'

'If they only board in an emergency,' said Alex, 'then the

380

battery story makes good sense to me. A dead battery – that's an emergency. It kind of shores up his story.'

'Oh, come on,' said Edith Twardzik. 'Harlan's right about the battery story. Miyamoto didn't anytime loan one to Carl Heine, otherwise he'd only a had one himself. That battery story just won't wash.'

'It was a sucker's ruse,' Burke Latham explained. 'Just like the prosecutor said. Miyamoto pretended he was dead in the water, drifted right down on top of Carl and took advantage of him. That's exactly what happened.'

'Wouldn't put it past him,' said Roger Porter. 'The man looks damn sly to me.'

'That sucker's ruse story,' said Alex Van Ness. 'To me that's just a stretch too far. Drifting down out of the fog like that and exactly into the very man you've got it in your mind to kill. Here it is the middle of the night, fog as thick as pea soup, thicker, and you're expecting you'll just neatly drift in and find the boat you're looking for? That, to me, is a stretch.'

At six o'clock Ed Soames made the announcement: the jurors had adjourned for the night. No verdict had been reached thus far. The courthouse was going to be closed, he added. Everybody should go on home and get a good night's rest, turn up their electric heaters. They could return at nine o'clock in the morning if they wished to know where matters stood.

The jurors ate dinner at the Amity Harbor Hotel and talked of other matters. Alexander Van Ness ate meticulously, wiping his hands on his napkin often and smiling at the others, saying nothing.

31

The power was not yet on along South Beach, and as Ishmael Chambers drove through the snow he glanced into the candlelit windows of the homes he'd known since childhood. The Englunds, Gunnar Torval, Verda Carmichael, Arnold Kruger, the Hansens, the Syvertsens, Bob Timmons, the Crows, Dale Papineau, Virginia Gatewood and the Etheringtons from Seattle who seven years ago had moved to the island for good; he supposed they regretted it now. Foot-long icicles hung from their eaves and the snow lay in drifts against the north side of their house: they should have gone on being summer people. The Crows had both passed away years before, and now their son Nicholas inhabited the place, steadfastly carrying on the border war with Bob Timmons, who had phlebitis in his legs these days and walked stiffly to clear the branches from where they fell among his cedar trees. Nothing had changed and everything had changed. Dale Papineau still drank too much and had no money to speak of. Verda Carmichael was gone.

Ishmael found his mother at her kitchen table once again, reading the last chapter of *Sense and Sensibility* by lantern light and drinking tea with sugar and lemon concentrate. She wore a coat and boots in the house, and her face looked bland and old with no mascara, for which she asked Ishmael's forgiveness. 'I'm getting to be so old,' she admitted. 'There just isn't any way around it.' Then just as before she gave him soup to eat, and he told her how the jurors had not reached a verdict and how the lights were on once more in town and how the docks had been destroyed by storm winds. His mother railed against the possibility that the jurors would be driven by hatred and prejudice; she hoped that in such an eventuality Ishmael would write an editorial. His newspaper, she said, had a responsibility at such times; his father before him had known that. Ishmael nodded and agreed with her; he would write a strong editorial. Then he suggested they pass the night at his apartment with its electric heat and hot water. His mother shook her head and claimed she was content to stick it out at South Beach; they could go to Amity Harbor in the morning if they wanted. So Ishmael loaded the cookstove with firewood and hung his coat in the hall closet. Philip Milholland's notes stayed in his pants pocket.

At eight o'clock the power came on again, and he flipped the furnace switch. He roamed through the house turning off lights and turning up the baseboard heaters. The pipes, he knew, would begin to thaw now, and he decided to sit and listen to the house while it came back to itself. He made tea and took it into his father's old study, a room with a view of the water in daylight and of his father's much-loved rhododendrons. And he sat in silence at his father's desk, in his father's chair, with a single light on. He waited while the furnace gradually warmed the house, and then Ishmael heard water moving in the pipes and the drip from the taps he'd left open. He waited awhile longer before moving through the house again to see that the pressure was strong everywhere, and then he shut down the taps. Everything seemed to have held up.

At nine o'clock his mother kissed his cheek and said she was going to bed. Ishmael returned to his tea in the study, where he pondered his father's books. His father had been, like his mother, a reader, though his idea of good literature differed from hers; he was far less given to novels, in the main, though he read his fair share of them, too. His books stood neatly along the glassed-in shelves of four vaultlike oak bookcases: the collected Shakespeare, Jefferson's essays, Thoreau, Paine, Rousseau, Crèvecoeur, Locke, Emerson, Hawthorne, Melville, Twain, Dickens, Tolstoy. Henri Bergson, William James, Darwin, Buffon, Lyell, Charles Lamb, Sir Francis Bacon, Lord

Chesterton. Swift, Pope, Defoe, Stevenson, Saint Augustine, Aristotle, Virgil, Plutarch. Plato, Sophocles, Homer, Dryden, Coleridge, Shelley, Shaw. *A History of Washington State, A History of the Olympic Peninsula, A History of Island County, Gardens and Gardening, Scientific Agriculture, The Care and Cultivation of Fruit Trees and Ornamental Shrubs.*

His father had loved his fruit trees. He'd tended quietly to his apples and rhododendrons, his chinaberries and mulberry hedges, his rows of vegetables and flowers. He could be found on fall afternoons with a rake in hand, or a splitting maul perhaps. One year he'd painted the eaves and dormers, the clapboards and the deep-shaded summer porch, taking his time, finding pleasure. He never hurried. He did not appear to wish for something else. There were his evenings reading and dozing by the fire or working slowly at his desk. In his study lay two large Karastan rugs, woven in a mountain village in Turkey, the gift of a soldier he'd fought beside at Belleau Wood long ago. Each had knotted, carefully combed tassels, fleur-de-lis borders, ornate medallion designs, and minute scalloping amid a motif of connected eight-spoked wheels, all in rust and fire orange. The desk, too, was pleasing – his father had built it himself. It was a vast expanse of cherry wood the size of an English baron's dining table; smoked glass covered most of its surface. Ishmael recollected his father at work here, his neatly arranged manila folders spread out before him, his yellow legal pad laid off to his right, an array of heavily scrawled index cards, onionskin typing paper in both goldenrod and white, a thick dictionary on a stand, a thicker thesaurus, and a heavy black Underwood typewriter, the desk lamp pulled down low over the keys and his father blinking through his bifocals, slow and expressionless, absorbed in his words, afloat in that pool of soft light. He'd had a cordial, lonely, persevering face, and Ishmael turned now to stare into it, for there was a portrait of Arthur hung on the wall just to the left of a bookcase. There he sat in his high, stiff collar, no more than twenty or twenty-one, a young logger on his day off from the woods. Ishmael knew his father had

384

come to logging with a romantic's sense of grandeur, viewing it at first as grandly heroic, in keeping with the spirit of manifest destiny. He'd come to outgrow this with the passing of time, and then he passed his evenings reading; sleep had seized him like a dark claw while other boys drank their hearts out. He'd educated himself in his spare time, had saved his money with the earnestness of a Horatio Alger, started his own newspaper, gone to war, come home, pressed on, moved forward. He'd built his own house, hauling river stone, milling lumber, a man prominently and wondrously strong far into his forties. He did not mind writing garden club features, school board reports, horse show notices, golden anniversary announcements – he pruned them as carefully as he pruned his hedges, rounding them toward perfection. He'd been, at best, an anguished editorialist; he was incapable of fully indulging himself when it came to condemnation. For he'd recognized limits and the grayness of the world, which is what endeared him to island life, limited as it was by surrounding waters, which imposed upon islanders certain duties and conditions foreign to mainlanders. An enemy on an island is an enemy forever, he'd been fond of reminding his son. There was no blending into an anonymous background, no neighboring society to shift toward. Islanders were required, by the very nature of their landscape, to watch their step moment by moment. No one trod easily upon the emotions of another where the sea licked everywhere against an endless shoreline. And this was excellent and poor at the same time – excellent because it meant most people took care, poor because it meant an inbreeding of the spirit, too much held in, regret and silent brooding, a world whose inhabitants walked in trepidation, in fear of opening up. Considered and considerate, formal at every turn, they were shut out and shut off from the deep interplay of their minds. They could not speak freely because they were cornered: everywhere they turned there was water and more water, a limitless expanse of it in which to drown. They held their breath and walked with care, and this made them who they were inside, constricted and small, good neighbors.

Arthur confessed to not liking them and at the same time loving them deeply. Was such a thing even possible? He hoped for the best from his fellow islanders, he claimed, and trusted God to guide their hearts, though he knew them to be vulnerable to hate.

Ishmael understood, sitting in his father's place, how he'd arrived at the same view of things. He was, it occurred to him, his father's son, and now he brooded in the same spindle-back Windsor chair his father had brooded in.

Ishmael remembered following his father one afternoon as he roamed the grounds of the Strawberry Festival in search of photographs and winning quotes. By three o'clock the sun had swung down over the west goalposts of the high school football field. The tug-of-war, sack hop, and three-legged races were over, and a languidness had inevitably crept over things, so that here and there grown men slept in the grass with newspapers over their faces. Many of the picnickers had eaten to excess and now sat heavy and dulled in the sun, which poured over the scene a clear, clean radiance, a piercing island summer light. The odor of baked salmon hung stale in the air, slightly bitter and slightly acrid from the long smoldering smoke of burning alder leaves, and lay like an invisible pall over the exhausted revelers.

Ishmael walked beside his father past the concession booths where shortcake, bagged popcorn, and caramel apples were sold and down toward the displays of strawberries. And then his father stopped to bring his camera to his eye and photograph the fruit that was the point of it all, and at the same time, peering through his lens, he held up his end of a conversation: 'Mr. Fukida,' he'd called out. 'A banner year for strawberries. How are prices holding up?'

Mr. Fukida, a leathery old farmer in overalls and a billed cap, answered in English that was too precise, too perfect. 'Prices are very good,' he said. 'In fact, excellent, berries selling very well. Mrs. Chambers just now purchased sixteen crates.'

'I see,' said Arthur. 'Sixteen crates. No doubt I'll be asked to help with them, then. Can I trouble you, Mr. Fukida, to move a little to your left? This should make an excellent photograph, you and your beautifully displayed strawberries.'

Mr. Fukida, Ishmael recalled, seemed to have no eyes. His lids had sealed themselves nearly together; occasionally a thin tear trailed out. Working its way along the cracks in his face, it would eventually end as a shine against his cheekbones, which were prominent high points in an otherwise gaunt set of features. He smelled of ginger and onion root tonic and, when he smiled – teeth large as old beach stones – of powdered garlic, too.

'Mrs. Chambers will put up some excellent jam,' Arthur had said, without pride. He shook his head now, admiring with genuine avidity the spread of fruit before him; strawberries arranged in turned-up cedar flats, heavy and pungent, deeply crimson and firm, a regal abundance of them. 'Fit for a queen,' Arthur had said. 'My hat is off to you.'

'Good soil. Good rain. Sunshine. Six children.'

'There must be a secret you're not mentioning. I've tried growing strawberries myself, a few times, and with most of the same ingredients.'

'More children,' said Mr. Fukida, and grinned so that his gold crowns glinted in the sun. 'More children, yes, that is the secret. That is important, Mr. Chambers.'

'Well, we've tried,' said Arthur. 'We've tried hard, Lord knows. But Ishmael here, my boy Ishmael here – he's a match, easily, for two lads, for three! We have high hopes for him.'

'Oh, yes,' Mr. Fukida had said. 'We wish good fortune for him, too. We believe his heart is strong, like his father's. Your son is very good boy.'

Ishmael went up the worn-out stairs to the room he'd slept in for so many years and dug the book on boatmanship out of its box in the closet. There was the envelope with Kenny Yamashita's return address, the upside-down stamp, her smooth handwriting. There was the letter written on rice paper, fast fading after all these years, as brittle as old leaves in winter. With his one hand it would be possible in seconds to squeeze Hatsue's letter into motes of dust and obliterate its message forever. '*I don't love you, Ishmael. . . . When we met that last time in the cedar tree and I felt your body move against mine, I knew with certainty that everything was wrong. I knew we could never be right together . . .*'

He read the letter a second time, gravitating now toward its final words: '*I wish you the very best, Ishmael. Your heart is large and you are gentle and kind, and I know you will do great things in this world, but now I must say good-bye to you. I am going to move on with my life as best I can, and I hope you will too.*'

But the war, his arm, the course of things – it had all made his heart much smaller. He had not moved on at all. He had not done anything great in the world but had instead reported on road-paving projects, garden club meetings, school athletes. He had coasted along for years now, filling the pages of his newspaper with words, burying himself in whatever was safe, typesetting the ferry schedule and the tide table and the classified advertisements. So perhaps that was what her eyes meant now on those rare occasions when she looked at him – he'd shrunk so thoroughly in her estimation, not lived up to who he was. He read her letter another time and understood that she had once admired him, there was something in him she was grateful for even if she could not love him. That was a part of himself he'd lost over the years, that was the part that was gone.

He put the letter away in its box and went down the stairs again. His mother, he found, was asleep in her bed, snoring a little, a rough rattling in her throat; she looked very old in the light from the hallway with her cheek buried against her pillow, a sleeping cap pulled low on her forehead. Her face was a map of wrinkles, and looking at them he felt more deeply how he would miss her when she was gone. It did not matter whether he agreed with her about God. It was only, instead, that she was finally his mother and she had not given up on loving him. His trips to South Beach, he understood now, were as much for his own heart as they were for hers; he had fooled himself for years into thinking otherwise. He had acted as if her death someday – for someday he would have to face the fact that her death would leave him alone in the world – would not pose a problem for him.

Beneath the stars, with his overcoat on, he wandered out into the cold. His feet took their own direction through the cedar woods and underneath the canopy of branches he smelled the old fragrance of the place of his youth and the clean scent of the newly fallen snow. Here under the trees it was fresh and untouched. The branches of the cedars were hung with it and beyond them the sky lay immaculate and decembral, the stars chilled points of light. He followed his feet to where the path met the beach – where a wall of honeysuckle bloomed in summer, intertwined with salmonberries and wild roses – and cut through the dell of snow-covered ferns to the hollowed cedar tree of his youth.

Ishmael sat inside for a brief time with his coat wrapped tightly around him. He listened to the world turned silent by the snow; there was absolutely nothing to hear. The silence of the world roared steadily in his ears while he came to recognize that he did not belong here, he had no place in the tree any longer. Some much younger people should find this tree, hold to it tightly as their deepest secret, as he and Hatsue had. For them it might stave off what he could not help but see with clarity: that the world was silent and cold and bare and that in this lay its terrible beauty.

He got up and walked and came out of the woods and into the Imadas' fields. The way was clear between the rows of buried strawberries and he followed it with the starlight striking off the snow, bathing everything in an aqueous light. And finally he was on the Imadas' porch and then in the Imadas' living room, sitting with Hatsue and her mother and father where he had never been before. Hatsue sat beside him, just beside him, close, wearing a nightgown and her father's old bathrobe, her hair awash in light along her back, falling in cascades around her hips, and he reached into his pocket and unfolded the notes Philip Milholland had written on September 16, and Ishmael explained what the shorthand meant and why he had come at ten-thirty in the night to speak to her after all these years.

32

There was no way to call Lew Fielding with the news because the phones were all dead along South Beach. So the four of them, cups of green tea in hand, the barrel stove murmuring and clicking in its corner, spoke quietly about the trial of Kabuo Miyamoto, which was for them the only subject possible, as it had been for many days. It was late now, the room very warm, the world outside frozen and bathed in starlight, and Ishmael told Hatsue and Hisao and Fujiko that as a reporter who had covered the courthouse in Seattle he felt comfortable offering a present conjecture: that Philip Milholland's notes would force Judge Fielding to call for retrying the case. That the judge would declare a mistrial.

Hatsue recalled that in the course of his testimony the sheriff had described finding a coffee cup – tipped on its side, the sheriff had explained – on the floor of Carl Heine's cabin. It meant, she said, that Carl's gill-netting boat had been rocked by a freighter in the middle of the night – *something* had knocked that coffee cup down, and since Carl had never picked it up it had to be that the very same something had knocked *him* down as well. It *had* to be, she repeated. Her husband's case should be thrown out.

Spilled coffee didn't really prove very much, Fujiko urged her daughter to see. Hisao shook his head in agreement. There had to be more than spilled coffee, he said. Kabuo was facing something very large. He would need more than a coffee cup tipped onto its side to get him out of jail.

Fujiko refilled Ishmael's teacup carefully and asked how his mother was faring. She said she had always thought highly of his family. She complimented Ishmael on the quality of his newspaper. She brought a plate of butter cookies and pleaded with him to eat one. Finally Hatsue's baby began to whimper – they could hear him plainly from one of the back rooms – and Fujiko disappeared.

Just after midnight Ishmael took his leave, shaking hands with Hisao and thanking him for the tea and asking him to thank Fujiko, too. Then he went out. Hatsue followed him onto the porch, wearing rubber boots and her father's old bathrobe, her hands deep in her pockets now, the fog of her breath streaming out of her mouth and billowing over her nose and cheeks. 'Ishmael,' she said. 'I'm grateful.'

'Look,' he replied. 'When you're old and thinking back on things, I hope you'll remember me just a little. I – '

'Yes,' said Hatsue. 'I will.'

She moved closer then, and with her hands still buried deep in her pockets kissed him so softly it was like a whisper against his cheekbone. 'Find someone to marry,' she said to him. 'Have children, Ishmael. Live.'

In the morning his mother roused him at six-fifty, saying that the wife of the accused man was here, waiting for him in the kitchen. Ishmael got up and splashed cold water against his face and put on his clothes and brushed his teeth. When he came down his mother was standing by the cookstove and Hatsue was at the table sipping coffee, and when he saw her he remembered once again how softly she had kissed him the night before. 'Do you want me to leave?' his mother asked from her place in front of the woodstove. 'I'll leave, of course, so you can talk.'

'We'll go in the study,' answered Ishmael. 'Why don't we try the study, Mrs. Miyamoto? Why don't we go in there?'

'Take your coffee,' his mother suggested. 'I'll top it off for you first.'

They made their way to the study, Ishmael leading. The first light of morning – a wintry orange hue dappling the sky – appeared high and far in the distance above the salt water, faint beyond the leaded windows. The rhododendrons were all

392

loaded down with snow; icicles hung from the eaves. Everything looked seized by a white stillness.

Hatsue had plaited her hair into a long braid, glistening, dark, and thick. She wore a thick-ribbed woolen sweater, a pair of navy dungarees, and a pair of calf-high fisherman's boots, and she stood now looking at the portrait of Arthur from long ago, in his logging days. 'You look just like him,' she said to Ishmael. 'I always thought you looked like your father – the eyes especially.'

'You didn't walk over here in the dark and snow just to tell me that,' answered Ishmael. 'What do you have on your mind?'

'I thought about it all night,' said Hatsue. 'Do you remember when my husband testified? He said that Carl had a lantern up. A kerosene lantern lashed to his mast. That he'd put it there because his lights weren't working. He'd lashed a hand-held kerosene lantern high up on his mast.'

Hatsue rubbed her hands together, then separated them again, lightly. 'My idea,' she said to Ishmael, 'is that if that lantern's still up there, right now, wouldn't it mean his batteries really *were* dead? Supposing you looked up Carl's mast and saw a kerosene lantern lashed up there, just like Kabuo said. Wouldn't that tell you something? That his lights were out and he'd lashed up a lantern as a sort of emergency measure? Don't you think that would prove something?'

Ishmael sat down on the edge of his father's desk, scratched his chin, and thought about it. Art Moran's report, the way he recalled it, hadn't said a word about a kerosene lantern lashed up high in Carl's mast, but on the other hand Art could have missed it. Such a thing was possible. At any rate, it was worth finding out.

'All right,' said Ishmael. 'Let's go into town. Let's go in and have a look.'

They took the DeSoto over snow-dazzled roads decorated with cracked and fallen branches and with the green twigs of cedars and hemlocks. The storm had passed and on the west side of

Lundgren Road five children stood at the crest of the hill with sleds and inner tubes at their feet, looking down at the run-out below, a bowl surrounded by slender alder trees and a thicket of low bare vine maple. Ishmael turned west on Indian Knob Hill Road, and they passed the Masuis' strawberry fields and then the Thorsens' milk cow barn and Patsy Larsen's chicken houses. Hatsue sat with her mittens in her lap and her hands held close to the car heater. 'We ought to go to see my husband first,' she said. 'We ought to tell him what's going on. I want to show him the coast guard notes.'

'The jury reconvenes at eight,' answered Ishmael. 'If we can get a look at Carl's boat first, we can go to the courthouse with everything. We can put a stop to the whole business. We can end it all,' he said.

She was silent for a long time, watching him. She looked at him closely and pulled her braid down over her shoulder so that it lay against the front of her sweater. 'You knew about that freighter,' she said finally. 'It wasn't something new, was it.'

'A day,' answered Ishmael. 'I sat on it for a day. I didn't know what I should do.'

She said nothing in the face of this and he turned toward her silence to see what it might mean. 'I'm sorry,' he said. 'It's inexcusable.'

'I understand it,' answered Hatsue.

She nodded and rubbed her hands together, then looked out at the sun-dappled snow. 'Everything looks so pure,' she said. 'It's so beautiful today.'

'Yes, it is,' agreed Ishmael.

At the sheriff's office in Amity Harbor they found Art Moran hunched down at his desk beside an electric heater. When Art saw the two of them come through the door, he dropped his pen at the edge of his desk blotter and stood and covered his eyes with his hands. 'Wait a minute, let me guess,' he said. 'You people are on a mission.'

Hatsue brought out the coast guard notes and, smoothing

them down with the palm of her hand, laid them in the center of his desk.

'Mr. Chambers discovered these,' she said. 'He brought these to me last night.'

'And?'

'A freighter out there,' said Ishmael. 'The night Carl Heine died, a freighter came through Ship Channel Bank, just like – '

'You playing detective?' Art said. 'You trying to be Sherlock Holmes? We got the mooring rope and that fishing gaff with Carl's blood on it – those things speak for themselves, don't they? What else does a body need?'

'Look, Art,' Ishmael answered. 'I suggest that if you're capable of reading shorthand you take a look at those notes there. I think they ought to make you consider at least going down to take another look at Carl's boat, okay? See if there's anything that's been missed, Art. In light of what's on your desk there.'

Art nodded. He nodded at Hatsue, too, for just a moment, and then he sat down beside the electric heater again and took the coast guard notes between his fingers. 'I kin read shorthand,' he said.

He was in the middle of reading the notes to himself, Ishmael and Hatsue watching him, when Abel Martinson came through the door in a pair of knee-high logger's caulk boots and a military issue polar parka, its fur-lined hood pulled tight around his head, his nose and chin a deep red. 'The phones are up,' he announced to the sheriff. 'They just got 'em up, about half the island. Town's got phones and south from there, all the way out to the lighthouse.'

'Listen,' replied the sheriff. 'Listen here, Abel. We're going down to Beason's Cannery dock, to Sommensen's warehouse, okay? You, me, Ishmael here, the lady'll wait at the cafe or something, get herself a breakfast. Can you get yourself a breakfast or something? 'Cause you're a little too close to all of this. You're a little too close to this already. I don't like the smell of it, okay?'

'It's me,' said Ishmael. 'It isn't her. This comes from me all the way.'

'Just the same,' said Art Moran. 'Go get yourself some eggs, Mrs. Miyamoto. Read the papers, maybe.'

Abel blew his warm breath against the lock before opening Sommensen's warehouse – a mildewed barn built of creosoted timbers, put up more than fifty years earlier. Even in the snowstorm it smelled of salt and tar and more faintly of diesel fuel and rotting lumber. Its sea doors opened onto the harbor so that boats could motor in and then out again once repairs were made. Its tin roof kept island rains out; with its two hoists, scaffolding, and wide-elbowed piers, it was a good place to overhaul a boat in winter. For the past two and a half months the sheriff's department had rented it from Arve Sommensen for the purpose of sequestering the *Susan Marie* and the *Islander* in berths side by side. It had been padlocked and on occasion patrolled by Abel Martinson, who kept the key in his pocket. Nothing, he insisted, had been tampered with. The boats had sat in the warehouse untouched since the seventeenth of September.

Abel opened the sea doors wide and a gray light flooded in. Ishmael looked immediately at the *Susan Marie's* mast and then all along her cross spar. No lantern hung anywhere.

They went into Carl Heine's cabin. Ishmael stood in the doorway looking out while the sheriff ran a flashlight across everything – the cased sausage beside the binnacle, the short bunk, the ship's wheel, the battery well. 'You know,' said Ishmael, 'when you were testifying, Art, you mentioned a coffee cup on the floor here, remember? Where was that exactly, the coffee cup? Do you remember exactly where it was?'

'I picked it up,' said Abel Martinson. 'It was right there, in the middle of the floor.'

'Everything else was neat and clean? Just the cup, that's all?'

'Like you see it,' said Abel. 'We didn't change anything – just the cup. I picked it up; a habit, I guess. Something's on the floor, a mess, I pick it up. Can't help myself.'

'Next time, help yourself,' said Art Moran. 'You're making a sheriff's investigation, don't change anything a-tall.'

'Okay,' answered Abel. 'I won't.'

'The cup,' said Ishmael. 'A cup on the floor. Doesn't it suggest this boat got waked? Don't you – '

'There's no *other* evidence,' cut in Art Moran. 'A guy gets waked hard enough to go overboard, you'd expect maybe more 'n a coffee cup on the floor. Everything's so neat and clean.'

They went out and stood just to port of the cabin door while Ishmael maneuvered a flashlight beam up and down the mast. 'You remember that business about the lantern?' said Ishmael. 'How Carl hung a lantern up there? Did you guys take that down?'

'Hold your flashlight still,' answered Abel. 'Just above the cross spar. There.'

He shone his own flashlight upward then, so that two beams shone against the mast now. There were cut lashings of net twine visible there, loose ends dangling, ten or twenty figure eights, cut through cleanly on an angle.

'That's where his lantern was hung,' said Ishmael. 'He'd hung a lantern up there, lashed it up, because all his lights were dead. That's where Carl hung his lantern.'

'We never took no lantern down,' said Art. 'What are you talking about?'

Abel Martinson hoisted himself on top of the cabin, propped one foot against the cowling, and shone his flashlight upward one more time. 'Mr. Chambers is right,' he said.

'Listen,' said the sheriff. 'Climb up there, Abel. Haul yourself up there and take a closer look. And don't touch *anything*.'

'I'll need to push off your hands,' said the deputy, shoving his flashlight in his pocket. 'Give me a boost and I'll go up.'

The sheriff gave Abel Martinson a boost, and he lunged in his polar coat toward the cross spar. He wrapped one arm over it and hung there, the boat rocking, while his other hand fished for the flashlight. 'Looks like a rust streak 'crost these lashings,' he said. 'Like it could be off the handle of a lantern, maybe. Where the handle rubbed against them, maybe.'

'Anything else?' said the sheriff.

'You can see where the lashings been cut,' observed Abel. 'Somebody took a knife to 'em. And hey – something else – this stuff on the mast? It looks like it might be blood.'

'From his hand,' said Ishmael. 'He cut his hand. It was in the coroner's report.'

'There's blood on the mast and the spar pole,' said Abel. 'Not much, but I think it's blood.'

'He cut his hand,' repeated Ishmael. 'He cut his hand making room for Kabuo's battery. Then he got his power back up. Then he climbed up there to take his lantern down because he didn't need it anymore.'

The deputy slid down and landed hard. 'What's with all this?' he said.

'Something else,' said Ishmael. 'You remember Horace's testimony? He said Carl had a shuttle of twine in one pocket and an empty knife sheath knotted to his belt. You remember Horace saying so, sheriff? How the knife sheath was empty, unbuckled? A shuttle of twine and an empty knife sheath. I – '

'He climbed up to take his lantern down,' said Abel. 'That freighter came along and knocked him from the mast. The knife and the lantern went overboard with him – the knife and the lantern were never found, right? – and – '

'Pipe down a minute, Abel,' said Art Moran. 'I can hardly hear myself think.'

'He hit his head on something,' said Abel. 'The freighter wake hit, the boat rolled over, and then he fell and hit his head on something and slid on out of the boat.'

Ten minutes later, in the port side gunnel just below the mast, they found a small fracture in the wood. Three small hairs were embedded in the crack, and Art Moran carved them free with his pocketknife and tucked them into the sheath in his wallet that also held his driver's license. They looked at the hairs in a flashlight beam and then they all fell silent. 'We'll take these up to Horace,' decided Art. 'If they end up to be from Carl Heine's head, the judge will have to take things from there.'

At ten o'clock Judge Fielding sat down with Alvin Hooks and Nels Gudmundsson. At ten forty-five the jurors were told that they were released from any further duties; the charges against the accused man had been dismissed; new evidence had come to light. The accused man himself was set free immediately and walked out of his cell without leg irons or handcuffs; standing just outside its door, he kissed his wife for a long time. Ishmael Chambers took a photograph of this; he watched their kiss through his viewfinder. Then he went back to his office, turned up the heat, and loaded paper in his typewriter. And he sat staring at it for some time.

Ishmael Chambers tried to imagine the truth of what had happened. He shut his eyes and exerted himself to see everything clearly.

The *Susan Marie* had gone dead in the water – the bolt shook loose in her alternator pulley bracket – on the night of September 15. In a drowning fog, impatiently drifting – and too proud to just lay hard on the air horn he carried in anticipation of times such as these – Carl Heine must have cursed his misfortune. Then he lit his two railroad lanterns, slipped his twine shuttle into his back pocket, and hauled himself up to the cross spar on the mast, a lantern slung temporarily down his back, his rubber bib overalls slipping. The cotton twine he used for mending net bound the lantern to the mast easily, but Carl put in extra lashings anyway, figure eights laid one over the other, pulled taut and finished crisply. He hung for a moment, his armpit against the spar, and knew that his light was futile against the fog; nevertheless he adjusted the flame higher before clambering down. And he stood in the cockpit listening, perhaps, with the fog closed in around him.

And perhaps after a while he took his other kerosene lantern and picked out the five-eighths wrench from his toolbox to tighten the alternator pulley belts, cursing again just under his breath: how was it possible he'd neglected this, failed to check it as a matter of course, come to such a pass as his present one (which ordinary seamanship might have prevented), and he a man who prided himself silently on the depth and purity of his seamanship? He tightened the belts, pressed his thumb against them, then went out once again and stood leaning against the port gunnel. Carl Heine listened to the fog and to the sea, to the other boats moving off the bank with their whistles sounding incessantly and to the water softly lapping against his boat as he drifted with the tide, moving east. He stood with one foot up, the kerosene lantern handy, the air horn clutched in his hand. Something in him would not use the horn, and for a good long time, an hour or more, he debated whether he should use it anyway, and he wondered if there were fish in his net. It was then that he heard a boat not far off, the sound of a foghorn blown deliberately, and he turned his ear in its direction. Six times it came, nearer at each blast, and with his watch he timed the precision of its intervals – one minute went by between each. When it drew inside of one hundred yards he gave a single blast on his air horn.

The *Islander*, her hold full of fish, and the *Susan Marie*, dark and dead on the water – a kerosene lantern lashed to her mast, her skipper poised in her bow with his chin set – came together in the fog. Then Kabuo's mooring lines were made fast to deck cleats in the efficiently wrought half hitches Carl Heine could lay out with no thought or hesitation. A battery changed hands, it was somewhat too large, a metal flange was beaten back. Carl's hand was sliced down the palm, there was blood on Kabuo's fishing gaff. An agreement was arrived at eventually. The things that needed to be said were said between them, and Kabuo pushed off into the night.

Maybe it had seemed to Kabuo Miyamoto, alone on the sea shortly afterward, a fortuitous thing to have come across Carl Heine in circumstances such as these. Perhaps it had seemed just the sort of luck he'd long thought he needed. His dream, after all, was close to him now, so close that while he fished he must have

400

imagined it: his strawberry land, the fragrance of fruit, the fold of the fields, the early-summer ripening, his children, Hatsue, his happiness. Oldest son of the Miyamotos, great-grandson of a samurai, and the first of his lineage to become an American in name, place, and heart, he had not given up on being who he was; he had never given up on his family's land or the claim they had to it by all that was right, the human claim that was bigger than hate or war or any smallness or enmity.

And all the while he was thinking this way, celebrating this sudden good fortune in his life and imagining the fragrance of ripening strawberries, he was drifting in the darkness, drifting in fog, with the low moan from the lighthouse barely audible and the steam whistle blasts from the S.S. *Corona* growing louder and coming closer with each moment. And a half mile to the south and west of the *Islander* Carl Heine stood in his cabin door and listened uncertainly to the same whistle blasts now penetrating through the fog. He had made black coffee and held his cup in one hand; the kettle had been stowed in its place. His net was out and running true behind as far as he could tell. All of his lights were burning strong now. His volt meter showed thirteen and a half volts charging, and the *Susan Marie* ran hard and steady, her spotlight suffused in the fog. It was twenty minutes before two o'clock in the morning, enough time left to catch plenty of fish – the coffee would keep him awake long enough to fill his hold with salmon.

Surely Carl had listened to his radio, the lighthouse radioman dispensing advice, the freighter's navigator calling in positions, taking readings off Lanheedron Island, then suddenly deciding on a bisecting dogleg right through Ship Channel Bank. Carl had tried listening into the fog, but the thrum of his own engines masked all other sound, and he had to shut down and drift. He stood again listening and waiting. At last there came another steam whistle blast, closer this time, definitely drawing closer, and he slammed his coffee cup to the table. He went outside then and considered getting hard waked, the big swell from the freighter going right through him, and it seemed to him he was secure to take it, there was nothing to get bounced around very much, everything was in its place.

Except the lantern lashed to the mast. A big freighter wake would smash it to pieces; Carl would have seen it that way.

And so he paid for his fastidious nature, his compulsion to keep things perfect. He paid because he had inherited from his mother a certain tightness through the purse strings. Drifting on the water, the *Corona* bearing down on him in the fogbound night, he figured he needed less than thirty seconds to haul himself up his mast. Save a lantern that way. What were the risks? Does a man ever believe in his own imminent death or in the possibility of accident?

And so because he was who he was – his mother's son, tidy by nature, survivor of the sinking of the U.S.S. *Canton* and thus immune to a fishing boat accident – he climbed his mast with confidence. He climbed it and in so doing opened the palm wound he'd incurred banging against the battery well's metal flange with Kabuo Miyamoto's fishing gaff. Now he hung by his armpit from the cross spar, bleeding and listening into the fog, working his knife from its sheath. Again there came the blast of the freighter's whistle, the low hum of its engines audible to port, so close he twitched in surprise at it, and then with his blade he exerted pressure through the figure-eight lashings he'd made a few hours earlier. Carl came away with the lantern's handle between his fingers and went to lock back his knife.

It must have been that in the ghost fog that night he never saw the wall of water the *Corona* threw at him. The sea rose up from behind the fog and welled underneath the *Susan Marie* so that the coffee cup on the cabin table fell to the floor, and the angle of deflection high up the mast was enough to jar loose the astonished man who hung there not grasping the nature of what was happening, and still he did not foresee his death. His bloody hand lost its grip on the mast, the rubber of his overalls ceased to grip, his arms flew out and his fingers opened, casting the lantern and the knife into the water, and Carl Heine fell swift and hard against the *Susan Marie*'s port gunnel. His head cracked open above the left ear and then he slid heavily beneath the waves, water seeping into his wristwatch, stopping it at 1:47. The *Susan Marie* rocked a full five minutes and while gradually she settled once again the body of her skipper settled, too, into his salmon net. He hung there in the phosphorescence of the sea, gathering light and undulating, and his boat moved now on the tidal current, brightly lit and silent in the fog.

The wall of water moved on. It traveled a half mile speedily and then gathered beneath the *Islander* so that Kabuo felt it, too. It traveled with nothing more to interrupt it and broke against the shore of Lanheedron Island just before two o'clock in the morning. The whistle of the freighter and the lighthouse diaphone sounded again in the fog. Kabuo Miyamoto, his net set, his radio off, the fog as palpable as cotton around him, replaced the line he'd left on Carl's boat with a reserve he kept stowed in his galley. Perhaps he'd squatted for a moment, building a bowline into the manila, and heard the steam whistle of the passing freighter sounding low across the water. It would have been as sorrowful a sound in that heavy fog as anyone could readily conjure or imagine, and as it grew louder – as the freighter drew closer – it would have sounded all the more forlorn. The freighter passed to the north still blowing, and Kabuo listened to it. Perhaps in that moment he remembered how his father had buried everything Japanese beneath the soil of his farm. Or perhaps he thought of Hatsue and of his children and the strawberry farm he would one day pass to them.

The steam whistle from the freighter faded eastward. It sounded at intervals with the fog whistle from the lighthouse, a higher note, more desolate. The fog closed it in, muffling it, and the freighter's note went deep enough so that it seemed otherworldly, not a steam whistle but a cacophony of bass notes rising from the bottom of the sea. Finally it merged with the lighthouse signal so that the two of them sounded at the same moment, a clash of sound, discordant. There was a dissonance, faint, every two minutes across the water, and finally even that disappeared.

Kabuo Miyamoto came home to embrace his wife and to tell her how their lives had changed; the lighthouse dogwatch drew to a close, and Philip Milholland stuffed his notes into a folder and threw himself into sleep. He and the radioman, Robert Miller, slept steadily into the afternoon. Then they awoke and left San Piedro Island, transferred to another station. And Art Moran made his arrest.

Well, thought Ishmael, bending over his typewriter, his fingertips poised just above the keys: the palpitations of Kabuo Miyamoto's heart were unknowable finally. And Hatsue's heart wasn't knowable, either, nor was Carl Heine's. The heart of *any* other, because it had a will, would remain forever mysterious.

Ishmael gave himself to the writing of it, and as he did so he understood this, too: that accident ruled every corner of the universe except the chambers of the human heart.

EAST OF THE MOUNTAINS

To Robin, always,
and for Henry Shain—he loved the mountains

There were ten thousand thousand fruit to touch,
Cherish in hand, lift down, and not let fall.

—ROBERT FROST, *After Apple Picking*

ONE

On the night he had appointed his last among the living, Dr. Ben Givens did not dream, for his sleep was restless and visited by phantoms who guarded the portal to the world of dreams by speaking relentlessly of this world. They spoke of his wife— now dead—and of his daughter, of silent canyons where he had hunted birds, of august peaks he had once ascended, of apples newly plucked from trees, and of vineyards in the foothills of the Apennines. They spoke of rows of campanino apples near Monte Della Torraccia; they spoke of cherry trees on river slopes and of pear blossoms in May sunlight. Now on the roof tiles and against his window a vast Seattle rain fell ceaselessly, as if to remind him that memories are illusions; the din of its beating against the world was in perfect harmony with his insomnia. Dr. Givens shrugged off his past to devote himself to the rain's steady cadence, but no dreams, no deliverance, came to him. Instead he only adjusted his legs—his bladder felt distressingly full—and lay tormented by the unassailable fact that he was dying—dying of colon cancer.

Three hours before first light in the east, wide awake and in defeat, he turned on his lamp, put his feet on the floor, and felt the pain bearing down in his side that plagued him through all his waking hours. He felt it where his colon, on the left, made a turn before dropping toward his pelvic cavity; if he pressed his hand into the flesh there, it produced a sensation of irritability seeping through his abdomen. Ben Givens put his fingers against it and began the insistent, delicate caress that had of late become his habit. He plucked his glasses from the side table, fitted their stems behind his ears, and once again probed his side.

To the west the city where he had passed his adult years lay incidental to the force of the rain, and mostly obscured by it. Eastward the rain fell hard against the hills, but higher up on the flanks of mountains it turned to snow dropping silent against glaciers, on slopes of broken talus rock, and on wind-worn buttresses and outcrops. East of the snow-covered crests of the mountains the sky lay almost clear of clouds; save for a few last spectral wisps of vapor floating beneath the chill points of stars, one's view of the heavens was unimpeded. October moonlight illuminated hay fields, vineyards, sagelands, and apple orchards, and the land lay dry and silent. On the sloping, dark verges of the Columbia River, where Ben Givens had entered the world, the apples hung heavily from fragrant trees, and the windfall fruit lay rotting in the night, gathering a pale sheen of frost.

Ben thought of lonely canyons, of how today he would travel eastward to wander in pale, autumnal light with his dogs quartering the ground in front of him and the quail holding when the dogs went on point—and then he rose with the unsteadiness of morning, shuffled to the bathroom still rubbing his side, propped one hand against the wall above his toilet, and waited with bitter, desolate impatience for the muscles of his pelvic region to recollect how to pass night water. He reminded himself that by dusk of that day—if everything went according to his plan—he would no longer be in this world.

Dr. Givens was a heart surgeon, retired, who had specialized in bypass operations. He had been admired by other doctors for his steadiness of hand, his precision, his endurance, his powers of concentration, and his grace. His assistants knew that when the heart was isolated—when everything human was erased from existence except that narrow antiseptic window through which another's heart could be manipulated—few were as adroit as Dr. Givens.

Now he lived in a much-contained fashion: a restrained, particular man. At seventy-three he had a thick chest and broad shoulders, though the muscles in his limbs had gone soft. Since youth he'd climbed mountains and more mountains, and hiked many miles in all seasons. He'd walked in the high country every winter and snowshoed into lonely canyons. These past nineteen months, since his wife died, he'd returned to a haunting, autumn pastime: he'd hunted birds to shoot on the wing for the first time since he was a teenager. This was a pursuit that stole his soul shortly after Rachel's death, after he'd turned from his work as a surgeon and found himself with too much idle time.

His face was weathered and furrowed, his eyes two dark shields. His coarse gray hair looked permanently wind-tousled, and he walked a bit gingerly, with a bowlegged gait, to keep the weight from his instep. He was so tall that, without thinking about it, he ducked his head to pass through doorways. His patients, in past years, had admired his hands: precise, large, and powerful. When he palpated their chests or listened to their hearts, they were infused with his professional confidence. Dr. Givens had believed fervently in medicine and deferred only grudgingly to its limitations. He had not readily accepted defeat and had struggled with the weaknesses of his patients' hearts as if those weaknesses were an affront to him personally. In this way he had removed himself so that when patients died on the operating table he did not have to feel unduly burdened. He did not have to feel haunted. The main questions for him had been tactical; the rest, he'd felt, was all mystery, and so beyond his governance.

None of this meant that Dr. Givens was devoid of tenderness. His heart wavered when the truth of another's lay exposed and irreparable before him. Always at work he had been aware of his divine power of intervention, and of his helplessness, too. He understood the mortality of human beings and the fallibility of their beating hearts, though these things had kept their distance from him, until his own diagnosis. Now he'd been told—it was the dark logic of the world—that he had months to live, no more. Like all physicians, he knew the truth of such a verdict; he knew full well the force of cancer and how inexorably it operated. He grasped that nothing could stop his death, no matter how hopeful he allowed himself to feel, no matter how deluded. Ben saw how his last months would be, the suffering that was inevitable, the meaningless trajectory his life would take into a meaningless grave. Better to end it now, he'd decided; better to avoid pain than engage it. Better to end his life swiftly, cleanly, and to accept that there would be no thwarting the onslaught of this disease.

As had been his practice since the death of his wife, Ben went out to let his dogs in the house immediately after rising. There were roses growing beside their kennel—summer damasks his wife had planted—and their stalks shone in the rain. The dogs were awake when he came their way to lift the latch to their fenced-in run, the wizened Tristan staring at him where he stood at four o'clock in the morning with an umbrella tightly over his head, the two-year-old Rex leaping high against the wire mesh as if to scrabble over with his forepaws. When Ben swung the gate wide, the young dog leaped and clutched him at the waist, then ran unbounded out into the rain, leaped at nothing, and returned.

They were brown-and-white Brittanies—Rex ran more toward a bronze hue—with fawn-colored noses, tapering muzzles, and eyes well set back in their heads. They were both broad and strong in the hindquarters, and had little feathering at the legs. Tristan, in another time, had been boundlessly energetic; he'd had the habit of pursuing birds with earnest, exuberant good intentions. Now, in his later years, he was increasingly deliberate, more reluctant to plunge into thorns, and generally stayed closer to hand. His tendency to range had been quieted.

When the dogs were coaxed in out of the rain, Ben fed them in the kitchen. He poured a tumbler half full with prune juice—constipation was one of his symptoms—then swallowed two capsules of Docusate sodium and set his tea water to boil. He was accustomed to reading a newspaper over breakfast, but at this hour the boy who brought it around was no doubt blithely sleeping. Ben laid out melba toast, orange marmalade, two small bags of lemon tea, and a jar of applesauce. He arranged a small plate, a knife and spoon, a bowl, and a cup and saucer. When the water boiled, he filled his thermos, then draped a tea bag over its lip to steep while he attended to breakfast. Despite his contest with sleeplessness, he felt keen of mind on this morning, as well as a calm, compelling urge to establish domestic order. There was a protocol to the day that would be pleasurable to follow, in spite of everything.

The dogs lay easily at his feet while he ate and were still there when he pushed his bowl away, gently rubbed his tender side, and sipped his lemon tea. Both of them rose at the same moment he did and followed him soberly into the bedroom, where he took his gun case from the corner of the closet and slid his shotgun free. At this the dogs froze and looked at him with uncertain curiosity.

Ben sighted down the barrels once, flicked the safety on and off, and broke the gun so as to hold it to the light and inspect the condition of the bores. It had once been his father's shotgun, a Winchester 21 side-by-side, choked for quail and chukars. It dropped an inch and a half at the comb, which was, as it turned out, right for Ben, but the length of pull that had worked for his father had not been entirely comfortable and Ben had added two inches to the stock butt. His father took him when he was eight years old to shoot mourning doves at the edge of the apple orchards. The doves flew up from the Columbia to feed, very swift and flocking wildly in the pale light of morning. Ben's father did not broach the subject of hunting's moral perplexity. He only showed Ben how to establish his lead, how to swing through smoothly and easily. Ben's mother, on the other hand, did not approve of bird hunting, and had made her sentiments known to them. Food for the table was necessary, she maintained, but pleasure in killing small birds on the wing was reprehensible in the eyes of God. Ben killed three mourning doves that day and watched them fall at the report of the .410 his father had placed in his hands. He buried their viscera, wings, and heads in a small hole in the ground. Their breast meat was dark and small in the frying pan, dusted with salted flour. He ate the meat with vague regret while his mother watched in silence from the sink, until after awhile she came near to touch his cheek. Then she went to the sink again and scrubbed the pan for him.

Now, in the bedroom, the Winchester in hand, Ben snapped the action closed. He shouldered the gun and swung it along the picture molding, and with his forefinger lightly against the front trigger he squeezed off a silent shot at the seam where the wall met another wall. Rex pranced, high-stepping.

Then Ben set the gun butt against his bed and wrapped his lips around both barrels, as though to fellate them. In this posture he ascertained that in fact the front trigger was just in reach; he had only to extend the full length of one arm, which pushed the sight bead against his palate. If he seized the shotgun in this way, wholly willing, embracing it, allowing the metal to prod his mouth, he could blow the top of his skull off without logistical difficulties. The knowledge that this was indeed possible, that such an act was not out of reach, suffused Dr. Givens with a glandular fear that washed through him like a wave.

Ben put the gun down and packed for his journey with the same judicious deliberation that had been his foremost professional trait: he weighed everything at immoderate length, but made few errors in judgment. He packed his duffel with his upland vest, a box of twenty-five number 8 shells, his shooting gloves, his shotgun sling, a canvas cap with a canted brim, and a whistle hung from a lanyard. He loaded his rucksack with a headlamp and battery pack, maps of Chelan and Douglas Counties, an altimeter, a compass, an aluminum cup, three paraffin fire starters, a roll of waterproof adhesive tape, a medical kit, a needle and thread, an entrenching tool, a folding camp saw, a rain poncho, a length of Manila cord, a pair of field glasses, a vial of lip balm, a tube of sunscreen, prescription sunglasses in their case, a cigarette lighter, insect repellent, a snap box of water-purifying tablets, and a sandwich bag full of toilet paper.

In the kitchen he filled his two water bottles, closed the thermos of tea securely, and turned all three on their heads briefly to check for leaks around the cap seals. He wiped them dry, wiped the table, and washed the breakfast dishes. He had hoped to move his bowels before leaving—the first hour in the car would stop them up firmly, sealing them closed for the length of the day—but he knew there would be no success to the enterprise should he endeavor to sit and wait on the toilet. That would swell his incipient hemorrhoids and encourage the frustration incited in his stomach when he could not void his bowels. Ben was sorry that at the heart of things this day he would carry the sensation of a poisoning fullness and a heavy reminder that he himself was now a blight on the world.

He had taken much of the previous night to page through photograph albums, to read his files of correspondence, and to hold in his hand the earrings and lockets his wife, Rachel, had worn. He had found, in a box, a jar of her sewing buttons, a bulbous-head lavender wand laced with ribbon, a pair of her shoes, a pack of foxglove seeds, and a sketch pad less than a quarter filled with her pencil drawings of trees. He had unzipped the garment bag in the storage room closet and, yielding to sentimentality, burrowed his face into the dresses there in order to retrieve the faint smell of her. He had done like things all evening long and so had found in the endpages of books his mother's neatly fountain-penned signature, and in a hinged cedar box his father's pocket watch, its face glass missing for fifty years. After midnight he came across photos long forgotten, at the bottom of a box, most of Renee, his daughter.

There were photos of him, too. He hadn't been handsome, but he'd been strong and tall, blue-eyed like his mother, lean-jawed like his father. There were photos taken in apple orchards, on the summits of peaks, in uniform, on leave in the mountains of northern Italy.

Now it was morning of the next day. And Ben could not bring himself to extinguish the kitchen light and turn away quite yet. He listened to the hum of the refrigerator and remembered how Rachel had habitually commented on the taste of things they ate together—Jerusalem artichokes dug from the ground, or apples at their sugared prime. He remembered her, too, slicing carrots with a paring knife, the ball of her thumb a stop. Ben shook off his memories, turned out the light, and called the dogs from the living room. It was time to go away from there. It was time to begin his journey.

Dr. Givens kept in his garage a 1969 International Scout, which he used as an adjunct to his sporting life. He had purchased it new twenty-eight years before, and although since then he'd bought and sold other cars, he had not been able to part with the Scout for reasons he could not readily give voice to. He was not a man who fell in love with cars or spoke of them in endearing terms; nevertheless, he felt for this one a certain enduring fondness. The Scout was modestly well-preserved, but idiosyncratic in keeping with its age, with the tics and uncertainties of passing time. It included a four-wheel transfer case and locking hubs one turned by hand after coming to a halt on the road verge. Its heater fan made a hollow din, and through the moldings where the doors met the windshield—the car's top could be removed in good weather—the wind whistled tonelessly. More disconcerting was that the driver's side window regulator had developed with time a modicum of play: the pane chattered at high speeds and irritated Ben deeply. Twice in three years he had taken the door apart and peeled back the plastic vapor shield in an effort to address the problem. To no avail, however. The play in the regulator was fundamentally ambiguous, or perhaps organic to the entire apparatus, which was deteriorating in all its particulars.

He slid his shotgun across the backseat and set his rucksack and duffel next to it. Then he slung down the rear door and entreated his dogs to load up, urging them to leap against their will. As it turned out, he had to lift Tristan in, because there was no room for a running start.

He opened his garage door to the beating rain, but then it occurred to him he had not made certain that the house was left in proper order—the home of a man who intended to return at the end of an ordinary bird-hunting trip—and he went inside once more. He moved methodically from room to room, until he felt secure in his impression that nothing could prompt a post-mortem inquiry, going so far as to leave on the kitchen table the 12-volt bird plucker he'd sent away for last Christmas but never used. He also pulled from a wall cabinet a small file-card recipe box and turned the recipe for quail on toast loosely on the diagonal. He left the box standing on the counter beside the sink with its hinged lid open.

This strategy had possibilities, he realized, so he programmed his VCR to record a show called *Great Railway Journeys* playing on public television, and turned back a copy of *Scientific American*—a Christmas gift from Renee, his daughter—which he placed on his bedside table. He wished he had reserved some bills unpaid to leave behind on top of his dresser: he might have arranged them artfully to appear artlessly strewn.

He had visited his family the evening before, eaten dinner with Renee and Chris, his grandson, in the pretense that everything was ordinary, but in fact to service his end-game ruse. He was going over the mountains, he'd said, to hunt for quail in willow canyons, he had no particular canyons in mind, he intended to return on Thursday evening, though possibly, if the hunting was good, he would return on Friday or Saturday. The lie was open-ended so that his family wouldn't start worrying until he'd been dead for as long as a week—so none would miss or seek him where he rotted silently in the sage. Ben imagined how it might be otherwise, his cancer a pestilent force in their lives, or a pall descending over them like ice, just as they'd begun to emerge from the pall of Rachel's death. The last thing they needed was for Ben to tell them of his terminal colon cancer.

He sat at Renee's table with a fork in his hand, admiring her durable, quiet beauty—at fifty she was slender, thoroughly gray, aging in a poignant, tender way—and taking note of Chris's forearms, which were vein-cabled, thickly corded. He asked after his granddaughter, Emma, who had married a man from Wellington, New Zealand, and was rarely seen in Seattle anymore; he asked after Renee's husband, John, who was on a business trip. Ben urged Renee to talk about her work—she wrote screenplays for children's movies and had penned two highly respected scripts—but she was, as usual, reticent about it out of a native modesty and preferred to deflect the conversation toward Chris, who had embarked on his third year of medical school. He'd begun his clinics, he told Ben. He was seeing patients for the first time, but only for the purpose of asking questions and to practice diagnosis: he found it more interesting than labs. "What about a climb?" he asked out of nowhere. "We haven't gone since August."

"Well, I don't know," answered Ben.

"What about Silver Peak?" insisted his grandson. "Up in the pass. A shakedown cruise. A tune-up run. A day hike."

"I don't know if I can do it anymore. My legs are beginning to wobble."

Chris held a piece of bread in his hand. "What are you talking about?" he demanded. "You're still the toughest old goat in the mountains. Don't start talking like that."

"I'm not the toughest goat in the mountains. That's you, Chris."

"Silver Peak," said his grandson.

They'd climbed together for fifteen years. Chris had been with him on fifty summits. They'd taken lunch on mountaintops, sprawled back easily on their elbows, peaks spread out before them. The boy was strong and confronted his climbs with an admirable good cheer. Ben enjoyed his company. Early he'd taken the boy to the mountains, but of late the boy took him.

"All right, Silver Peak," Ben said, and it was this lie he found most disturbing now, as he stood in his bedroom arranging more lies. "We'll go up there when I get home."

Ben decided he hadn't packed to produce the illusion he wanted. If this was at least a six-day hunting trip, beginning on a Saturday and ending on a Thursday, his outfit would certainly include more clothing, and so he gathered more together—socks, shirts, long underwear, and a worn pair of canvas-faced brush pants. In the bathroom he made up a full toilet kit, including a tube of hemorrhoid cream, a bottle of aspirin, his second pair of glasses, and his bottle of calcium gluconate pills for easing leg cramps at night.

The truth was that at the end of this day of hunting, he intended to set his dogs free on the sagelands, hang himself up between strands of barbed wire—as if he'd been making a low fence crossing—and shoot himself in the carotid artery: shoot himself in the neck. Only his doctor, Bill Ward, would suspect the truth, but even Bill wouldn't feel certain about it, given all the evidence to the contrary, and anyway he wouldn't want to hurt anyone by suggesting that Ben had committed suicide. For Bill, Ben knew, there was a protocol about such matters, a principle governing them. Unless obliged by a coroner's inquest or an insurance agent's inquiry, Bill Ward would keep Ben's cancer to himself.

Pausing in his bathroom, staring in the mirror, Ben recollected his pact with Rachel on the train from Mantua to Bressanone: that the ashes that were the remains of them both would someday make a bed for roses—his for a red rose, hers for a white: the two to grow and intertwine with the passing of many years. It had been the foolish desire of romantics, the sentimental vow of young lovers. It had been the sort of thing young people wish for in their recklessness and passion. He and Rachel, on growing older, had been amused by the idea of these roses, but had not let go of them, either. And he prayed now, thinking of her, that their pact might yet be consummated. He'd preserved her ashes in such a hope.

But perhaps the price of his suicide was that such a thing couldn't happen, and he imagined his bones bleached to dust in the sagelands, scattered about by coyotes. He imagined, too, that his dogs might wander into hunger, hardship, death. He hoped they would somehow fend for themselves and find their way to another hunter, yet he still felt he owed them more than to abandon them in that expanse of empty canyons. His last meal, too, he understood—the breast of a quail, spit-cooked on a fire—would go to nurture nothing but the worms and maggots feeding on a dead man.

When he returned, Rex had jumped across the car seat and had his forepaws over the rucksack. Ben had to prod against his haunches in an effort to force him rearward, Rex resisting stubbornly until Ben caught him at the throat. He spoke frankly to the dog about his behavior, then turned the Scout's engine over. As always it expired momentarily and required a half dozen strokes of the accelerator before the choke sustained itself.

Briefly, he sat idling in front of his house—a half-timbered Tudor, modest in scale—where the telephone answering machine was on, the heat set at fifty-five degrees, and the timers on the lamps in the living room and bedroom set at five and ten P.M., respectively. The rain beat hard so that the house seemed shrouded, beleaguered, and somehow reduced. A neighbor had been solicited to collect the daily newspapers and mail and to move the garbage out to the curb by eight A.M. Tuesday morning. Ben noted, to his satisfaction, that all had been left in proper order. He'd made his arrangements carefully, seeing that every detail was covered. To the last he'd attended to particulars.

Working himself into a seizure of purpose, Ben drove away

without looking back at his home of forty-three years. The rain rattled off the car roof, fell in long streaks through the arcs of streetlamps, and ran torrentially in the gutters. He could not see more than a few yards in front of him, even with the wipers barreling at full speed. Through the glass the streets he passed along seemed only half real, half formed. He leaned forward, squinting a little, switched on the defroster and made an adjustment to the heat lever. It was shy of six o'clock on a Saturday morning; no one else was on the road just yet. No other travelers, just Ben.

On the interstate he poured a cup of lemon tea, steadying it before him on the dashboard so that it shed a crescent of steam against the windshield, and settled back in his seat. There was the high smell of dogs in the car, the sharp odor of their animal digestive tracts, the rain evaporating from their rank fur. There were whitecaps southward on Lake Washington as he crossed the wind-wracked floating bridge. To the north the water was a black expanse, and on the east side, beyond Mercer Island, loomed half-built exit ramps dressed in skins of intricate concrete pouring forms. The wind tore tired leaves from the alders and blew them onto the freeway. The long shore of Lake Sammamish, once a place of marsh and cattails, now lay throttled by condominiums, their yard lamps bathing the valley. At Issaquah, there were more lights: a Triple X Root Beer, a Texaco gas station, a Dairy Queen, Boehm's Candies. Then the last of the suburbs dropped away, and he was climbing the grade above Issaquah Creek beneath the rain-embattled trees.

A tractor-trailer roared past on the right, and a sudden slap of road water, lashed from its tires, washed across his windshield. He could not make out the borders of the lanes or much beyond the rain in his headlights, as white as sleet and flashing rapidly like small electric sparks. Another truck passed, and then there was no one, and Ben took a sip from his lemon tea and fell into fretful meditation.

His cancer had metastasized, traveling from the mucosa of his colon to the lymph nodes close to his tumor, and from there to sites in his liver. Each day he fortified himself once again to accept this intractable state of affairs; each day he started over. He was, he knew, incurable; he had seen too much in his years as a doctor to delude himself that things were otherwise. He knew exactly what to expect and could not turn away from meeting. After the bed-sores and bone fractures, the bacterial infection from the catheter, the fluid accumulating between his viscera that would have to be expunged through a drainage tube; after the copious vomiting, the dehydration and lassitude, the cracked lips, dry mouth, tube feed-ings, and short breath, the dysphagia, pneumonia, and feverishness, the baldness and endgame sensation of strangling; after he had shrunk to eighty-five pounds and was gasping his last in a nursing-home bed—only at that point would Bill Ward put him down under a drip of death-inducing morphine. That was how his life would end if he did not end it first.

He was well aware of countervailing arguments, but these, he saw now, had been forwarded by people not yet confronted by death. He, too, had articulated at times the consolations of a gradual dying: how the trivial paled in the face of death, yet the veins in the tree leaves and the evening slant of light were brought to the forefront of existence. How all was intensified, heightened, compressed, vivified, transformed, appreciated. How love deepened and ordinary tribulations sank into insignificance. How one had time for a summing up, days on which to meditate in search of a divine composure. Yet what had he really known of these matters even as soothing words about them flowed easily from his mouth? What had he fathomed of dying? Ben knew there were regions of pain so bleak they could not be traveled without surgery to sever nerves in the spinal cord. There were re-gions of pain so terrible, they obliterated all argument. The cancer-ridden, often, preferred to die as the only antidote to their suffering. Such was predominantly the case at the end; such might be the case for him, too.

It did not seem to him cowardly to want to avoid pain. He had seen enough of it in his seventy-three years to understand its indifference to character, temperament, or virtue. There was no real bravery in enduring it, but only fear of pain's alternative, the cessation of everything.

The biology of the body, which he'd confronted every day, had not in the least taught Dr. Givens to disbelieve in God. On the contrary, he had seen that the body was divine, and he had witnessed the ceasing of its processes often enough to know that something holy left the body at the very moment of death.

It was sometimes possible—the perception came and went— to view the imminence of his own end with a calm, fearless detachment. In his grave he would experience nothing, the condition of death would not be painful, it was nothing, a kind of sleep. The problem, then, wasn't death but dying, and if the trial of dying could be got through—like any horrifying or painful ordeal—death, the other side, would be endurable. And so the best one could do, it seemed, was to remove the pain and horror from the process by choosing an intelligent suicide. A course well thought out, rational, the least of many possible evils. The worst of it was his present melancholy, and the illusion that after his end came, he would experience an eternal regret. In this netherlife he now endured, he experienced regret already. He felt no longer a part of the world. Everything reeked of the grave.

The rain fell even harder over Tiger Mountain, and by the time he had crossed the Raging River, he had slowed to fifty miles an hour. He passed Echo Lake and Rattlesnake Peak, and in the darkness of morning the hills all around—or what he could see of them through the veil of rain—were a bare shade darker than the sky. The faint first light from out of the east made the crests of the hills just distinguishable from the heavens, and as he traveled down the long grade to North Bend, the profile of Mount Si became visible. Ben had scaled it three dozen times, mostly to test his strength and endurance before more difficult ascents. Its abrupt black fault-scarp seemed to rise up directly from the lights of North Bend's main street, and the promontory of its summit—the Haystack, it was called—appeared forbidding against the sky.

The highway began to climb in earnest, following the south fork of the Snoqualmie River, past Harmon Heights, Cedar Butte, Grouse Ridge, and the low summit of Mount Washington. Here the trucks worked around one another and the wind whistled through the window moldings. Ben passed the cutoff to McClellan Butte—another promontory he had climbed often— and the Tinkham Road cutoff where in the growing light he could see the river steaming. The rain was pummeling the flats along its bank and melding into its currents. Power lines traveled over the hills. As the light of morning grew more expansive, the mist tucked low in the valleys was revealed, and the first snow dusting the high couloirs. It occurred to Ben to follow his present heart and on the spur of the moment change everything, hike in the rain to the summit of Silver Peak, and there simply lie on the crest of the Cascades and wait for the end to come. The plan had a soothing elegance, and the prospect of succumbing to a hypothermic torpor was not really so dreadful. It was less like taking one's life than allowing it to be taken. One just stopped living, that was all.

The mountains beckoned in this way, the green wet flanks of mountains breaking out into windswept scree and snow. Ben shrugged them off and continued on his way. He was bent on crossing into the country beyond. He had been born in the cradle of apple orchards, and it was this world he wanted to return to.

Past Humpback Mountain the road turned north and began to climb more steeply. A trio of haul trucks, convoy-fashion, took the grade at thirty miles an hour in the far right-hand lane. The darkness had mostly given way to the low gray light of early morning, and Ben could see red huckleberry brush and vine maples on the hillsides. Everything glistened and swam with rain, and the creeks plashing down their deep-cut ravines were white and fast with it. The Scout seemed to float for sudden interludes, as if riding weightlessly on shallow surf—there was the spatter of water beneath the wheels and the sense of being unmoored from the earth—and then it would seize the road again. And there were the headlights of a car behind him now, and the tail-lights of two cars in front of him, shimmering beyond his wind-shield. Ben slowed to forty miles an hour and leaned tautly forward. The rain, the wet pavement, the trucks to his right, the windows around him fogged with the breath of dogs—the mo-ment was so fraught with dangers that when Rex hurled suddenly over the seat to settle his forepaws again on the rucksack, Ben felt a surge of anger. The dog had to learn his place in things, as Tristan before him had. He had to understand how it was.

Ben spoke beseechingly at first, then with urgent command in his voice, then with the low melody of gentle threat. When nothing happened—Rex did not move—Ben took him firmly by the collar. "Get back there," he said between clenched teeth, exerting himself to pull the dog off the rucksack, but Rex only whimpered and held his ground.

Ben anchored himself against the Scout's steering wheel and tried to dislodge his dog. Half-turned in his seat, his hand be-hind him and locked at the dog's throat, he did not have time to correct or control matters when the Scout began to slide toward the median. He let go of the dog and swiveled forward, the car skating silently and as if in slow motion, and clutched the steering wheel. The Scout struck the concrete road barrier and rebounded across all four eastbound lanes, sliding miraculously between two haul trucks and down the summit exit ramp, where it slammed into a small fir tree.

TWO

The rain beat hard on the Scout's roof. A boy pulled open the driver's door and placed a hand on Ben's shoulder. "Are you okay?" he asked.

"I don't know," Ben answered. He was holding his head in his palms.

"You need some help? You need a doctor? You're bleeding pretty bad, it looks like."

"I am a doctor," said Ben.

The boy took his hand from Ben's shoulder and shut off the ignition. There was a squall of whimpering from the rear of the car—Tristan and Rex both sounding unnerved—and the boy urged them to settle down. Swinging his wet hair from his eyes, he squatted in the door of the Scout.

"You're going to need some help," he said. "It looks like you need stitches."

"My dogs," said Ben. "How are they?"

Suddenly there was a girl behind the boy, a tall girl in a yellow slicker. "Are you okay?" she asked.

"He's all right," the boy answered gently. "Everything's all right."

"I'm fine," said Ben, "but what about my dogs? How do they look back there?"

"They look good," the boy assured him. "It's you we're worried about."

Ben held the heel of a palm to his forehead, just above his left eyebrow. With his other hand, he slid free his glasses: one lens was broken, the other had popped out, the frames were twisted and mangled. Blood trickled into his left eye and along the left side of his nose with warm constancy. "Your head must've hit the wheel," the boy said. "Here you go. Use this."

From his hip pocket he slid a blue bandanna folded into a square. He leaned into the car and with no hesitation cleaned the blood from Ben's face; then, turning the bandanna inside out, he pressed it against Ben's forehead. "Drop your head back," he advised gently, "and hold this here for a minute."

Ben did. His neck hurt.

"Why don't we get him in the van?" asked the girl. "It's pouring out here and everything."

Ben couldn't see her or anything else with any power of distinction. A dense black shroud lay over his consciousness, and he felt that his brain had been jarred loose. At the same time, he felt startled awake, infused with adrenaline, raw. There was the giddy exhilaration experienced by those who survive accidents intact; there was a sense of freedom and good fortune, of his place among the blessed.

Without his glasses, on any given day, his sight was compromised. Now, with the blood running into his eye, he was vertiginously half blind. He could discern, in the foreground, a few stray details: the boy's long hair pasted against his scalp; the girl tall and slim in her rain gear, its hood pulled over her forehead. He guessed them to be in their early twenties. The boy wore a spindly goatee.

"How's the car?" Ben asked.

"Mangled," said the boy. "Wrapped around a tree. You want me to take a better look?"

"Is it drivable?"

"Your radiator's gone, at the very least. You don't have a cooling system." The boy shrugged and shook his head. "We were right behind you coming through the pass. It's like a miracle you're even alive."

"It's a total miracle," the girl added. "You slid between these two huge trucks. And they didn't even stop or anything. They just kept right on going."

"My dog," Ben said. "I turned because the dog jumped across the seat and . . . the road was wet. I lost control."

He leaned forward, took the bandanna from his forehead, and squinted at himself in the rearview mirror, tilting it in his direction. "That's right," the boy said. "Take a look."

There was a laceration just above his left eyebrow that would require three or four stitches. His glasses had pinched against his face, leaving several minor abrasions. The left eye's lower orbit suggested a tenderness that would darken rapidly into a bruise. He was going to look like a defeated boxer before this episode was over. His eye would swell shut, too.

"You had a little scuffle with your steering wheel," the boy said, squatting beside the car. "Looks like the wheel got the best of it."

"It could have been considerably worse. I actually feel very lucky."

"It's incredible," the girl agreed. "You could have been dead, you know."

"Yes, I could have," Ben said. "It's a kind of miracle."

He swiveled toward the door of the Scout and exerted himself to stand up. The boy assisted him, smoothly. Ben spun dizzily toward the rear of the car and slung down the tailgate. Rex bounded out—Ben cursed the dog as he leaped past—but Tristan stood still and sniffed the rain.

"You still alive, Tris?" Ben asked. And he ran his hands along the dog's flanks and held his muzzle gently. Searching with one eye shut, he found the tire iron. "I'd better pry open my hood," he told the boy, and set the tire iron on the tailgate.

Leaning gingerly through the driver's door, his neck and shoulders stiffening, Ben plucked his coat from the seat back. He rummaged through the rucksack for his spare pair of glasses and slid on his hunting cap. The glasses were antique, steel-rimmed ovals, very small and delicate, bought in 1954. He hadn't worn them in thirty-three years.

When Ben came out into the rain again, the boy had the Scout's hood levered open. He and the girl stood looking underneath it, the girl with her hands in the pockets of her raincoat, the boy holding the tire iron in one hand and rubbing his head with the other. "It doesn't look good," he warned.

The radiator had rammed into the fan shroud; the shroud had split and twisted sideways. The fan had been pushed against the water pump, which was fractured and leaking steadily. The front seal and pulley had bent, and the alternator had been torn from its mounting bracket. The battery had tipped over and lay against the steering box. It was cracked and slowly seeping acid.

The boy bent to peer beneath the car. "Bet your frame's been torqued," he said. "And I can see where you cracked your left front mount. Block could be cracked, too."

The girl had caught Rex by the slack in his collar and was caressing his throat and withers. "Let's go," she said. "We'll leave it here. Let's check out the Traveler's Rest."

"He doesn't deserve that," Ben told her. "Damn you, Rex," he added.

"There's a phone there," the boy said. "You can call a tow truck and everything. Deal with your forehead."

"Let me lock it up," said Ben. He shook his head as he looked things over. "I've had this car for twenty-eight years, and this is the first time it's been scratched."

"I know how you feel," the boy answered, easing the hood down against the rain. "I totalled my Travelall last year. It was the best car I ever had."

Ben looked at him for the first time with something approaching a proper interest. Through the old glasses he could see the world with only moderate, swimming clarity. The boy looked back at Ben earnestly, smiling with a charming ease. He was smooth-faced, brown-eyed, and handsome—as handsome as a movie star. The girl, too, was beautiful, kneeling beside the dog in her rain gear, graceful as a ballerina. Her hair was blond, her eyes blue, and she smiled directly at Ben, holding his gaze with a poise that stirred him. "I like your glasses," she said.

The girl's beauty was a torment. Her wet hand moving against the dog's throat and slowly down the length of the dog's chest filled Ben with a hollow yearning. He turned away from it.

They took him in their van toward the Traveler's Rest, a place he knew in Snoqualmie Pass, a haven for skiers and climbers. The rain beat hard off the windshield and roof, and the dogs were wet against his legs and boots. To the right Ben could see bare ski runs, their distant chair lifts idle; to the left rose slopes of huckleberry brush, subalpine fir, and vine maple. The van, he thought, smelled of lavender, but when he asked about it, the boy explained that the summer previous he and the girl had gone trekking in the Nepalese Himalaya and had come across this distinctive incense of sandalwood, musk, and saffron made by Tibetan monks. While the boy told of finding this fragrance in a village little visited by westerners, very close to the Sikkimese border, Ben sat patting the cut on his forehead and peering through his steel-rimmed glasses. The van had a sleeping berth cleverly up top, a built-in sink, a drop-leaf table, a refrigerator, and a chemical toilet. A length of purple climber's webbing hung in a loop from the rearview mirror, a well-worn carabiner clipped to it, dangling a ring-angle piton. On the dashboard sat an incense holder, an open bag of pumpkin seeds, and a few sprigs of ancient sage.

The girl eased off her yellow slicker—she wore a pile pullover underneath, her ponytail thick against it—and the boy sat drying his hair with one hand, driving easily down the summit road and talking over one shoulder. On the floor to Ben's left, in a cardboard box, were a white gas stove, two stainless steel cooking pots, a handheld water filter, and a candle lantern. Beside that was a grocery bag with the end of a long baguette poking out of it, and wedged in the corner were two sleeping bags inside nylon stuff sacks.

"How's your head?" the girl asked.

"I think it's okay," said Ben.

"You need anything? A drink of water? There's a water bottle in the cooler."

"I'm fine for now. Really."

"There's a first-aid kit," the boy remembered, then leaned across and popped open the glove compartment. "There's some Mercurochrome in there, I think. If you want to use it, go ahead."

The girl put the first-aid kit in her lap and found the Mercurochrome. She closed the glove compartment and smoothed her hair. Smiling, she turned to look at Ben, and at the same time flipped her ponytail deftly over one shoulder.

"We're just about to the Traveler's Rest," she said, as if he were in need of optimism. "We'll be there in just a few seconds."

"I know the place," said Ben.

"We ski up here," the boy explained. "If there's powder up here, we go."

"Otherwise we go over to Mission Ridge," the girl added with enthusiasm. "There's way more powder there, usually. It's way better snow."

"We hit the Rest for coffee," said the boy. "We've been there a million times."

He pulled up in front of it and shut down his engine. There were two other cars in the parking lot, the rain pounding off their roofs and hoods. The Traveler's Rest looked like an old-fashioned ski chalet—Ben remembered it from another time—but in fact it was mostly a convenience store. In the aftermath of hiking and climbing trips he had often stopped here to fill his thermos with tea for the dark westward drive home.

In the foyer, he stood beside a pay phone, where the business cards of towing companies were pinned to a bulletin board. On a placard a man named Steve advertised roof shoveling at "reasonable rates"; a '49 Studebaker was for sale. Plenty of mud had been brought into the foyer on the boots of mountain travelers. Ben held his head—his temples were throbbing—and waited with resigned patience while the phone rang seven times. Then a man answered in a curt, sleepy tone, as if in his life he'd fielded hundreds of such calls, and Ben told him what had happened.

"So what do you want me to do?" asked the man.

"I want you to tow the car," said Ben. "Get it out of there."

"You call the state patrol guys yet?"

"Not yet. But I'll get to it."

"You got insurance or anything?"

"Yes. But not for towing."

"Well, it's a hundred bucks for me to tow you, guy, so I need a credit card number."

"All right," said Ben. "A hundred." And he gave the man a credit card number, reading it from a sleeve in his wallet.

"You want us to make repairs?" said the man.

"I don't know yet. Maybe."

"Well, when will you know? For my information."

"I have to call the insurance agent. It's a Saturday morning and it may take awhile. Besides, it's a '69 International Scout. You'll have a hard time locating parts."

"We can find 'em," the man said. "We can get International, depending on what you need."

"I need a lot," Ben said. "The whole front end is totaled."

"Two days, probably, be my guess. Depends. We have to order from Chicago."

"I'll think about it some, okay?"

"It's five dollars a day to leave it in the yard. You're willing to pay five bucks a day, you can think about it a hundred years."

"That's perfect," Ben said. "You hold the car for me."

"Now what about you?" the man asked. "We've got twenty-four-hour taxi service I can have there in thirty minutes."

"That's okay," Ben heard himself say. "I won't be needing a ride."

"You won't be needing a ride," said the man. "You're up in the pass with a busted-down car. What are you going to do?"

"I have a ride. That's taken care of."

"All right," said the man. "I'm on my way. You say it's in the first summit exit?"

"Yes. Eastbound. Against a small tree."

"I'll see you there, then. About an hour."

"Maybe not. I need a couple stitches. So the key will be sitting on the driver's side leaf spring in case you need to get in."

"That's a good place for it," the man said.

In the rest room Ben leaned toward the mirror to inspect the wound in his forehead. He was surprised at himself for refusing the taxi service—but what did he have to go home to? And why shouldn't he continue with his journey? The young people would certainly give him a ride, and after that he could rent a car—in Ellensburg perhaps, there had to be a place—and continue to his destination.

Prying the wound open with his index fingers, he turned it toward the light. The boy entered with the first-aid kit and stood patiently beside Ben at first, then leaned against the wall with loose-jointed ease, one foot propped up behind him. "What do you think?" he asked.

"It needs to be sutured," Ben answered, though he knew sutures would be a waste of time, given his intentions. He removed his glasses delicately, slipping their stems from each ear with care, bent slowly, stiffly at the waist, cupped his hands beneath the tap, and doused his face, twice. He worked soap into the laceration. When he finished, the boy was at his side, handing him a paper towel.

"There's a couple of choices here," said the boy, rummaging through the first-aid kit. "There's the Mercurochrome. There's hydrogen peroxide. A tube of ointment. This dermal wound cleanser we got in Colorado, it's made from aloe vera."

"I could use some sterile gauze," Ben said. "What kind of ointment is it?"

The boy handed the tube to him. "It's bacitracin," he said.

Ben worked the bacitracin into his wound. After severing the gauze lengthwise with a small pair of scissors, he sliced it into narrow strips and laid them against the adhesive side of a length of waterproof tape. He pressed the dressing to his head and pressed it again, forcefully, with the tips of his index fingers. He put on his glasses, washed his hands, and ran his fingers through his hair, trying to arrange it neatly.

"What about stitches?" the boy asked.

"I know a doctor in Quincy," Ben lied. "It's another two hours east of here. I'd like to get him to do it."

"We're turning south at Vantage," said the boy, "but for sure we can get you that far."

"I could rent a car in Ellensburg. That way I'd be out of your hair."

"Little known fact," the boy said. "There's a rental place in Vantage at the RV campground. I had to use it once."

"You're sure?"

"For sure I'm sure."

"I never noticed it there before."

"It's a small place, but they'll rent you a car."

"All right," Ben said. "Let's do it."

The boy and girl in the Volkswagen van ferried Ben to his car again. He placed the key on the driver's side leaf spring and carefully sorted through his belongings, meditating on every item and casting off whatever seemed useless. He broke down the shotgun and put it in his duffel. He left all the extra clothing in the car—with the exception of two pairs of cotton socks and his thermal underwear—and he jettisoned the dog food and dog bowls. He considered the thermos but left it where it lay on the seat beside his broken glasses. The prescription sunglasses had dropped off the dashboard and fallen onto the floor mat. He slipped them inside his rucksack.

It would look, he hoped, as if he had decided to press on with a modified hunting trip. No one would read the truth, he felt, from the way he had left things here. He imagined his daughter trying to make sense of it: his car abandoned in Snoqualmie Pass, the credit card record of his car rental in Vantage, his corpse rotting in a sage canyon across the Columbia. She would trace his steps, or most of them, he hoped. She would see how naturally it had all unfolded. Her suspicions would be erased.

Ben hauled his duffel bag and rucksack to the van. He opened the side door and set his things on the floor. The two young people stared at him. He glanced at each and then stepped in. "I'm ready," he said. "Let's go."

He rode with them through Snoqualmie Pass to the east side of the mountains. He settled back with the dogs against his legs and let the terrain seep into him. To the northwest, he knew, was Denny Mountain. Twice before he'd walked the ridge to it from Chair Peak and The Tooth. He'd climbed Mount Wright and Preacher Mountain, the winter of 1959, in a pelting downpour of sleet. He remembered climbing Alta Mountain, and the brief, truncated glissades he'd made to work his way back down. He remembered a journey with his grandson to climb Mount Thompson and Kendall Peak, and the high camp they'd established in the lee of a ridge, where the cold caused Chris much misery. Ben had showed him how to warm his fingers by burying them in his armpits.

The girl in the front seat took a water bottle from between her thighs and extended it in Ben's direction. He thanked her for it and drank a little. He fingered the tape against his forehead and worked the vertebrae in his neck. Holding his side, he stared in silence out the window. The girl offered him some pumpkin seeds, and he let her pour them into his hand and ate them at the same rate she did. She'd roasted them, she said, in olive oil, and sprinkled them with sea salt. They were excellent, he told her, and she smiled at this and poured still more into his cupped palms.

"You must be bummed about your car," she said.

"Oh, well," said Ben.

"That's a pretty good attitude. That's what I try to do."

"Yeah," said the boy. "It's great."

"Now where were you going?" the girl asked. "Before you crashed and everything."

"Up near Rock Island," Ben said. "I was born up there. I'm going home."

"It's so beautiful," the girl answered. "All those apple orchards."

"Yes, it is," said Ben.

The boy reached out and touched the girl's cheek with the back of his index finger. She reached across and touched the boy's arm, and then she moved her hand to his shoulder, and from his shoulder to the muscle of his thigh, where she let it linger comfortably.

They were passing Keechelus Lake now. Its waters sat low at this time of year; the basin lay full of weathered stumps. On the far side, off to the south, the big hills were furrowed and deeply eroded, smooth, contoured, treeless. The land, already, was more arid than it had been. The rain had slowed considerably and had spent itself, as it always did, against the green mountains to the west.

"You're a doctor, you say," the boy asked.

"That's right," answered Ben.

"I kind of thought," the boy said, "that you had to hurry with stitches. Like if you waited too long, it didn't work."

"Not true," Ben lied again. "That's a misconception."

"I cut myself bad in the Dolomites," said the boy. "I took a header and laid my shoulder open. The doctor wouldn't even sew me up. He said it had been too long or something. He said it just had to heal."

"In the Dolomites," Ben repeated.

"Yeah."

"They don't know about stitches in the Dolomites," Ben lied. "They're living in the Middle Ages."

"It was incredible there," the girl said. "We totally loved the Dolomites."

"I've been there, too," said Ben.

"Did you go to Cortina?"

"Yes. Some. Mostly further north."

"What did you do?"

"I went hiking and climbing. Years ago. I had my honeymoon there."

"That's great," the girl said. "You don't meet a lot of climbers or anything that are, like, your age."

"This was years ago, " Ben said. "This was fifty-two years ago."

"We climbed the Marmolada," the boy replied. "We stayed at San Martino di Castrozza and went climbing every day. I totally loved the place."

"It's beautiful there," Ben agreed.

"We went up Sella Pass," said the boy. "We climbed all up around Cima Pardoi. We went over to Tre Cime di Laveredo and climbed up in there, too. We would have stayed forever," he added, "except that we ran out of bucks."

"That happens," Ben said. "Reality intrudes."

"Only if you let it," the boy said.

Ben made no answer. He sat with his right hand cupping his waist and his left fingering his bandaged temple. He remembered that long ago in the Dolomites, he and Rachel had taken the high trail from Vigo di Fassa to Ciampedie to see the glow of the setting sun against the Torre di Vaiolet spires. At their hotel on the Lago di Carezza, the electricity was unreliable. At Falzarego they'd bought wine and crostini and traversed uphill to Lagazuoi. At dusk a roseate glow had suffused the world. The mountain walls appeared buffed and polished. In the twilight they came to the Refugio Scotoni, a small inn in a narrow valley. They'd been married only ten days. The mountains were in the scent of Rachel's shoulder blades. The odor at her throat was salt and pine, the smell of her hair, wood smoke.

The Hotel Monte Sella in San Vigilio de Marebbe had been done up in the Jugendstil fashion: rough pine doors with wrought-iron grilles, grisaille tile in the corridors. The plaster had been painted to look like marble. In the vestibule, a lake pastoral, painted delicately against the walls: pleasure boats on turquoise waters, birds aloft over cypress trees, tranquil skies, pines. At midday, the headwaiter used his handbell with a delicate, calm persistence. Bruschetta and saltimbocca, consommé, tortellini filled with mashed potato, scallope di vitello with eggplant. In the lounge, late, card games. An atmosphere of pastoral extravagance. Bottles of grappa set out; carafes of the hotel's house wine—slightly bitter, tannic.

They'd bathed together in a claw-foot tub. The moon risen high over the mountaintops. On the chill, clean air, the chiming of the village bells. In the hall, late revelers moved toward sleep. The smell of the sheets, of bath soap; then no smell but hers. His mouth against her hairline, slow. A long descent toward those incidental places he found he did not want to neglect: the shallow channel in her lower back, the bones in her wrists, her heels. The rest of the world obliterated. Time arrested now. Everything possible, all manner of entanglement pleasurable. When they understood there was no choice anymore, they watched each other without shame.

He'd felt himself at the height of life. He told her so. He said that he loved her. He said that he wanted to hold her forever. He kissed her deeply, sweetly.

Sitting in the back of the Volkswagen van, Ben mistrusted his memories. Everything in memory achieved a truth that was only a brand of falsehood. He remembered what was beautiful—a torture unto itself, really—while all else receded and blurred, dwindled into insignificance. It pained him to think that with his death the narrative of his time with Rachel would disappear, the story of their love expire. He could not explain it to anyone. It would leave the earth when he did.

At the far end of Keechelus Lake, the sky eastward opened wide over distant coulees, buttes, and canyons, all swathed in morning light. Ahead lay a low film of red on the horizon where the sun was new; the road wound down through a stand of grand firs with long, broad, flat needles. Ben sat back and watched the country grow larger and more sparsely treed and gentle. They drove down out of Snoqualmie Pass and left the mountains behind. The girl gave Ben more pumpkin seeds; the boy flipped down his sun visor. They asked him his name, and he gave it to them, and the boy introduced himself as Kevin Lamont and the girl as Christine Reilly. The road ran straight and true into the southeast, the hills spread out beneath the sky, and there was no sign of rain now. Along the Yakima River, the cottonwoods had gone russet yellow. The light was huge and unadulterated. West of the mountains the light ran to gray, hushed and annealed by ocean clouds, but here on the east side the world yielded and lay unguarded beneath the sun.

They came down into the pine flats past the town of Easton, where half a dozen horses grazed on the north side of the highway. They passed the cutoff to Roslyn, the road grading down toward Cle Elum, the river twisting past gravel bars and islands, leaving sloughs and eddies behind, the tincture of autumn woodstove smoke hanging heavily on the air. As they climbed eastward into Elk Heights, the land was all pastures, hills, and range, the big hay sheds loaded to the rafters, the hay wintered under tin roofs. Off to the north was the Stuart Range, distant and ethereal as a mirage.

The country was given over to cattle graze, and the cotton-woods lay in folds and vales that rose toward the east horizon and north to the foothills of snowy peaks. Christine pointed out for Ben the autumnal beauty of all those trees, smoothing her hair just over one ear, and Ben quietly agreed. They climbed over Indian John Hill, where power wires marched west across the land as though cobbled together by the children of giants passing their time playfully. In Elk Heights Pass they saw to the east the hills of bitterbrush and ponderosa pine, and the rangelands of sage and bunchgrass. There were treeless, fruitless, sad buttes, their soil barren as the moon.

"You must be feeling better," said Christine. "You seem nice and mellow."

"I'm fine," said Ben. "I'm comfortable."

"We got the van for that," said Kevin. "It's nice to kind of stretch out."

"We travel a lot," Christine added.

"We're going climbing," Kevin explained. "We're going out to the Sawtooths for a while and then down into Sun Valley."

"If things work out, we'll ski all winter," Christine said hopefully. "That's what we did last season. There's this friend we know in Ketchum who can hook us into the ski patrol."

"Free lift tickets and a crash pad," said Kevin. "Only thing is, it's too crowded."

"We thought we'd get into heli-skiing," said Christine. "You guide people up in the backcountry, get away from the crowd."

"That's a few years off," said Kevin. "We don't have that focused yet."

"We're sort of poor right now," explained Christine. "We just have the cash to get there."

"Not even that," Kevin countered.

He opened the glove compartment, found his sunglasses, and slid them onto his face. They were mirrored glasses of the sort skiers wore, and he looked less handsome in them suddenly, with the mirrors concealing his brown eyes. "The sun," he said. "I'm driving straight into it."

"Better than rain," Christine said.

They passed the Thorp Fruit and Antique Mall. The hills in the distance were barren; eastward the land lay lifeless. They passed a grain silo, fenced pastureland, a row of willows planted as a windbreak beside a forlorn farmhouse. There were long wheeled irrigators lined up by ditches and canals full of runoff water. The river spilled broadly past cutbanks.

"Listen," said Ben. "It's apple season. If you're out of money, you could go up and pick. They'll be looking for people now."

"That's a good idea," Christine said.

"Yeah," said Kevin. "Maybe."

"You know what? It sounds really great."

"It does sounds great, you're right."

Christine put a hand on his thigh again. "I've always wanted to pick," she said.

"We ought to do it," agreed Kevin.

At Ellensburg they passed into the stench of a slaughter-house—the reek of blood spilled into the earth and of the exposed viscera of cows. The yards and gates stood empty now, the corrals deeply pocked by hooves and pools of muddy water. Plumes of steam rose off the ground; hundreds of cows fed until the last on a dirt hillside nearby.

"There's a good reason right there," said Christine, "to totally go vegetarian."

"We tried it once," Kevin said. "Then we sort of slipped."

"We made exceptions. It all fell apart."

"Thanksgiving," said Kevin. "We went to her mom's. What were we supposed to do?"

"We could have stuck to potatoes, you know. We just didn't, was all. We were weak."

They rolled on into the eastward country. The hills were more windswept and vast as they graded up out of the valley. A pig farm stood on the north side of the road, and the pigs wallowed in thick black mud beneath the shade of cottonwoods fast shedding their leaves. Ragged cover followed the fence lines, and the fields in the distance were muddy and furrowed, with the ditch water reflecting sunlight. They were leaving the cultivated, well-kept country and entering hills that had been there before the farms, hills dotted with islands of wheatgrass sprouting up between the sage.

"This stretch of road is spooky," said Christine. "Everything looks so old."

The country appeared bleaker, more desolate. WARNING! a sign read. NEXT EXIT 23 MILES. LAST CHANCE FOR FOOD OR GASOLINE. They drove on past the Kittitas exit, where cottonwoods stood on both sides of a ditch swollen with running water. Big irrigators loomed in the hayfields. Everything was still, silent, and sad; everything looked dilapidated. Against a fence grew Russian thistle, most of which had turned to tumbleweed. At the edge of the highway sat a run-down farmhouse, the ruins of a shed beside it. A swaybacked dog paced its front porch, halting to sniff at a sofa. The sage desert began in the farmhouse's sideyard and ran infinitely eastward.

Ben sat kneading the right side of his belly and staring out the window. The hills rose tan, olive, and brown, and the ribbon of asphalt cutting through them was the darkest thing on the landscape. They passed beneath a railroad trestle; they passed a concrete spillway. The power wires appeared feeble against the hills, like old telegraph lines. Now the road before them steepened, and as they ascended into Ryegrass Summit, Kevin downshifted into third gear. "Everything up here is crumbling," he said. "Erosion city or something."

"Basalt lava," Christine said.

"Old volcanoes."

"Very old volcanoes."

"Like fifty million years."

"Even older."

They made their way over Ryegrass. The country broke open into long barren slopes falling to the Columbia. Off in the distance, off to the east, Ben saw the breaks on the far side of the river shimmer in the October sunlight.

"We're coming into Vantage," said Kevin, moving into the right-hand lane, slowing to take the exit ramp. They emerged from the shadows of the talus buttes, where the river lay throttled behind Wanapum Dam, still and flat, a green lake. A flock of mallards, tightly packed, bobbed together in the lee of the bridge. A magpie perched on a stop sign.

Ben pointed north, upriver. "I was born out there about thirty miles," he said. "Up past the canyon and around a few bends. Back before there were any dams."

"Those were the good times," said Kevin.

Vantage sat sheltered behind windbreak trees—venerable Lombardy poplars. There was a Shell, a Texaco, an RV campground, a restaurant called the Golden Harvest. Kevin turned at the general store and stopped beside a phone booth. He came around and slid open the van's door, his sunglasses in his hand. "Stay," he said, pointing at Rex. "Just hold it right there, dog."

He gestured toward the campground office, through the break of poplars. "If you need to rent yourself a car, you can do it over there."

"Good," Ben said. "Thanks."

"We'd take you on," Kevin added, "but we're turning off toward Othello."

"It's all right," Ben said. "I'm glad to have gotten this far."

"Your eye's swelling up," Kevin observed. "Looks like you're going to have a black eye. It's going to be kind of gnarly."

"That's okay. I can live with that."

"Your neck looks pretty stiff, too. You better just take it easy."

Christine got out and stood in the sun with her hands in the front pockets of her jeans. "What about your dogs?" she asked. "Can we let them run loose out here? Or do you want to tie them up?"

"They can run," Ben said. "They won't go anywhere."

The boy and girl stood to one side and watched the dogs sidle out. Ben followed and slipped on his hunting cap. His side burned. His back hurt. He still couldn't see clearly.

"It's a great day," Kevin declared. "Everything smells like sage."

"It's warm out," added Christine.

The young couple stood by their van holding hands while Ben called his insurance company. He called the state patrol, too. The girl slipped her fingers into the boy's rear pocket, then around his slim waist. The boy pulled her to him, and they kissed briefly. They were seriously in love, Ben could see that. They were easy and familiar with each other. He turned from the sight of them, hung up the phone, and made his way to their van. He hauled his rucksack and duffel bag out, propped them beside the phone booth, and rummaged for the Manila cord he would need to leash Tristan and Rex.

"What's the deal?" asked Kevin.

"My friend's on his way," Ben said. "He'll pick me up right here."

"Okay," said Kevin. "Perfect."

"You forget anything in the van?" asked Christine. "You got everything out here?"

"I think so," Ben said. "I left your bandanna on the seat back there. It probably goes in the trash." He slid his wallet free of his pocket, plucked out four twenty-dollar bills, and thrust them into the girl's hand. "Don't argue," he said. "Just take it."

"We don't want your money," Christine said. "We didn't help you out for this."

"You can skip picking apples this way. That money will get you to the Sawtooths."

"Not a good reason," said Christine.

"Take it. You need it more than I do. So just take it and let's not talk about it."

"No way. Come on."

"Yeah," added Kevin. "Come on."

Ben backed away and put his wallet in his pocket. "You keep that money," he told them.

They stood for a moment looking at him. Then Kevin pulled open the van door. He came out with the bag of pumpkin seeds, a small carton of the Himalayan incense manufactured by Tibetan monks, and the length of purple climber's webbing, threaded with the carabiner and ring-angle piton, that had hung from the rearview mirror. "Here," he said. "Our gift."

"That 'biner is really good luck," explained Christine. "We found it up in the Dolomites."

"You're an old climber," Kevin added. "You ought to take this 'biner."

"I don't know," Ben said.

"Take it. We want you to have it." Christine took the webbing from the boy's hand and looped it over Ben's neck. "There," she said. "It's yours."

"It looks right," Kevin said. "It looks perfect on you."

"Take this other stuff, too," said Christine. And she gave him the incense and the pumpkin seeds. "It's not worth eighty bucks," she said. "But maybe it'll come in handy."

"Thank you," said Ben. "I appreciate it."

They stood looking at him awkwardly, uncertain about taking their leave. "You don't have to wait around," said Ben. "My friend's on his way. It's all taken care of. I can't thank you two enough."

"Okay," said Christine. "Good luck and all."

"Yeah," said Kevin. "Hope it goes well."

The girl reached back for her ponytail and laid it over her left shoulder. Her features, Ben saw, were much like Rachel's: her beauty was in her fine bones. Her beauty was not an ephemeral thing or a condition of her age alone. It would still be there in fifty years, underneath her aging skin. "If you haven't done it already," said Ben, "you two ought to get married."

Christine smiled and nudged Kevin, who put an arm around her neck. "I'm never going to leave her," he said. "I don't need a piece of paper."

"We're soulmates," Christine said. "We're forever."

When they had pulled away in their Volkswagen van, Ben sat down by his rucksack and perched his head against his hands. The van crossed the bridge in the distance, small against the rising hills.

Ben remembered that in Italy, he and Rachel had slipped down between rows of apple trees on the plain of the Po, deep into the cool and dark of orchards, and there they had kissed with the sadness of newlyweds who know that their kisses are too poignantly tender and that their good fortune is subject, like all things, to the crush of time, which remorselessly obliterates what is most desired and pervades all that is beautiful.

THREE

The wound in his forehead throbbed now. There was not a soul to be seen in Vantage; the town appeared lifeless, barren. Below was the silent highway and the river, and to the east spread a sky unfathomably vast, becalmed, devoid of clouds. Everything close, the stones and the grass, seemed hard-edged and vivid to Ben's eyes, but in the distance the clear substance of things gave way to mirages and shadows.

Tristan sidled over to lie at his feet and to rest his throat on Ben's boot. Ben put one hand on the dog's muzzle and with the other prodded his own wounded forehead and massaged his aching temples. He stayed that way for a long while, taking in the dark hills to the south; then he stood and leashed up the dogs with the length of Manila cord. He spoke to them gently, explaining the state of things, but the sound of his voice was strange to his ears and he retreated into silence. Stretching his neck, back, and shoulders, he tried to fend off the lassitude growing in him even at this hour of the morning. It seemed to him he had to move or risk falling into a pause that might become a stupor. At last, drumming up his energy, he maneuvered into the rucksack straps and, bearing his duffel over one shoulder, hiked up toward the campground with his dogs trailing, leashed.

The campground's office smelled of cigarettes, and on a shelf in the front window lay a dusty collection of quartz and petrified wood. On the counter sat a five-gallon aquarium of desultory neon tetras milling behind algae-tinted glass. There was a black velvet scroll, perhaps made in Hong Kong, of a sequined and benign-looking tiger. There were ceramic finger vases, ceramic snakes, and ceramic miniature flamingos. Behind the counter, on a couch in the corner, two small children, a boy and a girl, sat curled under a sleeping bag, watching a cartoon.

"Good morning," Ben said to them. "How are you?"

Neither child answered at first; instead they gawked at his swollen eye, the boy with the sleeping bag pulled up to his chin, the girl with a corner of it in her mouth. "Did somebody punch you?" she finally asked.

"Yes. But I don't want to talk about it."

The girl sat up to see his eye more closely. "What happened? You got busted good."

"I had a fight with a coyote."

"You didn't fight with any coyote."

Ben shook his head, as if disappointed. "Don't believe me," he said.

"I don't. Cuz you're just teasing."

"That's what they all say," said Ben.

She rose haughtily to leave the room, her torso thrust forward and misshapen. She had a severe case of scoliosis and was as bandy-legged as a cowboy. Yet she exited with the hauteur of a duchess who has been toyed with too often. The boy, younger, stared at Ben as if he were an apparition. "Really?" he asked. "For real?"

"Really."

"You should have climbed up a tree," said the boy, "or throwed rocks at him."

"There are a lot of things I should have done. But I didn't think straight."

"What happened?"

"He punched me, I punched him. You know." Ben shrugged.

The boy blinked and put his thumb in his mouth. "The coyote looks worse," Ben said.

The boy's mother came through the door then, trailing the girl behind. She was a heavy woman, not yet thirty, stout in the neck and shoulders. She wore a string of puka shells at her throat and a yellow hooded sweatshirt. "What do you need?" she asked Ben.

"I'd like to rent a car," Ben told her. "I've heard this is the place."

"Not really, not anymore. There was a guy in the campground used to rent a couple cars, but he's gone awhile."

She slid one hand into the pocket of her sweatshirt and inspected his damaged face. "What happened?" she asked. "That looks nasty."

Ben explained that he had crashed his car and banged his head on the steering wheel. "You were just teasing," said the boy. The girl put one hand against her hip, cocked her head, and sighed. "I knew you didn't fight any coyote. Can't nobody fight with a coyote."

Ben sighed in mimicry. "You win," he confessed. "I lied."

"You didn't even lie good. I never believed you for a second."

"You hush now," her mother said. She looked at Ben and shook her head. "She's just like a little grown-up sometimes. I can't figure out what to do with her."

"I have a daughter too," Ben said.

The woman nodded, leaned her weight on the counter, and yawned without embarrassment. There was probably a room at the motel, she said, if he wanted it. The Greyhound bus was coming through later that afternoon. He mentioned the two dogs waiting outside. She shook her head and explained that unless they were Seeing Eye dogs, the bus driver wouldn't let them board.

The motel, she suggested again. He could rest there, get his eye healed up, figure things out tomorrow. It wasn't any trouble for her to call over, let them know he was coming. Their rates were reasonable, she added.

Ben thanked her and picked up his duffel. "I think I'll just call a friend for a ride. But thanks for everything."

"Good-bye, liar," the girl said.

"You hush," said her mother.

Outside, his dogs sat impassively on the ground, watching him as if they expected something. Ben sat beside them, contemplative. The sun stippled the surface of the river, autumn-warm and pleasant. He reconsidered the attractions of a motel. But what would be the point of passing time in Vantage, sprawled out on some melancholy bed, watching television and dozing? It wasn't this he had come for. He patted Tristan's flank for a while, caressed Rex's belly and withers, until gradually he came to accept that his expedition had been thwarted by his accident, that it was time to get home any way he could—time to retreat, regroup, recuperate, then to reconsider this matter of how to meet his end.

He stood, and hauling his rucksack and duffel—his dogs straining on tightly held leashes—headed back to the highway. Ben hadn't hitchhiked in fifty-five years, but now it seemed unavoidable.

He climbed up onto the highway shoulder and stood there brazenly breaking the law with his bags sprawled on the ground next to him and his dogs restless at his side. Ben held his thumb out for a long time, but no one stopped for him. Who would stop for an old man with two dogs and a black eye? The drivers speeding past were from another universe—the universe he'd inhabited as a Seattle physician—and hurled past his extended thumb without concern or apology. One woman shrugged, but Ben couldn't translate the substance of her message. Perhaps she only meant to suggest that while half her heart wanted to serve, the other half was wary of strangers. Or perhaps she meant something more specific, that she was only going as far as the next exit and couldn't be of help to a traveler. Whichever it was, she didn't stop, and neither did other drivers. He was stuck outside of Vantage.

He hadn't reckoned with this possibility; he'd assumed his right to get home. After all, in times past, when he'd been a boy in orchard country, there was nothing illegitimate about hitchhiking or improvising a journey. He'd lived in a world of orchard tramps; a wanderer fell in with other wanderers. Though unwelcomed in settled places, they were not long scorned on paths or byways but generally treated to a ride. Now the cars flew by so fast, a driver could start in Seattle one morning and make North Dakota the next. No one waved or gestured. No one risked stopping at roadside. The world was full of madmen and strangers. Ben understood that he was one of them and that he had no chance of a ride.

Walking north on Wanapum Road, heading toward the Vantage Motel, he met another traveler. A long-haired drifter with thick tresses across his face, lean, tall, sun-burnished, he wore an oversized black leather jacket, its belt hanging limply from worn loops. He hadn't shaved recently, the hair sprouted mostly on his chin and upper lip, and he smoked a hand-rolled cigarette. "Hey, partner," he called to Ben. "I like those hunting dogs."

"Why don't you take them?" Ben answered.

"Can't," said the drifter. "I'm on the road." And he showed Ben his thumb, pointing east.

"I just spent an hour and a half doing that."

"It's the dogs, probably. Hide them in the bushes."

"Why didn't I think of that myself?"

The drifter shrugged. "Who knows?" he said. "Where are you trying to get to?"

"West," said Ben. "Across the mountains."

"The other side," the drifter said. "I haven't been over in a long time."

"Well, I was there a few hours ago. I came over earlier this morning."

The drifter shuffled his shoes in the dust, city shoes incongruous with the sagelands, his black leather jacket incongruous too, cut as if to be worn to a coffeehouse by a traveling blues musician. "Quick trip," he said to Ben. "You came over the pass this morning?"

"Three hours ago, about."

"Well, what are you going back for then?"

"It's a long story," said Ben.

The drifter tossed his cigarette in the road and perched his hands on his hips. "I hate to ask, but could you maybe spare a little change? I'm in need right now."

"I guess so," said Ben.

He set his bags on the road shoulder, experimentally fingered his forehead, then produced a twenty-dollar bill. The drifter took it in easy fashion. "Good man," he said.

"It's all right," Ben answered.

"Good man," the drifter said again. He folded the bill and slid it in his pocket. "So you're headed back, you say."

"I'm not headed anywhere," Ben replied. "I just had my thumb out for an hour and a half. Nobody even slowed down."

"Well, why don't you cross the river there? Go over and pick up Highway 26. People slow down at the intersection."

"It's the wrong way," Ben pointed out. "That's east, and I'm headed west."

"Well, maybe, but it's only a mile east. Put the thing in perspective."

"It's still the wrong way," Ben argued.

"There's no wrong way," the drifter said. "Whatever gets you there."

He propped Ben's duffel on his shoulder like a longshoreman, one arm looped over the top. "I've got this," he said. "Come on."

They set out toward the river. The drifter asked Ben about his damaged eye, and Ben told the story of his accident, the young people in the Volkswagen van, the attempt to rent a car. He said he'd come over the mountains to hunt quail, but with his eye swollen the way it was, he couldn't see well enough to shoot, so he may as well go home.

"Hey," said the drifter. "You can still hunt quail. A lot of people shoot one-eyed."

"It's not the best. No depth perception."

"Adjust," said the drifter. "You can do it."

They were at the west bank of the river now. They set out to cross the highway bridge, the drifter with Ben's duffel over his shoulder, Ben with his rucksack against his back, his dogs checked on tight leashes. The way was narrow, so they went single file, the drifter leading in silence. Ben followed him across the bridge. The Columbia here lay broad and flat. He was glad to see it, after all, glad to make this river crossing. To the east the breaks rose toward the plateau, and it occurred to Ben to hunt chukars. He had never hunted this stretch of country. It was all new terrain, unknown. But what difference could that make to him? Hunting birds in the open air was exactly what he'd come for.

They crossed on the north side with the traffic coming at

them, and as they did, the mallards in the lee of the bridge got up in a great slow easy flush and winged downriver, low, a hundred yards, where they settled again in long skating skids that raised pockets of white water. "Too bad you're not a duck hunter," said the drifter, calling back over one shoulder. "You'd be knocking 'em dead right now."

"Nothing against duck hunting. They're just not what I've come for."

"You're hunting other birds," observed the drifter.

On the far side the drifter stopped at the intersection with Highway 26. He eased Ben's duffel onto the ground. "You made it," he said. "All right."

"I'm here," said Ben. "I don't know exactly why. But anyway, I'm here."

The drifter lit another hand-rolled cigarette with a kitchen match struck off his pants zipper. "Park your dogs down there in the bushes," he said, "and try sticking your thumb out."

"I don't think I will. These breaks here might have chukar in them. I came to hunt. I'll hunt them."

"You changed your mind," said the drifter.

"I did," said Ben. "That happens."

"I change my mind all the time," said the drifter. "That's what's normal for me."

Ben tied his dogs to a fence post, spread his tin-cloth coat on the ground, opened the upland vest beside it, and laid out the items in the two bags neatly, where he could contemplate them one after the other. The drifter smoked, watching, and flipped the hair from his eyes. Ben turned the twin barrels of his shotgun to the sunlight, aligned the lug with the hinge pin, and snapped the gun together. "Winchester 21," said the drifter. "Top choice of heroes."

"I've had it forever," said Ben.

Deliberately, he pressed twenty-three number 8 shells into the loops in his upland vest and slipped the remaining two into a bellows pocket where he could bring them easily to hand. The tin-cloth coat he rolled up tightly and lashed it with the blanket and folded duffel against the bottom of his rucksack. Finally he put on the vest and the shooting gloves and pulled down his canvas cap tightly. He slid the whistle lanyard over his neck, then nestled the Winchester in the crook of his arm. "Hey," said the drifter. "Metamorphosis. You look like one ace hunter."

"Cyclops," said Ben. "Cyclops the hunter."

"Orion's the hunter," said the drifter.

Ben stood, looking up at the breaks. "You're out of here," the drifter told him. "Put your pack on, and you're free of it all. You're off into the hills."

"I'm dying of cancer," Ben told him. "So I guess I can do what I want."

The drifter drew on his cigarette, as if he'd heard nothing special. He spoke with the smoke streaming out of his mouth. "What kind of cancer?" he asked.

"The dying kind," Ben answered.

"We're all dying. You're just closer to it."

"You've been reading too many books. Or watching too many movies."

"Whatever," said the drifter. "But it's true."

"It's true, but it's like talking about the weather. I'm really dying. It's different."

The drifter picked up a stone and threw it into the Columbia. "No, it isn't," he insisted. "Except, maybe, that you're dealing with pain. Hey, wait—I've got something you can use, a little bit, along those lines."

He took from his jacket a breath-mint tin. He opened it and drew out three hand-rolled cigarettes. "You've heard about this," he said to Ben. "Medicinal marijuana. Joints."

"I don't want them."

"Yes, you do."

"I wouldn't use them."

"They've got magic powers."

"Put it away."

"It's a pain reliever."

"Put it away," repeated Ben.

The drifter slid the three marijuana cigarettes into his own jacket pocket. "This half is mine," he said. Then he knelt beside Ben's rucksack and stuffed the tin with its three other cigarettes into the cargo compartment. He stood again and smiled, snaggle-toothed. "You can toss them out in the desert," he said. "But I wouldn't, if I were you."

"I'm going to," said Ben.

"Well, either way, best of luck out there."

"I'll need more than luck, shooting with one eye. The hunting gods better be with me."

"They are," said the drifter. "I can feel it, partner. The hunting gods are with you."

"I hope so," said Ben.

A car approached from out of the east, and the drifter bounded up to the road shoulder. "We look like a tag team," he called to him. "You'd better get out of here."

"Okay," said Ben. "I'm sorry."

"Smoke that dope," the drifter advised. "And take care of those dogs. And happy hunting."

"I'll see what I can do," said Ben.

He set free his dogs and they quartered ahead, into the desert country. Ben went after them, traversing uphill, climbing the breaks above the river. Putting discomfort out of his mind, he passed between rough bands of basalt stained in pale streaks with bird droppings. Twice he stopped to ease his breath and rest half-bent with his palms against his knees. Far below lay the bridge he'd crossed and the silver-tinted river. He could see the dam at Wanapum, the sun pale in the southern sky, the canyon walls scalloped and scoured, the petrified drift of the basalt flows. He could see the drifter, still hitchhiking. To the north the river narrowed again and squeezed between bland rock walls before disappearing around a bend. The prairie smelled of sage and of the dampness held in the earth. Overhead the vast expanse of sky ran so deeply and unbroken to blue that he felt a momentary vertigo.

Ben knew he was leaving the world behind. He took courage from the pungent smell of the desert, and gradually—as he knew they would—his life and death became less disturbing, inconsequential somehow.

He hunted northward in open country, following the broken line of the ridge top, the river running below him in the west, the dogs working at a cross angle to the soft October breeze. Rabbit brush and purple sage festooned the bunchgrass prairie. A dozen times the dogs flushed flitting sparrows, who at the last minute bolted forward into far-off patches of cover. Rex would roust them out once more and send them in spurts of three or four, banging like popcorn out of the sage, then away across the hills. The shadow of a hawk passed over the land, and then the hawk bore down in lazy circles, caught the swelling river breezes, and rode broadside across the breaks, working south with ease. Ben stopped, slipped free of his rucksack, and drank from his water bottle. He felt broken in, less raw and fragile, though a ligament behind his left knee seemed bound up from the steepness of the climb, and in his left hip joint there was bone-against-bone clicking and sliding beneath the fascia. Yet vaguely he felt improved by the high air. The desert fragrance had cleaned his sinuses. He rested, fingered his side, and soon rose to hunt again over the breaks behind his pointing dogs.

He found a fire ring full of charred fence posts, a rusted coffee can holding dry, leached stones, and a plastic bucket turned upside down, tattered and torn along its flanks where shotgun pellets had passed through it. Two beer bottles were set against a strand of rusting, low barbed wire, and then no further sign of people. Ben felt right inside his loneliness. It was just as he had wanted.

He came across deer droppings against porous rock and beside them a patch of orange lichen. The sun came more laterally from west of southwest to burnish the left side of his face, and in the breeze his hands felt dry and worn. As he walked, he poked up under his sunglasses at the tender lower orbit of his eye and pulled and prodded gently against it to keep his depth of field intact, since the swelling had greatly reduced the world and unhinged his sense of distance. He knew that when it came to it, he would shoot the way beginners did, aiming deliberately with one eye shut. His view of the fleeing bird would be foreshortened, deluded, lacking in perspective.

Late in the day, he sat for a long time, drinking water in great swallows. He ate a handful of the pumpkin seeds the girl in the van had given him, worked the hinge on the Italian carabiner, and touched the ring-angle piton. He remembered using ring-angle pitons on the North Peak of Mount Index in 1957. He thought of Christine Reilly, then of Rachel in Italy: the train from Mantua. He and Rachel had boarded late, in sunlight that bathed the window of their sleeper car with a warm copper hue. It had inundated Rachel's face as they moved past the ocher and sienna walls of the flats on the edge of town.

He remembered it all so vividly: how the two of them sat in silence while the train gathered speed. The trembling of the train subsided gradually into a steady, pleasant vibration. The land outside seemed to travel with them, as did the sun and the violet sky, against which a church spire rose high, slim, pale as the moon.

Only the birds, swooping south from tree to tree, seemed free of the force that propelled the fabric of the world northward.

That night they lay in their mingled scent, in the heat of each other's breathing. At midnight they swallowed the last of their wine. He remembered taking her face in his hands. "Roses," she'd said. "Red and white. They'll make a single bush of pink roses."

"All right," Ben had said. "Roses."

She mentioned it a final time the day before she died. "Remember," she told him, two hours before her surgery. "You're red and I'm white."

"The mortality rate in a mitral-valve replacement for someone in your state of health is approximately one in a billion," Ben said. "You're going to be just fine."

"I'm not planning on dying, Ben. But if I do, remember about the roses. And remember how much I loved you."

It was early evening, the light fallen low, when he came across his first chukars. The air had cooled with the dying of the sun, and the birds were on the move to forage on the succulent blades and seeds of bunchgrass growing along the ridge crest. As they fed, they separated and called to one another reassuringly; Ben heard their gregarious, staccato clucking before his dogs could catch their scent riding on the wind. He stopped to listen and to fix their location. He cradled the shotgun in the crook of his arm and called the dogs in close. He listened with his palm cupped around his ear, turning his head down the long route of the horizon. The chukars, he thought, were feeding to the north, though with them there was no real certainty, for their low fast call always seemed to Ben to come from everywhere at once.

He had not pushed ahead more than thirty paces when Tristan became hotly agitated. The dog raised his snout to the breeze and trotted forward twenty yards, and with this the chukars stopped calling. Rex cut hard and fast behind Tristan, down into the breaks to follow scent where no doubt the birds had laid up through the heat before abandoning their cover for the ridge crest. It was silent now. Ben moved up between the dogs and dug in his thumb against the safety tang. Tristan had gone all stalkingly tight and was edging right and left again. Ben understood that when the birds broke at last, they would hurl themselves cleverly over the break and he would have the low sun in his eyes. He held his shotgun lightly. Rex bounded up into view from below with his withers flattened and his ears back. The dogs worked aprowl before him with their noses trailing fresh ground scent and Ben stopped to collect himself, should the birds suddenly flush. He relocated forward, set his feet, and adjusted the tilt of his sunglasses. He had just swung his rucksack onto the ground when Tristan halted twenty yards out and locked up high at both ends beautifully, classically gone on point.

Ben edged tensely forward. "Stay where you are," he said to Rex, who had not stopped pounding insatiably through the cover as if to put up all the birds. The dog, against his will, held up.

Then everything was still and silent. Ben had time to think. In his teenage years it had been his habit to pass on the initial shot at chukars, since they always posted a sentry, like the cow guard in a band of feeding elk. The first bird often flushed wild at a distance from where the feeding covey would flush outside of shooting range. More than that practicality, there was something poignant in passing on a first shot and standing in silence while the bird fled. There was something haunting in it.

When the lone bird got up at last, it held low to the purple sage, and in the late October light Ben saw plainly its dark barred markings, its vermilion feet, and its chestnut tail feathers. There was the quiet stirring of a single bird's wings while swiftly the chukar dropped over the breaks and sailed out freely above the river, where suddenly it grew incidental and disappeared down the hill.

Immediately the dogs moved forward, as though the flushed bird had been a shadow. Ben worked wide to his right and ahead so that the shots he might take would be more direct and less like passing shots. In the next moment, the dogs went on point together, a few yards apart in a patch of high bunchgrass, Rex pitched leftward with one paw raised, Tristan low and stretched solidly. Ben flicked off his safety and calmed his reeling heart.

It was always at this moment that he hesitated to take the life of a bird. It had been this way since he was eight years old, shooting mourning doves alongside his father. It had been easier for him in his teenage years, though still he had felt a flicker of doubt, been haunted by the feeling that something was amiss—and, of course, after the war, after killing was a part of him, he'd stopped hunting altogether. He had stopped fishing, too. He'd been done altogether with killing. Yet he'd embraced it again after Rachel died, the killing had become a substitute life, and in the past two autumns he'd taken up again the pastimes of his childhood— shooting small birds in canyons and sagelands, deceiving geese from cold pit-blinds, killing mallards in the bends of sloughs.

Ben stood waiting for the birds to flush. A chukar got up under Rex's nose, winging low toward the river breaks, and he shot it with the open barrel bored as if for shooting skeet, and suddenly chukars were everywhere, leaving cover in a bold flush, a dozen or more leaping from the bunchgrass while Ben was frozen by the weight of his astonishment and swung through on one bird and then another, and at last gave out with the second barrel, which was choked down tightly for a distant shot, and the chukar rose higher on the wing, as if assailed by a fast-rising breeze, and sailed wounded toward the sagebrush.

Ben broke open his Winchester and laid it over his forearm.

He was befuddled to have shot so well with the use of one eye only. There was a terrible injustice in it for him, as though shooting well were only luck. Or bad luck for the birds who fell at the hollow report of his father's gun.

Down the breaks below his feet, the remaining chukars settled. Ben knew they would sit for a lonesome interlude and finally in frantic desperation call with a yearning to meet again, until the covey reassembled. He wanted to hunt them while they were likely to hold, waiting for him to pass by.

He worked Tristan after the cripple. When the dog maneuvered close enough, the wounded chukar abandoned cover and dragged its left wing through the sage. Ben felt sullied by what had happened and watched helplessly while Tristan gave chase, pounced to seize the running bird, and clutched it softly between his teeth in a puff of gently floating feathers.

At the crest of the breaks Ben stood, bird in hand, and watched while Rex brought the other slain bird in and laid it neatly on the table rock. He praised his dogs, though not too profusely, as they stood panting at his side. Ben slid the first bird into his coat pocket and picked up the second to examine it, a young male with small, rounded spurs. He tucked it in beside the first.

The sun lay low against the mountains, but there was still good shooting light. He slid off his sunglasses, fingered the dressing over his eye, and worked on his steel-rimmed glasses. He drank some water—he emptied one bottle—and then he went after the singles slowly, leaving his rucksack behind on the ground, urging the dogs to stay close.

Last hunt, he told himself.

He hunted three hundred feet downhill. He missed on the first, but then there were others, and he felt satisfied. One bird he took straightaway on a second shot, staying beneath it as it barreled downhill; the next flushed from behind a stone tower and, unlike most chukars he'd seen as a boy, flew toward him along a steady contour twenty yards below his gun, so that he had to swing patiently for the longest time and kill it on the late going away.

He held this last bird in his hand. A dark band passed rakishly over its eyes, and the black bars along its flanks lay symmetrically, sleekly ruffled. The tail feathers were chestnut brown and the feathers elsewhere an olive color, in places darker or a blue-tinted gray; they lay well-ordered in delicate waves and were soft and thick against its breast. The warmth of life was still in it.

It was unfathomable to Ben that he had decided to die under circumstances so cruel. Odd not to have thought of this before—a death in the arid sageland, alone, in the aftermath of killing small birds. He could not understand the end he'd chosen except as an act of stoic machismo, and that was not enough. The shooting and the land were not enough. Hunting small birds as his final earthly act—it was inadequate, somehow, and misdirected, at odds with the life he had lived as a doctor, a husband, and a father. But so was the act of taking his own life instead of seeing it through. So was killing himself. Suicide was at odds with the life he knew, at odds with all he understood, of himself and of the world.

Ben put the bird in his coat pocket. He climbed the breaks in the last light of day with a steady pain in his side. The day was closing around him now. Things could not hold light any longer. Weary of climbing, short of breath, he paid no attention to his hunting dogs. The darkness seeped into and over the land, and inevitably into Ben too, as he saw the world swallowed by night.

He was too tired and in too much pain for the long hike back into Vantage. He sat and waited for things to improve, but there was only the sweep of the night wind blowing and the discord of his breathing. Reluctantly, he climbed fifty feet, and fifty more, until he came to his rucksack.

Somewhere in the night a coyote called, tremblingly high like a melancholy flautist, and with such ornate, long-winded insistence, it was impossible to know if it was one animal or many out toward the Frenchman Hills. A night music native to this country of Ben's birth; a grievous howling, as if the land mourned itself. Ben remembered a Wanapum man, with whom he'd boxed apples sixty years before, saying that the cry of a single coyote often sounded like the cry of many.

Now Ben breasted one of the chukars and fed the boned meat to his dogs. He tossed the remains of the bird down the hill; he watered his dogs from his aluminum cup, pouring a ration for each. He ate more of the pumpkin seeds Christine Reilly had given him and drank his own water ration. Then, digging in the rucksack for his headlamp, he came across the breath-mint tin of three marijuana cigarettes. Ben took one out and sniffed it. He pondered what he knew of *Cannabis sativa.* That it eased the pain of cancer was a well-established medical fact. And yet he remained adverse to it. Its associations were foreign to him. On the other hand, why not?

He got out his lighter and lit the cigarette against the grain of his principles, astonished at himself. The smell, inhaled, was pungent, raw. He felt the searing of the smoke in his lungs, and his windpipe rejected it. Exhaling, he gasped roughly. A veil soon dropped over the world. He brought the cigarette to his lips again and sucked on it until its tip glowed orange, then blew thick smoke through his nostrils in long double plumes.

Ben noted the strangeness of things. Nothing particularly troublesome, but certainly an odd difference—the desert poised, crystallized.

He drew again on the cigarette. Its acrid, green odor sweetened the chill air. He drew again deeply into his chest and held the smoke until his face turned a strangled red.

After that, he felt inured to pain but hungrier and thirstier than before. He ate more of the pumpkin seeds. He indulged in them and drank half of his water. He spread the duffel bag and the rain poncho on the ground, stuffed the remaining chukars in his rucksack, and lay down wrapped up tightly in his blanket like a nomad in the desert.

Ben's dogs excavated and maneuvered in the sand, settling in at his side. He urged them closer for the warmth they could provide. It was good to have them near, companions. They were sentinels, too, beside him there in the frigid, inhospitable night.

Resting his head on the folded hunting vest, he watched the stars with his one good eye, their light blurred through his glasses. His mind raced, his thoughts were rich, his memories vivid, graphic. He felt he could touch the past.

FOUR

Ben's parents had planted rows of apple trees on the east bank of the Columbia River. Their orchards were sheltered by Lombardy poplars and fell toward the river in an immaculate sweep, the rows full of irrigation ditches, sharp-bladed quack grass growing dense, and branch props leaning against forked limbs. There were thirteen acres of Golden Delicious, two of Winesaps, two of Rome Beauties, and eight of cherries and apricots. There were shanties for the pickers who came in June, a weathered shed for making boxes and for packing apples in oiled tissue, a barn loaded with hay to the rafters, a stable for the horses, a chicken house, an outhouse, an icehouse, and a small-well pump house. The Givenses' farmhouse sat on a knoll surrounded by shade elms and willows. Even inside, the world smelled of sage, and from the front window the setting sun bronzed the hills stretching westward. When the wind came up, the tops of trees swirled, so that with the windows flung open on summer evenings the crash of branches came startlingly loud. Year around was the wind in the trees, the drifting fragrance of sage.

Ben made apple boxes out of pine shook, pulled weeds in the kitchen garden, split cordwood for the fireplace, and milked cows twice a day. In the spring he helped his father and brother put out the pollinating hives. When the rains came, the sluice gates clogged with weeds, and Ben and Aidan stood in the ditches to clean them out by hand. There were also windbreak trees to plant and Jonathan pollinating trees. In April and May there were young trees to plant and finished trees to pull out. In early summer they disced between the rows to keep the mice from the orchards. In July they put spreader sticks in the yearling trees and strapped the branches back. Midsummer there was always fruit to thin and branches to prop and strap back carefully to keep them from cracking beneath the apples. In August came the picking season; in fall and winter there was pruning to do, and piles of water sprouts to burn.

Where the orchards ended, the desert began—buttes, coulees, unnamed canyons, arid expanses of infinite reach, sun-beaten, silent, and lonesome. Ben and Aidan took the dogs into this country in search of quail, chukars, and sage grouse, and occasionally got a shot at a jackrabbit. They rode on horseback when they had the chance, their shotguns slung across their backs, their canteens slapping against their saddles. Sometimes they camped in the sage at night, where they drew and spitted their birds carefully, stuffed sage sprigs inside the empty bellies, and cooked the meat on a twig fire. Then they lay back with their hands behind their heads and talked and watched the heavens.

Aidan was older than Ben by twenty months, stocky, sturdy, even-tempered. He worked with a pine sliver set between his teeth, a sheen of sweat on his collarbones, and the front of his shirt soaked in a line from breastbone to navel. Generally he wore his hat low on his forehead, so that his eyes were heavily shaded by its brim, but when somebody spoke to him he canted the brim up and listened with much animation around the eyes before answering.

Aidan was agreeable, amiable. His skin was brown, his eyes blue. He liked to swim in the river at dusk, just upstream from the ranch house, in the backwash of a small eddy. Ben and Aidan would strip on the bank, tossing their shirts and pants up high against the warm, polished shore rocks. They stretched their limbs and ran their hands along their bellies and through hair flecked with pollen dust, apple litterfall, or blossom petals. Then they splashed into the river. It rippled gently across their backs, and in the eddy they rode the current and swam against it while up the hill the orchards glowed in the last light.

In late fall the Givenses went mountain climbing. They took the train into Stevens Pass with a picnic lunch inside their knapsacks and walked open ridges in all weathers, ascending to unnamed summits. Their mother and father sat on a blanket while Ben and Aidan leaned against stones to look down on forests foreign to them in their density and reach. Ben claimed he could smell the salt of the sea, though it was off two hundred miles, carried on the mountain breeze. To the east the mountains gave way to sage, but westward loomed impenetrable forests, and they spoke of hiking into them to places no one had ever seen. They spoke of traveling for weeks in the mountains to see the uncharted high country, as though they were explorers or pioneers and not the sons of orchardists.

In Leavenworth, one year, they bought wooden skis with bent-metal toepieces and leather straps, to ski down Big Chief Mountain. Ben's mother taught them first to snowplow, then the trick of a telemark turn and stopping in a christy. They took their skis on winter trips, slaloming from summits on still afternoons, and tried the amateur ski-jump trestle near Leavenworth on Ski Hill Road, strapped to eight-foot hickory skis and falling badly and often. They skied along Peshastin Creek or up along the Chumstick River, then hiked uphill with their skis on their shoulders until they had earned a downhill run, or they took the railroad into Stevens Pass and telemarked back down.

Once they stood on the summit of Mission Peak with the December wind in their faces but the sky cloudless and lit by the pale sun low among the peaks. Ben was working his boots into the toe irons when Aidan pointed at a mountain goat risen out of drifts not twenty yards off, poised to flee with its head turned toward them, already certain of flight. It swiveled on its hind hooves and was gone in a puff of snow behind an outcropping, and Ben, closing his binding clamp, felt poised on the cusp of the world, as close to God as he might ever get, with no place higher but heaven itself, and nothing to obscure the truths of the wind, the sky, the snow, the winter sun.

At ten he rode horseback with his father and Aidan, deer hunting for the first time. They rode into the hills just after lunch, when new snow covered the ground. They crossed the river at Coleman's Landing and followed the Colockum Stagecoach Road, his father with his 270 Weatherby Magnum in a leather saddle scabbard at his right hand and a .22 pistol at his belt. It was dry-cold, winter-still; the land lay white and paralyzed. They saw no one and no deer sign in the clean snow of the road. When the stars were thick and brilliant in the sky, they stopped at a bench overlooking the river. Wright Givens buttoned his canvas coat and cupped his hands to light a cigarette, his jaw and mouth and the end of his nose glowing in the flaring match light. "This'll do," he said to them, and they stamped the snow down, staked out the tent, and hobbled the horses for the night. They started a fire of lodgepole pine slabs, on which their father boiled water for coffee, and they ate elk jerky from a leather bag and chewed dried apples and apricots.

Wright Givens smoked, his collar turned up, the brim of his hat turned down. He said that in the morning chances would be good, since deer were always nocturnal in their habits, moving at dusk and dawn. Deer watched their back trail as they moved to bed down, and traveled with their noses into the wind, but there was no wind now to assist them in their caution and they might well be approached from above. Then Wright settled in before the fire, tapped a pine ember with his boot, and said that in the early days it was hard along this stagecoach road where they were camped tonight. Wagons were lowered toward Wenatchee by rope; trees were dragged behind wagon axles to supplement the wheel brakes. A schoolhouse was pulled on skids from farm to farm each summer to spread justly the burden of heating it and of boarding the accompanying teacher.

Had they heard of the Rock Island wheat chute? At first the wheat smoldered and burned in the pipe because of its speed and friction. Before the railroad came through Rock Island, there'd been a tram between Waterville and Orondo for carrying gunny-sacks of wheat to the steamboat and for hauling coal back up. The Indians back then grew squashes and pumpkins in the bottom of Moses Coulee. They moved east when the sheep came in and farther east when the tractors came, the tractors fueled by sagebrush, bolts of pine, anything that burned, even greasewood. Ben's father had seen Hutterites up on the plateau who lived in hovels in the ground and boiled their soup on dung fires. He'd been to Soap Lake, where a sanatorium had been built by the muddy shore for sufferers from rheumatism, eczema, and gout. He'd been to the Yakima powwow at White Swan and to the Yakima horse races in the huckleberry country up in Indian

Heaven. He'd floated logs through the Yakima Canyon on the spring floodwaters past Ellensburg and down to the mill near Selah. He said that where his grandfather had lived, just outside of Walla Walla, freight was carried toward Hell Gate on the backs of African camels. There were channeled scablands down that way, where rich, kilted Scotsmen ran ten thousand sheep herded by indomitable miniature dogs and by men who spoke the Basque tongue. Ben's father had traveled by steamboat once all the way to the mouth of the Columbia and had seen the Pacific Ocean. He'd also been on the railroad to Minneapolis and had prospected the Black Hills in South Dakota. He'd passed a summer at a placer mine north of Ketchikan, Alaska. He'd been to Chinatown in San Francisco, where he ate raw sliced octopus and squid and baby eels.

Wright Givens told of how his grandfather led west a train of covered wagons in 1879. John Hale Givens was a fruit grower and nurseryman in the vicinity of Marion, Indiana, who built two wagons as soil beds in which he planted newly grafted fruit trees and bushes to bring across the plains. Apple starts, pears, cherries, plums, currants, gooseberries, peaches: they were canvased over for protection from weather, but on balmy days the canvases were removed and the traveling gardens bounced sun-drenched across the plains, hauled by teams of oxen. The Indians, Wright's grandfather claimed, had vouchsafed the westering party's passage in the belief that the traveling gardens were protected by the hand of the Great Spirit.

Wright Givens said that the boys' maternal grandfather had patented the Rainier Delicious apple. James Chandler purchased two dozen seedling trees from an itinerant peddler passing through Wenatchee—they turned out to be Golden Reinettes from Virginia—and when the offspring of one of these, sprung from a windfall, eventually produced an extraordinary fruit, huge apples growing mild yellow on each branch, he bought up the propagating rights. He built an iron cage around his tree to prevent the theft of bud sticks and took to promotion vigorously. In 1921, the American Pomological Society presented James Chandler with its Wilder Medal; in 1926, a carload of his apples was shipped to the men of the St. Louis Cardinals to honor their World Series triumph. The boys' grandfather had once been wealthy, but had invested with too much confidence in the stock market before it crashed in 1929.

The embers of the fire went quietly red while Ben sat listening. His father nodded across the coals, where Aidan was curled asleep on a log, his mouth hanging open. "Not interested," his father said, and shrugged.

"I am," said Ben. "Keep going."

"It's time for sleep," said his father.

In the morning they broke camp in the dark and rode up Stray Horse Canyon. Ben watched his breath boil off into the dawn, until his father motioned him alongside and pointed out the deep track of a buck, heart-shaped and split down the middle. The buck had passed the dark hours at the creek because there was no other running water, and now at first light was working west toward higher elevations. The track made an easy meander in the snow with the dewclaws readily visible, and finally they came across droppings in a pile, as if the buck had stopped unalerted. "This is good," said Ben's father. A quarter mile farther was an opening in the trees, but they held up below it in case the buck was watching his back track from a vantage point. They turned their horses directly up slope to keep the track below them.

They made the ridge top in gathering light and rode north, studying the hills on either side for signs that the buck had crossed ahead of them. They came to a saddle where no tracks showed, the world as still as if it had been painted, the snow loading up the boughs of pines in cumbersome white thick mantles. Wright Givens instructed his sons to tether the horses fifty yards downslope, then return to the ridge saddle. He took his Weatherby from its scabbard, turned up his coat collar, and pushed his hat down firmly. "This is good," he said again.

They sat with their backs to one another so that all points of the compass were covered. After forty minutes of waiting, Ben heard his father's rifle click as the hammer was brought back into full cock. Turning, he saw a buck of modest size, in high alert with its gaze full on them, seventy yards down the hill, its sleek left flank exposed. There was no time for Ben to ponder things or to wish they might be different. His father's Weatherby roared, and the buck buckled forward on tenuous forelegs, flailed weakly for a few seconds, and did not move anymore.

Ben's heart beat wildly. He leaned against his father, who put a hand on his shoulder. "Looks like we got one," his father said.

They approached the deer cautiously. Wright Givens touched a stick against its eye. Then he knelt, looked closely, and showed them the place where the bullet had passed through the buck's hide. He explained how his bullet had splintered the left shoulder joint, next the spine just below the neck, and finally the right shoulder. There was blood on the snow underneath the buck, and he said it was good for the blood to drain and for the meat to cool quickly. Pointing with the tip of his dressing knife, he showed them the sticking place on the buck's soft chest, and then with no warning he thrust in the knife, lifting its hilt until the artery was severed. The buck's eye remained open. More blood colored the snow.

Ben's father stepped back to look at his sons, pulled off his hat, and rubbed his chin. He was lean in the face, unshaven, wind-worn, with a head of neat black hair. He propped his Weatherby against a tree, knelt with one hand on the buck's warm flank, and motioned the boys to kneel. "I promised your mother," he sighed.

They took their hats off, as he had. They all three laid a hand on the buck, and their father began to pray. "Dear Lord," he said, "our thanks to you for this meat you have granted. Our thanks for your goodness and your bounty, Lord. In Jesus' name, amen."

He stood and worked his hat on. He cut the scent glands from the deer's hind legs, severed the testicles, and tied a knot in the penis so no urine would taint the meat. He explained what he was doing and why he was doing it, and Ben and Aidan watched. Then they brought the horses around, lashed the deer quarters over the saddles, and left the hide, the head, and the guts on the stained, snowy ground.

Five minutes later, riding down the ridge, their father halted his horse. There was blood across the front of his coat and on his jaw, nose, and hands.

"That's how it's done," he said to his sons. "That's the way you'll want to do it when I'm not around anymore."

At the Grade and Pack Conference in 1932, Ben's mother spoke against lowering standards. Dressed in black, her hair black, she was tall, confident, plain-speaking, her eyes a deep, strong blue. It was her contention that even C-grade apples should not be permitted to go out worm-stung, discolored, or pocked by hail. She said that culls sold at $3 a ton should go directly to vinegar plants because the brokers in Spokane and Portland were flooding the C market with high-grade culls, driving prices down. Worse, the price for Winter Bananas had fallen to $1.25 a box, too little to cover picking and packing, not to mention freight and auction. Half the shippers in the industry, she guessed, had gone broke after the stock market crash, and this threatened all orchardists because shipping contracts were the necessary collateral for a bank to cover growing costs. Did everyone grasp this? she asked. Did all support the shippers? She favored a lobbying effort made through the shippers to bring the Great Northern into line at

$1.25 per hundred pounds, and she insisted that apples could be shipped at sea from rail points on Puget Sound as a counterbalance to the railroads. Otherwise, she warned, there would be a lot of orchards out of business within two seasons. There would be a tightening of belts no matter what they did, but the belt would hold and they could endure it and eventually things would improve. In the meantime, she said, picking wages would have to be set at somewhere near 15 cents. The fixed wage for the construction of boxes should be no more than 75 cents per 100; to pay more was worse than folly. She encouraged everybody gathered there to consider the Crop Production Loan Office plan for the purchase of spray and fertilizer. She explained how the Agricultural Credit Corporation could do what the banks had once done. She spoke from the floor, not from the podium, after sitting for two hours beside her sons and husband listening to men joust bitterly, and she announced herself as the wife of Wright Givens, whose grandfather had brought the first fruit stock across the plains, and as the daughter of the founder of the Rainier Delicious apple, and the gathering held silent while she spoke and remained silent afterward. When she was done, she sat with her eyes fixed ahead, fanning herself with a Yakima newspaper, and her husband reached calmly across her lap and took her right hand in his.

Once every month she took Ben and Aidan on her market trip to Wenatchee. The avenues were paved with large fir blocks that froze and buckled in winter, giving horses trouble. The boys accompanied their mother to the bank, the courthouse, and the post office, and to pay the bill at the utility office. They went to the market for bacon, salt, flour, rice, beans, pepper, corn syrup, and sugar. They stopped at the apothecary and the fabric shop on Miller Street, and they visited the nickel-and-dime store. At a fountain shop on Kittitas Avenue, they stopped for a hamburger and ice cream at the counter; the boys sat on either side of their mother, who ate neatly and slowly. When their errands were done, they sat in the city library, combing through magazines and newspapers from Seattle, Boston, and San Francisco. The Wenatchee people spoke to their mother about the progress of the new irrigation pipeline going in on the east side of the river, or asked for her estimate of where prices might fix for Rome Beauties or Stayman Winesaps. She answered everyone in the same way, with confidence but no trace of arrogance. She had attended a boarding school near Boston, had learned decorum there. She had come west enthusiastically, with her parents and her two sisters, in the spirit of an adventure. On coming of age, her sisters went east again, but Lenora Chandler stayed. Now she kept the books for the orchards and told her husband when to plow new land and when to plant new trees. After dinner nearly every evening she sat for an hour at her rolltop desk with a ledger book in front of her. With one hand she held her hair behind an ear; with the other she scrawled neat figures. She worked, generally, with the Victrola playing the music of string quartets. Violins, she told her sons, were in perfect accord with the orchard landscape. She liked to have a half hour in the evening to sit in an armchair with her needlework and with the Victrola playing quietly. The orchard air came softly through the screens, and she would stop, shut her eyes, breathe in the world, and sometimes fall asleep with her feet up and the violin music playing.

In the summer she worked with Ben and Aidan in the packing shed, making apple boxes. They bought box shook from the mill at Malaga and ferried it across the river. They bought a hundred-pound wooden keg full of five-and-a-half-penny nails. The sun filtered in and lit up the pine dust slowly rising on the air. Ben's mother drove nails with a box hatchet, humming while she worked. She wore her kitchen dress with the sleeves rolled up, wiped sweat from her face with the hem of her apron, and hammered with either hand. His father could make sixty boxes in an hour, but his mother could make sixty-five. She held ten nails in her hand at once, as if they were sewing needles. In picking season she wrapped apples in oiled tissue before packing them tightly, nailing down the lids, and loading up the wagon. On each box she glued the label she'd designed: their orchard by the river, hung heavily with fruit, bordered by pink apple blossoms.

Once, at the end of the workday, Ben sat with her in the orchard shade, watching the dusk flight of doves to the river and drinking from a canteen. His mother kneaded the small of her back, sighed and brushed the dust from her hair, then settled back against a tree. "I'd better see to dinner," she said, but didn't get up to leave.

"I'll help," Ben offered.

"I'd rather you read a book," his mother said. "You've got time before dinner."

"There's ditches to clear," said Ben.

His mother watched the doves for a while. "Someday," she said, "you'll grow up and leave. So you'd better get in the reading habit before that day arrives."

"I'll never leave," Ben told her.

"You'll leave. You'll be ready to leave. You'll have your own work, somewhere."

"I don't know what I'd do except apples."

"You'll do whatever is in the spirit of who you are," his mother said matter-of-factly. "Some kind of gift you'll have to give. Whatever God plans for you."

Ben was silent now. His mother was a dyed-in-the-wool Presbyterian who could lecture at length on the life of Calvin, on the sacrament of baptism, or on predestination; she took her sons to church each Sunday, where they heard the minister Joseph Miles declare—when all the congregation was weary of picking apples—that God had ordained their sweat from the outset, on thrusting Adam and Eve from the garden. *Cursed is the earth in thy work*, proclaimed God, *with labor and toil shalt thou eat thereof all the days of thy life. Thorns and thistles shall it bring forth to thee and thou shalt eat the herbs of the earth. By the sweat of thy brow thou shalt eat bread.* His mother, riding home, had revised the sermon, in keeping with her own interpretation of the *Westminster Shorter Catechism:* that work was an expression of love for God, that work was the path toward knowledge of Him, that we are here to do God's work. Our life, she said, was full of worthy tasks to accomplish in accordance with our particular design, in such a way that we are lifted up, to ascend by the work God means for us to do toward a higher love of Him. We know ourselves through the work we do—Ben's mother insisted on this.

Ben was twelve—it was just after Christmas—when he noticed a yellow cast to her eyes. His mother acknowledged noting it too, and said that Ben's father had commented on it, asking her to visit Dr. Williams. She went and was told that her jaundiced condition was difficult to understand and might derive from many sources. For a few days she held to the hope that the problem would simply vanish; then after New Year's she went again to the doctor, and this time he drew blood, collected urine, and concurred with her that the yellowing had grown deeper, pervading the skin around her eyes. By the middle of January her skin was green, and when she cut herself with a paring knife one day—a shallow slice through her index finger—it was difficult to stanch the bleeding. Her blood ran thin, darkly colored. By February she had seen two specialists in Spokane, but despite their efforts she grew more green, gaunt, and hollow-cheeked. She took to bed one afternoon and could not rise to attend to dinner, but lay curled beneath the comforter. The next day she went again to Spokane. She was hospitalized for nearly a week, then sent home with tincture of opium.

After that she lay in a torpor or sat in an armchair wearing her bathrobe, and twice a week Dr. Williams came to dole out more tincture of opium. She had no appetite. The mere smell of food sickened her. She sometimes vomited in the early mornings, battling fever and chills. Her skin was now tinted orange.

On the tenth of April, she turned thirty-seven. That evening blood trickled from her mouth; Dr. Williams came at midnight. He rolled up his sleeves, loosened his tie, and gave Ben's mother a sponge bath. He explained to Ben's father how to move her carefully and change the sheets one side at a time. She was very thin now, and moaned with every breath. Dr. Williams increased her dose of opium. She quieted, and they left her room to sit in the parlor at midnight.

Dr. Williams warmed his back at the fire, a snifter of brandy in his hand, his sleeves rolled up, his face tired. He was a tall man with thick glasses, his jaw long and prominent. He had brought Ben and Aidan into the world, had treated their father for a rattlesnake bite, had stitched up Aidan's hand when he cut it making an apple box. Now he sipped from his brandy and sighed. He set the snifter on the mantel.

Dr. Williams walked to the window and looked out into the darkness of the hills. He paused there with his hands in his pockets. He pressed his glasses against his temples, but then suddenly pried them off, took a handkerchief from his pocket, and began to polish their lenses. "Sit down, boys," he said.

Ben and Aidan perched on the sofa. Their father wouldn't look at them.

Dr. Williams lowered himself to the edge of the rocker and set his elbows against his knees. He held his glasses to the light briefly, then slid them onto his face. "Your father has asked me to talk to you," he said, "because it's hard for him to do it himself."

"That's okay," said Aidan.

"Your mother can't be cured," said the doctor. "That's what we found out over in Spokane. She has a tumor, a cancer of the pancreas. There's nothing we can do to cure her."

"But you're a doctor," Ben said.

Dr. Williams fingered his chin. "A doctor isn't a magician, you know. I wish I was, believe me, Ben. If I was, I'd cure your mother."

"What do you mean you can't cure her?"

"I mean I'm just a man with a little learning and some medicines in an old black bag. I can't stop cancer of the pancreas."

"Yes, you can. You have to."

Ben's father raised his head. He looked gaunt and deeply tired. "There's no point in arguing with Dr. Williams," he said. "You hush now, Ben."

Ben turned his face to the floor. "I thought you were a good doctor," he whispered.

Dr. Williams took Ben by the chin, tilted his head, and looked at him. The light reflected in his glasses. "I'm neither good nor bad," he said, so close that Ben felt the warmth of his breath. "I wish I could make you see that."

"Make her better."

"I can't, Ben."

"You have to make her better."

"I can't."

Dr. Williams went to the rocker. He pulled his black bag close to him and looked inside it, silent.

"The opium," Ben's father said. "There must be some amount that's too much."

"That's for you to decide," said the doctor. "A question of how much pain she can bear, and of when enough is enough."

"I don't know how far that goes. I don't know what that means."

"I know just what you're saying," Dr. Williams said. "That's the hell of it."

Mrs. Emery came to help first, then Mrs. Fisk and Mrs. Elginhurst. At church women organized to help and spelled one another in the day hours. Evenings, after work in the orchard, Ben, Aidan, and their father took over. Ben's mother often lay on her side, looking out over the dark, cool trees stretching down toward the river. In the last light of evening the world looked haunted, as though on the verge of disappearing, solid, into the night.

"Are you scared?" Ben asked his mother once.

"I believe in God," she said. "But yes, I'm scared, to be honest."

He did not know what to say to this, so he said nothing; he waited. "It's the pain I'm scared of," she confessed.

He still had no idea how to respond. He had never heard her this way.

"This isn't any way to live," said his mother. "I miss the world, Ben."

"We could take your bed outside, though. Put it on the porch, maybe."

"It isn't that." She turned to look at him. "It's more that my work on earth isn't finished. Raising you, I'm not done with that. You and Aidan both."

He wished she wouldn't say these things. "Mom," he said. That was all.

"I wanted to see you as men. What you would be like as men. What you would do in the world."

"I don't know," said Ben.

"Do something fine," his mother said. "Do something grand and wonderful. Whatever your heart desires."

"I'll try," he said.

Later that week, her moaning turned into a faint wheeze, and she curled up like a fist, a leaf, curled up like a baby in the end, and died at 6:35 in the morning on the twenty-eighth of June, 1938. Ben, Aidan, and their father were sitting on kitchen chairs brought into the room, their father with his elbows on his knees, his forehead low, close to hers, and then her wheezing came to a stop, and he dropped his cheek to her heart. "Lenora," he said. "Lenora."

They buried her on a knoll above the river, her parents and the Fisks and Coles looking on, and the Robinsons and Knoxes and Elginhursts, and Dr. Williams and the Gilchrists and Cochranes, and the Emerys with their four small children, and twenty-three Givenses from up and down the river—from Kennewick, Wenatchee, Brewster, Kettle Falls—and that evening came a thunderstorm, and the rain beat across his mother's grave.

That summer, nothing was the same. They worked their apples with a hollow feeling, and the orchard fell into a decline.

Wright Givens wandered on foot, hunting birds in the willow canyons. He walked the hills for long hours, carrying his Winchester and following his Black Labs, returning at dusk with his coat pockets full of quail, chukars, and grouse. He'd dump them all in the kitchen sink and sit at the table, smoking. He'd scratch his unshaven jaw aimlessly or pull burrs from the dogs. Finally he'd throw his vest across a chair and stand at the sink with his sleeves rolled up, dressing birds as if in an assembly line. He pinched off their heads, twisted off their wings, severed the tendons in their knee joints, and threw their clawed feet in a metal pail. Rolling the meat in salted flour, he fried it in a cast-iron skillet, which he set on the dinner table. They ate the birds with fried potatoes, the shotgun set in the corner by the door, the dogs curled by his father's boots, asleep with their heads on their paws. All July his father hunted, returning at dusk with dead birds.

The migrant pickers came. They were mostly from Oklahoma and Arkansas, sometimes from Missouri or Texas. Single men and drifters, loners and vagabonds, also families with eight or nine children, they made the fruit run in pickup trucks, hopped freight trains, or walked the roads. In April they picked strawberries in California, then worked northward through plums and pears, arriving in June for sweet cherries and peaches, followed by yet more plums and pears, and finally the apple harvest. The men arrived at the Givenses' place sun-darkened and lean-jawed, bedrolls slung from Manila twine across their backs, unshaven under broad-rimmed hats and smoking hand-rolled cigarettes. In the rows of apples, high in their ladders, nestling fruit into canvas bags slung from suspenders and belted at their waists, they regaled Ben and Aidan with fabulous tales: dust storms, stabbings, arrests, brawls, riding the rails in Arizona or crossing into Mexico at El Paso for the whores in Cuidad Juarez. Herding sheep in the Sierra Nevada, riding roundup in Idaho. The impossible wastes of the Cactus Range, the Amargosa Desert, Death Valley. Condensed milk poured into a radiator to plug a slow-running leak; a crankshaft brought into round again with a shim made out of a bacon rind.

There was a family that came when Ben was fifteen, and one night deep in the rows of trees—they had been with the Givenses exactly a week—he kissed their sixteen-year-old daughter. Her skin smelled of dust, her mouth of apples, and when he pressed against her urgently, the girl wrenched free and ran away. Her name was Nora Ellerby, from Milfay, Oklahoma, and her skin was sun-polished to the color of dark pine wood, and her hair lay long and flat against her cheeks with the tips of her ears poking out of it. Her eyes were shallow and her chin very strong, but her fingers were long, brown, and smooth. Ben watched her hands plucking apples, then spoke to her quietly when no one was listening, and that night she met him in the orchard. They kissed, pushing against each other. The next night they lay beneath the apple trees, where he ran his hands along her waist and touched her breasts through the fabric of her shirt, until Nora, coming to her senses, ran away from him again.

On the following night, the moon rose addled and yellow. They went hand-in-hand to the river secretly and sat in the night shadow of a fine-grained butte pillared along its summit but graced by warm sand at its base. They lay in the sand, holding each other. The girl's breath blew warm against his face, and she spoke with a soft winsome twang. She spoke of a boy in Shingletown, California, who had not kissed nearly as well as Ben and had promised to buy her a brand-new dress if she ran off with him to Canada. She said that she had some money saved and that one day she would live in Sacramento or Chico or Redding or someplace civilized. She would shop in town, live in a house, keep fresh milk in an icebox. She'd been to the county fair in Klamath Falls, to the circus when it came to Yakima, and at a swap meet in Yuba City, California, she saw a man with a tattooed belly swallow a blazing sword. She paid three cents to a fortune-teller there, who told Nora she would have seven children and warned her to be suspicious of men who promised to buy her things. The boy in Shingletown had promised her a dress, but no one else had promised her anything, so what was the point of that prophecy? She had hoped for more from the fortune-teller.

Ben and Nora kissed for a half hour. Then he put his fingers between her legs and touched her where she told him to, until, three times, she shivered breathlessly in small persistent shudders. As if in return, she unbuttoned his pants and clutched him so that he flooded thickly against her arm and fingers. The next day, Nora left to pick fruit in Okanogan County.

School started after picking season. There were fifteen children on the Rock Island Road, and their schoolhouse sat on a knoll above the river a half mile downstream from the Fisk orchards, close to the Palisades junction. It was a small single room built of river stones and heated by apple cordwood. The orchardists up and down the road kept its slope-roofed woodshed filled in winter, and the older children kept the stove going strong by stoking it high when the embers glowed and leaving the draft open. The county ran power to the schoolhouse for a string of lights nailed over the desks so the children could write their assignments and see their maps and primers. The place was tidy and smelled of wood smoke, ink, and wet woolen clothes.

The teacher, Ruth Dietrich, lived with the Cochranes, an elderly couple with children long grown and an extra room to let. She was a lively woman, large, with glasses on a chain, and she peered at her charges over wire frames and then down through swimming lenses to read aloud from *Ivanhoe* or *Alice in Wonderland*. Miss Dietrich wore her gray hair pinned tightly to her head, and a cream-colored lace shawl draped across her shoulders, fastened with a brooch at her breast. Her face was coarse, lined, and thick; two long hairs sprouted from a mole on the left side of her chin. Miss Dietrich collected Wanapum arrowheads, petrified wood, and opals. She knew her medieval history, could recite the chronology of British kings and queens, and could render from memory "Frost at Midnight," "The Passionate Shepherd to His Love," and "The Nymph's Reply to the Shepherd." She was prone to poetry at the slightest provocation, so that the rising of the river breeze was a just occasion for orating an impeccable "Ode to the West Wind," and the various hues of apples on her desk for a rendition of "Pied Beauty." Upon the announcement by a student one day that the Rock Island Dam had been completed, she recited "Ozymandias," then gave a short lecture on the sin of hubris. Miss Dietrich could discourse knowledgeably on the agriculture of Mesopotamia, the habits and mores of the Egyptian pharaohs, and the scientific notions of the Greeks. She knew all about the religion of the Incas, the travels of Charles Darwin to the Galapagos, the Boxer Rebellion, the Potala in Lhasa, and the invasions of the Mongol Khans.

Ben took pleasure in listening to her. He read with zeal the story of Macbeth, *Canterbury Tales, David Copperfield, The Pickwick*

Papers, and *Heart of Darkness*—all loaned to him by Miss Dietrich. He learned the periodic table, the primary theorems governing geometry, and the Latin names for plants and animals as classified by Linnaeus. He learned about the exploration of the poles, the formation of crystals and of sedimentary rock, and the propagation of light.

Miss Dietrich was at home in the orchard country and had an expansive knowledge of apples: the fruit, she told them, *Pyrus malus,* had taken its name from Aphrodite's priest, who was turned into an apple tree after the impaling of Adonis. When her students, in the fall, bobbed for apples, she explained to them, while their faces were wet, that the druids had once done likewise—bobbing—as an act of divination. The apple tree, she told them one day, had been sacred to Apollo and Venus both, and was, of course, the fruit of discord that started the war at Troy. And it wasn't just pagans and pantheists who worshiped apples; in Bulgaria there were paintings of the Virgin Mary with Jesus cradled in one hand, an apple held in the other. When a student misbehaved, she quoted sternly from Chaucer—*The rotten apple injures its neighbors*—or she might borrow from Shakespeare—*An apple cleft in two is no more twin than these two creatures*—in reponse to an argument between the Gilchrist sisters. A student who complained of the burden of homework was reminded that Hercules, for his eleventh labor, traveled to the far western end of the earth in order to bring back golden apples, stolen from the Hesperides, and that he walked a thousand miles for them, and slew a dragon along the way, and if Hercules could do all this, why couldn't they read just ten pages from *Huckleberry Finn*? Once a girl asked Miss Dietrich if it was true that her husband had died at the Battle of Gettysburg, and Miss Dietrich laughed with such sustained force that tears gathered in her eyes, then uttered something about Asgard and apples of immortality. Another girl told her in class one day that a woman who washed her face and hands in water mixed with the sap of an apple was sure to bear a child, and Miss Dietrich smiled and nodded at this and said that a girl in search of a husband should squeeze apple seeds between her fingers: if any struck the ceiling, she was sure to be happy in her quest, for apples were the fruit of love.

One spring Miss Dietrich took ten students on a field trip to identify plants: Ben, Aidan, Billy Lawrence, Willy Griffin, Owen and Clare Goodall, Caitlin and Amelia Burns, and Hannah and Gillon Crichton. The students spread out with their pocket-knives and cut snowberry, wild rose, and boxwood twigs, arranging them in a grid on a square of canvas laid across a slab of table rock. Miss Dietrich showed them the red osier dogwood, used by the Shuswaps for fishing weirs and pipe stems, though she preferred a pipe of elderberry, a wood also good for an elk call whistle, a peashooter, or a drinking straw. She peeled back the layers of a mallow ninebark and explained that where you found this plant, ocean spray could be found, too; the Indians made fishing spears from it.

At noon they moved higher to eat in a meadow, and Miss Dietrich, between bites of her tomato sandwich, extolled the virtues of the surrounding larches: how they were hardier than pines or firs, stubbornly surviving winter weather; how their needles in the early fall turned a brilliant, gilded yellow. She thought of them as inherently old, as dying one small piece at a time but nevertheless showing new leaf each spring, and this in the parched, unheralded places no other tree much wanted. Miss Dietrich was moved to poetry by them and recited Housman's "Loveliest of Trees" and "Far in a Western Brookland."

She held Ben after school one day and told him he was her brightest hope in twenty-seven years on the western plains and a candidate for a good university, should he decide on such a path—a path she urged him toward greatly. A path he should have no fear about; a path he should walk with confidence. Ben answered that his father needed him to work the apple orchard. Couldn't he do that later? Miss Dietrich asked. Wouldn't it be both an adventure and a test? Didn't he owe it to himself? Wasn't the larger world waiting?

He thanked her again and went out to his brother, who was waiting propped against the wall of the schoolhouse, chewing on a stem of wheatgrass. The January wind blew hard off the river, and Aidan had his back turned to it.

"What did she want?"

"She said I should go to college."

"You going to do it?"

"I don't know."

"Probably you're smart enough."

"Maybe, maybe not."

"You ought to go, Ben."

Aidan pulled his hat brim low and rose, still chewing on his grass stem. "Come on," he said. "Let's get on home. We've got horses to feed."

Fifteen months after Pearl Harbor, Aidan was drafted into the Army. He packed his bag three days before leaving and said he wanted one last ride up in the Colockum country.

At dawn Ben and Aidan saddled the horses and crossed the river at Coleman's Landing. They rode on empty stomachs until nine; then they sat at the lip of a spring and ate in the sun from their saddlebags. They turned the horses up Dry Springs Canyon and rode southeasterly through the afternoon, sometimes at a canter over meadow ruts, or at a side-by-side trot over ridges. At dusk Aidan shot a pair of blue grouse from where they had lit on low tree limbs after kicking up before the horses. They made camp just north of Spring Gulch, near a grove of hoary willows. They sat in their blankets with the pair of grouse spitted, the wind railing hard at their backs, the fire's smoke streaming away. It was a chill evening. There were no stars in the sky. The night air was sweet and promised rain: Aidan said he could smell it coming as surely as if he had seen dark clouds borne toward him on the breeze, as surely as if he could see rain just upwind already.

They ate and banked the fire extravagantly, until the flames caused them to sweat. At midnight came a thunderstorm, and they lay with the lantern turned out in the tent to watch the lightning flicker. The rain fell with such fervor that the world disappeared.

They measured the rain's tapering by the quality of its sound against the canvas, and finally there came silence. Out beyond the dripping, dark willows, they took in the stars and the sliver of moon, calm and pale, as if the rain had never happened. "I don't want to go," Aidan said. "You're the one person I can say it to. Truth is, I'm not cut out for the Army. I'd rather be right here."

"I wish you were staying," said Ben.

They were quiet standing wrapped in their blankets in the darkness of the hills. "I don't know nothing but apples," said Aidan, and kicked, hard, at a loose stone on the ground. "What do they want with me anyway? I'm nothing but an apple farmer."

"Anyway, you have to go."

"I don't have to like it," said Aidan.

In the morning they ate the last of the apricots. They rode out onto the ridge top together to take in the long view across the river toward the sage plateau. The high country was March cold, the morning bright, the brush wet. The horses nickered and threw their heads when the riders stood them high on the summit reach by a field of huckleberry. Steam chuffed from their mouths. To the southwest were the big mountains in mantles of snow, and to the southeast the river coiling. "We ought to have climbed those mountains," said Ben. "How come we never did?"

"They're too far off," said Aidan. "They're one hell of a long ride."

"But they look like you might reach out to them."

"They're too far off," repeated Aidan.

They rode back all day to the Columbia, traversed it on the Colockum Ferry, and at dusk came into their orchard tired, on empty stomachs, their hats tipped back, to walk the horses between the rows of trees in a silent kind of processional, and Aidan ran his hands over limbs as he passed them with his horse behind him, the limbs trembling in the wake of his passing, and on, then, to the barn.

A letter arrived for Ben in May from a man named Willard Anderson, president of the Leavenworth Ski Club. Mr. Anderson remembered Ben from the time he'd passed on the jump at Ski Hill and urged him now to sign on with the mountain troops being raised by the Army. The 87th Mountain Infantry Regiment, he wrote, had been activated at Fort Lewis on the day after the attack on Pearl Harbor. There had been much training on the slopes of Mt. Rainier, and various advances had been made. The 87th had been followed by the 10th Mountain Division, and it was this division that was now recruiting, in part with the help of the National Ski Patrol, of which Mr. Anderson was the local chairman, so he was writing to boys of fighting age with an enthusiasm for the high country, in the hope they would find it an honor and a privilege to join the Army's mountain troops at this time of dire need.

Ben's alternative, Mr. Anderson wrote, was to go where the draft took him. Wasn't it preferable, his letter argued, to take matters into his own hands and "meet the war on your own terms, and wearing skis as well?"

Ben's father said that if he had to go, he may as well go as a mountain trooper. "I wish you wouldn't go at all," he said. "I wish you could stay. I need you."

"You'll get along."

"No, I won't."

"You can hire somebody."

"That's not what I mean."

"Well, anyway, I have to go."

"I wish you didn't," said his father.

That June the cherries ripened early, and Wright Givens set the eleventh of the month as the day to begin their harvest. At first light the pickers met by the siding: Ben, his father, and nine migrant workers, the Emerys and their four young children, and finally Mrs. Emery's niece, Rachel Lake from Waterville, Maine, who—as Mrs. Emery explained—had come to stay for the harvest. She'd come, it appeared, not fully prepared, and so wore Mrs. Emery's work clothes, denim pants and a flannel shirt, both many sizes too large.

Ben's father lined them out down the rows, assigning each a set of trees and a picking bucket and ladder. Before long came the sound of cherries striking the bottoms of buckets like hailstones and the voices of pickers beyond the branches. Ben left the woody spurs behind, clearing his bucket of leaves as he went, stripping the limbs of their every fruit, careful to take them with their stems intact, gathering them in clusters. The harvest season lay in front of him now, miles and miles of fruit ahead, ten thousand trees to be gleaned of their yield, days, weeks, and months of fruit, until one dreamed at night of cherries, of apples and pears plucked loose from trees, of moving hands and moving leaves.

When the sun was up and the dew had dried, Ben sprawled in the grass to eat breakfast—three eggs he'd boiled that morning—and looked down the row at the heaped cherry crates waiting under the trees. He could see, not far off, Mrs. Emery's niece, high in her ladder, picking. Most of Rachel Lake disappeared in the leaves, but he noticed that she'd cinched Mrs. Emery's denim pants around her waist with Manila twine. The belt loops in back were tied together. He saw her stand on the toes of her boots to reach into the branches. She stepped up onto a higher rung, and her makeshift belt disappeared.

In the afternoon the heat came up so that the cherries went soft and left their stems behind. Ben's father called off picking for the day, and they loaded the fruit on the flatbed truck, hauled their ladders and buckets to the siding, and lined out the boxes for pickup by the Consolidated Cherry Packing Company. Ben was busy picking leaves from the boxes when Rachel came out of the orchard shade with her flannel shirttail loose. She paused to wipe her face with it. The barest shadow of her belly showed, a dark bar of flesh revealed for a half second. She tucked in her shirt and ran her hands through her hair—neck-length, unadorned, the color of walnut shells. Tilting her head up, shutting her eyes, she drank steadily from a water jug, wiped her lips with the back of her hand, then drank again, pulling hard, the cords in her throat working. He couldn't help noting the shape of her head, her nose, lips, chin. Her face was made of fine bones. She glistened with the sweat of her work. It was hard not to look at her, inside her oversized clothes.

One time they rode in the flatbed together with a half dozen other pickers. The orange sunset glowed in her pores, and her hair was flailed by the breeze. Another time he picked in the tree beside hers. She was fast not because her hands were agile but because she was undistracted. Her forearms emerged from the leaves unscathed, unscratched by twigs and branches. Her wrists were flat, her elbows pointed, her arms brown and long in the sun, her hair flecked with bits of leaf. He had glimpses of her at odd moments—leveling cherries in their crates, perched in a ladder near the top of a tree, bent to drink from a barn spigot with her hair checked by one hand. One evening he saw her at the bend in the river, wearing nothing but her winter union suit, her hair pasted against her head, performing cannonballs from a ledge. Another time he saw her beneath pear trees, weaving dandelion chains with a cousin to hang from the freighted limbs. He saw her one noon at lunch in the orchard, in a contest to spit a cherry pit farthest; she was animated in victory, raising her fists toward the sun. He saw her currying a horse in the barnyard, walking it in the river road, at dusk riding with solitary leisure across the sage-studded ridge tops. She galloped hatless beneath the early moon, easy and still in the saddle.

Later that month came rain showers. They had to wait a full day to let the cherries dry out. Ben took the Black Labs up in a willow canyon to hunt for quail in the wild rose and sumac. It had rained all morning, but now, at noon, the air was fresh and the sun so strong that the dogs worked with their tongues hanging out, stopping at springs to lap at the muddy ground. A game trail threaded in and out of the draw, and the dogs followed it steadily, crashing into thickets now and then without Ben's urging them.

An hour out, they flushed a small covey laying up in bramble and thorn. After that they worked the singles uphill, the birds funneling out across the sage but coiling back into the canyon's cover, seeking the shade of willows. Ben brought four birds to earth in the course of a half hour. In the high heat, he rested at a spring, the orchard country spread out below, the river silver and holding sunlight, the mountains still snowbound on their north faces. Ben lay back to take it all in, as he had many times before. Aidan and he had rested here often. There were the charred remains of the fire ring where they'd sometimes spit-cooked birds.

He rested long in the shade of the spring with his hands behind his head. The ache of the climb was in his limbs, as well as the ache of picking, and it was good to rest in the cool of the willows, the damp smell of the earth beneath him, slightly bitter, alive. He shut his eyes and listened to the wind. He dozed for a while and then turned on his side to look down the ridge.

He saw Rachel there, in the distance, on horseback, riding toward the plateau. A girl at liberty beneath the sun, making her way through the sage. She sat easily in the rhythm of the horse. She climbed to the ridge, turned, paused, and took in the view of the mountains. The horse circled under her, and she worked it around again. Then she disappeared into the east.

They were well into the heat of cherry season when at last he spoke to her. He was unloading cherries onto the siding, and she suddenly stepped in next to him to clean leaves from the crates. Her hands moved through the fruit lightly. The river wind blew against their faces. She'd turned sun-burnished in ten days of picking and had gone to Wenatchee for work clothes that fit— denim pants and a boy's white T-shirt—but they were already stained with cherry juice, as were her teeth and lips.

Rachel said, "What's gotten into the bees today? They're all over the place."

"I don't know. It's strange."

He didn't look at her, just at her hands, swift among the fruit.

"This one's perfect," she said, and popped a cherry in her mouth.

"You're not tired of cherries?"

"I love them."

"Me, too."

"These are the best."

She ate a second and a third. He watched her spit out the pits.

"I've seen you riding," Ben told her. "Up there, toward the plateau."

"That's one place," Rachel said. "But along the river is good too, and up in those little canyons with the willows."

"There's rattlesnakes in the canyons," said Ben.

"I'm not scared of snakes," she answered.

"They're bad this time of year," said Ben.

"I'm still not scared," Rachel told him.

She moved along the row of crates, their conversation finished. He felt certain he'd made a bad impression. A boy living in orchard country, a font of information on rattlesnakes.

The apricots ripened before the cherries were done, and there were two crops to pick. Thirteen pickers lived on the place and at dawn moved out to their ladder sets with their buckets and water jugs over their shoulders, the Emery children and Rachel with them, starting before the heat came up, finishing when the fruit went soft. Ben rose from bed before anyone else, dressed, and went out into the darkness. He laid out crates for the pickers. He put in apple branch props, mowed the quack grass in the orchard rows, and pruned summer suckers out of treetops. Then there was the problem of the codling moth. A man named Kevin Lawrence in Wenatchee, who worked for the Bureau of Entomology, had convinced Ben's father that time and money could be saved with the construction of an elaborate stationary spray system, as opposed to the leaky, wagon-mounted pump sprayer—hauled about by a pair of mules—they'd long gotten by on. Now, at picking time, they were still laboring with laying the base line of one-inch pipe and the lateral lines of three-quarter-inch pipe, driving in the many standpipes, mounting the proper fittings for the spraying hoses, pouring the concrete for the holding tank, and getting in the pump. And then the horses and mules must eat, the windbreak poplars needed water in the heat, more fruit boxes needed working up, and the wire bindings on the wood water pipes were coming loose in the south orchard and had to be replaced. And there was a place where moles were diverting water and no time to see about changing this, and in the evening was the accounting to see to and all the record keeping.

On the last day of June, he spoke with Rachel again. He was standing knee-deep in a feeder ditch, cleaning the weeds from a lateral screen, when she came along with her picking bucket, and he stopped what he was doing and looked at her, weeds dripping in his hand. "Hey," she said.

"Hey yourself," Ben said.

"Is that algae?"

"We just call it ditch weed."

"That isn't any official name."

"I don't know the official name. The Latin name or anything."

"Maybe you know these berries," she said. "Up there growing in the willow canyon. The little red berries you see in the wet places. Not really red but closer to orange. Clusters of them. Little."

"Those are currants," Ben told her.

"Currants," she said. "I've been eating them."

"We used to make them into jelly sometimes."

"I've had currant jelly. It tastes like gooseberry."

"We don't have gooseberry out here," said Ben. "But up in the canyon there's something called serviceberry. They look, sort of, like little purple apples. You've probably seen those, too."

"If I did, I didn't notice." She smoothed her hair, which had turned a lighter shade at the ears since they'd last talked. "I'll let you get back to your ditch weed. Or whatever it's called—ditch weed."

"It could be algae," said Ben.

There was a respite on the Fourth of July, and the pickers lolled through the heat of the day, keeping well in the shade. At dusk they brought out a guitar and accordion, and hollered long across the hills to hear their voices echo. They traded empty curses too, and screamed senseless insults. Ben and his father sat on the porch with the doors and windows open behind them and the Victrola playing the music of violins, which mingled with the noise from the pickers' camp. It was one of Lenora Givens's records, a slow, piercing concerto that her husband played from time to time, though it seemed to Ben an odd choice for Independence Day. They sat and listened anyway. The light fell and blurred the contours of shadows. The stifling air of the river basin cooled, and an evening balminess settled in, the sort that people in orchard country coveted all day.

"You oughtn't to just set here with me," Wright Givens said after awhile. "Whyn't you wander up to the Emerys and see that niece of theirs?"

"Why should I?" said Ben.

Ben's father nodded and grinned. "You waste too much time, she'll be gone," he warned. "Girl like that gets tired of picking fruit, she's going to leave this place."

"Let her," said Ben. "I don't care."

They could see across the way to the Emery Orchard. Most of the lights were on in the house. A pool of light in the glower of dusk overtaking the sage hills.

"She's just right there." Ben's father pointed. "Not any more than a ten-minute walk. And probably thinking on you, too, girl like that, your age."

"Lay off," said Ben.

"It's the Fourth of July. A night natural for festivities. It's reasonable to wander over there."

"She doesn't mean anything to me, okay? I don't care about her one way or the other."

"All right. Sit around here with your old man all night if that's what you want to do, Ben. You damn-fool-greenhorn-wet-behind-the-ears-little-stubborn-lamebrained-mule."

Ben went down toward the pickers' camp. In the dusty clearing in front of the cabins a pair of kerosene lanterns burned, and in their incandescent glare the accordion player and the guitarists crooned, stomping their feet and hopping like puppets, throwing their shadows across the ground, and all about them worn, weathered men shuffled and spun on bandy legs, men who limped and moved gingerly. Men were cursing and jostling, playing cards, rolling dice on the dusty ground, howling like coyotes at the moon. Ben made his way around them to the butte where once he'd lain with Nora Ellerby and run his hand up between her legs. The sand still held the last of the day's heat. The light of the moon illuminated rock faces. Ben sat listening to the hilarity of the pickers honoring the birth of their nation, and beyond it his mother's violin music.

When he returned, his father had a bottle of bourbon on the porch boards beside his chair. His boots were propped on the porch railing, his hat tipped down over his eyes, his hands clasped behind his head. "No luck, sailor?" he said.

"I didn't go over there."

Ben sat down, too, and put his feet up. His father groped on the floor beside him, then took a pull from the bourbon. "Do you know how old I am?" he asked.

"Forty-nine," said Ben.

"Forty-nine's right."

"So?"

"So nothing."

"You ought not to drink that hooch," said Ben. "It just garbles up your mind."

His father took another pull from the bottle. "It's a holiday," he countered.

There were more cries from the fruit pickers. Ululations, mock wolf howls, war whoops, and drunken bluster. "Those men are having a time," said Ben's father. "I just hope they don't go on all night or burn the cabins down."

Ben didn't answer. He looked at the moon. A gibbous moon in the western sky, as bright as though on fire.

"Those men had families, it'd be altogether different," Ben's father said. "They wouldn't be carrying on such. They'd have a different take."

"Probably so," answered Ben.

He heard them long after midnight from his bed, the pickers stuporous but still celebratory, still railing away at the firmament, a passel of travelers who'd stopped in this place long enough to glean it of fruit. Then there was nothing but a scratching from the Victrola. He got up to turn it off. Moonlight over everything. He saw his father out on the porch, hard asleep in his rocking chair, his head tipped back, his mouth open, the bottle between his thighs. He was thoroughly gray now—his whiskers and hair. His face was cross-hatched with wrinkles.

Mid-July, the apricots were done, but the pears not quite ready. They were still hard and green in every tree, and not heavy enough to need propping. Mr. Emery put the pickers to work at making apple and pear boxes, pruning summer suckers from his apples, and scything away at the orchard grass. Ben and his father made progress on the spray system. The evenings were warm and windless. The field crickets resounded at night, and the bats worked over the orchards. In the morning, after the dew had dried, viceroy butterfly larvae fed on the poplar leaves. A red-tailed hawk rode afternoon breezes, languidly circling in a featureless sky. Starlings and robins pecked at the fruit. The coyotes came down at dusk, too. Their calls echoed across the hills, under the wide palette of the stars.

Ben spoke for a third time with Mrs. Emery's niece. He'd gone up into the willow canyon with the dogs and the Winchester 21 and found her with her horse tied, kneeling to drink at the lip of a spring—down on both knees as if to pray with her ankles turned up under her, her hands formed into a dipper. It was early in the morning. The water seeped between her fingers. Her hair spilled past her downturned face; she wore a pair of snake chaps. Ben emerged from between two willows and saw first the curve of her back, her chaps clipped to her belt loops. His dogs paused to consider the horse, then trotted up to drink beside Rachel. "It's you," she said, turning. "Don't shoot me."

"It isn't loaded."

"Supposing it was. Are you saying you'd shoot me?"

"No, of course not."

"That's a relief."

Ben called his dogs away from her, but they insisted on drinking at the spring, lapping at the water vigorously, showing their thick pink tongues. "We had a Golden Lab at home," Rachel said. "She died when I was fourteen."

Ben nodded. "They're always thirsty."

"Well, this is good water. From deep in the earth."

"I like this spring," said Ben.

Rachel drank from her cupped hands. She rose, wiped her lips, and seemed to appraise him and the shotgun broke open across his forearm. He propped it in the brush and looked at her horse, as if that were his primary interest. It was a sorrel mare worn down with the years, swaybacked and scraped and scarred by time, but her cannon bones still straight and clean and her mane and tail well groomed. "Your uncle's horse," Ben observed.

"He lets me ride it," said Rachel.

"He just about sold it last spring, I think, but then he changed his mind."

Ben knelt as she had at the spring, but on one knee only, his elbow against the other, and drank by raising the water in his free hand more than a dozen times. "You're out early," he said.

"It's not that early."

"You're wearing snake chaps."

"They're riding chaps."

"What's the difference?"

"These are longer."

"You always wear them?"

"They're smart to wear."

"I guess so," said Ben.

Rachel turned her back on him and went to her saddlebag. The riding chaps cut across her thighs and were clipped behind her calves. The seat of her pants was worn, dusty. She spoke to him from over one shoulder, so that he saw her face and neck in profile, the fine shape of her chin. "I've got a couple of short-cakes," she said. "Help me eat them, why don't you."

"I won't say no, I guess."

"There's cherries, too, if you're not tired of those."

"I'm not," said Ben.

They sat on the ground, out in the open, where the heat of the sun could reach them. The dogs probed aimlessly along the verge of willows, went their way, and came again. Rachel unclasped and set aside her chaps. She slapped the dust from the seat of her pants and folded the chaps to sit tailor-fashion on them, but then changed her mind and settled instead with her legs folded to one side.

They ate the shortcakes together. Ben pointed to a place in the canyon where she could find serviceberry. "The petals are white," he explained.

"I guess you remember the last time we talked. That time you were standing in the ditch, remember? You mentioned this ser-viceberry."

"That's right," Ben said. "And ditch weed."

Rachel nodded and smiled. "You have a pretty fair memory."

"My memory's bad. I can't remember anything. You're the one with the memory."

"Mine's fair. Close things, I forget. Faraway things, I remember better. I was three when my mom died, but I remember her."

"I can't do that," Ben answered. "I don't know what happened when."

Rachel lay down with one hip against the chaps and propped her head on her hand.

"My mom died, too," Ben told her. "But I was twelve, so I remember it."

"That's worse, being twelve like that. I don't really remember her, so it doesn't affect me like it does you. I'm guessing, anyway."

"It does affect me," Ben answered.

They were silent for a while. Ben ate the last of the shortcake in his hand. Rachel sat up again and reached behind with the ball of her thumb to scratch the middle of her back.

"I'm curious," Ben said. "Why did you come out here?"

"Out here?"

"To your cousins, I mean."

"To help with the picking."

"But you're from Maine, way back east. It's a long way to come to pick fruit."

"September I go to nursing school. In San Francisco."

"Nursing school?"

"The Cadet Nurse Corps."

"You're going to be—you want to be—a nurse?"

"I hope so," said Rachel.

She had one boot crossed over the other, both drumming the ground idly, her free hand resting on her hip. The fingers of her other hand disappeared in her hair, and her long torso rose with her breathing just beneath her T-shirt.

"You'll end up in the war," said Ben. "That's where they're sending nurses."

"That's the plan," answered Rachel.

They followed a cowpath down from the sage hills—Rachel

with her horse on a Manila tether, Ben's dogs ranging far and wide—and he showed her small mats of stonecrop and white stickseed flowers. Beyond rose mountains in the west, blue against the horizon. "I'd like to ride up there," said Rachel.

"You'd need time. After picking's done. Maybe late in October."

"I'll be gone before then, though."

They came down into orchards after ten o'clock. They walked between trees with the sorrel mare and the Labs, apples growing overhead. The light fell soft and diffused between the limbs, and the smell was of ripening fruit. "This is where it's just so beautiful," said Rachel. "This is what really just kills me."

"I feel the same," Ben answered.

A letter came for Ben one afternoon from the adjutant general's office in Washington: an order to report for active service in the 10th Mountain Division. Ben read it closely, twice; his heart began to pound. Then he turned between the trees to find his father in the south orchard, where he was laying new irrigating pipe.

Ben's father read, squinting a little, and scratched his weathered forehead. It was a clear day, windless and hot. The afternoon light fell full and strong, piercing the orchard shade. His father had the Farmall idling—he'd been using it to haul pipe about—but now he shut the motor down and hopped free of the seat. "Well," he said. That was all.

"I'm all accepted," answered Ben.

"I guess you are," said his father.

They leaned together against the Farmall while his father put one boot up behind him and read the letter again. "I don't like this," he said finally. "I don't want you to go."

"I have to go."

"I know that."

"It'll mostly be skiing."

"No, it won't." His father slowly measured his beard stubble. "I don't guess it'll mostly be skiing. But I hope it is, for your sake."

"Me too," Ben answered.

His father sighed, handed him the letter, and beat one heel against the grass.

"Anyway," said Ben, "where could they send me? Norway, or someplace like that. Finland or Sweden, maybe."

"It doesn't matter where they send you. It's still a war, Ben."

"I guess so."

"It is."

His father put a hand on Ben's shoulder and squeezed. "It just doesn't seem like it ought to be, you going off to fight a war."

"Well," said Ben. "I have to go anyway."

"You're seventeen," said his father.

The season of pears was upon them soon, at that point in August when nothing tangible suggests the demise of summer, except our apprehension. They pulled the props from the limbs as they picked, leaning them in the forks of trees, and picked the Bartletts with a steady insistence, easing them out of picking sacks as though pears were delicate as eggs. Ladders stood up and down the rows with the pickers perched in them loading bags by laying fruit on other fruit, the weight of pears gently pulling them forward, their bags swelling deep and low. In silhouette they resembled pregnant women.

On the third day of pears, Ben went with a blade of grass between his teeth and stood under Rachel's ladder. He could see her in among the leaves. She seemed self-contained, absorbed in her silent picking world. "Hey," he called. "It's me."

"Hey," she answered, and stopped working. She turned on her ladder and faced him, her bag of pears against her belly. "What are you doing?" she asked.

Ben pulled the blade of grass from his mouth. "I don't know," he answered. "Just saying hey, I guess."

"Well hey to you, too."

"Hey."

She worked down the ladder, walked past him. She unhooked the ties of her picking bag and unloaded her pears, a slow slide, so that none would bruise or dent. "It's hot today," she said.

"It is," he said. "A day like this, sometimes, I swim in the river after work. Just down there where it eddies."

"I know where it is."

She hooked the straps of her bag into place, then worked the ladder into a new set, in between the pear branches.

"What time will you go?"

"At dusk. In the dark."

"That sounds good," said Rachel.

He met her at the river bend, in the soft sand of the talus butte, to watch the setting of the August sun over the Colockum Hills. In the dark they went down to the edge of the water with the stars spread wide and high overhead, and stood on the rocks together. Ben stripped down to his trousers, Rachel to the union suit he'd seen her in before. She stood with her arms across her chest, her hands in fists at her collarbones, and hesitated with her toes in the river. "There's a strong eddy," she said.

"My brother and I used to come here," said Ben. "Almost every day, after work."

"What brother?"

"He's in the Army."

"What about you?"

"I joined up."

"When do you go?"

"End of October."

"That isn't a lot of time, is it?"

"More than you," answered Ben.

They stood in the river with some distance between them, the water swirling past their legs. "You know what?" Rachel said, pinching the fabric of her union suit. "I'm embarrassed to swim in this thing."

"It's okay," Ben told her. "We don't have to swim or anything. Whatever you want is okay."

"But that's it. I don't know what I want."

"Well, wait until you do."

"Does that point come?"

"I don't know any better than you."

She looked at him, a long gaze, then took her arms from her chest. He turned away and squatted against the shore rocks, looking out across the river so as not to embarrass her further. "I'm going in," she said.

He watched her wade into the river. The union suit revealed her waist and shoulders. The river was running hard for August, and the light washed just where her legs met it in a phosphorescent surge. Then, thigh deep, she dove in and rose a little downstream. She swept her hair back and rubbed her eyes. The union suit clung to her torso now. "The water's perfect," she announced.

He dove in too, and they swam against the current. The water divided and flowed around her. It shone on the skin of her face.

Afterward, still in their wet clothes, they built a fire out of drifts. The drifts burned white and smokeless enough that they could sit close beside them in a bright womb of heat. The world beyond disappeared. Darkness lay beyond the firelight. The stars appeared awash in pale ether. There was a hound, faintly distant, calling. Venus had risen low in the west, as brilliant as the moon.

Ben shoved a limb deeper into the fire. "Why do you want to be a nurse?"

"It's something I think I can do, I guess. Something I can put my hands on."

"I'm not sure I follow that."

"Like Florence Nightingale. Clara Barton. I don't know, maybe I'm stupid. I just have this picture of it."

"It might not be that way, though."

"Probably. I don't know."

She sat with her hands and feet toward the fire. The light played across her face.

"How long do you train for?"

"Nine months. They've compressed the courses."

"Then what?"

"I go to the Army."

"Where exactly?"

"I don't know."

"You could go anywhere."

"I guess I could."

"Me, too," he said.

Ben turned once more to take in her face, richly lit by firelight. While he watched, she pressed the hair at her neck to squeeze the river water from it.

"So you go at the end of October," she said. "Didn't you say October?"

"The twenty-seventh," answered Ben.

"Why are you going? Why do you want to fight?"

"I don't want to fight," he told her. "But I also don't want to be drafted and end up peeling potatoes."

"Well, you shouldn't enlist if you don't want to fight. You should train as a medic or something."

"A medic?"

"Yes."

"First aid?"

"Yes."

"What if everyone wanted to do that?"

"Then we wouldn't have a war," said Rachel.

Ben placed another drift on the fire and worked it into the flames.

"You could die, you know," said Rachel. "You're putting your life on the line."

"I try not to think about things like that."

"You should, though."

"I don't."

He thought about dying, not seeing her anymore. "I wouldn't want any regrets," he said. "So I guess I should just say it."

"What do you mean? You'd better say what?"

"That I like you, Rachel. That's all."

"I like you, too," she answered.

They kissed by the heat of the fire. He was surprised at the human smell of her flesh, the human smell of her mouth. It was not something he would have thought to predict, because for so long he'd imagined her sweetly perfumed—but here she was, mysteriously human, so that it seemed to him, with his lips against hers, that he grasped her mortality. "I don't know," he whispered in her ear. "This might be a mistake."

"I don't think so," said Rachel.

"We ought to think about this," said Ben.

"I already have," said Rachel.

There were evenings together in apple orchards laden bountifully. The apples hung heavy in the late-day sun, the leaves stirred in the wind. The green orchards were cool and inviting against the dun-colored sagelands. Thousands of apple trees gathered light and heat, on every branch a profusion of fruit, so many apples growing there it seemed an impossibility, a feat of nature rightly to be met with astonishment and awe. Ben and Rachel took a picnic basket deep into the coolest rows, where there were trees, quack grass, and sky. The sun came low from out of the west to filter in between the limbs, and it lit her face, arms, and throat as she sat with her legs tucked under her, searching inside their picnic basket—tomato sandwiches, spearmint tea, celery stuffed with peanut butter, cherries in syrup, walnuts. The light fell and blurred the contours of shadows. The late summer air of the orchard cooled. They lay on their blanket and stared up between branches with their hands behind their heads. They watched it come dark more swiftly than it had the month before. The sky passed from dusk to night. There were bats about in the orchard now. The apples in the trees hung black and still, poised above their heads.

In the darkness, Rachel spoke easily. Her father, she said, was a farmhand and millwright. She had two sisters, one older, one younger. They grew up south of Waterville, Maine, in five rooms heated by a barrel stove, on the property of a one-legged dairy farmer. Her father's mother cared for them; she was stern and demanded discipline. Each morning they milked a half dozen cows and fed chickens, geese, and ducks. Her father acted as stable keeper; Rachel and her sisters groomed and fed horses and cleaned out stalls every day. Her older sister had married last June, to a man who owned a bakery in town; she worked nights rolling and kneading dough and brought them day-old loaves. Over the course of the past school year, the dairy farmer's son courted Rachel. She wasn't interested in him, though. She had it in mind now to be a nurse. A girl she knew, an acquaintance at school, had signed up to join the Cadet Nurse Corps—free tuition, she told Rachel, a free uniform, free room and board, and fifteen dollars a month. Rachel signed up, too.

She saved money for train fare and traveled west with her belongings stowed in a battered leather grip. She got her sleep curled up on a wooden bench and watched the land pass behind her. All of it was foreign and beautiful. She had never really been anywhere before, except to Boston, twice. On the train she decided that nursing was good, that caring for the ill was a worthwhile thing and not merely an excuse to flee Waterville. She began to look forward to the work of nursing, to her training in San Francisco. She felt liberated.

A soldier had flirted with Rachel on the train, and she'd agreed to lunch in the dining car, but nothing came of it. Later she sat with two other girls who had heard there was work in Seattle. The three of them drank from a bottle of gin while crossing eastern Montana. Rachel vomited in the toilet stall, twice. She slept, and when she woke again, they were crossing the Rocky Mountains. The train passed across the wheat plateau and at last came down into the river country, where the apple orchards were in spring bloom, their white blossoms brilliant. Seeing this, she had no regrets, or felt she wanted to be elsewhere. She believed that a better life was starting.

But now it was time for Rachel to leave. They went to the river and stood knee-deep, embracing there in the current. Her skin felt smooth and cool to his touch. "I'm going to miss you," she said.

Her uncle's car idled in the yard. They kissed hidden in the orchard rows, and she promised to write from San Francisco. There was even a telephone in the dormitory, and she left the number with him. "This is it," she said firmly. "Wish me luck, Ben."

"I do," he said. "Good luck, Rachel."

"You too. Good luck."

She brought her fingers gently to his face. "I'm memorizing your features," she said. "I want to remember you."

"Don't say that," Ben pleaded. "It sounds like I'm dead already."

"You do it with me," answered Rachel. "Memorize my face."

Ben left the apple country when the picking was done, the bins and ladders put away, the canvas bags hung up. All the apples had been taken from the trees, the orchards brought to silence now, the transient pickers moving on, disappearing down the river road, leaving the country hushed and lonely: not even an evening breeze.

His father took him to the bus station in Wenatchee. He gave Ben six five-dollar bills and a new pocketknife. They milled about in silence for a while, then sat waiting with their hats in their laps, outside, in the loading bay.

"I'm going to worry," said his father. "Just like I do with Aidan."

"It won't do him or me any good."

"Just the same, I'm going to worry."

"There's too much to do to waste time on that."

"Picking's over," said his father. "I've got time on my hands."

They paused to watch the bus pull in. It came to a stop in front of them. "You take care," said Ben.

"Never mind," said his father.

"You keep yourself away from that hooch."

"I'm not on it."

"Yes, you are."

His father knocked a boot heel against the ground. "No, I'm not," he said.

In the open doorway of the bus they embraced, and Ben smelled his father's hair. "Thanks," he said. "For everything."

His father hugged him harder in reply. "Jesus," he said, "don't go."

Ben rode the bus to Cashmere, where he stepped off thinking

to hitchhike west in order to save on bus fare. He stood by the road with his whole life in front of him. He stood with his thumb out and his duffel bag beside him while a few dry flakes of snow descended from a strange, cloudless sky. A truck pulled over, and he rode to Peshastin, where at noon sheets of lightning crossed the orchards. He sat beneath an apple tree, waiting for the storm to pass, leaning against his duffel bag with the rain beating the leaves around him, his canvas coat pulled tightly against his neck, his hat low on his forehead. When the sun emerged, he went again to the road and took a ride with a farmer from Omak hauling hay to Gold Bar.

He passed the night in a wood of fir trees close to the Skykomish River. It was dense, dark, and silent there, wet and uninviting. But in the early morning he rose from dreams to find the river pale and lovely, mist steaming off its waters, the fog thick on its distant bank, and he went down in the cold dawn light to wash his face at a riffle, where he saw a kingfisher flash by. Then he packed, went back to the road, and got a lift in a log truck bound for Monroe, with a driver who carefully looked him over, snapped his metal lunchbox open, and handed Ben a piece of chocolate cake his wife had baked the night before.

At noon Ben made Seattle. He walked with his duffel bag over his shoulder until he found a diner on Occidental advertising specials in its window. He ate a plate of eggs and toast and drank a glass of milk. He sat with his plate pushed away from him and watched two men sitting low at the counter in hats and city over-coats, slouched over their stools. They drank their coffee and smoked in silence. The waitress stood tipped against the wall with a dishrag clutched between her fingers, hobnobbing with the short-order cook through the glare of the heat lamps in the pickup window. There was the low drone of her city voice, tired and cynical.

After breakfast he walked until he came to the salt water. He set his bag by a creosoted piling crusted with mussels and barnacles and descended a pier-side ladder to dip his fingers in the sea. He tasted it while hanging from the tide-bleached rungs like a sailor from mainsail rigging. Then he rinsed his face in a baptism and looked out over the water to the west.

Ben took a room in Pioneer Square, on the second floor of a flophouse. It was lonely and desolate in his paltry room with its dirt-encrusted window. All night through the lights burned glaringly along the street outside. In the morning, tired, he hiked to the bus station and bought a ticket to Fort Lewis. There was a chance for it while he waited for the bus, so for the first time in his life he used a pay phone, getting help from the operator, stuffing coins into the slot. He had to ask the bus clerk for change and try a second time. But when at last he had Rachel on the line, he told her simply that he loved her. It was easier to say it on the telephone. She told him that she felt the same. The time he had bought with his change ran out, and he hung up the receiver in the Seattle bus station and sat in the hall on his duffel bag, waiting with other travelers now, at the outset of a strange, new life.

FIVE

Tristan nudged insistently: a warm muzzle against Ben's ear, a whining deep in the dog's throat. Ben stirred with the moon overhead—tremulous, improbably large, as though while he slept it had stolen closer to the earth—but with no desire to leave his dreams. The languid serenity of marijuana was preferable, its hallucinatory depths transporting him away from a present in which he was sprawled in the desert, afflicted by a terminal disease. Yet he found himself wakened against his will, and the pain of his cancer, put away for a few hours, became, once more, chief.

Ben took stock. He was in the sagelands, alone but for his dogs, in the deepest hour of night. The cold had entered his long-suffering joints, and his bladder pressed for attention. He was as stiff in his back as if the vertebrae were fused, his left eye was swollen shut, and his fingers were numb and useless. More, his left knee seemed incapable of bending, and his arthritic ankle throbbed. Ben rose on one elbow, put his hand on Tristan's head, and berated the dog for rousing him.

Rex, he saw, was out at thirty yards, head high in the sageland. The dog pranced ahead another five yards, stopped to cast for scent and listen, then turned in Ben's direction, gazed at him, and whined.

Ben didn't know what to make of his dogs or of their present animation. He'd seen Rex and Tristan fidget in the presence of porcupines, moles, skunks, owls, voles, and rattlesnakes, but he could not surmise what bothered them now, out here in the placid desert. There were only the stars and that rich, prominent moon, its surface broken by shadows, pocked by enormous craters. And moonlight silver over everything.

Propped on one elbow, immobilized by doubt, Ben watched his agitated dogs. He wanted to lie down again wrapped in his blanket and leave them to face, without his help, whatever was so disconcerting. Ben recollected hearing somewhere that coyotes sometimes worked in packs to lure dogs to untimely deaths, attacking viciously. For a moment he was certain there were coyotes about, and he peered nearsightedly into the desert as though to spot one against the sage. Then, thoroughly exasperated with himself for indulging his fear of shadows—of shapes that were nothing more than wraiths produced by a marijuana-addled mind—he drank from his water bottle. He hoped no effort would be required, that he might sleep again without interruption if his dogs would only settle down, stem their animal fear of the night. "Pipe down," he told them. "That's enough."

Tristan whimpered louder in reply and came to nuzzle Ben's face again with greater urgency.

Ben rose bitterly, then peed long and hard against the earth. It was satisfying to him here at the end of his days to pee with so much vigor. It was a ridiculous thing to be satisfied about, but still he was satisfied. His stream splashed against the ground. He stretched his back and revolved his head so that the bones in his neck cracked a little. He cleaned his glasses with his handkerchief, and when he slipped them on again, the moon appeared through his one good eye like highly polished marble. Everything it illuminated melted into shadows and was softly, darkly beautiful.

Ben pressed the heel of his palm against his head and hawked spit into the desert. Out to the north, as he stood beside Tristan with his blanket wrapped around him, he heard what he thought was the baying of hounds, a restless din far off somewhere, a chorus of dogs just audible, and he cupped his strong ear to listen. They were hounds all right, Ben decided, and they seemed to be moving closer, coming in his direction, perhaps, though not yet visible in shape or motion, instead a wild singing in the night, a yapping, frantic tumult. "Heel," he called to Rex then. "You get in here now."

He repeated himself more forcefully, until Rex, against his will, fell in beside Tristan, whimpering a little. The dog made several false starts to the north, turned in a circle, and whined. The baying of the hounds, though distant and faint across the hills, was audible now not just as a chorus but as a number of distinct hard-trailing hounds in the throes of heated pursuit. "Stay," said Ben. "Just stay there. We'll let them run right past us."

He regretted, deeply, the marijuana. The world was a viscous dream. He felt inhabited by a listlessness ill-suited to what might be needed. His limbs, he knew, would resist what he asked. He was too numb with cold, too much in ruins, unprepared for a pack of hounds bounding in from nowhere. Ben hoped that nothing would come of them. He hoped they would pass, a night tableau, a spectacle, something merely to be witnessed. He hoped Rex and Tristan would keep out of their way. But his dogs, barking maniacally, bolted into the night.

He called with threat and anger in his voice, but they ran off with a heedless certainty, beyond the sphere of his influence. He thought to call a second time, but they were moved, he saw, beyond his command, and in the next seconds he better understood them—for a shadow slid across the desert, a coyote, he saw, at a full-out run, and his dogs were giving chase.

Ben caught only a fleeting glance: the dark coyote swift in flight, its tail low, its ears tucked back, hurtling along like a ghost in the sage, approximately the size and shape of his Brittanies but with a bottle-shaped tail and longer muzzle. The shadow of motion passed before him and disappeared without warning, suddenly gone into a dip in the terrain, out of his line of sight. A spirit soundless across the desert, his dogs in clamorous pursuit of it, and Ben uncertain if what he had seen was real or a deception of the night.

He dropped his blanket into the sand and took up his side-by-side. He pried two shells from their vest loops, broke the gun open, nudged them in, and snapped the action shut. The shotgun, like the world itself, seemed part of a dope-inspired dream, an object flooded by silver moonlight. It was his father's gun, also the gun he had put in his own mouth earlier that morning. For a moment he regretted every gun he'd ever held in his hands, but he shook off the urge to stand pondering this, rolled his blanket, folded his poncho, and lashed them together with the empty duffel to the bottom of his rucksack. Finally he wrestled his arms through the straps and set off in pursuit of his dogs.

East of the breaks the land flattened out into gentle, unbroken prairie. There was moon and starlight enough to travel by as Ben twined between islands of sage, carrying his gun like the infantryman he'd been in Italy fifty-three years before. The baying grew closer, and his own dogs barked in the distance. He exhorted himself to overtake them, but the back of his left knee soon bound up, and he had to stop to knead it.

He came on a pair of wheel ruts across the sage. Probably they'd been made by rolling stock trucks releasing and rounding up cattle, but they seemed to have no reason to be there, like most human sign in the desert. He followed them for their easy walking and because they tended in the right direction—his dogs were off to the southeast, he guessed, though he couldn't know with certainty. The ruts hairpinned and he followed them for a while, until they hairpinned again. He stopped in their bend to listen for his dogs, but the baying hounds were so close now, their cries mingled with his dogs' barking, and he found himself confused. He stood listening to no avail, and again he regretted the marijuana, its discombobulating effect.

Ben stood as though waiting for the flush of birds, and watched the ridge line a quarter mile north, where the stars disappeared behind crenellated rock, for it seemed to him that from just out there the cry of hounds was gathering. A star plummeted down the length of the heavens, and then a roiling shadow broke over the hill, bursting forth in a duststorm of sorts, hounds pell-mell and hell-bent southward, a sinuous, frenetic pack of them barreling down the ridge. They were too far off for Ben to identify, but he took them to be a half dozen or more, and he guessed from their rolling, leaping gait—gracefully fast, like cheetahs or antelopes—that these were Irish wolfhounds, the coyote hunters of his youth.

A potato farmer up the river road, a man named Dale Saunders, Jr., had run a pack of them when called upon by ranchers whose lambs or calves were disappearing. Saunders was known in the orchard country as a trapper, hunter, and prospector, and also a government bounty man, paid to poison coyotes and to gas coyote pups in their dens. His arsenal included spring-loaded cyanide canisters, leghold traps, and strychnine. Ben had heard Saunders holding forth on coyote killing at the county fair, where he sold his handmade coyote calls, home-welded coyote traps, and a device he called a coyote-getter, which when sprung delivered cyanide to a coyote's nose and mouth. Saunders demonstrated the range of his call, which he claimed mimicked the cry of a jackrabbit impaled on a barbed-wire fence. Any coyote deceived by such a call he dispatched point-blank with his ten-gauge; otherwise he picked them off with his .22-250 Remington, which, he added, was shot from a prone position, such was its immense precision. Still, he said, no method yet devised could match his Irish coursing hounds (which he displayed to fairgoers in a chicken-wire cage mounted on the back of his pickup truck) for pure sport and sheer drama. They were huge, confident, rangy dogs, and capable, Saunders claimed, of leaping twenty feet. Four times faster than a coyote, and also adept at treeing cougars and bringing bears to bay.

It had been fifty years since Ben had seen Dale Saunders's Irish wolfhounds, but he remembered their vaguely terrifying size, their power and lithesome restlessness, and it seemed to him in the desert now, that these shadowy creatures spilling through the night—like wild horses under the moon—had just that sort of galloping height, that equine size and speed. They sprinted across the broken terrain without the slightest hindrance. They killed, Ben knew, for the pleasure of it. They were thought by some to be valorous dogs, desirable as guardians and companions, clever, trustworthy, gentle with children, well-disposed and tolerant, but Ben had no faith in their goodness and didn't count himself among their admirers. They were too much enamored of killing.

They surged toward him—a pack of Irish wolfhounds—though at an angle to miss him narrowly, so that he had time to count their number and note their stride and size. Among the six he saw at least two as large as wild yearling colts, and the pack of dogs in their fury and noise reminded him of desert mustangs. In a panic he raised his side-by-side, his thumb against the safety tang, to kill the lead dog in its tracks should the pack turn full in his direction. He had no reason to believe it would, only an inchoate fear born of nothing distinct.

Time seemed fragmented. The distance between moments was greater than usual, so that he saw the hounds at their close approach with a particular detail prominent—the bubbling slather and foam hanging from the jaws of the lead dog, glistening in the moonlight, strands of silvery mucus flying from its teeth and gums. Then all was a blur until the passing of the hounds resolved itself into a crystalline frieze: the last hound's high-speed gait broken down into two clear frames of suspension, of airy, springing levitation, the acrobatic feat of touching the ground with only one paw—impossible—at any given moment. Even as Ben made all this out, the hounds went by him as though he was nothing but an apparition in the desert. He lowered his gun and checked the safety.

Then they were gone, fading to the south, their baying squalls still trailing them, and Ben, suspended briefly in their wake, stirred himself into action. He fell in behind and gave chase with as much zeal as he could muster.

It was a matter of proceeding as if on a forced march. He couldn't hear beyond his own breathing, nor could he stop to let it subside, since speed, he felt, was essential, his dogs had innocently tossed themselves between these hounds and their quarry. Spurred on by thoughts of the worst that could be, he gave himself to a fretful haste that magnified his pains. He limped ahead as fast as he could, making his way by the light of the moon and squinting into the distance.

It occurred to Ben that his feverish anxiety made no sense at all. What could it matter to him in the next world if he submitted to the will of this one instead of plunging on against it? Why exert himself painfully to alter the course of things? There was solid ground for apathy. He had no duty to recover his dogs. He was bound to leave them soon anyway. Let them wander where they would; when finished, they would find him again. And if they did not, so be it.

But out of long habit, he pushed ahead. It was not so much his dogs as his conscience that would not allow him to give up. He did not want to be careless, or transgress against his obligations: he wanted to be himself, a doctor seeing to every detail, a man tuned to his duties in life, and he found that even in the shadow of death it was not easy to be otherwise. In this frame of mind, bent on clarity, he stumbled awkwardly in the sage. With only one good eye he had a false sense of distance and caught his boot against a wrinkle in the sand, then lurched to his knees so that his lower back twisted, causing him a sudden pain. He dropped his head against his chest and set the butt of his shotgun down to lean on its length. Ben rubbed his back for a long while, and then, absently, his side. His breathing subsided. Again he heard the cries of hounds. Struggling to his feet, he pressed on.

In fifteen or maybe fifty minutes, he worked his way to the bottom of a draw choked with sumac and willows. The place was mad with the noise of hounds, their guttural fury and desperation, and as he thrashed through the thickets it seemed to him he was in their very midst. He could see no sign of them, only hear, though the full moon poured over everything, illuminating close details. He felt certain the doomed coyote was here, having found a covert where trickery might triumph over speed. The hounds were trying to roust it out, rooting and tearing at the bramble to expose it lying low. Like any animal brought to bay, the coyote had nothing to lose by waiting. It would cling to the earth, deep in its covert, its smallness now its only salvation, while beyond the thorns its enemies thrashed to get it by the throat.

Ben beat his way to the lip of the draw, stood above it in the open sage, then dropped wearily to one knee and called for Tristan and Rex, beseeching each by name. He wished he could catch a glimpse of them. His apprehension was greater now. They should have come at the sound of his voice. He had no trust in the wolfhounds, and the cries emanating from the thickets below were fraught with cruelty.

A dark shape plunged from the sumac thicket not twenty yards from where he knelt, a soundless shadow low to the ground and almost formless in its haste, though Ben noted its bottle-shaped tail, canted left and deployed like a rudder, as the animal became aware of his presence and instantly changed course. He watched it twist off in a puff of dust and disappear into the sage. Behind it, three times as large, with arched loins and pointed muzzle, a wolfhound cleared the tangled draw with as much loud bucking as a lassoed horse, and charged after it. Then four more hounds emerged, and amid them he saw Rex.

Ben stumbled to higher ground. Out in the sage the hounds held moonlight, their flanks shimmering as they ate up ground, their long tails curled. Rex, already, had fallen far behind, while the distance between the hounds and the coyote diminished with astonishing speed. The lead hound surged, the coyote veered in a twisting evasion, the hound found it smoothly. The coyote wheeled to face them all with its teeth bared, snarling.

Two hounds leaped to hamstring the coyote; a third locked jaws between its shoulder blades, while the lead dog spun and drove in low to seize it by the throat. The coyote cartwheeled in a spray of dust but the hounds clung heedlessly to it, addressing its death from various angles, thrashing as though to rend the animal, pinning it to the dusty ground. Then Rex drove into the fray.

Ben, struggling free of his rucksack, plunged downhill with his gun. At the same moment, off to the east, he spotted a light on the ridge crest—the solitary headlamp of a vehicle—and then he recognized the silhouette of a dirt bike raising dust in a high channel as it careened in his direction.

He saw the world through his one good eye, through the wire-rimmed glasses from another time, appearing as though underwater as he stumbled down toward the welter of dogs, the dirt bike approaching through the sage. There was no time to ponder anything. The hounds, he saw, had finished with the coyote and were turning their attention to Rex.

His dog seemed astonished to find matters so, wheeling back against the tide of hounds, growling and baring his teeth. The hounds advanced with mad insistence and sent Rex sprawling into the dust, and then one seized him firmly at the hindquarters, another sunk his teeth into his withers, and a third clutched him at the throat.

Ben lashed into their midst yelling, raised his shotgun toward the stars, and fired a deafening warning. Immediately, the hounds desisted, tongues hanging, whimpering, except that one still had Rex by the throat and tossed him left and right.

Ben waded forward and slammed the butt of his shotgun against the ribs of this hound. He saw how desperate Rex was now, pinned by the throat against the earth, his breathing hollow, reedy. Ben kicked the wolfhound as hard as he could, first in the ribs and next in the head, swearing at it under his breath, but it was as though he hadn't kicked at all. And now there was no time for anything else, Rex was dying as he stood and watched, and he had to act without compromise and in a way he had much resisted acting in the years since his war ended. He set his teeth, grimacing, then pushed the barrel of his Winchester home against the ribs he'd kicked before, and squeezed the gun's front trigger.

He had no time to contemplate the outcome or to deliberate with morbid revulsion on the destructive force of his shotgun. Instead, he knelt to look at Rex.

Rex, on his side, twisted slowly in the dust, exerting himself like a drunk man. He meant to rise but could not find the means, and howled a note of pain such as Ben had never heard issue from the throat of any dog. Something like human suffering was in it—a high, piercing wail. The dog's hindquarters were clearly ravaged, and Ben feared his spine was broken. "I'm sorry, Rex," he said.

He tried to put a hand on Rex's flank, but the dog writhed, his howl surged higher, and Ben thought better of it. The wolf-hounds leered at him uncertainly, keeping a respectful distance. Ben swore at one, and it loped away.

The dirt bike stopped in front of him, throwing sand from under its tires, and the rider, whom he could not see—he had his headlamp aimed in Ben's direction—cut the low-throated motor. Ben caught a glimpse of one heavy boot as it came to rest against the sand, its steel toe protruding through the leather. He threw his free hand over his forehead and tried to make out the face of the rider, but to no avail: he was jacklighted. He was as blind and incapacitated as a deer in a car's high beams.

"Supposing you put out that light," he said. "The thing is blinding me."

"It's my coyote spotter," the rider called.

The light stayed on, blindingly. "Your dog looks pretty torn up," said the rider. "But mine there looks plain dead."

Rex howled, but the tenor of it had changed, as if he'd made an adjustment.

"I had to shoot him," Ben explained. "He was tearing up my dog."

"Whyn't you just kick him off?"

"I tried that. It didn't work."

"Always works with me," said the rider. "I don't know why it wouldn't."

"Your dog had mine by the throat," Ben said. "He was stran-gling him. I didn't have a choice."

"Well, you're too damn fast to use your shotgun," the rider admonished him. "I've kicked every one of these dogs before. You give 'em a kick, they listen."

"All right," said Ben. "Turn that light out."

"Hey," the rider answered firmly. "You don't have a right to be out here, so you don't have any leg to stand on, do you, asking me to put out my light. Not while you're on private property, out here trespassing, damn it."

His voice was that of the country around them, flat and laden with certainty and an intention to get things done. Ben recognized it as the voice of men he'd known in his youth and childhood, the voice of the farmers and ranchers of the basin, and he knew there was no arguing with it.

"I'm sorry," said Ben. "It shouldn't have happened. But like I said, I didn't have a choice."

The rider seemed to contemplate this. "Damn," he said. "Listen here. You pick up that gun of yours. Carefully."

Ben did so, holding it by the breechblock, in his right hand, away from him.

"It's a side-by-side," the rider said. "I believe I can see that from here."

"You're right," Ben answered. "It is."

"Well, you fired two shots," the rider said. "So unless you reloaded after shooting my dog, the barrels are empty right now."

"I didn't reload," Ben said. "Why don't I break the gun open?"

"No," said the rider. "I don't want that. I want you to toss it out in front of you. With one hand, as far as you can. And I want you to do it now."

Ben hesitated. The Winchester had been his father's gun. "Look," he said. "Throwing it that way might damage it. What if I just put it down?"

Again there was a pause from behind the light, the disembodied voice gone silent. "All right," the rider said at last. "You set it down there in front of you. I'm watching. You go ahead."

Ben set the gun down gently. "There," he said. "That's that now. I'm going to see to my dog."

"Hold on," said the rider. "I want you to go on over there and get beside that dog you killed and take a look at him for me."

"What?"

"Get over there and take a look. Just go on now. Do it."

"Listen," said Ben. "I'm sorry he's dead. But it's my dog who needs attending to, if—"

"That dog's going to be all right. You get over there."

"Listen," said Ben. "I—"

"Look," the rider said firmly. "Just you do like you're told. I got my gun pointed at your head and I want you over there."

"All right," Ben told him. "I'm going."

He stumbled to the dead wolfhound. It lay on its side about five feet off, where the force of the shot had thrown it. Its midsection, its withers and flanks, were bright with viscera and bits of white bone, and its head lay tilted at an unnatural angle, as if it had been severed and then reconnected incorrectly. "Okay," Ben said. "Now what?"

The rider adjusted his dirt bike slightly so as to throw a full light on Ben. "Read his collar there for me," he demanded. "The tag's at his throat. Read it."

Ben dropped stiffly to one knee and took the slain dog's collar. He worked it around until he found the tag. He squinted for a long moment. "Jim," he said. "I think it reads Jim. I can't tell. My eyes are bad."

"Jim," said the rider. "Damn."

"I'm sorry," Ben said. "I am."

The rider again fell silent. "Jim," he said after awhile.

"He had my dog by the throat," Ben explained.

"You shouldn't have done it," the rider said. "I don't want to hear about it."

"Fine," said Ben. "You won't."

"Damn," said the rider. "Come out in front now. And keep your hands up high."

Ben rose and stepped around the dog, his face averted from the light.

"On the ground, now. Face down, go on. And spread everything out."

"What for?"

"Just do like you're told."

"I have to look after my dog now."

"He can look after himself, damn it. You get down on the ground."

Ben lay down on his belly. He rested his cheek against the sand.

"All right," said the rider. "You turn your head. Look off toward the west there."

Ben did so.

"Just so you don't get nervous," said the rider. "I'm going to take a walk out here and pick your gun off the ground."

"Go ahead," said Ben.

"And this coyote here," the rider said. "I'm going to take his tail."

"All right," said Ben. "Go ahead."

He waited while the rider went about his business. One of the wolfhounds sat in Ben's view, dour and bored-looking. Ben listened to Rex's whimpering and the sound of the rider's boots. Then to the sound of his shotgun broke open, the metallic snap of the action. "Say," said the rider. "A regular antique. And some fancy looking engraving."

"It's a Winchester 21," said Ben.

"What do you figure it's worth?" said the rider. "Because replacing Jim'll cost me some. A dog like that isn't cheap."

"I don't really know," said Ben.

"Anyway," the rider informed him. "I can't exactly leave this here. You're liable to shoot me in the back with it. So I'm going to sell your shotgun off and get myself a new hound."

"Now wait a minute," Ben said. "That's highway robbery."

"Shut your mouth," said the rider. "You just shut your mouth now." He snapped the gun's action closed again. "Smooth," he said. "You just stay right there. Don't you move a muscle."

Ben made no reply.

The rider whistled his hounds in about him. Ben heard the soft trotting sounds of their feet. "I ought to make you bury Jim," the rider announced bitterly. "I ought to make you paw out a hole and give Jim a decent grave."

"I didn't have a choice," Ben said again. "Jim was strangling my Brittany."

He struggled to his feet, brushed the dirt from his jacket. "Shoot me if you want," he told the rider. "I'm looking after my dog."

"Shooting you'd just be more trouble," the rider answered him. "If shooting you could bring Jim back, I wouldn't even think to hesitate."

"It couldn't be helped," Ben said. "He was killing my dog, like I told you. I didn't have a choice."

"Well, now you don't have a shotgun," said the rider. "So it can't happen again."

"Go to hell," Ben said.

In the nimbus of light around the rider his remaining wolf-hounds milled. Ben could see them in silhouette, turning restlessly.

"I'll tell you what's got me worried," said the rider. "Maybe while I'm tearing out of here, you'll try'n plug me in the back."

"With what?" said Ben. "You stole my gun."

"With whatever else you got on you. Hidden down your pant leg."

The rider started up his bike with a hard shove that registered beyond the light. "I'll tell you what," he said above its roar. "If you can draw that fast and hit a moving target, 'specially blinded the way you are, you deserve to get your gun back."

He spun out suddenly in a spray of sand aimed in Ben's direction. The dirt bike turned, gathered speed, and found its way between clumps of sage, the pack of wolfhounds following it as though on a casual training run, the rider intentionally veering to and fro in an effort to dodge the bullets he imagined Ben was aiming at his back. But, of course, there were no such bullets. Ben had already turned away to kneel, a doctor, beside his dog.

SIX

Rex had ceased to struggle. He seemed languid in a way that suggested shock, yet his breathing came neither rapid nor shallow, nor did he heave with a racing pulse, nor did he seem submerged in a torpor, but merely patient with the state of things, containing his distress in some private space, yielding himself to fate.

Ben rose and located his rucksack, uphill in the sage. Then he knelt beside his dog, and with his medical kit propped open beside him, his headlamp fixed just over his eyes, took stock of Rex's wounds.

"I'm sorry, Rex," he whispered.

Using moist towelettes from his kit, he scrubbed his fingers thoroughly. He unraveled a length of sterile gauze and draped it over one shoulder. Gently he put one knee on the dog's head, the other in his rib cage. Rex lurched with a feeble resistance, growled, and lurched again. Ben formed the gauze into a hanging loop and maneuvered it over Rex's muzzle. "I'm sorry," he said. "I know it's not pleasant," and then he snugged it moderately tight, crossed the ends beneath the dog's chin, brought them up behind his ears and tied them off at the top of his head, so that Rex looked like a soldier with a head wound dressed on the field of battle. "There," said Ben. "We're done now."

Lifting his pinning weight from the dog, he lay a hand against Rex's flank and stroked him soothingly. "You're all right," he said. The dog whimpered through the makeshift muzzle. He did not seem entirely resigned; there was a hint of anxiety in his voice.

"You're all right," Ben said again. "I'm just going to look."

Under the headlamp, working through the fur, following the evidence of blood matted there, he took account of Rex's wounds: the left hamstring, between the hip and stifle, was punctured and swollen from hemorrhage; from shoulder to shoulder, low across the withers, a long run of skin had been ripped open, a gaping tear he could retract with his fingers to reveal the transparent fascia, the blunt tips of the spinal column, and the neat bone of the shoulder blades; and finally a broad tearing of the skin at Rex's throat, exposing one jugular.

For many years Ben had played, informally, the role of climbing expedition doctor, and his kit testified to that. He carried Compazine, erythromycin, butterfly bandages, roller gauze, Telfa and adhesive bandages. He also carried a scalpel with a set of blades and suture material in packets. Ben had field-stitched pocketknife cuts and an ice-ax laceration. He had, in the field, set a fractured arm, had reduced both shoulder and hip dislocations, and had seen to the construction of makeshift litters, transport slings, and crutches. Yet he had never field-stitched a dog before, and that was needed now. Rex had a desert journey in front of him. He would need his wounds closed first.

There was plenty of downed willow on the bank of the draw, and Ben dragged out what he could in ten minutes and with his spearpoint blade cut shavings. His cigarette lighter sparked sluggishly, so he squeezed it inside his armpit. He lit one of the paraffin fire starters and built, quickly, an extravagant blaze. The wizened willow burned hot and clean. He heaped long branches of it on, then sat by Rex, watching him, one hand brushing his coat. He hoped Tristan would smell the blaze and come to it soon, unharmed.

Ben drank again from his water bottle. He had not passed a night so physically taxing since the assault on the tunnels at Lago di Garda and the counterattacks the retreating Germans made against the town of Torbole. He sat close to the fire's heat, his body seeking to balance itself after the surges of marijuana and adrenaline that had coursed through it these past hours. His exertions and the tension of confronting the shotgun thief had been at war with his drug-induced reveries, the dream world he'd inhabited. But he felt at last that he was coming loose of his addled, soporific haze. He had entered a place of tired clarity. He was alert in some enervated, worn-out fashion, with the kind of acuity one arrives at in the aftermath of fever.

After awhile, when the dog seemed calm, he washed his hands a second time, drew out his suture needle, opened a packet of two-ought nylon suture—the only sort he had on hand—and rinsed the needle in antiseptic.

"All right," he said. "It'll hurt a little, Rex. A lot less than what you've been through, though. We'll just go at it carefully."

He pulled up his coat sleeves, adjusted his headlamp. He pinned Rex again beneath his knees, and held him down firmly with his left hand, which seemed the only workable position. He would have to throw stitches in a one-handed fashion, in a continuous pattern, like a seamstress. "Here we go," he whispered.

Rex heaved beneath him when he threw the first stitch and again when he tied the anchor, but after that the dog surrendered. He was braver than Ben had anticipated, more patient in the face of pain. Rex had always seemed too brash, too headlong and imprudently eager, but now he acquitted himself with a decorous restraint, and endured nobly. Ben felt a grudging admiration.

When the dog had been sutured at the throat and back, he slept as though to obliterate the truth of the various insults he'd suffered. Ben worked the muzzle free and caressed Rex's flank while examining his handiwork. The stitches, he concluded, were not too bad, given the conditions under which they'd been thrown. They gave him a curious pleasure.

He banked up his fire. He was hungry now, hungrier than he'd been in a long while, and he pulled the chukars out of his rucksack and skinned each in the light of his headlamp, cutting the backs and viscera out along with the second joints of the wings and culling the small legs and thighs. He skewered the breasts and the dark meat on willow sticks; the rest he buried in the sand. He drew himself up to the fire, into the smoke and light and heat, and with a slow care not to burn the meat, grilled it much as he'd done long ago, camping in the sage hills with Aidan.

Ben ate indulgently. He devoured the birds to the bones. They tasted better than anything he'd eaten in weeks, many weeks. He drank a little water, with an eye toward conserving; Rex, he knew, would need some. There were the blond girl's pumpkin seeds, and he ate them too, and thought of her with a distant ache and a faint trace of desire. It was not so much her as the thought of her, of having been once young himself, of Rachel's skin against his own, the smell of Rachel's mouth and throat—everything he could not replace or easily let go of. And why couldn't he detach

himself from this earthly, mad desire? Why did he go on wanting a woman who no longer lived in this world? Her hold on him
was still great, a need with roots in his core. To die, he thought,
was to escape passion's grasp, but that was the last thing he
wanted. Instead he wished to be seized by passion and pinioned,
held in its palm forever—he could not imagine any other existence as embracing any real happiness.

Ben reserved some meat for Rex and limped to the draw for
more willow branches. He worked slowly at the gathering of
wood. It was important now to marshal his energies. A long journey lay ahead of him.

He stumbled onto the corpse of the coyote, its neck distended
by the whiplashings of the hounds, its tail cut off by the dirt-
bike rider who'd stolen his father's shotgun. Then he remembered
the dead wolfhound and went to it, his headlamp a grisly spotlight. The picture before him gave him pause, inspiring a stab of
regret. The dog's abdomen was an abraded pulp of raw muscle,
splintered bone, and purple, glistening viscera smelling of half-
digested food. It was an unkind thing to look on, but worse to
consider that he himself was the agent of this destruction. Ben
dropped to one knee, penitent.

He took the chain from the dog's neck and read the tag's in-
scription. The dog's name, JIM, was in capital letters, but underneath it, in smaller type, was the name of his owner, the rider in
the sage, and his address and telephone number. William C.
Harden. He lived out of Malaga on Joe Miller Road. Ben
squeezed the tag in his fist and raised his head to look into the
east, where the sky now showed a paler hue, a cerulean tint on the
horizon, the stars fading away. Dawn, he understood, was imminent, and he'd survived to witness it.

With the light he knew there was no choice left but to go in
search of Tristan. He walked the rim of the willow draw, crossed

at a swale of low wheatgrass that wet his boots with morning dew, and reconnoitered up the farther side with the steam puffing from his mouth. Twice he stopped to call into the silence, and in the heightened stillness that followed, he listened carefully. No answer came from any quarter, nor did he really expect one. For hours, now, he'd sensed the dog's fate, and it angered him to imagine it, this dog he had known for ten full years as a placid, sober, sensible companion, this dog he had brought home at seven weeks, not to hunt birds—he was not hunting then—but because he had wanted a dog in his life as a vestige of childhood. He'd seen Tristan through ringworm, coccidiosis, cherry eye, yeast otitis, then through a series of old-age maladies—gastroenteritis, a perineal hernia, a dislocating kneecap. He'd observed the dog's steady decline, his need to sit whenever possible, his waning zeal to cut up cover or pound his way through heavy brush, his great thoroughness everywhere to make up for an advancing sloth. That was when Ben brought home Rex, in the hope that the young dog might learn what he could in the seasons before Tristan died.

Another twenty minutes passed before Ben found Tristan at the base of a willow, sprawled in the position in which he slept, so that at first Ben hoped it was only sleep, until he saw Tristan's broken neck. The dog's head had been wrenched and distended, the skin at the throat torn open, the jugulars both severed. A penumbra of blood surrounded Tristan's head and stained the ground under him. Already his upturned eye had clouded, entirely obscuring the lens.

Ben carried Tristan up into the sageland, and at a little distance from his willow fire dug up the ground with the entrenching tool he carried in his rucksack. The grave was shallow and imperfect, but he had no strength to give Tristan more, and he laid him to rest with a little less care than he might have mustered at better times. Nevertheless, it was a grave of sorts, and the dog deserved at least that. He knelt beside it for a moment, then pressed the dog's eyes closed and shoveled the sand back over him.

It was that odd morning hour when clouds roll over after a clear fall night has passed, clouds that would douse the sage for an hour before marching eastward across the desert toward the Selkirk Mountains. Sitting beside his willow fire, Ben noted them, first and foremost, as a transformation in the texture of the air and a subduing of the morning light, as something imminent to be felt in all things, a sensation he remembered from childhood. He watched the sky and then, a third time, tucked his fingers under Rex's right hindleg to press against the femoral artery, measuring the dog's resting pulse, which seemed satisfactory enough. Then, his back warmed by the flames, he turned to watch the clouds come. They were high, dark plumes, fully massed in vertical columns like the ramparts of battleships, their lower reaches dense with rain. Ben, in the face of them, stirred himself and urgently loaded his rucksack.

He stood with his compass in his palm and estimated that in three miles of walking, shading slightly northeast, he would hit a piece of section road, or perhaps the reclamation project's West Canal, and then he could follow the roads or the canal another five miles into George. It was shorter, he guessed, than the walk into Vantage, and while he could not outrun the rain, he could get a jump on it if he set out now, and with luck he might even hail a ride, though chances were slim, in the Frenchman Hills, that many cars would be on the roads. George, Ben decided, might be ten miles off, which in his state of health and with the dog to carry meant the better part of the day ahead. His work stood starkly cut out for him.

He spread his blanket on the sand and, after a moment's hesitation, put one hand on Rex. The dog didn't move except to lift his head—but as if this were part of some bird-hunting dream—nor did he move when Ben took him by the forelegs and right hindleg, worked him gently into the center of the blanket, took up the corners in a jury-rigged sling, and devised himself a thick carrying knot against which to settle his hands.

He drank the last of his water. He would have to find more water soon, somewhere in the sage. He slipped his arms into the rucksack, hoisted the dog over one shoulder, and adjusted Rex's weight carefully, so as to not cause him pain. Bent under his burden, Ben doubted he could endure it. But he set out anyway, an old beleaguered man in the desert shuffling along on a cold fall morning with the rain clouds bearing down from the west, his back straining beneath his load. His chin was gray with stubble, his left eye swollen shut. He felt himself a node for travail, a gathering up of suffering into a single point. It was something he'd known long ago at war and on steep hard windy glaciers, where endless meditation on pain served only to deepen it. In desiring always not to suffer, one only heightened suffering. So now he employed the climber's trick, which was also the slogging infantryman's trick, of working to detach his mind from his body, of standing aside as best he could, observing his labored, torturous progress instead of enduring it. Yet he found, at his age, no relief in this. He was too downtrodden, beaten to the core. He stopped beside the next willow draw, eased the dog into the sand, and collapsed beside him, defeated.

Ben lay staring up at the sky, fiddling with the Italian carabiner. He worked its hinge aimlessly. He deliberated for a long time, until he came to a solution. Then, with his folding saw, he went down into the draw and cut two willow poles. He brought them out, smoothed them patiently, then lay one on either side of the dog, drew them into the shape of a V, and lashed their ends together. It took time to adjust things to his standards, but eventually he tied in Rex's blanket sling at the carrying knot he'd made earlier. Finally he ran a loop from the pole ends, clipped the Italian carabiner in, and slung the webbing over his shoulder to use as a makeshift harness.

It was a travois of the sort once used by Indians to move loads over the plains. As Ben pulled it, Rex swayed where he hung, snared like so much cargo. Still, it worked acceptably. The lashings held up sufficiently. The ring-angle piton, threaded on the carabiner, bobbled as Ben hauled his dog across the desert, and his travois scored the sand.

He felt a damp wind blowing at his back, and the first large raindrops began slapping hard against his shoulders. He remembered the poncho in his rucksack, but it seemed impossible to wear it and pull Rex without overheating. Ben was already drenched in a sweat that turned cold whenever he stopped, so he pushed on under the rain, pausing often to catch his breath with his elbows against his knees. The cold rain soaked the crown of his head, his neck, back, and ears.

Sometimes, journeying, he thought of other things, but mostly his mind was returned to the present by his agonized discomfort. He was worn-out, utterly exhausted, and at times his discipline fragmented and he felt himself begin to cave. The rain moved east, leaving the morning dour, the desert sand darkly stained with water, the sagebrush dripping wet. Ben's periods of rest lengthened. There was a rhythm to his thoughts when he struggled forward—panic alternating with redoubled efforts to cultivate detachment. Finally he rested on his back for so long that he had to quell the urge to rest permanently before setting out once more.

In two hours Ben left the sage behind and entered into a vast, dreary field, turned to lie fallow for the cold season. He crossed its unbroken, sodden expanse, traveling toward a line of power pylons and carefully keeping the big river bluffs over his shoulder to the southwest. Tucked under a ridge stood a stack of moldering hay bales five times as large as any farmhouse and covered with black tarpaulins. Ben came down into wheel ruts and a sign—HUNTING BY PERMIT ONLY—nailed into a fence post, and another that said LEASED HUNTING. The weeds at roadside had been burned off. It occurred to him that yes, he had trespassed last night, as the rider in the sage had indicated. He cleared a rise and south, toward Royal Slope, lay blond, sweeping, dry wheat fields and north toward the Caliche Lakes grew trellised apple trees stretching geometrically across the plateau reach.

He came down out of the Frenchman Hills, tortured beneath his burden. Below stretched big fields all disced under, and standing fields of grain corn. On the slope grew Gala apples trained on spindles in the European fashion, and a broad neat swath of Red Delicious trees in umbrella form, with centers open. The branch props were stacked by the orchard. There were no bins in sight.

At last he found a branch canal, which he knew to be laden with pathogens and the excreta of cattle, water he would never imagine drinking at any but desperate times. Now he filled his bottles with it, dropped into each an iodine pill, waited for the crystals to dissolve, and drank with steady greed. The taste was abhorrent; he spat it out. He untied Rex's traveling hammock, let him lap water from his palm, and fed him the remaining chukar meat.

Ben stroked the dog's coat softly. Rex sat on the blanket looking about, pawing tentatively. Finally, he pushed into a standing position, and keeping one foot free of the ground, hobbled forward on the other three.

"You're looking good," Ben called after him. "You're looking better, Rex."

The dog limped off about twenty yards, and with considerable trouble, whining a little, defecated in the sand. He tried for a time to lick his wounds. He turned, hopping, ran his tongue along his hamstring, poked his nose into folds of his coat, then hobbled off another ten yards and urinated feebly, stumbling in the midst of his stream. Licking his wounds again, he limped to the blanket, where Ben was already dismantling the travois. "Looks like you can walk," Ben said.

He looped the carabiner once more around his neck. It bounced against his sternum as he walked.

They limped on, two invalids, two lame wanderers in the desert. They hobbled across the plateau reach and at noon came out on a section road. They passed a pile of rubble in a ditch—stone, bricks, slab concrete—and then a draw strewn with worn-out tires and the rusting hulks of appliances—refrigerators, freezers, dryers. There were dusty side roads, irrigation pumps, the canal water drifting lazily in its course of half-round concrete. A sign sat mounted on a metal post, PURPLE LOOSESTRIFE HARMS WETLANDS AND WATERWAYS, and a few cattails grew here and there where the irrigating water spilled over. They'd come into true farm country. There were mobile homes with satellite dishes. There were lines of poplars, irrigated fields, and newly planted orchards. They came to an intersection with a paved two-lane that Ben guessed was the Beverly-Burke Road as it cut north from Low Gap Pass back in the Frenchman Hills.

They traveled on across the plateau, past mailboxes, newspaper flutes, and big aluminum silos. They surprised three coots on a brackish pond, who began to swim as Ben and Rex approached, paddling silently around a corner. The plain lay broken by shade trees and silhouetted farm buildings far into the east. There were no cars anywhere. Some time after two o'clock they passed what remained of the George Feed Store with its window frames devoid of glass, a mobile-home park laid out behind poplars, a gravel yard full of irrigating pipe, and finally a street of unkempt homes with ragged squares of lawn. They passed the Church of the Assembly of God and the George Community Hall. There was a sign in English and then in Spanish: WARNING NEIGHBOR-HOOD CRIME WATCH. ALERTA SE ESTA VIGILANDO LE VECINDAD. They limped on into the town of George, the doctor first and behind him his dog, and when they came across a boy behind a chain-link fence who was changing an excavator's hydraulic hose—a boy dressed in a mechanic's grease suit, haggard-thin, his hair worn long, a cigarette hanging from his lips—Ben asked in a weary voice if there was a vet somewhere in town. The boy replied that he didn't know, cast an eye briefly over them, and then, adjusting his cigarette, went back to his labors.

At the Colonial Market, Ben selected a can of dog food, a gallon of spring water, a quart of prune juice, five bags of salted peanuts, a banana, and a Winesap apple. It was warm inside, and he lingered; there were no other customers. One clerk worked the checkout stand and another the video counter. All the shelves seemed a quarter stocked, as if the place was going out of business. There were mostly canned goods and little that was fresh—two heads of iceberg lettuce, a clutch of bananas, a few tomatoes, some apples, a handful of pears. A glass case displayed cheap souvenirs—spoons, mugs, postcards, American flags, painted plates.

The checkstand clerk, a teenage girl, was unfriendly in a neutral fashion, offering nothing in the way of pleasantries when he approached her with his armload of goods, though she gawked at his swollen eye. "Is there a vet in town?" he asked.

"Quincy," she answered. "Eleven miles."

"I don't have a way to get to Quincy," Ben explained to her. "You don't have a vet here, do you—someone right here in town?"

"Only on Tuesdays," replied the girl. "The vet comes Tuesdays, runs a clinic."

He paid with a twenty-dollar bill, and she grew more comfortable. "It's a doctor you need, not a vet," she said. " 'Cept we don't have one of those, either. Closest doctor's up in Quincy."

"I don't need a doctor," Ben said.

He found Rex where he'd left him, splayed out in front of the store. They made their way to a copse of willows, where there were two hubcaps just behind a log, among desiccated roof tiles and rotting sheaves of particleboard, and here he opened the can of dog food and dislodged the meat into one of the hubcaps with the length of his spear-point blade.

The dog choked the food down instantly. Ben watered him and thought of Tristan buried out there in the sage. The night previous seemed unreal. Except that his shotgun and Tristan were missing, it might have been only a nightmare.

Examining the stitches he'd put in Rex that morning, he decided they'd held together sufficiently during the desert crossing. He rinsed them a little with the spring water, then sat on the ground with his back against the log, sighed, and drank long and hard.

Ben ate a small bag of peanuts. The salt and oil tasted good, and he ate a second bag. He drank half the prune juice, but it didn't slake his thirst, so he followed it with long draughts of spring water. He ate the banana and the Winesap apple. It was a good apple for store-bought, sweet and properly ripened. He ate it to its core, happily, and wished he had another.

A farmer passed in a mud-splashed pickup and gaped at him through the side window. Another truck rumbled by and the people in it, a boy and a girl, leaned forward to gawk at him. In his dishevelment, Ben understood, he cut a disconcerting figure, a transient pauper, a graybeard drifter, a derelict or vagrant. A rootless old bum who had wandered into town to die in a corner or sleep in a barn, piss against the tire of a car, eat an apple squatting on the ground, feed his dog from a cast-off hubcap. He knew what he looked like suddenly, and for a moment he wanted to laugh.

Sitting there with his jug in his lap, he thought of those Hindu wanderers he'd seen on a public television documentary, mendicants abroad with begging bowls, dressed in rags and clutching staffs, divested of all other property, seeking to meet the world unencumbered, aspiring, always, toward—what did they call it?—atman, the self, God. They had a better chance when liberated from possessions, moving freely through the world. There were no distractions in this way of life, everything pared to the barest essentials: food, water, rumination. It wasn't the life he had chosen to live, but it seemed more comprehensible now, as he sat on the ground reduced by exhaustion to an appreciation of simple pleasures. He recalled reading once that the Hindus saw life in four progressive stages: twenty years a youth, twenty years a fighter—one needed nothing martial to pursue this phase—twenty years as head of a household, and twenty in the cultivation of the spirit. It was part of this final stage that he was going to miss by dying of colon cancer, as if the last movement of a symphony had been truncated, rendering all before it pointless, stripping it of fundamental meanings and preventing it from achieving its effect of harmony and completeness. A few more years of twilight, melancholy perhaps, but beautiful.

Ben and Rex shuffled on. They hiked along Montmorency Boulevard with its median grass and poplar trees. They passed a sign for a Lutheran Church declaring its membership in the Missouri Synod. The leaves had come down everywhere, and the wind had whisked them into the gutters, where they were ground to an auburn paste.

Out by the interstate, at Martha's Inn, a stock truck sat in a parking lot of dark, wind-rippled puddles. Underneath the highway sign, starkly gargantuan up on its pole—

MARTHA'S INN
CAFE, FAMILY DINING, LOUNGE
CREDIT CARDS ACCEPTED

—sat two more gaudy tractor-trailers, one inscribed with the name *Glory*, the other painted pearl-black with jaunty purple roof faring. Ben crossed in front of them, tied Rex near the inn's doorway, and settled him on the blanket. "Wait right here," he said softly. "I'm going to get you to a vet."

He pushed into the foyer with its Pepsi machine and inert, still video games. He pressed on through to the heat of the place—a snug, agreeable cookstove heat—and holding his rucksack at his side, waited in front of the glass cashier's counter where a painting of a black Lab was displayed for sale, another of three elk poised in a field, a third of an iridescent waterfall.

Ben drew off his cap and entered the dining room. A mother and daughter were playing cards and eating a plate of onion rings. A man with a gray high pompadour scrutinized Ben with what looked to be a casual ill will for strangers. A wind-furrowed farmer in a flannel shirt trembled over his coffee cup and worked on a wedge of pie. At a table nearby sat a crowd of young people eating hamburgers and french fries. One was swellingly pregnant. She pulled on her soft drink, then on a cigarette. A name was tattooed on her shoulder.

Ben washed in the bathroom. A vaultlike dispensary sold glow-in-the-dark condoms, the directions for their purchase inscribed on a decal in both Spanish and English. Ben combed his hair, brushed his teeth, and cleaned the lenses of his glasses. He dried his face and hands on paper towels, then paused to look at himself. His eye had blackened obscenely now. He looked, he thought, horribly old, as smashed and bruised as a boxer.

It was difficult to accept that the face in the mirror belonged to him and could not be altered, the ravages of time reversed. But he gathered himself, pressed his hair into place, and tried to appear presentable. He dried his neck with a paper towel and examined his face in profile. His clothes were still wet from that morning's rain, and in the heat of the place he felt chilled.

He strode onto the restaurant floor, set his rucksack against his leg, worked his wallet free of his pocket, and holding three twenty-dollar bills high, announced in the firmest voice he could muster that his dog waited, injured, outside, that he needed to get him to a vet right away, and for anyone willing to take him up to Quincy there was sixty dollars in it.

A man stood up. Tall, thin, and hollow-eyed, he wore pointed, black sideburns. He wiped his lips with a napkin as he rose, then dropped it on his table. "I'll do it," he said. "Let's go."

His name was Stu Robinson. He shook Ben's hand in his tall lanky way. He wore cowboy boots and a tight red windbreaker with the name of a saloon in Arizona printed in white across its back. "What happened to your eye?" he asked.

"I was in a car wreck," Ben explained. "Up in Snoqualmie Pass."

"Christ," Stu Robinson said with a wince. "Don't even tell me about it."

They went outside. It was late in the day now. The light had begun to fade.

Robinson was interested in Rex's wounds and in the story of the dog fight. He listened to Ben's brief, colorless account with no sign of questioning its omissions. He took the story of the dusk chukar hunt and the desert camp and the coursing hounds at face value, it appeared. Then he bent over Rex on his storklike legs to examine the stitches more closely. "I had a German short-hair fell off a cliff once and broke one of his hind legs. Out hunting quail."

"Where was this?"

"West Texas."

"Is that where you're from?"

"Montana."

"Rex is a pretty good quail dog and adequate on pheasant, too."

"I always kept shorthairs," Robinson said. "But I know Brittanies to be good dogs. I was just partial to shorthairs."

He knelt a moment longer beside Rex, fingering his pock-marked chin. Robinson was acne-scarred in a raw, infected, graphic way, his face broken out in virulent eruptions of scarlet, blue, and purple. "I'm driving that tractor-trailer," he explained. "We can put him up in the sleeper, maybe. He'll ride comfort-able there."

"I appreciate that," said Ben.

The truck's refrigeration was running—overworked, rattling compressors. "Restaurant salad," Robinson said, when Ben asked him about it. "Twenty-pound sacks of restaurant salad I'm tak-ing to Calgary."

He had christened his truck the *Sweet Dreams Express,* a Freight-liner painted freshly blue, loud racing stripes across its flanks, im-maculate, pristine.

Robinson scrabbled up the passenger-side steps and pulled back the door to the sleeper. He set Ben's rucksack inside, then took the dog bundled up in the blanket. Rex gave no fight.

They climbed into the cab—it smelled faintly of diesel fuel—and Robinson pressured up the air brakes. The cab had the look and feel of a sarcophagus constructed out of gray plas-tic. It was high off the road and efficiently compact, like the cockpit of a jetliner. The roof and walls were covered with gray fabric, and everything seemed fastidiously kept, except that the windshield was much bug-bitten for this late in the fall.

Ben turned to survey Rex's situation. The dog lay staring back at him, as though these circumstances were dubious, beyond all understanding. The sleeper unit was like a motel room, clean, sterile, claustrophobic. A neatly made bed, a refrigerator, a closet, and a television set mounted in one corner. A remote-control channel switcher lay squarely in the middle of Robinson's plumped pillow. "This is something," Ben said. "I've never seen this before."

Robinson shook his head, rubbed his jaw, and picked at the tip of one sideburn. "What you see back there is my home," he said. "This is where I live."

"All year round?"

"Just about."

"You don't have a house?"

"This is it."

"You don't have a family waiting somewhere?"

"This is it," Robinson repeated.

"Well," said Ben. "I've never seen this before."

"It's a good rig," said Robinson.

Ben's heart recoiled. The lean, spare life of the wanderer, which had held some attraction an hour before, held no attraction now. It was time, he thought, to head home, defeated. What in God's name was he doing out here, beaten the way he was? He tried to embrace some other end than the one he'd chosen for himself— he thought of dying in a hospital room, imagined languishing in one. He fell silent and stared out the window. There were no good answers to important questions. He tried to picture the shape of Stu Robinson's final days, but he couldn't even begin.

Robinson shifted gears, let out the clutch, and teased his truck from its spot. He turned to the left, then leaned to his right to check his rearview mirrors. The *Sweet Dreams Express* bounced over deep potholes and onto the Frontage Road. They passed a field of wind-blown corn, beyond which cars flew by on the highway, toward Vantage and Moses Lake, toward both Seattle and Spokane. Robinson ground patiently through the gears, and the truck crossed over the interstate and onto Highway 281, the way north to Quincy.

The road made a bend just after the interstate, then straightened to run through fields of seed peas, potatoes, alfalfa, peppermint, and wheat. There was a stand of low bare walnut trees and a feed lot thronged with cattle. It was not familiar as the country of Ben's youth, because it had been so deeply alchemized by the coming of irrigated water. What he recalled as wastes of sagebrush broken by coulees and willow draws was now fields and orchards. The river of his youth had been diverted and poured out broadly across the land to seep through dirt to the roots of crops instead of running in its bed. The river was no longer a river, and the desert was no longer a desert. Nothing was as it had been.

He knew what had happened to the sagelands. He himself had helped burn them. Then men like his father had seized the river without a trace of evil in their hearts, sure of themselves but ignorant, and children of their time entirely, with no other bearings to rely on. Irrigators and fruit-tree growers, they believed the river to be theirs. His own life spanned that time and this, and so he believed in the old fast river as much as he believed in apple orchards, and yet he saw that the two were at odds, the river defeated that apples might grow as far away as Royal Slope. It made no more sense to love the river and at the same time kill it growing apples than it made sense to love small birds on the wing and shoot them over pointing dogs. But he'd come into the world in another time, a time immune to these contradictions, and in the end he couldn't shake old ways any more than he could shake his name.

He was coming into the place he'd sought when he'd set out on his journey. From Quincy it was six miles to the Columbia. Over the crest of Babcock Ridge and across the mouth of Lynch Coulee, beyond the trading post at Trinidad, and then upriver toward Rock Island. Northwest of Baird and Willow Springs, but southwest of Moses Coulee. Southwest of the Burlington Northern Line and the road to Palisades. It was the place Ben wanted to end his life, if he could only get to it. A surcease from living where his life had started. A neat, uncomplicated end.

SEVEN

Just before dusk they pulled into Quincy at the junction with Highway 28, the Ephrata-Wenatchee Road. Robinson asked a boy at a gas station where a veterinarian might be found, and the boy, without any hesitation, gave elaborate directions. Then they drove west down 28 until they were opposite the Quincy cemetery, not far from a cold-storage warehouse as cavernous as an airplane hangar. Robinson pulled into the parking lot of a low building made of cinder blocks, the Quincy Veterinary Clinic. Its lights were out, it was late on a Sunday, but posted on the window just left of the door was the after-hours telephone number, which Robinson wrote down. "We'll get this thing licked," he said.

They found a phone booth at the Quincy Deli-Mart. Ben climbed down the ladder steps while Robinson sat with the engine running, clawing his chin and cheeks. In the parking lot Ben drew his hunting coat close and looked across at the cold-storage warehouse, then at the gate of the cemetery. The October wind blew east across the headstones. Darkness was settling in.

He dialed the after-hours number, but it gave him only a recorded voice instructing him to call a cellular phone number or a second number Ben took to be the veterinarian's home. He dialed the latter, and a woman answered; he asked for the vet and she said, flatly, "I *am* the vet. Is this an emergency?" Ben said it definitely was, he was standing in front of the deli-mart, his dog was severely wounded. "How severely is severely?" asked the vet, and he explained to her that he was a doctor and detailed the nature of the dog's wounds, the treatment he'd administered, and the distance he and the dog had traveled, from Vantage to George, on foot. "Go back over to my office," said the vet, "and wait for me, right out front. Give me fifteen minutes."

"All right," said Ben. "I appreciate it."

"Fifteen minutes," said the vet.

Robinson drove Ben back to the clinic, and they sat in the cab with the engine running while the darkness deepened outside. The *Sweet Dreams Express* hummed extravagantly: its cab felt snug and warm. Ben gave Robinson the sixty dollars, which Robinson said would buy enough diesel fuel to get him five miles up the road, maybe ten if the price of fuel hadn't gone up in the last three minutes. They laughed at this and drank Robinson's coffee, thick and overly sugared. Holding plastic cups in hand, they turned together to check on Rex, who looked content to be where he was, asleep sprawled on the floor. Robinson tuned in the radio traffic and lit a cigarette. He said he'd come up north from The Dalles on Highway 97, but at Ellensburg he'd headed east in order to avoid Swauk Pass. It was all the same to him, he said, if he hit the 97 at Wenatchee or followed the 28 to Soap

Lake and caught the 17 to Brewster. He could make Wenatchee or Ephrata for the night or drive on up into the Okanogan and pass the night at Omak. He could stop anywhere, he said. It didn't really make any difference. He had a bed and enough food— salad to feed two armies. Sitting here didn't mean anything, twenty, thirty minutes either way.

"You're not on a schedule?"

"There's leeway in it."

"How many years have you been driving like this?"

"Sixteen. I quit for a couple once."

"What did you do?"

"I tried out a day job. Down in Texas."

"How was that?"

"Not so good."

"You didn't like it?"

"I don't know. It wasn't the job so much, I guess. It was being married did me in, put me back on the road."

Ben looked at him. "Married?"

"Not even for seven months. If you want to call that married."

"I don't know," answered Ben.

Robinson picked at a sideburn. He adjusted the heat in the cab.

"I was married for fifty years," said Ben. But he couldn't think what he might add to this. He didn't even know why he'd offered it.

"*Was* married," Robinson said. "Now you've moved along?"

"No, I haven't," Ben replied. "My wife died nineteen months ago."

Robinson nodded and held a respectful silence. "How's your eye?" he said finally.

"It's doing all right."

"Dog seems comfortable."

"I'd just as soon see the vet show up. He needs attending to."

"We can wait," Robinson assured him. "However long it takes."

"You don't have to," Ben said.

When the vet pulled in, Robinson helped; from the door of the sleeper unit he lowered the dog's blanket-sling as though from a helicopter cable. Then he looked down on both of them, rubbing his ravaged face. "All right," he called, with an air of finality. "The best of luck with everything." And he cast his eyes in a far-off direction, as if something there drew his attention.

"How far is it up to Calgary?" Ben asked.

"Not too far. Maybe five hundred miles."

"All right," said Ben. "Good luck with it."

"All right," answered Robinson. "Same to you."

The veterinarian was a solid young woman with the sturdy hands and face of a farmgirl and thick, soda-bottle glasses. She spoke in the direct, firm way of the country, with the vigorous practicality and certainty that had remade the sage desert into fields. Kneeling in the parking lot, she examined Rex, and Ben guessed she was not yet thirty, even though her professional manner suggested years of experience. There was something irrepressibly young in her, some vague crack in her doctorly demeanor through which her private self seeped as she introduced herself as Dr. Peterson and made note of his blackened eye without commenting on it. He had the idea she was shelving small talk until some later, less critical time, after the dog was treated. There were Petersons, he knew, up and down the plateau, from Manson south to Royal Slope—more Peter*sons* than Peter*sens*— and he guessed that she was a daughter of this clan, born and raised in the river basin amid the builders of the dams and farms and the fruit and potato growers. He guessed she rode horses from an early age and had decided as a child to become a vet, staunchly sticking with her girlhood plan even as the romance wore off and she found it to be hard work. She must have been admired for her perseverance, praised by her grandparents, aunts and uncles, her church pastor, Bible class instructor, the leader of her 4-H group—all, perhaps, had smiled on her pursuit of a profession both honorable and useful. Now there was no hint of hesitation in her as she turned the lock to the clinic door and held it open wide for him so he could haul Rex inside. He found, despite her youth, that he trusted her. She was just the sort to do well by Rex. She communicated proficiency, as all good doctors must.

"There's a registration form on the counter," she said. "Go ahead and fill one out, and I'll get things started back here."

She left, and Ben collapsed on a bench, where he massaged the ache in his side for a while before filling in the form. Rex lay sprawled at his feet.

On the counter he found her business card: ILSE PETERSON, DVM, DEDICATED AND CARING. A bubbling aquarium full of angelfish, an orange canary in a spacious cage, pamphlets on canine parvovirus and enterotoxemia in sheep, copies of *Cat Fancy* magazine. The room was orderly, efficient, well lit, with a pill dispensary behind the counter and notices posted high on the walls: *Does Your Pet Have Bad Breath? Ask about Our Dental Program. Tired of Getting Scratched? We Have Safe Pet Carriers. Member Quincy Valley Chamber of Commerce—Promised Land of the Columbia Basin. Please Keep Your Pet Leashed.*

Ilse Peterson hurried around a corner and opened a file cabinet. "You can bring him in," she called.

Ben took Rex up in the blanket sling and followed her into a warren of rooms, past an office with shelves of neat veterinary texts, past a tiny operating theater, finally into an examining room—an anesthesia machine on wheels, a stainless steel table with a drain hole and bucket, a bright, adjustable light overhead, and an electric razor poised high, hung from a retractable cord.

"Good, then," Dr. Peterson said. "Let's take a look at him."

Ben set Rex on the stainless steel table and assessed, critically, the equipment on hand: a blood cell counter, a blood chemistry unit, a high-powered tissue microscope, an X-ray machine with folded lead drapes, a pair of sealed plastic bins for the safe disposal of waste. "Just relax now," the vet said to Rex, one hand stroking the top of his head, the other patting his dusty side. "We'll find out what your problem is and see what we can do about it."

There was no condescension in her voice. She did not pretend the dog was a child or a difficult human being. She pressed her glasses against the bridge of her nose, pulled her light closer. Then she checked Rex's feet for warmth. She pressed on his gums, pinched the skin at his forehead, palpated his chest, stroked him. "So you're a doctor," she said.

"I was a doctor," Ben told her. "I've been retired for a while."

"Where at?"

"Over in Seattle."

"General practice?"

"Thoracic surgeon."

She nodded a bemused assent. "I hate to say it," she said over her shoulder, "but you don't much look like anyone's idea of a surgeon just now."

"It's a long story," Ben said. "I was in a car wreck yesterday."

"You can tell me later," Dr. Peterson said. "In the meantime, I could use some help. There's a lot of resuturing that'll have to be done. I'm going to have to put him under, set up his IV support. And you're going to have to sign a consent form. We're looking at two or three hours here—a hundred fifty to three hundred dollars."

"I'll stay," said Ben. "I want to."

"It'll get him off the table quicker."

"Whatever I can do," said Ben.

He unbuttoned his field jacket, peeled it off, and set it on the floor in a corner. It had been nineteen months since his last surgery—repairing a human heart in trouble, not this work of assisting a veterinarian in sewing up a dog. Nevertheless, he felt a twinge of excitement. He rolled up his sleeves and washed his hands. He had not expected anything like this. Strange and stranger still, he thought, that at a moment in which he'd intended to be dead, rotting and eaten by flies in the sage country, he was instead scrubbing for surgery as he had thousands of times.

Dr. Peterson asked Ben to hold Rex down while she administered ketamine and Valium, leaving the needle in the dog's cephalic vein and taping the catheter to his foreleg. They watched while Rex succumbed to the Valium and fell into a wide-eyed haze. Dr. Peterson set up an IV; Ben held the dog's maw gently open while she fed in an endotracheal tube, inflated the cuff to tighten it, and tied it securely in place. She pulled the anesthesia machine closer, opened the valves to the oxygen and isoflurane canisters, then hooked up Rex's tube. Watching the meters, she made her adjustments. She leaned in close, adjusted her glasses, and finely tuned the valves. Rex went under swiftly, sagging low against the beanbag mattress, his eyelids fluttering closed. Peterson checked the valves again. "All right," she said. "Now 500 milligrams of Keflin by slow injection in the access port of the IV tube, if you want to do that."

"I'll take care of it," said Ben.

While he administered the antibiotic, Dr. Peterson injected a painkiller, butorphanol, subcutaneously. Then she plunged into a thorough evaluation, bringing a strong light close to her work and cutting away the field stitches. "These are very well done," she said. "They kept most of the dirt out."

"I had to throw them one-handed," said Ben. "Otherwise, they'd be better."

"They're good," she said. "They're excellent."

She palpated the ligaments and tendons of the left hamstring, then pulled the razor on its retractable cord and shaved away the hair. Ben ran the hand suction for her. The skin looked badly punctured and hemorrhaged. She palpated everything one more time. "I'm looking for laxity in the joint," she said. "It seems all right. It feels pretty good. I don't think there's serious damage."

"That's good," said Ben.

He brushed the stitches down the drain hole. At the vet's direction, he eased the blanket free, and replaced it with a thick padded mattress of polystyrene beads. Peterson flushed the punctures with saline and scrubbed them with an iodine solution, painting the skin a garish orange. She retracted the largest hole—a true laceration, not merely a puncture—and peered inside, blinking.

"I'll tell you what we've got here," she said. "The semitendinosus muscle is pretty badly torn up, but there's no damage to the Achilles tendon. He's a lucky dog on that score. This is something that will heal."

"Which muscle?"

"The semitendinosus."

"The tendon is all right?"

"It seems fine."

Peterson doused the wound with more saline and applied a wet dressing of sterile gauze. Then she addressed the other wounds. "Skin-deep," she assured Ben. "There's no problem anywhere here. It's a sewing job, and we're done."

She asked Ben to do the skin prep. He lavaged copiously with saline and scrubbed the wounds with the iodine until the skin gleamed brightly. Peterson took the dog's pulse and listened to his breathing. "All right," she said. "We're moving into my operating room. Why don't you carry the dog and the mattress? I'll wheel the anesthesia and bring along the IV bags."

They settled Rex in the operating room and hooked up the heart monitor. Peterson applied the final Betadine prep and filled the lavage basin with saline. Then they opened the sterile surgery packs, the gown packs, and the lid to the cold tray, scrubbed up, put on cloth caps, and wrestled into masks, gowns, and gloves. Peterson laid blue drapes over Rex, framing the hamstring wound. From the cold tray she selected the Metzenbaum scissors. Then she went about debriding the skin, laying it asunder.

Ben assisted with the retractors. There were bits of sand and strands of hair inside, and the vet picked at them methodically, with her fingers first and then with tweezers, breathing roughly through her nose. "In a minute here I'll irrigate," she said. "Sixty cc's at a time will do. And a 14-gauge needle."

"I'll put it together," Ben said.

He set it up for her. She made sure he'd done it right, and after that seemed to settle on a basic trust in him. She irrigated, watching for debris, then flushed the wound again. "It's plenty clean," she concluded. "I think we've doused the road dust here from all the way back to Vantage."

"It looks good," Ben agreed.

Peterson selected a sterile packet of single-ought suture material. They discussed the merits of two stitching approaches and settled on a mattress pattern. Then he watched her take the stitches, with pleasure and no small admiration for her precise and vigorous work. She threw them with adroit small turns of the wrist and took up the tension smoothly. She was accomplished in a plain and steady way. Her fingers were strong but surprisingly fluid. She didn't flag or grow restless, and she paid attention to the lay of each stitch, making fine adjustments, leaving no dimples or wrinkles.

Ben assisted in the placing of the Penrose drain. She irrigated liberally while he opened a packet of three-ought suture for her to use subcutaneously. Standing back, she checked the meters on the anesthesia canisters. "The hard part's over," she said.

"You're an accomplished doctor."

"It isn't heart surgery."

"It's not that different."

"Not technically." She pushed, again, at the bridge of her glasses with the back of her wrist. "But I imagine it was probably more difficult for you to face whoever was out there in the waiting room when you had to deliver bad news."

"I never liked that very much," said Ben.

"I don't like it, either," said Dr. Peterson. "But I would guess it's harder for a doctor than a vet. As much as people love their dogs."

She used three-ought suture to bring together the subcutaneous tissue and closed the skin with a stapler. She moved on to the shoulder blades, scrubbing again with iodine, debriding the wound to leave clean edges and irrigating with saline. She closed the shoulder blades and then the throat, while Ben watched and rubbed his side. He admired the patient tidiness of it. Dr. Peterson, the last staple inserted, surveyed her handiwork critically. Then she gave Rex a half cc of butorphanol and a dose of acepromazine, disconnected the heart monitor, backed down the valves on the anesthesia machine and, when Rex began to blink and swallow, slid the tube from his throat. Prying open an eyelid, she looked at the dog's pupil. "He'll come around soon," she said.

They dropped their caps and gowns in a bin, and Dr. Peterson gave Ben a ten-day supply of an antibiotic, and five days' worth of a pain reliever. Then they washed and went to her office. She sat at her desk writing copious notes and spoke to him in a preoccupied fashion, her glasses low on her nose. The dog would stay overnight with her. She recommended thorough rest for the leg. The staples could be removed by his vet in Seattle, after he got home. Ten days later, limited exercise. The drains were due out in forty-eight hours, something Ben could do himself, unless he wanted his vet to. The antibiotic should run to the end, he shouldn't stop it short. Eat and drink as normal, but rest, no hunting for a while. Perhaps, with luck, come Thanksgiving, Rex would hunt birds again.

"The dog lives to hunt," Ben told her. "It's all he ever wants to do."

"Well, six weeks or so and he'll be doing it. But maybe you're anthropomorphizing. Maybe you live to hunt."

"Not really," said Ben.

Peterson slid off her glasses, rubbed her eyes with the palms of her hands, and massaged her eyelids with her fingertips, the pen still between her fingers. "So what happened to you?" she asked.

"I just about killed myself. In Snoqualmie Pass."

"You what, now?"

"I hit a tree. Right at the summit. Some kids in a Volkswagen van came along and took me down to Vantage."

"You and the dog."

"Me and two dogs. I lost the other. I was hunting chukars out on the breaks. They ran off with some coursing hounds, and my other dog was killed."

"Coursing hounds?"

"Irish wolfhounds, a pack of them. They were coursing coyotes on the river breaks."

"Irish wolfhounds," Dr. Peterson said. "That'd be Bill Harden's dogs. He's the only one around here who keeps Irish wolfhounds."

"Bill Harden. Rides a dirt bike?"

"I don't know. Could be. But anyway he's got a pack of wolfhounds. I've seen them out at dog shows."

"He's breeding them?"

"I'm not sure. Used to, I think. They have a good-size orchard, the Hardens, out back of Malaga there. Wolfhound Orchard, they call it."

"Wolfhound Orchard," Ben said.

She slid her glasses back into place and finally put her pen down. "Wolfhounds," she said. "That makes a lot of sense. The way your dog was ripped up—exactly what I'd expect to see from a run-in with Irish wolfhounds. That or a broken neck."

"That's what happened to my other dog," said Ben. "He was too old to fight back, I guess. It might be just as well."

"I don't know," Dr. Peterson answered. "Better old than dead."

"Maybe," said Ben. "It's a question."

She rocked back in her desk chair. "So you walked up here?" she asked.

"I stitched up Rex and carried him to George. Most of the way. He walked some."

"It's a long walk."

"I didn't have a choice."

"The whole thing sounds crazy."

"It is crazy."

"This is what you get for killing little birds. Maybe you should take up golf."

"That's a lot of walking, too, from what I understand."

Dr. Peterson smiled. "You're up a creek," she said. "Do you have any kind of plan?"

"Sleep," said Ben. "My plan is to sleep, like a dead man."

"Sleep," she repeated. "Your best bet's probably two doors east, the motel just down the street over here." She pointed at the wall as if it meant something to him. "You take a right, and you're there."

"That sounds perfect," said Ben.

"Come by here when you wake up. It'll be two hundred and fifty dollars. And I don't take credit cards."

"All right," said Ben. "Two fifty."

"Two minutes' worth of open heart surgery is two hours' worth of dog surgery," Ilse Peterson declared. "That's one difference between dogs and people we didn't talk about."

"Malpractice is bigger, too," said Ben.

She nodded and smiled. "I'll drive you over to the motel," she said. "You look like you're ready to collapse."

She dropped him off, and he thanked her for it, and by way of an answer she advised rest and no fretting about the dog. When he stepped from her car, a wind from the mountains struck him in the face, dry and carrying the smell of apples and of alfalfa fields put to sleep for the winter. It was a smell Ben remembered from childhood.

He went in and set his rucksack on the floor. The boy at the front desk greeted him crisply. Young, pudgy, manicured, he moved bits of paper about with a flourish, conducting the ritual of a motel check-in as though its details were pleasurable. He took pains to angle his stapler, and laid the strips from the computer paper neatly in a plastic garbage pail. "Free coffee," he told Ben, "is right behind you. Help yourself, anytime."

He put the room key on the counter. "What happened to your eye?" he asked.

"I'm a boxer," Ben told him. "The senior circuit. We had a tournament in Moses Lake. The other guy looks worse."

"I never heard of that," said the motel clerk. "Senior-circuit boxing."

"It's a new sport," Ben told him. "Just got started a couple years ago. Everyone who does it is crazy."

"It sounds like it," the clerk agreed.

In the room the alarm clock was off by an hour, as though someone had forgotten about daylight saving's time. A Gideon's bible had been left on the side table, beside a placard listing local churches. On the wall behind the bed hung an oil painting of seagulls, shells, driftwood, and dunes, from the other side of the mountains.

Ben turned the heater as high as it would go and sat on the bed in front of it. It made an enormous, clattering din, then blew cold air into the room. He still had his field jacket wrapped tightly around him, yet he felt the cold in his bones. Bent to work free of his hunting boots, their laces festooned with sharp burrs from the desert, he was suddenly aware of how much his feet hurt, of how much he wanted to get out of his boots, and he pried them off with considerable effort, then stripped off his wet socks. His feet, ghastly white, were chafed at the arches and red where his boots rubbed his heels. His toenails looked rotten.

The heater began to work better. Ben peeled off his glasses, rubbed his eyes, and massaged his side for a while. He worked his bad knee and his arthritic ankle, took the measure of the pain in his hip, touched the cut above his eye. Every muscle felt bound up, seized, his range of motion limited, and he considered simply collapsing on the bed without a shower or food. Instead, he found the remaining bags of peanuts and the half-empty bottle of prune juice, and sat by the heater eating and drinking. When he'd finished, he looked in the double cupboard, the drawers, and the two-shelf refrigerator, but there was nothing left behind or forgotten, only a small box of baking powder and a near-empty bottle of vinegar.

Ben ran the shower, switched on the heat lamp, and struggled out of his clothes. He took the Italian carabiner from his neck and set it on the counter. Without meaning to, he caught his image in the mirror: his naked form, at seventy-three, was not a kind thing to look on. His eye was a darkly swollen mass, the lower lid distended. His forehead, when he pulled free the bandage, looked almost as raw as it had when he'd cut it, the ruptured blood vessels still visible, the surrounding skin a sickly gray.

He was ghostly, pale, old. The hair sprouting from his chin and head was gray and as stiff as brush bristles; a few wisps, paltry and listless, sprouted from his rounded shoulders. He was bent forward, slack-heavy in the chest. His many moles showed dark against his skin. The tautness in his muscles was gone.

Ben stepped into the shower. The water felt so intensely hot, he stopped breathing for a moment. Yielding, he shut his eyes and let the stream wash over him. A simple, ordinary pleasure. He stayed that way, the water running down his chest, and then he washed indulgently, shampooing his hair three times.

There was some minor key of redemption in cleanliness Ben had noted before. When he was done, and dry, his teeth duly brushed, he sat on the toilet with his head between his knees, made use of the hemorrhoid cream, and lathered his cut with Neosporin. Fearing leg cramps, he took his calcium gluconate. He slid into his long underwear, switched off every light in the room except the one beside the bed, and lay down beneath the covers with a sigh.

It was good to be there, clean, revived, but still, at the core, he felt chilled. His side hurt, and he cursed it silently—a burning, prodding sensation. He drew up his knees to temper it and warmed his hands between his thighs, but the pain persisted despite his manipulations, and after awhile he rose. He peed and ran a fresh towel through his hair. He was suddenly occupied with the thought of his daughter, of how she might contemplate his sudden death on the arid side of the mountains. He saw her examining his credit card records, discovering that his car had been towed on Saturday, October 17, the transaction posted from North Bend, Washington, and finding that on the following day he'd taken a motel room in Quincy, 125 miles to the east. She would wonder how he had covered those miles. She would wonder what had become of his dogs. She would contact the Grant County coroner and sheriff and the man who had towed her father's car. Renee would piece together his final hours, the way in which he'd lived them. She would hear about his swollen eye and ask questions of Ilse Peterson, who would relate the story of the wolfhounds and of the death of Tristan and the recovery of Rex, and certainly it would all seem strange. Eventually Renee would want to see the place where her father had entangled himself in barbed wire, and perhaps she would even visit William Harden, to get his view of things. Everyone would recollect a similar image: a man in dust-bitten hunting gear, filthy, hauling an overloaded rucksack on his shoulders, as smashed up and broken as a vagrant or boxer, stinking of sweat and sage. Renee would feel troubled. Something in it would not add up. The county sheriff might become involved, and suspicions might fall on Harden. They would ask questions of Bill Ward. The truth of Ben's cancer might emerge.

So the thing to do was call her now and tell her what had happened. That all had finally settled down, that he was safely ensconced in his motel room, the long night of Tristan's death behind him, the car wreck details seen to. That he intended to hunt blue grouse west of the river—something he could do without a dog, allowing Rex time to convalesce. In a day or two, he'd tell Renee, he would bring Rex home in a rental car, they'd be back Tuesday or Wednesday. He would tell her, too, about his one good eye, how the other was swollen shut, and this would figure in her postmortem conjectures as the source of his error in spatial judgment while negotiating strands of barbed wire. His vision had been skewed, truncated, and as a result he'd bungled the fence crossing.

Dishonesty was his policy now; but dishonesty on behalf of the living, not for his own advantage. He lied in order to leave this world as quietly as he could. Yet at the moment—more than a technicality—he had no shotgun with which to exit. He thought of buying one up in Wenatchee, but this might seem curious to his daughter: her father dead with a new gun, his old Winchester missing. That would be a mystery to her, and it certainly would be to the county sheriff, and the investigation into Ben's death would deepen, and Bill Ward might be prompted to speak. Ben understood that he needed his Winchester, mainly as a prop for his suicide. But also because it had been his father's; he did not feel right losing it.

He picked up the phone to call Renee, but his grandson answered after one ring, and Ben wasn't ready for that. "Chris," he said, "It's you."

"I'm over here studying. My apartment's no good. People play music all the time."

"How is everything?"

"They're piling on homework."

"Merciless pedants."

"It isn't that bad."

Ben thought of the purpose of his call. But he didn't want to lose his grandson yet. "I remember the beginning of my third year," he said. "I don't think I slept very much."

"I get four or five hours when I'm not on night duty."

"That isn't enough."

"I'm doing all right."

"But you don't get outdoors."

"Not like you."

"So what are you going to do about it?"

"You and me. Silver Peak."

"Cakewalk for you, Chris."

"You, too. A tune-up."

Ben sat rubbing his temples, eyes shut. "You ought to go without me, somewhere. The Stuarts, maybe. Mount Stuart."

"Why couldn't you go?"

"Too tough these days."

"So what?"

"I'm out of shape, Chris."

"Work on it."

"My legs aren't under me."

"Yes, they are."

"Do Stuart without me."

"I've been up Stuart."

"Do something else, then."

"We'll do Silver Peak together."

"All right."

That seemed a note to end on. He didn't want to end on small talk. "Is your mother around?" he asked.

"Mom's at a meeting."

"Tell her I called."

"You want to leave a message?"

"I'll call in the morning."

"Where are you anyway?"

"East of the mountains."

"Any birds out there?"

"Chukars. A few."

"You've got legs for that, Pop."

"It's not uphill."

"So what?" Chris asked. "You're fine."

Afterward, Ben sat in his long johns, perched on the edge of his motel bed. He wiped his good eye with a fingertip, but the bad one leaked water onto his cheek. He dried it with a corner of the bedsheet.

EIGHT

Ben switched off the bedside lamp and absently massaged his side, as if to knead away the cancer. There was the din of the heater but no other sound. A rim of light showed around the curtains. The heat and darkness were just what he yearned for, but the pain in his gut was sharp, severe, and despite his weariness he couldn't sleep. Acquiescing, he turned on the light and dug in his rucksack for the marijuana cigarettes the drifter had given him at the river crossing. Ben thought of the night before, of the dysfunction of his mind through it, and it seemed to him a mistake to risk again that kind of folly and befuddlement. Yet in his motel bed, what could go wrong? What use here for a clear, sober mind? He needed relief from pain.

He slid one of the cigarettes between his lips and sat back

against the pillows, his lighter between his fingers. After the third deep inhalation, he recognized the feeling from the previous evening—a busy, relentless current of thought, a confusion about the meaning of things—and after the fifth, he felt paranoid. When he had smoked the entire cigarette, he worried that the room was thickly noxious with a sweet green pall that would seep outside to indict him as a criminal. Perhaps a guest in an adjoining room would catch a whiff of marijuana and call the Quincy police. There was no way to judge if this worry was valid—there was no way to know, now that he'd smoked—so he decided that, to cover himself, he should open the windows and run the bathroom fan. Then he remembered the carton of Himalayan incense the young people in the van had given him.

In his long johns, breathing roughly through his nose, he lit one of his parrafin fire starters, blew it out when the wax softened, set it beside the bathroom sink, and pierced it with a stick of lit incense. A fine line of smoke unfurled from the tip, rising in a fragrant helix. The smell of what he took to be saffron mingled with the marijuana, and he thought of the Himalaya Range, mountains he had never seen. It seemed profound that this incense had traveled from Tibetan monks on the Sikkimese border to a motel in sagebrush country. Its convoluted journey here seemed evidence of God's vast reach.

Ben crawled into bed, unhinged, dazed, and switched off the bedside lamp. The pain in his side felt bearable, but his mind traveled restlessly, and the fact of his death seemed pronounced and heightened, more real and more frightening. His limbs began to tremble. He felt neither awake nor asleep but, rather, in a curious limbo, a third form of consciousness. In this state of mind, ineluctably, he found himself thinking of his war. He tried to put it away, ward it off, but here it was again. For years he'd struggled with his memories of it, wishing they would go away, but here they were, unleashed by marijuana, welling up on the cusp of sleep.

At Camp Hale, in Colorado, he'd trained as an infantry rifleman. He'd arrived in a snowstorm on the Denver and Rio Grande Western line with six per diem dollars in his pocket and presented himself, his duffel bag on his shoulder, to the sergeant on duty at the train station at two-thirty in the morning. The sergeant passed him into the keeping of L Company, in the Third Battalion of the 86th Mountain Regiment, and Ben spent his first night sleepless in the barracks, fully dressed beneath two blankets, curled up with his hands in his armpits, thinking of Rachel Lake.

That first morning, the company assembled on the parade ground with the late fall wind driving down from the mountains, sodden snow underfoot. The cold seized Ben's face and hands and rose through his boots. The drill sergeant announced to the new recruits that in this place it was every man for himself, and then they began calisthenics. On the snow-covered drill field they stripped off their shirts to perform jumping jacks, knee bends, and push-ups at seven in the morning. They marched for three hours at 10,000 feet, on the Continental Divide, north of Leadville. They marched over Tennessee Pass in the coal smoke rising from the barracks stoves, and before noon it began to snow, a pelting snow, like rain. The new recruits buckled and wavered. Three went down and were left on the ground while L Company traveled on.

Ben suffered from a dull nausea, and his hands and feet grew numb. He marched in a stupor, short of breath; blood trickled from his nose. In the evening he was sent to the camp hospital. He could not get warm or stanch his nosebleed, and his temperature rose overnight to 103 degrees. In the hospital barracks he lay on his bunk and considered going to Denver, AWOL, as soon as he was sufficiently recovered, but for now he had cotton balls stuffed in his nostrils and a hacking, expectorating cough. A doctor assured him he would soon get better and explained that scores of men in the regiment had preceded Ben in altitude sickness—asthma, respiratory collapse, fever, nausea. "Things could be worse," the doctor said. "You could be fighting a war."

After three days his health improved, and Ben returned to training. He was a private first class and infantryman who served in L Company's Second Platoon, and as with everyone else at Camp Hale his lips were cracked, his eyes stung, and he wheezed with every breath. The camp air reeked of coal smoke, not only from the barracks stoves but from the locomotives in Tennessee Pass, striving up the basin's grade in great black plumes of exhaust. At taps the men sloshed water underfoot for the humidity it might provide. By dawn the floorboards were sheets of ice, and the men arose to reveille in the dark with the windowpanes frozen from their breath. Under stars they went in silence to the parade ground for shirtless calisthenics and close-drill marching, the wind blowing in their faces.

Ben was transferred to N Company for no apparent reason. They assigned him to a weapons platoon, perhaps because he'd scored high at firing the .30-caliber light machine gun. The sergeant placed him among the machine gunners, but then the company commander transferred Ben to a rifle platoon, where the lieutenant handed him a BAR to carry—the Browning automatic rifle—assigning him two ammunition bearers, Bill Stackhouse and Kelly Lastenpole, to haul the extra clips. Carrying this weapon in training, on top of his field pack and his own extra clips, Ben floundered in the snow.

After two months, the regiment embarked on winter field maneuvers. They started in the dark, shouldering ninety-pound packs, skins on their skis, steam chuffing from their mouths, and herringboned into Tennessee Pass, then toward Ptarmigan Peak.

They traversed uphill in single file, the mortars lashed on toboggans, the mules hauling artillery. Ben carried a canvas mountain tent, white felt boots, camouflage gear, pile jacket, and double sleeping bag. At dark the company made rough camp in the lee of a ridge at twelve thousand feet and ate K rations from boxes: cans of veal loaf warmed on gas stoves, bouillon, and powdered coffee. Ben passed the night with his socks, insoles, and canteens of water warming against his belly. Between the linings of his sleeping bag, he kept his boots and bindings.

In the morning it was twenty below. They ate a frozen biscuit each and broke camp wearing chamois masks, the air stabbing their lungs. No one could remember cold like this—it was cold on a mythic scale. A corporal removed his glasses from their case, and the frames shattered in his hand; another man's eyelashes froze solid and pulled free in white shards. The batteries in the field radios turned to ice. The M1 rifles wouldn't fire.

On the third day out, the temperature fell again, and those who felt too ill to push on were lashed to toboggans and hauled back to camp like so many frozen corpses. On bivouac that night, Ben heard around him the explosive frost-checking of the mountain birches; in the morning fresh snow had inundated the tents, whisked over them like sand. A radioman closed up his tent with two cookstoves going inside, and for a moment he had a working radio to call for tracked Snow Weasels. None came for them.

A blizzard was general to the mountains now, but no one of rank would call off the maneuvers, and the company fumbled toward Ptarmigan Peak on empty stomachs, sleepless. Ben's feet bled from the gusseting of his shoepacs. His fingers cracked open inside his gloves and the blood froze against his nails. Welts formed along his back from the pressure of his pack straps. Yet he slogged on through frozen trees, snow roiling under his skis, clouds of white suspended dust. That night, at Ptarmigan Peak, the hoarfrost grew like mold on the tent he shared with Bill Stackhouse. Their own breathing melted it.

They were ambushed that night—their guards having burrowed themselves into snow caves—and taken prisoner. Ben was lying in his sleeping bag with the drawstring pulled around his head when the hypothetical enemy attacked in the quiet hour before dawn. One of them tore open the tent door and knelt there pointing his M1 at Ben, telling him to sit up cautiously and do nothing to inspire an itchy trigger finger. Ben was in no mood for war games. His Browning rifle had frozen solid, and the pistol he normally kept between his thighs had been left, overnight, in his field pack.

The air warmed to 35 degrees that day, and Ben's clothes grew wet with melting snow, but at dusk the temperature dropped again, and his pants and shirt froze against him. A heavy snow fell fast in the darkness, and there was nothing left to eat or drink but snow scooped up with a mitten, and no fuel left to melt it. In the morning they followed the order to dig out and with packs loaded marched through a pass, under an armed guard. Sidehilling on their sealskinned skis, they made a bitter ascent.

On the open slope, flailing in new snow, the wind tearing off the mountain summits so that he couldn't look any place but down to where his skis disappeared altogether, Ben came to understand what it meant to freeze to death. There was nothing to it but to wait in one place, and he saw that by doing nothing he could escape from all the suffering of the past interminable days. He paused to get the feel of it, this death by default, this seductive surrender, and then shrugged off his attraction to it and flailed grimly in the snow again, with a new and desperate resolve.

To live, Ben felt, was to be on fire, lest one turn to ice.

In the summer they left the mountains behind to inhabit the flatlands at Camp Swift, Texas, a land of chiggers and copperheads, poison ivy, cockroaches, dust, and scorpions. There was no explanation as to why mountain troops should be stationed in such an arid place, and they languished there unhappily. Ben wrote Rachel about army life, confessing that the imminence of war filled him with the fear of an awful death, or worse, of permanent wounds. She wrote back to say that in her training she had seen much that was terrible and disturbing. She had seen men legless, armless, and blind, their faces seared beyond recognition, their backs riddled with shrapnel, their feet blown off by land mines. She did not wish by describing these injuries to inspire in Ben a hindering fear, but on the other hand she thought it wise to tell painful truths. And she asked him bluntly to reconsider—couldn't he serve as a medic? Did he want to participate in killing? Ben replied that they'd made him a gunner, that from this there was no turning. On the issue of war they traded letters, Rachel insisting that the work of healing was better than the work of killing, Ben replying that his feelings compelled him to fight the war directly.

In the middle of June, Rachel finished classes and was sworn into the Army Nurse Corps. She volunteered for overseas service and despite her inexperience was accepted. She wrote Ben again from Fort Devens, Massachusetts, where she'd been transferred for an eight-week orientation in the art of military nursing. Once she wrote from Waterville, where she'd gone on leave to visit her family, and once she sent a card from Manhattan, where her unit was on standby, awaiting orders to embark. By mid-August she was on a transport ship, headed for the coast of France.

In the fall Ben's orders came, too, and in late November, after Thanksgiving, the Third Battalion of the 86th went by train across the South, living in Pullmans for three days, eating standing up in the kitchen cars, washing mess kits in cavalry cans in which the dishwater sloshed and churned as the steam engine negotiated bends. They passed through Arkansas and Mississippi,

Ben staring vacantly at fields turned fallow and at bleak, drab pine forests.

They passed through Norfolk, Virginia. At Camp Patrick Henry, they slept in tar-papered barracks, played rounds of five-card draw, and read dog-eared novels borrowed from the camp's library. German prisoners manned the chow lines, and in the camp stockade, sequestered behind a high double fence, were draftees who had refused their orders to board ships for Europe.

Ben sailed aboard the *SS Argentina*, a converted luxury liner. It was part of a convoy of troop transport ships escorted by destroyers through Hampton Roads and out into the winter swells along the Virginia coast. The destroyers took gunnery practice with their aft-mounted antiaircraft guns, shooting at enormous gas-filled balloons ascending into winter skies—as deafening an exercise as Ben had been party to, setting up a ringing in his ears. Within a few hours men fell ill who had no stomach for rolling seas. That night they lay in bunks six deep, thousands of men in the hold of the ship, many of them retching, the floors slick with vomit. Ben could keep nothing down, either, and lined up in the gangways for seasickness pills that didn't solve his problem. At night he stood guard with a life vest on and leaned over the rail heaving, salt spray dashing his face. There were sudden, irrational submarine drills, and drills to determine if all knew their lifeboat stations, and at dawn more deafening gunnery practice while the convoy plowed through twenty-foot swells, over waves boiling with sea spume. It was a fogbound crossing, sunless. Soldiers played craps and blackjack in stairwells, in companionways deep in the hold of the ship, or lolled in their hammocks morosely, meditating on private omens.

Word was that they would land in Naples, and on the seventh day out they saw in the distance the green coast of Africa. They were detained briefly at the Strait of Gibraltar while an escort of four destroyers assembled, supported by a phalanx of PBYs, blister-gun ports aft of their wings, transparent gun turrets in their bows. Passing into the Mediterranean, they stood on deck in an African breeze, the water placid off their bow and blue in a lushly textured way that reminded Ben of the sky at home on certain midsummer afternoons. He leaned over the rail. Bill Stackhouse appeared beside him and said he'd won almost five hundred dollars playing craps in the hold.

"I'm spending it all," Stackhouse said, "as soon as we get into port."

"It's a lot of money," Ben said.

"I'm buying Italian women," said Stackhouse. "I might not get another chance."

"Yes, you will."

"I might not."

"You're not going to die."

"We might, Givens."

They passed close to the Isle of Capri, and on the ninth day, in dismal weather, entered the Bay of Naples. They were directed to anchor on the south side of the harbor to wait their turn to disembark, and from there they saw sunken German ships resting on the harbor mud, their superstructures and upper decks breaking the surface like reefs. Some of the harbor buildings had been bombed and stood windowless with gaping walls, rubbish piled against them. Between rain squalls the air freshened; beyond the city sat Vesuvius. On the dockside street milled young women Stackhouse took to be prostitutes. Kelly Lastenpole explained to Bill how appropriate it was that here the sirens had lured wayfarers of antiquity to a death on distant shores.

The *Empress of Australia* anchored beside them, at such close quarters as to block their view; they saw only the curve of its hull. That night Ben tossed sleepless in his hammock, and in the morning felt weary as he packed his rucksack and hauled his duffel topside. No military band hailed them, like the band at embarkation in Virginia, playing "Over There." Instead there was rain and a throng of beggars, Red Cross girls in overcoats cheerily handing out stale doughnuts, and a line of army trucks waiting in the street to take them God knew where.

Ben made his way down the narrow gangplank and was disgorged into Italy. The day before Christmas, 1944. Bailey bridges spanned the pier's bomb gaps, a catwalk crawled over a capsized ship: the docks at Naples were a giant staging area choked with newly arrived soldiers. Ben deployed into a quartermaster truck that had been refitted to carry troops, and from it saw the wreckage of Naples with its streetcar tracks bombed loose and twisted, the facades of apartments dropped away. A girl squatted in the street to defecate, half-concealed by her coat. At the edge of town Stackhouse threw a small boy a chocolate bar, which landed at his feet.

Christmas Eve they staged at Bagnoli in the remains of a bombed-out orphanage the Germans had earlier occupied. Ben's company was assigned to its school, a cold building with no lights or furnishings, where the rain slanted through the broken windows and spattered against the stone floors. Ben wore his trenchcoat and beneath it his field jacket, wrapped his blankets tightly around him, and tried to sleep sitting up in a corner, like fruit pickers he remembered who'd slept against tree trunks on nights the ground was too cold or damp for sleeping in the grass. Sleepless, bored, and shivering, he thought of home and Rachel Lake.

At noon they ate turkey and potatoes from their mess kits in celebration of Christmas. The next day they boarded the SS Sestriere and debarked in darkness at Livorno. They went by convoy northeast to Pisa to bivouac at a muddy staging area where the sound of distant artillery was audible, the flash of it visible at night. They encamped in the Tenuta di San Rossore, which had once been the picnic ground of kings, a place to hunt wild boar. Now under handsome poplar trees, men played five-card draw.

Ben shared a pup tent with Lastenpole, who came from Syracuse. Ben told him about the orchard country, and Lastenpole remembered picking apples in orchards along Lake Ontario. Every year, his father made cider.

They lined a #10 can with sand, poured it full of gasoline, and tossed a lit wooden match inside to make a lantern of sorts. Then they lolled in their pup tents, while the rain beat hard outside. Lastenpole drew on a hand-rolled cigarette, at rest with an arm behind his head, blowing smoke toward the tent canvas. He insisted that the real action was in Belgium and France: the goal here was to force the German military to divert resources southward. He'd read in *Stars and Stripes* that a German offensive had been repelled in Luxembourg, that the Russians were closing on Warsaw and Budapest, that at Bastogne the 101st Airborne Division stood face-to-face with the German Fifth Army—but there was no mention of hill towns in the Apennines, or even of Italy. The war, said Lastenpole, would be won when the Rhine was crossed, when the Russians pushed their way into Berlin; the smart thing to do in the meantime, he argued, was to keep out of harm's way.

They convoyed again out of Pisa to the south and made a fresh bivouac at Quercianella, putting up tents by the coastal road along the Ligurian Sea. In the new year the *Stars and Stripes* reported that the Germans had been halted and routed in the Ardennes; it ran photographs of Montgomery and Patton, and one of Eisenhower in Paris. Lastenpole pronounced the war all but over; everything that happened hereafter, he said, was a mere denouement. Montgomery was about to cross the Rhine.

A bag of mail was distributed, the letters in it weeks old and full of Christmas salutations. Rachel wrote to Ben from Revigny, where she was billeted in a concrete barn: she and twenty-five other nurses were huddled in the servants' quarters with a charcoal brazier and an array of candles, cutting snowflakes and stars from tin cans in preparation for Christmas. They were stringing red berries, cutting out angels, and making paper snowflakes for children convalescing in the hospital. There were plans afoot for a talent show. They'd salvaged foil wrappers as tinsel, and they were going to eat turkey and fruitcake.

Arriving that summer in Normandy, she reported, they'd bivouacked in an apple orchard throttled by swags of mistletoe and inundated by hornets. Their camp covered sixty acres, a city of tents laid out in muddy rows, German prisoners of war watching them from behind a barbed-wire stockade. They lived in floorless ward tents and slept on flea-ridden straw. They killed field mice with their GI shoes and ate C and K rations, Spam, hardtack, tins of cheese spread, fruit bars, raisins, canned corn. Their luggage had been lost en route from England, so they had no change of clothes. They had their musette bags and dungarees, but not their class-A uniforms. They sampled the brandy of that region, made from windfall apples. Rachel couldn't stomach calvados, but other nurses were fond of it.

The hospital ran on kerosene lights. Its first patients were two village children who'd strayed, at play, into land mines. Women came in for difficult births; farmhands appeared with blistered feet, jaundice, and tuberculosis. Soon soldiers from the front arrived. Rachel saw cases of trenchfoot, hepatitis, pneumonia, and gangrene. The burn cases were terrible; at night dark moans could be heard from the ward that made Rachel feel helpless. She was pressed into surgery service and had learned to administer a blood transfusion, start an IV, suction a lung wound, and perform a secondary skin closure. She'd also learned to dig a foxhole and shoot a carbine rifle.

Paris was liberated while she was stationed in Normandy. The rains began, their tents collapsed, and all were perpetually soaked. They bathed in their helmets, worked double shifts. They chlorinated their drinking water in Lister bags and tinctured it with lemon crystals. Soon it grew cold enough to coat their tents with a thin film of ice. They warmed themselves at coal burners. They could no longer get the *Stars and Stripes,* but there was the BBC on the radio and a movie tent with leaky seams.

Late in the fall, they were transferred. They moved closer to the war. During the fighting near Bastogne, Rachel was evacuated—she climbed into the back of an ambulance that soon mired itself in mud, and had to cling to the rear of a half-track all the way to a clearing station in the town of Malmedy. Now here they were in Revigny, her post for the foreseeable future. At the hospital, they were inundated: men lay swaddled in blankets on the floor, in the hallways, even in the boiler room. It was so cold, the morphine froze, as did the plasma supply. There were men in the wards with their spinal cords severed, others who had lost their arms and legs, others whose faces were wrapped in gauze with no holes for their eyes. Rachel remained in the surgery service. She thought of Ben all the time, she confessed. She remembered her summer in the orchard country. Those days seemed like a dream to her now. She missed him very much. She loved him.

Ben's company practiced digging foxholes, despite the fact that a foot beneath their boots lay an immense slab of marble. They were ordered to remove their insignia, cut away their stripes of rank, and were forbidden to salute outdoors anymore, in order to minimize the exposure of officers to potential sniper fire. This, said Lastenpole, was an ominous sign. It meant they were going into combat.

It was raining hard on January 8 when they set out for the front in quartermaster trucks and battalion supply vehicles. They traveled through uplands far to the northeast, into the Apennines. The rain became snow settling slowly over fields, and it was cold and still in these gentle, low mountains broken by fallow farmland.

Higher up, the roads were more difficult, filled with heavy, wet snow. Snow fell steadily out of a still gray sky, as heavy and fast as spring rain, and by afternoon the hills lay shrouded, there was no way to see any distance. They heard muffled artillery as the road wound up through forests, its sharp bends rising steeply through fields and quiet hill towns.

They came to the village of San Marcello. Ben's rifle platoon was billeted in an abandoned primary school for girls. They slept on a concrete classroom floor and burned slabs of pine on the portico. Overnight, more snow fell, and in the morning the valley opening below sat beneath a foot of it, with vineyard trellises showing. Children waited with wooden pails near the tent kitchen set up in the town square. The muffled, distant artillery had stopped. The world was tense and silent.

For three nights they patrolled the hillsides. Stackhouse complained about the weight of the BAR clips, since not a round had been fired. Lastenpole smoked his cigarettes and made entries in his journal. Ben went with Stackhouse to drink grappa at a tavèrna. As promised, Stackhouse had spent all his money on whores, so Ben paid for both their drinks and for a bag of figs as well. They ate them looking out over the country, their helmets in their laps. Stackhouse was from Baltimore. He hadn't finished high school. He had begun training to be a machinist and had worked delivering ice. Stackhouse confessed to hating the Army. He was drunk from the grappa and wanted to go home. The whores had been bleak. In Pisa he'd found one who spoke English and paid her to talk with him all night.

Orders came, and they moved north, first to Lizzano in Belvedere, then toward the town of Querciola, traveling in the dark under heavy loads, working uphill through snow-blown vineyards, fields, and apple orchards. Querciola lay deserted by its citizens because it sat in range of German shells, and the company established surveillance there and probed the countryside. On their fifth night in Querciola, a German patrol in white camouflage penetrated the foxhole perimeter. Ben lay on the ground with other men while the telephone operator called for reinforcements, and in ten minutes reserves came up from positions to the south. They, too, lay on the ground while the telephone operator called for artillery, but the reserve unit sergeant grew impatient and ordered his squads to fight. They spilled out toward the German fire, and a Private Zwickert was shot in the back by a BAR man of another rifle squad who had not understood the reserve's intentions and had assumed Zwickert was a German. This was the first of Ben's company to be killed in Italy.

Afterward, the sergeant of the reserves railed long at them, calling out the name of the dead man, telling them all it was John Zwickert they'd killed in their cowardice and stupidity. Then the perimeter fell quiet. They set up trip wires to deliver flares in case the Germans tried again, and they manned their foxholes by the book. At dawn they were shelled by 88s that cut through the trees like scythes. In a lull they were replaced by other men and withdrew to Vidiciatico, where they passed long hours in coal-heated rooms, sleeping or lying about. It was damp in Vidiciatico, the wind coming down from Riva Ridge, the snow melting at the height of day, turning the roads to mud. The jeeps traveled up to their axles in mud, and the men coming up from back of the lines reported that southward it was nearing spring—in the lowlands the air smelled of lemon blossoms.

Ben was shaved by an Italian barber with large, callused hands. He acquired new woolen underwear and a new helmet liner. With Lastenpole and Stackhouse he went to a trattoria and ate polenta and farina of chestnut and drank the wine of the country. A boy of twelve in a jersey of sheep's wool followed them to where they were quartered, until Bill gave him cigarettes. At Ben's request the boy named trees—the abete, the pini, and the castagno, which Ben recognized as a chestnut. In pidgin English the boy explained that the clay of the region made excellent plates, that the wild pears tasted sour, and that the berries growing in summer on the ginepro were especially good for one's digestion. Bill gave him more cigarettes, and the boy showed them the biancospino bush, whose berries, he made theatrically evident, were a chore to gather but delicious.

The weather turned sharply cold thereafter, and the snow fell hard overnight. Powder settled in the ravines and defiles, and the cliffs turned to ice. Ordered to patrol, the men went out in mattress covers sewn into snow tunics and in creepers made of tightly knotted rope. In darkness they crossed the Dardagna torrent and climbed by way of gullies and buttresses onto outcroppings of crumbling shale, searching for a route up Cappelbusso to serve as a supply trail. Lastenpole complained of frozen fingers. He insisted that their endeavor was useless, until the sergeant told him to shut up.

In the second week of February, the snow began to melt. The south slopes of hills were laid partially bare, and the air felt comfortable, balmy. At night a fog rose thick from the earth and concealed the movement of troops. All along the roads now, behind turns and under banks, lay stocks of rations, gasoline cans, and crates of ammunition. Ben and Stackhouse were sent to the rear on a mission to retrieve white phosphorus grenades, rucksacks, K rations, and mountain jackets. In the curves above Lizzano-in-Belvedere they encountered trucks and men moving up, mules driven slowly by Italian alpini sporting jaunty Tyrol hats, more big guns being hauled toward the front, and tractors sent by engineers to scour out the road mud. Farther to the rear, the boxes of materiel—rations, wire, ammunition, GI cans of drinking water—were stacked openly along the roads, where they resembled a kind of wooden hedge too high to see over. In the fields below were the encampments of the engineers, the signal corps, the truck companies, and the armored infantry. By the following night Vidiciatico was thronged with concealed soldiers and munitions, and there were new gun emplacements hidden in the hillside facing the long-entrenched German positions on the ridge from Spigolino northeast toward Mount Belvedere. Ben and Stackhouse sat with an infantry map, memorizing the names of promontories—Mancinello, Serrasiccia, Cappelbusso, and finally Campiano, where the ridge fell away toward Rocca Corneta, a hamlet occupied by the Germans. Through field glasses they watched the place: stucco peeling from the stone walls of a barn, willows hanging over a road, red roof tiles fallen from a house, a shutter dangling against a wall of crumbling white plaster. Bare earth showed in the pockets of snowmelt, and the hillsides were covered with leafless chestnuts. The main road, now that the snow had cleared, revealed last year's layer of fine white sand where it wound downhill to Lizzano.

On a frigid night of low-lying fog, Ben's company left Vidiciatico and traveled in refitted quartermaster trucks to the foot of Mount Belvedere. From there they hiked to the line of departure, and in the dark they dug slit trenches in the rocky earth. Fresh snow had fallen earlier that day against the steep rock faces. The valley was a bowl of darkness. The wind from the ridge bore down on them.

After one o'clock, Ben heard the far-off crack of gunfire and the detonations of mortars. A blister on his left heel troubled him, and he treated it with Mercurochrome, bandaged it and adjusted the boot, tightening the laces a little. He drank long from his canteen. Stackhouse chewed on his fingernails, checked his watch from time to time, and sat on his knees to relieve himself.

At first light, word came down the line that Riva Ridge had been taken. Yet they stayed in their slit trenches all day long, stiffening in the February cold, hearing the German counterbarrage and the artillery fire to the north, which finally quieted at dusk. Ben field-stripped and cleaned his BAR, then ate the tinned cornbread and peaches in his pack. In the dark he defecated on his entrenching tool blade and flipped its contents into the night; later, Stackhouse did the same.

The sky was lit by brilliant flares, and the German artillery began firing. Stackhouse directed the light from his headlamp on the face of his watch and timed the rockets fired down Belvedere by the Germans on the summit. They were smoke throwers, he said—six rounds every ninety seconds—and later in the night he announced with a curse that the Germans had gone to 88s, which traveled hard for twelve miles and weighed twenty pounds.

They stayed in their trenches while tracers behind them lit the slopes high above. The 88s arrived without warning, roaring directly overhead, while the grinding rise and fall of the smoke throwers—screaming meemies, Stackhouse called them—caused Ben to hold his breath. Later, shards of hot steel fell out of the illuminated sky, and beyond the dark silhouette of limbs, trees toppled and settled against other trees, into the forks of branches. Ben blew into his numb fingers and felt himself drawn tight. Stackhouse held silent beneath his helmet, but whenever the long low moan of a shell grew ominously loud in their direction, he swore under his breath.

At dawn, P-47s roared over, shadowy bombs beneath their wings, which they dropped on the summit of Belvedere. Ben's company was ordered to move up the slope and secure itself behind the front. The men did so and hunkered behind chestnut trees, and at 0700 the company commander issued the news that Mount Belvedere had been taken by the 85th, and shortly thereafter Gorgolesco, and the Third and First of the 85th had been ordered by General Hays to defend these new gains at all cost against counterattacks. The Third of the 86th, Ben's unit, was to move up through the lines at the front to take Monte Della Torraccia.

They came out of the pines in single file and slogged toward Mazzancana. On the trail they met a party of mules with dead GIs lashed across their backs, driven by Italian alpini. As the mules picked their way down the pocked, hard slope, the corpses pitched and settled. The line of infantrymen moving to the front slowed to watch the procession. The dead were skewed and twisted unnaturally on the backs of the silent mules.

Ben's heart beat harder. He climbed upslope past trees sheared high where 88s had slashed through them, then under chestnuts where wounded men sprawled, some of them smoking stuporously, others prone with their heads on their helmets, awaiting escort to the aid station by litter-bearing squads. Later they passed a dead German sitting upright, his back against a tree, a neatly rolled cigarette in the corner of his mouth; then a GI with his left foot, inside its boot, severed from the rest of him. When someone turned him over to have a look, it was Gavin Neiderhoff. He'd tripped a mine, plainly; he lay in a perfectly round depression, his helmet tipped to one side. At midday they found Leonard Campbell, whom Ben knew from chess at the Camp Hale Service Club: he'd been hit in the throat and chest by mortar fire, and the snow around him, pierced by artillery, was strewn here and there with pine twigs. Leonard had bared his wound to the sky and died with his dog tag twisted.

They passed through beeches ravaged by mortar fire, some splintered, cracked, and toppled, others sheared of prominent branches, which speared and festooned the ground. They passed through a snow-covered pasture, always climbing steadily. In the trees beyond, men were digging in, and the company paused behind them to check orders by telephone lines laid up the mountain. They sat waiting in the damp woods, where Ben changed the bandage on his foot. The blister had opened and oozed a clear fluid. He dressed it carefully, laced up his boot, and examined the sear on his BAR.

The platoon leader, Lieutenant Daniels, told them that at dusk they would proceed across the shoulder of Hill 1018 and onto the slopes of Della Torraccia, where they were authorized to hold until daybreak in the thick pines there. The front lay directly forward, he said. There were no more troops between them and the enemy. In the morning they would make their assault, but only after artillery fire had prepared the way for them. The Second of the 85th, previously covering the ground before them, had taken considerable casualties; now their unit composed a second wave aimed at the defended crest. They would move up at dusk and dig in for the night. It was advisable to go deep, if possible; otherwise, to dig a slit trench. The BAR men should be prepared for the task of providing heavy fire in full support of a frontal attack, and the ammo bearers should stay close, since the guns were useless without them.

Ben rested against a tree, watching the light seep away. The pines all stood in silhouette when Kelly Lastenpole sat down beside him and tilted back his helmet. The dark humor was gone from his eyes. He smoked with his hand cupped around his cigarette. "This is crap," he said.

"Have you seen Bill?"

"He's back that way."

"He's supposed to be here."

"Forget about that."

"Come on, Kelly."

"It's crap," said Lastenpole, and flicked his cigarette away. "I'm not going to put myself out there."

In the night they took over foxhole positions from the men of the 85th. At dawn Lastenpole squeezed shut his eyes while mortars sailed overhead toward the German positions. When the order came to advance upslope, he vomited on his knees in the hole. Strands of it hung from his mouth.

Ben heard the sound of his own breathing as he vaulted out of his foxhole, struggled into his field pack, and took up his Browning rifle. While he shrugged his pack higher into place, he heard the whine of a shell hurling by just to the left of his face. It came so close that he felt the wind from it.

For a moment he stood behind a tree, Lastenpole on his knees beside him, and then he moved into the open, hurrying uphill with other men. Lastenpole stayed until Ben called, saying he needed the extra clips, and then Lastenpole, gathering himself, dashed up the hill.

They stepped over bodies, some of them from the Second of the 85th, others in German uniforms, but there was no time to ponder the nature of the wounds or how the dead had met their ends, since more 88s were raining in. Some men clung to the shell-pocked ground, others scrabbled on their hands and knees to dig into the hillside. Ben moved unthinkingly, because other men were moving. He ascended a ridge but at its crest was met by machine-gun fire. A radioman sprawled beside Ben to report their position through his headset but received only static for his efforts and swore incessantly, the side of his face against the earth. More 88s slammed in at their left, canceling out all sound. Ben, in a pause, set up his BAR and began to fire at nothing in particular, simply forward of his position.

P-47s came in low and sought to clear the way for them with fragmentation bombs. Men ran wildly down the slope while the planes passed closely overhead, and Ben, hauling his BAR along, followed them into a north-facing hay field still ankle-deep with snow. He moved into sheltering pines, advancing along the edge of the field—the snow hard in the shadows here—set up his BAR a second time, and fired into the trees. Again it was indiscriminate;

he fired merely to fire. No one from his squad was near. The ammunition bearers had not shown up—Lastenpole or Stackhouse. There was no sign of Lieutenant Daniels.

Sheltered by trees, he held his ground until a staff sergeant came along who was organizing the company for an assault on the German line. Spittle hung from the sergeant's mouth, and he'd lost his helmet and sidearm. Ben advanced behind other men, following a mule path etched into a side hill; and as he climbed it in a long traverse, an 88 blew two soldiers off the trail in a plume of smoke. Ben abandoned the mule path and scaled the ridge in a direct ascent, where he found Lastenpole and Stackhouse, stopped by a tangle of trip wires. They passed through it under fire and staggered down into beeches, where they lay breathing hard on the ground, struggling out of their packs.

Ben heard only the ringing in his ears. Stackhouse, rolling onto his back, put his canteen to his lips; the water ran across his face and down into his shirt. He wiped his forehead a couple of times, twisted over onto his belly, and lay one cheek against the ground. "Goddamn," he breathed.

"Where is everyone?" asked Lastenpole. "What the hell is going on?"

He slid on his elbows between the trees as if to survey their position. With the first shot, a sprig of pine needles dropped on his back. With the next, he clutched his shoulder and twisted onto his side. The third entered behind his ear and passed through his skull below the eye. Lastenpole brought his hand to his cheek, turned on his back against the ground, and lay facing the tops of the trees, blood between his fingers. "Oh, Goddamn it," he said.

He died quickly, shuddering. Blood ran out of his mouth.

Stackhouse lay low, staring. Ben crawled to the cover of a tree, lodged himself between two roots, and stayed there for over an hour. Three Germans passed, one waving a white rag tied to a pine branch, the other helping a comrade whose intestines were falling out of his abdomen; he held them in as best he could, but purple loops slipped between his fingers and slithered against the snow. It occurred to Ben to shoot all three in return for the death of Lastenpole, but Stackhouse counseled strongly against it, and when one of the Germans looked at them, Stackhouse waved them toward their rear.

Later there came another German, limping through the woods without a helmet, a bloody bandage around his forehead. A tall, gangly man in glasses, he appeared thoroughly dazed. Bringing his hand up to press against his head, he grimaced and closed his eyes wearily, then staggered forward ten more steps and stopped nearly in front of them. He wore fingerless gloves and a stained, tattered field jacket—a German in his middle thirties, perhaps forty, gray stubble on his chin. His field pants were tucked into his boots. The lenses of his glasses were misted by vapor, flecked by damp green needles. The canteen at his belt was missing its top, and beside it was a pistol in a muddy holster.

Ben set his finger against the BAR's trigger, hoping that Stackhouse would decide matters. He felt frozen, unable to act. The German doubled over beside a tree, one hand against the bark. Head hung, he steadied himself, hawking spit on the ground. Then he turned to look to his left and squinted through the interstices of bramble—one end of his bandage coming loose—where Stackhouse lay fumbling with his rifle, trying to pull the safety back, the German noting this commotion in the brush and saying something in his language, at the same moment scrabbling for his muddy pistol, clawing to pull it free of its holster, with Stackhouse screaming at Ben to shoot the man—*Shoot him! Shoot him! Goddamn it, shoot him!*—and Ben still paralyzed while the German brought his pistol up and fired three rounds into the underbrush. Stackhouse groaned, and Ben shot, squeezing down hard on the BAR's trigger. He severed the man at the waist.

The German's legs pitched forward, but the rest of him toppled backward and lay twitching against the ground.

Ben pulled his hands from the BAR and moved away from it. The German was still alive. The eyes behind the glasses met Ben's. He lurched and shuddered, and a whistle came from his throat. His legs shivered; one foot trembled. "Christ," cried Bill Stackhouse. "I'm shot up. Christ."

Ben pulled Stackhouse's field jacket up, ripped his trousers open at the hip, and found a gaping bullet wound flecked with splinters and shards of bone, dark blood spilling from it. "I'm sorry," Ben said. "Jesus."

"Goddamn," said Stackhouse. He spoke wincingly, his teeth set. He grunted each time he exhaled. "My shoulder, too," he said.

"We need litter bearers," Ben said.

"The guy goddamn shot me."

Ben pulled the first-aid kit from his pack, opened it, and hesitated. Eighty-eights sailed over the trees to crash on the slopes behind. He mopped the blood with a compress, then poked a sulfa pill into Stackhouse's mouth and tried to make him swallow it, but the water leaked between his lips, and the pill would not go down. "I'm sorry," Ben repeated. "Jesus."

He put the compress over the hip wound and yelled, without hope, for a medic. He passed a roll of gauze around Bill's hip to hold the compress in place and watched it darken with blood. There was no point in merely watching. Watching didn't change things. Ben hurried out onto the open slope and yelled again for help.

He saw himself from a distance now, or as if at some watery remove. A loud hum echoed inside his head he could not shake or stop. He was aware in some detached way of the trembling in his shoulders. He couldn't keep from trembling. A mortar sailed overhead, then another, and a third, and all the while he screamed for a medic, hearing his own strained, high-pitched voice, which seemed to come from elsewhere. The air smelled of gunfire.

In the end he carried Stackhouse toward the rear draped across his shoulder. Stackhouse grunted with each step as Ben labored through the pines, sweating hard beneath his load. Soldiers passed him in both directions. When he saw one with the Red Cross brassard, he lay Stackhouse at his feet.

The medic cut holes in the arm of Stackhouse's jacket, shirt, and long underwear. Then he stuck him with a morphine styrette, poured sulfa powder into the wound, stuffed a compress tightly in, and bandaged it—coat and all—to stem the flow of blood. He tore open the gash in Stackhouse's field pants, tossed the blood-soaked gauze aside, and mopped the blood before pouring in sulfa powder and applying another compress.

"Hey," he said. "Are you there?"

"Nnn," Stackhouse answered, ashen. His face glistened with sweat.

"You're all right," the medic told him. "We're getting you out of here."

There were no litter bearers anywhere in sight, and they could not wait for any. The medic slipped a wound tag around Stackhouse's ankle. They knotted a blanket over either end of a pine pole and carried Stackhouse in the hammock it formed, the medic leading the way downhill, Stackhouse slung between him and Ben something like a ceremonial pig slaughtered and spitted for the fire.

The battalion aid station was at a place called Carge, which was no more than a solitary farmhouse at the far end of a tree-studded meadow. The chestnuts beyond it were bare of leaves, and the whole area was strewn with shell crates, discarded K-ration boxes and cans, a muzzle snow-cover left behind, an infantryman's forgotten ammo bag, an empty first-aid dressing carton, a stack of litters, an entrenching tool, a pair of muddy tin cups. A netted helmet with a wet leather liner, the strap frayed off, top down in the snow. Beside it, a shooting mitten.

Litter bearers sprawled near the aid station with their hobnailed soles propped on rocks, beside a trail of boot prints etched raggedly through the mud and bloodstained snow. Next to the farmhouse with its tile roof, a chestnut tree stood starkly outlined against a sky of cirrus clouds and against a lofty ridge to the south dusted with sparse new snow. There was hay put up in the animal pens, dark and dense as peat. The upper reaches of the farmhouse had been shelled, but its thick stone walls remained intact. Its windows were blacked with tar paper.

Inside, the wounded slouched against the walls, some seated with their heads hung, others prone on the dirt floor. Medical technicians worked among them, carrying flashlights and kerosene lanterns, and none took note of Ben and the medic as they hauled Stackhouse inside and lowered him onto a vacant litter. While the medic caught his breath, Ben cut the blanket free with the scissors; then they hefted Stackhouse's litter and set it down on crates and bins arrayed beneath a gas lamp to serve as an operating table.

The light here shone fierce and glaring, a hard, garish cone of light, and the battalion surgeon stood in it, a broad-faced man with a salt-and-pepper mustache, fresh blood on his hands. He was bent over a soldier's Adam's apple, and the soldier was coughing bright blood.

The surgeon turned to look at Stackhouse; the medic exposed the wounded shoulder for him and ripped Bill's pants open. The pants and blankets were saturated, and the shoulder stained with blood. Stackhouse's eyes were open but glazed, and he didn't move at all. "I gave him morphine," the medic explained. "The guy's going fast."

"Does he have a pulse?"

"I think so."

"Don't think, know," said the surgeon. "And get a blood-pressure cuff on him. You," he said, across the room. "Get some saline in this guy. Start him on an IV, quick. And get some plasma going."

He looked at Ben, then turned away. He seemed both angry and tired. He went back to working on the throat of the other soldier, whose head was held down by a medical technician Ben recognized from Camp Hale. "Put some pressure on that hip for him," the surgeon said without turning. "Otherwise, get out of here. There's too many people around."

"You mean me?" Ben asked.

"Put some pressure on it for him, soldier. Go to it already."

"Okay," said Ben. "All right."

They cut Stackhouse free of his field jacket, combat shirt, and T-shirt. They cut away his pants, too, so that Stackhouse had on only his filthy underpants, muddy boots, and socks. The technician couldn't get the IV started, because Stackhouse's veins had collapsed: his blood wouldn't keep them open. The surgeon turned from his other work and with a scalpel cut through the skin and fat at the inside of Stackhouse's elbow. While the sergeant retracted the skin for him, he isolated the vein with a hemostat and passed a suture under it. Then he nicked the collapsed vein open, ran a large-bore needle in, and fixed it in place by tightening the suture. "There," he said. "Now tie off that vein. And put a stitch in when you get the chance." And abruptly he went back to the soldier with the wounded throat, taking a clamp in his hand.

The surgeon pushed his glasses snugly against the bridge of his nose. "Listen," he said to a medical technician, in the same direct, emphatic tone he used for everyone in the room. "I've got to work on this new guy over here. He won't make it if I don't. So I want you to watch this clamp I've got until I can get back to it. Just make sure he doesn't work it loose."

The technician took hold of the clamp. "I've got it," he said.

The surgeon turned again to Stackhouse, and gave orders to all in the room. "Move," he said. "Let's get moving. Get that plasma I asked for brewed in the next two seconds or so."

The sergeant technician ran saline through Stackhouse with the valve cock turned all the way open and started a new bag immediately. "It's going right through him," he said.

"I'll do a second cut-down," said the surgeon. "Get his pulse again for me. And take a pressure reading."

He cut through the flesh in Stackhouse's other arm and again isolated a vein with a hemostat, ran a needle into it, fixed it, and tied it off. "I don't have a pulse," the sergeant said. "I don't think he has one anymore. Not that I can find." But the surgeon continued with his work. Ben watched his hands move swiftly. He kept his own hand against Stackhouse's hip, which looked stark white in the light of the gas lantern hissing overhead. "Plasma," the surgeon called. "This needle's ready and waiting here. Fill the poor bastard with plasma."

The sergeant technician hooked up the plasma, which had been reconstituted by a medic in the corner who was busy reconstituting more. The sergeant opened the valve fully. The surgeon placed two fingers against Stackhouse's neck. He moved them around, stopped, moved again. "I'm on the carotid now," he said. "Not a thing. Nothing."

"Jesus," Ben said weakly.

The surgeon made no reply to this. "You," he called to a second technician, "get into that crate and find the epinephrine." He paused over Stackhouse, whose chest and belly had turned a sallow blue. The face was empty, the eyes wide open, the pupils enormously dilated. "This guy's dead," said the surgeon.

He hit Stackhouse in the chest with no small violence. Nothing happened, and he hit him again. He hit him a third time, harder still, and Stackhouse bounced a little. A medic handed him the epinephrine, and the surgeon filled a syringe with it. Aiming deliberately between two ribs, he plunged the needle through Stackhouse's chest, and with no hesitation drove it forcefully, using his arm and shoulder, into Stackhouse's heart.

"Nothing at all," said the surgeon.

The surgeon struck Stackhouse's chest twice more, as if it were made of wood. "Zero," he said, with his fingers at Stackhouse's neck. "I can't get anything."

"No," said Ben. "Please."

The surgeon ignored him. "Sergeant," he said. "You let Waterman man the IVs and ventilate this soldier for me. Can you do that for me, no matter what?"

"Yes, sir," said the sergeant.

"Just keep him ventilated," the surgeon ordered.

The sergeant tilted Stackhouse's head back, pulling him by the chin. He slid an airway into the mouth to hold back the tongue. He laid an anesthesia mask over the lower half of the face, wrapped his lips around the blow tube, bent low, and went to work. He blew forcefully.

The surgeon turned to Ben now. "There's a packet of sterile gloves behind you. Hand them over to me."

"All right," answered Ben.

"Hurry up," said the surgeon.

Ben found and opened the packet. While the surgeon worked his hands into the gloves, he went on giving orders. He asked that the surgical retractors in the equipment chest be doused thoroughly with alcohol and brought to the operating table. He told

Ben and the medic to stand by until he showed them what to do. He said he was going to cut the man open and would need them to manipulate the retractors.

Ben felt a tremor in his shoulders. The idea of opening Stackhouse's chest as he lay before them dead on the litter with his eyes blank and his face blue was horrible to contemplate. But the medic brought the retractors, and the surgeon with his gloved fingers counted the gaps in Stackhouse's rib cage and plunged in his scalpel. He swept it gracefully along the shadow of a rib, cutting slightly longer than a hand's width two inches below the left nipple. Contrary to what Ben expected, there was no blood to speak of, only beads of it. The surgeon handed his scalpel to the medic. "Give me the retractors," he said.

He inserted them into the lips of the cut, against the exposed ribs. Ben saw the pink of a lung. It deflated while he looked at it, and then it rose again, swelling and glistening, when the sergeant exhaled through the blow tube. The medic took one retractor in hand and Ben took the other. "Pull hard," said the surgeon. "Open him up."

They pulled, and the surgeon turned to face Stackhouse's head. With his left hand he reached through the incised gap so that his palm and wrist disappeared. It seemed to Ben a kind of illusion, one man's forearm disappearing inside another man's chest. The surgeon rotated his arm to the left, until it slipped a little farther in, and then rotated it back again, wriggled, and bent even lower. "I'm there," he announced. "I've got it now. You keep that plasma coming fast, run plasma through both arms, take him off the saline. Sergeant, stay with that blow tube."

The surgeon turned to Ben next, his forearm pumping rhythmically. "Pull a little harder," he said. "It's biting into my arm." He nodded when Ben put leverage on Stackhouse's rib and pulled it out of the way. "This is much easier for left-handed guys," the surgeon said matter-of-factly. "I don't have the same finesse."

"Is he dead?" Ben asked.

"He's been out for less than a minute," said the surgeon. "I'm trying to compress his heart and get him started again."

"You're doing what?" Ben asked.

"I've got his heart in my hand," said the surgeon. "It isn't too much of a trick, really. You just want to make sure you palm it correctly, don't try to do the work with your fingers, and especially not with the ball of your thumb, which is very tempting and seems right, but what you want is to cup the thing and squeeze it hard and evenly, as if you were wringing a sponge."

"So he's not dead," Ben said.

"He was dead," the surgeon said. "I don't know right now."

"This is a helluva thing," said the medic. "I haven't seen this before."

"It's the last resort," said the surgeon, the muscle in his forearm still working rhythmically where it disappeared between the retractors. "It's a relatively basic thing. I'm pumping his heart for him."

"Yeah, but still," said the medic.

"Sometimes," said the surgeon, "this actually works. If everything goes just right."

He was true to his word in this regard. Stackhouse's heart began to beat again, quite irregularly for more than two minutes, but then with a racing, regular rhythm, so that the surgeon slid his hand out, pressed it hard against the incision, and with the other checked the carotid artery. Stackhouse's pulse ran thready and wild; his blood pressure was coming up. The sergeant pulled away from his ventilating work, and they all looked at Stackhouse's eyes. The pupils had constricted again, and the surgeon immediately ordered more morphine, lest the patient, stirring toward consciousness, find himself with his chest cut open on a litter in an Italian farmhouse.

The surgeon did not stop his work, slow down, or relax. Keeping his hand pressed against the incision, he commended the sergeant for his endurance in ventilating the wounded man and urged him to continue for a while longer until he could sew things up. He ordered a urinary catheter and told the technician to cut openings in it and douse it with alcohol. He asked the medic to find a can and half-fill it with water. Without hesitating in his delivery of commands, he told Ben to rinse the scalpel, and when he had it in his free right hand, he made a hole in Stackhouse's chest and plunged a hemostat through it. A technician took over compressing the incision, and the surgeon fed the catheter in, trapping it in the hemostat's jaws in order to draw it out. He tied it off with purse-string sutures, attached a length of IV tubing, and ran the end to the floor. "Tape this in here," he told Ben, pointing at the can of water. "There's some tape in the crate over there. Tape the tube against the inside of the can so the end of it stays in the water."

He took a deep breath, checked Stackhouse's pulse again—it was racing still, in frantic fashion—and urged the technician with his hand on the incision to apply a sealing pressure. "Just a little longer," he said. "Then we'll sew him up."

The surgeon leaned over Stackhouse's hip and removed the medic's dressing. "This guy took it in the femoral artery," the surgeon observed, adjusting his glasses. "He took it right in the bone, too—opened the marrow cavity."

He turned his attention to Stackhouse's shoulder, pulling the dressing aside. "Same kind of problem here," he said. "The subclavian vein has been torn."

A litter team hurried into the room and deposited another

wounded soldier on the bins and crates behind the surgeon. The soldier's left leg was missing below the knee. A tourniquet had been applied, stained red with blood. The doctor turned to examine it, then ordered the medic to twist it tighter and returned his attention to Stackhouse.

"All right," he said. "We have to turn this man on his side and get this wound taken care of."

They pulled Stackhouse's right arm over his head so that the side of his face lay against his bicep, and they passed the IV around the sergeant technician, who knelt, red-faced, at the blow tube. The surgeon ordered a rolled blanket placed beneath Stackhouse's neck and head to free the right arm for the passage of plasma. Then he swabbed clear Stackhouse's hip. The blood welled up immediately. "This guy's down to no clotting factors," the surgeon observed, compressing the wound. "He's bleeding out pure plasma here. There's nothing left to coagulate. He's just lost too much good stuff."

He opened the hip a bit more with his scalpel, to drain the accumulated blood. He took a closer look inside, made a tamponade of gauze, tucked it firmly into the wound—packing it tightly at the edges—and taped a compress over it. Next he did the same with the shoulder. "Like sticking your finger in a dike," he said. "That should work for a while."

He turned his attention to the boy behind him, whose leg had been blown off. He tightened the tourniquet and swiveled again. "Okay," he said. "Tell you what. I want this guy"—he pointed at Ben—"to wash his hands over there. Then he can keep a seal on that incision while you"—he pointed at the technician—"get this new man an IV."

"All right," the technician said.

"You get this soldier in shape," said the surgeon. "Get him some plasma, take his pulse, get a blood-pressure reading."

"Yes, sir," the technician said. "The problem is, I'm stuck right here until this man"—he gestured at Ben—"gets his ass in gear. You're just standing there, Private."

Ben washed his hands and took over the technician's job of sealing Stackhouse's incision. It pushed against his palm a little each time the sergeant blew into the tube. "How is he?" Ben asked. "Will he live?"

"His heart's beating," the surgeon said. "But he won't coagulate anymore. He needs real blood, quickly."

"Well, I'm his friend," Ben said. "Maybe he should take some of mine."

"You O-positive?"

"I am, yes."

"Okay," the surgeon answered. "Right now we'd better sew him up. Then we'll draw a pint out of you and drop it into him."

"Take more," Ben told him.

The surgeon used sutures of heavy black silk, working rapidly. He pierced the skin and looped around the ribs to draw the incision together. "This is dicey," he said to the sergeant. "If you don't sew things good and tight, you end up with an air leak."

"Hey," the sergeant answered, pulling the anesthesia mask aside. "The guy's breathing again."

The surgeon anchored the catheter to the skin with three sutures around it. "Air-tight," he announced. He called for a fifty-milliliter syringe, attached it to the catheter, and suctioned air from Stackhouse's thorax. He broke the syringe free and attached the catheter to the IV tube snaking into the bucket. "Take a look," he said to the sergeant, rubbing his face with the back of his wrist. "We've got air coming out of the chest now. See those bubbles in the water?"

"My God," said the sergeant. "What a miracle."

He drew a blanket over Stackhouse, tucking in its edges. "Christ," he said. "It's a miracle. It's a goddamn resurrection."

"Call it what you will," the surgeon said, still rubbing his face and scratching his nose with the back of his hairy wrist. "But you could learn to do it, too. It isn't something from a Bible story. You go to med school, you can do it."

"Look at that," said the sergeant. "The guy's back from the dead."

"It's a miracle," Ben agreed.

"We'll talk about it after the war," said the surgeon, turning to the boy behind him with the tourniquet on his leg. He checked his pulse, two fingers at his throat. "In the meantime, sergeant, I again need plasma to throw at this other poor bastard."

They drew two pints of Ben's blood, and he sat in a daze while the technician disconnected the plasma line and started Ben's blood into Stackhouse. A third soldier was hauled in on a litter, but Ben didn't look at him. Instead he cradled his head in his hands and stayed that way until they passed him into the keeping of Father Carr, the Third Battalion chaplain. Father Carr consoled him a little, but seemed himself at a loss. Then they went into the night, down the hill with other men, toward the rear, away.

For three days Ben stayed in the rear, wrapped in blankets on a cot. The division psychiatrist interviewed him twice to determine if he was fit for service, and in the end they put him back in the line with recruits brought in from the replacement depot. Ben spoke to none of them. It was better that they remain nameless—they would leave less of a wake.

He made no pretense of fighting as the regiment advanced over the plain of the Po to liberate Bomporto, San Benedetto Po, Villafranca, and Verona. Fortunately, he was not much called upon except in the fighting to liberate Torbole, and there he squatted behind a wall and didn't participate. When the surrender came, they sent him to Bolzano, where men from his company commandeered shotguns and pistols from the Beretta factory, and guarded a warehouse in which the Germans had hidden paintings plundered from the galleries of Florence. In the distance rose the Dolomites.

On the train to Livorno he had nothing to say, though other men were loud and raucous in expectation of going home. They steamed down the spine of Italy in boxcars, and men drank wine, leaned from the cars, and waved to the peasants in the fields. It was July-hot and oppressively humid, but nobody seemed to mind very much and the general atmosphere was one of mirth. They passed fields of battle, towns shelled, farmhouses shattered, the plains strewn with burned tanks.

Ben sent a letter to Rachel in Marseilles, and she came to Livorno aboard a hospital ship on a leave of twenty days. He looked for her in a makeshift encampment of army tents by the Ligurian Sea, just north of the city. It was midafternoon, a day of still heat, and he was sweating, unshaven, and filthy, dressed in military issue khakis and a military tank-top undershirt, his skin darkened from his days in Italy, his lips chafed by the wind. He asked around and was told by a nurse that Rachel had gone down to the sea to swim, and he went in search of her.

He found her wet, her hair in flat strands, wearing a plain blue bathing suit. A lean woman with amber skin, older than he remembered. But the smell of her mouth was as he recalled. She wept a little, looking at him. She, too, was harder, darker. She held him tightly and stroked his hair. "Never you mind," she whispered to him. "Never you mind now, Ben."

That night they took a room in town, over a bakery. The toilet stall was two flights down. There were mice about, and from the street outside came the clamor of wee-hour drunks. Without a fan, they flung open their window, and yet there was no relief from the heat, and the mattress beneath them was soaked. The noxious smell of the town's sewers, the exhaust of cars, the smell of the bakery, the lamps in flats across the narrow way, the clattering passage of motorcycles over the ancient cobbles. They dragged the mattress onto the floor. Ben lay on his back gazing up at her face, held lightly in his hands. Very close, her hair falling into the space between them, the girl he remembered from the orchard country, a woman now in a foreign country, her long arms on either side of his head, Rachel sweating over him at five A.M., at dawn.

They were married the next morning by an army chaplain glad to dispense with regulations. No blood tests required, he said, nor did he care that the bride was an officer, the groom an enlisted man. There were many such weddings afoot, it seemed, and the chaplain performed them with a generosity consistent with the circumstances. The end of the fighting, he explained to them, had inspired many couples with love, and who was he to thwart them? God worked in strange ways, he droned: out of the cinders of ten million deaths were born the seeds of marriage. And how to explain that except as God's will at work among us in this world? The divine hand lay in it; God used the attraction between two people to further the unfolding of His scheme. The chaplain wished them the very best, bade them exchange vows of mutual fidelity in good times and bad, in all such conditions as the years might bestow, instructed them in signing the documents, and sent them on their way. Ben and Rachel, once outside, requisitioned the chaplain's jeep, in which he'd left the keys.

They bought two bottles of chianti and took the road to Florence. They passed a night in Pontedera. In Florence they left the jeep with a motor pool in front of the Palazzo Strozzi. They rode a train north into forested valleys. It was on the train to Bressanone that Rachel thought of roses: their ashes, she said, should lie side by side, his for a red rose, hers for a white, until with time they merged into one, a soft and delicate pink. It was a story she'd read, of two lovers, the final flowering of their passion. She could not remember their names now, it was something from very long ago, a book of tales from the library, illustrated: she might have been ten years old. Ben had wondered in teasing fashion if in fact it worked that way. Did the two roses mingle into one pink bush, or did their blooms tangle and intertwine, red and white, for eternity? There was no guarantee of pink, they decided. Who knew the outcome of such a thing? They would have their ashes interred side by side, leaving the rest to fate.

They disembarked, rode west in a supply truck, then set off on foot into the mountains. He told her about the German he'd killed, the man's eyes, his legs in front of him, the twitching, rattling death. "I didn't think," he confessed.

"It's difficult in a situation like that."

"It didn't have to be that way."

"It's done now," said Rachel.

They were resting in a rock-and-timber hut where a rough-framed painting of a beneficent Christ had been hung in one corner. Ben sat back with Rachel against him, looking out at wooden ladders bolted to a cliff.

"I wonder who he was."

"That makes things worse."

"I think about him."

"Try not to, Ben."

"Maybe he had a wife. A family."

"It's in the past," said Rachel.

That afternoon they came to a hamlet of Ladin homes and barns. They hiked uphill past potato patches and rested under a plum tree. A farmhouse stood open to travelers, and they presented themselves to the woman there, who wore a green apron and a hat of plaited straw and was busy lofting hay over racks. She led them through a low door, into a room made of pine boards. The floor had been painted in a floral pattern wearing away underfoot. They sat by a window in hand-hewn pine chairs, at a table painted in wildflowers—calendula and edelweiss—and looked out over long hay slopes falling away to the south. The woman brought a bottle of wine, diluted and chilled by spring water. She brought dumplings flecked with chives, polenta, and roe deer goulash.

Ben told Rachel about the field surgeon who had saved Bill Stackhouse's life. "You were right," he said. "I should have been a medic. I should have listened to you."

"This place is a dream," Rachel said. "A fairy tale or a dream."

"You warned me. You tried to warn me."

"There's green onion in the dumplings, too, mixed in with the chives."

"I want to be like that surgeon," said Ben. "A person like that, a doctor."

"I'm with you all the way," answered Rachel.

NINE

Ben opened his one good eye to a still and empty October morning in a motel room in Quincy, Washington. A nimbus of light, a gray corona, formed a halo at the curtains. The heater fan made a terrible racket, and outside, in the parking lot, someone was warming the engine of a car by repeatedly revving it. The air smelled of saffron, and from the bathroom the toilet sang. Ben felt mired from the marijuana, his limbs immovable. He couldn't rise with his war still in him, and he lay there feeling troubled by it as he had for fifty-three years. He'd returned home from Italy to the news that Aidan had died at Peleliu, hit in the neck by mortar fire. That fall, the apples rotted on the ground. Ben's father sold ten acres to the Fisks before Christmas. In the spring, he sold the rest to a Wenatchee man, young and starting out, and moved into a cabin on the outskirts of town. He did odd jobs, hired on with the railroad. He moved to Spokane, then Yakima.

Ben thought of the miracle of Stackhouse's heart: Bill had come away with a limp and a shoulder that ached in cold weather; was retired from a position in sales at an office-supply company in Bethlehem, Pennsylvania; and had, to date, eleven grandchildren, photographs of whom he'd sent to Ben with letters over the years. Ben had seen him three times at reunions of the Tenth Mountain Division. They'd spoken at length about what had happened. Stackhouse was slowly writing his memoirs, so that his progeny would know about it, too.

Ben thought of the hearts of other men and women in all their naked, exposed truth—muscles about the size of fists, pulsing at the center of living forms. The heart that was for poets and priests the seat of all things beautiful, the house of love, the host for God, the chamber of sadness, rage, discord, envy, despair, glee. Ben knew the heart as a muscle first, designed for the work of pumping blood, not so terribly intricate that it couldn't be duplicated. Parts of it were replaceable: a heart valve could be made from titanium, or lifted from a hog. In knowing the heart in this cold way, he had lost all innocence about it. It was not that he didn't believe in love, but first he was a scientist, a physician, and a man of reason. He had manipulated the hearts of human beings, and he thought he understood that when we speak of love, we speak of something transitory, something gone when we go. The heart, for Ben, was tangible—and nothing tangible remains.

There were few things more depressing he could think of than to be alone in a cheap motel room, dying of cancer at seventy-three, the smell of fallow fields outside, gruff voices in the parking lot; a bleakness grew in him he couldn't face, couldn't abide or accept. He rose from bed, limped to the bathroom, and sat on the toilet with his head dropped between his knees, noting his thin and flaccid thighs, but nothing passed from his obstructed bowels except for a foul dark squirt of water that antagonized his hemorrhoids. An old man, terminally ill, thoroughly humbled on the toilet. An old man fallen from grace.

He was driven out before eleven by hunger, and walked toward town with his hat pulled low, his hands deep in his coat pockets. The sun rode high and pale in the east, but a hard wind gusted from the mountains. A train whistled, gaining speed, churning toward the Rock Island crossing. The grit in the gutter rose and boiled whenever a truck flew past at high speed, and he was surprised once by the hiss of brakes when a freight truck slowed alongside him to turn at the Central Bean Company. To the south stretched a long row of mobile homes and trailers, some with windows broken and patched with duct tape and cardboard. In a packed-dirt yard of sparse weeds, a school bus dispensed kindergartners—the children of fruit pickers, Ben guessed—raising dust as they went. A mangy dog, yellow and slat-ribbed, came out to fend off Ben as he passed, stopping warily at thirty feet, its tongue spilling from its mouth.

Ben had no desire to face the world. He longed to be in bed again with the heat turned high, the sheets pulled close, his head resting on a pillow. But hunger urged him forward. He limped toward town, barren fields to his right, past the cemetery, a fruit warehouse, a nursery full of apple-tree rootstock, a ditch full of roadside cattails. The night had settled the wounds of his journey into a general soreness. He felt, as he walked, each of yesterday's miles, carrying them in his bones.

At Akins Foods, a chain-link fence kept the firewood out front from the hands of sneaks and thieves. A dozen cars were parked near the double doors, but the rest of the lot was littered with beer cans, food wrappers, broken bottles, a pair of overturned shopping carts, a brown paper bag ripped apart by dogs—the refuse of the previous night.

Inside, at the automatic teller machine, Ben withdrew two hundred and sixty dollars to pay Ilse Peterson's bill. It was warm in the store and smelled of donuts and of the bread for sale in the bakery. There was a rug-cleaning apparatus for rent and a Lotto Scratch Ticket machine beside it, bags of bulk-size dog food, toilet paper in cut-open cartons, a pyramid mound of Presto-Logs, and a display of canning jars. There were sunglasses, cigarettes, bags of ice, and a rack of romance paperbacks: men with oily, puffed-up bodies, women shorn of half their clothes, grappling together on sunny beaches or posed in front of palm trees.

At the end of the aisle of Mexican food—pozole, mole, yucca root—a girl gawked indiscreetly at his eye as he fumbled past with his shopping cart: the bruised and swollen violence of it, he saw, aroused her curiosity and disgust. Padding about uncertainly, deliberating on what he might stomach, he selected a can of chicken soup, a box of rye crackers, a pint of vanilla yogurt, a liter of prune juice, a half gallon of spring water, a bag of fig bars, two Winesap apples, and a ripe-looking mango. He found a plastic spoon at the deli counter and hauled everything to the checkout stand, where the cashier glanced at his eye twice before asking him about it.

"A game of croquet," Ben answered. "It got out of control."

"What a crock," the cashier said. "Hah, hah. Very funny."

"These people take it seriously," insisted Ben. "I got cracked with a mallet."

"I always know when somebody's lying."

"Croquet," said Ben, "with the wrong people."

"If you say so."

"All right. I'll confess. I walked into a door."

The cashier, a girl of twenty-five, laughed derisively. There was a splotch of red between her eyebrows, and her hair had been stiffly frosted. "Oh, my God," she said to him. "You should have opened it first."

"You're right," said Ben. "Next time."

"It's not that hard, opening a door." The cashier shoved his things aside. "$12.78," she said.

He limped out into the cold again with his shoddy plastic bags in tow, one in each hand. They felt heavy, heavier than they should have: his shoulders ached from carrying Rex, as did the tendons in his forearms. He passed the forlorn trailer court and a placard urging dieters to call a toll-free number for the secret to loosing thirty pounds a month. MAGIC! it read. GUARANTEED! The sky was cloudless across the broad plain, tender with morning sunlight. Beneath its expanse, Ben felt alone. The cashier had been devoid of compassion, and he took her heartlessness with him. But how was she to know of his condition, his need for kinder treatment? He felt like going back to tell her that she ought to be careful about what she said, but he could not summon the strength it would take, and at any rate it would cause a scene: a crazy old man with a black eye ranting away in Akins Foods, embarrassing everybody.

There was no way to explain himself. He felt removed from the world. Suffering suffused everything. The sadness in the October wind was also the sadness in the cashier's mouth—different notes struck from the same chord.

Ben hung the DO NOT DISTURB sign on his door and choked down the overripe, dripping mango in an excess of appetite. He wiped his chin and, still ravenous, devoured the vanilla yogurt. Next he poured the chicken soup into the plastic ice bucket beside the sink and warmed it in the microwave oven. The bucket melted and warped slightly, but he saw no reason to worry about it and sat down in front of the television. Rifling through stations aimlessly, he ate the soup, blowing at his spoon and dropping crackers in. He tried to take an interest in something, the midday talk shows with their amicable hosts, but none of it appealed to him, it was all puerile gibberish, and he muted the sound with the remote controller and picked up the Bible on the bedside table left there by the Gideons. He had not read the Bible for a long time. He turned to the Book of Job:

> *Days of affliction have taken hold*
> *upon me.*
> *In the night my bones are pierced*
> *and fall from me,*
> *And my sinews take no rest.*
> *By the great force of my disease*
> *is my garment disfigured;*
> *It bindeth me about as the collar*
> *of my coat.*
> *He hath cast me into the mire,*
> *And I am become like dust and*
> *ashes.*

It struck him how Satan and God conversed with such indifference and arrogance about their experiment. It was disturbing, too, that God punished Eliphaz the Temanite, Bildad the Shuhite, and Zophar the Naamathite—all come to comfort Job—simply for misunderstanding Him in the course of delivering comfort. That Job himself recovered his health and lived a hundred forty years more, with fourteen thousand sheep on hand, six thousand camels, a thousand yoke of oxen, a thousand she asses, three new sons—not to mention the fairest daughters in the land—seemed too much of a happy ending, until Ben came to the book's final passage, where Job died.

He looked up from the pages of the Holy Book to find the television still on. He fumbled for a moment with the remote, then turned the volume up. A married couple sat on a stage, ordinary people, overweight, the man with a handlebar mustache and side-burns, the woman's dress revealing the cleavage of slack, pendulous breasts. They were swingers, the man was saying. They were twenty-seven and had no children. They had sex with members of a swingers association at weekend conventions and get-togethers. There were also weeknight rendezvous. They were happily married, said the man. He enjoyed the thought of his wife that way. She, too, liked the arrangement. She thought about sex all day at work. He did, too—the coming of evening. He was in marketing with an auto parts company, she a receptionist for a floral distributor. They labored, he said, to pay their bills—their real lives were all about swinging. They saw no need to change this. They saw a future of endless sex, so why should they change anything? They were the happiest people they knew of. It seemed to them they shared a secret. In restaurants full of ordinary people they groped each other under the table, as randy as seventeen-year-olds. Why would they want to be any different? Why would they want ordinary sex, the garden variety most suffered through? They held the key to living, said the man. Sex, said the woman, was the heart of things. What else was there as wonderful?

Chewing on a Winesap, Ben changed the station. A pale man near his own age was bowling, and Ben watched him toss his ball down the lane with as much force as he could muster. The man, poised, watched the course of the ball, anguish creasing his face. For a moment the world was brought to a halt, the bowling ball arresting time, the bowler wholly unaware that elsewhere swingers were pawing each other with a desperate, blinding passion. For the bowler there were no swingers, the course of the ball was everything. He followed it with a yearning heart. Ben switched off the television.

He called the Greyhound 800 number to get the schedule for the bus run upriver, then a Wenatchee company to reserve a rental car. His plan was to drive to Malaga, find William Harden's

Wolfhound Orchard, and try to pry his gun, somehow, out of Harden's hands. After that, he would walk for grouse in the Colockum country, find a barbed-wire fence somewhere, and shoot himself in the neck.

Ben sat mulling the difficulty of retrieving his gun from Harden. He could not present himself at the man's door and expect a hospitable reception. If he pressed his case for rightful ownership, made an entreaty invoking fair play, or apologized again for the wolfhound's death, he would only be turned away. He couldn't just ask for the gun's return, though the notion of acting in some other fashion—as a burglar or thief—was beyond imagining.

Ben thought through what he had to say, then called his daughter in Seattle. "I thought you were hunting," she said.

"I am," said Ben. "I'm over in Quincy. What are you doing, dear?"

"Nothing, really. Working on my screenplay. Chris said you called."

"Working on a screenplay isn't nothing," said Ben. "What's this one about?"

"It's a children's movie."

"What's it about?"

"It's complicated."

"In a nutshell, then."

"A boy on a journey."

"What happens to him?"

"He loses his dog and goes after it. A lot of things. It's complicated."

"Well," said Ben. "What a coincidence. That's the reason I called."

There was a pause on the other end of the line. He could hear Renee breathing into the receiver. "What?" she said. "I don't get it."

"I had an accident," Ben told her. "Saturday morning. I crashed the car."

"You what?"

"I crashed the car in Snoqualmie Pass. But I'm fine, I didn't get injured."

"You crashed the car? Your four-wheel-drive car?"

"That's the one," said Ben.

"You're kidding, Dad. Did you hit anyone?"

"I hit a tree. In the summit exit. The road was wet, and I lost control. It could have been much worse."

"You didn't get hurt?"

"One eye is swollen and bruised a little. Other than that, nothing."

"You ought to have it checked, Dad. You don't want to take a chance."

"It's fine," said Ben. "It's nothing."

"Wait a second," Renee said. "How did you get up to Quincy?"

"Some people stopped and gave me a ride. A couple of very nice people."

"You hitchhiked?"

"No."

"Who were they, then?"

"Two kids in a Volkswagen van."

"You're kidding me."

"What's wrong with that?"

"That's just so funny. It's hard to imagine. That's so funny," she repeated.

"Anyway," said Ben, "they took me to Vantage."

"I thought you said you're in Quincy."

"I am in Quincy."

"So how did you get there?"

"Believe it or not," Ben said, "I ended up walking from Vantage to George. Cross country. Hunting chukars."

"Hunting what?"

"Little birds. Chukars."

"You walked all that way to hunt little birds?"

"Not exactly. I had some problems. There was a fellow out there chasing coyotes, and my dogs got tangled up with his dogs. And Tristan got himself killed."

"No," said Renee.

"I'm afraid so."

"Wait a minute. What happened?"

"A dog fight, a bad fight. His dogs attacked mine, and I found Tristan killed."

"Dad," said Renee. "That's terrible."

"What can you do?" Ben asked.

"You can sue the guy. He killed your dog."

"I don't even know who he is, though. Besides, it wouldn't bring Tris back."

"That's terrible," Renee said again.

"I hate to think about it," said Ben.

There was another pause, a long one. Ben shifted the receiver to his right ear because his arm was falling asleep.

"This is a really weird story," said Renee. "I can't believe I'm hearing this."

"I know," said Ben. "It's weird."

"So you walked from Vantage all the way to George? That's fifteen miles, uphill."

"Not quite. Not really."

"Dad, this is so crazy."

"There's more," said Ben. "Rex was injured. I brought him up here to the vet."

"What?"

"Those coyote dogs went after Rex. But he made it through. He's all right. I got him up here to the vet."

"Rex—that's your other dog, the one you got last year?"

"You know Rex," Ben said.

"Now wait," said Renee. "Wait a minute. How did you get up to Quincy?"

"A trucker," said Ben. "At Martha's Inn. I met him at Martha's Inn."

"A trucker took you from George to Quincy?"

"That's how it went, yes."

"You rode with a trucker."

"Rex, too. We got him up here to an excellent vet. His wounds were mostly skin wounds."

"This is bizarre," said Renee.

"It is," said Ben. "It's crazy."

"So where are you?"

"I'm at a motel."

"That's good," she said.

Ben sat rubbing his side as he spoke. He had eaten too much, and his stomach was in turmoil. He was curled on the bed with the jar of prune juice open on the nightstand.

"What are you going to do?" asked Renee. "Dad, this is just so crazy."

"I don't know," he said. "I'm so far into this thing now, there's no reason not to continue. So my plan is to wander a little and see if I can find some blue grouse."

"You're nuts, Dad. You're completely nuts. You ought to go home and rest."

"I don't want to go home and rest. I came over here to hunt."

"You can hunt anytime."

"No, I can't."

"You shouldn't hunt anyway. Go hiking with Chris."

"I like hunting."

"It's awful. It's blood sport."

"Let's change the subject," said Ben.

At the end, and in an easy way, he told Renee that he loved her. He sent his best to his son-in-law and grandson. He told her not to worry about things. He wished her the best of luck with her screenplay. He convinced her he was all right.

Afterward, he curled up but, seized by nausea, hurried to the bathroom. He sat on the toilet passing fluid from his bowels, waves of peristaltic cramping seizing his abdomen. The mango, he thought, had been too acidic. Or perhaps it was the Winesap he'd eaten. The obstruction in his colon was growing, swelling, narrowing the path of ordinary digestion—he was in need of palliative surgery; either that or stop eating altogether. But especially, he should stay away from fruit. He could not afford to eat fruit anymore. His apple days were over.

Ben left his room key by the bathroom sink and set out with his rucksack on his back, his carabiner around his neck, a traveler once more. His respite at the motel lay behind him. It was time to push toward his destination. He trudged down the road with his face to the asphalt, the wind slinging grit and sand. He passed the Custom Apple Packers warehouse, where bins were stacked six high outside and forklifts scurried about. It was the height of harvest season in the river country. The wind would shake loose apples from the trees. In a week the limbs would be bare of fruit. The orchards would look desolate, unsettling.

In five minutes he came to the veterinary clinic: inside a woman held a cat in her lap, while another clutched a small white terrier. A man sat rubbing his beard stubble, yawned, licked his lips, and stretched dramatically, twining his arms above his head.

The receptionist seated behind the counter wore a sleeveless denim shirt with pearl buttons and a necklace made of rhinestones—a woman of thirty or thirty-five who was not afraid to show her shoulders and arms and whose river-country beauty had started to fade, which made her all the more beguiling. "My God," she said. "How nasty."

"Don't ask," said Ben. "I'm here to see Rex. The Brittany, in back there."

He paid for Rex's surgery. She stood, and he took her immediately for a horsewoman, a dusty horsewoman who actually rode, who curried, combed, and lived among horses. It was in the way she moved, the economical fit of her jeans as she transferred a file from one place to another and paper-clipped ledger sheets. He followed her to the recovery room, where they stood looking into Rex's kennel. The dog twitched and shivered in his dreams, and there was something depleted in his sleeping face, something vulnerable. Reaching through the wire mesh of the kennel, Ben lay two fingers on Rex's head. "It's all right," he whispered.

Calmly examining her fingernails, the lengths of her arms sleek and honey brown, the receptionist said that Rex had been awake when she opened the clinic at eight-thirty, had taken water and food readily with every sign of returning health, but now he slept as might be expected, given all he'd been through. Dr. Peterson had examined his stitches, and things were as they might expect. Meat, she added, was good for a black eye. A thawing slab of red meat would draw the bruise right out.

"Listen," said Ben. "I can't take him right now. I have to go up to Wenatchee."

The receptionist slid her fingertips into the rear pockets of her jeans. It caused her shoulders to rotate back and exposed the blue veins branching in them. "Not a problem," she said to Ben. "He can stay with us today."

"I appreciate that."

"It's not a problem."

"I'm heading up there now," said Ben. "I'll be back before you close."

"We're open 'til five, but I'm here 'til five-thirty, so swing by when you get back." She stood with her fists against her hips and again appraised his swollen eye. "Did you see a doctor?" she asked.

"I am a doctor."

"I'm surprised you didn't take a stitch or two. Looks like you could have used it."

He followed her out of the recovery room. She was long-legged and well curved, the small of her back a deep, dark secret, and the shadow of her bra beneath her denim shirt inspired in him not desire but sadness. One of the bra's straps with its little adjuster had slipped into the open and ran over her brown shoulder in a delicate, taut white line.

Ben left and pressed on, past the United Church of Christ, past Verdah's Department Store and the Quincy water tower. The town lay sleepy and leaden, and except for the shade trees raging in the wind there was no other sound. On C Street he passed El Molino Bakery—TORTILLERIA Y PANADERIA it read in the dusty plate-glass window. There were no customers there, and none at Royer's Home Furnishing or any of the other stores. The town seemed uninhabited, yet as he crossed Central, a yard dog came out, a blunt, tough-looking stump of a dog who barked at him threateningly. Ben walked by with one hand on his hat to keep it from flying off.

The bus stop was at the edge of town, out near the Great Northern railroad tracks, beyond which lay a liquid fertilizer plant and a big diatomite processor. Tumbleweed skittered down B Street toward him, and three children huddled underneath a blanket in the backseat of a rusting, dilapidated Buick parked at the Quincy Food Bank. Across the street stood a fence hand-crafted out of stray bits of corrugated roofing metal salvaged or plundered from a refuse yard. Its gate chattered raspingly when the wind rippled through it.

At the bus stop all the planter boxes were empty. There was the red, white, and blue image of a greyhound overhead, a sign advertising WESTERN UNION, another PACKAGE EXPRESS. All were attached to a slatternly storefront, and through its grimy window Ben saw rows of unpainted ceramic figurines—dinosaurs, Indians, Pilgrims, ghosts, tigers, dwarfs, elephants—some of a size to stand in gardens, others more appropriate as mantel knick-knacks or to adorn tabletops and shelves. He pushed his way through the heavy door, pulled off his hat, set his rucksack on the floor, and bought a bus ticket from the clerk at the counter, a woman dressed in purple warm-ups and a patriotic-print nylon windbreaker, who was hard at work with a razor blade, shaving clay from a figurine of Snow White. Broad liver spots mottled her hands. She was neither friendly nor discourteous to him. She expressed no curiosity about his eye, and he guessed she knew, from long experience, that there might be trouble inquiring. She made out his ticket for the Wenatchee run with a slow, troubled inefficiency, as if writing was a trial. Her letters were tall, with shaky, large loops. She paused, adjusted the set of her glasses, then finished writing his ticket. A pottery kiln gave heat beside her. The rest of the room was cold.

"Bus ought to be here in about three minutes," she told Ben, handing him the ticket. "You can wait in the doorway, if you want."

Ben half-turned to take in the displays of angels, baying wolves, Indians on horseback, impressively antlered elk and deer, fringed frontiersmen, and wood fairies. "Did you make all these?" he asked.

"I did," said the woman. "All of them."

"Can you sell them here? Do you get customers?"

"Not really," said the woman. "No."

She took up her razor blade again and went back to cutting small shavings of clay from the crown of Snow White's head. "There's no money in this," she said. "That's the way it goes."

"They're really good," Ben said.

"I've been doing it a long time."

"That's the way to get good at something."

"Well, I don't know what else I'd do. Too much time on my hands."

"It's a good hobby," Ben told her.

The woman looked up. "Hobby," she said. "I hate that word."

"Sorry," said Ben. "Me, too."

They looked at each other warily. The bus pulled up to the curb outside, raising dust in the street. The brakes gave a hydraulic gasp, and the door hinged open noisily. The driver bounded down the steps with theatrical resolve and energy, a crisp, neat man of thirty-five, his hairline prominently receding. He wore wrap-around sunglasses and carried a pair of leather driving gloves. Pushing through the door of the little shop, he swung off his cap, high-stepped and saluted, snapping it low off one eyebrow. He said to Ben, "Hi-dee ho!"

"Hi-dee ho," Ben answered.

"Stow your bag?"

"I'll keep it with me."

"Where to?"

"Just to Wenatchee."

"Trip to the doctor?"

"Maybe, maybe not."

"Boxing practice?"

"Sure. You and me."

The driver whipped off his sunglasses. "Whenever you're ready," he said, grinning. "I'll tag that other eye."

The shop clerk laughed—the twitter of a bird—and her exasperation was evident. "Men," she said, shaking her head, her wrists turned back against her hips. "My God. What is it with men? Whatever will we do with you?"

To Ben's surprise, the bus was crowded. Most of the passengers looked wan, road-weary. Small televisions sat mounted on high, but no one had them on. A wastebasket, clinched by a bungee cord to the back of the driver's seat, was full of hamburger and candy wrappers, cola cans, paper cups—all the refuse of travelers passing tedious, interminable miles in a ruinous highway torpor. A teenager in the front row slept against the window, his mouth gaping wide. A bag of Cheetos lay open beside him, as well as a plastic bottle of Coca-Cola and a gaudy paperback with a submarine on its cover. Behind him sat a black man with his hair in shiny ringlets, eating an Almond Joy. On his knees was a briefcase with a combination lock. He spoke softly with another black man, who wore a Nike Air billed cap and sat with his legs crossed effeminately. In the next row a fat man with headphones clutched a tiny cassette player, drummed his prominent belly, and occasionally stopped beating rhythm to the music to caress his long gray locks. There was a cheerless couple of approximately Ben's age, looking washed-out and diminished by their journey, and even vaguely humiliated, as if riding the Greyhound was beneath them. Farther along was a very young woman traveling with three small children. A baby slept on the seat beside her, and the other two children wriggled, slouched, and slithered about as if underwater—first with their feet running up the backrests, then coiled like fraternizing sea snakes, then curled like small human seals. A coloring book lay on the floor beneath them, crayons scattered about. In the back of the bus rode three young men Ben guessed were apple pickers coming in late for the harvest, migrants following the crop even now, this far into the fall. They were all nut-brown and dusty. One sat tightly wrapped in a blanket, shivering and sweating from a fever, wracked by a sputum-filled cough.

Ben sat down amid these strangers and looked up at the bus driver, who stood before them pulling on his leather gloves, securing them against his fingertips as if he were a gunslinger or a surgeon. YOUR OPERATOR, read a sign above his head. SAFE, RELIABLE, COURTEOUS. The driver made a final adjustment at the thumbs, flicked a lever that shut the door—it gave a soft, hydraulic sigh—then took his palm-sized microphone in hand, working its handset cord. His eyes were still concealed from view behind his sunglasses. "Hey, all right," he said in the voice of a man who considers himself a stand-up comic. "We have a new passenger riding to Wenatchee, and that's good, that's excellent, so why don't we all just sit back now and enjoy the ride, let me do the driving, relax and we'll all go Greyhound together—let's get this show on the road!"

The driver adjusted himself on his throne. He pulled out, rumbled through town, and turned onto the highway. The bus shook as it picked up speed. Its ventilators hummed with a steady insistence. The passengers were jostled and stirred a little, readjusting their legs or heads or turning to look out the windows. Opposite Ben a girl slept with her face beneath her upper arm, a hardbound book propped open beside her, pages down, spine showing. *The Philosophy of Freedom*, by Rudolf Steiner. Subtitled *The Basis for a Modern World Conception*. She wore blue jeans many sizes too large, and when she moved her arm and half-sat up, he saw the ring impaling her nose. A compact girl, her hair tinted green, freckles on her cheeks and nose, fundamentally pleasing to look at. When she noticed that he was staring her way, he pretended to look past her at the orchards along the road, but she straightened up, stared back at him, and asked what happened to his eye.

"I took a baseball bat to it," Ben said, "so I'd have a conversation starter."

"It's gross," said the girl. "I mean, really."

"True, but it's been worth it," Ben said. "I've had interesting conversations."

The girl smiled, and he saw crooked teeth, but their asymmetry was a quiet thing and carried with it a certain charm. Her smile was unguarded and suggested to Ben that she was not afraid to speak to a stranger, an old and battered vagabond. "You look totally wasted," she said to him.

"I am wasted," he agreed. "That's a good way of putting it."

The bus slowed for a crew of linemen unspooling cable at roadside. There were low sloughs of water, aluminum silos, and rows of trellised apples. The sunlight pooled over everything, and the wind blew briskly in the trees. He could hear it whistling through the windows.

In the back of the bus, the sick fruit picker began to cough. A phlegm-filled cough, coarse and rough, so that Ben turned to look at him. The picker wore his blanket like a hood.

"Your book," Ben said, "looks a little profound. Not really typical bus reading, is it? *The Philosophy of Freedom*?"

"I'm just reading it," the girl replied, handing it across the aisle. "It looked kind of interesting."

"*The Philosophy of Freedom*," Ben repeated. "Are you a college student?"

The girl touched a pimple festering on her chin. "I'm working on my master's," she said. "At WSU, on Goethe, his poetry. The author of this book—Rudolf Steiner—edited Goethe's scientific writings. I've gotten kind of sidetracked into him. Have you heard of anthroposophy?"

"I have," said Ben. "I know the term. But I don't know what it means."

"It's from Steiner here," the girl said. "It's a spiritual thing, a philosophy. And I really relate to what he's saying. To the point where I'm thinking of changing my thesis, focusing more on Steiner."

"Why not? It's your thesis, after all."

"It's just kind of late. I'm so far into Goethe."

"You've got your whole life, though."

"I don't know."

"Believe me," said Ben. "You do."

The girl turned fully toward him now. "Where are you from?" she asked.

"Here. Hereabouts. A little north of here."

"You mean you live here?"

"No, I was born here."

"You live somewhere else."

"Over in Seattle."

"Me, too. I grew up over there."

"Two west-siders," Ben said.

There was the chatter of the children in the row behind them and the hacking of the apple picker. The bus dropped toward the Columbia. A steep draw gaped beside the road, throttled by sage and sumac. In the distance ran the railroad tracks and a stark web of power lines against the dry, auburn hills.

"Anthroposophy," Ben said. "Now you've got me curious. You have to tell me about it."

"That guy," the girl said, lowering her voice. "He's been coughing like that for hours now."

"It doesn't sound good," Ben agreed.

"Well, anyway," the girl went on, "it's this spiritual thing, I guess is how to put it. It's like there's this spiritual dimension people just don't see. Because they're so occupied with the material world. And in anthroposophy you try to reach it. You train your consciousness to rise above the physical. It's mostly an intellectual thing. You use your mind, you train yourself."

"That—to me—doesn't sound so unusual. I'm no expert on these matters, but I'd guess most religions would say the same— that it takes mental discipline to find spiritual truth. This anthroposophy, as you describe it, doesn't sound so unique."

"I guess," said the girl. "Yeah, okay. But this was back around the turn of the century. People weren't thinking the same way then. Materialism had no counterbalance, except a few intellectuals like Steiner."

"Tell me," Ben said. "This spiritual realm. This dimension you use your mind to discover. Is it life after death? What most people would call heaven?"

"I can't say," the girl replied. "But no, Steiner doesn't put it like that. Angels playing harps in the clouds, if that's what you mean, no."

"But does he describe it, this spiritual place? In some other way? Not angels?"

"I haven't finished the book yet. It might be in a later chapter."

"I wonder if he will," Ben said. "And I wonder how he'll claim to know."

"You get there with your mind. You don't have to die first."

"So it isn't life after death, then. It's something else, not heaven."

"It's something else," the girl agreed. "Steiner doesn't talk about angels."

"Well, angels wouldn't be bad," said Ben, handing back the book.

She took it and set it on the seat beside her, rested her forearms on her knees, and dangled her loose hands in front of her. "You're a skeptic," she said accusingly. "You're way too analytical."

"Skeptic, yes," Ben said. "I don't accept things easily, I have questions, I'm a skeptic. Analytical—maybe, but no more than Rudolf Steiner. Didn't you say gaining the spiritual realm was a matter of using your mind?"

"Yeah, but it's also spiritual. You have to accept that it isn't just intellectual. You have to believe it's out there."

"What's out there?"

"The other world."

"I'll believe it when I see it."

"That's circular logic."

"Circular is good. It keeps me here."

"If you like going in circles," said the girl. "Okay, fine, you're here."

"Where else would I want to be? Out there with the stars?"

"If you feel that way, death is too scary. But if you believe there's this spiritual realm, you're not afraid to die."

"You're not afraid?"

"No. I'm not."

"That's good. I'm terrified."

"That's because you don't believe in something."

"No," said Ben. "It's because I'm older. Death isn't real at your age."

The girl leaned toward him, animated now. "Yes, it is. I've thought about it. Death is totally real for me. Don't say that. Death is real."

"It's easy to say," Ben said. "But try to imagine it."

"I have," said the girl. "I'm not afraid."

Ben smiled and rubbed the back of his neck. "This is why I smashed my eye," he said. "You see what I mean? It works."

The girl laughed and took her foot in her hands; she was limber in an easy, unathletic way and looked comfortable sitting tailor-fashion. "It's weird," she said, "but you remind me a lot of this doctor I had when I was growing up."

"Did he have a black eye?"

"He had glasses like yours."

"I was a doctor, too," said Ben. "I retired a year and a half ago."

"Well, maybe you should look at that guy back there, then. He's really sick, I think."

"Maybe you're right," Ben agreed. "But what if he speaks only Spanish? I won't know what to say."

"That's all right," the girl said. "I took Spanish as an undergrad."

"Are you pretty good?"

"I read *Don Quixote*."

"What did you think?"

"I loved it," said the girl.

"Quixote's mad."

"Much madness is divinest sense." She admonished him with a forefinger. "That's Emily Dickinson."

"Much madness can just be madness, too. What is it Sancho Panza calls him? Knight of the Mournful Countenance?"

"I wouldn't talk," the girl warned, "with your eye swollen that way."

Ben looked at the picker again. One of his companions looked back at Ben, calmly, showing nothing. He wore a cap emblazoned with the name of a fruit company, DOLE.

"Come on," said the girl. "The guy's messed up. Take a look at him."

Ben felt a surge of affection for her. He wanted her to believe in decency. "If you'll translate," he said.

She stood up with no hesitation. She smiled at him, her hands in her pockets. "Come on," she said.

"You keep yourself back a little. You don't want him breathing on you."

"You look out, too. Wear a mask or something."

"I don't have one."

"Use a handkerchief."

"I'll be fine. I know what to do."

"What's your name, by the way?" said the girl. "Just in case they ask."

Ben told her. Then she gave him hers. "Catherine," she said. "Catherine Donnelly."

She led the way. She stood in the aisle next to the pickers who, up close, looked to Ben like boys younger than seventeen. "*Es doctor,*" said Catherine, pointing at Ben. "*Es médico. Quiere ayudar.*"

All three looked at her, then at Ben, then away again. The one by the window stared out with no expression—a dark boy with a thick pug nose, his black hair swept up and pomaded, a faint mustache above his lip. The sick one shut his eyes with a listless resignation, the blanket draped closely over his head so that only his mouth, nose, and brow showed. The one in the Dole cap removed it from his head and set it gently in his lap. His hair was shorn close to his skull, except for a long black ponytail sprouting from the base of his neck. "*No se preocupe,*" he replied. "*Un resfriado. Nada más.*"

"He thinks it's just a cold," said Catherine. "What do you want me to tell them?"

"Tell him it isn't just a cold," said Ben. "Tell him the coughing is serious. And tell him he doesn't have to pay me."

"*Es muy serio,*" said Catherine. "*Pulmonia. Tuberculoso. Es muy serio. El médico, no va a cobrarle. Es gratis, entiende?*"

There was no answer. The one by the window appraised her with suspicion. "*El médico generoso,*" she said. "*Gratuito. Un hombre de Dios. Un ángel de Dios. Muy bien.*" She touched the sick one's shoulder, lightly. "*Hace cuánto tiempo que usted está así?*" she asked. "I asked him how long he's been sick," she told Ben. "Just to get things started."

"That's good," said Ben. "Keep it going."

The sick boy didn't answer. Ben looked up the aisle of the bus. A number of the passengers had turned around and were watching him and Catherine. The driver watched through his rearview mirror. They were passing along the river now, not far from the place where Ben had been born. Orchards stretched away north and south. The poplars stood tall in the wind.

Catherine sat down across the aisle. Ben could see the boy better now. His eyes were bloodshot, his eyelids crusted, his cheeks gleamed with sweat.

"Catherine," the girl said, pointing at herself. Then she put a hand on Ben's arm. *"Este es el Doctor Ben Givens. No habla mucho español. Comprende?"*

There was no answer. They didn't look at her. The one with the Dole cap in his lap began to finger its bill a little and pulled on his ponytail. The one with the pomaded hair looked studiously out his window. The sick boy began to cough again. He leaned forward and gagged.

"Qué le ocurre?" said Catherine. *"Hace cuánto tiempo que está usted así?"*

"No me siento bien," said the boy. *"Estoy enfermo. Tengo escalofríos. Tengo fiebre. Me duele la cabeza y la espalda y todo el cuerpo. Me cuesta respirar. Pero no quiero un doctor. Muchas gracias."*

"He's really sick," said Catherine. "He says he's got a chill and a fever and his head and back hurt a lot. Plus, it's hard for him to breathe. But he doesn't want a doctor."

"Tell him he doesn't have to pay," said Ben. "Tell him we won't ask to see papers. We won't even ask his name."

Catherine translated these things. They all three looked at Ben again. *"Un ángel de Dios,"* she assured them again. *"Un buen hombre. No es nada como para preocuparse. Un médico de Dios."*

The boy with the Dole cap studied her face, then began to speak in a whisper. Catherine leaned toward him.

Ben recognized place-names: Boardman and Milton-Freewater, Pasco and Walla Walla. The boy spoke evenly, rapidly, until

Catherine stopped him with the palm of her hand. "It's his brother," she said. "The sick one's his brother. He hasn't worked in three weeks. It started out he had a cold. Anyway, they thought it was a cold. They bought him some aspirin in Walla Walla. Still, he's always coughing and sweating. He can't work, he's always tired, he gets hot, his body aches. They've been all over looking for work. Pasco, Milton-Freewater."

"The coughing," asked Ben. "Does it hurt?"

She translated. *"Sí,"* said the boy. *"Me duele mucho el pecho."* He patted his chest. *"Aquí."*

"Ask him if he's coughed up blood. Even just a little. Ask him."

She did. The travelers conferred among themselves. The answer was no, no blood, none anyone could recall.

Ben massaged his forehead. The night sweats in particular interested him. He guessed it was a case of tuberculosis, though he could not rule out pneumonia, or coccidioidomycosis, or a host of other possibilities.

He stared out the window. They were passing a dirt yard, carved from bench land, where a thousand cows thronged a feed trough, yellow tags stapled to their ears. Beyond was the old Fisk orchard, which was now Bartlett pears. Then came his family's old orchard. The house had been torn down and replaced. The Lombardy poplars were stately sentinels. In the south orchard, the ladders were up. The bins stood between the rows. He could see someone picking in the wind.

"That's where I was raised," he told Catherine. "That was our orchard, there."

"Really great," she answered. "But this guy's kind of suffering. You can't just look out the window."

Ben sighed. "I was a heart surgeon," he said. "I'm sort of shooting in the dark here."

"Well, keep shooting," Catherine said. "What should we ask them next?"

"Ask them what kind of work they've been doing."

"What's that got to do with anything?"

"Maybe he ingested a pesticide, or maybe they've been working around barnyard animals. I don't know, just ask."

She asked them about the nature of their work. The one with the ponytail answered at length. Asparagus at first, for almost four weeks. Then, in June, no work for a while. They lived at the bottom of an onion field, waiting. In July, three weeks of sweet onions. They went into Oregon for raspberries. Afterward, no work again. Then, finally, hoeing potatoes. They waited more. They picked apples near Yakima. Now they were heading north.

"De dónde es usted?" asked Catherine. *"Sonora? Chihuahua? Jalisco?"*

The one by the window answered. *"Tejas,"* he said. *"Somos de Tejas."*

"De qué parte de Tejas es usted?"

There was no answer. The boy shrugged and looked out his window. "He says they're from Texas," said Catherine. "But he can't say what part of Texas, or maybe he didn't understand me."

"They're here without green cards," Ben said. "They're afraid they're going to be deported. Tell them again we're not the police. We're not going to turn them in—stress that. Promise them or something."

Catherine turned again to the travellers. *"No somos policía,"* she said. *"Les prometo. No se preocupen."*

There was no answer from the one by the window, but the one with the Dole hat in his lap faced her earnestly.

"Ask them," said Ben. "Before they came here. Was anyone sick at home?"

No, none had been sick at home, not especially.

"What about in their travels?" asked Ben. "Have they met others sick like him? Anywhere? Picking raspberries in Oregon? Somewhere? Hoeing potatoes?"

Yes, there had been others ill. But there were always a few ill workers in the fields. Colds, fevers, it was to be expected. Nothing that stood out.

"Sprays," said Ben. "Pesticides. Chemical fertilizers."

"Líquido para rociar," Catherine tried. *"Cebolla. Papas. Espárragos. En la hacienda . . . abono para la tierra.* I don't know. *Químicos. Respiraba quími-cos, acaso?"*

The one by the window seemed to understand. In animated fashion, he explained it to the others. They nodded in their understanding. But no, they said, there had been no chemicals, none that they could recollect.

"All right," said Ben. "What about skin rashes? Ask him about his skin."

There had been no rashes, no stiff, sore neck, no swollen throat. He had no lumps in his neck or armpits. He didn't smoke cigarettes and never had. He did not eat much, but in the last few days he'd had refried beans, a ham sandwich with salsa and onion, a stew of chicken backs, tortillas. He'd had coffee with sugar and milk that morning, some Kool-Aid and a Pepsi Cola. As much water as he could drink. Yes, they drank irrigation water at first. No, they didn't often wash their hands. Yes, they had all felt ill at times, mildly ill, from traveling. But the sick one had really begun to suffer about three weeks ago. He began to ache in his muscles and joints and was light-headed in the fields. He felt sleepy most of the time. Now he couldn't keep from coughing, especially in the night hours. They didn't know what to do with him.

"This is a mystery," Ben said. "If I had to guess, I'd say TB, possible TB versus pneumonia. But there are all kinds of viruses around out here, fungal infections, bacterial diseases, any number of things."

"Still," said Catherine. "We have to do something."

"He needs care," Ben told her. "He needs a clinic or a hospital. Myself, I can't make a diagnosis, much less offer treatment.

I'm out here on this bus without anything—I don't even have a stethoscope. Tell him this is serious. Tell him he should go to the hospital as soon as we reach Wenatchee."

"Now wait a second," said Catherine. "If he goes to a hospital, they'll ask for papers, won't they? Identification. A visa or something. And then he'll maybe get kicked out of the country. We can't do that to him."

"Look," said Ben. "He's seriously ill. If he doesn't get some help soon, he's going to get even worse than he is. He could even die from it."

"We promised him," said Catherine. "We promised he wouldn't get deported."

"He won't get deported," said Ben. "The main thing is, he needs treatment right away. That's all there is to it. A hospital. As soon as we get off the bus."

"You have to help him from outside the system."

"There isn't any help outside the system."

"Then what'll we do?" asked Catherine.

The boy threw another coughing fit, which brought her exhortations to a halt. He lurched forward spasmodically, whipping his head against the seat back before him, and brought up a bolus of blood-tinged sputum that spattered his blanket, red.

It was as though a demon had seized his chest. He wheezed and labored to move air through his lungs. His brother put a hand around his shoulder. *"Ángelito,"* he said. *"Quédate tranquilo. Ya va a pasar. Dios nos va a ayudar."*

"What did he say?" Ben asked.

"He said God will help them."

TEN

The bus went past the Rock Island Dam, a silicon plant, and an aluminum smelter, and on the east side of the road a cherry orchard barren in this season. The apple orchards, though, were laden heavily, the pickers filling their canvas bags, the tractors busy pulling bins, the apples waiting at pull-outs and sidings, the branch props stacked in the crooks of trees, and everywhere on the road to Wenatchee the haul trucks ran fully loaded. Along the river course the wind blew downstream: the flag on the basalt island just south of Hurst Landing stood stiffly battered by it. The river here was a frothing lake with a few fall whitecaps blown up like tufts of scudding ocean foam.

The bus passed the Rock Island Hydro Park with its ball fields silent this time of year and its stark NO SWIMMING signs. It passed a trailer park laid out formally above the river. Across the water lay South Wenatchee with its dingy railroad freight yard, poplar trees, and more mobile homes. The rail yard had once been thronged by apples, but now it was desolate and little used, its buildings skeletal. Fruit pickers squatted in makeshift camps. One had a warming fire sparking in the wind. Children sat by the river's edge.

The bus crossed the bridge to Mission Street and came into Wenatchee. Some of the passengers began to stir and gather their belongings. It was a prosperous town—more than twenty thousand people—the preeminent city of the apple country. It sat in a bowl between bleached hills that rose a thousand feet above the river. To the east they were colored in auburns and tans, their summits and ridges forming the rim of the vast wheat plateau. To the north the hills fell steeply to the river in rippling, undulant, shadowed draws, and the river ran with the sun on it, its sinuous surface broken by bridges and by the dams at Rock Island and Rocky Reach. Everywhere on the edges of town were orchards ascending into arid heights, including the Wenatchee Pinnacles, summits Ben had scaled as a boy—Castle Rock, Squaw Saddle, and Old Butte, sun-beaten peaks of eroding basalt, tall spires against the skyline. The outlying neighborhoods were tidy and quiet, the homes with deep porches and sheltering willows, but downtown were stoplights in inordinate number, hamburger and taco joints, crowded parking lots and strip malls. The streets ran wide, two lanes in each direction. There were more trucks than passenger cars. Wenatchee hummed with fast-moving vehicles, with tractor-trailers, four-wheel-drive cars, and late-model crew-cab pickup trucks riding high above the asphalt. On the sidewalks some men wore cowboy hats, shambling along with their hands in their pockets or cupping cigarettes against the wind; they were ranchers of the sort Ben remembered from childhood, basin men with leathery faces, pearl-button shirts, cowboy boots, and emaciated backsides.

At First Street the bus careened into a covered loading bay with a broken skylight in its high roof. The driver announced a fifteen-minute pause and suggested that passengers use the station bathroom, buy coffee at Cecil's Cafe, or simply stretch their legs outside before taking to the westward road again at 2:55 P.M. He swung open the cargo compartment as the passengers filed off. The apple pickers put their heads together and spoke in a soft, rapid Spanish. From under their seats they pulled grocery bags overstuffed with their belongings. The sick one, Angel, waited wrapped in his blanket, his mouth open, sweating. His brother slipped his Dole cap on, adjusting its bill to throw a shadow across his eyes. *"Donde estamos?"* he asked.

"Wenatchee," answered Catherine Donnelly. "Wenatchee, Washington."

"Guanache," he repeated. *"Cuándo vamos a llegar a Orondo?"*

"Este bus no va a Orondo. Usted tiene que tomar otro bus para ir a Orondo. Es necesario bajarse aquí y cambiar de bus."

"Ho-kay, muchas gracias," the picker said, rose and took up his bags. The one by the window stood up, too. They helped Angel to his feet.

"They say they're going to Orondo," said Catherine. "What do you think we should tell them?"

"Ask them why they're going up there. Ask them about Orondo."

"Tienen ustedes trabajo alli?"

"Si. Acaso."

"Cosechando manzanas?"

"Si."

"Y su hermano? No puede trabajar. Necesita ir al hospital."

"No. El está bien. Por favor, no se preocupe."

"He says," said Catherine, "that in Orondo they have a job. They're going up to Orondo to pick apples. He insists Angel is doing fine. We shouldn't worry about him."

Ben looked at Angel now, directly into his eyes. *"No hos-pi-tole,"* he said to him. *"Muerte, sí? Comprende, Angel? No hos-pi-tole, muerte."*

Angel, in answer, drew his blanket closer and turned his bloodshot eyes to the floor.

They filed off the bus with the other passengers, the fruit pickers with their plastic bags, Catherine with her sunglasses on, Angel shrouded in his stained blanket, Ben with his rucksack on his shoulder. The wind blew loud, a sudden whirlwind hurling dust down the loading bay. The driver stood with his back to it, clutching his cap to the top of his head, his pant legs billowing and his coat flailing, so that he looked as if he might blow away. A garbage pail fell over and rolled toward Chelan Street, refuse spilling onto the ground—cans, bottles, candy wrappers—and they, too, were wind-whipped north and up against the brick facade of the Labor Union Temple.

"El remolino," said one of the pickers. *"El viento del Diablo."*

"I'm calling 911," said Ben. "They'll take Angel to the hospital here, and that'll be the end of that."

"I don't know," said Catherine. "I'm back on the bus in fifteen minutes and heading over the mountains."

"You are?" said Ben. "I didn't know that."

"I just hope you're doing the right thing and all. I hope you don't get him deported."

"Better deported than dead, you know."

"That's true," said Catherine.

In the station, a girl in a pink, oversized shirt worked the joystick of a video game. A map of the country displayed Greyhound's routes as an arterial system of blue lines. Beside the map was a lost-children poster; beneath it, at the corner of the counter, sat a box of baggage tags and a stack of Gospel tracts. There was a ceiling fan, inert and dusty, a soft-drink machine, and three telephone booths, two with the phones ripped out. A hand-scrawled sign was taped to the bathroom door, NO BEER: THIS IS NOT A TAV-

ERN, and at the fountain counter—Cecil's Cafe—the stools were bolted to the floor. From behind the ticket and baggage desk, feeble radio strains could be heard, a melody Ben faintly recognized, a homely ballad, a love-gone-wrong song, a country lament from the fifties.

Angel collapsed on a wooden bench, coughing incessantly. His brother put a hand around his shoulders and spoke softly in his ear.

Ben called the emergency operator. He said he was a doctor traveling on the Greyhound, had come across a young man seriously ill, and was now in the bus station at First and Chelan. In his opinion as a thoracic surgeon, the situation was an emergency, the young man in question had coughed up blood and needed immediate assistance. The operator dispatched an ambulance and kept Ben standing by on the line to answer plodding questions: Ben's name, the sick person's name, Ben's address, more about the sick person's symptoms, more about Ben's credentials as a doctor, more about the Quincy bus ride. In three minutes, an ambulance pulled in, lurching to a halt in the loading bay. "They're here," said Ben, and hung up.

Everyone in the station gave their attention to the ambulance, a spectacle to break up the boredom. Ben raised a hand at the emergency technicians as they came through the door with their medical bags. "Over here," he called. "Right here."

They were stalwart-looking, both of them, in blue uniforms and polished shoes. Their name tags read COLEMAN and ODLE. Coleman stood as tall as Ben, at least six-foot-four. Odle was short, with tight curls at his brow and thick, veiny forearms. Ben pointed to Angel and said he suspected tuberculosis. The boy had expelled a bloody bolus and needed a workup immediately, and good hospital care. Coleman, listening, set his medical bag down. "What happened to your eye?" he asked.

"Car accident," Ben said.

"Looks like you should have had it stitched," said Coleman. "It's going to leave a scar."

"The boy," said Ben. "Come on now."

The apple pickers whispered among themselves, their bags against their legs. Catherine squatted on the floor with them, as if she were a picker herself. "*No se preocupe,*" she said. "*No es la policía. Les prometo.*"

Angel's brother replied, at length, eyeing the EMTs.

"They don't have money for a hospital," said Catherine, coming across the room. "He says he won't let Angel go. He's Angel's brother, he can't let him go. He feels responsible for him."

"Tell him they don't have to pay," said Ben. "Tell them it'll all be taken care of. It won't cost them a dime."

"But they do have to pay," said Coleman. "We'd better be clear about it."

"No, they don't," Ben said. "There's federal assistance for this. But anyway, that's irrelevant. The important point is to get him treatment." He put a hand on Catherine's arm. "Just tell them they don't have to pay anything, that's all they need to know."

Coleman shook his head emphatically. "There's no federal assistance for wetbacks," he said. "I've been through this before."

"Now wait," Odle countered. "That isn't really right, is it? The hospital can apply for welfare assistance with the Emergency Medical Office."

"Not for these guys," Coleman said. "These guys are wet, it's obvious. They don't have permission to be in the country. Like I said, I've been through this."

"They still get assistance," said Odle.

"All right, forget it," Coleman said, snatching up his medical bag. "Fine with me. Let's go."

The technicians slipped on filter masks and pulled on rubber gloves. Odle eased Angel down against the bench, put a thermometer in his mouth, and took a blood-pressure reading and a pulse while Coleman wheeled in a chrome gurney. The passengers in the station watched in silence. "The bus for Seattle waits for no man," the driver announced from the doorway. "Let's wish this fellow the best of luck and hit the westbound highway."

Catherine anchored her hair behind her ear and began to hop in place. "Hey," she said. "This looks good. You think he's going to get better?"

"He should," said Ben. "With antibiotics. If he has what I think he has."

"Just so they don't get deported or something."

"You really ought to stop worrying about that."

"All right," Catherine sighed. "I guess I better go. It was nice meeting you and everything. Later on, I guess."

She turned to the boy with the long black ponytail, the brother of Angel. "*Hasta luego,*" she said. She nodded at the other boy, the one with the pug nose and pomaded hair, and he nodded back at her. *"Angel,"* she called. *"Buena suerte. Ahora vas a mejorarte."* Angel smiled weakly.

"What did you say?" Ben asked.

"I told him he's going to get better."

"You'd better catch your bus now."

"Okay," said Catherine. "Later on."

She left then, without looking back, her jeans hems scraping the ground. The driver hopped onboard behind her. The door closed, the air brakes gasped, and the bus pulled out of its covered bay, described a wide and steady arc, and disappeared into the west.

Angel's brother got in the ambulance, but despite Ben's polite entreaties, Coleman refused to take the other boy. There was no legal place for him to ride, they couldn't stow him in the back with Angel, and besides the hospital was on Fuller Street, he could walk it in less than an hour. The ambulance pulled out with Angel and his brother, and the third boy watched it go. He stood in the loading bay with his plastic bags, his collar turned against the cold. To Ben, the cold seemed to rise from within. He felt sick to his stomach, feeble, and listless. The wind had subsided, the sun was out, the bay stood empty of passengers; there was only the boy with the pomaded hair standing there, scratching his chin. Ben watched him and then, sighing, limped back into the bus station. He slumped on a bench, rubbed his side, and watched the boy beyond the window, who seemed content to stare down the bay where the ambulance had disappeared. After some time, the boy trudged through the door and stood by the window with his bags beside him. He didn't look at Ben.

"*No hablo español,*" said Ben. "*Habla* you *inglés?*"

"*No,*" said the boy. "*No inglés.*"

"*No inglés,*" Ben said. "That makes things difficult."

They watched each other. The boy shrugged. He was short and sturdy, with a smoky complexion. "*Hos-pi-tole,*" Ben said. "Your *amigos* went to the *hos-pi-tole.* Do you think you might want to go there?"

"*No hospital.* Apples. *Trabajo.*" The boy's fingers plucked invisible apples, placing each in an invisible picking bag belted at his waist. "*Manzanas,*" he said. "*Trabajo.*"

He swiped his brow in stylized fashion, then flicked his wrist toward the bus-station floor, as though flinging sweat away. "*Trabajo, trabajo.*" He tapped at his chest. "*Quiero trabajar.* Apples."

"Okay," said Ben.

They went out into the loading bay and walked down First Street with the wind at their backs, the boy trailing slightly behind as if in deference to the gringo doctor, Ben limping and laboring beneath his rucksack, stopping twice to lean against streetlamps while the boy waited patiently. In the bookstore on Wenatchee Avenue, Ben bought a copy of *Spanish for Travelers* and an English-Spanish dictionary. Then he and the boy sat down on the sidewalk, their traveling gear against their legs, while Ben leafed through the books. Through his one good eye, the print wavered, but he found the word *to harvest.* "*Cosechar manzanas?*" he asked the boy. "Is that what you want to do?"

"*Si,*" said the boy. "*Manzanas.*"

"*Cosechar manzanas,*" Ben repeated. "*Muy bien.* Okay."

He pawed through the gear in his rucksack carefully until he found the map of Chelan County rolled up in its cardboard tube. Then he unfurled it against the sidewalk, where the boy held two of its corners down, and pointed out the town of Wenatchee— "*aquí*" he said, "Wenatchee, *aquí*"—and with a finger Ben followed Highway 2 until it reached Orondo. "Orondo," he said. "*Amigos?*"

"*No le comprendo a usted,*" the boy answered. "*Orondo? Sí? Orondo?*"

"Do you want to go there? *Cosechar manzanas in Orondo? Amigos* in Orondo?"

"*No,*" said the boy. "*No amigos aquí.*" He tapped his chest, his breastbone. "*Solo,*" he said. "*No amigos aquí. Solo, comprende usted?*"

"*Comprende,*" said Ben. "Me too."

He sat for a moment looking at the boy's shoes—battered black chukkas coming apart at the welts, probably salvaged from a Dumpster. The boy's odyssey, clearly, had been much longer than Ben's brief trip across the apple country. He was dusty, sun-beaten, and smelled of earth; his plastic bags were tattered. He had probably traveled a thousand miles, sleeping under trees and bridges, out in the open country. Ben paged through his dictionary again, looking for the right words. "*Hambre,*" he said, after some time.

"*Hambriento. Restaurante. Alimento.* Something like that. Let's go eat, okay?"

They went to a restaurant on Wenatchee Avenue, mostly empty at that hour of the day, a close place smelling of cigarettes. Ben ordered tea for himself and a T-bone steak with fried potatoes for the boy, and while the boy ate a roll and butter, Ben struggled with his Spanish books and tossed garbled questions across the table. The boy's name was Emilio—he offered only that, no surname. He was not a brother to the other two, whom he'd met picking pears near Yakima. The others knew of apple-picking work, so Emilio had accompanied them northward. Now they were gone, but he still wanted to work. In Orondo, somewhere else, anywhere.

His plate of steak and potatoes arrived, and Emilio pondered it. "*Muchas gracias, señor,*" he said, then rained salt and pepper over the potatoes, steak, and boiled green beans. He ate neatly, unhurried, using his knife deftly. Scratches—white streaks—crossed the backs of his hands. His fingers were thick and callused, blunt and cracked at the nails.

Ben sipped his tea and asked no more questions. The hardship of communicating allowed for silence, as did the boy's reserve. Ben didn't ask Emilio, though he wondered, how he'd come to be alone, how he happened to be separated from his family, if he had any family to speak of. What sort of world he'd left behind, what sort of life he'd lived until now, how it felt to be rootless and adrift, always in pursuit of work, unable to speak the language. These things were beyond telling, certainly beyond Ben's *Spanish for Travelers*, since the life of the boy—of anyone—was a life, in the end, and no mere story to be told across the table. The essentials could not be culled from the rest without divesting both of certain meanings.

As he watched Emilio at work on his food, cutting and eating with instinctive dignity, Ben accepted that the boy wouldn't trade his story for a meal. It was really a desirable thing in a companion, this reticence, this taut reserve, because if it meant no answers, it also meant no questions. The boy had not used his talents as a mime—as a wielder of gesture, expression, and signs—to interrogate Ben about his black eye, as if to suggest that Ben, too, was entitled to his secrets. So if Emilio preferred to have no story, Ben was happy to oblige. Just a boy eating a lucky meal, a thousand miles from home.

Ben bought him a piece of apple pie a la mode and a second glass of milk. Then he went to the phone booth by the rest rooms and called the Job Services Office. "Apple-picking work," he told the receptionist, and she transferred his call to a job specialist, who introduced himself as Hector Martinez. Yes, there were jobs in agricultural labor, but these were all of short duration, the apple harvest was nearly over, the work would be done in days. "Where?" said Ben. "Where do I go?" "That depends," answered Martinez. "Where are you right now?"

"I'm at a phone booth here in Wenatchee. Wenatchee Avenue."

"Okay," Hector Martinez said, in the tone of a public servant trained to be empathetic, within limits. "Have you been into our office before, or have you registered with us recently, or did we refer you in the last twelve months or anything like that?"

"No," said Ben. "None of the above."

"Okay," said Martinez. "Just let me get to the right screen on my computer and . . . okay, your name."

"Larry Miller," Ben told him. "L, A, double R, Y. Miller as in the beer."

"As in Miller beer, okay. Your social security number?"

Ben made one up. He invented a date of birth, too, and an address and telephone number. The act of formulating a false identity with such ease and authority made him feel pleased with himself. "A few years back I was out here," he said. "Up by

Malaga, the Wolfhound Orchard. Something like that. Wolfhound."

"Wolfhound Orchard," said Martinez. "Let me check my job
list."

"I'd like to get there again, if I could. It was out of Malaga, I
think."

"Wolfhound Orchard. It's not a problem. They have some positions. We can do you a referral."

"I appreciate that," said Ben.

When he was done on the phone, he limped back to the table
and nodded at Emilio. *"Trabajo,"* he said. *"Manzanas. Trabajo.* There's
work for you *en* Malaga." He dug out his map of Chelan County,
unfurled it across the table, and traced for the boy the route to
Malaga, down the west side of the Columbia on the Malaga-Alcoa
Highway. *"Cosechar manzanas,"* he said. *"Manzanas* to pick, *aquí."*

They walked up Wenatchee Avenue, passed Kim's Tae Kwan
Do School, the Central Washington Water office, assorted furniture and auto parts stores, a tavern called Brews And Cues. Outside the Valley Pawn Shop, Ben slung his rucksack onto the
sidewalk and leaned over a newspaper vending machine with his
head propped against his forearm. The urge to vomit swelled and
subsided while he rubbed his side in that stooped posture and
gradually came to feel up to the task of pushing forward once
more. But the boy reached for the rucksack when Ben did, and
looked at him inquiringly. *"Muchas gracias,"* Ben said, putting a
hand on his shoulder. *"De nada,"* the boy answered.

They continued up the avenue, Emilio hauling both their bags,
Ben shivering in his tin-cloth coat, until they came to the U-Save
Auto Rental. The clerk eyed them suspiciously—an old man with
a battered eye, at his side a dust-bitten apple picker, shoes split
open at the toes, loaded down like a hobo. She could not conceal
her disdain, but she rented them a half-ton Ford for thirty-seven
dollars a day with a reminder to return it full, lest there be a sur-

charge for gasoline they wouldn't feel happy about. When she dropped the keys into Ben's hands, she made certain not to touch him. "We expect the truck back clean," she said. "I don't know what you're planning with it, but we expect to get it back clean."

"Medical waste," Ben said. "Plus landfill runs for a rendering plant, and some organic fertilizer."

The woman blanched and touched her hair with the tips of her painted fingers. "Well, I don't know," she said.

It was a new truck with cloth seats and big padded armrests, its cab done up in royal maroon, and as they drove down Wenatchee Avenue, luxuriating in the motor's smooth silence, Emilio tried the power window. He worked it down a few inches at a time, then up until it sealed out the road noise. Next he worked the power locks and felt the nap of the seat. "Try the radio," Ben suggested. "*Música,* or something like that." He turned it on and searched the channels until he found a station broadcasting in Spanish. "*Aquí,*" he said. "Okay?"

"Okay," the boy said. "*Gracias.*"

"*De nada,*" said Ben. "*Está bien.*"

They came to the river bridge but didn't cross, and passed into South Wenatchee. There was laundry hung to dry in the wind, a car without wheels on jacks in a yard, a tractor-trailer parked in front of a dilapidated two-story warehouse. The road ran high above the old rail yard and looked down onto the decrepit roundhouse, icehouse, and sand house, the turntable with weeds growing through it, abandoned boxcars of the old Great Northern and Burlington lines, and a web of iron tracks. The Appleyard Terminal Ben remembered from long ago was empty of apples now. Glass insulators still decorated the power stanchion cross beams. In a corner of the yard sat dry, weathered bins stacked six and seven high. The paint had peeled in scabrous blisters, and the plywood beneath had been bleached by the sun to a washed and pale gray.

They passed the Shaw Orchard and the Atwood Orchard—full bins waited at the sidings there—and came to the Stemilt Creek–West Malaga cutoff, where Ben paused at roadside, idling, to consider the way to Joe Miller Road. The country before him lay dense with fruit trees, all the way to Jump-Off Ridge, the roads winding among canyons and draws and up through the manicured Stemilt Hill orchards, which looked as graceful as the plain of the Po, as undulant as the vineyards of the Apennines. A listless pond sat in the shade of Russian olives where Stemilt Creek ran out of the mountains. A brace of widgeon milled on the far shore, feeding in the interstices of marsh weed.

"Madre y padre hacienda," Ben said, pointing east and south across the river. "I grew up right over there."

"Bien," said Emilio, and smiled.

They drove up into the Stemilt Hills, the orchards large and well kept, the hills above Malaga that had once been in grapes, English walnuts, and pears. They gained a thousand feet until they were high above the river and traversing switchbacks and tight-loop turns through orchards cut into the sides of hills; past a tarp encampment of fruit pickers and a few worn trailers along a creek; past a row of pickers' cabins; past a silent cherry-packing shed tucked under a turn in the road; up to the crest of Stemilt Hill, where the wind blew hard across cemetery stones and beat against the windows of the Grange Hall. Here the view gave out to the east, a long vista over the tops of trees and beyond the river to the wheat plateau, and all down the hill were pickers on their ladders, working in the apples. *"Manzanas,"* Ben said to Emilio. *"Aquí, manzanas. Cosechar manzanas aquí."*

Emilio nodded and scratched his head. *"Está muy bien,"* he said.

Ben pulled over at the community church and sat with the engine idling. He didn't feel he could continue. His side felt as if it might burst, and it was painful merely to sit upright.

"I have to get out for a few minutes," he said. "*Un momento, Emilio*. Okay?"

He stumbled out into the cherry trees behind the Stemilt Hill Community Church and lay in the grass battling the urge to vomit and slowly rubbing his side. In this position, curiously, his nausea felt endurable. He curled up around his tumor and suspended it there at the heart of his viscera as gently as he could. He understood that the cancer in his gut had a mass and density, a friction and gravity. A dark stone weighing in among his organs, a rotten pit nestled in his flesh. The cause of his illness was something tangible: a festering object in the mucosa of his colon, penetrating through the muscle wall but also narrowing the bowel lumen, causing serious constipation. He was headed for perforation, with its accompanying infection and septic death; his colon would be split open like a banana skin, its contents would spill into his abdomen—his watery excrement, his meager diarrhea, curdling and sloshing between his organs.

There was a quiet, humble fluttering—small birds on distant limbs. There was the pale heat of the sun against his cheek, the smell of orchard grass. Ben became aware of his breathing, and of the steady rhythm of his heart. He became aware that he wanted to live, to have and hold such things as a cherry orchard in midautumn in river country. It was this world he wanted and no other. There was no sweeter world he knew of.

Despite himself, he vomited, slouched on his hands and knees. Stomach acid burned hot in his throat. His nostrils stung, and he panted heavily, at the mercy of his body. The pits of cherries were everywhere. Fallen leaves stirred in the wind.

On Joe Miller Road, Ben slowed to a crawl to pass by sidings bristling with apples, the trees flowing down and out across the hills, the rungs of ladders disappearing among leaves, the bins laid out between the shaded rows, the tractors hauling bins to the sidings. In some places, at the edge of the trees, pickers rested in groups of three or four, but mostly they worked with dogged persistence, with the patient madness of harvest. It was the time of year when the silence of the orchards was subsumed by the voices of pickers. Hung from limbs were coats and hats; propped between branches were canteens and bottles. In the orchard grass the dogs lay about; children sprawled in sunlight, dreaming; men and women stood high in their ladders, reaching into the tops of trees, leaving limbs bereft of fruit. They pulled the branch props one by one and descended rungs with their bags bursting-full, easing the apples into the bins for fear of bruising them.

Ben asked a woman at her mailbox if this was the way to the Wolfhound Orchard, then drove another mile south. On the west side of the road was the Hardens' mailbox, just before a siding thronged with bins, two men laying hands on the fruit. A tractor emerged from between the trees to set another bin in place, and a forklift loaded a truck. Ben pulled over and, though the hour was late, slid his sunglasses on. He felt ridiculous, doing it. He felt he must look like a blind man, wearing sunglasses at dusk, in October, with the sun behind the hills. But one of these workers—the tractor driver, say, or the man on the forklift—might be the night rider who had stolen his shotgun, the thief Ben had come looking for, yet whose face he had never seen. This William Harden who ran his wolfhounds after coyotes in the moonlight. Harden would remember the battered eye, Ben's signature feature of late, Ben's calling card in the world.

He recognized his entire day as a kind of protracted stall. Things had gone awry, aslant, but now he was back on course. There was no turning back now, nothing to lose that wasn't lost. What could Harden do to him? In the morning, when he had rested enough to gain the strength, he would find Harden and take his gun back.

Ben parked the rented truck around a bend and stepped into Joe Miller Road, one arm wrapped across his gut. Emilio emerged from the truck, too, and hauled out their traveling gear. Ben paused to button his jacket and to take in the color of the sky in the west, which had gone purple now. The shadows were deepening across the hills. The timbre of the light was quieting. The orchards that had looked so inviting in the sun were sullen now in the desert gloaming. The world lay altered by the imminence of night, as though a curtain was dropping over it. Yet out on the low rim of the western horizon the sun streamed into the high eastern sky, which held its unearthly light.

ELEVEN

The contractor at the Wolfhound Orchard, a man named Lyle
Parmenter, squatted with his clipboard and a carpenter's pencil,
filling in the blanks on a Department of Justice Employment El-
igibility form. He pondered Emilio's employment card, tattered
and worn along its edges and bearing the name Raul Ramirez; he
examined Ben's Washington State driver's license and social security card. Parmenter eyed Ben's photograph, scratched his forehead, scrutinized Ben—who wore dark glasses at the hour of
dusk—then considered the license once more. "There were
Givens," he said, "other side of the river. You related to them?"

"No," said Ben. "I'm not."

"You ever picked apples?"

"I have, yes."

"Where at?"

"All over. You name it."

"But you're from t'other side of the mountains."

"I can still pick," said Ben.

Parmenter tapped his nose with the pencil. He was a red-skinned man with pointed sideburns and a chapped, cross-hatched neck. "This is a young man's work," he said. "It's harder than it looks."

"I'm old for picking, that's true," said Ben. "But you can figure at my age I know better than most how to do it right."

Parmenter seemed to take this as a challenge. "We'll see about that," he replied. He turned to size up Emilio. "You speak English, señor?"

"No," answered Ben. "He doesn't."

"Raul Ramirez," Parmenter read. "Does he know what he's doing with apples?"

"Yes," said Ben. "He's good at it."

"How do you know?"

"I've seen Raul pick."

"Where was that?"

"In Yakima."

"Well, I don't know how they do it down there, but here I don't want any broken branches or crashing around with the ladders. And I want people handling the fruit gentle. You start bird-dogging or bottoming trees, I'll pull you off your ladder fast and send you down the road."

"Understood," Ben answered.

"We've got to be this way," said Parmenter. "Better to make it clear beforehand than have trouble because we didn't."

"I'd do the same," Ben assured him.

Parmenter handed Ben the clipboard and showed him where to sign. "It's late for them sunglasses, isn't it?" he asked. "There's not much light anymore."

"I've got cataracts," Ben answered. "In both eyes."

Ben and Emilio were passed into the hands of a field boss introduced as Sanchez, who was told to show them to the pickers' camp. A small, crisp man in cowboy boots, Sanchez wore a rawhide belt with a silver buckle embossed to depict a bucking bronc. He wore a lightweight cowboy hat high on his bronzed smooth forehead. The hair at his neck was closely cropped. His breath smelled of menthol cough drops.

Ben, walking, took off his sunglasses, but when he went to tuck them in his pocket, they tumbled to the ground. Emilio picked them up for him, and they hiked on toward the pickers' camp. "Wolfhound Orchard," Ben said to Sanchez. "That's a peculiar name."

Sanchez nodded, inaccessible. He was quiet in a perturbing way and would not look at Ben's face.

"Are there wolfhounds out here or something?" prodded Ben. "Or did they just make it up?"

"There are wolfhounds," Sanchez answered.

"A lot of them? A pack or something?"

"Yes," said Sanchez. "Twelve."

"Twelve hounds," Ben said. "You'd think a guy with an orchard this size wouldn't have time for that."

"His brother is the keeper of the dogs," said Sanchez. "His brother is always the dog man. We have to turn left on the path right there and go down that hill."

They followed Sanchez along a dirt track, past dark orchards and stacks of pear branches ravaged by fire blight. The camp lay in a hollow of hoary pines, cottonwoods, and tall poplars. There was a row of cabins sheathed in graying plywood, a cinder-block washhouse beside a creek, and a vast, dilapidated equipment shed thronged with the rusting detritus, the trim and tackle, of an orchard. In a flat, dusty field beyond the pines sat a ragged arc of pickers' trailers, moonlight playing off their sides through the vertical lines of the trees. Sanchez led them past a shed half full of neat apple cordwood. It was cold now, with the sun's descent. A girl labored at a chopping block, splitting stove wood with a short-handled ax; she didn't look at them, resolutely, as though it was dangerous to look.

Sanchez showed them the features of the washhouse: hot-water tank, two shower stalls, a wall heater, a washing machine, a Manila line for drying clothes. He and Emilio spoke in Spanish, then stopped when Ben collapsed on a bench. "You look pretty sick," said Sanchez.

"It's nothing," said Ben. "Indigestion."

"I hope it isn't contagious or nothing."

"It isn't," said Ben. "Indigestion."

Emilio helped Ben to his feet again by pulling on his left arm. They left the washhouse and walked the row of cabins, which Sanchez explained were the dwelling places of the unmarried pickers. Lights glowed in most of these; smoke blew from cinder-block chimneys. Ladders and bins lay scattered about. Two cars sat parked in front, one with a crucifix, one with foam dice hung from their rearview mirrors. On each small porch sat a hatchet and cutting block, pine kindling and scrap wood. A man emerged onto his porch as they passed—a shirtless man, in jeans and slippers—hung a mesh bag of onions from a hook, and spoke to Sanchez in Spanish. Sanchez answered, and they talked for a while. From the man's open door came the hiss of meat frying, the smell of onions simmering. A cat slipped noiselessly between the man's slippers, rubbed its flank against his leg, and stalked out into the pines. A car pulled in beside another cabin, and two young men piled out of it, laden with groceries. Ben heard the blaring of the car radio while the doors stood open. There was the smell of wood smoke and pine needles; the heat and light from the man's cabin spilled into the night.

Sanchez unlocked the next cabin and handed the key to Ben. He pulled a beaded chain inside to switch on the overhead light.

Emilio surveyed things at Ben's shoulder, his face impassive, neutral. They stood together, taking everything in, the lightbulb swinging on its cord. The cabin was the size of a garden shed, with a buckling, warped linoleum floor and slap-painted walls of plywood. A scanty, red-checked gingham curtain was drawn across a small window. A cast-iron cookstove sat on a fire pad; oilcloth covered the little table. From hooks just over the sink hung a fly swatter, a potato masher, and a ladle. Sanchez waited with one hand on the doorknob. "You have to be careful with that hot plate," he advised. "We don't want to have any fires."

"I don't plan on cooking," Ben said.

"There's a little trail across from the washhouse. You walk up there at six A.M., and we'll put you up in a ladder."

Ben nodded. "I'll be there."

"This is a cabin for one person only. They don't want more in here."

"What about my *compadre*, though?"

"He sleeps next door," answered Sanchez.

He said something to Emilio in Spanish, and they all said *buenas noches* to one another, and *gracias*, and see you in the morning, and finally the two others left.

Ben collapsed on the cot. A paltry mattress on a loose web of springs, it put him in mind of Camp Hale. Pulling his knees up toward his chest, he wrapped his arms around his gut and moaned softly with each breath. The moaning soothed him a little. He didn't have the energy to pry off his boots, so he untied them and left them on. It was silent except for a bluebottle fly that landed on him now and then. The naked bulb had ceased its swaying and cast a bald white light.

Ben sat up and fumbled in his rucksack for the drifter's breath-mint tin. There was one marijuana cigarette left, and he lodged its tip between his lips and lit it with a kitchen match he found in a dish on the cookstove. Standing in the doorway, Ben blew smoke toward the pines. The moon's glow lay over the world. The girl splitting wood had left the ax in the chopping block. A light was on in Emilio's cabin. Ben drew smoke into his lungs again, and while he kept it there, holding his breath, an owl hooted in the hollow. A strident and mysterious call, somehow disconcerting.

He turned out the light, lay on the bed, and in his thick, slow, narcotic way, took note of disconnected details. The stovepipe had a right-angle bend above the damper key. On an open shelf stood a candle, a flashlight, and a spray can of Barbasol. The ceiling was made of square fiber tiles coming loose in two corners. A bottle of castor oil stood beside the sink, slightly less than half full. Ben weighed the merit of taking some, desiring its purgative effect, but chances were it was rancid, old, and in the end he decided against it.

His mind shifted, dancing. He thought of Catherine Donnelly, then of Christine Reilly. He thought of the horsewoman at the veterinary clinic, the blue veins in her shoulders. He was half in dreams, mired in marijuana, when someone knocked on the cabin door and opened it tentatively. In the darkness Ben made out only a shape, a figure hovering silently, and his heart raced, panicked. "Who is it?" he called. "Who's there?"

The answer came, indecipherably, in Spanish, but Ben was familiar with its pleasant lilt, and the figure resolved into someone he recognized—Emilio, or Raul Ramirez, whatever his name was, it didn't matter. Stove wood heaped in the crook of his arm. He waited patiently by the door. *"Qué pasa?"* Ben asked. "What is it?"

"Hace mucho frío," the boy answered.

He set the wood on the floor by the stove and brushed his shirtfront clean. In the darkness he moved about silently. He put Ben's rucksack on the room's only chair, lay a blanket over Ben's legs. Next he built a warming fire, slowly feeding the flames. The light reflected against his face, the cleft in his chin, his bold forehead. He sat on his ankles comfortably, a stick in his hand, poking. Ben lay listening to the spit of the kindling. The boy looked contemplative with the fire's glow in his pores. *"Gracias,"* Ben said. *"Muchas gracias.* I appreciate the fire."

"De nada," Emilio answered.

He adjusted the damper, closed the firebox, and fine-tuned the draft. He sat for a moment looking about, then took the candle from the shelf, set it in the sink, and lit it. Candlelight fluttered across the room. Trembling shadows, the borders of things muted. Emilio came to Ben's cot and knelt. "Okay, *señor,"* he said.

Ben lifted an age-mottled hand and settled it on the boy's forearm. "Thank you," he said. *"Muchas gracias."*

Emilio nodded and made the sign of the cross in the air in front of Ben. Then he rose and went to the door. In silhouette he was featureless, dark. The shape of a boy, slender and easy. *"Buenas noches,"* he whispered.

But a good night wasn't possible. In this world of shifting, quivering shadows, Ben fought with his disease. The chill of death was upon him, he felt, though it might have been something less than that, mere exhaustion, nausea—marijuana obscured the truth. Marijuana stood between him and knowledge of his condition. Yet to the best of Ben's ability to perceive, he felt the blowing of the Last Wind, heard the scraping of the scythe, smelled the grave. And for how long had he anticipated this, expecting it with dread? How long afraid of its coming? Outwardly he'd been stalwart and stoic, but privately he'd quaked like a child, trembled in apprehension, lived with a constant, quiet fear below the surface of everything.

Ben lay on his cot in the fruit pickers' hut, listening to the ticking of the fire in the cookstove, and felt the carabiner against his chest and the length of the ring-angle piton. In their classic application, they held a climber in the throes of ascent fixed to a wall of rock. Bits of human ingenuity standing between the climber and death. As if death was a game, as if challenging it was recreation. Ben thought of the young people in the Volkswagen van, eagerly headed for the Sawtooth Range, the mean, sheer faces there. The two of them thought of death romantically. They hadn't reached their apex yet. In their blood they had no inkling of decline, could hardly imagine it.

Dazed, Ben sought some view of death that made leaving the world endurable. No matter how often he'd turned it over, no matter the years he'd passed with it, there was still no answer to the final riddle, or an answer lay beyond his reach. Always his search had led him nowhere, and the next day he was one day older, with no greater wisdom as a shield against death, no revelation to pit against its strength. And this was how a person aged. Suffering in astonishment the progress of the days. One moment puffed up by a blustery denial, the next drowsing in blessed forgetfulness. Ben's life was an ocean of fear punctuated by islands of calm acquiescence, by well-lit places in which he forgot because his work or love or the mere light distracted him from the truth.

He had not found any way to proceed beyond such distractions. It was not the life of the spirit at all, in which mortality inspires a course of right action and humility. It had been instead a willful turning from the true conditions of existence. And, for the most part, this had been fine. He'd partaken of life with appetite. But now he found—he'd known it since Rachel's death—that this forgetting couldn't sustain him to the grave. The interludes of ignorance had grown shorter. And now there were none, there was only knowledge, and he wasn't ready for it.

Ben recalled how, on ten thousand nights, he'd watched Rachel undress at her armoire—turned from him, her long torso in the lamplight, her hands reversed at the small of her back swiftly and deftly to unclasp her bra—and the memory deepened his sadness. It was something that had never ceased to move him or to prompt in him a momentary reflection on the nature of love's good fortune. He did not take such a thing for granted, even after fifty years: always he celebrated what he'd been granted and admired what he saw. When they'd argued or carried some silent grievance or were divided temporarily by ill-chosen words—still Ben clung to her. She'd carried a tranquil grace at her center. A poise he could not limn, in the end, which had kept him turned toward her.

Now her poise had left the world. In the seasons since, he hadn't learned to live—he hadn't let go of mourning. The arc of his grief had been willfully long. He had indulged and extended its trajectory.

His death would solve that problem. It was nice to think of it that way. But death presented a thousand other faces. His thoughts on it were madly circuitous. Inevitably, there was no other subject, and he forced himself to muse on death as though it were simply a form of sleep, warm and full of dreams.

His musings finally gave way to sleep, and Ben dreamed he was traveling in the desert. On a journey whose purpose he couldn't guess. Underfoot, a fine sand shifted and confounded his progress. A strange apprehension haunted his limbs. He changed his direction twice, three times. Low, barren mountains appeared on the horizon. A lunar barrenness, the topography of dreams, stones strewn artfully down an arroyo as if laid by a Japanese gardener, a sinuous bend in the dry bed of stones, one stone, two, a stone carved in runes, the inordinate size of his walking shoes, an anxiety over the lack of water, he carried nothing, went empty-handed, looked out over the land from a ridge where the desert shuddered and disappeared, trembled and folded into itself: waves of heat, burning sheaves of air, a pall obscuring his view. He followed a trail of cobbles then, and knelt beside a rivulet. Christine Reilly knelt there, too, and placed the lucky carabiner once more around his neck. Which made no sense, since he wore it already. The illogic of that jarred him loose. He was in the fruit pickers' cabin, he was at the Wolfhound Orchard. The fire in the cookstove ticked and popped. The candle in the sink cast a wavering light. He thought of the girl with the nose ring, Catherine Donnelly with her book by Steiner, a pimple on her chin, the hems of her jeans dragging. What he wanted was gently to hold her, nothing more than that.

The boy, Emilio, knelt at his side, uttering repeatedly the word *señor*, until Ben opened his eyes. "*Necesito un medico—rapidamente*," said the boy. "*Rapidamente, señor, rapidamente, por favor.*"

The field boss, Sanchez, was in the cabin, too. He pulled the cord on the overhead light, and its white glare blinded Ben. "He says you are a doctor," explained Sanchez. "There is a woman in the camp having a baby tonight. Maybe there is something you can do."

"Okay," said Ben. "I'm with you."

"Please hurry," answered Sanchez. "That baby is stuck tight in her. It's trapped there. It doesn't move."

"Okay," said Ben. "Let's go."

Beneath stars, as in a dream—Emilio before him, Sanchez at his back—he stumbled through pines and into an orchard where the dark apples had not yet been picked, on between rows of silent trees, until he emerged in a dusty field. The lights of a dozen trailer homes burned; pickers stood about. The place seemed blurred, but flat and still, as in a photograph.

They hurried past the first three trailers, where pickers gawked like spectators at a race, men and women standing in the cold, their hands stuffed in their coat pockets, their hats pulled low on their foreheads. It was clear that few were abed in the camp, dogs wandered in agitation, children ran footloose and dumbfounded in the night, their faces tired, quizzical. Emilio ran through without stopping to speak, without apology or explanation, and the pickers moved to make room for him and for the strange-looking doctor with one eye swollen shut, wearing steel-rimmed spectacles, his boots untied, limping. Emilio pressed on toward a silver trailer hulking in the dark like a dry-docked submarine or airplane fuselage. Its low door was thrown open, and a woman waited there, in vigil.

As they approached, she clasped her hands beneath her chin. She was fat and wore a parka patched with duct tape. "You are the doctor?" she asked.

"Let us through," said Sanchez.

"Thanks to our God," the woman said. "I have been praying for you."

"Let us through," repeated Sanchez.

Ben put his head in the trailer door. The room had the feel of a cave or chamber; distorted shadows shimmered against walls of riveted, contoured aluminum. The spectral light of a kerosene lantern illuminated a macabre scene. At one end of the trailer, on a bare mattress thrown there as if by a tornado, a woman—a girl—was in the throes of labor, naked and twisting on a nest of blankets, bucking and swaying on her hands and knees, her eyes shut, her belly heaving. Her hair had matted to her shining face, obscuring half of it. She tucked her head between her breasts and groaned until the cords in her neck bulged; then she fell onto the lengths of her forearms and paused to catch her breath. Her feet kicked spasmodically, she cradled her head in the palms of her hands, her face lay against the rough mattress. She rolled on her side, flailing, and a wail escaped from her lips.

A young man in stocking feet knelt beside her, brushing the hair from her cheek with his fingernails. A woman knelt on the mattress, too, speaking urgently in Spanish. A second woman, short and large—a dwarf, Ben realized: she was four feet tall— stood with rolled sleeves at a propane stove, dipping a towel into a kettle of steaming water, then wringing it with muscular vigor. "It's good you're here," she said to Ben.

"How long has she been in labor?"

"A long time. Too long," said the dwarf.

Ben ducked inside, carefully. The ceiling loomed claustrophobically low, and he couldn't stand without stooping deeply, which hurt his neck and back. He moved closer, knelt beside the mattress. The girl, he saw, was very young, a child giving birth to a child. "What's your name?" he asked.

"Her name is Doris," the boy answered, and draped a blanket over her.

"How old?"

"Fifteen."

"Are you the father?"

The boy nodded.

"What's your name?"

"Jimmy Perez."

"This is her first?"

"Her first, yes."

"Okay," said Ben.

The woman on the mattress caressed the girl's damp forehead. She seemed to Ben to have an eye of glass, or a wandering, unfocused, dead pupil—he couldn't tell which. He couldn't tell if she was looking at him. She seemed to look sideways, or through him, or beyond. "Are you her mother?" he asked.

"No," said the woman, her eye roaming.

"How long have you been here?"

"I came last night."

"Twenty-four hours?"

"More than that."

"She's been in labor twenty-four hours?"

"Longer," said the woman.

Ben shook his head. "Are you a midwife?"

"I don't know anything," the woman answered.

Ben put a hand to his forehead, pausing. He had not attended a woman in labor since his internship in obstetrics forty-four years earlier. For six weeks in 1954 he'd assisted in delivering babies. "We need to call for an ambulance," he said. "She needs to go to a hospital."

As if in response, Doris heaved painfully onto her back, seized the hands of the glass-eyed woman, and bore down with so much force, her lips whitened, her eyes squeezed shut, tears leaked from their corners. She flung her legs wide unabashedly— a seething mass of dark tissue, her purple rectum swollen. The vulva had stretched to the limit; her perineum might rupture. An episiotomy would have helped, but that was impossible now.

"Can you do anything?" asked the glass-eyed woman. "What are you supposed to do?"

Ben didn't answer. He kept his hand on his forehead. The girl panted, gasped, and grunted, then bore down again. Ben saw the swelling of the baby's head, the wet, dark oval of its hair. "The head is showing," he said.

"What does that mean?" asked Jimmy.

"It means it's too late for the hospital." Ben turned to the propane stove. "How hot is that water?" he asked.

"It's too hot," the dwarf said. "I'll put some cold in it."

Ben took off his hunting coat and rolled up his shirtsleeves. The dwarf poured dish soap into his hands, and he washed, adjusted his glasses on his face, and knelt again by the girl. "You're all right," he said.

"Are you a doctor?"

"Do I look like one?"

"No," said Doris.

"Well, I am."

As if in answer, she pulled at her thighs to spread them as wide as possible. Then she buried her chin against her chest and bore down with the concentrated force of a woman trying to move the earth. Her skin went from gray to blue, her brow furrowed, her eyes narrowed, it appeared as though she was being crushed by something enormous and invisible. Ben watched while the baby's head crowned, and then Doris's perineum ruptured. There was blood now, but not very much. The tear looked relatively superficial, involved the fourchette and mucus membrane but not the underlying fascia. "Your baby's coming," said Ben.

The dark wet head emerged gradually. It came face down, then turned sideways—a natural restitution. The features were scrunched, constricted, crabbed, the eyes clenched, the mouth closed, the skin tinted a shade of blue far darker than the blood of veins. The head stopped, came no farther, and seemed to retract or shrink again, like the head of a turtle or snail. An odd, swollen, parasitical growth attached to the girl's groin. Her gaping legs with a head between them—a neckless, embryonic head. It hung suspended, a third appendage, Doris impaled on it. Ben lay on the floor beside the mattress to wipe its strictured face with a towel and swab its mouth with his forefinger. He wished he had an aspirating syringe, and even more, a fetoscope. The baby wasn't breathing, it was stuck at the shoulders. He wasn't sure what to do about it, but he knew there was no time to lose. The cord might be fatally compressed.

Ben pulled up Doris's left knee until it pressed against her swollen belly, and then he brought up the right. Doris held them there. Awkwardly, low against the mattress, he pried hard at the baby's head, stretching the neck unnaturally, then gave up and slid two fingers in, next to the baby's ear. Doris shrieked and swore at him in Spanish, and Jimmy Perez put a hand on her back and leaned close to her. Ben was relieved to find that the umbilicus wasn't tangled, but he still felt time was running out. He slid in a third finger and tried to twist the baby, turn it in some subtle fashion, unlock it as though the passage to birth were a Chinese puzzle of sorts. He tried clockwise and counterclockwise. He couldn't think what else to do. He withdrew his fingers and pressed on the girl's pubis, as though the baby might be popped free, as in a Heimlich maneuver. It didn't work, and he pried again, gripping it behind the ears. The baby remained intractable.

"Is it dead?" asked Jimmy Perez.

"No," said Ben. "We'll get it out."

"Its face is blue."

"It isn't breathing yet."

"It's dead," said Jimmy.

"No, it isn't," said Ben. "It's still getting blood from the umbilical cord. That blue will go away."

"It's dead," said Jimmy. "I know it."

"No," Ben repeated.

He slid his fingers past the baby's neck—slid them into Doris's vagina. He knew he was hurting her—she was trying to pull away and shrieked at him in Spanish—but he had no choice anymore. His hand was in, now, to the third set of knuckles. Doris winced, holding her breath; her face blanched, her eyes closed. Ben crouched with his fingers inside her, seeking with his fingertips. He followed the length of the baby's upper arm, which was folded across its collarbones, until he came to the little elbow. It took awhile. He searched. Finally he found what he was looking for. When he drew out his hand, he had the baby's small blue fist trapped between two of his fingers, as in a magic trick.

The baby's arm hung quivering near its head while Ben popped the shoulder free in a gradual release of traction. The other shoulder came much more easily, and the baby—a girl—slid out like a fish, awash in blood and amniotic fluid, the umbilicus wrapped around her. "You have a new baby," announced Ben.

Catching her, he trembled. He held her, a jewel, in his palms. "It's a girl," he said. "She's beautiful."

"A girl," said Jimmy Perez.

"Thank God you were here," exclaimed the glass-eyed woman, her pupil crackling with light.

"Let me," said Doris. "Let me see her."

Ben ran a finger inside the baby's mouth, then blew in her face to startle her. Next he turned her upside down, his hand locked around her ankles, flicked the bottoms of her feet gently, then slapped her on the back. The girl began to wriggle in his grasp and made small squawking noises. She turned pink gradually. When she started to cry, her father crossed himself. "A miracle," he said.

Ben was still trembling. With a towel he swabbed the baby clean, then set her, covered, on Doris's belly. Jimmy lay down to look at his daughter. He covered his mouth in disbelief.

"What do you need?" the dwarf asked.

"A sharp knife," said Ben. "And some twine."

Sanchez, from the doorway, produced a lock-back blade. Ben sterilized it in rubbing alcohol brought from a neighboring trailer. Then he tied the umbilicus in two places, using bits of Manila twine, and made his cut between them. The placenta delivered of its own accord. Ben made sure it was all there, then dropped it into a plastic bag the dwarf held open for him. He washed and looked again at the child, who was nursing vigorously. Her color was substantially better now. She had a lot of dark hair, and a cowlick.

Ben pressed gently on Doris's lower belly, assessing the condition of her uterus. It was hard to the touch and had contracted swiftly to the size of a small grapefruit. She was not bleeding, and he felt satisfied that there was no immediate danger. "You should take them both to see a doctor," he said, addressing Jimmy Perez. "After she's rested, but as soon as possible. Just to make sure everything's all right. That there aren't any problems."

"Okay," said Jimmy. "Thank you."

"There should be a clinic in Wenatchee," said Ben. "They'll have a doctor who knows about this, who knows about newborn babies. And someone for Doris. She needs stitches."

"Okay," said Jimmy. "We'll go."

"It's dangerous not to," Ben warned.

When he went outside, it was first light. The orchards nearby were hung with ripe apples. The broad sky was pale, cloudless. Things looked different now.

TWELVE

He slept all morning in the picker's cabin. At ten Sanchez came,
bringing a woman. They stood in the doorway looking at Ben.
"This is the doctor," said Sanchez.

"This man here?"

"Yes."

Ben put on his glasses. He had folded his hunting coat into a
pillow and lay with the side of his face against it, in the smell of
blood and bird feathers. "Excuse me," he said. "I'm not very well.
Excuse me for not getting up."

"Please," said the woman. "Don't."

She was almost his age, Ben guessed, a gray-haired woman with
deep wrinkles and liver spots who wore a housedress, a cardigan
sweater, and calf-high rubber boots. Her hair was amiss, her dress
front stained, and there was hay stuck to her. She looked as if

she'd been milking cows or working in a stable. The handles of a pair of pruning shears stuck out of her sweater pocket.

Sanchez took off his cowboy hat and held it by its crown. "This is the woman of the house," he said. "This is Mrs. Harden."

"I'm Ben Givens," said Ben.

"I'm Bea," said the woman.

Sanchez put on his hat again. "I'm going to head back to my pickers," he said. "Unless you need me for something."

"You go ahead," said Bea.

Sanchez walked to the door and turned. His face was as quiet, as inaccessible, as it had been the evening before. "We just went to look at the baby," he told Ben. "She was sleeping, and so was her mother."

"What did they name her?"

"Ellen Dolores."

"Remind them to go to a doctor, okay? Mother and baby both."

Sanchez nodded and went out. Bea Harden took her pruning shears and put them in the opposite pocket. "I heard all about it," she said.

"Heard about what?"

"You and the baby. Gustavo told me." Bea rubbed her nostrils with a handkerchief. "I heard it was stuck at the shoulders for a while. That can be dangerous."

"You're right. It's very dangerous."

"Then it's lucky you were there."

"It was lucky," said Ben.

Bea stuffed her handkerchief away. Her nostrils looked inflamed and tender. She had an equine, pop-eyed face. The space between her lips and nose was deeply etched with wrinkles.

"Your name," she said. "I know it."

"Plenty of Givenses used to live around here."

"But you used to live across the river when I was growing up in Wenatchee. My name then was Beatrice Cade."

"Cade," said Ben. "I don't remember."

Bea kneaded the fingers of her left hand, which were bent, knobby, arthritic. "My dad worked with your dad on the Icicle Ditch. And we had the milliner's shop in town. Your mother used to come there sometimes."

"My memory's bad," said Ben.

"Her name was Lenora. One of the Chandlers. I knew your aunts, too."

Ben didn't answer. He tried to remember. Where had the milliner's shop been in Wenatchee? He thought back sixty years.

"Lily," said Bea. "That was my sister. She was your age—one year younger. And my brother was Andy. He worked for the utility. You remember him. Andy Cade."

"Andy," said Ben. "No."

"They're gone," said Bea. "But you had a brother. Aidan—wasn't it Aidan?"

"He's gone, too," said Ben.

Bea picked the hay from her sweater. Her large, worn fingers worked slowly at the task, absently, as she spoke. "I knew there was something going on last night. There were so many lights on down in the hollow. They said there was a picker delivered the baby. A picker who was a doctor, maybe. Why would a doctor be picking apples? It didn't make any sense."

"It doesn't make sense," answered Ben.

"So why are you picking?"

"It's a long story."

Bea poured a cup of water at the sink. Ben sat up and drank all of it. "Is your husband named William?" he asked.

"William is my brother-in-law."

"Does he have wolfhounds?"

"He raises them."

"He stole my gun," said Ben.

Bea took the cup again. "He's always been the terror of the country," she said. "Nothing he does surprises me."

"A varmint hunter."

"Worse than that."

"He sends his hounds out after coyotes."

"He sends them after anything that moves."

Ben nodded. "Like my Brittanies," he said. "His hounds killed one and maimed the other."

Bea shook her head regretfully. "I wish he had another hobby."

"I killed the one that got after mine."

"You killed one of Bill's hounds?"

"That's why he stole my gun."

Bea put the cup in the sink. She grimaced, angry, and shook her head. "I'm going to talk to him," she said.

Ben rubbed his side. It hurt relentlessly. "Don't bring it up. He can have the gun. I don't want it back. Forget it."

"It's yours, though."

"I don't want it anymore."

"It's the principle."

"Just let him have it."

"We'll get it back."

"I don't want it, though. The only thing I want is to go home."

Bea, again, kneaded her fingers, the swollen, misshapen knuckles. "Where is home?" she asked.

"I live on the other side of the mountains."

"You're a transplant, then."

"I guess I am."

"Can I bring you an aspirin?"

"Aspirin doesn't help."

"What does?"

"Nothing, really."

"What do you have?"

"Cancer. Of the colon."

"Oh, no," said Bea.

She took him in her car, an El Dorado, up past an orchard of trellised Fujis and another laden with Granny Smiths. A day of full sun, warm and well lit, the pickers working in their shirtsleeves. There were orchards rolling across the hills, a vast plot of spindled Galas, Braeburns on vertical trellises, seasoned Red Delicious. Off in the distance, across the river, a delicate web of power wires ran over the hills. In the hard light they looked as fragile as gossamer, their pylons and stanchions complicated, and at the crest of the breaks they disappeared across the wheat plateau.

Bea, driving, offered comfort—people she knew in remission. A cousin who'd outlasted lymphoma, the daughter of a friend who'd licked Hodgkin's Disease, an orchardist in Mattawa who'd overcome lung cancer on a diet of raw calf's liver juice and organic Winesaps from Manson. "I hadn't heard about the Winesaps," said Ben. "But the calf's liver juice sounds familiar."

"Well, what about it?"

"It's not for me."

"Why shouldn't it be?"

"Because it doesn't work."

Bea gave him a crestfallen look. "You sound like a doctor," she said.

They passed a weathered maintenance shed, then mesh-wire kennels housing Bill Harden's wolfhounds, who lolled about in their cramped dark cages like circus animals. Around the corner was a barn, a shop—ladders stacked up under its eaves—and a clapboard house with dormer windows and a broad, wraparound porch. There were stacked bins in front of it, a forklift and Farmall tractor. A box of tools sat on the ground, and a case of motor oil.

Bea urged Ben to come in for breakfast, to rest on the couch, use the bathroom. He told her about the rented truck, parked overnight on Joe Miller Road. If she could drop him there, he asked.

"You can't drive, the way you are."

"I can, too. Once I'm settled at the wheel."

"No, you can't. I'm not going to let you."

Ben frowned stubbornly, but Bea only put her open hand out. "Give me your keys," she told him. "I'll make sure we get your truck back to the U-Save in town."

"I don't have any other way home."

"I'll drive you across. Don't you worry about that."

"It's a long way."

"I'm a good samaritan."

"You don't even know me."

"It doesn't matter."

She got out and spoke through the window frame. "Give me about five minutes," she said. "My husband is up in the orchard somewhere. I'm going to tell him about driving you."

"But you really shouldn't," said Ben.

She walked away, to the house. Ben watched her go. She had a vegetable garden laid out in tidy rows, free of weeds, bountiful, the plants poking up out of black tarp. The potatoes grew inside of old tires. The tomatoes were staked with twine to tall poles. Purple grapes hung from a willow arbor. A rototiller sat in the yard, beside a pile of bark mulch.

Ben sat with his window open, smelling apples on the air. The five minutes became fifteen. He shut his eyes and dozed a little. He was worried that Doris could hemorrhage still. He decided to tell Bea about that possibility. The girl should see a doctor right away, go to the clinic in town.

He heard the racing of an engine behind him, and then a crew-cab pickup pulled in, a little fast, raising dust. A man got out, big, in his fifties, gray and weather-furrowed. He wore his hair cropped close to his head, suspenders over a sweatshirt, stagged logging jeans, and worn boots: the steel toes showing through the leather. In one hand he carried a power drill, in the other a leather carpenter's belt and a plastic bag of nails. Walking, he spat into the grass.

He had taken ten steps toward the maintenance shed when Ben struggled out of the car awkwardly, stood in its door with his arms around his gut, and called to him, weakly, by name. "William Harden," Ben said.

Harden turned and looked at him. His eyes were small, his shoulders sloped, his face tense, pale. "What the hell?" he said.

"It's me," said Ben. "Remember me? The hunter you stole the Winchester from a couple of nights ago."

William Harden spat again, then wiped his lips with the back of his hand. "'Stole' ain't the right word," he said.

"I came to get my gun back," said Ben. "But I've changed my mind."

Harden snorted. "Good," he said. "Then get the hell out of here."

Ben walked toward him, limping. It was hard for him to walk. He came close enough to see Harden clearly through the old, steel-rimmed glasses. Harden's eyes were uncertain, but he held the power drill firmly, like a weapon, something to club Ben with. He set down the nails and the carpenter's belt. "It's your call, old man," he said.

"My call is this," said Ben. "That gun was in my family sixty years. My father used it before I did, hunting birds. He killed a lot of birds with it. After him, I killed my share, too. But you know something about that gun? It was never anything but bad, really. A bad thing, that gun."

Harden didn't answer. He wiped his mouth instead.

"That gun is cursed," Ben said. "All guns are cursed."

He moved closer, pulled off his glasses. Harden raised the drill. "You go ahead and take it," said Ben. "I pass that gun on to you, Harden, and wash my hands of it."

Bea drove the El Dorado upriver, and they crossed the Columbia at East Wenatchee. There were apple trucks going both ways on the road. There were pickers working the last of the fruit. Bea drove past Rock Island and came down into the country Ben had lived in as a boy, orchards spread out on both sides of the wide water, sagebrush and groves of Russian olive. "Where was your place?" she asked.

He pointed it out when they came to it. The apple trees fell in a sweep toward the riverbank, the tan hills rose in the west. The new house sat behind willows grown to splendor with the passing of the years. Bea slowed and sat on the road shoulder. "It's pretty," she said. "All those poplars."

"Things have changed. A lot of things."

"It's good to get to see it anyway."

"It's still beautiful."

"That it is."

They lingered there a little too long. Bea made no move to drive on. "Let's go," Ben said finally.

In Quincy they picked up Rex at the clinic. Ilse Peterson was occupied, but the horsewoman at the reception desk promised to relay Ben's gratitude and brought the dog for him. Ben checked the staples, stroked Rex's coat, and carried him outside. He arranged the dog across the backseat, on a blanket. "We're going home," he whispered.

The road to George, at noon, was sunlit, and the big irrigators sat in the fields. The vacancy and magnitude of the land struck Ben, and its fertility—false—struck him, too. The edges where the fields met the desert were sudden: clean lines of demarcation. Whatever was not cultivated was steppe, haunted and beautiful. The arid plateau lay under the fields. The sage had been pulled out whole, by the roots. When the water no longer arrived here, the fecund crops would die of thirst. The land desired dryness.

Long before George, Bea asked about his eye, and Ben began at the beginning. Rachel's death, first of all. His daughter and his grandson. He didn't go into the details, but he did tell, in linear fashion, the story of how he had come to this pass, his shotgun lost, his dog wounded, his eye blackened, his transience. It felt good to speak of it all. She seemed the right person, a stranger.

"Suicide," Bea said when he was done. "I couldn't imagine it."

They passed a feed lot, peppermint fields, a walnut grove, a new orchard. Ben, experimentally, pressed on his eyelid. "I didn't want to burden my family," he said. "Put them through nine months of it. I didn't want to make them miserable."

"It isn't a burden," Bea said firmly. "Think what they'll learn from it."

"That sounds good, in principle."

"It is good," Bea insisted. "Seeing you die, it'll make them compassionate. It'll help them be more compassionate."

They came to the interstate and turned toward the Columbia. Bea kept to the right-hand lane, both hands high on the steering wheel. "What did your wife do?" she asked.

"My wife was a nurse. She started in the war. For thirty-four years, a hospital nurse. In a burn unit, for a long time. The worst cases. Burns."

"A doctor and a nurse," said Bea.

"She took off eight years when our daughter was born, but then she went back to work."

"She must have liked it."

"She did like it."

"I admire that," said Bea.

Ben fell silent. "I admired her, too," he said after awhile. "She was a better person than I am."

Bea nodded. She made a small adjustment to her rearview mirror and changed lanes to pass a truck. "Well, I don't really know," she said.

"She was," said Ben. "She gave everything."

"I guess you'd have to, being a nurse."

"A burn-unit nurse."

"It's so."

They came to the bend where the plateau broke, high above the Columbia. Ben looked toward the Frenchman Hills. A flight of ducks passed over them. To the south lay endless sagelands.

"So why did you change your mind?" asked Bea. "What made you change your mind?"

"Cowardice, mainly. Try shooting yourself. It isn't easy."

"There's sleeping pills."

"I couldn't do it."

"You didn't really want to."

Ben shrugged.

"Think of this," Bea said. "You saved a baby last night."

There were geese on the river, three dozen of them, down toward the Wanapum Dam. The wind blew north, up the canyon. The light lay bronze on the hills. Beyond rose the Saddle Mountains.

When they had crossed the river, Ben spoke again. "When we married, we made a pact," he said, "to bury our ashes together."

"That's very romantic."

"Well, we felt so."

"I like the idea."

"I like it, too. And if I'd gone through with shooting myself, it probably wouldn't ever happen."

"Coyotes and worms instead, you're right."

"So I'm going home because of that, too."

"I understand," said Bea.

They came up over Ryegrass Summit, into the Quilomene, then the Kittitas Valley. The trees along Manastash Ridge had gone russet red and yellow. "October," said Bea, "is a beautiful month on this side of the mountains."

"The fall is more vivid over here," said Ben.

"On the coast you just don't get the same colors."

"It's a trade-off," said Ben. "Our weather's more temperate. We don't have quite the extremes."

"There's a price for everything," said Bea.

They came into a country of evergreen trees and left the sage and canyons behind. The mountains rose in front of them, snow-swathed, in the west. Forests covered Easton Ridge; already the light had softened. They came up toward the Stampede Pass cutoff, between slopes of Cascade blueberries. There were fields of burnished, dying red where the berries grew among mountain heathers. The old clear-cuts were full of them. They made a kind of heath.

In Snoqualmie Pass—the crest of the mountains—they stopped at the Traveler's Rest. Bea had to use the rest room, she said. She was going to get a cup of coffee and a donut. She could bring him something, if he wanted it. He answered that he had no appetite. He thanked her for her attentions to him, and thanked her again for her generosity in taking him back home. "It's nothing," said Bea. "It's useful to you, and interesting for me. I don't ask more from any day."

She went into the Traveler's Rest, and Ben turned to check on Rex. "You look okay back there," he said. "Better than me, really."

He rolled down his window with effort. He wanted to smell the mountains. It was getting on toward midafternoon, and an alpine chill was in the air. He remembered walking the crest of the Cascades from Windy Gap to here. Silver Peak was a few miles off. He thought of his promise to climb it with Chris. He would have to explain that now.

It was a long way down to the west side, home—almost three thousand feet. Bea drove with her coffee in one hand, a maple bar on a napkin in her lap. The sky here was a muted gray. There was nothing to see but mountains, forest. By North Bend, it was raining gently. Mount Si lay veiled by clouds.

Everything at home was as Ben had left it; nothing had gone awry. His neighbor had taken out the garbage that morning and had seen to the newspapers and mail. The VCR had made its recording of *Great Railway Journeys*. The bird plucker sat on the kitchen table; the recipe for quail on toast poked from the recipe box. There were four messages on the answering machine: Bill Ward's nurse confirming an appointment, another doctor Ben sometimes hiked with, the auto shop that had towed his Scout, his car insurance company. He would have all these calls to return, but not now.

He fed Rex, and while the dog ate, he slumped at the kitchen table, his head against his arm. Through the window he could see the dog kennel and the Summer Damasks his wife had planted between the pad for the garbage can and the wall of the neighbor's house. A few leaves were left on them, and the unpicked blossoms had turned to hips. The plants were tall now, profuse.

Ben turned up the heat in the house and made his way to the bedroom, where he had left the copy of *Scientific American* open on the side table. He pried off his boots, settled back on the bed. He curled up as comfortably as he could. His dusty hunting clothes smelled of sage. There were bloodstains on the front of his coat and feathers in his pockets.

Rex limped in, looked at him, and lay down on the throw rug beside the bed. Ben rested a hand on his flank. "I guess you can stay," he whispered.

After awhile he took the telephone receiver and punched in his daughter's number. "Hello," she said. "Renee Givens-Kane."

"It's me," said Ben. "I'm home."

ACKNOWLEDGMENTS

For generosity in Washington's apple country, Doug and Sue Clarke, Ed and Virginia Clarke, Thyra and Doyle Fleming, Mike Robinson, Brian Vincent, Grady Auvil, and Mary Pat and Jerry Scofield. For assistance in historical research, Barbara Walton and Karen Ashley of the Denver Public Library, Moya Hansen of the Colorado Historical Society, Franco Polegato, Frank Chuk, Ken Hanson, Bob Ellis, Ken MacDonald, and Matteo Bavestrelli. For help with medical and veterinary questions, Will Toth, David Cowan, Bob and Bea Bourdeau, Mike Hobbs, Carol Riley, Laura Hoyt, and Mark Swaney. For expertise regarding medicine and war, Dr. Albert H. Meinke. For days afield east of the Cascades, Ralph Cheadle, Trip Goodall; Taylor, Travis and Henry Guterson; Ellensburg writer Joe Powell; Tess, Jack, Thorn, Gus, and Sam.

For kindness and help in Italy, Norbert and Pepe Cristofolini. For information on migrant workers, Victor Rodriguez and Dr. Patricia Ortiz. For assistance with Spanish translation, Sue and Luis Koch and Karla Sullivan. For help regarding birth and shoulder dystocia, Susan Anemone. For expertise on the flora of Central Washington, Bill Barker. For office help, Angelica Guterson.

I am grateful to Drenka Willen for her help in shaping this book and to Anne and Georges Borchardt.

Sources include Dr. Albert Meinke's *Mountain Troops and Medics: Wartime Stories of a Surgeon in the U.S. Ski Troops*; Robert Ellis's *See Naples and Die*; H. Robert Krear's *Journal of a U.S. Army Mountain Trooper in World War II*; Ken MacDonald's unpublished memoirs; Diane Burke Fessler's *No Time for Fear: Voices of American Military*

Nurses in World War II; Barbara Brooks Tomblin's *G.I. Nightingales: The Army Nurse Corps in World War II*; Lt. Col. Marjorie Peto's *Women Were Not Expected*; Al C. Bright's *Apples Galore*; Isabel Valle's *Fields of Toil*; Ronald J. Taylor's *Sagebrush Country: A Wildflower Sanctuary*; Toby F. Sonneman and Rick Steigmeyer's *Fruit Fields in My Blood: Okie Migrants in the West*; and Daniel Mathews's *Cascade-Olympic Natural History: A Trailside Reference.*

To those I have neglected to mention from sheer failure of memory or character, please accept my apologies. I owe all a great debt.

A NOTE ON THE AUTHOR

David Guterson is the author of *Our Lady of the Forest* and a
collection of short stories, *The Country Ahead of Us, The Country
Behind*. *Snow Falling on Cedars* won the PEN/Faulkner Award.
He lives in Washington State.